The Kookaburra Bird

S. E. Jenkins

Published by FeedARead.com Publishing – Arts Council funded.

A CIP catalogue record for this title is available from the British Library.

For my father, George,
and in memory of my mother,
Eileen Young.

Author's Notes

During the twentieth century successive British Governments sent over a hundred and thirty thousand children from British orphanages and children's homes to live in Canada, South Africa, Zimbabwe [formerly Rhodesia], New Zealand and Australia, and of these more than seven thousand boys and girls aged four to sixteen were sent to orphanages and farm schools in Australia. It is clear from reading the literature, including published government reports, that many were traumatised and left emotionally and, in some cases, physically scarred by the treatment they received, but there were others who benefited and thrived in the countries they had been sent to as children.

The kookaburra is not indigenous to Western Australia but was introduced from Eastern Australia in the mid 1890s by the Director of the Zoological Gardens in South Perth. By 1948 the kookaburra could be found as far east as Northam to Kellerberrin; however, for purposes of the storyline I have placed these birds further inland than they would have been in the late 1940s.

PART I

CHAPTER 1

Jon Cadwallader spat out dust and grit thrown up by the wheels as the truck bounced over the corrugated road. He shifted his position, easing the cramp in his back and legs. Charlestown couldn't be much further. Freddie reckoned it was a two hour drive, so why weren't they there yet?

He cursed Freddie Fitzpatrick and his mad idea to stow away on Ed Scally's delivery truck. But it was a good plan: get to Charlestown, hitch a lift to a remote cattle station, keep their heads down for a couple of months and then travel on to the goldfields where the real money was to be made, enough for their tickets home to England – not that Freddie was going anywhere now. Jon's fingers tightened around a metal cross-strut as he recalled the sound of earth peppering the coffin lid – it could have been him, not Freddie, buried six feet down half a world away from Liverpool and home. He banished the thought; the past was the past and better forgotten.

A quarter of an hour later the truck jerked as Scally changed down through the gears and brought it to a halt. The engine died and Scally jumped down from the cab, his feet hitting the ground with a thud. Jon caught a glimpse of boots disappearing into deep shadow, and of a brindled mongrel lying flat out in the shade of a water trough. Was this Charlestown?

Minutes slipped by, his ears ached from listening but nothing moved in the deadening midday heat. He stretched his stiff legs and his boot caught the edge of the steel brace that normally supported the spare wheels. The metal pinged.

The dog lifted its head, listened for a moment, snapped at the halo of flies and flopped back onto the dust.

Voices! Jon tensed. And footsteps! Someone riffling through a sheaf of paper.

'Jeez, Les, two in one day, it's a bit rich,' said Scally, 'can't it wait until tomorra?'

'No, you've got the Cavanagh's Creek run tomorrow, and Mrs Macarthur's stuff's already overdue.'

His luck was in. Scally was down for another delivery. Some place run by a woman by the sound of it. Fingers clicked. The dog dragged itself to its feet. Seconds later came the familiar rasp and flare of a match struck against the metal banding on the trailer's wooden sides and the sweet, pungent scent of tobacco drifted on the air. Mam had always liked a cigarette with a cup of tea. He pressed his eyes with his thumb and forefinger and clenched his teeth. It didn't do to think too much of home.

Scally struck up the truck and rammed it into gear. The wagon snatched and juddered as he reversed it up to the dry-store depot.

Knuckles rapped on the flatbed trailer. 'Whoa, mate!'

Scally switched off the engine. 'Where's Gerry?'

'He's crook.'

'Skivin' more like.' Scally slammed the truck door. 'Y'want to give him the push, Les. He's more trouble than he's worth. Likes his grog too much.'

The dog sniffed at a back wheel two feet from Jon's hiding place. Any minute it'd catch his scent and then what? Jon held his breath as it lowered its brown and yellow head for a better look. Its bright eyes locked on to him. He waited for it to bark, willing it gone, he waved it away, but it just stood there in a semi-crouched position, like a pointer flagging up game. Les took a swing at it and caught it four-square in the ribs. The dog yelped.

'Y'can load up the wagon,' said Scally, 'I'm off to the bar.'

'I want this delivered today, Scal.' Les returned to the store, picked up a sack, lugged it over to the truck and humped it on the flatbed.

From beneath the wagon Jon heard Scally mutter an obscenity as he hauled himself onto the trailer. Neither man spoke as they loaded the truck. The dog, now a safe distance from Les's boot, watched the proceedings, and Jon, in silence.

'Is that it, Les?' asked Scally after a while.

Les disappeared into the store again and returned with a canvas bag and a brown paper parcel tied with thick string. 'Don't forget the mail and put this box of spare parts somewhere safe. They're for the Samuels' generator. They're waiting on the delivery.' He tossed them up and Jon felt the wagon rock as Scally moved to catch them and then two or three jerks as he tightened the ropes to secure the packages.

Les glanced at his watch. 'You'll be at the Macarthur place by three and the Samuels' by five if you don't hang about.'

'I tell ya, Les, I ain't going anywhere with this throat. It's as parched as a galah's gizzard.' Scally jumped down off the truck and bashed his hat against his thigh. 'You can lash down the load. I'll be in the bar.'

Jon licked his dry lips. The water bottle he'd brought with him was empty but he couldn't risk discovery now, he'd have to stick it out and pray that the Macarthur place wasn't too far away.

Scally swerved off the graded road onto a rutted track. Jon hung on, terrified of falling off, of being crushed by the back wheels as the truck jumped and jerked over the rough ground. Then, after half an hour of hell, the truck stopped and he caught a glimpse of wood and iron sheds – a homestead.

He waited for a while listening as Scally walked away from the truck, then, shakily, he lowered himself to the ground, muscles screaming in protest as he shuffled, crab-like, towards a large patch of wanderric grass and cotton bush. He lay still, flattening his body to the ground, waiting for Scally's irate yell, his breath creating tiny whorls in the dust. An inch from his nose meat ants struggled with a centipede carcass. His belly squished and rumbled, breakfast was hours ago.

'Mail, Alice.' Scally hammered on the fly-screen door. 'Anyone about?'

Beyond the truck a ramshackle bungalow stood on two-foot high stone pillars with broad, shallow steps leading up to a verandah five or six feet deep. The red corrugated-iron roof was rusting in places. To the left was a fenced off paddock with a type of tree he didn't recognise and a couple of spindly eucalypts, the silver-grey leaves drooping in the heat. A few chooks fluffed in dust baths in what little shade there was, while an old rooster stood guard and scratched about for insects. Further back still stood a lifeless windmill towering over galvanised water tanks while to the right of them was a row of derelict sheds.

Jon breathed easy – the place was perfect, run down and remote, at least sixty miles from Charlestown and by the look of things Mrs Macarthur wouldn't say no to an extra stockman.

'Alice! Y'okay?'

'That you, Ed?' The fly screen banged again.

'God, Alice, y'had me worried.'

'Thought I'd croaked, did ya?'

Jon could see her legs. They were thin and as straight and mottled as the red gums that grew alongside the creek at Karundah. She shuffled along in a pair of old carpet slippers, her stick tap-tapping on the scrubbed boards.

'Too right, I did,' said Scally. 'Where are the blacks?'

'Gone walkabout,' she said.

'Y'need a manager, Alice, no job for a woman, especially–'

'A cripple–'

'Aw, I didn't say that–'

'But that's what you thought, isn't it, Ed?'

'Nah, Alice, I didn't, but a dislocated hip takes some getting over and y're not getting any younger.'

'That a fact,' snapped Alice.

'Yeah, it is. Now is that kettle on? I could do with a cuppa.'

The door slammed and Scally walked back to the truck. He drove over to the shed at the side of the bungalow and unloaded the dry goods and margarine and then lugged the jerrycans and oil drums over to one of the buildings beyond the post and rail fencing.

Jon muttered a quick Hail Mary. He'd fallen lucky. The bastard, O'Leary, wouldn't think to look for him this far out. He'd rest up for a month or two and work for Mrs Macarthur, get some cash together then hitch a ride east to the goldfields.

After Scally had gone Jon left the safety of the wanderrie grass and cotton bush cover and, shielded by the great jarrah trees bordering the creek, headed for the nearest old shed and squatted down behind an empty barrel, listening. The station was quiet, not even the kookaburra resting in the silver gum disturbed the silence. Jon eyed the bird, if what Father William said was true it shouldn't be in Western Australia either. He banished the bitter thought as the kookaburra shook its feathers and settled back on the branch, watching, as he edged along the building as fast as he could. When he reached the door he opened it an inch, scanned the room and slipped inside. Sixteen iron beds with horsehair mattresses were ranged along both sides of the bunkhouse. The place stank of mildew; no one had slept in the room for weeks. Had he made a mistake? Had he ended up on a derelict station with no stockmen and no prospect of work? A door slammed away to his right, out of his sight line.

Jon crossed to the window and spotted a grey-haired Aborigine padding across the yard wearing a grubby vest stretched tight across her chest and a patterned skirt flapping around her ankles. A heavily pregnant dingo-cross bitch followed her then flopped down in the shade of the verandah when she disappeared into the bungalow.

He sat on the nearest mattress – an Aborigine, that meant there'd be others, a station this far out, there must be. Scally had asked about the blacks and the old woman had said 'gone walkabout' whatever that meant.

Minutes later the smell of pan-fried beef drifted across the yard. Tea! Saliva flooded his mouth. He spat it out and wiped his mouth with the back of his hand. He glanced down at his filthy clothes, finger-combed his dusty hair, and then chewed at the corner of his thumbnail. Should he go straight across or wait until Mrs Macarthur had eaten?

He'd wait – folk were always more amenable after a meal. He prowled round the bunkhouse, killing time, listening out for the rattle and bounce of the fly screen. When it came he took deep breaths between each *sluff sluff* as the black woman shuffled back across the yard. No worries. Mrs Macarthur was old. In any case, there wasn't much she could do, was there?

Jon stepped out into the late-afternoon sunshine. The dying heat prickled his bare arms after the chill of the bunkhouse. To his right a couple of horses leaned against the fence posts. In the silver gum the kookaburra cackled a greeting while the dingo-cross bitch watched from the verandah. He expected the dog to bark; instead, she dragged her swollen belly off the boarding, waddled across to him and sniffed his arm. Her warm tongue rasped the back of his hand as he leaned forward to stroke her. Satisfied she was friendly, he crossed to the fly screen and hammered on the door. He rapped again, pulled it open and stepped inside.

The kitchen stank of stale fat, fried meat and fresh coffee. A rough pine table buried under ketchup bottles, mugs and other kitchen paraphernalia stood in the middle of the room. Over by the window was an old stove coated in grease – he recognised the make – and, next to it, a sink piled high with dirty pots and pans. Flies swarmed around the wire-gauze meat safe, and a gently turning spiral flypaper rotated one way, hung for a moment and spiralled back, the amber surface all but obliterated by dead and dying insects. Next to the meat safe was a wooden cupboard, and next to that a dresser with plates and mugs that didn't match, whilst in the corner stood an ancient, rusting, kerosene refrigerator. The walls, covered in a browny-yellow paint, hadn't been touched in years.

'Anyone home?'

A muffled squawk came from the room on his right. He knocked tentatively, opened the door and blinked, forcing his eyes to adjust to the gloom.

The room smelt of frowsty old woman and stale tobacco smoke. The only light came through the worn curtains covering the window. She was sitting in an overstuffed chair on the far side of the room. His eyes widened as he took in the sulphur-crested cockatoo perched on a wooden stand next to her.

'Can I come in?'

'Looks like you're already in.'

He remembered the hard, rasping voice from earlier. 'I did knock.' He resisted the urge to run and stepped into the room. Take it easy, he thought, speak slow and clear.

She leaned forward in her seat. 'What're you doing at Jarrahlong?'

So that's what the place was called. 'I'm looking for work.'

Her hooded eyes glinted in the half-light. Her brown face crinkled even more when she squinted at him – she was one of the ugliest women he'd ever seen.

'What makes you think I'm looking for ringers?'

He guessed she meant farm hands.

'Where're you from?' she asked.

He racked his brain for places far enough away. 'Leonora...in the–'

'I know where Leonora is. You take me for a fool or something?' Her cold, hard eyes bored into him like Mrs Mainwaring's used to at the children's home in Liverpool. 'And what are you doing hiding in my quarters?'

The Aborigine had told on him!

'How did you get here?'

'Hitched and walked.'

'Hitched all the way more like. I'm half inclined to send Adie into town.'

The muscles in his neck eased. So, Adie was the black. She didn't look like she could make it any distance, never mind into town.

'You a runaway?'

'No.' He'd answered too quickly.

Her blue eyes, faded with age, looked deep into his soul seeking out the truth from the lies. He didn't flinch, after seven years of living with the good Catholic Brothers at Karundah he could cope with anything.

'How old are you?'

'Sixteen.' It was close enough, come December he would be, besides, he was big for his age.

'What can you do?'

He shrugged.

'Can you rope a poddy?'

What the hell was a poddy? He nodded.

'You can, can you? What about sheep?'

He didn't answer.

'You hungry?'

She leaned sideways and grabbed the large brass bell on the side table and jangled it. He saw the shotgun leaning against the chair, the oiled wood and steel glistening in the dim light. He looked into her eyes.

'You never know who might come visiting,' she said.

The fly screen banged, and the black shuffled into the kitchen.

'Steak and eggs and coffee, Belle.'

He kept his eyes fixed on Mrs Macarthur. Belle? So who was Adie? He heard the black woman bang a pan down on the stove, the hiss of gas, the rasp of a match, and the pop as the gas ignited.

'Your family come from Leonora?'

He hesitated, sweat rolling down his sides.

'I don't have no truck with liars, if you can't be telling the truth then keep your mouth shut, understand?' She picked up the carpet-bag at her feet and rummaged through it.

He glanced at the shotgun again. There was no way she'd use it, was there? If she did, they'd never find him. No police around for miles. And what was a runaway Pom to an Aussie anyway? She could have him dumped in the outback leaving his body for the dingoes, she looked mean enough.

Alice pulled out a pair of steel-rimmed spectacles, put them on and scrutinised him for a long moment, then she took them off and replaced them in an embroidered case. 'You'd better go and eat your tea and wash up your plate after, I can't stand a messy kitchen.'

A slab of steak topped with three fried eggs swam on a greasy chipped plate. The meat made his jaws ache but it tasted indescribably good after the stew he was used to, he'd never had food like it, ever, even in England. He wolfed it down, wiped the plate clean with a hunk of bread and drank the bitter, black coffee.

He leaned back in his chair enjoying the bloated feeling, and belched. He'd fallen on his feet – just Mrs Macarthur, Belle, and Adie, another Aborigine, most like. He glanced at the stacked sink – unpleasant tasks were best done with the mind in neutral. He set to and washed the dirty plates, scoured out the pans with steel wool, cleared the table and wiped down the surface with a dish-cloth that had seen better days, then, after one last look around, he knocked on the parlour door and went in leaving the door wide open behind him. He was in. All he needed to do was to be respectful.

'You can't stay in the bunkhouse.'

'I'm a worker, Mrs Macarthur.'

'So, you know my name do you, lad?' Her pale eyes glittered and her mouth was a hard line.

He felt the blood drain from his face – he sounded like a con man – the best he could hope for now was that she'd let him go and say nothing. He stared at the cockatoo picking its foot; he'd head out to the graded road and hitch a ride east. 'Thanks for the grub, missus.' He turned to go.

'It's a long walk to Charlestown,' she said.

'I'm not afraid of walking.'

'Then you're a bloody fool,' she snapped, 'it's a harsh place, the outback; it'll bleach your bones faster 'n lye.'

He averted his eyes not wanting her to see his disappointment.

'There's a spare bed in the lean-to, next to the manager's place, behind the barn.' She waved a mottled hand in the general direction of left. 'I'm between managers at the moment so you needn't try to take any liberties, when I get a manager that's where he'll be living.'

'Thanks Mrs Macar–'

'Alice, my name's Alice. In the morning go and find Adie. Tell him I said you're to help check the sheep; he could do with another pair of hands. And tell him you're to ride Daisy.'

'Righto.'

'What's your name, lad?'

'Jon.'

'Jon what?'

'Just Jon.'

'Okay, Jon Just, now get the hell out of my sight.'

CHAPTER 2

Adie's skin glistened like bitumen. His bush hat was tilted back revealing a deeply lined forehead, grizzled eyebrows, and a broad nose. He sat on an upturned bucket mending tack. He didn't look up.

'Mrs Macarthur says I'm to go with you and check the sheep.'

Adie continued to work the leather before punching a new hole in it with a crude awl fashioned from a piece of iron.

'She says I'm to ride Daisy.'

Adie punched another hole. 'Y'need hat.' He glanced at Jon and then nodded in the direction of the far wall.

Jon selected a hat from off one of the pegs, the leather, black and greasy around the inner rim, smelt worse that a sweaty armpit but only fools went out in the sun without hats.

'Y'ride?'

'A bit,' he lied.

Adie lifted a saddle off the nearest wall peg, walked outside into the morning sun, saddled one of the horses and tossed the reins to Jon.

Jon stared at the animal's backside, at its tail switching at flies. He'd never ridden a horse in his life but he knew how to do it from the pictures – it looked easy enough. He waited until Adie went back into the barn and clambered into the saddle.

Once he was on the mare he knew it was going to be all right, the saddle was high at the back and at the front and it also had raised flanges that pressed against his thighs holding him in place. He felt safe and it was comfortable too, a bit like the moquette easy chair in the parlour back home.

Adie led the way on the other horse, past the jarrahs, following the dried-up creek bed, weaving along the line of scrubby acacia trees, keeping to the shade as much as he could. The bush around the orphanage was nothing like the barren landscape before him – he'd heard the Brothers talk about the drought and knew everywhere was dry in the outback, but not this dry.

Close to the homestead they passed a thin cow with her calf and saw a couple of scrawny kangaroos bounding off into the distance. Later they rode past the rotted carcass of a scrub bull, its sweet stench still tainting the air.

After an hour Jon leaned forward on the pommel, taking the weight on his arms, easing the cramp tightening his thigh muscles, but by the time they reached the billabong the strength in his arms had gone and he just sat slumped in the saddle staring at the scene before him, shocked at the appalling sight – a flock of emaciated sheep and everywhere small mounds of fleece and bone, the remains of carcasses picked clean by crows and dingoes, littering the landscape.

Adie dismounted, flipped the bridle over his horse's head and handed it to Jon. He pushed his way through the mob towards the billabong, the ground beneath him baked hard, the surface crazed like dried orange peel.

In the shimmering heat a dozen or more sheep were bogged down in the rapidly drying quagmire, belly deep in the putrid mud, too weak to extract themselves from their graves. A crow, perched on a sheep's head pecking at the eyes, stopped what it was doing, glanced at Adie and resumed its gory meal oblivious of the animal's feeble struggles. Two more sheep stared out of empty sockets thick with flies.

A few feet away bloated corpses of sheep and a half-grown brumby lay along the water's muddy edge, their legs in the air, crows already squabbling over rotting entrails. The animals closest to the water just stood, dull-eyed, bones sharp under their fleeces, heads down, nosing the dust. The whole area was foetid and thick with flies that rose and fell in dark clouds above the decomposing carcasses and putrid water.

Jon retched while Adie waded into the sticky mud and hauled out those animals that were still alive. He pulled out the hammer he'd tucked under his belt and killed the three blind sheep with a sickening thwack to their skulls.

A weak, half-grown, kangaroo struggled to free itself from the mire, but the effort was too much, it flopped backward, its head unrecognisable in a coating of thick slime. Adie killed it and four more sheep that were too far gone to save, and then he lashed a rope to the back legs of the newly dead animals and dragged their bodies away from the water. Finally, he hauled the putrefying carcasses clear of the sludge leaving trails of white wriggling maggots in the dust.

Nausea rose up Jon's gullet and flooded his mouth with acid, sweat beaded his brow, and then when the second wave came he leaned sideways in the saddle and vomited gouts of undigested breakfast and bitter yellow bile into the dust.

'How long will the water hold out?' Jon asked. They were sitting in the shade of some scrubby gum trees well away from the billabong and the emaciated sheep. The hard packed earth felt like a feather bed after the saddle.

'Water'll last, grazin's the problem, there's nothing left for them to eat. Need to get the mob to the well up at the top end – plenty grazin' there, then after, move 'em on to the two-mile paddock. Reckon that'll see 'em through to the summer rains,' said Adie.

'That's weeks off. Why don't we move them now?'

'No stockmen.'

'How many sheep are there?'

Adie tilted his bush hat back, and scratched his deeply furrowed brow. 'Reckon she got about three thousand left. Lost over a hundred last week, reckon she'll lose more this.'

Jon lay on his back and closed his eyes, the light behind his lids turned red as he tilted his face to the sun. He could hear Adie sorting through his knapsack.

'Y'want pigsnout?'

Jon opened his eyes. 'Pigsnout?'

'It's what Belle calls 'em.' Adie held out a doorstop of a sandwich filled with cold, fried mutton.

Jon took it and chewed on the leather-like meat. Talk of moving the mob bothered him. He didn't want the sheep to die but more men about the place meant trouble. People talked. They'd guess he was a runaway and he'd be sent back to the orphanage to help finish building O'Leary's blasted church and then it could be years before he'd get another chance to return home.

He swallowed the last of his sandwich. Maybe Alice had sent him off with Adie while she got word to O'Leary. He leaned back against a gum tree and scrutinised Adie through half-closed eyes. Was Adie in on it? He couldn't make up his mind; Adie's face was unreadable, so best stay on the alert and at the first sign of trouble head for the main road and hitch a lift to Kalgoorlie.

* * *

Jagged pain stabbed through his thighs while beads of perspiration stung his eyes and blurred his vision as they made their way back to Jarrahlong. Jon ignored Adie's broad grin, ground his teeth and forced his body to ride with the horse, refusing to give in to the agony. By the time they got back to the homestead he didn't care if Scally was waiting for him, or Father O'Leary, all he wanted was a bed.

He slid off the sweat-soaked saddle, clung to the horse for a moment or two, and then staggered across to the railings. He edged like a drunk to the lean-to using the fence for support, flopped onto the cot, and slept.

Hours later a sharp rap on the door woke him and there was Alice silhouetted against the morning sun. Behind her was Belle.

'Twelve hours you've had. Feeling better?' asked Alice.

He blinked sleep out of his eyes.

'You've got guts, I'll give you that.'

Alice stood aside while Belle placed a bucket of water and a carry-all bag next to the bed. The black's muskiness prickled his nose as she leaned over to remove the blanket.

'Take your britches down,' said Alice, 'or shall we cut 'em off?'

He didn't move.

'For God's sake, lad, Belle's had four of her own and I'm old enough to be your grandmother. You haven't got anything we haven't seen.'

Biting his lip against the pain he stripped off his britches and stared, wide-eyed, at his inner thighs, the flesh red raw and weeping where his sweaty skin had chaffed against the saddle.

Alice clicked her tongue. 'It'll hurt, but you've no option unless you want those sores to turn septic.'

The warm water stung like ants. He clamped his jaws together and swore through his teeth as Belle washed away caked dust and sweat and patted his legs dry. Then came the soothing salve, a revolting smelling grey paste that she smeared over his raw flesh with a touch lighter than a mimosa flower.

'Old family remedy,' said Alice as Belle bandaged his thighs using strips of well-worn sheeting, then, when the Aborigine bent to pick up his filthy trousers, Alice pointed to a pile of clean clothes on the floor. 'Put those on and Belle'll wash yours.'

He sat up.

'And your jocks.'

Jon reddened. His clothes stank. He turned his back on them, slipped off his underpants and dragged on the clean ones.

'Looks like you fell on barbed wire.'

He didn't comment. What was the point? No one would believe him. He still felt the humiliation of bending over a table, his trousers round his ankles, while O'Leary beat the shit out of him with a length of bamboo until it split leaving him with his skin in ribbons.

The sun had already set and he could smell cooking as he rubbed sleep out of his eyes. He eased himself off the bed and inspected the ointment-stained bandages. He flexed his legs, gingerly bending each at the knee in turn. Whatever was in the grey salve had killed the pain.

In the kitchen Belle placed a plate of cold mutton and fried potatoes in front of him. He nodded his thanks and chewed the meat slowly, listening out for Alice and her cockatoo. What was she planning? Maybe he should leave, except he wasn't fit the state his legs were in. And, anyway, what was she doing all the way out here living with just a couple of blacks for company?

A short volley of raps interrupted his thoughts. A command! And from the sound of it she was used to getting her own way. In the parlour he noticed the glow of a cigarette first and then the pungent smell. He sneezed.

'Cheroot,' she said, 'I always buy myself a box of 'em for Christmas, want one?'

Jon shook his head.

She dragged on the cigar; the foul-smelling smoke spiralling upwards made her squint. 'Don't just stand there like a yard of pump water, sit yourself down, or perhaps you'd rather stand.'

He sat on the nearest chair, his face an impassive mask.

'From Leonora, you said?' She peered at him. 'Hate me, do you, lad! Well, you can't afford the luxury; I'm all that stands between you and those Catholic Brothers. It's lucky for you I'm not partial to Catholics, or any other denomination come to that, but I don't hate them so much as to compromise my own position.'

She knew where he was from! He avoided her eyes and stared at a chessboard half hidden beneath a pile of magazines. Was she telling him to go? It sounded like it. He didn't want to stay anyway.

She caught his eye. 'You can have free board and lodge, but I'm not paying a penny until I see what you can do. Take it or leave it.'

CHAPTER 3

The next morning Jon hobbled, stiff-legged, across to the bungalow for breakfast. He wolfed down the food Belle had cooked for him, washed up and knocked on the parlour door.

'Come in,' came Alice's voice.

He opened the door and stepped into the room.

Alice dropped the magazine she was reading and tossed him a key – he had to stretch to catch it and swore under his breath.

'Reckon it'll take a week for those sores to heal and, as I said, I'm not running a charitable institution so you can start by getting the place spruced up a bit. There's red-oxide paint and brushes in the store and when it gets too hot to work on the bunk-house iron you can creosote the insides of the shearing shed, and in your spare time repair the fences, they're looking a bit crook.' She paused for breath. 'Go on then, lad, get on with it, you're wasting my time hanging around like a dag on a sheep's bum, time's money, and shut the door after you.'

At the bottom of the verandah steps he stood for a moment, his back to the bungalow, the key Alice had given him heavy in his hand. He'd wanted to fling it at her feet, tell her to go to hell, but that's what she'd expected, instead he'd bitten back his retort. Now the hairs on the back of his neck were prickling, she was watching him, he could feel her gimlet eyes boring into his back waiting for him to quit.

He straightened his shoulders, he was damned if he'd give her the satisfaction. He gritted his teeth, blocking the pain in his chapped thighs and headed across to the store.

The key screeched against the metal as he rammed it into the rusting padlock, a sharp twist and he felt the lock give. The wooden door shrieked as he yanked it open. He picked up a screwdriver, felt its weight and imagined it doing damage until the white-hot rage subsided. As soon as his legs were healed he'd leave and find some of those gold nuggets Freddie Fitzpatrick and

Binky Brent had talked about.

On the shelf were half a dozen rusting tins with labels so faded it was impossible to make out the words. He flipped the nearest tin from the shelf and prised off the lid, broke the leathery skin in a dozen places and peeled it back. The oxide paint gleamed glossy red and the colour reminded him of his sister's hair.

Kathy would be twelve now. Would they recognise each other after so long apart? She'd been five when he last saw her, tears streaming down her cheeks, her fingers in her mouth, snot dripping off her chin. He'd promised his dying mother that he'd look after her and he hadn't. He'd been too carried away by the excitement of going to Australia to realise Kathy wasn't on the emigration list. Well, God had punished him for his selfishness, he'd put him in the care of the good Catholic Brothers at Karundah.

He jabbed at the viscous paint and swore. He'd been a fool to listen to the superintendent at the children's home when he spoke of golden opportunities in Australia, of good food, sun and healthy outdoor living and the chance to make something of himself, but he'd been a kid then, only eight years old, and by the time he knew the truth of it he was nine thousand miles away from home and trapped. He dragged the screwdriver round and round in the paint, loosening it, until the pain in his chest eased.

Over the next five days he painted the bunkhouse corrugated-iron roof, creosoted the shearing shed and mended fencing. There was no shortage of tools and equipment, just the men to use them. There was even an old utility truck with a two-seater cab, and an older flatbed lorry like Scally's, but with a broken back spring, mouldering in a stock shed.

'Are you staying?' Alice asked when he'd completed the tasks, her pale eyes never leaving his face.

'What you paying?'

'What d'you want the money for?'

'My passage home to England.'

Her eyes glinted as she studied his deadpan face. 'I'll pay you a jackaroo's wage, but you'll have to earn it. The boys'll be back any day, when they are you're to go with them and move the mob up to the top end before I lose the lot. You up to it?'

'When do I get my pay?'

'End of next month.' The tone left no room for argument. 'Well?'

He hesitated. Eight weeks! Could he wait that long? His mind slid to the utility truck in the shed, maybe it was a runner. He nodded.

'And you listen to what Adie says, he might be black but there's nothing Adie doesn't know about stock…and another thing.'

'What?'

'You're to come over Friday evenings for a game of chess.'

'But I'm no good.'

'You'll improve. We start after tea tomorrow, six sharp.'

On Alice's side of the table was a cut-glass tumbler with two fingers of dark, amber liquid, next to the chessboard, on his side, a bottle of beer and a bottle opener. The beer fizzed and frothed, and the gassy, malty smell reminded him of Saturday nights, his dad home from the pub.

He moved his pawn.

'How long're you planning on staying?' asked Alice.

'Depends,' he lied. No point in letting her know his plans.

'On?' She moved her knight. 'What's so special about England anyway? It's overcrowded, blitzed to hell and back, then there's rationing, not to mention the cold, wet winters, you'd be better off carving a new life for yourself here. What's your name, lad, your real name?'

'Cadwallader.'

'Fancy name for a Pom.' She studied his face for a moment. 'So, what're you doing out here if you hate the place so much?'

'It was supposed to be a better life. And they told us we could go home if we didn't like it.'

'Quitter, eh?'

'No.'

'Going gets tough and you run away,' she commented. 'You're a bigger fool than I thought not seeing an opportunity when one's staring you in the face.'

He gazed sightlessly at the chessboard. She sounded just like Father O'Leary. He was always going on about opportunity, not that there'd be any opportunities for Freddie Fitzpatrick – the sarcastic, sadistic slave-driver O'Leary had seen to that.

He glanced at Alice, saw the hard lines running down to the corners of her mouth and her thin lips pressed together in concentration. He'd made a mistake stopping off at Jarrahlong, the sooner he moved on the better. 'Is it all right if I take a look at the utility truck?'

'Mechanically minded, are you?'

'Sort of.' He'd spent enough time helping Brother Francis with the orphanage car to know the basics and driving shouldn't be too difficult.

'You don't stand a chance, lad, it hasn't run in years.'

Jon scowled. She was short-staffed and determined to keep him, and he needed the money.

Alice didn't speak for the next hour as they battled over the chessboard but he knew he was no match for the sharp-eyed old woman. He watched her considering her next move while idly stroking the cockatoo's chest feathers and caught the slight smile creasing her cheeks. He looked back at the board and saw his mistake.

'Checkmate,' she said, leaning back in her seat. 'The ute manual's on the shelf next to the stock magazines. You'd better take a couple of those too. In your own time, mind. Not mine.'

Jon rose at dawn over the next two days and worked through till midday, until it became too hot to work on the iron, and then he collected his sandwich from Belle and took it out to the shed.

He tried starting the engine. Nothing, not even a cough! He began with the basics just as Brother Francis had taught him to do. He cleaned the engine first and then the spark plugs, he topped up the battery, checked the oil, filled up the radiator, put air in the tyres, and petrol in the tank – once it was running again he'd be off. Alice could look after her own sheep.

He wiped his hands clean and switched on the ignition, grabbed the starting handle and fed it through the hole in the bumper into the engine. He muttered three Hail Marys, crossed himself and then gave a sharp turn on the starting handle.

Nothing!

He turned it again, and again.

Still nothing!

He looked under the bonnet, checked the spark plugs, whacked the carburettor with a spanner and gave the starting handle another yank.

Sweat dripped off his chin. He opened the shed doors wider to pick up the breeze and saw three black stockmen he hadn't seen before sitting on the bunkhouse steps taking a smoko and watching him from beneath their greasy bush hats – Adie's mates, most like, maybe they'd help to push-start it.

He cranked the engine over a few more times getting hotter and sweatier and shorter tempered by the minute. Suddenly the engine coughed, spluttered for a moment and died.

He punched the air, tweaked the carburettor, said another Hail Mary and yanked the starting handle upward in a single sharp jerk.

The engine fired.

He dashed round to the cab and eased his foot onto the accelerator, gentling the engine, smoothing out the splutter, praying that it wouldn't die on him.

Adie strode into the shed and leaned on the off-side mudguard. 'Missus Macarthur wants a word,' he said.

Jon ignored him. Couldn't Adie see he was busy? Alice's bell jangled – he heard the insistent ringing over the sound of the engine – she could wait a moment, he was damned if he was going to drop everything the minute she rang her blasted bell. As Adie left him the engine coughed again and then died.

Jon hammered at the steering wheel with his fist and swore, the bloody bell still clanging in his ears. He got out of the truck, swore again, and kicked at a tyre. What did she want now? He wiped his brow and hands on an oily rag as he crossed the yard behind Adie.

'Mick back yet?' she asked before Adie's foot touched the first step.

'His old man's sick, he's taking him back to ancestor place. Reckon he'll be gone a while.'

'So, who have we got?'

'Just Jimmi, Sammo and Curly.'

'They'll have to do.' She thumped the floor with her stick. 'Tucker, now, Belle, the boys are back out,' she shouted loud enough for the Aborigine to hear and then she turned her attention to Jon. 'Saddle up Daisy.'

He flung the oily rag at her feet and pointed back to the shed. 'But I've just–'

'Don't you *just* me, lad. I've fifty sheep dying every day, they need moving to fresh pasture and that's what I'm paying you to do not tinker with a clapped-out ute, now get out of my sight and take that mucky rag with you.' The cold stare didn't waver.

He swept up the oily cloth and stalked across the yard ignoring the black stockmen enjoying their break. They'd be gone days shifting stinking, dying sheep in the sweltering heat. Stupid time to be going out now anyway, they wouldn't even get to the billabong before nightfall, was she expecting them to start moving the mob in the dark? He kicked out at one of Alice's chooks scattering the lot of them. All he'd needed was a few more minutes; a couple more turns on the handle would have got the ute going.

Adie led the way while Jon followed at the rear on Daisy. He glowered at the four ahead of him and at their horses kicking up dust – he had better things to do with his time than spending days with a bunch of blacks driving a flock of stupid sheep across the outback.

The sweet, sickly stench of death hung in the air long before they could see or hear the animals. The men and the station dogs rounded up the sheep and herded them together. Adie circled his horse around and rode over to Jon. 'You folla mob,' he said, and held out his hammer.

Jon stared at the ugly, stained head, the handle worn smooth from use, not wanting to believe what was expected of him.

'Here.' Adie thrust the hammer into his hand and rode off towards the others.

Jon reined Daisy back, he wouldn't do it; he'd never killed anything in his life. Ahead of him the sheep, covering the ground like a dirty blanket, shambled west stirring up a cloud of red dust. Lit by the dying rays of the sun it seemed as if the whole mob was heading into hell.

Jon looked around him in despair, already the first of the stragglers had collapsed. Should he stay or head back to the homestead and tell Alice what she could do with her job? The sun dropped to the horizon, the decision made for him. 'Sod you!' he yelled after Adie, the words swallowed up in the dry air. He kicked Daisy's flanks and walked her over to the dying animal, a bag of skin and bones, its legs folded under, its head resting in the dust.

He dismounted and led Daisy a short distance from the sheep. He took his time wrapping the bridle around a sprout of mallee scrub, conscious of the heavy hammer rubbing against his thigh, trying to recall what Adie had done at the billabong. One swift blow – that was all it took. He approached the ewe. Sick to the stomach he lifted the hammer above his shoulder and brought it down on the animal's head. It grunted as the hammer made contact; the startled eyes stared at him.

Anger, horror and revulsion engulfed him, he couldn't even put it out of its misery properly – he had to finish the job and there must be no mistake. He lifted the hammer higher and brought it down with all his weight behind it. The steel head sank into the skull, the animal shuddered and slumped; he saw the blood and brain on the metal and cursed Alice Macarthur.

As soon as the moon came up and flooded the land with light they pushed the mob hard, the muffled drumming of hooves drowning out other night-time noises. At three in the morning they reached the top end. The windmill, standing sentinel over holding tanks, gleamed in the moonlight. Beneath its silver skeleton stronger sheep jostled for water while the weak waited. For speed the stockmen filled and refilled the free-standing troughs and then drove the sheep out to pasture. Finally, they saw to the horses and the dogs, unrolled their swags and slept.

Next morning he awoke to the smell of woodsmoke and breakfast. Sammo leaned over the cast-iron oven suspended over the fire testing the damper with a stick. A billy hung from another stick gently stewing the tea. The rocky overhang, blackened by earlier campfires, shaded them from the sun. Chilled to the bone Jon rolled out from under his blanket, headed to the nearest trough and sluiced off the last night's dust. He straightened up and looked across the plain at the grazing sheep – only the dead and the dying remained close by already food for crows.

He ate his portion of damper and dried meat and sat back against the rock with his battered enamel mug cradled in his hands as he studied Jimmi, Sammo and Curly from over the rim.

There'd been no blacks at Karundah, but plenty in Liverpool, West Indian mostly. One of his best friends, Albert White, was black, his dad drove a tram; they'd come over from Jamaica when Al was a nipper. Then there were the West Africans from off the boats, and the Chinese, but none of them looked like these fellas.

He wondered whether Sammo and Jimmi were brothers; they had the same blue-black skin, furrowed brows, broad noses, and wide mouths. Sammo was the elder and the stockier of the two, his khaki shirt and cord breeches fitted where they touched, moulding his muscular frame. Jimmi was taller, more grizzled, and slimmer, and he sported a close-clipped beard, his teeth were brown and a missing front tooth gave him a lop-sided look – he could have been anything from twenty-five to forty-five.

Curly caught his eye and grinned, his gappy front teeth gleamed. 'Family,' he said, nodding in Sammo and Jimmi's direction. He flung his tea dregs into the ash as he stood.

Sammo spoke to Curly in a language Jon didn't understand and soon after Curly untied the boomerang and spear lashed to his saddle and disappeared over the ridge into the valley beyond. Overhead the windmill clanked and ticked in the breeze lifting the water into the holding tanks which, in turn, gravity fed the permanent troughs through the network of iron pipework. The rest of them spent the morning checking the equipment and the sheep out on the plain, then they returned to camp, and Curly, as the sun reached its zenith.

A four-foot-long charred spike of something peculiar looking straddled the campfire.

'Roo tail,' said Curly. A keyboard grin lit up his face when he saw Jon's expression. He smacked his lips. 'Good bush tucker.'

Jon's stomach lurched. Where was the rest of the animal? He'd have preferred roo steak. Curly tipped out fresh damper on a flat stone, hacked the roo tail into portions and handed Jon a middle bit.

It tasted of charred meat and not much else. He spat out the bones and gristly bits for the dogs and filled up on damper.

'Y'swim?' asked Curly after they'd eaten.

They left the others sleeping off tucker in the shade of an old eucalyptus tree, their heads resting on their saddles, hats tilted over their noses. Curly led the way through the mallee and onto higher ground. Once above the scrub line the going was easier, they walked for an hour, until they reached a quartz outcrop. Curly scrambled up the steep sides like a rock wallaby and stood on the top, his slim black shape silhouetted against a cobalt sky. Jon followed, hauling himself up the stacked rocks layered like birthday cake, glad of the regular hand and foot holds afforded by the strata, until he stood next to Curly.

Below them, in a narrow gorge, lay a pool of still, green water. Weeping gum trees grew out of the rock and arched over, their delicate fronds like trailing ribbons floating on its smooth surface. Snaking downwards a narrow path, half buried in scree, disappeared between thin brush. The sun beat down on them; heat bounced off the rock face; not a breath of wind disturbed the air or the corellas dozing in the ghost gums. Suddenly, Curly whooped and skittered helter-skelter down the slope at break-neck speed. The corellas rose like handkerchiefs tossed in the air, shrieking their protest as Jon followed behind, slithering and sliding on his backside, skinning his shins on jagged rocks as he careered after the Aborigine.

At the bottom Curly stood waiting for him, stark naked, his wire-thin bronzed body gleaming in the afternoon sun. Jon joined him on a rocky outcrop and looked down into the green depths. Curly dived in one smooth, sleek movement, his body as curved and streamlined as a platypus. Jon stripped off, stood on the lip of the boulder for a moment, pinched his nose, and jumped, feet first, into the pool.

The water, ice-cold and satin-smooth, closed over his head. Air bubbles tickled his cheeks. His feet touched the bottom and he pushed off, cork-screwing to the surface in a spluttering shower of crystal droplets.

'How did you find this place?' gasped Jon.

'It's me back yard, mate.'

Jon's teeth chattered. He trod water to warm up.

'Where y'from?' asked Curly.

'Liverpool and my backyard ain't no bigger than this place.'

Curly's arm arced round taking in the whole gorge. 'Cor, mate, how d'y'breathe?'

'No. This.' Jon slapped the surface of the pool.

Curly grinned, his teeth a white slash in his black face. 'Nah, mate, y'havin' me on.'

Would Curly understand the word 'terrace'? He hadn't seen any in Australia, only bungalows, and shanty homesteads.

'This place y' live in, called Liver?'

'Liverpool.'

'Like Charlestown?'

Jon laughed. 'Nah! Liverpool's huge, bigger 'n Fremantle.'

He floated on his back, eyes closed to the bright sky, remembering the city, its docks with the cargo boats and liners, the Liver Building with its soot-streaked Liver birds, the stone lions in front of St George's Hall, the cinema queues for the Saturday matinée, and the police wearing white gloves directing traffic on Church Street, and the noise, and the bustle, and the trams, and the terraced streets where he played footie with his friends.

'This's a bonzer place, mate. Plenty bush tucker,' said Curly.

Jon grinned, imagining Gran trying to cook roo tail in the oven.

'Y'stayin' long?'

'Nah, I'm heading for Kalgoorlie.' He rolled over onto his belly and swam lazily to the edge of the pool, although maybe he'd be better off staying a while, give O'Leary and the others time to forget about him. Alice wouldn't say anything. She needed an extra pair of hands, and besides, it couldn't get any worse. There'd be no more dying now the sheep had grazing and water. As he saw it there were worse places to hole up and with luck he'd get the utility up and running in no time.

Jon pulled himself out of the water; after seven years a few weeks wouldn't make much difference and by then they'd think he was long gone. He sat on a rock and dabbled a toe in the water. At Jarrahlong he'd got a bed, food in his belly and Alice said she'd pay him. He could stick the place, and Alice, for another couple of months.

He looked down at Curly and grinned. 'You're right, mate, it's a bonzer place.'

CHAPTER 4

Jon leaned on the verandah rail next to Alice watching the bitch play with her three pups. The last puppies he'd seen were black and tan mongrels in St John's market when he was eight and Mam was still alive. He'd wanted one, but, as Mam said, you can't feed a dog on thin air.

The pups rolled in the dust and fought over their mother's tail; they chewed her ears and each other until the game turned rough and the dog pup lost his temper. He bounced up and down, growling and snapping at the loose skin on his mother's neck with his needle-sharp teeth, but the bitch wasn't having it; she rolled him over in the dust and kept rolling him over until he was exhausted, then, when he'd given up, she turned him onto his back and topped and tailed him. It was a sight to see.

Alice sipped her tea. 'They're blue heelers. Best cattle dogs this side of the black stump – half Scottish collie and half dingo with a bit of Dalmatian and a bit of kelpie thrown in for good measure. They're on the big side for working the sheep but they'll work till they drop, and they're loyal.' She glanced at him. 'You want the dog pup or one of the bitches?'

He hadn't been angling for a dog, a dog meant ties, and anyway he was out of the place as soon as he could fix the ute; he'd stayed too long already, eight weeks, and was getting too comfortable. It was time to leave. He didn't answer.

'Find anything interesting in those magazines?'

'Adverts for improving the stock.'

'You can't improve on Merinos for this country. What else?'

'Artesian wells.'

'Can't afford to drill.'

'You could keep more sheep.'

Water hadn't been a problem at Karundah. Only last year they'd spent the autumn building a dam across the creek to conserve water for the farm school. 'You could dam the creek at Cranston Gap.'

'Oh aye! Know about damming do you?'

Seven years of hard graft, blasting stone at the quarry, loading it onto trucks, carting it, unloading it and then building with it qualified him. The administration block, and the kitchen had been built before he arrived, but then there'd been the dormitories, the farm buildings, and after that O'Leary's bloody church to build. He'd never forget the stench of dynamite, the taste of chalk dust, and the raw fingers and ragged nails torn to shreds from lifting heavy rocks, and after, his bare feet burned by the cement as they built with the stone they had quarried. 'You'll need dynamite. Blow up a bit of the rock on the ridge overlooking the creek, cart it down and build your dam.'

'I'll think about it.'

'How big's the station?'

'Nine hundred and fifty thousand acres, or thereabouts.'

Jon whistled.

'There are bigger. Some of the stations up in the Northern Territory are two or three million acres, but here it's marginal land; most of it isn't worth having. You've seen for yourself what happens in a drought. We were lucky to keep two or three thousand alive in the worst years, but Jack, my husband, made a go of it, he'd drive the stock out to fresh grazing, then ferry water out to them with the flatbed.'

Jack must have died years ago if the dust on the lorry was anything to go by, so why didn't she sell up and move into town and live a normal life? What was keeping her at Jarrahlong?

'I've ordered a new battery.'

A battery would do the trick – he could be away from the place in days. The significance of Alice's words sank in. He glanced across at her.

'Radio transmitter and receiver; have to keep in touch somehow.' The creases round her eyes deepened.

'But you've no—'

'Mast? It blew down so Jack nailed it to the gum tree.'

Jon leaned forward and saw the cable. What else had he missed?

'I've a delivery due. You'd better say you're a relative. I'll tell Ed you're from home and that you're helping out for a few months.'

Scally! Scally would recognise him straight off.

'What's the matter, lad? You look like you've eaten something that doesn't agree with you.'

Jon swallowed the saliva flooding his mouth.

'Ed owes me. He won't say anything if I tell him not to,' said Alice. 'And if anyone else asks you questions you can say you're Walter's grandson. What was your father's name?'

'James,' he said, remembering the peroxide blonde his dad had run off with just after Mam got sick.

'James then, better keep it simple,' said Alice.

Gerry Worrall, a buffalo of a fella with a ruddy complexion and sour breath, delivered the dry goods, cooking fat, and kerosene a couple of days later. He stood, one foot on the lowest verandah step, waiting to be introduced.

'Meet Walter's grandson, Jon,' said Alice.

'Walter?'

'Jack's brother. You won't remember. He came out to stay with us once, a couple of years after we moved here, 1910 or thereabouts, if my memory serves.'

Gerry didn't reply. His eyes narrowed and it wasn't against the glare. He swept Jon, top to bottom and bottom up. 'So, y're a Pom are ya, lad?'

'That's about it,' said Jon, listening for clues. Did he know the man?

Jimmi ambled over and shouldered the heavy black battery Gerry had on the truck. Gerry's lip curled in distaste; he hawked up phlegm and spat it out at Jimmi's feet. 'Don't know why y'put up with them buggers, Alice. Y'niver know what the black bastards is thinking.'

Jon avoided Jimmi's eyes, conscious of the heat in his cheeks. The Aborigine adjusted the position of the battery. Jon expected him to lob it at Gerry's head, it was what he deserved; instead, Jimmi turned on his heels and headed back to the outbuildings.

'Vermin,' said Gerry, 'that's what they is, vermin.'

'Any post?' asked Alice.

'Nope, just a note from Rachel.' He fished in his trouser pocket and handed over a dog-eared postcard. 'Scal's gone and busted his leg unloading metal piping, got careless, he did. Les's in a pig of a mood about it, he had to get his backside out of the office and do a bit of work for a change. How's things here, Alice? Y'managing a'right?'

'I'm fine, Gerry.'

Gerry swung his bulk around towards Jon and hitched his britches over his beer gut. 'Y'look out for her and don't tek no strife from off them blackfellas. They give y'grief y'know where to find me. Right?'

'Right.'

'Tea?' asked Alice.

'Wouldn't say no to a beer.'

Alice thumped her stick on the verandah. 'Belle, fetch a beer,' she called over her shoulder. She turned back to Jon. 'There's a letter for posting in the parlour, mind getting it?'

The letter lay on the side table addressed in a neat copperplate hand. He flipped the envelope over and read the address, Mrs B. M. Morton, Thornwood Farm, South Sutton, Lincolnshire, England. Was she Alice's sister or a friend? He turned and held it up towards the light and caught a glimpse of Belle in the kitchen spitting into an open bottle of beer.

'Hope you don't do that to mine, Belle.'

She grinned. 'Nah, only nasty buggers.'

Alice stood in the shed doorway leaning on her stick, listening to Jon turning over the engine. The new battery hadn't made any difference, the truck still wouldn't start.

'I'll get Ed to tow you into Charlestown. Wes'll fix it.'

'Wes?'

'Wesley Chapman. He runs a garage business out of a quarter-section of the old shearing shed on the edge of town. Born with a spanner in his hand, was Wes.' She crossed to the truck and ran her hand over the chrome wing mirror. 'I remember the day we bought it. Wool was selling at a premium and we paid for it in pound notes.' She chuckled to herself. 'We were like dogs with two tails driving back from Perth.'

He wished she'd shut up about buying the damn vehicle. The problem was getting it fixed. He closed the bonnet and secured it. 'Can't Adie take it?'

'They won't be looking for you this far out,' she said. 'They'll think you've gone to Perth or Fremantle. No one in their right mind would head for Charlestown, there's nothing out this way except the ranges and the desert unless you're heading for the goldfields out Kalgoorlie way.' She watched him wipe his hands on a bit of rag. 'Was it that bad?'

Jon looked up. Her hooded eyes were slits as she squinted at him. He didn't want to go down that road. He returned her stare. What did she want from him apart from a bit of company? Then there was her offer of a pup. He couldn't work her out.

Suddenly she started to laugh. 'Don't fool yourself lad, you're not indispensable.'

Alice sent for him a few days later. Scally was sitting on the verandah next to her, smoking.

Jon's stomach tensed, he kept his gaze level and his face blank. Alice wouldn't turn him in, she needed stockmen.

Scally frowned as he drew on his cigarette. 'Didn't realise y'd lose yer marbles so young, Alice.'

'Adie rates him.'

'That makes him right?' Scally leaned sideways in his seat and looked at Jon full on. 'Tanned up pretty quick for a Pom, ain't ya?'

Jon ignored the sarcasm and glared at the pair of them discussing him as if he wasn't there, treating him like shit, like it was a game. He reached out to stroke the cockatoo. It bit him. Blood welled up and dripped on the floor.

'That bird never was no good with strangers, was he, Alice?'

'Jon's here to work and he's not bad at chess either.'

'Is that so?'

'Aye, it is,' snapped Alice. 'I want him and the ute back in one piece, so you better look after him for me.'

Scally drew on his cigarette again and the end glowed like a rat's eye. 'Aye, I'll take care of him for ya, Alice.'

CHAPTER 5

Wes's garage was as Alice had described it. Rusted corrugated iron fronted the building, the peeling white paint stating the owner's name was barely legible, even in bright sunlight. Faded posters advertising oil, a dance in Merredin, and various quick-fix remedies clung to the walls like geckos. Two battered red and cream petrol pumps stood to attention in front of the open double doors, whilst out the back sprawled a collection of partially cannibalised lorries, utility trucks and trailers.

Scally parked, unhitched the towing rope, dropped his cigarette butt on the forecourt, crushed it with his boot and entered the garage. He squatted down and spoke to the feet sticking out from under a car.

Wes, a heavily built sixty-year-old, pushed himself out from under the engine and rolled to his feet. He stretched his back, and then extended a hand the size of a dinner plate. 'Scal says you're from Liverpool,' he said as they shook hands. 'I remember when your granddad visited, back in the early days.' He glanced across the yard to Alice's utility truck that they'd towed into town. 'What's wrong with it?'

'Dunno, it won't go,' said Jon.

'Probably needs a good clean. Let's roll it on the ramp and I'll take a look, and then you can make yourself useful and brew up a tea. There's a tin of condensed milk on the side.'

By the time Jon made the tea Wes had the bonnet up and the carburettor lid off.

'Reckon the whole banshee's clogged up with residue,' he said. 'The petrol's evaporated, left a sticky mess everywhere – got to clean out the whole system if we want to get her running.' He fiddled with a length of pipe and washed it in a petrol bath. 'It should be ready midday tomorrow.'

Scally finished his tea and threw the dregs in the dust. 'Get yer gear, lad. See ya, Wes.'

Jon got into the passenger's seat. At the crossroads they turned off the main street into a side road lined with four small square bungalows, each constructed of wood on a brick base with corrugated-iron roofs and wide verandahs. They parked in front of the last bungalow in the row. Scally got out, strode up the path and yanked open the fly-screen so it bashed against the wall.

'Y'coming or not?' he yelled.

Blue gingham curtains framed the small window behind the stone sink and the same fabric hid the space beneath the worktops. A hand-knotted rug in blue, similar to the ones Gran made from rags, softened the scrubbed boards, and in the middle of the room was a square table with two ancient bentwood chairs. The whole place smelt of carbolic soap and bleach. Jon kept his expression neutral – Scally didn't strike him as the gingham type.

Scally disappeared through the other door. Minutes later he returned with a rolled-up kapok mattress and an old army blanket.

'Let's get one thing straight, lad. You take advantage of Alice and I'll have ya and no mistake, y'understand?'

Jon nodded. There was no point in telling rat-face that Alice was the one taking advantage.

'Y'can bed down on the verandah. It'll be better than y're used to wain't it?' He tossed the bedding at Jon.

Jon ignored the jibe, dumped the bedding on the verandah and returned to the kitchen.

'Here,' Scally fished in his back pocket and pulled out a battered brown-leather wallet. The button popped when he flipped it open. He counted out five Australian one-pound notes and dropped them on the table.

'I don't want your money,' said Jon.

'It ain't mine, y'big galah. Alice said y're to have it for some new britches. And there's no point in getting any ideas, it's an advance on y'pay.' He pocketed his wallet and left the room.

Jon picked up the notes and held them to his nose breathing in the scent – his first wages.

Scally returned wearing clean trousers and a check shirt, his black curly hair dripping water onto his shoulders. He gestured with his thumb. 'There's a pump out back.'

Jon picked up his bag and went through the inner door into a short passage. On the left was the parlour with a sofa and an easy chair with an antimacassar and, on the floor, a flowery rug. On the right were two closed doors. Bedrooms? Ahead, a half-glazed door led into the back yard.

He stepped onto a crazy-paving path that led down the centre of the yard to the dunny in the far corner. To the left, on a patch of hard standing, was a hand pump with a large enamel bucket catching the drips and next to that was a bench with a chipped china bowl. On the far fence a willy-wagtail watched for flies, darting here and there when it spotted one.

Jon stripped to the waist and washed. Indoors he could hear a kettle whistling. Did Scally owe Alice money or did she have some other hold over him? Whatever it was, it was enough to keep Scally quiet and give him a bed for the night. He took a deep breath and opened the kitchen door.

The young woman standing next to the sink turned towards him. 'Hello! You must be Jon. I'm Rachel.'

He noticed her breasts, the way the fabric stretched over them, moulding them, like Rita Hayworth's. Her brown curly hair framed a pretty face and her grey eyes sparkled with amusement – she was laughing at him. He blushed.

'Haven't you seen a girl before?'

'Course I have.'

'You weren't expecting one, that it?'

Was she Scally's wife?

'Sit down. You want a drink?'

She reached up and took a glass from off the shelf above the draining board. 'Dad'll be back soon. He always goes for a couple of beers before tea.'

She was Scally's daughter!

She leaned across the table and placed a glass of lemon squash in front of him and he got a whiff of Lifebuoy soap. She returned to the sink and the pan she was scrubbing. Her bottom jiggled below the apron bow. The blush crept up his neck again and he looked away.

'Where're you from?'

'What?'

'Where're you from?' she asked over her shoulder. 'Dad said you're visiting from England.'

'Liverpool.' At least he didn't have to lie about where he came from.

'We have family in England. The Watsons, they live near Manchester, maybe you know them?'

Jon stared at her bottom.

'It's not that far from Liverpool, is it? It's practically down the road…Dad said.'

'Manchester's a big place, bigger than Perth.'
'So, you don't know them then?' She tipped tinned potatoes into the pan and put them on to boil. 'Hope you like cold mutton.' She made herself a drink and sat opposite him. 'Tell me about England. It's a place I'd like to visit one day.'
The squash tasted strange, but drinking it gave him time to think.
'Mum's grandparents emigrated when her father was twelve. She always talked about going home...Dad worked all hours to get the money together so we could go, but Mum was taken sick, and then she died...so we didn't.'
'I'm sorry.'
'No need,' she said, 'it was a long time ago. I was only four so I don't remember it.'
The pan lid lifted. Cloudy water bubbled, then hissed and spat like a cat when it dribbled onto the hot-plate. Rachel got up and turned the heat down. She tilted the lid to let the steam escape. 'There's only me and Dad now. What about you?'
'A sister, Kathleen.'
'What about your mum?'
'She's dead.'
'So, you're just like me then?'
His glance slid over her breasts again. Maybe he shouldn't have mentioned Kathy.
'What do you think of Australia?'
'What?'
'Australia.'
He hesitated. He could hardly tell her he hated the place. 'It's hotter, dustier, more flies.'
'You're not wrong there.'
The door opened and Scally lurched into the room.
'Where's me tea?'
'It'll be ready in a tick, Dad.' Rachel jumped up, opened a tin of carrots, put them on to heat and strained the potatoes.
Scally sat down at the table and scowled. 'Suppose you're used to silver plate and bone china, y'being a member of the Macarthur clan an' all.'
Jon didn't reply; it was safest. It had been the same with his father when he'd had a drink or two.
'An' y'can keep yer eyes to yerself. My Rachel don't mix with the likes of you.'
'Dad!'
'Don't you *Dad* me. I know what's best for ya and this young

pup is trouble, trying to get his feet under Alice's table.'

'Don't be daft, Dad.'

Jon smiled. Alice didn't have anything he wanted.

Scally sprang to his feet. He grabbed Jon's shirt and pulled him forward until their faces were only inches apart. Scally's beery breath wafted over him.

'Y'can wipe that smirk off y'face, lad. I've got yer measure. Y'treat Alice bad and y've me to answer to. Got it?' He thrust Jon away and flopped back onto his seat.

Shocked, Jon sank back onto his chair avoiding Rachel's glance, conscious that his face was scarlet.

They ate the rest of the meal in silence. Afterwards, Scally went out onto the verandah with his tea and tobacco and left them to clear away the pots.

Rachel flung him a tea towel. 'Don't take any notice of Dad. He's soft as butter.' She caught Jon's look and laughed. 'The crockery goes behind the curtain next to the cooker, and the cutlery in the right-hand drawer in the dresser.'

He stacked the mugs and plates and then put the knives into the right compartment. A faded photograph of a dark-haired woman smiled at him out of a cheap wooden frame.

'It's Dad's favourite, not that we've got that many photographs of her.'

She looked like a film star. She could have done better than the tight-lipped, rat-faced bastard she'd ended up with, but, there and again, Mam married Dad and they didn't come any worse than him either. 'What did your mum die of?'

'Tuberculosis.'

He'd heard gran talk about sanatoriums where everyone slept in cold wards with the windows wide open, even in winter. People talked about the white death like they did about cancer, in hushed tones.

'She was only twenty-four when she died. She had the best treatment, private and all, but it was no good, she had the galloping consumption.'

'Must have cost a packet,' said Jon.

'Alice paid. Dad wasn't happy, but he was desperate.'

'Alice family?'

'No, just a friend.' She smiled. 'It's nice, you visiting. She gets lonely with only blacks for company, but she won't come and stay.'

Scally opened the door and stepped back into the kitchen. He glared at Jon as he dumped his empty mug on the draining board. 'Bedtime, Rachel, I've an early start in the morning.'

Later, Jon lay on the lumpy mattress, his feet next to the bungalow wall and his head near the edge of the verandah. He hadn't seen a girl for seven years, not since he'd arrived at Karundah. Pity she was Scally's daughter. Was Kathy as pretty? He couldn't imagine his sister grown up. He stared at the Southern Cross high above him, waiting for sleep.

When he first arrived in Australia the stars were a comfort. He imagined Gran looking at the same stars, the ones she'd shown him in the night sky – the Great Bear, the Little Bear, Orion's Belt and the Pole Star. Then Father William spoilt it when he told him the constellations in the Southern Hemisphere weren't all the same as the ones back home in Liverpool. He'd stopped believing in God for a while and he still had his doubts. Father William had doubts too. The memory of the priest's body hanging from a cross-beam troubled him as he drifted off into uneasy sleep.

Scally woke him at seven. Breakfast was a bowl of cereal and a mug of strong tea. Out back he could hear a wireless playing Glen Miller. Maybe in a few years, when Kathleen was old enough, they'd emigrate to Pennsylvania, or maybe Chattanooga, wherever that was.

'Wes reckoned the ute'll be ready later. Y'know y'way back, don't ya?' Scally's dark eyes glittered with hostility. 'Take it y'can drive?'

'Yes.' It couldn't be that difficult.

'Right then, Rachel will teck you to the store and fix y'up with britches, then y'go straight to Wes's. Righto?'

'Right,' muttered Jon as they set off for Simpson's Store.

Charlestown was a dead-end place with a single, wide street and one intersection. Next to the hotel was an empty plot and then a derelict building, adjacent to that was a brick-built lock-up and then the bank. Behind a ramshackle row of wood and corrugated-iron sheds lay the emergency airstrip and beyond that was the sprawling cemetery. On the opposite side of the road to the hotel was Simpson's Clothing Store, more disused building plots, derelict buildings and the town hall, and at the intersection, the Charlestown Agricultural Supplies and General Store, the wooden doors wide open for business. A battered utility truck was parked in front of the doors, the tailgate down ready for loading.

The brindled dog sitting next to the horse trough watched their progress down the street. It didn't seem two months since he'd escaped from the orphanage. His stomach churned. Had they forgotten about him at Karundah?

'Many people live here?' he asked.

'Eleven at the last count,' said Rachel, 'at the turn of the century it was booming – the gold rush; now there's nothing to do around here except read, listen to the wireless or drink – if you're old enough. Friday, Saturday nights it's busy, men come in from the stations for a beer and a game of two-up.'

John glanced across to The Grand Hotel, an ornate building with an upper verandah and, at ground level, broad steps leading up to a fancy iron-colonnaded lower verandah and the double swing doors. It was the only two-storey building in the town and despite its faded paintwork it still looked imposing.

'It must be lovely, Liverpool...,' she said the name as if she were savouring chocolate, '...the dancehalls, cinemas and shops. Dad reckons it looks like Fremantle.'

Jon tried to remember Fremantle. He'd been a few weeks short of his ninth birthday and scared. He remembered standing on the dockside with the others for what seemed like hours, each of them with a small case containing the bare essentials, waiting to be fingerprinted like criminals; and the people checking names against lists and sending them in different directions, to trucks waiting to take them to the orphanages deep in the outback. Theirs had been one of the last to leave and the sun had been low in the sky as he'd sat in the back with the others as the driver headed out into the bush. It was all so long ago now and he couldn't recall that much, just the feel of the place, and the unbearable heat of the late Australian spring, and the town bathed in an orange glow, as if on fire, as he looked back at his last link with home. But he did remember the huge, ornate Victorian buildings beyond the docks, like the ones in Liverpool, and the surge of homesickness he'd felt when he saw them. 'Yes,' he said, 'but Liverpool's bigger.'

'I want to go to England one day,' said Rachel wistfully.

You're not the only one, thought Jon as they made their way to Simpson's shop.

Simpson's carried just about anything anyone could want in the clothing line, and it was where Rachel worked. Larry, an older bloke, balding, with a thin neck and rotting teeth, measured his waist and inside leg and then unfolded cords and drills for him to look at. Jon chose the khaki drills, and a blue and green check shirt to go with them. He considered buying a pair of boots but they were expensive and the ones Alice had given him fitted fine, best save his money, not fritter it away on fancy clothes. He paid and Rachel gave him his change.

'I'll see you when you're next in town, then,' she said with a broad smile as she held the shop door open for him.

Wes had his head under the bonnet when Jon arrived at the garage.

'Put the kettle on, son. I'm ready for a brew.'

Jon tossed his new britches and shirt onto the passenger seat and boiled up a kettle.

'Not so much tea this time, the last one was a bit strong, even for me.' Wes wiped his hands on a clean rag and sat on one heel, the other leg extended for balance, like the Aborigines did. He offered Jon a biscuit from a battered tin. 'Pretty gal, Rachel.'

Jon's cheeks burned.

Wes grinned. 'Better not let Scally see you're interested. Worships the ground she walks on, he does. He's scared sick she'll go off and leave him. That's the trouble with the outback, kids get to fifteen and they're itching to leave, especially gals. Crook place, Charlestown, for a gal. There's only the bar, it's not a place to take the women. So what do you think of Australia?'

Why did everyone want to know what he thought of the place? Couldn't they see for themselves? The heat and the flies – he didn't know which was worst. Then there were the vast distances, you couldn't get anywhere in a hurry. He glanced at Wes, saw his open, friendly smile and bit back a smart answer. 'Big.'

'Too right! Bet you folks back home can't imagine driving for three hours to go to a dance or see a film, but I can't complain, I like the outback. We moved out here in nineteen hundred when I was a youngster. Me dad loved it too, reckoned there was space to breathe, but me mother never settled, always hankering after the shops and the beach, so, when I took over the business they moved back to the coast, got a nice little bungalow over Geraldton way. Is your dad a bank manager, like Walter?'

He could hardly tell Wes his dad was a riveter. Bankers' sons didn't become riveters – even he had the nouse to know that. 'Engineer,' he lied, 'he's an engineer.'

'What sort of an engineer?'

'On ships.'

'He keeps the big turbines running, I suppose,' said Wes.

'Something like that.'

'Is that the career for you?'

'No, I'm not one for engines.'

'Not like me then, nothing I like more than fixing an engine, so, what are you doing here then?'

Jon's heart pounded in his chest. He was sick of all these questions. 'Dad thought it would do me good to get away for a bit.'

'Don't blame him,' said Wes. 'I've heard the Old Country took a bit of a battering in the war what with the bombing and the food shortages. You look like you could do with a few square meals in you. Six months and Alice'll fatten you up. How long're you staying?'

'A couple of months or so.'

'Pity.' Wes stood up and put his empty mug on the bench. 'Reckon you'd take to the place like a duck to water, young fella like you. You're just what we need out here. There aren't many eligible blokes under twenty-five between here and Southern Cross since Ray Keeley's and Burt Morran's lads were killed in Indonesia, only Jeb Samuels' boys.'

Jon glanced at Wes and saw the sincerity in his face. Wes meant it! He hadn't considered making a life for himself in Australia; he'd been too obsessed with hating the place and thoughts of Liverpool. He recalled his conversation with Curly at the green pool. Perhaps there was more to the outback than he first thought, maybe life wasn't so bad here if you weren't hankering after someplace else.

Wes fished in his pocket and tossed him a set of keys. 'Here, you'd better reverse it off the ramp.'

The keys clattered onto the concrete. Wes looked at them for a moment.

'Bloody hell, son, don't they teach you anything in England?' He bent over, swept up the keys, got into the cab and reversed the utility onto the forecourt, and then moved across to the passenger seat. 'Jump in.'

Jon slid into the driver's seat.

'You'll soon get the hang of it. Put your left foot on the clutch and slip her into first.'

Jon jammed the gearstick into first.

'Relax, son! Relax! Now, lift your foot off the clutch and with your other foot push down slowly onto the accelerator.'

The truck lurched forward in a series of kangaroo hops, and then crept along at five miles per hour, the engine screaming.

'Right,' shouted Wes above the noise of the engine, 'you have to double the clutch on these. Put your foot on the clutch...left pedal...left pedal...left pedal,' he yelled. 'Keep your right foot on the accelerator. Take the gearstick out of first...good...good. Now, take your left foot off the clutch, and rev the engine gently with your right foot...gently. Gently! Now, foot on the clutch and slip the gearstick into second.'

The truck kangarooed less and within fifteen minutes he'd got the hang of it. He parked on the forecourt and switched off the engine.

'Damn good job you're not planning on driving any distance on graded roads, you'd get me arrested, there's nothing surer. Now, reckon you can manage? Or shall I get Scally to take you home?'

'No, I'll be all right, thanks, Wes.'

Wes got out of the ute and loaded the back with a jerrycan of fuel, two of water, and a spare wheel. 'Just remember, son, treat the outback with respect, don't even think of going anywhere without spares of everything and always make sure you've plenty of water. And if you do breakdown sit it out 'til someone finds you. Don't go trying to walk out.' Wes lashed the jerrycans down and threw a heavy tarpaulin over them. 'Rig up a shelter for yourself with the tarp and keep out of the sun, it's a killer. Right! Remember what I've told you, and if you meet another truck, which isn't likely, but if you do make sure you keep to the left-hand side of the road. And slow right down to a stop 'til it's gone past, all right?'

'All right.'

'And next time I see you I expect to see an expert,' said Wes. 'Practise reversing and for pity's sake don't go and run over Alice, or Belle, or Adie for that matter, otherwise you'll be seeing the inside of an Aussie lock-up for the next ten years, right!'

CHAPTER 6

A big red lay in the middle of the road, its back legs smashed, blood and flies blackening the dust. Jon jumped down from the cab and saw the fear in the animal's eyes as it scrabbled with its front paws trying to drag itself away from him. He returned to the truck for the lump hammer and dispatched the kangaroo the same way he did the sheep. The action still sickened him but there was nothing else to be done for the creature.

Skid marks in the dust led his eye to the old salmon gum marking the turn off for Jarrahlong. He followed the line, saw the deep scoring on the bark and then the black sedan ten feet from the road, partially hidden by mallee scrub, lying in the run-off gully at a forty-five degree angle, its off-side wing and bumper badly crumpled, the damaged wing mirror winking in the sunlight, sending out random Morse code.

The driver lay slumped across the gearstick, his head tilted forward, facing the passenger-seat footwell. The black jacket and grey shirt looked familiar. Jon kneeled on the running board and leaned in; he grabbed the man's jacket and heaved the dead weight upright. Then, keeping tight hold of the jacket, he stepped back and allowed the body to flop towards him revealing the man's moon face.

Father O'Leary!

Jon rocked back on his heels, blood roaring in his ears. For a long moment he stared at the face, mindlessly taking in the lump on the forehead the size of an emu's egg, the bloody, blackened gash, revealing the bone underneath, and then at the shirt and jacket sticky with congealed blood. He glanced along the road, then back to the priest. Maybe O'Leary was dead. He looked pale enough. A clout like that should have killed him, ought to have killed him if there was any justice in the world, but how could he tell for sure? Pulse, that's what they checked first. He shuddered as his fingers sank into the still-warm flesh feeling for the blood pulsing through the jugular vein. The bastard was still alive!

He stepped back. Now what? He stood for a long moment looking at the man he hated more than he did his own father. He could pretend he'd never seen him. With luck no one would travel along this road for days, and by then he'd be long dead, the meat ants would have got to him. A pretty fitting end, ants, they reckoned death was agony.

Jon climbed back into his ute and stared at the dashboard. The road wasn't that deserted and Scally would be along before too long. He'd seen it in his eyes, heard it in his voice: I'll be seeing ya, mate, tell Alice I'll be over tomorra.

Jon chewed at his lip. O'Leary looked crook, maybe he'd die soon, but what if he didn't? He pictured O'Leary's pudgy hands, the beautifully manicured fingernails, and glanced at his own, barely recovered from the days when he and the others worked in the quarry lugging rocks twice their own weight onto carts for transportation to the building site, and all for O'Leary's damned church. He saw Freddie's broken body in the dust, remembered the anguish, the despair. Suddenly, white-hot rage exploded in his chest, hatred engulfed him – the bastard didn't deserve to live.

He ran back to the car and hauled the priest out. Sweat poured off him as he dragged the body onto the ground, manhandled him over to the ute, and shouldered him onto the flatbed. He slammed the tailgate shut and looked about him, listening for the rumble of an approaching vehicle. Nothing! A flock of parakeets flew over, their strident calls mocking his momentary indecision.

The kangaroo, he had to get rid of that as well. He grasped the back legs, the broken bones grating as he dragged the carcass off the road and into the bush. Back on the road he kicked dust onto the congealed blood scattering the manic flies crazed by the sickly scent. Now he needed bearings.

The mallee either side of the road obscured his view, but to the left a rocky outcrop offered a vantage point. He scrambled to the summit and surveyed the terrain. North-east, perhaps a mile away, the outcrop he was standing on continued in a long escarpment, with cuts. The lie suggested a valley lay through the cut, the bush thinned too; he'd have a better view once he was clear of the denser scrub.

A couple of miles down the road he turned off onto an overgrown track. The ground was rutted and littered with rocks; he picked his way carefully avoiding anything that could hole the sump.

Once he reached the valley he realised he'd stumbled on the perfect location. Disused mines were dotted along the base of the escarpment. Large mounds of discarded rubble, scree and the spoil from old mine workings partially overgrown with scrubby trees and wispy grass littered the valley. He reversed the truck as close as he could get to a likely looking shaft and switched off the engine. The place hadn't been mined in decades, along the way a rusting derrick leaned drunkenly, the pulleys a tangle of wire and old rope.

Jon cocked his head to one side and listened. A mob of galahs squawked in the bushes and two families of kookaburras argued over boundary lines whilst on the yellow shale a thorny devil basked in the sun, watching. He wiped a forearm over his brow. He needed a drink. The place was like a bakehouse, hot and airless, well over one hundred degrees, he calculated, hot enough to desiccate a coconut. The place gave him the jitters. Quietly, he unhitched the tailgate, scanning the valley the while. The thorny devil hadn't moved – a good sign. Above, the kookaburras had quit their discordant argument, the granddaddy of the family sat on a branch not fifty feet away, its head sunk down in its shoulders, also watching.

He grabbed the priest's sleeve, dragged him to the edge of the trailer, lifted him by the shoulders and pulled him off the truck. O'Leary's feet thudded to the ground. Sweat dripped off Jon's chin as he dragged the dead weight up to the shaft.

At the shaft lip Jon slumped to his knees, his body shielding the priest from the worst of the sun, and paused. A wisp of grey hair clung to O'Leary's damp cheek; the monster looked almost angelic. Jon shut his ears to the faint asthmatic whistle that he'd heard for half his life. O'Leary's chest rose and fell gently with each shallow breath and his words from earlier days rang in Jon's ears: Boys, thou shalt not commit any mortal sin. And a gentler voice, Father William's, whispering: Thou shalt not kill.

Jon hesitated, he was getting soft, a shove that was all it needed, one little push and he'd be rid of the bastard for life. He'd be doing others a favour, Jannek, and Smithson; they were O'Leary's current favourites, weren't they? They'd want him to do it. But what if he was wrong? And what if God was out there somewhere?

He looked about him furtively, shivering despite the heat. Father William was watching from beyond the grave, he was sure of it, the prickling sensation on his neck told him so. Father William had murdered himself. Was he still in purgatory? Could a soul ever be purged after premeditated murder? He wished he knew.

He listened to O'Leary's rattling breath. O'Leary was going to die anyway. He was just helping the Lord do his work, wasn't he?

Jon shivered. He wished he wasn't Catholic; surely it would be easier if he was a Protestant. Protestants were used to blood on their hands, burning Catholics at the stake, stretching them on the rack. Being Catholic he'd be eternally damned, saying half a dozen Hail Marys wouldn't put things right no matter how sorry he was later. Except he'd never be sorry, he wanted O'Leary dead; he wanted him in Hell, forever. An eye for an eye it said in Leviticus, well, this was an eye for an eye for Freddie.

Jon sat back on his heels, letting the midday sun beat down on the priest's face. He recalled O'Leary's shouts of encouragement on the cricket pitch, the pat on the back when he'd first arrived at Karundah, and the time O'Leary prayed all night in the chapel when they all went down with scarlet fever and Jeremy Hodges died. Jon stared into the bruised and battered moon face. He couldn't do it; it was one thing to kill a man in the heat of the moment but another thing altogether to do it in cold blood, to leave a man to die a lingering death down a disused mineshaft. It would be kinder to use the lump hammer.

He vented his frustration with a string of expletives, and, grabbing the priest's ankles, pulled him away from the edge. 'You deserve it, you bastard,' Jon muttered savagely through gritted teeth as he felt O'Leary's head bounce over the rough ground, 'I hope it kills you.'

A double click like a dry twig snapping interrupted his efforts. He turned. Not thirty feet away a hunched figure stood on a pile of yellow scree, his arms resting on a huge boulder half buried in the spoil. Deep-set eyes watched him from behind the cocked hammers of a double-barrelled shotgun.

Jon dropped O'Leary's feet and stood up. The man too pulled himself upright and, with the raised gun pointing directly at Jon's chest, he half walked, half slithered down the scree. The shale-like spoil rattled and hissed as it rolled and settled lower down the slope. Jon kept his eyes fixed on the fella's face expecting death at any moment. The deeply lined face registered no emotion, no surprise, no fear, not even idle curiosity.

'Ain't the cemetery good enough for him?' His harsh voice, like glass paper on rusting metal, grated in Jon's ears. 'Or is it murder?'

'He's not dead.'

The old fella didn't comment, instead he jerked the gun twice in the direction of the truck.

Jon hesitated.

The gun jerked again.

The distance between them was too great to rush him, and the old fella was wiry, like a coiled spring, no telling what he might do. One squeeze of the trigger and that would be that. Dead! Another, sharper jerk on the gun ended the stand-off.

Jon heaved O'Leary back onto the flatbed and jammed the rolled-up tarpaulin against his body conscious of the old fella's faded blue eyes watching his every move. The gun jerked in the direction of the cab door. Jon followed the instruction, sidled around the side of the truck and got into the driving seat. When he glanced in the rear-view mirror the old codger was already seated on the tarpaulin, his feet resting next to the priest's inert body, the gun still pointing at him through the ute's rear window.

Jon drove slowly taking care to avoid ruts and rocks, one jolt and he'd have his head blown off, there was nothing more certain.

Scally's truck was parked outside the hotel. Jon parked next to it. The utility rocked as the old fella jumped down and made his way into the bar. Jon stepped out onto the road. The game was up. He'd be arrested and thrown into the double-brick cell he'd seen between the derelict shop and the bank. Did they still have the death penalty in Australia? He reckoned they did, hanging most like, same as in England.

Scally, Wes, and a chap Jon took to be a barman followed the old fella out of the saloon and over to the ute. They stared at the priest in silence.

'Trying to kill the poor bastard, were ya, lad?' asked Scally eventually.

'He hit a big red.'

'My arse,' said Scally.

'He looks a bit crook,' said the barman, wiping his hands on a towel.

'Just concussion, Al,' said Wes. 'He'll have a mother of a headache when he comes round.'

'If he comes round,' said Scally.

To Jon's mind, the conversation around O'Leary's inert body was bizarre. Why weren't they yelling for a doctor, or the constable? It didn't make sense.

'What's a priest doing this far out? I haven't seen one in these parts in months,' said Wes.

'He's from Karundah, out Merredin way,' said Scally.

'He's a long way from home,' commented Al.

'Y're not wrong there,' said Scally, his eyes never leaving Jon's face.

'Aren't you fellas going to get him inside or are you going to leave him out here all night?' A tall, good-looking woman wearing a floral dress and red shoes clattered down the hotel steps. The men stood aside to let her pass.

'He's fit for nothing, Connie,' said Al. 'You'd not even raise a smile.'

'He's a priest for God's sake,' snapped Connie. She glanced at her watch and then at Al. 'If you're quick you'll catch the evening schedule. Tell them we need the doctor that we've a priest here and he looks crook, lump the size of a rock with a gash that'll need stitches.'

'Poor bugger,' said Wes, easing him to the edge of the truck.

'Gently,' ordered Connie. 'Carry him through to the parlour, put him on the daybed and lay him on his side in case he vomits.'

The four of them lifted the unconscious priest off the flatbed and into the bar. Walking sideways, hunched over to avoid jolting the body, they looked like a grotesque centipede. Connie went ahead, opening doors through to the parlour, fussing, yelling at them to be more careful.

They stood in a ragged group watching while she fetched water, bathed the wound and put on a clean dressing. 'Reckon he'll live.' She turned to Jon. 'Good of you to bring him in. You're Mrs Macarthur's great-nephew, aren't you? What's your name?'

'Jon.'

'Bit late to drive back. I can give you a bed for the night.'

Jon hesitated.

'No charge. One neighbourly act deserves another.'

'It's all right, Connie, he's driving me back to my place.' The old fella nudged Jon in the ribs, 'Aren't you, son?'

'You sure, Stan? I can find a bed for you too.'

Stan waved his thanks and ushered Jon out of the bar. 'You drive,' he ordered and got into the passenger seat.

Sixty miles out they reached the overturned car. Jon pulled over and they pushed the saloon upright and towed it back onto the road.

'Wes'll collect it,' said Stan, dusting off his hands as he got back into the utility truck. 'Take the third turn on the right, I'll direct you after.'

The light had gone by the time they left the graded road. Using headlights Jon negotiated a dirt track through a valley thick with mulga scrub, mallee and ghost gums, their bleached boles and branches standing like skeletons in the bright beams. At the head of the valley the headlights picked out a wooden shack with a stone chimney stack and a narrow verandah on the front elevation. Two dogs rose to their feet as the utility truck approached, both sets of eyes white in the high beam.

'You'll have to sleep here tonight,' said Stan, picking his way between rusting engines, old buckets, spades and jerrycans, the dogs at his heels. When he reached the shack he turned and waited. Jon switched off the engine and the lights and pocketed the ignition key.

A single kerosene lamp, similar to the ones Alice used, lit the interior. Stan stood in front of a blackened stove set in the cavity beneath the chimney stack and an equally black aluminium pan sat on the hot plate. On the deal table an empty tin of haricot beans stood next to a small tin of corned beef. Stan attached the key and wound the tin open. 'You like bully?' he asked as he emptied the can into the pan of beans.

'Yes,' said Jon.

Stan turned back to the table and sliced half a dozen cold potatoes into chunks and added them to the mix. 'Irons,' he indicated in the direction of the sink.

Jon picked up a couple of dirty forks and plates and dunked them in the soupy water that they'd been soaking in. There was no tap.

'Stand pipe's outside to your left.'

Jon collected the two plates and forks, rinsed them and shook them dry.

Five minutes later they ate, not looking at each other, concentrating on the food they were shovelling into their mouths. At the end of the meal Stan made two mugs of tea and handed one to Jon. 'What're you doing with Alice's truck?'

'Getting it fixed.'

'Wes's?'

Jon nodded.

'Where're you from?'

Jon hesitated. Stan hadn't said anything in town and he could have done. He looked into Stan's eyes, and read nothing. The game was up anyway; once O'Leary was better he'd be back, like as not he was on his way to Jarrahlong when he hit the roo. Bloody

Scally! 'Liverpool.'

'Aye, that may be, but not in the last ten years, not with that mongrel accent. You from the orphanage out Merredin way?'

Jon didn't answer, the less said the better. He took another sip of scalding brew and concentrated on the bitter flavour. Original Billy Tea, it said on the package. He could feel it gnawing his belly.

'Met a bloke once who told me the kids were treated nothing better than slave labour, little uns working in the quarry, humping rock all day to build the place; he said one priest in particular was a sadistic bastard, liked his boys pretty.' Stan took a sip of tea, straining the black leaves through his teeth. He spat a couple on the floor. 'Lucky you're an ugly bugger.'

Jon thought of Stephen Hicks and tears sprang into his eyes. He blinked them back and gulped down the scalding tea to take the pain away, welcoming the burning sensation as the bitter liquid flowed down his gullet and into his belly, conscious of Stan's disinterest in his discomfort.

'So, what happened to you then? What made you run away?'

'A boy was killed,' he said, choking on the words.

Stan took another swig. 'A brother was it, or a friend?'

The muscles in Jon's neck ached. He unclenched his jaws. 'A mate, I suppose.'

Stan's eyebrows arched.

Jon picked up the mug again and finished the bitter tea. He hadn't even liked Freddie Fitzpatrick that much, but he didn't deserve to die half a world away from home. Sweat prickled his brow at the memory – Freddie steadying the huge piece of rock, the altar stone, when everyone could see it wasn't safe. But O'Leary had insisted it was. God's altar stone won't fall, he'd shouted. Hold it steady, lad. Stop ballet dancing and do a proper job, he'd yelled.

Then the trailer's nearside back wheel slipped into the rut and the truck's whole back end tilted. God's altar stone ground inexorably towards the edge, teetered on the lip, and then, with a gut-wrenching screech, slid off the trailer. He remembered yelling and yelling, but Freddie, wrong-footed, pirouetted, his ankle bent at an unnatural angle. He'd flung his body sideways, his arms flailing for balance, but it was too late, he was pinned to the ground, his arms and legs splayed in the dust, the blood, spreading out beneath him like wings, darkening the red earth. It could so easily have been him crushed by the rock and then he would never have had the chance to put things right, to get home to England, to take care of Kathy.

Stan prised his fingers off the mug. 'You'll dent the enamel if you're not careful,' he said. 'Here!' He unscrewed a bottle of rum and poured a shot. 'Get that down you. It'll do you good even if there's nothing wrong with you.'

Jon choked it down, tears pricked his eyelids and he coughed.

'Better?' asked Stan after a moment or two. 'It always works.' He poured himself three fingers. 'It doesn't do to dwell on the past. How's Alice?'

'She's all right.'

'And the sheep?'

'All right now we've got them to the well up at the top end.'

'1939 was the worst. She tell you? Neither of them got much sleep and they were no spring chickens, even then. They reckon it was killing the sheep that got to Jack, turned the gun on himself, he did, and blew his brains out. Alice went looking for him when he didn't come home.' He nodded in the direction of the yard. 'Brought his body back in that ute, then she parked it up and never drove it again. She's lived like a recluse ever since, even given up chess for the most part.'

'She hasn't.'

'Well, I'll be damned!' Stan grinned when he caught Jon's expression. 'I'd drive over now and again for a game of chess but we haven't spoken in six months. Fell out over a questionable move. We ought to have our heads knocked together.' He chuckled. 'I've got books belonging to her. You'd better take them with you and tell her I'd like to borrow a couple more, if she's half a mind.'

'You a prospector?'

'What d'you want to know for?'

'Just interested.'

'No such thing as *just interested* when it comes to gold.' Stan's pale blue eyes hardened. 'More blokes lost a claim to fellas who were *just interested* than I've had hot dinners.'

'I was only asking,' said Jon.

'You ever seen real gold?'

'Mam's wedding ring.'

Stan laughed. He pulled a sizeable lump of rock out of his pocket and dropped it on the table. The piece clunked as it landed and rolled leadenly for two stops.

'It's raw gold, son, just as Mother Nature made it.'

Jon poked it, rolled it with his index finger, and noted the indents packed with dirty reddish-brown earth. The gold bloomed, but not with the sparkle of a wedding ring, more like the gleam of a covetous eye. Jon weighed the surprisingly heavy nugget in his hand. 'How much is it worth?'

'A hundred pounds give or take a tenner.' Stan pocketed the nugget then took out a fob watch, read the dial and wound it up. 'There's a truckle bed in the corner and a blanket.' He scraped his chair back and banked down the stove, refilled the kettle and placed it on the hot plate. 'There's no dunny, shovel's to the right of the door.'

Jon stepped outside and headed across to the scrub, away from the shack, followed by both dogs. So the old fella was prospecting – working the old spoil. On the way in he'd noticed the derelict foundations of an engine house and a fallen chimney stack; the rush hadn't lasted, that was for sure, it wasn't a big enough place for a town, just a settlement of maybe half a dozen shacks. Binky reckoned folk found nuggets lying on the ground just waiting to be picked up. Was that how Stan had found his?

That's what he needed, a big nugget. He unbuttoned his flies and peed scattering the dogs with a well-aimed stream. A big nugget would see him right – five hundred pounds would set him and Kathy up for life.

At first light Jon struck up his ute. Stan stood on the verandah watching him, a bucket at his feet laden with a trowel, lump hammer and a bolster chisel, in his hand a mattock, behind him the dogs milling at his heels.

Jon waved as he drove off. On the seat beside him lay four books for Alice.

CHAPTER 7

Jon steered Daisy round the mob, his mind on Stan Colley, Stan on his verandah, dogs milling at his feet, a day of prospecting ahead of him. He mentally weighed Stan's gold nugget as he checked the state of the flock and drove them east to Jack's well and fresh pasture.

Gold, that was the fastest ticket home and he wanted to find out more, the best places to look, how to pan for it, or whether digging it out of the ground was more efficient. He wished he'd listened to Binky Brent; he'd always got his nose in one of the library books reading up about gold-bearing rock and refining processes. But Stan would tell him, the old fella liked him, wouldn't have shown him his precious nugget if he hadn't. What he needed was time off. He'd have to work on Alice.

So he wants more books, does he? Well, he can whistle, she'd said when he'd returned the four Stan had borrowed. She had that hard, stubborn look etched on her face which also said, and don't raise the subject again. The rest of last Friday night had been tense. They'd barely spoken and Alice had taken savage delight when she'd thrashed him at chess, yet again.

He kicked Daisy in the flanks and trotted across to Adie, spoke briefly to him, waved to the others and headed south, back to Jarrahlong. He glanced up at the sun – midday; if he didn't hang around he'd be back by four. He rehearsed a few chess moves in his head. Since he'd got back from Stan's place he'd spent every spare minute studying the game from the book Alice had lent him weeks ago, memorizing a few new strategies; for once he was keen to play.

At Jarrahlong he unsaddled Daisy, rubbed her down, fed her, and turned her loose in the paddock. He grabbed clean clothes and headed for the makeshift shower, an old forty-four-gallon drum with a perforated base. He stepped under the water watched by a mob of chattering budgerigars decorating the iron wind pump like fairground bunting, waiting to paddle in the mud like kids on a beach. He ignored the birds and concentrated on the rusty warm water washing off the dust; he soaped his hair and scrubbed his scalp, conscious of the cooking smells wafting over from the kitchen – mutton stew and nothing like the scouse Gran made with thick rings of potato layered over scrag-end, with plenty of onion and carrot for flavour. Belle's mutton stew always left a film on his teeth and made him belch for hours after he'd eaten.

What was wrong with him these days? Eight weeks of freedom with more food than he could eat and he was getting picky. He ought to be more grateful. What was it Alice and Wes said about rationing in England? Did it mean people back home were going short even though the war had been over for a year? He would ask Alice, maybe Mrs B. M. Morton, whoever she was, wrote to her about it.

He grabbed a scrap of rough, threadbare towel, stiff as starched linen, flung it over his shoulder, grabbed the end from behind and sawed it over his back until the skin tingled and the stiffness in his muscles eased. When he was dry he dragged on khaki drills and a clean shirt and headed towards the kitchen and tucker.

While he ate he could hear Alice talking to her parrot. He couldn't make out the words, they were too indistinct, but she sounded cheerful enough.

'What time Adie back?' asked Belle.

'Sometime tomorrow. Is Alice in a good mood?'

Belle turned towards him still scrubbing a pan, the whites of her eyes a disconcerting yellow and the irises deep brown. He never knew what she was thinking and she rarely spoke unless he spoke to her, but he reckoned she was okay about him ever since he'd caught her spitting into Gerry's beer. She stopped scrubbing and flapped at a bluebottle buzzing round her head. 'Bout same,' she said, 'I say she born sour, like green quandong.'

Jon grinned. Curly had given him a handful to chew once and had laughed his head off at the sight of his mouth puckered as a cat's bum as the bitter fruit turned his saliva to sawdust.

'Y'finished?' She didn't wait for a reply; she whipped his plate away and washed up, dropped it back into the rack next to the others and shuffled over to the door. 'Y'cun git yer own beer,' she said over her shoulder and out she waddled, over to the two-roomed stockman's shack beyond the shearing shed that she shared with Adie. Jon hadn't quite worked out their relationship. Alice referred to Belle as Adie's gin but he didn't know whether that was an Aboriginal word for wife or whether it meant Belle was Adie's bit on the side. It didn't matter either way; it wasn't any of his business and Alice wasn't bothered, he reckoned people's morals didn't come too high up on her list of priorities.

He got himself a beer from the refrigerator, knocked off the cap, tapped on the parlour door and entered. He'd been right; Alice was in a good mood, no frown lines for once and even the hint of a welcoming smile on her wrinkled face.

'Hope you're ready for another thrashing, lad.'

There never was a good time to broach a subject with Alice; better get it over with. 'I want tomorrow off, and Sunday.'

'Do you? Planning on going to church or something?'

'I haven't had a day off in six weeks.'

She looked at him sharply. 'Stock isn't a nine-to-five, five-day-a-week job, you know.'

He held her cold eyes. 'I'm entitled.'

She glanced away and arranged the pieces on the chessboard. 'You aren't entitled to anything in my book, so the answer's no. Now shut up and sit down and let's get on with the game.'

He remained standing. If he gave in now he was finished; she'd trample all over him with her demanding ways, the selfish old cow. He deliberately took a long swig of beer. 'I beat you at chess and I get two days off and Stan gets a few books to read.'

Her head whipped up, her eyes narrowed. 'So, you want to pick his brains, do you? Learn about gold, got an itch to get rich quick, have you, lad?'

'So?'

'How rich do you think Stan is?'

Jon shrugged.

'Spent his whole life searching for El Dorado like a lot of other idiots before him, convinced he's going to make the big time, find the mother of all lodes. Know how old he is? Seventy-six or thereabouts and he hasn't two pennies to rub together to show for thirty years of graft. Hand-to-mouth he lives, no wife, no kids, nothing. He'll die a lonely old man, probably be months before anyone notices he's not around, a dried-up bag of bones, that's what he'll be when they find him, skin tight across his skull like one of those Egyptian mummies.'

He sat down opposite her, picked up a pawn and held it in the air so she could see he meant business. 'I win I get two days off, all right?'

Alice leaned over and stroked the cockatoo's chest feathers, her

eyes watching his face. 'How long have you got?'
'As long as it takes.'
'We should make a start then.'

Jon yawned as he reversed the utility truck out of the shed at first light. It had been a long session, it had gone one o'clock before he got to bed. Conversation had been minimal whilst they'd battled it out on the chessboard. It was touch and go at one point, he thought he'd lost the game but then Alice made a silly mistake, tiredness probably, or the whiskey, and it was all over bar the shouting. She didn't say much at the finish and he'd half expected her to renege on the agreement, but she didn't, she'd hauled herself to her feet and told him to pick out a few books for Stan. I expect you back six sharp Sunday night, she'd said, you not here and you're fired.

He'd resisted the temptation to crow, to do what Alice usually did when she won a game; instead, he'd handed her her stick, opened the door for her and didn't forget to say thank you.

Alice had given him an odd look as she'd shuffled past him, a look he couldn't quite read and he'd wondered what was going on in that head of hers. One thing was for sure, she was a formidable opponent, she seemed to read his mind and she had an uncanny knack of wrong-footing him with her pointed questions and snide comments – she might be a semi-invalid but her brain was still nippy even if her feet weren't. Then there was the Charlestown mob, Scally, Rachel, Wes and Gerry, all of them looking out for her, especially Scally with his threats, and Gerry, worried that the Aborigines would take advantage. Jon smiled to himself; Gerry didn't know the half of it. Did Scally? Because he certainly didn't and the longer he was at Jarrahlong the more questions he had about Alice, maybe Stan would be able to answer some of them.

Chooks scattered in all directions when he drew up in front of Stan's shack over an hour later. The door opened and the old fella stood there in his singlet and long johns, a mug of tea in his hand. He looked like an old-timer out of an old cowboy film with his half-inch of stubble, his squint lines, and his white hair sticking out at right angles from his sun-burnt scalp.

'Didn't expect to see you again, son.'
Jon held up six books. 'From Alice.'
'How did you manage that?'
'It wasn't easy. Had to beat her at chess to get here.'
Stan raised a bushy eyebrow. 'You beat Alice?'

'Yeah.'

'Been playing long?'

'What's that supposed to mean?'

'Nothing.'

Jon frowned at the fleeting half smile he thought he saw on Stan's face.

'What do you want to know about prospecting?'

'Everything.'

'Stan tilted up his battered Akubra hat and scratched the scalp behind his ear. 'How long you got?'

'You're as bad as Alice.'

'What do you mean?'

'That's what she said last night, before the chess game.'

Stan grinned. 'That's Alice for you.'

'Yeah, and I've got to be back on Sunday, six o'clock.'

They were standing behind an old snub-nosed Bedford van. Stan pulled open the back doors and out jumped Bess and Bonny. 'Here!' He handed over a couple of shovels, two blackened iron pans and a drinking bowl for the dogs. He left the two jerrycans filled with water in the back of the van and picked up a galvanised bucket jammed full with lump hammers and trowels.

Behind them, back the way they had come, the bone-dry valley was littered with the remains of partially collapsed wooden head-frames and iron winding wheels on crumbling foundations tilting drunkenly over disused mineshafts. All around were mounds of spoil as well as the brick remains of an old mining office, engine housing and sheds. Tyre tracks, like tramlines, marked the easy route between the dried-up creek bed and collapsed winding gear.

The valley hadn't been mined intensively for decades. It smelt of scrubby mulga and baked earth. There wasn't a breath of wind and even the raucous native birds were oddly subdued as if the effort was too much trouble in the dry, morning heat.

'We going down there?' asked Jon, looking back at the mineshaft with its wood and metal head-frame still in one piece.

'No, too dangerous, all the props are rotten, if they collapse there's no coming back. No, we'll start with panning. We should do it in water, but the bloody drought's put paid to that.'

Jon looked from Stan to the dried-up creek bed. 'Where do we start?'

'First, you have to study the creek and work out where the water would have slowed a bit. See here?' he indicated the gravel bar across the width of the creek. 'That's what you're looking for. Fast water carries gold, slow water dumps it, so you dig where you think the gold dropped. It's a sight easier when the water's flowing.'

Jon scanned the creek bed for likely looking spots.

Stan grinned. 'Now comes the graft, son. You have to dig down below the sandy gravel to the muddy sludge bit that's baked as hard as a mud brick till you hit the ironstone underneath. The stuff above the bedrock is what you pan. If there's gold that's where it'll be.'

Digging the baked earth was hard going, he put his back into it like a navvy, throwing the gravel back onto the bank until he reached the layer above the bedrock. He filled his pan and crushed the silt with his boot heel. 'Nothing here,' he yelled.

Stan eased himself upright, hands braced against his hips. 'You haven't looked yet; you've got to pan it with water. First, make the soil friable again, then chuck in a pint or so and pick out the floaters and you're ready to start panning. Swirl the water round and let the light stuff tip over the edge. What you're aiming for is to keep all the heavy bits in the bottom; that's where the gold will be if you haven't been too cack-handed.'

Jon bent over the pan holding it at the angle Stan had shown him. He stirred the soupy water and swirled it, concentrating on the sludge and the muddy old-socks smell of sour, compacted earth and rotting vegetation. Water and dissolved soil slipped over the edge and trickled down his hands and arms onto his legs, but he barely noticed. An hour slipped by and the pan was empty save for a curve of gravel in the bottom, hissing like a cornered snake as he rolled the gritty bits round and round.

'Now what, Stan?'

'More water and start on the gravel.'

Jon tried to straighten up but his back had locked; he put the pan down and with both hands on hips eased himself upright like Stan had done an hour earlier. He added another pint of water. This time he half knelt, one knee at a right angle, the other on the ground, one arm supported on the raised knee. He braced the pan and found it easier. 'What's this gritty stuff?'

'Ironstone,' said Stan, 'that's what you need to look for if you want gold – ironstone and quartz together, it gets the blood running in the brain when you see that.'

Jon worked slowly and methodically, but nothing glittered or gleamed in the pan. 'Reckon there's nothing here,' he said.

'Then you start over with another pan. Maybe next time.'

By the end of the third pan Jon had found nothing and was hooked; swirling the water and sludge around was hypnotic.

Stan found three flakes no bigger than rice grains among the grit in his pan, the metal as distinctive as luminous paint on a black watch-face.

For his last pan of the day Jon moved further back along the creek closer to the heaps of spoil scarring the landscape. He dug down in front of a big boulder half buried in the bank and began the process all over again.

He mixed the mud with the water, swirled the lot around rapidly and tilted the pan sharply left, then right, allowing the silt to slide across the pan and back. Bright caught his eye. Gold?

Jon repeated the exercise. Nothing! Not even a glint. But he was sure he'd seen something. He started the process again, slowly, carefully.

Stan was sitting on the bank, watching him. 'It can take days to find something worth while and then you find a good spot and you're on a roll. Tomorrow, we can try further along the creek if you like and I'll show you how to use the dry-blower.'

Jon hadn't realised it was going to be so tough. Binky Brent hadn't said anything about it taking days to find gold, listening to him the stuff was just lying around on the surface waiting to be picked up.

Stan tapped him on the shoulder, 'Try swirling it the other way, gently like, then back again.'

The weight of the pan made his shoulders ache and reversing the direction made the muscles in his neck scream but he obeyed and caught a glimpse of bright again. 'Did you see that, Stan? Did you see that?' Another gentle swirl and he saw the same brightness glinting.

'That's more than a flake,' said Stan. 'Easy now. Don't rush it'

Another half hour of intense concentration and gold, the size of a coffee bean, sparkled in the bottom of the pan.

'Well, I'll be damned,' said Stan as the two of them stared at the irregular lump of pure gold winking at them from among the grains of ironstone. He took out a small glass vial with a tiny cork stopper from his pocket. 'Pick it up on the end of your finger and drop it in here.'

Jon dried his hands on his shirt and lightly touched the top of the golden bean. It clung to his damp skin as he gently curled his finger towards himself while carefully keeping his hand over the pan. He studied his first find fascinated by the depth of colour and its irregular shape, like a dimpled new moon.

'It's a beaut,' said Stan. He held the vial steady. The gold gave a satisfying clink as it dropped into the bottom of the small glass bottle.

After tea Stan threw a couple of slow-burning mulga logs into the stove and slammed the door shut. 'Drag a pew over, son, and take the weight off your feet. Rum?'

Jon eased himself onto a hard chair, leaned his aching back against the slats and accepted a mug with a generous tot of rum in the bottom.

'Do you have to have a lease or something to go prospecting for gold, Stan?'

'Too right you do, and you have to pay for it.'

'So, how do you go about getting a lease?'

'First you find a patch where the lease has run out, or lapsed, or maybe never even had a lease, then you peg it and head off to the Department of Minerals and file an application. If it's available it's yours so long as you work it and maintain the lease, but if you don't work it or you don't maintain the lease then some other bugger can move in.'

'How long've you been mining this patch?'

'Twenty-seven years, or thereabouts.'

Jon frowned. Why would anyone want to spend twenty-seven years working the same ground if they weren't making any money out of it, unless Stan was two ounces short of a pound? He stole a look at Stan relaxed and easy in the flickering light, feet propped up on the stove, mug resting on his belly, contentment etched on his old face. Maybe Alice was wrong and the old fella was loaded, perhaps he had a cache somewhere and was just the miserly type who'd end up a dead millionaire. He went fishing.

'So there's a seam in the valley?'

'Yeah.'

'But you haven't found it.'

'Not yet.'

'So, how do you know?'

'I've a gut feeling about it.'

Jon sipped his rum – twenty-seven years following a dream! Gran always said there was nothing queerer than folk. He decided she was right. 'How can you be so sure?'

'Because the place is rich in ironstone and quartz. A geologist, Geoff Hardman, found a couple of nuggets in 1900, said there was a seam just waiting to be discovered so he took out a lease. Anyway, he spent a fortune looking; all the mine workings, engine housing, winding gear, the lot were built by him. He sank everything into it for fifteen years, even employed blokes from Charlestown. Then he went bust and didn't work the lease for a while, he tried to raise money, get backers, but it was just after the war finished and no one was interested. I'd just returned from France and decided to have a go. I jumped the lapsed lease and I've been here ever since.'

'Hardman ever come back?'

'Nah, they say he died a pauper.'

'Alice says you're wasting your time.'

'She mention El Dorado?'

'She says you'll end up like an Egyptian mummy – that they'll find you dried up and desiccated with a shovel in one hand and an empty pan in the other.'

'That's the trouble with Alice, too vivid an imagination.'

They sat staring at the pot-belly stove sipping rum together, ignoring the fumes rising from the dogs silently farting at their feet.

'You known Alice long?'

'Since about 1903. I got to know Jack first; he was managing a cattle station over Gwalia way. I met him in the State Hotel just after they built it. He'd come in most weeks and we became drinking pals, soon after that I met Alice and their little lad, then later, after the war, I took out a lease like Jack had done in 1908 except Jack's was a pastoral lease at Jarrahlong and I took over Hardman's lapsed mineral lease here.'

'Alice has a son?'

'Had. While I was in the trenches in France he was getting himself shot in the Gallipoli Campaign, poor bugger. He was barely eighteen when he was killed.'

No wonder she was so cold, thought Jon, losing her lad like that explained a lot. 'She had no other kids, then?'

'No, just David.'

'Jack hit the bottle in the years after David died. He'd drive himself into Charlestown on a Friday and drink himself to the floor so I took to driving him home. Alice was a handsome woman in those days, tall and straight as a Norfolk pine and just as prickly till she got to know you – never trusted anyone, even then.' He took a quick swig of rum, a faraway look in his eyes. 'Most of the time she wore Jack's shirts and britches when they were working the sheep, but when they took off to Perth for a few days she'd knock your eye out – always scrubbed up well, did Alice.'

'You soft on her or something?'

'Too right I was and so was every other hot-blooded male who met her. Pretty as paint she was and she knew it, but she never looked at another fella. She liked a bit of banter, slick, silver tongue she had, you couldn't get one over on Alice. Aye, son, she was some woman. I'd have jumped Jack's claim in a shot had he let it lapse.'

Jon caught the gleam in Stan's rheumy old eyes. 'You still flippin' fancy her, don't you?'

'The young don't have a monopoly on fancy,' snapped Stan. 'Just because a bloke's a bit long in the tooth doesn't mean his tackle don't work.'

CHAPTER 8

Heat pounded through his body. Rachel was kissing him; her hair was tickling his face. He brushed it aside and turned to kiss her back, but the feeling wasn't right, he opened his eyes and looked directly into brown ones. Rachel's were grey. Bonny!

The dog's pink tongue lolled out of the corner of her mouth as she panted, her whole body pressed against his, just an old army blanket between them. He tried to turn over on the narrow truckle bed and couldn't. Bess lay across his feet – three of them on a cot two-foot wide – no wonder he'd woken up in a muck sweat!

He shoved both dogs onto the floor and stretched. How long had they been there? Bloody ages by the smell of the bed! He rolled onto his side and glanced across towards Stan flat out on his pallet, the old iron bedstead jammed into the little cubbyhole he called the boudoir. Fast asleep still, his rasping snores matching the rise and fall of the old eiderdown draped across him.

Steely light filtering through the dusty windowpanes brightened the room as Bonny edged over to the side of the bed and crawled back onto the warm spot where Bess had been.

Watching the dog's technique he could understand why she hadn't woken him the first time around. What was it about dogs and him? – most seemed to make a beeline for him. Old Yella had taken up residence on the verandah outside his shack along with her pups and every time she saw him her mangy tail thumped the boards like a carpet beater. He'd done his best to ignore her but in the end he'd taken to saving her some of his steak, for which she was pathetically grateful, ravenously swallowing it whole while the pups milled about hassling for milk.

The dog at the orphanage had followed him about like a shadow too until the poor thing was found dead next to the swill bins, its mouth pulled back in a rictus grimace, poisoned by the strychnine-laced bait Brother Tobias used to kill the rats. Binky suggested they bury Dog next to Father William. They'd snuck out at dead of night to do it after they'd rescued Dog's body from the manure heap where Brother Tobias had dumped it.

Jon unclenched his fists; it didn't do to carry so much hate. He tried to think of something else, but the image of Dog was too clear in his mind, its white coat covered in red dust and cow shit, the brown eyes sunken and dull. He'd wiped off as much of the muck as he could but the animal's pelt was stained green and the body was beginning to stink. After the dog died Brother Tobias told them animals didn't have souls that the best place for it was the muck heap where the carcass would rot down so the nutrients could be spread on the land again.

They didn't put a cross on the grave; they didn't want the priests to know in case they dug him up. They said a prayer for Dog and both of them agreed that they'd rather be like a dog with no soul than a human with a soul like Brother Tobias's. Binky said that when he died he hoped he'd never leave purgatory because then there would be no chance of bumping into any of the Brothers. Jon wasn't so sure. According to Father O'Leary, Father William was in hell, but if anyone deserved hell then it was O'Leary, he was the one supposed to be looking after them, and yet all he cared about was impressing the dignitaries who came to admire the orphanage or the church they were building, or the plans for the next project – a huge statue of the Lord with outstretched arms that he was going to have built on the hill overlooking Karundah.

Unease wrapped itself around him like a stinking blanket. No one, Stan, Scally or Alice, had mentioned O'Leary and he didn't dare ask. It had been over a month since the accident, long enough for the constable to be informed. Perhaps O'Leary was still in hospital; maybe he'd lost his memory, maybe neither. He couldn't afford the luxury of relaxing, the sooner he gathered some money together the better.

At nine they were back down in the valley again and Stan was inspecting the dry-blower.

'Bloody thing's broken,' muttered Stan. 'Dry-blowing'll have to wait for another time.'

'How does it work?'

'It's the same principle as a sieve except you're letting the wind do all the work. You dig out the alluvial cement, crush it down as fine as you can and then pass it through the blower, as the soil tumbles down the light stuff blows away and the solid, heavier stuff is left behind and that's where the gold'll be if there is any.'

'What about mining?' asked Jon.

'What do you want to know about it?'

'Will you show me what to look for?'

'How do I know you won't try and jump my claim?'

'I wouldn't do that, Stan, you've got a gun and I haven't.'

'Tell you what, I'll show you a no-hoper. What are you like in confined spaces?'

'Don't know.' He couldn't ever remember being in a confined space.

'Follow me.' Stan led the way up the valley carrying a lamp and a small chipping hammer until they reached a cave-like entrance. There was no winding-gear at the adit only a huge pile of loose slag and yellow scree spilling down the valley side. The entrance was small, about the size of a bloke Stan's height, and the sides and roof were braced with props of rough-hewn mulga wood. Jon had to bend down to follow.

Within minutes he started to feel uneasy, the dank, musty smell was rank in his nostrils. No-hoper Stan said, did that mean it was a worked out mine? He reckoned it would be. Stan would be mad to show him the real thing. He'd said greed made people do daft things that blokes out in the goldfields had died over a nugget of pure gold.

The light from Stan's miner's lamp barely lit the way, blocked as it was by the old man's slight body. Jon kept close, trying hard not to imagine a rockfall and a slow death from asphyxiation.

The tunnel seemed to go straight into the rock and there were galleries, some barely two feet high, branching off. Jon shuddered. How did men do it? He pictured them working by candlelight, chipping away, a mountain of rock above them. He didn't want to think about it but couldn't stop. His chest tightened, it was difficult to breathe – they were running out of air, he was sure. Sweat prickled his top lip and in his armpits. He felt light-headed and sick. He wanted to go back, but that meant leaving Stan and the light, besides he could get lost – the place was a warren of tunnels and passageways – then the old chap veered left, shuffling along an even narrower passageway than the one they had been following. When his own shoulders brushed against the rock he shuddered so violently he was sure Stan could hear his teeth rattling in his head. Suddenly, the light ahead appeared bigger and cast longer shadows on the walls, the claustrophobia eased as they stepped into a small rectangular chamber with a ceiling that barely cleared his head, six feet high, he calculated, by six feet by six feet. Faint with relief he fell to his knees, dragging air into his tight lungs, forcing away the pinpricks of light that danced behind his eyes.

'Are you all right, son?' Stan squatted next to him and rested a hand on his shoulder. 'Take it easy. Breathe slow and deep…that's it…slow and deep.'

Gradually the bright spots faded and the tight feeling eased.

'Looks to me like you're not cut out to be a miner, son. Takes some like that. Some get over the fear, others don't.'

Jon felt a fool, and a coward. 'Now you've got me here you might as well show me what we're looking for.'

Stan held up the lamp and peered into his face. Satisfied with what he saw he swung round and directed the beam on the back wall. 'See that?' The beam picked up a lighter looking seam that zigzagged like lightning through the reddish rock. 'That's quartz and the brown stuff is ironstone. By rights there should be gold here but no one's found it.'

Jon touched the rock, ran his fingers over the rougher, wetter feel of the ironstone and then felt the smooth hard edges of the quartz. So that's what he needed to look for if he ever got to go mining for gold!

'I suppose mining the stuff's the only way to get rich?'

'About right, you can make a living from panning for alluvial gold, or dry-blowing and sometimes you might make a packet but the real money comes from mining, finding a mother lode, a bloody great reef.'

'Like Lasseter's?'

Stan laughed, a deep belly laugh, 'Aye, like Lasseter's.'

Lasseter's mountain of gold! Binky Brent was always going on about it. According to Binky, Lasseter's body was found near Shaw Creek in 1931. In his diaries he said he'd found a reef of solid gold but he'd left no coordinates, no directions as to how to find it. Some said the man was barking mad, but Binky believed the reef was out there waiting to be rediscovered.

Jon stepped out into sunshine, eyes squinting against the brightness, and shivered. How could blokes like Stan spend their whole lives in holes in the ground, in tight, cramped spaces with hundreds of tons of rock above them looking for elusive reefs?

Depression settled on him like wet fog. There were no quick fixes in this life, hard graft, that's what it took. No one ever gave you anything for free; even the free gold in the creek bed had to be

panned for – hours of back-breaking work for a nugget the size
coffee bean – only lucky buggers found big nuggets lying on
ground. You make your own luck Mam always said.

'Gone off the idea, have you?' asked Stan.

Jon didn't answer. What was the point?

'I knew a bloke once who tramped off into the bush for a du
Dug a hole, squatted over it, mind miles away, waiting for
bowels to move and what did he see, a yard in front of him, ly
on the ground, a nugget the size of a cricket ball.'

'Crap,' said Jon.

'No,' said Stan, 'gold.'

Jon looked at Stan's deadpan face. They both started to lau
'You're having me on.'

'You need an open mind about this place,' said Stan.

'Or a gyppy belly,' added Jon, laughing fit to burst.

They spent the rest of the day panning for gold. Stan told him m
about the gold rush days, about Hardman and his run-in with
blackfellas over a sacred site at the far end of the valley oppo
No Hope mine, and about the good and the bad times and old pr
pecting tales he'd heard over the years. While they talked S
found more flakes and Jon a few pinheads of bright but nothing
compare with his solid gold crescent-shaped bean. With no
find to keep them they finished up early and headed back to Sta
shack.

'All right if I visit again, Stan? Maybe next time you'll show
how the dry-blower works.'

'Any time, son, any time, so long as you're not intent on jump
my claim the minute I get sick.'

'You're a mate, Stan. I wouldn't do that.'

'What do you want gold for?'

'I told you, my little sister, Kathleen, she's in a children's ho
in Liverpool. If I can get enough money together I can get u
place, look after her myself.'

'No family?'

'None to speak of,' said Jon. 'Mam died in 1939 and Gran
too sick to care for us.'

'What about your dad? Killed in the war, was he?'

'He ran off with Rose Butler, a floosie from Prince Street.
skipped across to Canada, or so Gran said.'

'No wonder you're driven,' muttered Stan.

'What do you mean?'
'Nothing, son, just saying life can be a bit of a bastard at times.'

CHAPTER 9

It was dusk as Jon pulled into the yard. On the seat next to him was a brown paper packet from Stan for Alice. He parked the utility in the shed, lifted the packet off the passenger seat and headed across to the bungalow, Old Yella at his heels.

Alice watched him approach from her favourite seat on the verandah. What was she thinking? Did she have plans up her sleeve to make him pay for taking time off or would she behave as if nothing had happened?

'Rachel came to see you,' she said before he'd reached the steps. 'Nice girl, Rachel, make some fella a fine wife one day.'

He ignored the comments and handed over the parcel.

'What's this?'

'Don't know. Stan said it was for you.'

She took it off him and stripped away the brown paper covering. She grinned when she read the title and then dropped the book on the floor. Jon craned his head, trying to read the upside-down title – *Advanced Chess*. What were the two of them playing at?

'Find any gold?'

'A bit.'

'Come on then, what does *a bit* look like? Show me.'

Jon took out the glass vial and handed it over.

She held it up against the light and rattled the gold bean. 'Won't buy a ticket home to Liverpool, will it? Are you planning on going prospecting again?' She sat there watching him like a cat with a mouse, a half smile playing on her lips; she tilted her head to one side waiting for his reply. For a fleeting moment he had a glimpse of a younger Alice – the Alice Stan had fallen for forty years earlier.

He felt colour flooding his cheeks. 'Yeah,' he said shortly.

'Well, seeing as you've a yen to go gallivanting you can take the ute into Charlestown tomorrow and pick up the supplies. Don't see the point in paying Les Harper's delivery charges. And while you're at it you can deliver this letter to Rachel, pick up the new frock I ordered, and then call in at the bank.' She dropped a couple of envelopes on his lap.

Knots twisted Jon's stomach; breakfast was like lumpen lead in his belly. He took a couple of long, slow, deep breaths and mentally rehearsed the words – Alice's great-nephew, Walter's grandson – in case anyone asked.

A soft patch on the dirt road grabbed the wheels, the ute yawed left then right when he spun the steering wheel trying to correct the slewing vehicle. Curly hung on to the dashboard, knuckles paler under his dark skin. For a moment Jon thought he'd lost control, then the tyres gripped and hauled them out of the hole.

He glanced in the mirror and looked into the red dust thrown up by the backdraught. Red fog, that's what his brain felt like sometimes when he couldn't see any way out of the mess he'd got himself into, and lying to folk was a sure way to get tied up in knots. Suddenly, England seemed very far away.

He pulled up outside the Agricultural Stores and waved the envelopes in Curly's face. 'Reckon I'll be about half an hour. Will you be all right?'

Curly grinned. 'No sweat. I'll keep me nose clean and stay out of Gerry's way.' He leaned back in the seat and propped his feet up on the dashboard.

It was dark inside the store. Jon made his way through piled-up blocks of salt lick, rolls of bailer binder, skeins of rope and tightly rolled barbed wire wrapped around small, sturdy wooden frames. On the walls to the left were saddles, bridles, horse blankets, and stacked underneath, horse feed, drenches for horses, cattle and sheep, sheep dip, shearing equipment and all the other paraphernalia needed on the local cattle and sheep stations. On the right were five-gallon tins of tar, creosote, red-oxide paint, and buckets full of galvanised nails, nuts, bolts and staples. Hammers, saws, chisels, and similar equipment were laid out on steel shelving. Through a door on the right was the General Store annex where Les stored tinned food, cooking fat and dry goods such as rice, dried peas and flour.

Jon heard Les's 'G'day' before he saw him.

'I've come for Alice's order,' he said, handing over the shopping list.

Les read through it, occasionally glancing to the left or right, checking the stock. 'I haven't heard a word from that priest,' he said at last, 'have you?'

Jon shook his head.

'He must have pulled through. We'd have heard on the bush telegraph if he hadn't and the constable would have been out to Wes's checking the saloon.'

'It's still at Wes's?'

'Aye, Scally's told them where it is, but no one's been out to collect it and Wes says it's drivable. I'll have this loaded by...' he glanced at his watch, 'half past eleven. Got anything else to do?'

'Bank,' said Jon. 'I've got a letter from Alice for a fella called Maurice Cato.'

'Righto! While you're in the bank I'll get Gerry to load this stuff for you.'

Jon left Les to it and crossed the road. It was marginally cooler inside the bank. An aluminium fan that had once been painted sage green clanked above him, churning the soupy air and making life difficult for the flies zigzagging between the rotating blades.

'Mr Cato?' said Jon to the middle-aged bloke behind the counter.

'Yes?' Cato flicked back a stand of jet-black Vaselined hair. It stayed where it landed accentuating the pronounced widow's peak and frown lines creasing his damp forehead.

Jon flapped dust off the envelope and handed it over.

Cato's sweaty fingers marked the envelope and smeared the counter where his hand had rested. He sliced open the envelope with a paper knife, removed the single page and read it. He glanced at Jon and re-read it. 'And who are you?' he asked.

Cato knew who he was; Alice would have put it in the letter. 'I'm Mrs Macarthur's great-nephew from England.'

'It'll take a while to deal with this,' said Cato. He stretched his neck and pulled at the stiff collar with a damp finger. 'Will you wait or call back?'

Jon felt hotter watching Cato sweat. 'Half an hour?'

'Half an hour will do fine,' said Cato.

Jon stepped back into the rising heat and crossed over to Simpson's. He didn't know who Alice was fooling asking him to deliver a letter to Rachel. Rachel was nice enough, but he wasn't staying at Jarrahlong. He peered through the shop window and saw her folding garments and stacking them in one of the pine drawers that lined the back wall of the store.

He pushed the door open. The bell jangled.

Rachel smiled when she saw him and in her best posh voice she mimicked Simpson's, 'And what can I get for you, Sir?'

Jon grinned and in his best accent joined in the game. 'I'd like to see your neckerchiefs please, Miss.'

Rachel bobbed him a curtsey, 'Certainly, Sir.' Then she burst into a fit of giggles. 'You need a haircut,' she said, 'you look like a girl. All the blokes'll fancy you.'

'Hardly any to choose from.'

'You wait until the shearing...the place'll be busy. The hotel'll make a packet for a few weeks.'

Jon ran his fingers through his hair.

'There's a barber down the road, he'll make a half-decent job for a price. You still want that neckerchief? We have a good selection.' She turned round and pulled out a pine drawer and placed it on the counter in front of him.

'Alice asked me to give you this.' He handed her the letter.

She took it, and their fingers touched. Her hands were warm and dry, not like Cato's.

'You find any gold then?'

So, she had visited Alice. 'Not much, just a piece the size of a coffee bean.'

'That's not bad, is it? Not for a first attempt. Are you still planning on heading off to the goldfields?'

What else had Alice said about him? 'Yes.'

'You don't want a neckerchief, do you?' She put the drawer back.

Jon didn't know what to say. He felt himself redden. 'I better be going then.'

'You'll call in next time, won't you?' She looked at him, her cheeks pinking-up even as she spoke.

He didn't know what to say.

'Only there isn't anyone else our age hereabouts.' She waited. 'Look, I'll tell Dad to go easy on the sarcasm.' She shifted her weight from one foot to the other still waiting for him to speak. 'Oh, just forget it; I was only being friendly, not proposing marriage or anything.' Her face scarlet she turned and flounced through the door marked 'Storeroom'.

Jon couldn't get out of the shop fast enough. What the hell had Alice said? Had she encouraged Rachel? The red fog descended again, and another feeling he couldn't quite identify. Despair, or was it embarrassment? He wasn't sure, but one thing was certain – the sooner he left Jarrahlong the better.

He was still thinking about Rachel as he re-entered the bank. He didn't notice Mr Cato sitting at the desk in the corner of the room until he spoke.

'Mrs Macarthur has asked for this package from her safe deposit box. You'll need to sign for it and I'll need your signature for the money too.'

Money! Mr Cato handed him the two release forms and a black and silver fountain pen. Jon sat down. On the desk lay the safe deposit package and a wad of notes. He stared at the money. Wages for all the stockmen and himself, and he guessed the rest was to pay the shearers. His hand shook as he signed J. Macarthur as Alice had instructed him to do.

He picked up the notes, now bundled up in a brown envelope, and felt the weight of them. He could head for Fremantle. He'd have no trouble getting on a ship. He could bribe his way on board if necessary and he'd have enough to keep him going in England until he could get a proper job.

Mr Cato's voice cut through his thoughts. He jumped. Had Cato read his mind?

'Have you somewhere safe to put this?' Cato held out a package. 'These are valuable documents. It wouldn't do to lose them.'

Jon swung the small haversack off his shoulder and unfastened the holding clips. He pulled out the sandwiches Belle had made and, ignoring the disdain on Cato's face, laid the greasy packet on the counter while he stashed the money and the package in the bottom of the bag.

Jarrahlong wages – a king's ransom! He thought about Liverpool and his sister. He could be home in six weeks.

Mr Cato handed him a brown paper bag. 'For your sandwiches.'

Jon took the hint. 'Thanks.' He hitched the haversack onto his shoulder conscious of the weight and didn't register Mr. Cato's clipped 'Good day' until he was out of the bank; he was too busy planning what to do with Curly.

He'd drop him off at the edge of town, give him plenty of water, he could make his own way back – Aborigines knew the land and according to Alice they were always going walkabout. But what if he was caught? Jailed for theft? He'd never stolen anything before – only penny liquorice sticks and chewing gum from the corner shop when he was seven and that didn't count; he'd only done it once for a dare.

He turned off the deserted main street and cut down alongside the dry store to the back entrance where he'd left the truck. The flatbed sat low on its axles. Curly, stooped under a half-hundredweight sack of flour, looked up when he heard Jon and bumped into Gerry as he went to off-load it on to the truck.

'Watch what you're doing, y'black bastard,' slurred Gerry.

Curly steadied himself and shrugged the heavy sack onto the truck trailer. It landed with a flat thump.

Gerry swayed, legs spread, his chin jutting forward. 'I told y'to mind yerself, y'black bastard.' He slammed Curly hard against the tailgate. 'Y'hear me?'

Jon heard Curly gasp and saw the fear in his eyes.

Gerry's left hand shot out; he grabbed hold of Curly's shirt, dragged him forward and smashed his fist into his face.

Jon felt Curly's blood splatter his cheek. He wiped it away, the stickiness slick against his fingers. He stared at it and smelt its cloying sweetness. He couldn't move. He was back in the orphanage. He clenched his fists until the knuckles ached and the rage kicked in.

'Let go!' he yelled. He grabbed Gerry's right arm and dragged it down.

Gerry staggered. He let go of Curly's shirt and in an uncoordinated, clumsy movement took a swing at Jon.

Jon was too quick. He dodged Gerry's fist and shoved him, pushing him away from Curly and himself.

Gerry recovered faster than Jon expected and his face reddened as surprise turned to fury. He didn't waste time talking; he grabbed a handful of Jon's hair. At six foot two Gerry stood three inches taller and he had a long reach.

Jon sensed, rather than saw, the fist heading for his face. Stinging pain exploded behind his eyes and nose. He forgot where he was. Everything started to spin. He didn't feel the second fist; by the third he'd got his addled brain together. Gerry's piggy eyes had glazed over – Jon recognised the signs, he had to act and act fast if he wasn't to be beaten into a pulp. He yanked his head free leaving Gerry staring at a handful of blond hair.

The drunkard's ruddy face split into a grin as he balanced on his toes, rocking gently, as he prepared to attack.

The two circled each other eye-to-eye like a pair of fighting cocks. Neither spoke. Gerry's heavy breathing rasped in the dry air; his sour breath fanned Jon's face. Their boots scraped the hard-packed earth.

Jon feigned a jab with his right fist but Gerry's ugly smile told him everything, Gerry wasn't afraid: he was pacing himself and he was going to do a thorough job.

He watched Gerry move forward, cat-like, his hand low and his fingers curled ready to deliver a crippling uppercut to the belly. Jon sidestepped at the last moment and, taking advantage of Gerry's bulk and momentum, grabbed his arm and swung him around and shoved. Disorientated, wrong-footed and carried by his own body weight, Gerry fell heavily against the dry-store door and cracked the back of his head against the large metal hinge closest to the ground. Jon winced.

Gerry lay with his head at an unnatural angle, his arms splayed like a discarded rag doll. Jon stood over him panting and gathering himself for the next onslaught, but Gerry didn't move.

Jon sensed Curly standing behind him even before he spoke.

'Is he dead, Jon?'

'Don't be daft. He's just out cold.' Jon felt the short hairs on the back of his neck prickle and he shivered even though he was sweating heavily.

'What do we do now?'

Jon dropped to his knees and shook Gerry; the Australian's head tilted sideways and thudded onto the earth, his sightless eyes stared into the dust.

'Bloody hell, Jon, he's dead!'

Jon stood up. 'He's not, he's just out cold.' He stared at the body lying at his feet, conscious of the horrified expression on Curly's face. He tried to think and couldn't. He glanced down the street, then back to Gerry. He wiped his brow and then peered into the back of the dry store. Where was Les? Where was everyone?

Jon licked the sweat off his lip, knelt down again and felt for Gerry's pulse. It was there, but it was weak, he was still alive! He rolled Gerry onto his side and tried to haul him into a semi-seated position, then, without warning, Gerry vomited.

Jon jerked backwards. When Gerry came to he'd be dangerous. He'd call the constable. He'd have him clapped in jail and if he wasn't sent to prison for assault he'd be sent back to Karundah. The colour was returning to Gerry's ashen face. He'd got to act.

'Get into the truck,' he said to Curly, slamming the tailgate closed. He yanked open the cab door, threw his haversack behind the driver's seat, grabbed the starting handle and muttered a Hail Mary. The engine turned over first time. Without a backward glance he tossed the starting handle into the cab, jumped in and drove like a maniac with Curly hanging on to the dashboard as the ute bounced over the corrugated road.

When they were clear of the town Jon glanced at Curly. 'He

tripped,' he said, 'I didn't touch him, okay? He was drunk and he tripped and banged his head on the door. Okay, Curly?'

Alice Macarthur sat on the verandah, smoking a cheroot; a thin ribbon of blue smoke spiralled upward.

'What's wrong, lad? What've you done to your face?'

He had to tell her. He didn't know what else to do. 'Gerry.'

'What about him?'

'He started shoving Curly around. He was beating his brains out.'

'And?'

'And...' He squared his shoulders. He should have taken the road west and kept going for Fremantle and the docks.

'And?'

'I tried to stop him...he was drunk...unsteady and he staggered, he hit his head.'

Alice stared at him for a long moment. Her pet cockatoo, its sulphur-yellow crest bright against the bleached wood, squawked then shat, adding to the mess under the perch. 'Is he dead?'

'Don't think so.'

'What do you mean, you don't think so?'

'No...I don't know...I don't think so.'

'For God's sake, lad, why didn't you go and find Les?'

'He wasn't there...I...I... '

'You panicked.'

Jon nodded. He wished he hadn't, but he had, and now he'd got to live with the mistake. 'It'll be his word against mine.'

'So?'

'Well, they won't believe me, not against Gerry.'

'Why not?'

'Because—'

'Because you're a runaway from the orphanage?'

Jon gazed into cold blue eyes, heard the scorn in her voice.

'Did you remember to go to the bank?'

Jon dropped the money and the package onto the seat next to her, avoiding her eyes – she'd know straight off he'd planned to do a runner. He was surprised she'd trusted him, he wouldn't have.

'I ain't opened it.' He sounded guilty as hell, and defensive. He should have kept his big mouth shut. When in doubt say nothing Gran always used to say. He wished he was back at home in Liverpool instead of stuck out in the back of beyond with a hard-faced, hard-hearted old woman and her bloody cockatoo.

He knew he was being unfair. Alice had given him a roof over his head and then there was Rachel. Rachel talked about her with real affection. He'd heard it in her voice and he suspected it wasn't because of the doctor's fees Alice had paid either.

'What about my frock?' She saw the look on his face. 'Not to worry, it'll wait till next time.' She leaned back in her chair and drew on the cheroot as the sound of a vehicle came to them carried on the breeze. She exhaled the pungent smoke. 'Looks like I've got a visitor.'

Red dust lifted by the backdraught billowed out behind the truck like an eerie vapour trail.

'You'd best make yourself scarce, lad.'

Jon ducked into the shade of the verandah.

'Hold up a minute.' Alice peered hard at the approaching vehicle. 'It's okay, it's Ed. You'd better stay.'

'Is he on his own?'

'Probably, Ed's not one for company.'

Scally drove the ute right up to the homestead. He jumped down and didn't bother stuffing his hands into his jeans pockets as he usually did. This time they hung loose at his sides as he strode the few yards between them.

'Y'blethering idiot,' he yelled. 'Haven't y'got any sense?'

Jon stood behind Alice.

'I told ya y'couldn't trust him, Alice. Y'should've sent the bastard packing. Bloody Poms, sending us their dregs, the only reason they're here is because their own families don't want them. Old habits die hard,' said Scally savagely, 'convicts first and now scummy kids.'

Jon's nails dug into the palms of his hands, so that was what the locals thought, that was why Scally hated him and all the other kids at the orphanage – he saw them all as good for nothing...scum...the kids that Britain wanted shut of, kids like him who'd been shipped out and dumped halfway around the world to be looked after by the good Catholic Brothers.

Jon sagged. He stared blindly at Scally. Maybe he was right. Maybe they were scum. Their families didn't want them and their Government couldn't get rid of them fast enough.

'How's Gerry?' asked Alice.

'Headache,' said Scally, 'and a bloody great lump on his head the size of an emu's egg. The idiot could've killed him.'

'What did Gerry say?'

'He said this young thug set about him, that Jon lost his temper because he wasn't loading the truck fast enough.'

'He's a liar,' snapped Jon, his hands fists as he struggled to control his temper. 'It was nothing to do with that. It was Gerry. He was picking on Curly, calling him a black bastard—'

'So,' said Scally with a shrug. 'Curly *is* a black bastard. Don't give y'reason to nearly kill the bloke.'

'He was drunk,' said Jon. He'd always hated Scally and now he knew why. It had nothing to do with his link to the orphanage, his morose nature, or his attitude to Poms. It was the shrug. It reminded him of his dad when his mam learned about Rose Butler. His dad was always saying, so what? And he was a self-centred bastard too, walking out on Mam like he did.

'Hold on, Ed. Just look at the lad.'

Scally looked at Jon. 'What about him?'

'He's well beaten up wouldn't you say? Curly doesn't look any prettier. Strong, beefy lad like Jon here, I'd say Gerry's got a black eye at the very least.'

Scally glanced from Jon's badly bruised face to his clean, unmarked fists.

'Was Gerry drunk?' asked Alice.

'Gerry's always got a skinful, y'know Gerry.'

'Aye,' said Alice, 'and what about Gerry and blackfellas?'

'What about them?'

'He hates em. Says they should be shot like rabbits.'

'He ain't the only one to think that.'

'No, grant you that, but it all hangs together. Jon says Gerry attacked Curly and you know Curly, easy-going's his middle name. Never known Curly lay a finger on anyone and certainly not on a white fella, and not Gerry. Gerry'd make two of Curly, he's a big fella.' She leaned back in her chair, her eyes slits as she watched Scally think things through.

Scally shrugged again, the familiar 'so what?' look on his face.

'Jon and Curly are mates, Ed. Stands to reason he'd stick up for him and I'll grant you, he *is* an idiot. It would've made more sense if they'd left Gerry to it and gone back later.'

'Yeah, well, they didn't and Gerry's pride's hurt. And now he's shooting his mouth off and threatening to call in the constable.'

'Warn him off,' said Alice, 'and tell him if he isn't careful we'll be the ones pressing charges for assault and battery.'

Scally looked up from his cigarette and scowled. 'Why're y'so bothered about this young pup? We both know what he is.'

'Aye, but he's not afraid of hard work and the likes of him are in short supply around here. You ask Rachel.'

Scally glared at Jon. 'He needn't get any ideas about sniffing around my Rachel or I'll do what Gerry couldn't.'

Jon's body tensed. He imagined shoving his fist down Scally's gullet.

'Go and fetch Curly,' said Alice.

Jon stared at her, his mouth open.

'Now,' she bellowed.

'Why? It wasn't Curly's fault.'

'Just fetch him,' she said, a hard glint in her eye.

Jon turned his back on them. There was no way Scally would be able to force them both into his ute. If it came to it he'd punch his way out. He was already in trouble over Gerry; one more fight wouldn't make any difference.

He found Curly sitting on the bunkhouse verandah steps with the other stockmen.

'Mrs Macarthur wants a word,' he said, nodding in Curly's direction.

'Me in trouble?'

'You and me both,' said Jon.

They didn't speak as they made their way across the yard. The scent of burning tobacco drifted on the air, Scally's roll-up; Jon smelt it as they rounded the corner.

Alice waited until they stood before her. 'Where's your family, Curly?'

'Me mother?'

'Yes. Where is she?'

'With me sisters up Murrin Murrin way, unless she go walkabout.'

'I want you to go and visit her until this trouble with Gerry blows over, you understand, Curly? And take Jon with you. Leave tonight, you can ride out as far as Denman Creek. Adie'll bring the horses back.'

Curly turned to leave. Jon barred his way. 'But I don't—'

'Close y'mouth, lad,' growled Scally, his face contorted with menace. 'If I'd've had my way I'd've had y'back in Charlestown tonight.'

Jon shut up but he didn't see why he should. He didn't want to go bush. They hadn't done anything wrong and now they were going on the run like a pair of criminals.

Alice leaned back in her chair. 'It's just a precaution. Call it a holiday.' She chuckled at her own joke. 'I should think four or five weeks will do and by then Gerry will have got over it.'

Jon didn't comment. Resentment gagged him. He hated being told what to do and the very idea of going walkabout for a month appalled him. It was a harsh land out there; they'd end up dead, desiccated bundles in the middle of the outback just like the sheep he'd seen when he'd first arrived at Jarrahlong.

'You're to be back for the shearing, we'll be needing extra hands,' said Alice. 'Now go and find Belle, get her to sort you out some grub.'

CHAPTER 10

Adie left them at Denman Creek, heading north-east, deeper into the desert. They'd followed the watercourse at first, camping near the muddy pools and living off the land, on rabbits, emu chicks and goannas. The further east they travelled the drier the land became. Scrub gave way to huge expanses of red earth and saltbush and then came the plains with spinifex so dense it scratched and prickled the skin on their calves and ankles as they picked their way through the razor-sharp grassland.

Jon listened to Curly, mesmerized by his continuous, melodious mumbling, like a Catholic telling his rosary. He flapped at the flies. Bloody dangerous place, the outback, especially in the dry months if you didn't know where the permanent waterholes were. Alice had hammered it home, stick with Curly and you'll be fine, she'd said when he'd cut-up rough about going walkabout. But it was two days since they'd refilled their bottles, if they didn't find water soon they'd end up like the camel they'd found at the dried-up lake picked clean by dingoes. He should have stood his ground, taken his chance back at the homestead.

In the ashes of the campfire they cooked pebble-sized frogs that Curly dug out of the ground. When the lake dries they dig in, he'd told him, they sit it out till the rains come and the lake fills up. Jon loosened the last of the succulent meat with his index finger and savoured the chickeny flavour. It tasted a damn sight better than the snake they'd eaten the day before even though it didn't fill the hole in his belly.

'Where are we heading, Curly?'

'Told ya.'

'Murrin Murrin,' muttered Jon. Murrin Murrin was the standard answer. 'So where's Murrin Murrin?'

Curly held up eight fingers.

Eight more nights! Jon kicked at a column of ants scavenging for food. They'd be dead in three. He crouched over the dying embers, soaking up the last of the heat, fear a tight knot in his belly. He'd been stupid to leave the station, stupid to follow Curly. Maybe tomorrow he should strike out on his own and try and follow the trail back to Jarrahlong.

'We're lost aren't we?'

Curly stopped chewing. Jon felt uncomfortable under the intensity of his gaze.

'Aren't we?' he repeated.

'Nah, we're not lost.' Curly turned his attention back to his food, sucked a bone clean and tossed it into the ashes. 'How'd y'find y'way round back home?'

'I follow the road signs,' Jon snapped.

'That's what we're doin'.'

'There aren't any road signs.'

Curly grinned. 'Just cos it don't have a wooden marker with Murrin Murrin painted on it don't mean it's not a road. We're follerin' the ancestor footprint.' He nodded in the direction of a narrow spit of brown rock that rose about three feet out of the earth. It was long, fifty yards maybe, snaking its way deeper into the outback like a king brown.

'You mean you're wandering about looking out for rocks and stuff?'

'Nah, I'm singin' the trail.'

'You've been this way before then?'

Curly shook his head. Jon stared at him. Was this some sort of Aboriginal joke?

'In the Dreaming, first time Perentie Man foller this trail he make up a song about what he see: desert, salt pans, creek bed, spinifex, sandhills, rock, mulga scrub. We learn the songs so we know the way.'

'Perentie?'

'Big lizard, Perentie Man, clan ancestor.'

'What if you forget the words?'

'You're in deep trouble, mate.' Curly drew a line across his throat. His black face split into a broad grin that showed off a row of perfect, white teeth.

Jon thought about the ten-day trek across the vast, barren plain, the harsh, unforgiving land sucking moisture out of everything like a giant sponge. 'So, if you forget the words you can't find the waterholes and if you can't find them you die. Right?'

'More than that, mate. Y'can't sing the piece y'undo the Dreaming, mess up what ancestor did. It's important – life or death stuff.

When the clan gets together to sing the footprint y'have to know y'bit. Big crime not to. Clan take y'life if y'don't respect ancestor footprints.'

Jon tried to read the expression on Curly's face. Was Curly spinning a yarn, or was that mumbling he'd been doing ever since Denman Creek, singing? Maybe the heat had got to him, addled his brain. Jon shivered. How the hell could anyone sing on and on about mulga scrub and spinifex plain, mile after mile? And how did he know which direction to take?

'Well, you'd better get singing again because we need water.'

Curly gazed at him, his face untroubled.

Jon flopped back and stared at the Southern Cross, the stars brightening in the evening sky. Was Curly telling the truth? Did Aborigines have a weird way of remembering old trails across the desert, some way of finding permanent water in a desert ten times bigger than England?

He sat bolt upright. What if Curly forgot the words or missed a marker? He glanced sideways at Curly. Perhaps he ought to start paying closer attention, maybe leaving a few markers of his own. Perhaps he should shut up, he didn't want Curly to go and forget the tune or anything; he didn't fancy dying of thirst in the outback just because he couldn't keep his big mouth closed.

They'd been walking in the baking heat for days, crossing salt pans, a vast claypan, and interminable sandhills that sapped energy and dragged at the muscles in his legs. The flat, arid, stony plain stretching to the raised ground in the distance had been a welcome relief, but that was hours ago. He'd stopped listening to Curly miles back; instead, he fixed his eyes on a mountainous plateau floating on the horizon and the watery mirage shimmering in the distance. Bloody things mirages, they fooled you even when you knew they weren't real. Days ago he'd caught tantalizing glimpses of black, stalk-like men way out across the claypan. He'd walked faster hoping to catch up with them until Curly yelled at him to slow down, told him they weren't real.

He sucked on the pebble Curly had given him, but it didn't quench his maddening thirst and by the time they reached the base of the plateau he no longer cared whether Curly sang the footprint or not. He dropped his haversack and flopped down next to it while Curly dug into a depression not far from some acacia bushes. The red sandy soil darkened and, at about two feet deep, water collected in the bottom of the hole.

Jon sucked in the smell. 'Perentie footprint?' he asked.

'Nah, creek bed.'

Jon noted the dogleg of scrubby bush leading away from them. 'Why here?'

Curly pointed to the one green acacia bush among the brown and grinned.

In a surprisingly quick time Curly filled a bottle and passed it over to Jon. The water was discoloured and gritty, but it slid down his parched throat like nectar. That night they went to sleep hungry, huddled in an old army blanket against a big rock for warmth.

When Jon woke, water was already bubbling in the billy. Curly threw in a handful of dried leaves and watched the concoction simmer. Scattered at his feet were green, yellow and red feathers. Mulga parrots! A couple of birds were already skewered onto a cooking stick. Breakfast!

'Where did you find them?'

Curly nodded behind him towards the mallee scrub, a dense thickety mass of silver-grey brush that stretched as far as the eye could see along the base of the plateau.

'Is this an ancestor footprint?'

Curly waved his arm indicating different directions. 'This big place, many ancestor footprints. Clans meet and sing the Dreamings.'

'Bloody hell, Curly! You mean it's a sort of crossroads, right here, in the middle of nowhere? Is this Ayers Rock or something?'

'Nah,' said Curly, 'that one's up by Alice.'

After they'd eaten Curly led the way through the mallee brush to a wide cleft in the base of the ironstone escarpment. They followed a dried-up creek bed, walking in single file into deep shade through a network of purple-blue gorges and then they climbed to a vantage point high on the plateau.

A hidden paradise lay in the gorge below them. A necklace of pools followed a watercourse that seemed to rise from the rock. Majestic ghost gums were dotted along its length and jewel-bright parrots sat among the branches like ripe fruit.

'Where does the water come from?' asked Jon.

'Underground, where the ancestor sleeps.'

'Where does it go?'
'Back to the ancestor,' said Curly, pointing to a clump of eucalyptus at the edge of a rocky outcrop far below them at the other end of the gorge.
High on the plateau the temperature was hovering around the hundred-degree mark, Jon could feel the sun biting through his shirt, below him, on the shady side of the gorge, it looked cooler, inviting after the heat of the desert they had crossed.
He batted away the flies circling his sweaty brow and flopped his hat back on his head wondering how the great rent in the rock had been formed, an earthquake perhaps, back when the earth was still young and then maybe water eroding the softer stone – was there any way of telling? Far in the distance more dark smudges on the plateau suggested other gorges formed part of a chain along the flattish backbone that he and Curly were standing on.
Jon leaned over and peered down. A hundred and fifty feet below he could see the first of the pools.
'How do we get down there?' he asked as he scanned the sheer sides of ironstone layered like streaky bacon.
'Folla that path,' said Curly, nodding in the direction of a precipitous route down into the canyon.
'Is it safe?'
'So long as you don't do anything daft,' said Curly, a grin splitting his face.
'No helter-skeltering then,' said Jon.
'You what?'
'Like we did at the green pool…on Jarrahlong,' he added when he saw the puzzled expression on Curly's face.
Curly's face cleared. 'That what you call it?'
'Yeah, what do you call it?'
'It don't have no name, mate,' said Curly over his shoulder.
Jon followed Curly as he picked his way down to the bottom of the gorge. Even on the sunny side Jon was conscious of the temperature dropping from the baking heat high on the plateau to pleasantly warm the closer they got to the canyon floor.
When they reached the bottom they stood on flat rocks and there Jon saw carvings of lizard footprints and zigzags scratched deep into the stone.
'Perentie Man,' said Curly when he saw Jon tracing his fingers over the man-made marks.
He led Jon down towards the first pool. It was no bigger than a basin with animal and bird tracks baked into the mud at the water's

edge. Ten yards away another pool, this time the size of a bath, led the eye to yet another and another meandering along the gorge.

'The creek's dry,' said Curly. 'Sometimes it's full.'

Jon recalled the marks on the rock and saw the perentie footprints, the dragging tail and imagined Perentie Man making the zigzag of glittering silver water in the Dreaming.

'Where does the water come from?'

Curly turned and pointed to the canyon wall behind them, to the water seeping out from between the strata. It glistened against the red rock; tiny rivulets of water sparkled and cascaded down to the next layer, bounced off a ledge, caught the light and fell again to the next, and the next.

'Pretty dry now but it's always wet, usually it pours out.'

'Like a waterfall?'

Curly nodded. Jon looked up at the rock face again, to the level where the water was seeping through the rock a good hundred feet above them; it would be some waterfall, he decided. Even now in the middle of a drought he could hear the water tinkling as it cascaded and bounced its way to the bottom and collected in the first of the pools.

Curly touched him on the shoulder and led him along a well-trodden path through the grasses and bushes growing beside the water's edge, past a profusion of butterflies and huge dragonflies that flitted across the glistening surface.

They pushed through thicker growth into an open patch of scrubby grass leading to a sandy spit. On their right a pile of large, red ironstone rocks banded in gunmetal-blue provided a sunning spot for two rock wallabies. High above was the scar in the rock face from where the stone had fallen.

The canyon took Jon's breath away; it was an Eden in the middle of a desert. He sat down on one of the blue and red rocks and soaked up the beauty of the place. Above him, high overhead in a ghost gum, a muddle of rose-splashed galahs chattered. There was nothing like this back home and no Dreaming. The sounds in Australia were also different; the harsh calls of the parakeets, galahs and corellas were nothing like blackbirds and robins. And the smells were different too: the singeing dry heat, the peppery-oily scent of eucalyptus, the sweet acacia flowers, and the arid, red earth. Even after seven years the country was still alien to him, and strange, and yet it had a beauty of its own. At sunset the colours were deep vibrant orange-reds, purple-blacks and eye-watering blues; in contrast, at midday, the sun leached out the colour leaving paler tints that shimmered in the unrelenting heat.

He pinched his eyes and turned away, scanning the rest of the valley, letting his eyes follow the strange question mark shape of the gorge.

'What's that?' Jon squinted in the bright light. 'Over there.' He pointed towards another large rockfall further along the canyon. 'It looks like mirror or glass.'

'A plane,' said Curly.

'A plane?'

'It crashed.'

'When?'

'Ten years back, maybe. Some fella tried to land on the plateau and ran out of ground.'

'Anyone in it?'

Curly shrugged.

'You mean the pilot's still in there?' The idea of a dessicated corpse still strapped into the pilot's seat fascinated and horrified him.

'Nah, reckon he had a go at walkin' out.'

Jon thought of the distance they had travelled and of the inhospitable terrain. 'Did he make it?'

'Don't reckon. He never came back for his clobber,' said Curly as he collected wood for a fire.

Jon wanted to see for himself. Leaving Curly behind him he scrambled down from the rock he'd been sitting on and skirted the mulga thicket between him and the far cliff where the crumpled wreckage lay. He clambered over more rocks and as he approached the remains he saw the nose was flattened and the wooden spars were kindling. The plane had cartwheeled after it nosedived onto the rockfall and had slithered the rest of the way on its back ending up close to the gully floor. Both wings, smashed to smithereens, littered the surrounding boulders. One wheel, still attached to the axle, hung at a drunken angle. Red dust covered the whole apart from one half of the windscreen that had survived the impact, its surface wiped by the scrubby bush next to it. It was amazing it had survived the crash as well as it had and the pilot had been lucky to get out alive.

Up close Jon saw it was small, a single-seater. He crouched down to look inside the cockpit. Old webbing from the seat belt dangled down like spirals of dirty flypaper. The wooden dashboard with its fuel and altimeter dials was splintered, the glass broken. He twisted over and lay on his back looking for clues, something to tell him who the plane belonged to. He traced a brown smear with his finger – blood? Then he probed, feeling for stowed maps, documents, anything. In the space between the floor and the bottom of the brittle leather-covered seat something moved – a small box. It wouldn't budge. He fished for his penknife. The extra leverage helped and eventually he waggled it free.

He laid it carefully on his stomach, and wriggled out of the confined space.

The tin box had rusted a little. The once blue label was almost unreadable; he could just make out 'London' in small print. There was no hinge, only a tight fitting lid, a bigger version of the tins containing Oxo cubes that Mam used to buy.

He flipped open his knife again and with care inserted the blade under the lid flap and dragged it along to loosen it, lifting as he did so. When he least expected it the lid popped off and clattered on the rock. He jumped and then laughed at himself.

Inside the box were pieces of ore, irregular in shape and the size of sugar cubes. Gold! He was sure they were gold nuggets – unless they were just lumps of fool's gold. The lads back at Karundah told tales of prospectors who had paid a fortune for a stake and ended up with a worthless seam of iron pyrites. He counted out the nuggets. A dozen in all plus two lumps of black rock that looked different from the others. In the strong sunlight they glinted like fire. He turned the two stones over and watched the red, violet and green facets change and glow, the vibrant colours reminding him of blue wrens, red-tailed black cockatoos and parrakeets on the wing. They weren't emeralds or rubies, nothing like, but they were pretty.

Swan matches and an unopened packet of ten cigarettes like the ones Mam smoked were also in the box. He caressed the cellophane. His mam bought Craven A for the lucky black cat. Odd the pilot hadn't taken them. Lastly, in the bottom lay a piece of grubby paper. Unfolded, it revealed a neat hand-drawn map. He recognised it instantly. It showed the zigzag creek not yards from where he was sitting and in the top corner were map references and obscure notes written in some sort of code.

He packed everything back into the tin and went looking for Curly. He found him down by one of the dried-up pools where he'd built a fire to roast yabbies and a few dusty, brown roots that looked like shrivelled carrots.

Curly looked up. 'What y'got?'

'A tin box, found it jammed under the seat.' He opened it and tossed Curly the matches.

Curly grinned. 'Y'might have fetched 'em sooner, mate. Easier that way.'

'Look at these. Reckon it's gold.' Jon picked up the nuggets and tossed them up like jacks and caught them. The gold gleamed in the sunlight. If it was gold he'd have more than enough to get back to Liverpool. 'We can go halves.'

Curly turned away. The silence lay heavy between them.

What had he said? Jon dismissed the uneasy feeling that swept over him and dropped the nuggets into his pocket. Perhaps he should hand them in, claim a reward, it didn't need to be a lot, just enough for a one-way ticket back on a boat – steerage would do. 'We'll tell the authorities then.'

'No.'

'What d'you mean?'

'Reckon he's forgotten by now,' said Curly. 'If the fella's dead it don't matter, if he's good he's had plenty time to come back for it.'

'Maybe he doesn't know where to look.'

'We ain't sayin' nothin', this is ancestor place.'

Jon sucked the moisture out of his last yabby and tossed the remains over his shoulder. He glanced across at Curly. The Aborigine's face was a mask of concentration as he picked meat out of a claw. Selfish bastard! He could see that now. Curly wanted to keep the place secret; he didn't want the likes of him tramping over it prospecting for gold. Well, it wasn't on. There was plenty of space for everyone. The outback was vast. Curly and the rest of them would have to get used to it. Everyone had a right to what lay in the earth, didn't they? Especially out here! He hadn't seen any fences or boundary markers. And Curly didn't want it.

After they'd eaten Curly got up and indicated for Jon to follow. He led the way back to the wreckage, skirted around it and followed a gully leading off from the canyon until the sides closed over their heads and they could touch both rock faces with outstretched arms.

Suddenly, Curly vanished.

Jon waited.

'Curly!'

His voice echoed in the enclosed space.

Bloody stupid name for an Aborigine!

'Cuuurly!'

Still no answer!

He pressed forward, edging his way round a bulge in the rock face. Ahead, he saw another cleft, a cave entrance? Must be! There was nowhere else for Curly to go.

Jon hesitated. Cold, dark places gave him the willies, made him think of Karundah and the cooling-off room. He shuddered. It was ten degrees colder in the shade, and dark. He felt for the floor with his feet, scared it might vanish. A slight, metallic-scented breeze drew him forward, deeper into the narrowing passageway. He stopped and listened. He could hear breathing. Ahead, a grey-white pearl of light danced and grew larger and brighter. He stumbled towards it and stepped into a huge cavern.

Curly stood facing away from him, his black body an exclamation mark in a shaft of pure sunlight spilling down from a gaping hole high in the cavern roof.

The hair on Jon's neck prickled. He murmured a Hail Mary and crossed himself. Somewhere deep in the cavern water burbled gently, like a sleeping cat. He stepped closer to Curly. Was it the ancestor he could hear? He wiped clammy hands on his trousers and peered through the stream of light, forcing his eyes to adjust, ready to bolt, following Curly's gaze, and gasped.

A huge monitor lizard, its body decorated with intricate patterns in red and yellow ochre, dominated the wall: the Perentie Man. Above it and below paintings covered the rock face to a height of twenty feet; he recognised the Perentie footprints with the zigzag trail. There were white saltpan circles and the reddish-brown squiggle of the king brown rock, and other symbols that he couldn't read. Was this an ancient map of Perentie Man's travels in the Dreaming?

He stared at the patterns and the fabulous creatures, some he'd only ever seen in books, their x-ray images drawn in fascinating detail: kangaroo, wallaby, possum, bandicoot, echidna, snakes, lizards and fish and then there were the handprints, hundreds of them, painted in the same three colours.

Curly stepped closer. Jon could smell his musky warmth.

'Is this what you've been singing?'

Curly nodded.

Jon shivered and took a step backwards. The place was sacred to Perentie Man, a sort of rock cathedral. Was it why Curly had brought him here? There was so much he wanted to know, so much he didn't understand. He turned to ask but Curly was studying the cavern wall. At first Jon thought he was praying but then he started to clamber up the rock face, clinging to small outcrops, feeling for hand and foot holds as he went.

'What're you doing?' he asked as Curly neared the painted head of the giant Perentie. Was it some sort of Aboriginal ritual? Was he going to kiss the image or something? Then he spotted a natural fissure in the rock just as Curly reached up and retrieved an object from it. Curly lowered himself a level and then dropped to the cavern floor clutching a dirty bundle to his chest.

Jon stepped forward to steady his landing and caught a glimpse of golden rock gleaming dully in the shadows of the cavern. Shocked, he took a step forward, his eyes fixed on the wall behind the Aborigine. 'Holy Mary, Mother of God, it's a reef!'

He pushed past Curly, stumbling as he stepped towards the reef, and ran his hand along the cold, glinting surface.

There was more gold than in the Bank of England. Was this Binky's famous Lasseter's reef? His eyes took in its golden length and rested on the cavern floor, on a neatly folded bundle and a prospector's pickaxe.

Jon frowned. Spoil, scattered and ugly, littered the cavern floor, fragments of bright rock gleamed among the discarded ore. He dropped to his knees and lifted a piece marbled with pure gold. He held it for a moment, conscious of its weight and of the nuggets in his pocket pressing against his thigh.

The pilot had stolen the gold, had violated a holy place. He looked into Curly's impassive eyes. 'It wasn't his to take, was it?'

The gold nuggets were hard against his fingertips. His ticket home gone almost as soon as he'd had it. Slowly he pulled them out of his pocket and laid them among the rubble at Curly's feet.

Curly bent down and picked up two. 'They're not from here, Jon.'

Jon looked at the fire-bright nuggets. His sister would like them if he ever got back to England. He dropped them back into his pocket. They were pretty, but they weren't the same as gold.

CHAPTER 11

Ten days after finding the plane Curly and Jon arrived at Murrin Murrin, an area dominated by mulga bush and wanderrie grasses. All that was left of the old gold-mining community was a partially demolished chimney stack, the brick foundations of a hotel, and footprints of old homesteads – squares of hard-packed earth beaten smooth fifty years earlier when Murrin Murrin was a gold-rush town and folk were throwing shacks up as fast as time and labour allowed.

The land about Mount Murrin Murrin was riddled with gold-mine workings and scrapes. They crossed the railway line behind a locomotive hauling laden wagons heading south and soon after came upon a graded road and heavy lorries going to Kalgoorlie, Jon supposed, from one of the many mines in the area. They turned back to the creek, dry even before summer took hold, and followed a chain of red gums dog-legging through the acacia bush to a rubbish dump a mile or so from town.

A wood and corrugated-iron shed stood a distance from the creek at the end of a dirt track. A cannibalised saloon, a black carapace minus its windscreen, doors, bootlid, wheels and seats, squatted on its belly; next to it was an untidy heap of blackened and rusting forty-four-gallon drums and the metalled rims of burnt-out car tyres. Humpies, single sheets of arced corrugated iron, were dotted about. Empty tins and discarded and broken bottles littered the landscape whilst shredded paper and rags flapped in the stiffening breeze. Jon stood for a moment, stock-still, shocked. Was this where Curly's family lived? Like diddicoys?

A scrawny-looking dog threw back its head and howled. Three others woken from their afternoon nap bounded over towards them their heads lowered and hackles up until Curly spoke to them in his own language. Human heads poked out from the humpies. Folk roused themselves from their shelters into the heat of the day.

A youngster, no more than four years old, ran over to them first.

The rest of the family, an old man, three more children and four women, followed.

'Where y'bin?' asked one of the older women.

'Mrs Macarthur's place.'

'Y'walkabout?'

'Yeah.'

'Y'had tucker?'

Curly shook his head.

'Lucky you find us. We goin' up Mullin Soak tomorra. Find us a nice fat kangaroo. Ain't had no roo tail in—'

'Roo-tail stew,' muttered the old fella, smacking his leathery lips as if he'd just supped a bowl full.

Jon's stomach squelched, roo-tail sounded just fine. He wasn't accustomed to the small portions he and Curly had survived on for the past three weeks. He'd lost weight; he was nearly as rangy looking as Curly.

Curly made a half-hearted attempt at introductions; Jigger, the old man, skinny as a lath and with a straggly white beard that dusted his chest every time he coughed or spoke; Rube, who had done all the talking, and Myrtle were the older women; and Curly's sisters, Maisie and Jinny – the four kids were theirs although which child belonged to which woman wasn't clear.

Jon's stomach squelched and rumbled for another four hours while everyone else lazed about in the shade under the humpies or by the red gums. Late afternoon one of Curly's sisters wandered off and returned with an armful of brushwood. In no time the dying embers were revived, the billycan set up, damper made and a giant tin of bully beef opened, the block of pink meat rimmed with yellow solidified fat.

Rube, Curly's mother, doled out the food – damper topped with a slab of meat. When the tin was empty she flung it over her shoulder. All four dogs chased after it, squabbling over its razor-sharp, meaty edges. Afterwards everyone lay sprawled around the fire like a heap of pups, scratching and farting until the sun went down and the night chill set in. That night, and for the next four, Jon and Curly slept in the old saloon with just a blanket each for warmth.

After five days Jon was sick of damper and bully beef. Every morning he expected everyone to pack up and move off; instead, they idled the day away, lazing around camp doing nothing, Mullin Soak and roo-tail forgotten.

Midday blasting shook the ground and rattled the one remaining sheet of glass in the Buick. Budgerigars and zebra finches lifted from the acacias, swooped overhead and settled in the red-gum canopy. Jon rolled to his feet, stepped over sleeping kids and dogs and headed towards the mine, Curly following at his heels. They stopped at the edge of the opencast mine watching vehicles entering and leaving. It looked dog-rough, a worked-out site, the men struggling to make a living from gold that wasn't there.

Jon took in the ramshackle, single-storey timber and iron huts, the rusting carts and discarded waste; he saw the mounds of ore piled close to battered hoppers and wide conveyor belts carrying it to the processing plant or to waiting lorries. 'Ugly, ain't it,' he said.

'Didn't used to be.'

Jon looked at Curly's grim face. 'What're you saying?'

'This ancestor place too 'til mining company said there was money to be made. They didn't listen to the old men. They just filed a claim and started digging. They disturbed the ancestor an' destroyed his Dreaming.'

The two of them stood side-by-side, hidden from sight by acacia bushes, watching, listening to machinery chewing into the earth, eating the guts out of the ground.

Jon glanced across at Curly, saw the hard look on his face and sensed his anger and despair. 'Why can't you stop them?'

'We don't have no bit of paper to say it's ours.'

'But if you own it.'

'We do, but not like Alice or the mining company that've got the land marked out in a square.'

'What have you got then, if you haven't any papers?'

Curly turned his back on the mine and squatted down next to the fence. 'Y'remember the salt pans?'

'Yeah.'

'That's my bit.'

'What do you mean?'

'Big place the outback, you have to know the lines through the country. We've all got bits that're ours to memorize and share with others. Add all the bits together and remember them and that gives y'a line across the land. I know my brother's bits and they know mine and we share 'em with cousins and people from other mobs.'

'You mean everyone learns a bit of the road, except it isn't a graded road?'

'Yeah,' said Curly, and grinned. 'There's roads all over, y'can get anywhere singing the footprint.'

'And all the lines are learnt by someone?'

'Too right, mate, as I said, y'have to know y'bit, big crime not to.'

'What about the bits in between?'

'What about them?'

Jon couldn't get his head around what Curly was saying – that clan ownership of the land depended on knowing the words. 'Is this to do with that ancestor footprint thing and the Dreaming you were on about the other day?'

'You're right.'

'Why haven't you told the authorities?'

'We tried, but they don't want to know...says we need paper with writing on it.'

'So what's the Dreaming here?'

'It's gone,' said Curly. 'They dug up the ancestor, destroyed his Dreaming, when the land's not here y'can't sing it.'

Jon woke at dawn to find the whole camp being dismantled around him, cooking pots, old grey blankets and other camping paraphernalia already being bundled up, the kids standing around, thumbs in mouths, listening to their mamas haranguing them.

He'd never seen anyone pack so fast. Not fifteen minutes after they'd started they set off in a straggling group leaving their humpies behind them, the campfire doused and the ash scrubbed away, only the corrugated-iron sheeting and the rubbish a reminder of their presence.

The journey to the new camp took five days. The mob set off early each morning and travelled during the cooler hours. During the hotter midday heat they rested in the shade of scrubby bushes and ghost gums or under the dingo hides that the women carried. When the day cooled the women went foraging for roots, seeds and berries while Curly caught goannas, rabbits, half-grown emus or snakes.

When the others dozed after setting up camp Jon headed towards the far ridge for a look about. The landscape, semi-arid and barren, glowed gold as he made his way to higher ground, skirting the prickly grasses, his feet sinking into the soft red sand until it thinned into rock. Shrubby acacia, a type of mulga he wasn't familiar with, clung to craggy scree. Small lizards basked in the summer sunshine. Jon kept his eyes peeled for desert death adders or king brown snakes, the venomous variety that frightened even the most stoic Aborigines, and searched for goannas.

An ochre-coloured lizard with a regular brown pattern along its back and of a type he hadn't come across before, and larger than most, dozed in the late sun. Supper! He crouched down, lizards were fast bastards and watchful. This one lazed on the edge of a rocky outcrop, one leg and its tail dangling over the edge. He watched it for a moment or two and it didn't even twitch. Oblivious to everything but the sleeping reptile Jon advanced inch by inch, a sizeable rock in his hand. Kill it and he'd pay his way for once and make Curly proud of him.

The lizard didn't move until the last moment and by then it was too late. The rock crushed its skull, the tail flicked, the legs splayed, the mouth gaped and the purple-pink tongue lolled as it gasped its last. Jubilant he grabbed it by its tail and lifted the three-foot-long lizard into the air. Roast goanna! He could taste it already.

He found Curly dozing next to a dingo hide propped up on four sticks. Jon stood over him, shading him from the late afternoon sun, the reptile's elongated shadow, taller than a man, lay across him and the sand he slept on. Fleeting unease flickered in Jon's brain, the shadowy shape reminiscent of…of what?

'Supper,' he said when Curly opened his eyes.

He waited for the look of surprise, of pleasure, but he saw neither. Curly sat bolt upright, shock and then horror etched on his black face.

'What's the matter?'

'Where y'been?'

'Up there,' Jon indicated the ridge behind him. He waggled the reptile, 'Caught him napping. Roast goanna.' He smacked his lips like Jigger did, waiting for Curly's keyboard grin. It didn't happen. Jon dropped the lizard; it flopped on the ground at his feet. 'What's the matter?'

'Perentie.'

'Nah,' said Jon, 'it's just a blue-tongue.'

Curly shook his head and pointed at the carcass. 'He monitor lizard.'

The blood seemed to pool in Jon's feet, he felt light-headed, scared. Perentie was Curly's clan ancestor, his totem. He looked at the animal again. Saw a smaller version of the cave painting. Why hadn't he recognised it? 'It's too small,' he said, realising he'd killed a juvenile – a baby monitor lizard, a perentie.

Curly ignored him for the rest of the afternoon and at supper he disappeared into the bush and didn't return. Rube prepared dinner but Jon didn't taste the food, and no one spoke. The others didn't seem as bothered so why was Curly so upset? Grace told him they didn't all share the same totem and that the totem was sacred. When he tried to question her further she clammed up and turned her back on him. The others were frosty too. That night Jon sat by himself wrapped in his blanket staring at the southern sky while the others slept. There was so much to learn, so much he didn't know about what Curly believed, about the Dreaming, the ancestor footprints, ownership of the land and totems. It was a whole other world, and he didn't fit in.

CHAPTER 12

The following evening they reached the rabbit fence. That night they camped alongside it and after breakfast Curly announced that they were leaving the mob.

'What about your family?' asked Jon soon after they'd set off.

'They're going back to the depot.'

Jon hitched Curly's swag over his shoulder while Curly plucked the supper he'd caught earlier. 'Where is it?'

'Over Leonora way. It's where they stay a lot of the time, there and Mullin Soak,' said Curly, 'they're almost out of billy tea and baccy and me mother wants corned beef. She says she's sick of bush tucker.'

Jon imagined the depot to be some sort of huge warehouse packed to the rafters with tins of bully beef, packets of billy tea and hard-packed blocks of chewing tobacco.

'It's a hut the constable uses,' added Curly. 'You can get rations there from the Government.'

'Corned beef?'

'Yup.'

'Your mob live there all the time?' He was asking questions for the sake of it, trying to jolt Curly out of his depression, anything to keep him talking, to avoid the long silences between them.

'Nah. Sometimes they go into the bush. They go walkabout when they're fed up with corned beef.'

'I thought Aborigines didn't like whites that much.'

'Old Colman's okay, he leaves us be, not like Dawson. He was a bastard, right enough. He took me Ma's two sisters away to the Settlement School and she never saw 'em again. They ended up working as maids for white women in Victoria.'

'Why?'

'They's half-castes.'

Jon frowned.

'Their dad was white; he was a manager on one of the big stations. Government said all half-castes had to be taught white ways, how to read English and write.'

'Why didn't your mob go back into the bush and live there?'

'The old folk had had enough. In the big dry we was starving. Not enough bush tucker to keep a kid alive never mind a mob of us and there was Government supplies at the depot.' He flapped away a fly. 'Now we got the best of everything. Roo-tail when we fancy it and corned beef when we don't. Dawson reckoned we never had it so good.'

Jon walked for a bit, slashing at the fence with a piece of stick he'd found. 'He sounds like O'Leary.'

'Who's O'Leary?'

'A priest.'

Curly tossed another handful of underbelly feathers into the air. 'Y'any brothers or sisters?'

The feathers floated down in front of Jon and he batted at them with his stick. 'A sister.'

Curly stopped plucking. 'With y'mother?'

'She's dead. Me sister's in a children's home.'

'What's a children's home?'

'Place you get sent to when there's no one to look after you.'

'Y'no aunties and uncles?'

Jon laughed bitterly. 'None to speak of.'

'What y'doin' here? Why ain't y'lookin' after y'sister?'

'The bloody superintendent at the children's home sent me, said he was doing me a favour.'

Curly plucked more feathers. 'Y'sound like me mother. She hates the Government, blames them for splitting up her family.' He held the half-grown emu at arm's length. 'Reckon y'better off on y'own.'

Was Curly right? He recalled the initial feeling of excitement after Gibson told them about Australia and then the panic as the time came to leave and all the while he was nursing the faint hope that someone would turn up and take them home. Every day he watched and waited and everyday came disappointment when no familiar faces appeared to claim them or even visit. Gran was sick, he knew that, it even crossed his mind that she'd died like Mam had done, suddenly, with no warning. But there was Aunt Marg, why hadn't she taken them to live with her? He didn't like Marg, but she was family and family was important, wasn't it?

Even now he could remember the abandoned feeling that grew until it became a knot in his belly and he couldn't eat. Matron had summonsed the doctor who said he was worrying about the voyage, that the sooner he was on the boat to Australia the better. When they'd told him Kathy wasn't going he'd shouted and screamed and swore at everyone until Gibson took out the cane and gave him a thrashing for his bad language, and after that he'd given up. He knew now he should have run away while he was still in England, but he'd been eight years old and hadn't realised just how far Australia was, that it would take six weeks to reach Fremantle.

He looked about him at the land as flat as a plate as far as the eye could see, with low-growing saltbush, bluebush and turpentines, and some plants Alice called cassia interspersed with mulla mulla and daisies, and everywhere the cushiony looking spinifex that was anything but cushiony if you were daft enough to sit on it. None of it was like anything in England, except for the daisies. A wave of nostalgia swept through him as he pictured his terraced home in Liverpool, where he'd lived with his mam and his sister, and the backstreets where he played football with Billy Wainwright and the others. He gazed over the flat land and then looked at Curly still plucking the half-grown emu and hated the overwhelming feeling of loneliness that Curly's aloofness stirred in him. If only he hadn't killed the perentie.

Overhead a flock of bronzewings muttered past and Jon caught a glimpse of the vivid, metallic-colour of their plumage. He wondered where they had come from and where they were going, to water most likely, and it was probably miles away. He kicked at a couple of stones; he'd had no idea of the distances involved until he'd run away from Karundah and then he'd learnt fast enough. No wonder the British Government had thought the place ideal for convicts and unwanted kids.

They followed the fence south and then they crossed it and cut a trail south-west. Four days after they left the others they stopped for the night at the bottom of a gorge and set up camp. The same evening, after they'd killed and roasted a rabbit that wasn't supposed to be their side of the fence, they sat around the fire watching the flames lick and curl around an old acacia stump.

The air was heavy and oppressive, even Curly had broken into a sweat chasing the rabbit. On the horizon, under a blanket of cloud, flashes of lightning temporarily lit up the sky and thunder rolled over the plain.

'Is it going to rain?'

Curly sniffed the air. ‘Nah.’

‘The day after?’

‘Maybe.’

‘Sometime, never?’

‘Sometime,’ said Curly, ‘not never. Get the build-up lastin’ days, sometimes it rains, sometimes it don’t, it depends.’ He poked at the fire, his shoulders stooped like an old man and then he pulled his blanket about him and turned away.

Jon unrolled his swag miserably conscious of Curly’s continued detachment, the old easiness between them gone. He lay for ages staring into the overcast night sky trying to understand why it was all right to kill and eat rabbits, goannas and emus but not monitor lizards, and why Curly had taken it so much to heart; it was almost as if a light had gone out in him. He watched Curly’s back, the rise and fall as he breathed. What was so special about a totem animal anyway? It wasn’t Curly who’d killed the bloody thing. He hadn’t eaten it.

He hadn’t said sorry properly. Maybe that was why Curly was still upset. ‘Sorry about Perentie,’ he said quietly, ‘I wouldn’t have killed him if I’d known.’ He shivered. ‘Can we be mates again?’

When Curly didn’t answer Jon rolled onto his back knowing that sleep wouldn’t come easily. Suddenly, he saw Stephen Hicks’s face before him and he remembered the other time he’d felt the same sick feeling in the pit of his stomach when he knew he’d let a mate down.

He closed his eyes, blanked out his thoughts and concentrated on the night noises, the tiny creatures scuttling through the undergrowth, but the soft rustling reminded him of Father O’Brien’s worn soutane brushing against the horsehair mattresses as he sidled down the length of the dormitory to Stephen Hicks’s bed.

Jon pulled his blanket closer, hot tears pricking his eyes. He’d pulled a blanket over his ears that night, but he hadn’t looked away. He’d seen the terror on Stephen’s face, he’d watched the priest roll Stephen onto his belly, his fat hand clamped over Stephen’s mouth and all the while Stephen’s cheek was pressed against the mattress, his eyes locked on to his, begging him, beseeching him to do something, anything, to stop the unspeakable act.

He scrubbed his face with the rough blanket. Why couldn’t he forget? But he knew the answer. Guilt. He’d not intervened, he’d been too afraid, and to his shame he’d been glad that it was Stephen and not him the priest had chosen.

Jon gazed at the camp fire, the flames shimmering through fresh tears as he remembered Stephen sobbing into his pillow and how, the next morning, he couldn't face his friend.

He wasn't fit to be a mate, he was a selfish bastard. He hadn't listened when Curly told him about his clan ancestor; and he should have recognised the monitor lizard, the perentie, from the cave painting. But he hadn't, and now he'd hurt Curly in a way he couldn't understand.

He turned and looked at Curly rolled up in his blanket and leaned across and lightly touched him on the shoulder. 'I'm really sorry. I'll never kill another perentie, I promise.' He waited for Curly's answer; he was still waiting as he fell into troubled asleep.

When he woke the next morning Curly was already up and gone. The fire had been rekindled and damper was cooking in the ashes. He sat for a moment or two, his head in his hands, allowing the warmth to seep into his bones and then he pulled the damper out of the ash and left it to cool on a flat rock.

A magpie flew past and landed in the acacia, a ruffed lizard caught the movement and scuttled into the shade, hesitated a moment, one foot raised, flicking the air with its tongue. Did magpies eat lizards? He didn't know. One for sorrow, two for joy Mam used to say. He looked for the magpie's partner. The lizard made a dash for it.

The gorge was smaller than the last one – the place he thought of as Paradise Canyon – in this gorge the rock sides were sheer and straight and the river that had cut its way through the rock had long disappeared underground, the only sign of its existence a straggly line of gum trees dotted along its length.

Scrapes, where the euros, the small, rough-coated wallaroos, had dug down for water, pockmarked the ground. And a deeper, darker patch, where Curly had filled their water bottles, attracted the magpie, galahs, parakeets and a flock of bronzewings, probably the mob he'd seen earlier, he thought idly as he watched the birds take the sandy water, dipping and tossing their heads like the Russian pecking-bird toy his dad had given Kathy for her third birthday.

Movement caught his eye. A python, its short fat body like dappled shade, slithered down from a rotting eucalypt and hesitated; it tasted the air with a narrow tongue and then it slid across the sandy creek bed and disappeared into the long grasses. He hated snakes, all snakes, even pythons. He tossed a rock after it. Curly had been gone for too long.

A knot of anxiety tightened in his belly as he made his way along the bottom of the ridge. He had visions of Curly dying somewhere, bitten by a king brown – the mulga snake, or even the deadly death adder.

He called.

There was no answer.

Had Curly abandoned him, left him to find his own way home, punishment for killing Perentie?

'Cuuurly!' His voice echoed along the rock face bouncing fear around the valley. He scanned the edge of the escarpment rising thirty feet above him.

Sweat trickled down his back. He stepped away from the rock face hoping for a better view. Away to his left, and fifteen feet above the ground, bushes growing out of the cliff side lay flattened and battered by dislodged rocks, and next to them was a brown arm draped over the ledge.

Curly!

He scaled the rock face, oblivious of scraped knees and elbows, feeling his way, afraid of more rockfalls, fearful of what he would find.

Curly lay on a narrow ledge, his right leg twisted under him, his left cheek pressed against the rock, another fifteen feet above him was more broken acacia. He'd been lucky not to fall the whole thirty feet from the escarpment – the vast and barren sheet of sandstone they'd spent the last two days crossing.

Curly's breathing was ragged and shallow. Jon shook him. Nothing! He sat back on his heels and tried to think. Fifteen feet was a long drop, but somehow he had to get Curly on the ground before he regained consciousness. He took out a knife and split the trouser seam. The leg was broken and although it was badly swollen and bruised, no bones protruded, the only breaks in the skin, as far as he could see, were a couple of deep scratches just above the ankle.

He shrugged Curly across his shoulder in a fireman's lift and, while hanging on to him with his right hand, crawled awkwardly along the ledge until he reached a narrow cleft, a safer route down. He peered over the ledge. A smooth landing, it was the best he could hope for. He swapped hands and hung on to Curly as he eased them both over the ledge. They fell the last few feet. Jon landed with a jolt and bit his tongue, blood flooded his mouth and tears spiked his eyes. Curly grunted as his body hit the sand.

Jon rested a moment, catching his breath, his heart pounding from the effort. They were in deep trouble and miles from anywhere, and no one knew where they were. He looked down at his friend's body lying in the dust. What if Curly didn't regain consciousness? He imagined crows pecking at their eyes, dingoes sniffing the tainted air, squabbling over their remains, and later their bones bleached white, their skulls grinning at the sky, and swore. How could Curly have been so damn careless? He bit back angry words and heaved Curly onto his shoulder again and shrugged him into a better position. Curly groaned. Groans were good; groans meant they'd make it.

Sweat poured off him, ran into his eyes and made them sting as he staggered under Curly's weight. He clamped his jaws together, breath hissing through his teeth, the distance back to camp interminable.

Curly's foot flopped sideways when he laid him on the ground. Jon knew Curly's leg needed a splint and bandages and he soon found a suitable eucalyptus branch which he snapped to length, then he ripped his shirt tail into strips and tied them together with reef knots. Ratty had howled for his mam when Father William pulled his busted leg straight, at least Curly was out cold, in any case he was almost an adult, not a kid, if he came to he'd just have to grit his teeth and bear it like a man.

Jon dropped to his knees and gripped Curly's ankle, he pulled, feeling for the bones grating into place, and then he tied the leg to the splint above and below the break. He sat back on his heels, the leg didn't look right. He didn't remember the flesh looking so black back on the ledge. Had moving him started it bleeding again?

He paced about, and poked the fire. The eastern sky was turning dark blue. Was it best to wait till morning or travel at night? One thing was for certain, Curly's broken leg needed treatment and the sooner the better by the look of it. But perhaps if he waited another day Curly would come round and get enough strength back to walk with a crutch.

That night and all the next day Jon kept the fire going; he trickled water down Curly's throat and watched the ominous sky rumbling overhead. Come evening he chewed his nails – he'd wasted a whole day and Curly was getting worse, his leg looked bad too, swollen and puffy and it smelt. He shouldn't have waited.

Long, purple shadows filled the valley and birds flew in to roost in nearby trees. Curly was drifting now, talking in an Aboriginal language, muttering and waving his arms about. Jon trickled more water down his throat, shouted at him and shook him and made him open his eyes.

'I'm going to try and find help, okay?' He shook Curly again, slapping him awake. 'Okay?'

Curly managed a nod.

'What do I look for?'

When Curly didn't answer he repeated the question, slapping Curly's face harder as he did so. 'Jarrahlong, what do I look for?'

'The babies,' mumbled Curly, 'the babies...notch...the ranges.'

'What're you on about?'

'Notch...the ranges...notch...straight.'

'What babies?' yelled Jon in frustration. 'What babies?'

But Curly was out of it. His hand seemed to flutter, making a sort of wavy double M sign and he was gone again.

Jon squatted down to refill the bottles. He didn't want to be alone in the outback. He wasn't an Aborigine. He didn't have Curly's knowledge, his skills or his confidence. The place was a bloody nightmare. Bloody Gerry...the bastard, and Scally, and Alice, they were all bastards. If he got out of the desert alive he'd pack his bag and work his passage home on a tramp ship. Australia could keep its gold, its sheep, its mad people and its Dreaming.

He screwed down the bottle tops tightly and then collected dead wood and dumped it next to the fire. He looked at the darkening sky – he had to work fast. He split the uneaten damper and left half next to the water bottle. Then he laid his own blanket over Curly's unconscious body, tucked it in and added an old canvas sheet for protection against the penetrating night chill. He leaned over Curly, willing him to hear, to understand. 'I'm going now; I'll be back as soon as I can.'

A clammy hand clasped his and drew him down. Curly opened his eyes, the whites enormous, the pupils clouded with pain and fear, his grey skin slick with sweat. Curly tried to lick his lips but spasms shook his slim frame and when he moved a sickly stench tainted the air.

'What do you want, Curly? Water?'

Curly waved feebly at his swag.

Jon fetched it and watched as Curly tugged at the piece of rolled-up blanket he always carried with him, desperation shining through his pain.

'In here?' asked Jon.

Curly struggled to sit up, but the effort exhausted him.

Jon opened out the scrap of worn blanket. In the middle, wrapped in a piece of dirty cloth, was an oval-shaped object, the object

Curly had retrieved from the cleft in Perentie's cavern. He held the bundle up. 'This?' When Curly didn't answer he unwrapped the carved, foot-long, mulga-wood plank covered in incised marks: concentric circles, zigzags and parallel lines, patterns similar to the ones he'd seen in the cave in Paradise Canyon.

Curly lifted his head. 'Tjuringa', he whispered. He plucked at Jon's sleeve and then indicated the piece of wood, 'Tjuringa.'

Jon knelt down close to Curly's side holding the object so that Curly could see it and touch it. Curly reached out and ran his hand over the carved surface as if caressing a loved one. Then he grasped one edge of it and thrust it against Jon's chest. He licked his dry lips, 'Tjuringa – you keep safe.'

'Don't be daft; you'll be right as rain in no time, mate. We'll soon have you out of here.' He went to re-wrap the object.

Curly heaved his body upright and grasped Jon's arm again. Sweat prickled his upper lip and forehead and his hot breath fanned Jon's cheek when he repeated the words, 'You keep safe.' His finger nails bit deep and he wouldn't let go. For a long moment he held Jon's gaze, the effort clear in his strained features.

'I'll keep it safe for you,' said Jon, unease filling him with a sense of dread, but still Curly clung to him. 'I promise,' he added. 'I promise.'

Curly flopped back on the ground and tried to remove the blankets covering his body.

'Are you too hot?' asked Jon glad that the moment had passed. He laid the carved wood down, removed the blanket covering Curly and stared horrified at the flesh below the knee, blacker now and puffier, the muscle above the ankle already decomposing. The stench made him gag. Gangrene!

Snakebite! Too late, he realised he'd done all the wrong things. He stared at the gangrenous leg, at Curly's face, at his body in toxic shock, and vomited.

Minutes stretched into hours, his fear a growing knot in his belly, not knowing what to do for the best. He waited and watched, dreading the long night that lay ahead. He kept the chill at bay with fire and sat listening to Curly's rattling breath, grateful for the company of tiny animals and their nocturnal rustlings in the scrubby bush.

For hours he held Curly's clammy hand and used a small piece of cloth moistened with some of their precious water to wipe Curly's brow. When Curly tried to fling off his blanket Jon covered him against the bitter cold then sat back against a rock, keeping his vigil, watching his own breath fog the air, counting off the minutes and hours, knowing it was the worst thing to do to pass the time.

Unbidden, his thoughts drifted to Karundah and his friends there. Stephen Hicks would have left the orphanage by now, and Binky Brent. Had Binky found the gold he hankered after? He thought of all the other, older boys he'd known over the years and wondered how many of them had returned to England. A few might have, the determined ones, but too many of them had given up, you could tell, the fire had gone out of their eyes; they were just living, taking one day at a time. That was how Stephen Hicks would be, whereas Binky Brent would make something of his life.

Binky's mam had drummed it into him before she'd given him up. She was mental, Binky had told him once, she couldn't look after me no more, and she said she was doing it for me own good. He remembered asking Binky how he knew. Because she was crying, he'd said, she wanted a better life for me. She told me to take me opportunities, to get a good job and be happy.

He smiled as he remembered Binky leafing through books on gold mining in the orphanage library. Binky would do that all right. He planned to stay in Australia and make his fortune in the goldfields. Nothing for me in England, he'd said. Me mam's dead, she killed herself a few months after she put me in the children's home. Brother Tobias reckons she's in hell, he says it's where all suicides go, but I don't believe him. Mam was sick; she did her best but there wasn't no one there to help her.

Maybe Binky was right, maybe Binky's mam and Father William were together in heaven. Maybe God was more understanding than the good Catholic Brothers.

Curly stirred and flung off the blanket. Jon mopped Curly's brow again and trickled water into his twisted mouth and held him until the agony eased.

When Curly fell into fitful sleep he gentled the blanket over his fevered body, and then leaned back against a rock, his eyes closed. He was afraid. Curly was dying, he knew that now. In one lucid moment he had come to realise that Curly wasn't going to make it, that the two of them were never going to walk out of the God forsaken outback together.

The urge to run away was overpowering. He didn't want to stay and see Curly die. He looked down at Curly's sweating face, the pallid flesh that had turned his dark skin grey. How long would it take for the agony to end, hours, days? He wished he knew. He gazed at the brick-sized rock at his feet and then back at Curly. He could end all the suffering, he'd done it often enough before with dying sheep.

He tried to pray, but he had no words; besides, what good had praying to God ever done him? Tears of self-pity rolled down his face and he angrily brushed them away. He had to stay. This time he couldn't abandon a friend as he had Stephen Hicks. But he knew his resolve was weak, his fear overwhelming.

He shut his eyes and ears to blot out everything. He didn't want to look at Curly's sweat-filmed face, see his shivering body, see the terror in his sunken eyes, or hear his laboured, sobbing breath. He had no words of comfort. He crossed himself and leaned forward to pick up the rock.

Yea, though I walk through the valley of the shadow of death, I shall fear no evil, came Father William's familiar voice in his head.

'Liar,' shouted Jon, shocked by the unexpected memory. He looked about him half expecting to see Father William's ghost and saw no one. 'Liar! Liar!' he shouted into the night. Who could he believe in now? Not the priest, the gentle, caring priest who couldn't live with Karundah's shadows, with the floggings and worse, and the sound of little boys crying into wet pillows. 'Liar!' he whispered to keep the devils away.

When Curly roused again he trickled more water into his parched mouth and reassured him when the shakes started and the terrors drained colour from his dark skin. Jon shivered, convinced that Perentie looked over his shoulder, his purplish tongue tasting the tainted air, waiting for revenge.

In the small hours Curly called out to Rube and Jigger, and then later came the monotone chanting, singing the ancestor footprint, journeying across the outback, his words incoherent, muddled and desperate, his eyes bright with fear, his hands clammy and trembling as the poison leeched into his body and into his brain.

The fire burned low, the wood exhausted. Jon fetched more and laid it on the dying embers, listening to the snap and crackle as the flames gently licked the dry timber.

He took his own covering and shook it free of sand and twigs and wrapped Curly's chilled frame in the second blanket.

'Jon,' the word barely formed on Curly's lips.

'I'm here,' he whispered in Curly ear.

'Tjur—'

'I know, your tjuringa. I won't forget.'

Curly's eyes opened and he looked up into Jon's face. He struggled to find the words that wouldn't come, his mind too confused, the effort too great. His brown eyes shone with fever, and Jon could feel Curly's heart pounding as he held him close.

He gazed into Curly's frightened eyes and knew the end was not so far away. He brushed away hot tears. Curly was too young to die. It should be Alice dying, or Stan, they'd lived their lives but Curly hadn't, his death was senseless. God doesn't care, he raged.

All night and through the long hours before dawn Jon rocked Curly in his arms when the spasms racked his fevered body and fear paralysed him.

In the quiet moments he remembered their time at the green pool, Curly's bronzed body, tall and sleek, diving into cool water, and Curly's laughter, his smiling face, his friendship. Overwhelming sadness engulfed him and he choked back sobs – there would be no more hunting kangaroo together, no more storytelling around the campfire, no wife for Curly, no family, no more time to grow into a man. Where was Father William's God now?

Despair racked him. For the first time in months he prayed to God, and cursed Him, his face wet with tears.

And then, at first light, as the dawn eased fingertips over the horizon and turned the rock face red, Curly died.

CHAPTER 13

It took all day for Jon to dig a grave and when it was ready he wrapped Curly's body in a blanket, his ragged fingers leaving bloody marks on the wool, and laid him in the ground with his arms folded across his chest, facing the morning sun.

He covered the grave with boulders the dingoes couldn't move, weeping as he did so, for Curly and for himself, and then he slept. At first light he wrapped Curly's tjuringa in its dirty rag and stowed it in his haversack, packed the rest of the damper and the water bottles, and headed south.

Five days Curly said when he'd asked him how far to Jarrahlong and Jon knew his two bottles of water wouldn't last that long – he'd have to travel fast, three days maximum! He tried to remember Curly's words, his actions, the double M, the notch, the ranges, and what the hell were the babies? Was it something to do with Aboriginal Dreaming...a rock formation...something odd about the lie of the land?

Once out on the open plain Jon fixed his eyes on a marker on the horizon and set off, ignoring the growl in his belly. The damper he'd eaten hadn't been enough, but it had to last him all day.

He sang as he walked, silly songs, at the top of his voice until his throat dried, keeping a watchful eye out for king brown snakes and death adders, terrified of dying like Curly had died.

The sun climbed higher, scorching his body and the earth, cooking the soles of his feet even through his boots. Escarpment gave way to sandy plain, and sandy plain to stony ground carpeted with pink and white everlasting flowers and yellow billy-buttons, and at midday he sheltered under stunted bushes and dreamed of home.

It was easier travelling by night and cooler. The moonlight silvered the landscape creating shadows, purple tongues that seemed to vanish when he looked at them. He ate his damper and finished the second bottle of water as he marched and, when the sun came up, he saw a mound of rocks in the distance, the only landmark in a plain of arid scrub punctuated with sheoaks. Were those rocks the babies that Curly had spoken of?

The sun rose higher, sweat trickled down his forehead and into his eyes making them sting and blurring his vision. He sucked on a pebble to forget his thirst, the sleep his body craved, and the heat, trying to keep a rhythm, thinking of England and home, of pavements, people and traffic, of Lime Street railway station and the smell of the trains, of the Majestic cinema and Billy Wainwright with his round, cherubic face and his love of rude limericks. What was Billy doing now?

He stumbled and fell face down on the ground, winded, his cheek stinging, and his lip. He pushed himself to his feet and brushed off the gravel embedded in his palms, ran his hand over his face and felt slickness. Blood?

Dazed, Jon stared at his wet fingers – colourless! Only a graze then! His lip doubled in size. 'Watch where you put your bloody feet,' he muttered, focussing his eyes blindly on the horizon and thinking of pleasanter things – of the Majestic, its deep-pile carpet soft beneath his feet, the smooth brass handrails cool to the touch, the usher's torch leaching the colour from his ticket, the sloping aisle, the torch flashing an empty seat, whey-faced kids turning and grinning when the usher yelled at them to take their feet off the furniture. But all too soon the heat and thirst pulled him out of his reverie. He felt his lip again and winced.

A thorny devil, its bright yellow and brown skin shocking against the red earth, watched him, its eyes unblinking, its body prickly, like thistles, and then it turned away and scuttled into the spinifex.

Jon reached the rocky outcrop in the afternoon. Close up the smooth, rounded rocks looked like babies' bottoms. The babies! He'd found the babies.

He scrambled up them and scanned the horizon for a notch, his head pounding in the heat, mirages making the distance shimmer and jump. Nausea overwhelmed him and he retched until his belly ached. Heatstroke! Bleary-eyed he looked about him; there was no shade, no dried-up creek bed in which to dig for water, no birds, no animals, just silence and mile upon mile of spinifex plain.

He rested his eyes for a moment, brushing away tears, waiting for his vision to return to normal after squinting into the sun and then he scanned the plain again, shading his eyes against the relentless glare and spotted what he was looking for. The cut or notch that Curly had spoken of was a rough V shape on the horizon to the south but he couldn't be sure, it kept merging into the shimmering heat, the watery mirage a tantalising joke. He slithered off the rocks, a sick, pounding headache like a tight band around his head, knowing he must focus on the notch and not let confusion overwhelm him. He concentrated on his feet, one foot in front of the other, then another step, and another. He mustn't stop, stopping would mean certain death on the stony plain, he knows that…but how does he know it? He can't think…better to keep going…

…His legs and feet ache, razor spinifex punctures his skin – a thousand tiny cuts – his feet squelch inside his boots. Blood? Sweat? He's not sure which and he can hear singing in his ears, Evensong perhaps, or Curly's voice chanting the footprint? His skin feels like fire. He pulls the haversack off his back, strips off his shirt, wipes his brow on it and looks at it trying to remember why he is wearing it. He tosses it away and feels better, cooler, he should have done it miles back. He looks into the eye of the sun and blinks, waiting for the black to fade to colour…soft dragging breath swooshes in his ears as he walks…time passes…and passes…

Later, Perentie Man, his ochre-coloured body with its light-brown pattern, his purple-pink tongue tasting the air, keeps pace beside him.

He blinks away the mirage.

Curly smiles. 'Not long now, mate,' he whispers. His gappy grin fades and his lips move methodically chanting the Perentie footprint.

He stops, shocked at the sight of Curly, but can't remember why he should be so surprised. 'Nice to see you, mate,' he mutters, his words sluggish, sticky and fat.

'You can't stop now,' murmurs Curly, 'folla me.'

His feet chafe and rub and feel like lead, the boots dead weights. He kicks them off and feels the burning sand between his toes. The haversack is sandpaper scraping off layers of skin, but he knows he cannot let it go, he promised. Who did he promise? Curly? Perentie? He can't remember.

He's burning up, his trousers and his jocks sear his flesh, the pain exquisite, like nettle rash or ant bites. He sheds them as he walks, hopping first on one foot and then the other, laughing maniacally at his ungainly lope as he chases after Curly.

He squints at the sun, then at the stones and the spinifex. He glances at Curly. What are they doing? Where are they going? Have they both lost their senses? He doesn't know and he can't think.

Ahead of them a watery mirage shimmers, merging the sky and the plain. Unrelenting heat beats his head and back and sucks the breath out of his lungs. He blinks the blur away and concentrates on his feet, on walking, one foot, then the other foot. He's never noticed his toes before. Where are his boots?...his britches? He glances at Curly's black toes, the rotting flesh dissolving even as he looks, the white bones treading delicately between the razor grasses, skipping over stones, sticky threads of flesh trailing behind him like ribbons.

'You all right, Curly?' The words slur, his thick tongue sticks to the sides of his mouth. He takes the silence for yes.

A brown snake slithers at his feet, the zigzag shape leaves tide marks in the sand, its scales rasp softly. Then it rises up, its upper half a lazy S, its brown head poised, its black eyes unblinking.

The image fades.

He turns blind eyes to the sun and wipes his brow, his skin as papery dry as snake skin, and shrugs the haversack over his shoulder scrubbing blisters off his back.

He thinks of singing, the silent sounds echo in his head. Curly beckons him, draws him forward, urges him on and makes him put one weary foot in front of the other. Tiredness overwhelms him. Can't do it, Curly, he says wordlessly.

He sinks to his knees and then to his belly and slithers like a king brown, curling his body around a boulder, feeling the warmth against his bare skin. The light in his head closes in, darkness wraps around him like a blanket, and he smiles as Curly sings the footprint in his ear...

So, this is the Dreaming – purple-tongued Perentie Man running over the baked earth, Curly after him, the ground littered with their bones picked clean by crows. He smiles as the image changes. In the distance Kathy calls to him and beckons, when he looks again it is Alice's face and then Stan's...

...Someone called his name and shook him.

'You all right, mate, y'still with us?'

He wanted to sleep and brushed away the hand on his shoulder shaking him awake.

'Can't leave y'here, mate.'

The voice was familiar. Curly, he tried to say, and couldn't, his tongue a sandbag in his mouth.

The cool water that splashed over his face and trickled down his throat made him cough. Then strong arms lifted him and carried him like a baby cradled against a chest, his arms flopped and bounced with each step, the scent of musk, of dry sweat filled his nose, the smell comforting, reassuring…

Later, he came to again, confused, the light now dark. He blinked away the blur and forced himself to remember. Close by he heard a bird flapping its wings and someone rising from a creaking chair and footsteps crossing to his bed. An old, lined face looked down at him – Alice! She stood watching him for a moment, not speaking, then she rapped on the floor, two short raps. Belle appeared next to her; the old Aborigine folded back the sheet covering his burning body and smoothed cooling gel on his back, his buttocks and his legs – the scent reminding him of cucumber and an English summer day – then her strong arms lifted him upright.

'Drink,' Alice ordered as water filled his mouth.

'Now sleep,' she said as she pulled the sheet over him and soon he felt himself drifting…drifting…

CHAPTER 14

When he could walk again he went to find Jimmi. The black man's face split into a lop-sided grin. 'Y're a lucky bugger, mate.'

Jon nodded, a lump in his throat. He swallowed. 'How did you find me?'

'Y'mate told me.'

'Curly!' He tried to read the expression on the Aborigine's face and failed. Alice had told him Jimmi had saved his life, that one more day and he'd have been a goner. When he asked her how Jimmi had known where to look she'd shrugged. I don't know, she'd said, telepathy, chance, your guess is as good as mine, he just took up his swag, saddled his horse and set off to find you, said he'd be gone five days.

'Did you find Curly's grave, Jimmi?'

'Yup, I did.'

'I didn't know what to do.'

The Aborigine looked him in the eye. 'Wasn't much y'could do, mate.'

'What about his mother?'

'Sammo's with her.'

'You know I'm going home?'

'Adie said. When you leaving?'

'Next week. But I want to go and see Stan first, let him know what I'm doing.'

'He the old fella out Yaringa Creek way?'

'That's him.'

'He been there years now, Adie say he's a fool, ain't nothing there but disappointment.'

Jon forced a smiled, that about summed it up. 'See you Jimmi; I'll have a word before I go.'

'You're not planning on walking there?'

Jon smiled briefly. 'No, I'm taking the ute, no more walking for me for a while.'

He went back to the bungalow for the books Alice had packed and the basket of food she'd ordered Belle to prepare.

Alice looked up as he entered the parlour. 'Now you be careful, no going down that mine of his, and keep out of the sun. How long are you planning on staying?'
'Just till tomorrow, if that's all right with you.'
'It'll have to be, you're not fit to be out in a saddle all day anyway.'
There was no smile to soften the harsh tone. She didn't want him to go but she knew argument was useless. He was leaving anyway.
'Tell Stan it's about time he came over for a game of chess.'

Halfway along the valley, in the section Stan rarely worked, the old man was busy dry-blowing. Jon parked his ute on a flat patch of alluvial ground and got out of the cab. Bess and Bonny wandered over and they both nuzzled his hand as he leaned down to stroke them.
'What're you up to, Stan? Got fed up with being a mole?'
Stan stopped what he was doing and leaned on the shovel handle. 'You could say that, I fancied a change of scenery.' He pulled out his hip flask and took a swig, coughed to clear his throat and offered the flask to Jon.
'No thanks, Stan, it's a bit early for me.'
'What's the matter, son? You look like you lost half a crown and found sixpence.'
'Just a bit tired, that's all. I'm not sleeping so well these days.'
'I hear you've been keeping out of Gerry's way these last few weeks.'
'Who told you?'
'Scally. He reckons you laid Gerry out cold.'
'Gerry was drunk and took a swing at me. I never thought he'd hit his head like he did.'
'So that's what happened. Scally didn't elaborate, you know Scally.'
Stan ran a hand down his face and then tilted his head forward and vigorously brushed dust out of his hair with his fingers. He straightened and glanced at the sun. 'I reckon it's about time for some grub…and I could do with a bath, what do y'say?'
'Sounds about right to me, Stan.' He indicated the dry-blower, 'Was it worth it?'
Stan crossed over to the machine, inspected the cloth filter and ran his fingers through the grit and dust that had collected along the leading edges of the laths.

Gold glinted in the late afternoon sun as Stan transferred the result of his effort into a canvas bag. 'Not bad for a day's work, enough to pay for me grog,' he said.

Later, they sat on kitchen chairs watching the water heating in the old tin bath, their bodies warmed by the last of the sun, sipping rum from a pair of mismatched tumblers.

'You're like a cat on tacks,' said Stan after a while. 'What've you gone and done now?'

Jon's knuckles whitened as he gripped the tumbler tighter before tossing back the fiery liquid. 'I killed Curly, Stan.'

'What do you mean, you killed Curly?'

Jon stared desolately into the bottom of his empty glass – guilt was like a rat in his belly, chewing and clawing his guts, and it was wearing him out. It had been bad after Mam died, but nothing like the anguish he was suffering now. 'I killed his totem, Stan,' he said in a quiet voice, 'except I didn't know it was his totem, and that's why Curly died.'

After a while Stan leaned forward and poured them both another shot of rum. 'You want to talk about it?'

Jon shook his head.

'So what are you planning on doing now?'

'I'm going home, Stan.'

'Will it solve anything?'

'It won't change what's happened to Curly,' said Jon quietly, 'but I'll be able to keep the promise I made to Mam and look after Kathy. I'm old enough now.'

'Aye, I reckon you are, but I don't know whether you're doing the right thing.'

'Well, that's what I'm doing and that's the end of it.' Jon tossed back the second tot of rum; the liquid burned its way down his throat and made him cough.

Stan finished his. 'Here, give me a hand with this bath; I should think it'll be warm enough by now.' Together they lifted the tin bath off the fire and lowered it onto the ground. 'There's a towel over there on the sawing horse and while I'm seeing to my ablutions you can get the tea ready.'

An hour later Jon looked at the food on his plate and felt his stomach turn over. Since he'd returned from the walkabout he hadn't been able to face eating.

He picked at the stew, each mouthful like a ball of cotton wool sticking in his gullet. He forced it down, holding back the nausea. Why did everything smell of putrefying flesh? What was wrong with him?

After half an hour Stan took their plates and laid Jon's on the verandah for the dogs to finish. Then he poured out two generous tots of rum and handed one to him.

'You'll have me drunk, Stan.'

'Get it down you, it might help.'

Jon gulped a mouthful; tears pricked his eyes as the spirit burned a hole in his belly and suffused his stomach with heat. He took another swig.

'How long've you been off your food?'

'Since Curly died…everything smells of rotting flesh.'

'Anything else?'

Jon glanced at Stan. What did he want him to say? Did he really want to know the rest of it?

Stan looked him straight in the eyes, 'What else, son?'

'Nightmares about dead people. I see them, hear them and smell them. They are real and I can't look away. And it's not just people, Stan, it's animals too, sheep and lizards, perenties, and Dog…'

'What dog?' asked Stan.

'Dog,' Jon repeated half to himself as he remembered the friendly white mongrel that had turned up at the orphanage and died soon after, in agony, from strychnine poisoning.

'You need to come to terms with what's happened then the nightmares will go and so will everything else, the churning belly, the jitters, and the squitters.'

'Oh yeah!'

'I've been where you're at, son. Reckon you're suffering from a sort of shell shock.'

Jon choked on the last of the rum. 'Don't be daft, Stan. I've not been anywhere near a battlefield.'

'You don't have to be in a war to suffer from what I'm talking about. And you've been in a few bad places these last few months. You think about it.'

Jon shrugged off the suggestion. The old fella was talking rubbish.

'You ran away from the orphanage after seeing a mate die under a bloody great rock, didn't you? Then you come to this place in the middle of a drought, you see all the dead and dying animals and end up having to kill more than a few yourself, and after that there was O'Leary.'

Jon looked across at Stan, appalled. 'He had an accident, it wasn't my fault he crashed his car.'

'I know that—'

'I was taking him back to Charlestown,' snapped Jon.

'I know, son. But the fact is you were pretty close to finishing him off. Ask yourself, what drove you to even think about it? And then there was the walkabout with Curly. It's bad enough in the outback at the best of times, but during a drought!' Stan shook his head.

'Curly knew what he was doing.'

'Aye, I know he did, but then he went and died on you, a pretty gruesome death from what you say. The journey home can't have been easy either. Reckon you nearly bought it out there. Am I right?'

Jon nodded.

'Psychological trauma is the word for it if you don't like the term shell shock and that's what you're suffering from.'

'And you know, I suppose.'

'Aye, I do.'

Jon looked up sharply.

'No one knew what to do for blokes like us after the Great War and, I can tell you, there was one hell of a lot of us. They tried all sorts of treatment, some of it pretty barbaric.'

'So how did you get shell shock?'

'Same as every other bugger, having to see and do things that no human being should have to see and do, that's what. You see, son, everyone has a breaking point and when you reach it that's when you've got shell shock.'

'Where were you fighting, Stan?'

'At the battle of Fromelles at first.'

'Where's Fromelles?'

'France,' said Stan bitterly. 'Well over five thousand Aussies were killed, wounded or taken prisoner in one day and for what? – a diversionary tactic that didn't work. The place was a blood bath.'

Stan stared into the distance and Jon guessed his thoughts were back in France.

'The air was thick with bullets – I could hear them whining past my ear and all around me blokes were dropping like flies, caught in the crossfire. I'm telling you, son, it was a battle that no one should have had to fight.'

'Were you wounded?'

'Yep, a bullet through my side.' Stan pulled up his shirt and showed Jon a deep indentation at waist level. 'Came out the back, it did and took a chunk of fresh with it.'

'Then what?'

'They patched me up and sent me to Ypres. I was with my division fighting near Polygon Wood in the battle of Passchendaele.'

'I've heard of that place, my granddad is buried somewhere near there except he hasn't got a grave, only his name on the Menin Gate.'

'Aye, there're a fair few names I know of on that memorial, and on a few others.'

'What was the tipping point for you, Stan?'

'I reckon it was a bit like you really, just an accumulation of things all piling up on top of each other, the sheer terror of being shot at, the stink of the trenches, seeing men blown to smithereens, the stench of gas gangrene and rotting corpses. And on top of all that there was the killing. It's one thing firing blind at the enemy and hoping you've got one of the bastards, but it's harder killing them face-to-face even when it's either them or you.'

Stan took another slug of rum, 'Aye, I reckon that was the thing that pushed me over the edge, all those fellas I bayoneted or shot.'

He roused himself from old memories. 'It was all a long time ago, but if you want my advice the best thing to do is to face your demons, there wasn't owt you could do about your mate at that orphanage, and it was the drought that killed them sheep, not you, and as for Curly, it was just one of those things, a bit of bad luck.'

Jon sat hunched over his empty glass, 'But—'

'No buts,' said Stan, 'as I see it you've nothing to reproach youself for, you did your best, there wasn't anyone could have saved Curly, so don't you go blaming yourself. And the sooner you let yourself off the hook the sooner those nightmares'll stop, and everything else you're experiencing, but right now the best thing for you is a good night's sleep.'

'It's no good, Stan; I'll just wake up in a muck sweat—'

'No, not tonight you won't, not with me here.'

'You sure?'

'Sure! My word, course I'm sure, no sweat.'

Stan cleared the truckle bed of boxes and threw on a blanket. He refilled the stove with keepers to last till morning, lit the kerosene lamp, drew up a chair and opened one of the books Alice had sent while Jon settled down for the night.

'You don't need to stay up, Stan. I'll be fine.'

'Yes, I do, son. I'll be watching over you. You can sleep safe tonight.'

Jon closed his eyes, and felt his body relax for the first time in days. Stan was like his gran had been when his mam was sick, before she went into hospital; Gran had been there for him then, sitting by his bedside until he went to sleep, but he wasn't a kid anymore so why did he need Stan to watch over him? He was still mulling over the question when he fell asleep.

CHAPTER 15

'Stan well?' asked Alice when he pulled into the yard the next day.

'Yes, and he sent back the books you lent him last time.'

'Is he going to come over for chess next week?'

Jon grinned. 'He said who was he to deprive you of a thrashing.'

'Did he now, we'll see about that. I hope you are ready for our last game?'

'Of course, Alice, I'm looking forward to it.'

'Straight after tea do, seeing as you'll need an early night?'

'That's fine with me, and it'll give me time to have a word with Jimmi.'

'You'll have a job, he isn't here. He said he was going over to Mullin Soak to see Curly's family.'

Jon frowned.

'What's the problem?'

'Nothing, I just wanted a word with him before I left.'

'Well, he's not likely to be back before tomorrow. I can give him a message if you want.'

'No, it's all right, Alice. I'll see you later then.'

He crossed the yard to his lean-to to start packing, cursing himself. He'd intended asking Jimmi to return the tjuringa to Curly's grandfather, Jigger, but he'd been in too much of a hurry to see Stan and now he was stuck with it – he could hardly leave it behind for the white ants to destroy, not after his promise to Curly.

He rewrapped the carved wood and carefully stowed it in his bag alongside the rest of his belongings then sat back on his bed looking around the tiny, wooden shed. Five months he'd been at Jarrahlong if he counted the six weeks roaming the outback with Curly, and it felt like a lifetime. Now he had enough money for his passage to England on a tramp ship, if he could get a berth without papers.

It didn't do to look back; even so, he knew he'd miss the place. Here he'd made something of himself, learnt new skills, earned a living wage, made friends, but the time was right to move on, he needed to build a new life for himself, and for Kathy, at home in England.

He pricked up his ears as Belle shuffled past in her old slippers. Dinner wouldn't be long, pan-fried beef and fried potatoes probably, the same as they usually had on Friday night. He supposed he wouldn't be able to afford beef in England; according to Alice, they still had rationing in Britain.

Alice sipped her favourite bourbon whiskey and, as usual, a bottle of beer stood on the side table.

'So, this is our last time,' she said as she watched him from over the rim of the cut-glass glass she was holding. A wisp of blue smoke curled and twisted upward from her cheroot while the old cockatoo sat on its perch preening itself. 'What's your plan?'

Jon looked at her.

'I reckon you don't have any papers.'

She was right, he didn't. There hadn't been any in his file at Karundah, only a note from the superintendent at the children's home in Liverpool with his name and date of birth. For family it simply said 'Deceased'. And in the destination box it just said 'Australia'. Even the vaccination certificate, which they'd taken off him when he boarded the ship in Southampton, was missing.

'How are you planning to provide for this sister of yours?'

He couldn't answer for a moment. He'd never mentioned Kathleen to her, ever. Keeping his mouth shut had become second nature with Alice. He'd only told Curly, Rachel and Stan.

'Rachel,' said Alice, reading his mind. 'Rachel said. What's her name, Kath, Kathleen?'

'Kathleen.'

'And how old is she?'

'Twelve.'

'Like I said, how are you planning to look after her?'

'I'll get a job.'

'Doing what?'

'I'll find something.'

'Sure you will, lad.'

She was as bad as Stan, he'd said something similar. He listened to the hiss of the kerosene lamp, worrying about the future, while Alice took her time finishing her cheroot. There were no Jarrahlongs in Liverpool, just docks, and shops, and jobs he couldn't imagine, but were Alice and Stan right, were their unspoken doubts justified? Well, sod them both, he was old enough, plenty of lads his age had well-paid jobs didn't they? Somehow he'd make enough for them both to live on, even if they couldn't afford steak on a Friday night.

'I've arranged for Ed to take you to Ken Bates out at Cavanagh's Creek. Pass me that box will you?' She pointed in the direction of the daybed.

He carried the fancy cigar box over to her. She rummaged through the contents and passed him a folded sheet of paper, yellowed at the edges, and creased – David Macarthur's birth certificate.

'He'd have been rising fifty by now had he lived,' she said. 'He was only eighteen when he died. Killed at Gallipoli in the first war fighting the Turks and Germans.' She leaned back in her chair and watched him read the document for a moment. 'Ken can touch it up, make a few changes here and there – good enough for what you need. He's pretty decrepit these days but his mind's sharp and his hand is still steady…he worked for the Government in the war, secret stuff.'

'How much will it cost to do it?'

'It's taken care of,' she said, 'call it a leaving present, and after Ed'll drive you to Fremantle. You'll be on a boat and on your way home inside a week. And before you ask I've taken care of Ed too. You won't have to use your precious money.'

There was no point in protesting. She had that hard, closed look on her face that he'd first seen when he'd arrived.

Jon sat staring at the piece of paper in his hand. Why was she doing this if she didn't want anything in return? Folk didn't usually do something for nothing. Except here they did. First Stan, then Curly, and now Alice had turned his world upside down.

Over the years he'd steeled himself against people. Everyone let him down in the end. Even his mam had when she went and died like she did. He knew it was unreasonable to think like that but reason didn't come into it, not where feelings were concerned.

'Call it reparation,' said Alice.

He didn't know what she meant.

'Did Stan tell you?'

'Tell me what?'

'That before David was killed he was injured. A local family found him, and his best mate, and took care of them. But the Turks found them. They dragged them both outside and stood them against the wall and made them watch while they shot the whole family – all seven of them, the couple who took them in, their four children and the grandmother. Shot the lot, including the baby. Cut them down in a hail of bullets in front of them. Cockeyed, I know,' she said, 'but that family did their best for my lad and the least I can do is my best for someone else's who has a need. And before you ask you don't owe me anything.'

'Stan talked about the war last night. He says he suffered shell shock.'

'Did he!'

He picked up the tone. 'Didn't you know?'

'No, the war wasn't something we talked about. Too many good young men lost their lives, or came back maimed from that bloody conflict. And none of the survivors wanted to talk about it. So we didn't.'

The hard, angry look on her face stopped him asking further questions. He finished the last of his beer and put the empty bottle back onto the table.

'Sixty thousand killed fighting for the mother country and a hundred and fifty thousand maimed or taken prisoner in the Great War, that was the price Australia paid for freedom in Europe,' she said bitterly. She drew on the last of the cheroot. 'And God knows know many died in this last one.' She stubbed out the cigar. 'You'd better go and pack. It'll be an early start tomorrow.'

The bungalow doors were shut. Alice's empty chair stood on the verandah, only Belle waited on the steps, Old Yella at her feet.

The rains still hadn't arrived, but the thick cloud low on the horizon looked promising. The thunder and lightning had rumbled on for days, the muggy, sticky atmosphere making everyone tired and bad-tempered. And in the last few hours the wind had risen, whipping willy-willies across the paddock, the spirals of dust, sticks, grass, and loose litter swirling fast as a man could run. Windows rattled, and doors, as sand-laden wind battered the buildings. The spare horses were spooked too, chasing about the paddock with their tails up, noses flaring, sniffing the air.

'Y'ready?' snapped Scally.

Jon dithered then hurried up the steps and let himself into the stifling kitchen still hot from Belle's shift at the stove.

Alice was where she usually was, sitting in the stuffy room, feeding the cockatoo.

'I thought you'd gone.'

'I can stay longer, if you want. A couple of months...if you need—'

'No, lad, one more hand won't make any difference here nor there, besides...' She looked away and delicately stroked the bird's sulphur crest with a tobacco-stained finger. 'You got that birth certificate safe?'

Jon patted his shirt pocket. He didn't know what else to say. The wind howling round the building said it for him, it was time to leave. 'Thanks, Alice.'

She waved a mottled hand at him. 'Just remember what I said, and don't go worrying about Old Yella if that's what's bothering you, she'll be fine, Adie'll look after her. Now bugger off, you're upsetting the bird.'

He closed the door on the hot, dark room and Alice and her pet cockatoo. He didn't know why he'd got a lump in his throat. It was only a bit of paper she'd given him. She was a hard woman and she'd had her money's worth out of him. In any case, he'd got what he wanted, hadn't he? There was nothing else left but to shake the dust off his feet as he got on the boat so why had he made the daft offer?

Belle handed him two sandwiches wrapped in a checked cloth.

'Thanks, Belle.'

'Don't thank me, Missus said to do it.'

'Get yer arse on this seat,' yelled Scally, 'I'm getting sand in me eyes.'

Old Yella stood at the foot of the steps, her tail half wagging, her head held low. Jon knelt and grabbed her around the neck and buried his face into scraggy fur, breathing in the old-dog scent. Then he let her go, avoiding her sad, brown eyes, glad he couldn't hear the gentle rasps of her tail sweeping back and forth in the dust above the noise of the wind.

'Fer Gawd's sake, lad, it's only a bloody dog.' Scally slammed his foot down and pulled away before Jon had shut the ute door.

The land slipped by – ochre-red hills covered in grey gum, mulga scrub, gidgee and gimlets, and open land with clumps of spinifex, saltbush, and wanderrie grass. Jon saw it all and noticed the darkening sky, the unnatural light enhancing the colours, and felt the hot northerly winds driving the temperature higher, whipping up dust storms, cutting the humidity. He couldn't remember autumn weather like it and shivered despite the heat.

Sand peppered the windscreen and Scally turned on the headlights. Sweat dripped off their chins, ninety degrees Fahrenheit and rising, Jon reckoned. It'd be late spring in England, and cold, raining most probably. He imagined the cool wet on his face and vowed never to complain about rain like Mam used to. It'd be strange building a new life and seeing Gran again, and his sister, after being away from home for so long.

He glanced at Scally. 'Do you mind if we stop in Charlestown?'

'What for?'

'I just want to see Wes and the others before I go.'

He knew what Wes's reaction would be, he'd try and persuade him to stay, but England was home, it was where he belonged.

'You keep well away from Rachel, lad. She's Aussie born and bred and I don't want y'invitin' her to visit, turning her head with fancy tales of Liverpool, paintin' a picture that don't exist – y'get me drift?'

Jon didn't answer; he hadn't given Rachel a thought.

'Yeah?' growled Scally, the word a threat.

'Yes,' said Jon, 'I get it.'

'Reckon yer making the right decision, lad. The outback's no place for a quitter. You need to be a man to survive out here.'

Jon didn't answer. What did he care anyway? Scally could think what he liked. He turned away from Scally's grim face, no wonder he'd agreed to drive him to Fremantle free of charge. He looked out across the bush. Away in the distance he could see a thick, dark mass boiling on the horizon and beneath it orange beads that danced and twinkled like fireflies. He tapped Scally on his arm and pointed.

'Oh my word,' Scally muttered even as they watched the beads of orange flare like firecrackers exploding in a night sky and the black smoke billowing ahead of the orange glow. 'It's a bush fire and the whole bloody lot's as dry as tinder.'

'Is that another one?' Jon pointed straight ahead and felt the truck lurch and yaw when Scally lost concentration. 'It'll burn itself out, won't it? There isn't anything out there anyway except mulga scrub.'

A nerve twitched in Scally's cheek. 'You're talking out of the back of yer head, lad. See those pretties?' Scally nodded as another column of flame flared and exploded into a million sparks. 'It's a bloody gum tree, the oil in 'em explodes and seeds itself and in these winds it can travel faster than y'can run.'

Scally chewed his lip and hung on to the steering wheel, his foot to the floor, the truck roller-coasting over ruts and slewing through the sandy patches as he fought to keep it out of the deeper holes.

The wind changed as they reached Charlestown, it swung round twenty degrees and the fire that had kept pace with them was advancing. A huge, black cloud of ash, sand and debris whipped up by the wind blew overhead like a vast cloud of locusts.

Scally drove straight to Wes's garage where the whole town had gathered. Above the roaring wind Gerry was yelling at Connie to take a truck and get herself out of the place. Scally pushed past him and grabbed the four-gallon water knapsacks that someone had filled; he dumped them in the trailer and threw in a dozen fire beaters.

Wes tossed a set of keys to Gerry. 'She's full of water,' he shouted, pointing at a water truck, 'folla me.' He fired up a bulldozer and set off in the direction of the fire.

'What're they going to do?' Jon yelled at Rachel.

'Cut a fire break through the bush, douse with water and try and stop it reaching the town,' she yelled back.

'Connie, fuel up Wes's wagon,' said Scally. 'Hold her ready. If the fire swings or she jumps we won't have long, and if we look like getting cut off don't mess about waiting.' He touched her arm. 'You look out for Rachel for me, Con. Rachel, you're to do as Connie sez, right?' He didn't wait for an answer.

Jon threw his haversack onto the bench in Wes's garage, grabbed a spare beater and sat down on the flatbed trailer floor between Al Green and Maurice Cato. Larry Simpson got into the passenger seat just as Scally slammed the truck into gear and drove after the bulldozer and water truck.

In the minutes since they'd arrived the day had turned black, the acrid scent of fire burnt the back of his throat, and the jewel-like string of ruby beads had become a yellow glow spreading across the sky to the north-west.

'How'd it start?' yelled Jon above the roar.

'Spontaneous combustion, most like,' shouted Al, his voice whipped away in the howling wind, 'there aren't any power lines to spark.' He saw the look on Jon's face. 'Sun,' he shouted, 'on a bit of quartz. In tinder conditions it doesn't take much for bone-dry scrub to catch fire. It's either that or an electrical storm, a streak of lightning and away it goes like a bloody train and in these surroundings you're lucky if you can contain it. You'd better start praying the wind doesn't shift again. Have you ever been in a bush fire before?'

'Never,' yelled Jon.

'You better listen close then,' said Al, 'first, you can't outrun a fire, leastways not this sort of fire, and not for long, and second, whatever you do never go uphill.' He wagged his finger in Jon's face to emphasise the point, 'Fires burn faster going up hill than they do going down, so if you've any choice at all go round, not over. Got it?'

'Got it,' mouthed Jon as the truck bounced over rough ground flinging him against the wooden sides of the trailer knocking the wind out of him.

'You, all right, boy?' shouted Al, recovering first.

Jon nodded vigorously, feeling his ribs, wondering if he'd managed to bust one before he'd even reached the fire front.

'And if you find yourself surrounded by flames look for burnt ground, it's safer – nothing left to burn. Or go for open plain where there's not so much to fuel the fire, it passes over quicker there.'

The three of them looked ahead at the great wall of black billowing smoke, at the sparks and flaming branches bowling through the air, and already they could feel the heat from the fire.

'Water'll protect you,' yelled Al as he shouldered his water knapsack, 'a dam or a creek but never take refuge in a water tank, the water can boil faster'n you'd imagine and you'll be cooked.'

Jon shuddered at the thought as he picked up a knapsack and grabbed tighter hold of his beater. At least out in the bush he wouldn't be tempted to jump into a tank, there weren't any, but there were no dams or creeks either, not that he knew of.

'And if the worst comes to the worst and you can't avoid the fire, choose the spot with the least combustible material and then get yourself in a hollow or behind a big rock, anything that will protect you against the heat, you could even bury yourself in the ground, that'd be better than nothing, and cover up your skin as far as you can. Right, son?'

'Right,' said Jon, wishing he were miles away.

Al jumped down first and Jon followed leaving Cato to sort himself out.

When they arrived at the front Les Harper was already there with half a dozen men he didn't recognise who were busy beating at the flames, concentrating on the left flank of the advancing fire. Les took the water knapsack off him and left him with the beater, he pointed him in the direction of the fire indicting he should join the others pounding the small flames creeping forward at walking pace in an attempt to prevent the fire reaching the gully.

‘It reaches that,’ yelled Les, ‘and we’ve had it, it’ll folla the creek and sweep along the valley and through the mallee and mulga faster than a horse can gallop.’ He stopped for a moment and wiped his brow, black streaks smeared his reddened face. ‘We keep it on the escarpment it’ll burn itself out, maybe.’

Jon’s boot leather smouldered; hot ash burned his arms and face. The fierce heat singed his eyebrows and lashes, and the hot air seared his lungs with every breath. He knew he must look like the rest of them with their red eyes and blackened faces and desperation etched into every facial line. He pounded the flames again, muscles screaming, lungs burning, back aching from the effort.

Behind them Wes manoeuvred the bulldozer, cutting great swathes through the bush and pushing away the smashed-up wood and brush to create a fire break some distance from the inferno. Gerry followed through with the water truck, two men riding in the back directing water onto the flattened brushwood.

‘Reckon we’re winning,’ shouted Scally. ‘If we can hold it till the wind drops we’ll have it under control.’

‘It’s a bloody big fire,’ yelled Al, ‘it’s gone through a few hundred acres already.’

Jon grafted for the next four hours beating away at the blackened scrub and then the worst happened, a seventy-foot-tall eucalypt exploded like a Chinese cracker, hot oil and burning twigs shot high into the air and seeded fire into the bush behind them. Flames licked their backsides and they had to retreat or be incinerated.

Scally came and found him. He grabbed his shoulder and pulled him round. Jon could barely hear him above the roar of the fire.

‘Y’gotta go back to Jarrahlong. Reckon there’s an outside chance it could swing round to the east and cut a swathe through Alice’s place.’ He pulled out a set of keys. ‘Take the truck. Get Alice and Belle and bring them back to town.’ He peered into Jon’s eyes. ‘Y’okay, lad?’

Jon nodded.

‘Good on ya. Can y’do it?’

Jon’s mouth was too dry to speak. He nodded again.

‘Don’t hang about now; it’s a foot down job. You’ve a two-hour window as long as we can hold her. Tell Alice, she’ll know what to do. Right, now get yer arse out of here.’

Even as Scally spoke another eucalypt exploded spewing out a mass of burning twigs and leaves, showering the pair of them.

Scally reacted fast; he beat out the burning debris, then ran, dragging Jon along with him, away from the fire front and bundled him into the truck.

In Charlestown Rachel flagged him down. 'What's happening?'

'Town's safe, fire's swinging east, going along the valley. Your dad says I'm to bring Alice and Belle into town.'

Rachel jumped into the passenger seat. 'I'm coming with you.'

'No, your dad said you were to stay safe.'

'Dad wouldn't have sent you if it wasn't safe.' She leaned out of the window and shouted to Connie, 'We're to get Alice and Belle, Connie.' She turned to Jon, 'Now drive.'

Half an hour from Jarrahlong they knew the worst. A chain of fire described a near-perfect arc between them and the town, and it was moving relentlessly in their direction fed by the forested land between Charlestown and the station, and driven ever faster by the winds created by the firestorm. Even at a distance smouldering twigs and ash rained down on them starting small, new fires wherever there was bone-dry tinder to ignite.

Jon leaned on the horn as they approached the homestead. Where the hell was everyone? There wasn't much time, Alice should know that. He left the engine running and jumped down from the truck. 'You get Belle,' he yelled at Rachel.

'Alice! Alice!' He took the steps in one bound and flung open the door to the kitchen. Empty! He looked into the living room and saw the pair of them over by the stone chimney breast, their backs to him.

'Alice! We have to go.'

She didn't answer.

Jon grabbed her arm and pulled her round ignoring the fury on her face. 'There's no time for this. We've got to hurry,' he yelled.

'I'm hurrying as fast as I can. Charlie,' she said, shuffling across the room to the bird. 'I'm not leaving Charlie.'

Belle didn't move.

The damn stupid pair, thought Jon. 'Get a move on, can't you.'

'It isn't the first bush fire and it won't be the last,' snapped Alice. 'It'll swing round and follow the creek, it always has.' She shuffled out onto the verandah and stood looking at the fire front less than a quarter of a mile away.

Jon threw his hands out in frustration. 'Doesn't mean it will this time, Alice.'

Belle joined them and for a moment the three of them stared at the huge curtain of orange advancing rapidly, the sky black with smoke and debris.

'Looks like you're right,' said Alice, 'but it's too late to do anything about it now, we'll just have to stick it out, dust off the Bible and pray.'

In the yard he could hear the horses whinnying, trampling the ground as they dashed about trying to find a way through the fencing, and Rachel yelling for Belle at the top of her voice.

'She's here,' he shouted, turning away from Alice.

He left the women and crossed the yard to the horses. One had a gash on its chest where it had run into the post and rail fence. He dropped the pole gate; better to let them loose, let them find their own way to safety. The horses stampeded and leapt the remaining bars, ears back, tails high.

He whistled for Old Yella and her pups. Had she run off frightened by the sound and the smell of the fire? He whistled again and thought he heard whining and scratching coming from the wood shed. Rachel heard it too and opened the door and the dogs piled out. He picked up Old Yella and put her in the back of the truck while Rachel gathered up the pups.

'What are we going to do now?' she asked.

Jon forced himself to think. They couldn't stay at Jarrahlong, there were no stone buildings, no cellars, no road out other than the one they'd come in on. The creek bed was almost dry and Al had warned him of the danger of taking shelter in water tanks. He looked at the bone-dry wood of the buildings, they'd withstand a flash fire, but this wasn't a flash fire as far as he could see, there was too much to burn and too much mallee and mulga around the homestead to risk it. Besides there wasn't time to douse down the buildings with water. They'd have to take their chance and head for the rocky ridge a mile to the north-east. He'd only ever ridden out that way, even Adie said it wasn't suitable for a truck but as he saw it, it was their only chance – there was a cave up there, if he could get them that far. He pointed to the ridge. 'We can shelter up there.'

He glanced back at Alice. She wasn't going to like it but they had no alternative. 'Get in the truck, Rachel, I'll get Alice and Belle.'

He joined the women on the verandah. 'Alice, we can't stay here.'

'I'll take my chance,' she snapped.

He glanced at the fire, closer now, the sound of it loud in their ears. 'You're coming with me, Alice.' He didn't wait for an answer. He picked her up and, staggering under her weight, half carried and half dragged her to Scally's truck, shutting his ears to the stream of invective she hurled at him.

'I'd rather die here,' she yelled.

'Well, I wouldn't,' Jon snapped, 'and I'm not leaving you behind.'

He put her down, opened the passenger door, lifted her bodily into the cab, and slammed it after her.

'Charlie!' she called.

Jon went back and collected the cockatoo. It squawked and struggled and tried to bite him.

Belle didn't say a word. She climbed into the back of the truck and sat next to Rachel and the dogs while Jon thrust the parrot through the cab window.

'What about the chooks?' fretted Alice.

'To hell with the chooks,' muttered Jon as he rammed the truck into gear. 'It's going to be a bumpy ride,' he yelled so Rachel and Belle could hear. 'Hang on.'

Tussocks of burning grass and spinifex bowled through the air like meteors. They created new spots of fire where they landed that soon blazed bright and spread the firestorm east. It was far worse than Jon had imagined. He had half a mile to drive, diagonal to the fire steaming towards them – hit a rock, smash a hole in the sump and they'd be charcoal.

He couldn't see Rachel or Belle in his rear-view mirror. They were crouched down, lying on the floor of the truck with Old Yella and her pups, a tarpaulin pulled over them to protect them from the sparks, gravel and small stones hammering down, carried by the fierce wind that buffeted the vehicle as they tried to out-run the fire.

Jon swerved to miss a rock. The engine screamed as the tyres chewed uselessly through bulldust. He prayed to Father William's God and still the truck sank, inexorably, deeper.

Alice leaned over and rested her hand on the back of his. 'Slower,' she said, her voice an oasis of calm amid the fury of the firestorm.

Her words penetrated his terror. He took his foot off the accelerator, lowered the revs and the truck eased forward, clear of the soft sand. See, he thought, there's no God out there, you get yourself into a mess and you have to find your own way out.

The wind, a shrieking, howling banshee, blasted sand through gaps in the doors. Would the engine last? Grit in the carburettor was the last thing they needed. They followed the line of the creek bed and, for the first time, turned away from the fire. Wind assisted the truck lurched forward at a faster rate.

Two hundred yards from the cave they reached the rocky outcrop. Rachel jumped down and gave Belle a hand while he helped Alice. She was still clutching the bloody parrot. 'Give me the bird, Alice.'

Halfway up the slope, half choked by Alice's arms wrapped round his neck, he started to laugh. What did they look like? – him giving Alice a piggy back and carrying a cockatoo; a girl, an Aborigine, and four dogs following behind – it was something out of a comic book.

Smoke choked them; their clothes were holed and their skin singed by flying cinders. He could hear Belle wheezing but he could only carry one at a time and he was having problems of his own. His eyes felt gritty and raw and the sweat trickling down from his brow made them sting. The thick, soupy air poisoned their lungs, making each breath an effort, starving their bodies of oxygen. We're dead anyway, Jon thought, but somehow, and together, they reached the cave entrance and safety.

Hours later the wind dropped and the fire burnt itself out. They stood at the entrance to the cave and looked at the devastation below them, at the fire-blackened landscape. The bigger eucalypts and sheoaks, now mutilated, blackened and twisted, stood like charred skeletons in a wasteland streaked with denuded red earth. Hell, thought Jon. It looks like hell. Why do folk live in this godforsaken place?

The ground burnt his feet. Scally's truck squatted on its chassis, the metal wheel rims digging into the earth, black stains were all that remained of the tyres – pools of melted rubber glistening in the sun. It was a burnt-out hulk, the cab and trailer twisted metal. Only one jerrycan of water had survived intact the rest ballooned by super-heated steam.

'What now?' asked Rachel.

'A long walk.'

'Dad'll come looking.'

If he survived, thought Jon unable to look her in the eyes. He lifted out the one good jerrycan and carried it to the cave.

'I don't know how long I'll be.'

Rachel smiled. She stood on tiptoe and kissed him on the cheek. 'Take care, won't you?'

He nodded. 'I will.'

Small animals littered the route, their bodies charred and unrecognisable. From a distance he could see that Jarrahlong was badly damaged. The wind pump, water tower and the stockmen's bunkhouse had survived and so had the shearing shed and the shearers' quarters over near the holding pens in the far paddock. The great jarrahs that gave the place its name were still standing too, but Belle and Adie's shack had gone, so had the barn, the store sheds, the fencing and the bungalow. Only the stone chimney stack and the stone piles on which the bungalow had been built remained.

A wagon stood in the yard. As Jon approached, Scally appeared from the stockmen's bunkhouse, his face ashen under the soot. He grabbed Jon's arms, his lips working, trying to get the words out.

She's safe,' said Jon. He swung round and pointed behind him, 'She's in a cave. Alice is there, and Belle, but they're in a bit of a state.'

'Git in,' said Scally. 'Show me.'

The next hours slipped by in a blur.

Alice, when she saw the state of her home, accepted Scally's offer of a place to stay, but Belle refused to leave Jarrahlong and insisted on waiting for Adie and Sammo to return. They sorted out a place for her to sleep in the stockmen's quarters, found water containers and some undamaged tins of bully-beef, potatoes and carrots, enough to last until Scally could make the trip again with the basics and then came the long drive to Charlestown in Scally's wagon, Alice in the front seat, Rachel riding in the back with him.

The fire had missed the town, but huge swathes of bush on three sides had vanished. Despite the conflagration no human life had been lost, although Harrison Station had suffered some damage and Jindalee had burnt to the ground. According to Al Green, the Samuels' sheep were greasy, blackened blobs covering their home paddock like fresh dollops of bitumen, and the few mobs that had survived the inferno were beyond saving.

Stan turned up for a beer and a natter. He told them that the firestorm had clean jumped the whole Yaringa valley and didn't singe a stick, one moment it was a freight train pounding towards him from the north-west, the sky white hot, next it was steaming away south-east, chewing up the bush like a kid eating candyfloss.

'You look done in,' said Stan in a quiet moment, 'ever been in a bush fire before?'

'No, and once is enough,' said Jon.

'It's a fact of life if you live in the outback, but they're not usually this bad.' He paid for two beers and handed one to Jon. 'Scally says he's driving you to Fremantle.'

'That's right, and he's taking me to Cavanagh's Creek first. Alice has given me David's birth certificate, says Ken Bates will 'doctor' it to make it look like mine so I can get a passport.'

'You haven't changed your mind about the place then?'

Jon shook his head.

'What about Rachel?'

'What about her?'

'From the look in her eyes I'd say she's taken a liking to you. Nice lass, Rachel. Do you reckon you'll be back this way?'

Jon shook his head, 'No, Stan, I won't be coming back and in any case, Rachel and me, we're just friends and I'm not—'

'In love with her? Maybe that's so, son. But you've an old head on you, and don't forget, friendship's not a bad basis for a relationship whether it's Rachel or some other lass.'

Jon stopped drinking and turned to Stan. 'I have to go home, Stan, and find my sister.'

'Aye, I know, I just don't want you to be disappointed, you've been separated a long time, things will have changed between you. You'll both be different people now.'

'In what way?'

'Maybe she'll want to stay where she is.'

'What, in a children's home! No she won't, no one in their right mind would want to stay in a children's home.'

'I just think that you need to keep an open mind, son. Things don't always turn out as we'd like them to. I wouldn't want to see you disappointed.' Stan stared into the distance nursing his beer, oblivious of the crowd alongside them downing beers as fast as Connie could line them up. 'I thought you might have understood the place a bit better after spending time with Alice and Curly, I thought you might have got a liking for the outback.'

Stan was serious; there wasn't a hint of a gleam in his eyes, no half smile on his lips. Jon didn't know what to say. The old fella was as bad as Alice; Stan didn't want him to go either by the sound of it.

'Give the place a chance and it'll be the making of you,' said Stan quietly.

You mean the killing of me, but he didn't bother to put the thought into words. Since Curly's death, and despite his long talk with Stan, his dreams were still haunted by decay and destruction and Perentie; his stomach still tensed, and anxiety was with him even in nightmares. He'd learned earlier than most that folk were never far from death in the outback, there were too many bleached bones out there in the desert if confirmation were needed. He stared sightlessly into the mirror behind the bar. The sooner he was away from the place the better. Once home in England he could put everything behind him and make a fresh start.

He fished in his pocket and pulled out one of the pretty nuggets from Paradise Canyon. 'It isn't much, I know, but will you give this to Alice for me, after I've left?'

Stan rolled it round in his hand. 'You didn't dig this out of the ground, leastways not around here. Last time I saw this I was out east, over at Coober Pedy. Know what it is, do you?'

'It's just a bit of rock.'

'It's a black opal, a type of silica, as I said, you can mine it in Coober Pedy, or the only other place I know of is at Lightning Ridge.' He turned the nugget over and it caught the light, a bush fire glowing in the stone, flashing red, purple and green. 'It's a fine piece.' He dropped it in his pocket. 'Aye, I'll do that for you.'

'And there's something else, Stan. Curly gave me a piece of wood.'

Stan frowned. 'What sort of wood?'

Jon looked at him surprised by the wariness in his voice. 'It's about a foot long, oval, lots of carved marks on it.'

'A tjuringa?'

'Yes, that's it. That's the word Curly used.'

'Strewth, son, what're you doing getting yourself mixed up in Aboriginal business?'

'Curly gave it to me when he was dying, he asked me to look after it.' He picked up his haversack. 'I was going to tell you about it when I saw you the other day and then I forgot. Here, I'll show you.'

Stan clamped a restraining hand on his arm. 'You leave it be. It's more than my life's worth to gaze on that.'

'But all I want you to do is pass it over to Jimmi when he gets back. I meant to do it before, but with one thing and another…and then he went off on walkabout while I was over at your place.'

Stan shook his head. 'No, son, I can't help you with this one. It's none of my business and it's a pity it's yours.'

'What do you mean?' asked Jon, trying to ignore the jitters suddenly flaring in his belly.

'Them tjuringa things are sort of sacred, and you know how touchy Aborigines are about sacred stuff, they ain't above killing folk who poke their noses into business that don't concern them.'

'But Curly gave it to me.'

'Ever heard of Aboriginal bone pointing? Strong magic that. An Aborigine points one at you and does his magic and nothing'll save you, Aborigine or no.' Stan took a long draught of beer and wiped his mouth with the back of his hand. 'If Curly's folk think you stole the tjuringa they might point the bone at you.'

'I don't believe that, Stan.'

'Suit yourself. But I'm not about to go upsetting blackfella sensibilities at this point in my life and if I were you I'd keep quiet about that lump of wood. Don't go telling folk you've got it. Better still, dump it somewhere where no one can find it, or burn it.'

'I can't do that, Stan. Curly asked me to look after it.'

'What else did he say?'

'He couldn't get the rest out. His mind kept drifting.'

'Probably trying to tell you where to take it,' said Stan.

Jon could feel the hardness of the mulga wood through the canvas side of the haversack. He shivered conscious of the warmth it seemed to generate. He pushed the bag away from his leg. You daft bugger, he thought, ignoring his unease, now you're getting as fanciful as the old fella. 'You want another beer, Stan? My shout.'

Two days later Scally drove him over to Ken Bates's place at Cavanagh's Creek and then on to Fremantle. At the docks Jon pulled his haversack out of the boot while Scally kept the engine running.

'Want me to stay a while?' Scally offered.

'No need. Thanks for the lift.'

'It's a pleasure.'

Jon didn't bother to look up. Sarcastic bugger! Let him have the last word – he always did. He hitched the haversack onto his back and walked round to the driver's door. He looked Scally in the eye. 'Thank Alice for me, will you?'

'Aye, I'll do that fer ya.'

Jon turned towards the shipping office.

Scally slammed the car into gear. 'Fer what it's worth, I was wrong,' he yelled as he pulled away.

Jon turned round, but Scally had his foot down and was already halfway to the gate.

PART II

CHAPTER 16

The lorry driver dropped Jon near Lime Street Station in Liverpool eight months after he'd left Fremantle on a tramp ship bound for Singapore. It had taken longer than he'd expected to reach England; the ship had been laid up in Jakarta for weeks and he'd had to find another boat when it became clear his was only fit for the breaker's yard.

In the city the people hurrying for buses, trams and trains jostled him as he stood for a moment getting his bearings. The familiar Liverpool dialect and the sight of the huge, stone lions crouching outside St George's Hall brought a lump to his throat – he was home! He searched the skyline for the Liver birds, looking for their soot-streaked wings lifted for take off, but the day was closing in. Fog hung over the city like a shroud blanking out the already dull grey sky, and only the lights from the Punch and Judy Café shone bright on his patch of pavement. Disappointed, he hitched his haversack over his shoulder and, dodging the heavy traffic and trams thundering along Lime Street, headed for the town centre.

The city smelt and looked different, dirty, battered, and dismal in the cold December light. Even the glow from Blacklers' windows didn't dispel the gloom. He joined the queue for a tram and stood in the aisle as it rattled along Renshaw Street and on up Great George Street and into Park Road. Great swathes of the city had vanished, bombed in the Blitz, would his home still be there, or had it been bombed too? He got off at the next stop onto the crowded pavement, listening in on friendly banter and the old familiar Liverpool expressions as folk hurried home wrapped up in dull overcoats and thick mufflers against the winter chill. He dog-legged his way through half-remembered streets and reached familiar ones, the rat runs he'd used as a kid, glad to leave the city noise and crowds behind as he crossed Jerry Road into St Micky's and home.

The street looked closed; it was turned in on itself and smaller than he remembered. The tired steps were scrubbed, but peeling paint, boarded-up windows and drunken guttering added to the air of neglect. The familiar terrace had a gap in it. Numbers four and six were missing! Shocked, he stopped to look, taking in the huge baulks of timber shoring up numbers two and eight, noting the ominous cracks in the brick work and the shreds of number four's flowered wallpaper that were still visible. An image of Billy Wainwright flashed into his mind, his round face and jet-black hair with its cowlick that never stayed flat no matter how much water he plastered on it. What had happened to Billy and his family? Had they been killed?

Number two was boarded up, but number eight was still occupied if the pot dog in the window was anything to go by.

A group of men overtook him, huddled against the cold, their heads down as snow started to fall.

'You lost, son?' asked the last in the group.

'Nah, just looking.'

'No charge for that, least not yet,' said another, and the rest laughed. 'Bloody government,' he heard one say, their steel studs rattling on the cobblestones as they tramped home. Dockers most like. He shivered, drew his coat closer, hunched his shoulders and breathed into his shirt.

Ahead, the door at number twenty opened and a woman wearing a revealing v-necked black jumper, a red skirt, black stockings and crocodile-leather shoes stepped out onto the pavement and pulled the door closed. She slung a fox-fur jacket over her shoulders – Jon caught a glimpse of gaudy lining – rummaged in her bag and pulled out a cigarette.

Her red mouth curved in a smile. Wavy, bottle-blonde hair done up in fashionable bangs framed her face.

'Home for Christmas, sailor?'

Jon adjusted his haversack. She was knocking twenty-five.

'Gorra light, luv?'

'Sorry.'

'Don't blame ya, it's a filthy habit.' The woman dropped her bag on the pavement, shrugged on the jacket and rubbed her arms briskly. 'Bloody brass-monkey weather, ain't it?' She looked him over, and smiled. 'Off the banana boat are ya?'

'No, hitched from Southampton.'

'Home for long?'

'Maybe.'

'Come up and see me sometime, hon.' She blew him a kiss, picked up her handbag and tottered off, her bottom swaying as she sashayed towards the bus stop.

Her face was familiar under all the make-up. He tried to recall the lads he knew who had older sisters: Graham Eastham, Barry Smith, Gerald McKinnon, but her face didn't fit.

He crossed to his grandmother's house, number twenty-seven. The once red door was now painted dark green and the new brass knocker in the shape of a clawed foot gleamed gaudily against the dark ground. He'd always liked the old one, the hinged black S-shape that gave a satisfying rat-a-tat-tat sound. He hammered twice – not a patch on the old one!

The door opened. A wizened face topped with iron-grey hair peered up at him from the crack. 'Yes?'

Jon stared at her. She looked familiar. 'Mrs Gregson in?'

Her eyes narrowed. 'She's dead. And who'll be wanting to see her?'

He grabbed the door jamb for support. Of course she was dead; she'd been sixty when he left, and sick. And all the time he'd been in Australia he'd never had a letter from her. So why had he never really considered the possibility? 'When?'

'Seven years ago or thereabouts.' She peered at him again. 'Don't I know your face? Aren't you Sarah's boy?' She waited for a reply and then clicked her tongue. 'You better come in, lad, you're looking a bit wan – shock was it?' She guided him into the hallway, her claw-like, arthritic fingers clamped around his arm.

The overriding smell was boiled cabbage – boiled cabbage and turpentine wax, and his gran was dead.

She led the way into the kitchen. The stone sink in the corner with shiny brass taps and, next to it, the old-fashioned, black-leaded range with a coal fire glowing in the grate were comfortingly familiar. The cooker was new and so was the row of painted cupboards.

'I'll make us a cuppa.' She flitted about the kitchen like a jenny-wren, collecting tea things together.

Jon sat and stared at the rag rug Gran had made. He recognised the old red-flannel shirt she'd used for the border.

'No one told you? About your gran, I mean?'

She busied herself with the teapot, rinsing it, pouring in the hot water, swirling it round to warm it, emptying it, two scoops of tea, then the boiling water, the lid, and the cosy. She fetched the teapot to the table and two mugs – Gran always used thick, white cups and saucers. She sat on the spare chair, took the biscuit tin and tipped out a few custard creams onto a small plate.

'It wasn't the emphysema, heart attack, in the end. Died in her sleep, she did.' She picked up the teapot and gave it a *yunck* and poured, *yuncked* again and, satisfied with the colour, filled her mug and then his. 'Nice way to go, here one minute, happy as Larry and dead the next. Milk?'

Jon nodded.

'So what've you been doing these past years, luv? Sunning yourself? Somewhere hot by the look of you.'

'Australia,' said Jon.

'Australia? What the heck were you doing in Australia?'

'Got sent out.'

'Sent out? Sent out from where?'

'The children's home.'

'When?'

'Thirty-nine.'

She sighed. 'Where do the years go?' She sipped her tea, a frown deepening the already deep lines on her forehead. 'What about your sister?'

'Still in the children's home.'

'And you've come back?'

'Going to get a job and a place for us to live.'

'Blood's thicker than water, I always say. Never understood that auntie of yours. You'd have thought she'd have taken you in when your mam died especially with your gran being poorly and all.' She took another sip. 'Still, according to Lizzie, there wasn't a lot of love lost between your mam and Marg. You know she moved?'

Jon shook his head.

'Aye, South Street wasn't good enough. She moved out Childwall way three months or so before your gran died. Lizzie never saw the place, not that it bothered her. She reckoned it'd be some fancy semi-detached house with a porch and a front garden and an inside lav. Chalk and cheese, your mam and Marg.'

'What happened to number four?'

'Bomb. Direct hit. 1942.'

'What about the Wainwrights?'

'Just Violet, God rest her soul.'

Violet was Billy's grandmother, he'd only met her once when he was seven and he couldn't remember much about her except she was bedridden even then. Billy used to run up and down the stairs with cups of tea and Garibaldi biscuits for her. And Billy's mam used to say, she'll be the death of me one of these fine days, outlive the lot of us she will. And now she was dead, killed by a German bomb.

'Where are they now?'

'The Wainwrights? Moved to the Dingle somewhere and the O'Hares went back to Ireland. They had family in Donegal and reckoned they'd be safer there, Ireland being neutral and all. Good riddance, I say. I never did like Patrick O'Hare even when he was a lad and the older he got the worse he was, always on the scrounge. So, lad, you got somewhere fixed up?'

'I only arrived home this afternoon. The boat docked last night. I had to hitch from Southampton.'

'Bit late to start looking. You can bed down in the spare bedroom if you want.'

'Thanks, Missus...?'

'Mrs Roberts, but call me Elsie, everyone else does.'

'Ta. I can pay me way.'

She waved him away. 'Geraway, your gran was my friend.'

The children's home with its high walls and railings was as he remembered it. He hesitated for a long moment then pushed the bell.

The young woman who opened the door took him aback. He glanced at her smart navy-blue uniform and then at her pretty face, everyone had been old before, fifty if they were a day.

She opened the door wider and invited him in. He stepped into the hall and the smell of carbolic soap, starch, and disinfectant transported him back seven years – the stink of institution made him gag. He controlled the urge to run and followed her along the familiar corridor into an empty office. Kathy was in the building somewhere, only yards away. She'd be in class having lessons. All he could imagine was the five-year-old child she had been. Would he recognise her? Would she recognise him? His mind and stomach churned over. He needed the lavatory.

The door opened. Jon jumped to his feet.

The superintendent nodded a greeting then crossed to the chair behind the desk. 'My name is Jones. I believe you are looking for a relative?'

'Yes,' said Jon, taking in the bloke's steel-rimmed glasses, slicked-back hair and clean-shaven chin.

'Whom do you wish to find?'

'Kathleen Cadwallader. She came here in early 1939. She'll be twelve now.'

'And what relation are you?'

'Her brother,' said Jon without taking his eyes off the superintendent's face. He wasn't from Liverpool, not with that accent.

The bloke scrutinised him over his glasses. Jon squared his shoulders refusing to be intimidated by the man's piercing stare. Jones looked away first.

'Wait here and I'll see what I can do.'

The stark room with its square desk, hard-backed chairs and the picture of King George on the wall gave him the creeps. The high, north-facing window was still barred. He shivered, remembering the austere dormitories, the dull green walls, the iron beds with their scratchy horsehair mattresses and grey bed sheets, and the tight-lipped woman who looked after them but never smiled.

Jones was taking his time. Was there a problem? Were they working out what to say to him? He shuddered. What had they done with Kathy?

Jones returned with an orange file in his hands. He placed it on the desk and then he opened a drawer and took out another pair of spectacles. He carefully removed the pair he was wearing, put them on the desk and then he polished the second pair and positioned them on his nose. He peered at Jon over the top of the half-moon frames. 'It seems your sister was adopted in 1940.'

'Adopted?'

The superintendent smiled briefly. 'We always try to find good placements for our youngsters.' He glanced at Jon. 'Take your good self.' He patted his tie.

Smarmy bastard! Jon knew the type, he was like Father Walter, and it didn't do to cross them. 'Where is she living now?'

'We can't divulge that information.'

'But she's my sister.'

Jones steepled his fingers and rested his chin on them.

'But I've come back to look after her.'

Jones closed the file. 'I'm afraid I can't help you.'

'Why not?'

'It's against the rules. Once a youngster is adopted they begin a new life with a new family.'

Jon's face felt stiff with shock. His mind refused to work. He couldn't think.

Jones filled the silence. 'In our experience children settle more quickly if the old ties are cut, a fresh start and all that. You understand?'

Jones's patronising tone angered him. 'Can I write to her?'

The superintendent stood up and extended a hand. 'I think it would be better if you let the whole matter drop.'

'Better for who?' said Jon bitterly.

Jones shrugged.

He wasn't going to let him get away with it. They couldn't just split a family up like that, have kids adopted without telling anyone. 'Is that all you're going to say?'

'I'm not at liberty to say more. She's none of your business now, Jonathan. She has a new family. She is happy and settled.' Jones crossed to the door and opened it.

Jon leapt to his feet and his chair crashed to the floor behind him. 'But you just can't do that; I'm her brother. She—'

'I think it best if you leave now, Jonathan.' Jones stood by the door an implacable expression hardening on his face.

Jon ignored the dismissal, his hands fists as he fought the rising panic, the growing fury.

'Good day, Jonathan,' said Jones, his tone steely as he ushered him out of the office. 'Thank you for calling, it's always nice to meet up with our old boys.'

The bastard! Jon brushed off the guiding hand and stalked out of the room conscious of Jones's eyes following him as his footsteps echoed down the corridor, checking that he left the premises. He yanked open the front door and stepped outside. The door clunked to behind him, the Yale lock clicked.

He stood for a moment in the chill December morning, frustration and rage souring his face. To hell with Jones! He thrust his hands deep into his pockets, hunched his shoulders against the cold, and clattered down the steps onto the slush-covered pavement. He'd find Kathy with or without the bastard's help. But where did he start? Who could he ask?

A blast on a horn and the driver's raised fist pulled him up short. 'You bloody fool! You'll be no good to her dead,' Jon muttered to himself as he stepped back onto the pavement. He let the van pass, crossed the road and headed back to the city centre with constant, gnawing hunger chewing his guts and clouding his brain. Maybe his aunt would know. Perhaps Kathy had written to her. Apart from Dad, Marg was their only living relative – he'd start with her.

Steam billowed out of a shabby café and the stale-fat stink wafting on the breeze made him feel hungry. A bacon sandwich, that's what he needed, he'd feel better with some food in his belly. He joined the queue at the counter waiting for the day's special, not bacon as he'd hoped but Spam.

He ordered a Spam sandwich and a mug of tea and carried them over to the window seat. He ate slowly, making each mouthful last, remembering Belle's enormous damper and steak sandwich that Adie gave him the first time at the billabong, and the quiet companionship beneath the blazing Australian sun. He glanced up at the dull grey sky heavy with snow and then at the folk in the café eating, smoking and chatting; he listened to their breathy speech, its distinctive intonation, conscious of his loneliness in the middle of the busy city.

Soon after he caught the tram to Park Road and walked the rest of the way. He hammered on number forty-five.

Two doors up the street a curtain twitched. He abandoned number forty-five and went to number forty-one and hammered again.

'Yes?'

'I'm looking for Mrs Graham.'

'She moved.'

'I know. I'm her nephew but I don't have her new address.'

The woman looked at him suspiciously.

'I've been in Australia for seven years.'

'Where in Australia?'

'Perth.' It was close enough.

Her sharp eyes bored into him as if she were trying to read his mind. 'Childwall, Kilbride Avenue.'

'Do you know the number?'

'No, but knowin' her, it'll have a fancy name like Dunroamin' or Journey's End.'

'Kilbride Avenue?'

'Aye. No guarantees she'll still be there though. Knowin' Marg she'll not rest until she's in a detached house.' She went to shut the door and then hesitated. 'You know she has a new fella? Harry Warrener. She married Harry Warrener soon after Fred was killed.'

Marg was prettier than he remembered. She'd had her hair done differently, softer, and she was wearing lipstick. Mam always said she was the good-looking one, maybe she was right, he had no way of telling, he'd half forgotten what his mam looked like.

'Yes?' she said.

'Auntie Marg?'

Her hand flew to her neck and she took a pace backward. 'Jonathan?'

Jon shifted his weight, wasn't she going to ask him in?

She glanced up the avenue and then at her watch. 'You'd better come in.'

She pulled the parlour door closed and led him into the kitchen. She hadn't changed much; she still thought he was too scruffy to sit in her smart front room, mucking up her posh couch, dirtying her fancy carpet with his muddy feet. He recalled the only time they'd been to tea at the other house when Fred was alive. She'd been like a cat on tacks then while they drank their orange squash and ate digestive biscuits – plain ones in case they smeared chocolate on the re-upholstered couch.

She avoided looking at him and busied herself filling the kettle. Her cheeks were pink. 'Well, this is a surprise. I didn't expect to see you again, Jonathan.'

Seeing him was a big shock. He hadn't taken her for the easily rattled type.

'What are you doing back here?'

'For Kathy. I've come back for Kathy.'

She agitated the tea with a spoon. For a few seconds the only sound was the chink of metal against pot as Jon absorbed her words. She knew! She knew he'd been sent to Australia! He unclenched his fists and forced himself to breathe normally. He had always thought she was an old bag, but she was family, she could have put a word in for him, kept him in Liverpool with Kathy.

'You knew?'

'They told me it would be a fresh start, that Australia needed young boys like you. It was for the best. They said it was a wonderful opportunity.'

'Yeah, well, it wasn't.' He wanted to add that she could have taken them in, or visited, but he didn't. 'Kathy's been adopted,' he said bitterly.

'How do you know that?'

'I went to the children's home.'

'Children's home?'

'Yeah, where Kathy and me were after Mam got sick, before she died.' He stared at her as he said the words, letting them sink in, and took savage delight in her unease. Serves her right, hope she can't sleep at night, he thought as the colour faded from her cheeks.

She opened a cake tin and lifted out a Battenberg cake and cut it into slices. Then she reached into a drawer and took out a crocheted doily and placed it on the plate. When the Battenberg slices were arranged in a half crescent she handed him a plate and a cake fork, a twee little thing that looked like a spoon with prongs. He didn't know why she bothered for someone as uncouth as him, and he never had liked marzipan. When she offered in that posh voice of hers he'd refuse.

'Has Kathy written to you?'

'Why?'

'I just thought she might.'

'No, she hasn't written.'

'So you don't know where she is?'

'Tea?' She poured a cup and handed it across to him and then she passed the sugar bowl with half a dozen sugar cubes in the bottom and a pair of silver sugar tongs. 'Did they say when she was adopted?'

'1940.'

'Perhaps things are better left.'

'That's what Jones said.'

'Jones?'

'The superintendent.'

'Cake?' She held out the plate.

Jon's stomach rumbled, maybe after all this time he'd like marzipan. He took two pieces, food was food when all said and done, he hadn't eaten since midday and the Spam sandwich hadn't been very filling.

'How did you find me?'

'The woman at number forty-one.' He didn't bother to mention asking at the newsagent's down the road.

'Dora Tulley. So you know I've remarried?'

The cake crumbled in his fingers and a pink square bounced off the plate and landed on the kitchen floor. He bent down, picked it up and stuffed it in his mouth enjoying the horror on her face. He still didn't like marzipan, too sickly sweet; after Jarrahlong and Belle's cooking he'd lost the taste for cakes and stuff. He caught her looking at the clock – quarter past three.

'You wouldn't speak to Jones, would you?'

'Who?'

'Jones…the superintendent.'

'Well, if he wouldn't tell you, he won't tell me, will he?'

Her voice was clipped with a hint of sarcasm. Why didn't she like him? 'He might.'

'No, these things are confidential, I believe.' The careful enunciation was back. She sipped her tea. 'Perhaps it would be for the best if you just forgot about her. You've made a new life for yourself now – in Australia.'

Slack jawed, he stared at her for a moment. 'I thought perhaps I could stay here.' He ignored the shocked look on her face. 'You know, until I can find a place of my own, a room or something, and a job…it wouldn't be for long…a week perhaps. I can pay my own way; I've plenty of money.'

'Harry wouldn't like it.'

'Harry?'

'My husband, he works long hours and needs peace and quiet when he gets home in the evening. You understand?'

'It'd only be for a few days. I'll be no trouble.'

She wouldn't meet his eyes. 'Sorry, Jonathan, but I think it's better if you leave now.' She started tidying things away. 'It's been nice seeing you again. Perhaps next time you're over you could stay and have tea with us or something.'

He didn't know how she managed it but less than three minutes later he was standing in the avenue looking back at the closed door. Nothing had changed. She hadn't liked him when he was a kid and she didn't like him now. Her own flesh and blood and all she'd offered him was a cup of tea and a piece of bloody Battenburg! She hadn't even taken him into the parlour but kept him sitting in the kitchen like some sort of tradesman. The bitch!

The earlier drizzle had turned into driving sleet; Jon pulled up his collar and walked. He couldn't make sense of Marg. It crossed his mind that Harry didn't know about him, or Kathleen, that Marg hadn't told him, which would explain the nerves and why she was so rattled when he asked to stay for a few days.

When he arrived back at Elsie's house he was soaked, hungry and depressed. Elsie sat him down in front of the old range to warm up and gave him a cardigan to wear while his jacket dried on the drying rack high above them. She didn't nag or probe, she just made a mug of tea and handed it to him with a slab of home-made bread and strawberry jam.

The taste of an English summer and her unobtrusive kindness made swallowing difficult. Had he made a mistake? Liverpool wasn't as he remembered even allowing for the bomb damage, and the people with their harsh, staccato accents and their banter, as they went about their business, was both familiar and yet strange. Then there was the grime and the noise and the rushing about, people, cars and trams all jostling for space in the battered city. But the worst was the weather, at least in Australia he'd been warm most of the time, often too warm, and even the winters weren't mind-blowingly cold like they were in England.

He finished eating, the heavy bread filling the hole in his stomach. Elsie knew what he needed, not like Marg with her posh house, china cups and fancy Battenberg cake.

'Got some nice scrag-end,' said Elsie, 'you look like you could do with a square meal. You like scouse? Course you do! I never made it for my Ted, he wasn't a mutton man, he'd eat beef or pork any day, but not mutton. Take it you like mutton.'

Jon grinned. At Jarrahlong he'd had plates piled high with mutton: mutton roast, boiled, hot, cold, sliced, minced, topped with eggs and served with spuds. He liked mutton. He watched as she packed the brown earthenware pot with onion, two scrag-end chops, thick slices of potato and the stock, and put it in the oven.

'So, what were you doing in Australia then?'

'Raising mutton,' said Jon and laughed.

'Well, I never! On one of them farms?'

'Stations, they call them stations.'

'No wonder you're as brown as boot polish, suppose you can ride a horse and all?'

'A bit.'

'Aye, and the rest. I've seen them boys on their horses bringing in the sheep for shearing.'

'The Pathé News,' said Jon.

'Aye, you get to know what's going on in the world from that Pathé News, so there's no need to mock.'

'Wasn't,' said Jon.

She topped up her cup with stewed tea and sat opposite him. 'I take it things didn't go well today?'

Jon shook his head. 'Kathy's been adopted but they won't say where she is. They say I should let her get on with her life, but that can't be right, I'm her brother. They didn't ask me.'

'I'm right sorry, lad.'

'And Marg doesn't care.'

'You found her?'

'34 Kilbride Avenue. I thought she might know where Kathy is, you know, that Kath might have written to her, but she hasn't. Marg said I should go back to Australia.'

'What're you going to do now?'

'I don't know. But I must find Kathy and make sure she's all right, make sure she's happy, and not being treated badly or anything.'

'That isn't likely, now is it? They have to check these people before they let them adopt, you can't have any Tom, Dick or Harry looking after children.'

'Yeah!'

She looked up sharply at the tone in his voice. 'What's that supposed to mean?'

'It isn't always like they say it is,' he said and turned away from her. He half expected her to ask him what he meant. He could sense her watching him, but she let him be and drank the last of her tea while he stared at the embers in the range grate.

'You're welcome to stay in the back bedroom, if you want to.'

Jon didn't know what to say.

'I'd be pleased to have the company until you get yourself sorted with something better.'

'Ta,' said Jon, 'I can pay, I've plenty of money.'

She waved her hand. 'The room's free but we need to get you sorted out with a ration book, and then we have to get you registered at the butcher's and the grocer's.'

He remembered Alice talking about rationing in England. 'But the war's over.'

'Yes, it is, but we've still got shortages and rationing means we all get our fair share of what's going, so long as you've the money to pay for it, that is.'

'So where do I get a ration book from?'

Elsie grinned. 'From a man I know.'

'Is that legal?'

'Needs must when the devil drives,' said Elsie tartly.

Jon smiled. 'You're just full of surprises, Elsie.'

'Well,' she said, 'them with a bit of money in their pockets don't go short, so if it's good enough for the toffs then it's good enough for the likes of us.'

'I wouldn't want you to get into trouble, Elsie.'

'Don't you worry about that. Anyway, it's about time they stopped all this rationing, after all, we did win the war, although you wouldn't think it sometimes. You finished your tea?'

She reached across the table and swept up the mug and empty plate. 'And while I remember you should try the Sally Ann. They're supposed to help trace lost souls and if they can't they should be able to point you in the right direction.'

CHAPTER 17

A week later Jon took a job as assistant delivery boy at George Henry Lee's Department Store working under Frank Cooper, a thirty-year-old bloke who had been demobbed from the army at the end of the war. Jon soon learned that Frank had been in the Royal Army Service Corps transporting ammunition and the like to the front line in France, Holland and Germany. Initially he reminded Jon of Scally, they both had the same stocky build, but there the similarity ended, Frank was as open as his smile. One of his front teeth was missing, like Jimmi's, he'd lost it in a brawl, and he chained smoked both on and off duty, waving each lighted cigarette around like a conductor's baton. He had a wife and three kids and he was on the look out for a better paid job so he could save up for an Austin Seven – a black one with red leather seats so he could take his family to Blackpool in style when petrol rationing ended.

Lunchtimes, Frank liked to park down near the Pier Head so they could eat their sandwiches and watch the ferryboat begin its journey across the river to Birkenhead.

'You don't say much, do you, lad? I'd get more out of a tailor's dummy,' said Frank between mouthfuls. 'I don't even know where you're from.'

'Liverpool.'

'Geroff, you don't sound like a Scouser to me.'

'I am. I was born here.'

'Is that a fact?' Frank stared out through the windscreen watching the grey water, choppy in the stiff breeze, and took another bite of his sandwich.

Frank didn't believe him! 'I've been in Australia for seven years,' said Jon.

'That's it, I knew something wasn't right.' Frank turned to him his mouth open in surprise. 'What're you doing back here, bomb damage, rationing and bad weather? You must be mad!'

'Australia's not all it's made out to be.'

'What, they ain't got no sun and no beaches?'

Jon scowled. 'There's plenty of sun, didn't see any beaches, not where I was.'

'Well, that's what they reckon. According to the adverts it's a great place – sun and sand and sea. I've been thinking of applying for this assisted passage scheme the government's going on about. They want blokes like me with a young family. Ten pounds a person, that's all it'll cost. Doris likes the idea, she says we could do with a change and we've no family to hold us back. So, what's it really like?'

'Hot.'

'Where were you?'

'About three hundred and fifty miles inland from Perth.'

'Where's that?'

'Western Australia.'

'You been to Adelaide? The wife fancies Adelaide.'

Jon shook his head.

'Didn't know they had assisted passage that far back,' said Frank, a grin splitting his face.

'We were told we were going to a better life,' said Jon bitterly, 'only it wasn't better, anything but. They sent us into the outback and we lived in tents and sheds and we had to build our own orphanage, every last block of it.'

'How old were you?'

'Eight.'

'Eight?' Frank stopped eating and nudged him. 'You got me goin' there for a couple of minutes.'

Jon shrugged.

'You're serious, ain't ya?'

'To blardy right, cobber,' Jon said in broad Aussie.

Frank whistled long and low.

'We had our own quarry and we built an orphanage and a church. Seven years it took and it's still not bloody finished.'

'You mean the government sent little kids on a boat halfway round the world to build an orphanage?'

'That's right.'

Frank grilled him and Jon told him everything, about the rotten food, the beatings, the accidents, the interference from some of the Brothers, the bed-wetting, everything. He told it straight in a deadpan voice that only cracked when he described how Freddie Fitzpatrick died.

'That was when I decided I couldn't stay any longer,' Jon added finally. The ferryboat held his attention briefly before he turned back to Frank. 'It could have been me and then Kathleen wouldn't have had anyone left.'

They both watched the ferry cutting through the murky water.

'Then what happened?' asked Frank.

'I ended up at Jarrahlong.'

'Jarrahlong?'

'A sheep station.'

Frank lit up a cigarette and sucked in a deep draught of smoke, held it and then exhaled slowly. 'So, what's wrong with the place? Wasn't there nothing you liked about it?'

'It's hot and dry out there, we lost over fifty head of sheep a day in the drought, then there was the bush fire that just about wiped out Jarrahlong, only the stockmen's quarters, the water tower and the wind pump were left standing,' said Jon. 'Everywhere was black as far as the eye could see, black and red and blue sky, you wouldn't like it.'

'Oh, I don't know, you get brassed off with all this damned weather we're havin' and the rationin'. What about grub?'

'Mutton: hot, cold, stewed, roasted, and steak,' said Jon.

'No rationin'?'

'No rationing, not that I saw.'

'What about the cities?'

'I only saw Perth and Fremantle – they've got big stone buildings like Liverpool.'

'When are you goin' back?'

'I'm not.'

'Geroff, you're missing the place, I can tell.'

'No, I'm not, my home's here.'

'Oh yeah!' said Frank, stubbing out his cigarette.

Jon chewed over their lunchtime conversation as they drove to the next job. Frank's questions had unsettled him, had forced too many comparisons. He'd never thought about it before and he didn't want to think about it now. He didn't want to admit that he found Liverpool dirty, dingy and claustrophobic after the vast open spaces of the outback. He didn't want to admit he missed the huge plates of roast mutton and potatoes, the steak and eggs. He couldn't tell Elsie that he was constantly hungry, that the tiny portions she served up wouldn't satisfy a five-year-old kid never mind a strapping youth like him.

The truth was he couldn't stop thinking about the place, and his disturbed dreams didn't help. He missed the life, the heat and the dust. He missed Alice, Adie, Belle, and Stan, and whenever he pictured Old Yella he drove out the image with inane chatter, anything to take his mind off the aching void in his chest.

It's not finding Kathy that's making me unsettled, he decided. When he found her things would be different. The minute they were together again thoughts of Australia would disappear like Mersey mist on a summer morning.

He vowed to renew his efforts. He'd been wasting too much time. The Salvation Army couldn't help. Captain Prescott had been nice enough. He'd offered him someone to talk to, but as far as Kathy was concerned he'd said adoption was the end of it, that they couldn't help him. Well, he didn't agree that that was the end of it. Just because it was the law it didn't make it right. Someone must know where she had gone to.

The children's home records, that's what he needed. Perhaps he should jemmy open a window into Jones's office, get his hands on those orange files. He pictured the high windows and saw the iron bars cemented into the stone block work. It was a non-starter; even he had the sense to see that. Maybe he should start asking around – perhaps his old mates might know something.

CHAPTER 18

Sefton Park hadn't changed. He cut along the side of the lake to the makeshift football pitch and stood near to three girls watching the kickabout. A bitter north-easterly wind cut through his clothing, chilling him to the marrow. He'd been back a fortnight and he still wasn't used to the weather: the snow, the ice and the sleety rain – it could be cold in Australia, but not like England. Two of the girls laughed and giggled, coats unbuttoned, cheeks rosy; the third was taller and she had dark straight hair hanging down her back to her waist. She stood looking away from him at the players, her hands buried deep in her pockets and, unlike the other two, her coat was buttoned up, and she wore a bright red scarf around her neck. The two blondes kept looking in his direction.

'Hi ya,' called the one with the cigarette, 'you gorra light?' She brushed a chin-length curl behind her ear.

He glanced at her, 'Sorry, I don't smoke.' She had a nice face, pretty, he supposed, shoulder-length curly hair and the bluest eyes he'd every seen in a girl.

'Don't ya?' commented her friend and giggled. 'Ask him his name,' she said in a loud whisper. 'Go on, Val, ask him.'

'You gorra name then?' called Val.

Jon pulled his jacket closer. He didn't like the whisperer, her eyes were too watchful and she liked to hide behind the curtain of hair that swept her face every time she tossed her head. He concentrated on the football certain that he knew two of the players. Suddenly the blonde with the cigarette was standing under his nose looking up at him.

'Tall, ent ya. Giz your name then. I'm Valerie, that's Dorothy,' she said, pointing at the whisperer, 'and she's Merle.' She didn't bother to look at Merle, and Merle didn't acknowledge them when her name was spoken. 'Cat got your tongue, has it?'

'Jon,' he said, watching the football match over her head. She smelt worse than an ashtray, stale cigarettes and something else, chip fat? He shuddered.

'You're not from round here, are ya?' said Val, blowing cigarette smoke over her shoulder. 'He's not from round here,' she said to the others. Her eyes narrowed, 'You off the banana boat?' She flapped her elbows up and down, 'Ugh! Ugh! Ugh!' and laughed.

She had a mellow, tinkling laugh and it made him smile.

She caught it and grinned. 'You one of them stuck-up snobs from Childwall or somethin'?'

He wished he hadn't bothered to come to his old stomping ground. 'No.'

'Where you from then?'

'South Street.'

'Geroff! You're havin' me on. Hey, Merle, he's from South Street.' She glanced over her shoulder to Merle and then back to him. 'Merle's from South Street.'

Merle turned and studied him for a moment. She had olive skin and arresting green eyes that held his and his stomach lurched at the sight of her. She was more beautiful than any of the Asian women he'd met in Jakarta and Singapore.

He realised he'd stared too long and looked away, embarrassed and confused. He knew her, he was sure he did. He cast his mind back seven years, thinking of all the families on South Street who had girls his age. 'I'm living in Bridge Street at the moment,' he said, acutely aware of Merle's presence.

Valerie's eyes widened, a small smile played around her lips and she fluttered her lashes at him. 'What number?'

'Twenty-seven.' He could see her brain working.

'You the sailor that's stayin' with Elsie Roberts? Mam said Elsie'd taken in a lodger. She told our Evelyn we should do the same.'

'You haven't any spare room in your house,' said Dorothy.

Val's eyes sparkled with laughter, 'We could make room for one like him.'

On the pitch the lads were picking up their jackets. Val waved both hands in the air above her head. Two of them ambled over towards them while the others headed for the bicycles over by the fence.

Jon smiled broadly when he recognised Pete McGhee and Barry Smith. Neither had changed that much. Baz still carried a splattering of freckles over the bridge of his nose but the pudding-basin haircut had gone; he now sported a smart short, back and sides reminiscent of the bloke in the Brylcreem advert.

Barry stood close to Merle. She glanced at him and smiled a welcome. Were they going together or just mates? Just mates, he hoped, burying a twinge of envy.

Barry grinned, and Jon saw he still had the chipped front tooth from when he fell out of Billy Wainwright's bedroom window onto the outhouse roof and rolled down it onto the bikes leaning against the wall.

Pete's green eyes swept Jon and he chuckled, revealing teeth as white as Curly's had been. 'Hey, Bill,' he yelled to one of the lads over by the fence, 'look who's here!'

Bill Wainwright spoke to the lads he was with and then wheeled his bike over, his brown hair with its cowlick flopping on his forehead as he walked. He let his bike drop to the ground. 'Jon! Me old mucker. Where you bin?'

'Australia.'

'Straight up?'

Jon nodded, 'Straight up.'

Bill stood back and looked him up and down. 'You've stretched.'

Jon couldn't keep the smile off his face. It felt like Christmas seeing Billy again. 'And you've shrunk.' They both laughed and he sensed Merle watching them.

'When did you get back?' asked Bill.

'Couple of weeks ago.'

'Why didn't you come and see me.'

'I'm here, aren't I? I've been getting sorted out with a job, and looking...you know?'

'So what you bin doin' in Australia?'

'It's a long story. What about you lot? I saw what happened to your house, Billy.'

'That's war for you,' said Bill.

'It's brass-monkey weather standin' out here,' said Val, 'let's go over there out the wind.' She nodded in the direction of the Palm House.

The six of them followed her and crowded in out of the chill wind.

'Come on then, spill,' said Billy. 'What have you been doing in Australia?'

'Remember when Mam had to go into hospital and Gran was sick with emphysema.'

'And your dad had done a runner with Rose Butler.'

'Who's Rose Butler?' asked Valerie.

'An old tart,' said Bill.

'Well, Kathy and me were put in the children's home. Temporary, Mam said, just till she got over the op. Anyway, when she died they sent me to Australia. I've been over there seven years.'

Barry whistled.

'Did you get bombed?' asked Dorothy. 'We did.'

'I've seen the mess,' said Jon.

'You ain't seen nothing,' rattled on Dorothy, 'you should have seen it at the time. London got it worst, but Liverpool was bad enough. They say that more than fifty thousand civilians bought it all told, but I reckon they exaggerated.'

'Elsie told me what happened, Billy. I'm really sorry about your gran. It must have been pretty grim,' said Jon.

'Scary,' interrupted Dot dryly.

'How do you know?' snapped Billy. 'You weren't here, your family didn't get bombed to blazes.'

'Mam told me. Anyways, I was at the beginnin', before we got evacuated.'

'Evacuated of what?' asked Jon.

Pete grinned. 'You weren't the only one who got to travel. Merle and me and Ben were evacuated to a farm in Wales.'

Jon glanced across at Merle. Pete's twin sister – he remembered her now. How could he have forgotten!

'Merle had to scrub the kitchen floor every night, and the outside lav. I had to look after the pigs, and Ben's job was to collect the eggs. Old Ma Williams had us up at six and in bed for six, and on top of that we had to walk two miles to school every day. Hated it, didn't we, Merle?'

'It wasn't that bad,' said Merle, 'Mrs Williams did her best.'

Pete sniffed. 'Like hell she did.'

'A pile of kids from the Dingle got sent to some place in North Wales called Colomendy,' said Billy. 'A mate of mine, Dougie Hamilton, was sent. He said it was miles from anywhere, on the edge of a forest, and they had to live in freezing wooden sheds and the food was horrible. Anyway, he ran away and hitch-hiked home, reckons he got into hell of a lot of trouble over it, but they didn't make him go back.'

'Mine were all right,' said Barry, 'I got an old couple with no kids and they spoilt me rotten. Mam said I'd not want to come home. We still visit Uncle Fred and Auntie Vi.'

'We didn't have to go anywhere,' said Billy. 'We stayed in Liverpool. According to me dad we'd had all our bad luck, he said he didn't want strangers looking after us, and me mam didn't argue, especially after the Benares sank.' He saw the look on Jon's face. 'A liner taking evacuees to Canada. A German U-boat sank it in mid-Atlantic. About eighty kids died. After that they never mentioned us being evacuated.'

'It's sunny in Australia, isn't it,' said Val. She pushed up her sleeve and held her bare arm alongside his hand. 'We didn't get evacuated either. Mam says if your number's up, it's up and there's nothin' you can do about it. So, what you doing back here then?'

'I came back to find my sister.'

'Where is she?' asked Bill.

'Don't know. She's been adopted and they won't say where she's living now. I don't suppose any of you know where she is, do you?'

'They can't do that, can they?' asked Val.

'They can,' said Jon, his tone sharp.

The others shuffled uneasily. No one spoke.

'I can ask my mum, if you like,' said Pete, eventually. 'She might have heard something.'

Val shivered despite the warmth in the Palm House.

Barry looked at his watch. 'I'll have to be getting back.' He grinned. 'You know me mam, five minutes late and she's told the police I'm missing. You lot staying?'

'I better go too,' said Dot.

'We'll catch up later, yeah?' said Barry.

'Yeah, see you later, Baz,' said Pete. 'We'll walk with Jon a bit. You coming, Merle?'

'I'm coming with you lot,' said Val, catching hold of Jon's arm.

The five of them headed home, taking the short cut through streets that had been bombed and the rubble cleared ready for re-development.

'The bombing was pretty bad, wasn't it?' commented Jon as they crossed a pocket of devastation, Val stumbling along beside him in her high heels.

'Yeah,' said Bill, 'it was a bit grim. May 1941 was the worst; took a real hammering, we did. The Jerries blitzed the place solid for a week, that's when Gran bought it.'

'Everywhere was rubble; all those streets next to Lord Street were flattened,' said Val. 'Bootle gorrit bad an' all; all the dock areas gorrit bad.'

'One hundred thousand houses were destroyed or damaged in Liverpool in that one week,' said Merle from behind them.

Pete turned to his sister. 'How do you know that?'

'A girl at school told me. Her dad's a reporter for the *Liverpool Daily Post and Echo*.'

'Those figures weren't in the paper,' said Pete.

'The censor,' said Merle, 'the authorities didn't want the people to panic.'

Pete snorted his derision. 'People knew; we were living through it, for God's sake.'

'We used to hide under the stairs mostly,' said Bill. 'Me Dad said it was the safest place. We'd hear the sirens and we had to run for shelter, everything would go quiet for a bit and then we'd hear anti-aircraft barrage and the bombs dropping. We used to sit with our fingers in our ears and the little 'un would be crying.'

Jon frowned. Was Kathy in the middle of it all or were orphans evacuated too? Was that why she'd been adopted, to get her out of the city? 'So how come you weren't all killed along with your grandma when the bomb dropped?'

'Because we'd gone to see me Auntie Harriet and her new baby. Me mam had stayed to wet the baby's head and then the sirens went so we had to go to the air-raid shelter with everyone else. You should've seen it. The fires were the worst. The city was glowing red from all the burning buildings and then you'd hear a big whumping sound when a building collapsed.' He nudged Jon in the ribs. 'See what a jammy kid you are living the life of Riley in the sunshine. Bet you didn't have rationing either by the size of you.'

'No,' said Jon, 'no rationing, not where I was. What's Albert doing these days?'

'You haven't heard, then?' said Pete. 'His dad bought it.'

'What happened?' asked Jon.

'Don't know exactly. Happened in 1942 or thereabouts. Anyway, his mum took Bert and his sister back home to Jamaica, said she'd had enough of war and England.'

Jon swallowed his disappointment. He'd always got on well with Albert. He'd been looking forward to seeing him again and hanging out like they used to do down the docks watching the banana boats come in. He kicked at a piece of wood and sent it skittering across to the remains of an out-building.

'What's that?' asked Merle.

Val looked about her. 'What's what?' she asked.

'That.' Merle pointed in the direction where the stick had landed. 'It's a cat!'

She crossed the uneven ground and knelt down on an icy patch next to where it lay stretched out, its black fur matted, its bones clearly visible through the pelt. It had a nasty gash in the right hind leg. She stroked its head as they stood over her and the cat.

'Wouldn't do that, it'll have fleas,' said Val.

'The poor thing's dying,' said Merle, glancing up at them. 'What are we going to do?'

'Nothing,' said Pete. He tried to pull his sister away. 'It stinks.'

Val held her nose, 'God, it *wronks*.'

'We should take it somewhere,' said Merle, looking up at Pete.

'Like where?'

'I don't know. The vet.'

'And who's going to pay?'

She jumped up and turned on him, hands on her slim hips. 'Well, we can't leave it here, can we? It'll freeze to death.'

Jon glanced down at the animal. He recognised the taint of death, Curly's smell in his dying hours. He picked up a house brick, crossed to the cat and brought it down swiftly on the cat's skull. He felt the bone break as the weight of the brick crushed the cat's head. He'd misjudged. Sheep skulls were much thicker, he should have realised.

Behind him Merle started screaming. He dropped the blood-stained brick and turned to the others. Merle looked at him, her hand clamped over her mouth, revulsion and horror in her eyes. There was disbelief on Bill's face, while Val's was expressionless, only her hand shook as she drew on her cigarette.

'Blooming heck, Jon,' said Bill finally.

Pete pulled himself together and put a protective arm around his sister's shaking shoulders. He looked at Jon. 'What did you do that for?'

'It was dying.'

'You a vet or something?' questioned Merle, shock making her voice brittle.

'You said it was dying too.' They all stared at him. Arguing wasn't going to work. He could see it in their eyes. 'I'll bury it,' he said instead. He picked up the cat and carried it across to an existing hole, dropped the animal in it and kicked frozen soil and rubble over the body.

'They're gone,' said Val when he'd finished burying the cat. 'Merle reckons you're cruel that you should go back to Australia.' She linked her arm through his and led the way. 'Was it dyin'?'

Jon stopped walking and pulled his arm away from her. 'Course it was!'

'Just askin', hon.'

'It'd got gangrene.'

'Oh,' she said and linked arms again. 'Tell me about Australia.'

'Nothing to tell.'

She laughed. 'Ooooh! Sulkin' are we?'

'No.'

'Yeah, you are.' She tickled him under the ribs.

He wished Val would shut up, if only they'd never seen the bloody cat. He couldn't block the image of Merle's shocked face or blot out her scream and felt sick; she was the first girl he'd ever really fancied and he'd messed it up.

He glanced down at Val, her blonde hair bouncing against her cheeks as she hurried to keep up with him. She was pretty enough, but she wasn't beautiful like Merle. Merle was different. From the moment her green eyes had held his and he'd felt his stomach do a loop he'd known she was the one for him.

'Slow down, can't ya, hon,' said Val, gasping for breath. 'You're goin' too fast.'

'Sorry,' he muttered, slowing his pace.

She clung on to his arm and bent over. 'Cor, I've gorra stitch now.' She giggled at the pain.

'You all right?' he asked.

'I will be,' she said, standing straighter, 'just as soon as you ask me out.' She grinned at him. 'How about tonight? I fancy seein' the Bogart and Bacall film.'

Jon walked on listening to her inane chatter, at her going on about Lauren Bacall, John Wayne and James Stewart and all her other favourite film stars. He didn't want to go. For a start she didn't stop talking and her breath stank of tobacco, furthermore, it was Merle he wanted.

She looked up at him. 'So, how about we go to the flicks?'

'Flicks?'

'The cinema. You aren't doing anything tonight, are ya?'

'What'll your Dad say?'

'I haven't gorra dad.'

'Your mam?'

'She won't care. She had our Evelyn at sixteen. She says I'm old enough to know me own mind.'

Their footsteps rang along the street, it was five o'clock, tea time, and folk were hurrying home, their faces tired, keen to get into the warmth. It was where he wanted to be, somewhere quiet with no one bending his ear.

'You don't have to pay for me. We can go Dutch,' said Val.

Jon stopped walking and looked down at her. 'I've got money.'

'Sorry, hon, I didn't want you to…'

He ignored her embarrassment and set off again at a brisk pace, irritated by the sound of her high heels clattering on the pavement.

'You've gorra job, then?'

'Delivery boy for George Henry's.'

'Ooooh, swank shop. Mam sez if you buy a pair of gloves from there you can have 'em delivered. I work in a bakery. Beaties on Brook Road. Know it?'

He shook his head.

'Behind the counter. It's okay and I can have the stale cakes and loaves for next to no coupons. We're never short of bread in our house. So, shall we go then?'

'Go?'

'The flicks.'

She glanced up at him. 'How tall are you?'

'Six foot one.'

She clung onto his arm even more tightly. 'I'm five four, five six in high heels. I like tall men. You haven't gorra girlfriend then, in Australia?'

An image of Rachel flashed into his mind, her bottom jiggling beneath the pinny bow as she scrubbed out a pan; she was a friend, but not a girlfriend. 'No.'

'That's all right then, isn't it?' She stopped outside number twenty and blew him a kiss. 'See you later, hon.' She opened the door and stepped inside. He gazed at the dull brass 20 on the door. So who was the woman he'd seen the night he arrived, Val's sister or her mother?

'I see you've met the Rayners then,' commented Elsie with a sniff.

'Val?'

'Humm. She's the best of the bunch, but give her two years and she'll be just like her mother and sister.'

'What's that supposed to mean?'

Elsie turned her back on him and busied herself preparing tea.

'She's asked me to take her to the pictures tonight.'

'Has she now! Well, I hope you're not going to get too involved with that one. There're plenty of lasses about, nice ones, for you to be wasting your time on the likes of her.'

'You sound just like me gran.'

'Well,' said Elsie tartly, 'perhaps you should think on. Your gran would turn in her grave if she thought you were soft on a Rayner.'

The next morning Jon changed his route to work. He walked down South Street hoping to catch a glimpse of Pete and Merle, but they weren't at the bus stop.

He'd completely forgotten Pete had a twin sister. At eight she'd been all pigtails and teeth, a swot according to Pete, and a bit of a loner, not like Pete who had been the class extrovert in the junior boys, the one who organised after-school football and decided what they'd all be doing in their spare time.

As a kid he'd looked up to Pete McGhee. Pete had been the most popular boy in the year; all the lads liked him and wanted to be in his team. Everyone said he would make something of himself, and so did Pete, he always said he was going to make scads of money and build himself a mansion over Meols way like the one out at Speke.

Jon glanced out of the bus window, at the terraced houses, with unseeing eyes. It was the look on Merle's face, not Pete's, that bothered him the most, a look of utter revulsion when he'd killed the cat.

'You all right?' asked the old fella sitting next to him.

'What?'

'Are you all right?'

Jon let go of the seat in front of him and flexed his fingers, allowing the blood to flow into the tips.

The old fella leaned closer to him. 'It's all right, son, I was at the Somme the first time around. If I were you I'd not think too deeply.' He stood up to leave, touching his cap by way of goodbye, and got off at the next stop.

Jon watched the old fella slipping and sliding along the snow-packed pavement. Stan had given him similar advice. He suddenly felt old and knew that what he wanted more than anything was stability in his life. He was sick of always looking over his shoulder, sick of being alone, sick of the nightmares and flashbacks and here he was, back in England, starting all over again, trying to find the sister he hadn't seen for seven years. Suddenly, doubt assailed him. Had he made a mistake coming home? Was he on a wild-goose chase that would end in disappointment and disillusionment?

He looked at his reflection in the window of the bus and saw the shock of streaked blond hair and a tanned face with watchful eyes that were grey in natural light, he took in the square jaw and the straight nose and didn't recognise himself; he looked careworn and older than his years. He'd changed, life had changed him and it wasn't for the better, and he wondered what had become of the happy, carefree kid he had once been.

CHAPTER 19

The following Sunday Jon crossed the road and entered the cemetery through ornate Victorian ironwork gates. There had been a heavy frost in the night; it rimed everything, softening the severe lines of the tombstones. His feet scrunched along the gravel path, disturbing a blackbird. It flew low over the ground, its melodic alarm call, so unlike the strident screeching of Australian birds, echoed and faded as the creature took shelter on a bare branch.

There was just him and the bird, and row upon row of decaying bones beneath the ground. There'd been so much death in his life. Since Curly died he hadn't been able to clear his mind.

These days his sleep was troubled. His dreams were dominated by the bleached bones of the dead. Sometimes the bones where his mother's, he knew they were hers because the voice asking after Kathy was hers. He recognised Curly's in the same way, and Father William's, but Perentie Man's bones spoke to him the most often in nightmares, calling to him for…for what? Curly's tjuringa? He shivered and drew his coat closer to him.

He followed the route Elsie had given him. Reading the inscriptions and looking at the ornate carving on the older graves, even the uncared for ones where the grass grew rank over the stone like old frayed rope, calmed him in a strange way. Towards the far corner of the cemetery, where the newest gravestones were, he read each and every inscription looking for Sarah Mary Cadwallader, née Gregson, and Elizabeth Ada Gregson, née Davies.

Some graves had flowers. He hadn't thought to bring any. He wished he had, flowers brightened a grave, made it look cared for. Worst were those where long-dead flowers had mouldered away, decomposing in the damp English weather, their grey-green stalks now stiff with frozen mildew, the earth bare where rotting flower heads had killed the grass beneath them.

Their graves were where Elsie said they'd be, the simple grey headstones stained green, their flower holders empty. Marg hadn't been recently. He didn't know what to make of that, graves were important weren't they, markers of a life lived, a place for the living to visit and remember? He would have thought his aunt was the type to bring flowers. There was so much else he didn't know about her. But he knew one thing, if it had been her lying here and not Mam, Mam would have brought flowers for her, just like Gran always brought flowers for Walter. Gran always laid them at the memorial to the fallen of the First World War because no one knew for sure where Granddad was buried, somewhere near Poperinge, in Belgium, they said, his name recorded on the Menin Gate, in Ypres.

Jon squatted down and started to pull at the long grass with sharp quick tugs, tidying around both graves, and then he wiped down the stones with a handful of frozen stalks. He rubbed the marble clean with his handkerchief, stood back and looked at what he'd done, waiting for the emotion to kick in, the pain he'd felt when they'd told him his mother was dead and his gran was seriously ill in hospital with emphysema. Instead he felt empty, devoid of all emotion. What was wrong with him that he couldn't cry for his mother, for his gran? It didn't make sense.

He remembered how he felt when Curly died, the ache in the middle of his chest as he'd dug a grave for Curly's body. The utter desolation, the sense of aloneness as he'd buried his friend under a blazing sky in the middle of the outback. He remembered the scalding tears; here the feelings were blunted, not sharp and raw like sunburnt skin. Mam had been gone eight years now. Could you cry for someone after that length of time, when they were no longer people but just bones mouldering away in the earth, six feet under? He should have brought flowers.

'Hello, Jon.'

He spun round. Merle stood behind him on the grass. She was wearing a navy gabardine macintosh belted at the waist, thick navy stockings and black shoes speckled with frost. In her gloved hands was a bunch of pompom-headed chrysanthemums, their russet-coloured heads bright against the dark of her coat. He forced the surprise off his face and closed his mouth.

'What are you doing here?' she asked.

'Visiting Mam's grave,' he said, his heart suddenly pounding in his chest like a jackhammer.

She glanced at the headstones behind him and then studied his face, her own expressionless. He wondered what she was thinking as she looked down at his dirty hands stained with grass, soil and green algae. 'I should have brought flowers…I didn't think,' he added.

'This your first visit?'

He nodded, not willing to trust his voice, not wanting her to hear the anger and hurt he'd been feeling.

'Mum went to her funeral, you know. She said it was the least she could do with your grandmother being so ill.'

He hadn't known that. They'd told him and Kathy nothing except their mam had died, that his grandmother was sick. They said funerals weren't suitable occasions for children.

They stood facing each other, not speaking, until the silence became uncomfortable. She held out the flowers she had in her hand. 'You can have these.'

'But you brought them for—'

'You know my mother, fresh flowers every Sunday without fail. I'm sure my grandmother wouldn't mind missing out for a week. Here,' she thrust them further forward until the bunch touched his chest. 'I'll get some water,' she said as he took the flowers.

He watched her walk back the way she'd come, her stride purposeful with no exaggerated sashaying of the hips like Val did. Her long dark hair, held back by a rubber band, swung from side to side as she walked and called attention to her narrow waist and slim hips. Minutes later she returned with a battered metal jug in her hands, slopping water over the rim as she picked her way over the rough ground. She knelt down and filled his mother's vase and then his grandmother's.

'There should be enough for two,' she said and held out her hand for the flowers.

Jon handed over half of the bunch she'd given him and watched as she arranged them, biting off the stems with her teeth when she couldn't break them, and then he handed over the rest.

'There,' she said when she'd finished. She looked up at him and smiled. 'Happy?'

A feeling of warmth washed over him, he felt the hair on the nape of his neck stand up and another feeling, desire, course through his veins as he looked down into her open face. Suddenly, he felt as old as he knew he looked, a man, now, in a man's body. She seemed so fragile kneeling at his mother's grave looking up at him. He wanted to touch her face, hold her, feel her warm breath on his cheek, crush her to him and protect her. He leaned forward to caress her and then stopped himself, colour flooding his cheeks.

'Will you go out with me?' he blurted, his cheeks burning as the blush rose up his neck and face.

She put her hands on the grassy grave, pushed herself up and dusted them dry on her coat. 'No.'

'Is it because of the cat?' When she didn't reply he knew he had to explain. 'It was the kindest thing to do.'

'Yes, I know,' she said. 'I realised that later, when I'd recovered from the shock. But knowing what you should do and doing it are two different things when it comes to killing.' She looked him straight in the eyes. 'How did you get to be able to do that so impassively?'

He hesitated. Would she understand that you never got over killing something unless you closed your mind to it, until you could begin to see it as a kindness and not a cruelty? What would she say if she knew he'd considered killing Curly at the end, but that he couldn't bring himself to do it even though he knew it was for the best? Before he could find the words she turned and walked away from him.

'You're going out with Val,' she called over her shoulder.

'No, I'm not.'

She turned back towards him. 'You went to the cinema.'

'She asked me,' he said lamely. 'She's not a girlfriend.'

'She thinks she is. She'd been telling everyone that she's going to go back to Australia with you when you go.'

'I never said that, I never said anything like it.'

She shrugged, and then smiled.

She didn't believe him. Damn it! 'Look! I'm not going back, ever. Why would I want to go back there, I was born here, in Liverpool, and I've come back to find Kathy, to make a home for us.'

'You sure?' she asked.

He took her arm and pulled her towards him. Her body felt warm through the cloth. The feelings he'd had earlier coursed through his body. He didn't want Val. Val was fun, but that's all she was. Merle, with her cool eyes and dark looks, unsettled him. Touching her was like touching fire; couldn't she feel it? Couldn't she feel the heat? Couldn't she feel the spark that jumped between them when they touched? 'Yes, I'm sure,' he said, holding her gaze.

She pulled away and walked towards the gates, he fell in beside her. Val would have grabbed his arm ages ago; she'd be clinging to him like a limpet, laughing at his attempts to shrug her off. He was fair looking, so why didn't Merle like him?

'I'll tell Val,' he said.

'You'll hurt her feelings.'

He hid his disappointment and annoyance.

'I should be getting home,' she said. 'Mum will have Sunday lunch on the table.'

'Can I walk with you?'

'If you want to,' she said, smiling at him.

He grinned. She did like him. 'Of course I want to.' He stuffed his hands deep into his pockets and fell in beside her.

They walked in silence for a time, Jon racking his brains for something interesting to say, but he suddenly felt tongue-tied and a kid again. 'What're you going to do when you leave school?' he asked finally.

'University.'

Her answer surprised him. Pete always said she was a clever clogs. Pete was clever too; if Pete had said he was going to university he wouldn't have thought anything of it, but Merle! He cast a sidelong glance at her. Folk like them didn't go to university; only the rich could afford it.

'I want to be a doctor,' she said.

Schooling hadn't been a priority in Australia; O'Leary's building programme was the important thing. But Mam had always nagged him about doing well at school although he'd never listened; he'd been too busy playing football with his mates to bother about schooling. His Mam had always had funny ideas about education. She'd read to him at bedtime. His favourite was Jack London's *The Call of the Wild.* Mam had never finished reading it; she was halfway through when she got sick. Maybe he should join a library and get himself educated. 'What about Pete?'

'Entrepreneur.' She laughed and her breath clouded the air between them. 'Mum says he should go to university too, but he's got other ideas. He thinks that in the years it takes to train he could make a bob or two. Dad calls him The Spiv, says if he's not careful he'll end up in jail before he's thirty. You know what he does on Sundays? He goes over on the boat and then cycles to Rock Ferry to buy rabbits from a fella who goes out lamping, and then he sells them along with his other black market stuff. Dad says Pete's already got a bigger post office account than he has and Pete hasn't left school yet.'

'He ought to go to Australia if he wants rabbits,' said Jon. 'They've more rabbits than they can deal with. They built a damn, great fence just to keep them out of Western Australia.'

Merle laughed, a deep, throaty laugh that matched her striking looks. 'I'll tell him. He's already talking about emigrating to Canada when he's twenty-one, maybe he'll change his mind and go to Australia instead.' She stopped outside her house and glanced at him. 'What about you?'

What did he want to be? He didn't see himself as a delivery boy for the rest of his life. He was already bored with the job. His trouble was that in Australia he'd been treated as an adult while here he was still a kid and it rankled. He didn't feel like a kid anymore. At Jarrahlong he'd had responsibility. Alice trusted him, treated him like a man, expected him to behave like one and ripped strips off him when he hadn't met her exacting standards. He and the blackfellas were responsible for thousands of sheep and two hundred head of cattle, for repairing fences, breaking in the wild horses, ordering sheep dip, salt licks and all the other paraphernalia needed to run the station. And she'd paid him well, jackaroo's rates. 'I don't know,' he said.

He glanced at Merle standing beside him. He really wanted to see her again and was damned if he'd take no for an answer. He took her arm and turned her towards him. 'But I do know one thing; it's you I want, Merle, not Val. So why won't you go out with me?'

She hesitated, a small smile playing round her lips.

'Go on, Merle, we can take the ferry to Seacombe like we did when we were kids and walk along the front to New Brighton.'

'In the middle of winter?'

'Why not? I'll go anywhere you fancy going so long as you say yes.'

It was a beautiful Saturday, bright and clear after another heavy frost, when Jon picked Merle up from South Street. They made their way to the pier head and took the boat to Seacombe. After paying for their fare they set off on foot for New Brighton, a couple of miles away, following the wide path alongside the coastal road, breathing in the freezing air along with the other day trippers who had decided to take advantage of the brighter weather.

He liked it when she took his arm, and he slowed his pace to suit hers, wanting to savour the few hours they'd got together.

'I'm glad you said yes, I thought you were going to refuse,' he admitted when they stopped briefly to take in the view.

'Did you tell Val you're seeing me?'

'No, it's none of her business who I go out with.'

'What about in Australia, were they queuing up for a date?' she asked, a smile on her face.

He laughed. 'No.'

'What's so funny?'

'You don't know Charlestown, it's a dead-end sort of a place and the only other person there my age is Rachel.'

'Is she pretty.'

'Yes, but I wouldn't call her beautiful, like you.'

'I wasn't fishing.'

'I know.'

'I bet she fancied you.'

He didn't reply. He didn't want to go down that road.

'What about on the journey home. You meet any nice girls then?'

'One or two,' said Jon, remembering the little Filipino whore the crew had fixed up for him in Jakarta. He changed the subject. 'So how come you and Val are friends?'

'I wouldn't call her a friend, we just hang around in the same crowd, you know how it is, and we were in the same class at school.' Merle glanced at him. 'Val doesn't look clever, does she, but take my word for it she's bright enough. She won a scholarship, like me, but her friend, Dorothy, didn't; when we went to the High School Dot went to the Secondary Modern, but Val never really fitted in, she always said we were a stuck-up bunch and soon as she could she left and got herself a job in a bread shop.'

'Beaties,' said Jon.

'So that's where she works,' said Merle, 'I never asked.'

He sensed she didn't want to talk about Val and changed the subject. 'Why medicine?'

'I want to help people, do something useful with my life.'

'We need doctors in the outback,' said Jon.

'What's it like out there?' she asked.

As they walked he told her about his life in Australia on Alice's sheep station. He described the land, and the people he worked with, he told her about Alice and Stan and the others in Charlestown, but he didn't talk about Curly, his memories and feelings about his Aboriginal friend were still too raw, Curly's death still too recent for him not to choke up. But he did tell her about the drought and of having to kill dying sheep to put them out of their misery, desperately wanting her not to think too badly of him for killing the cat.

They reached Egremont and stopped briefly, looking out over the sandy beach near the boathouse, along with the others. In summer the deckchairs would be out and kiddies would be playing and paddling, but not that day, sunny as it was it was still bitterly cold, too cold to stop for long and soon they were stepping out towards New Brighton.

The seaside resort was packed with day trippers from Liverpool. Some had arrived on the ferry while others, like them, had walked from Seacombe. The place was as he remembered it, the old fort standing guard at the entrance to the Mersey, the Pier and the imposing red-brick turreted remains of the Tower with its ballroom – once a smaller version of the famous tower at Blackpool. He remembered it all and the fairground where his dad and mam and gran had brought him and his little sister when he was a kid, before his dad ran off with Rose Butler and his mam got cancer. He recalled he'd eaten candyfloss and been sick on the ferryboat on the way home, and his dad had held him over the side so he didn't puke up on the deck. He smiled at the memory.

'Why are you smiling?' asked Merle.

He told her the story of the candyfloss and of being sick.

She laughed. 'My mother wouldn't let us eat candyfloss, she said it was only sugar and air, and it was bad for our teeth.'

'You've never eaten candyfloss! You haven't lived. Wait here a minute.' He crossed over the road and joined a queue at the candyfloss booth and bought two.

Soon they were giggling like kids as they sat on a wooden seat tearing off strips of spun sugar with their teeth. Jon felt the sugar dissolve in his mouth, the sickly sweetness sticky on his lips and cheeks and he couldn't believe he'd ever liked the stuff. 'What do you reckon?' he asked, licking his lips and wiping his mouth with the back of his hand.

'Ghastly stuff,' she said, finishing the last of hers. 'I'd say my mother was right.'

They walked along the front to the edge of town and then back again and bought fish and chips and ate them out of newspaper. In no time at all it was time to catch the ferry back from New Brighton. As he walked Merle home he asked her to go out with him again on the following Saturday and she said yes. That afternoon he kissed her for the first time and, later, he made his way home to Bridge Street thinking that life in Liverpool wasn't so bad after all.

CHAPTER 20

Ten days after the trip to New Brighton Jon and Frank were making their last delivery of the day, the air inside the van fuggy from damp clothes and body heat. The driving rain thudding on the metal roof like marbles, and the windscreen wipers hissing with monotonous regularity, made conversation difficult.

'Bloody weather,' muttered Frank, wiping the inside of the windscreen with the back of his arm, 'if it's not snow and ice it's freezing rain.'

Jon swept the side window with a sleeve and looked out. The rain-sodden streets were busy with mums and kids hurrying home from school, everyone dressed in drab blacks and browns with dull umbrellas tilted against the weather – it was as far removed from Australia and late summer as he could get. He tried to recall the scent of burning eucalyptus and mulga wood, of newly baked damper and billy tea stewing over a campfire, but the fuggy aroma blunted his memory and depressed him further.

'I'll be glad to get home tonight,' said Frank, clearing the windscreen yet again, while outside the wipers shrieked on the greasy glass. 'Bloody wipers, they're getting on my nerves,' complained Frank. He took his hand off the gearstick and squeezed the bridge of his nose.

Jon knew where Frank was coming from; the constant squeak had got on his nerves too until he applied the Karundah trick of shutting out the unpleasant. Now it bothered him less than a mob of Aussie flies, except shutting out the unpleasant didn't dispel the sense of despair that had crept up on him over the weeks since he'd heard of Kathy's adoption.

Frank cursed and swore at every driver who happened to be in front of him irrespective of the quality of the driving. He rolled the window down and shouted at two women who darted across the road in front of the van, skipping over puddles like kids on a day trip. 'Reckon they've left their brains at home,' he grumbled as he watched them wave their apologies and jump onto the tram heading into town. 'Any more stupid tricks like that and it won't be a tram they catch but a flippin' hearse,' he muttered. He leaned forward yet again and cleared the screen.

Jon saw her first. She stepped off the pavement without looking. She was hunched up against the lashing rain; her grey school hat banded in red – the carmine a bright splash in the drab street – hid her face.

Jon snatched at the steering wheel but Frank was faster. Time slowed. Sound was suddenly muffled. The windscreen wipers' shriek became a whisper and the marble raindrops a muted tattoo. Jon pressed his foot so hard on the imaginary brake that he could feel the ridged floor through the leather soles of his shoes. His fingers squeezed the metal dashboard until his knuckles whitened. His breathing ceased and his eyes bulged as he willed her to stop.

She looked up just before they hit her, her face moon white, her eyes huge and her mouth open. The thud, like a fist against a punch bag, barely registered inside the cab. She seemed to spreadeagle with her arms outstretched over the bonnet, hanging there for a moment, disbelief etched on her face. Their eyes locked, her pupils were dark saucers of shock, and then she slid off the bonnet like a rag doll, her eyes holding his until the last. The van aquaplaned, slewing on the wet, slick tarmac and stopped. Inside the vehicle the atmosphere was acrid with the scent of fear.

Frank sat glued to his seat, his hands gripping the steering wheel, his face an ashen mask. Jon heard screaming and then came hammering on the van door and the shouts of panic and rage. He shook Frank's arm and yelled at him, but it was no good, Frank was catatonic, paralysed with shock.

Jon jumped down from the van; he shoved his way through the crowd and stared at the girl lying between the front wheels. He knelt down next to her and took her cold, wet hand in his.

She lay on her side, her cheek pressed against the road, her hat pancaked by the nearside wheel. A small pool of blood stained an open exercise book, the rain diluting the black ink and blood a muddy pink.

'Is she all right?'

Jon saw Frank's boots and looked up into his stricken features. 'We need a doctor,' he said as he stood up, 'and an ambulance. Somebody call an ambulance,' he yelled at no one in particular. He leaned against the van and tried to roll the vehicle backwards to give them space. Frank hurried to release the handbrake and then helped to pull the van clear.

Jon stripped off his coat and laid it over the girl.

'Is she dead?' someone asked.

'She's dead,' screamed a girl, wearing the same school uniform, 'she's dead!'

'For pity's sake, shut up,' said Jon. 'What's her name?'

'Kath,' said the girl, 'Kath Warrener. She lives just down there.' She pointed away to the left, towards the next avenue.

'Go and get her mother,' said Jon.

The girl stared at him open-mouthed.

'You heard me,' he shouted. 'Go and get her.'

Jon knelt at the girl's side. It was like Karundah all over again, the white face, the blood, except this time it was a girl, but she looked the same, a goner, just like Freddie Fitzpatrick.

The rain was heavier; rivulets ran down his face and neck. The girl's hair turned to long rats' tails over her face. Jon leaned forward and moved them off her cheek and eyes.

'Has anyone got an umbrella?' He glanced up and caught the eye of a young mother standing at the back of the crowd, staring at the tableau, one hand on a pushchair handle the other holding an umbrella aloft. He held out his hand, pointedly. He saw a flicker of hesitation and then she coloured up. Without a word she handed it across and Jon held it over the girl's body shielding her from the worst of the downpour.

'Where's the damned doctor...and the ambulance?' muttered Frank.

Jon wondered too, and the police, why wasn't there someone else to take responsibility? It felt as if they'd been there half a lifetime. There'd been no doctor for Freddie either, he'd been lifted onto the back of a flatbed truck and bounced back to the orphanage infirmary. He still remembered the ride as if it were yesterday. But Freddie was already dead; he'd died under the altar stone with the midday sun beating down on him, drying the sweat on his brow even as they'd watched. He held the girl's hand, willing her to live, praying for the ambulance to come and then they heard it, its bell clanging as it wove through traffic.

A policeman arrived and ushered the crowd back, making space around the girl.

'What's her name?' asked the ambulance man.

'Kath Warrener,' called a girl from the crowd.

'Kath, you're going to be all right. We're going to take you to hospital,' he said. 'Have her parents been contacted?' he asked.

'Yes,' said the same girl, 'Jenny's gone to get her mother.'

'How did it happen?' asked the policeman, taking out his note book.

'She stepped out in front of me,' said Frank, 'I didn't stand a chance.' He stood palms upward, misery etched on his face.

'Did the wheels go over her, do you know?' asked the ambulance man.

'No,' said Jon, 'she was under the bonnet, between the wheels.'

The two ambulance men lifted her onto a stretcher and covered her with a blanket.

'Kathleen,' a woman screamed. 'Kathleen!' She barged Jon aside and leaned over the stretcher, walking by the side of it, holding the girl's hand through the blanket.

He watched his aunt not able to fully comprehend what he was seeing as she fussed and wept, her eyes wild, her hair flattened by the rain, her sodden dress clinging to her body as she bent over the stretcher. 'Kathleen,' she kept saying as she stroked the girl's face. Then the ambulance man closed the door on Kathleen and Marg and it pulled out into the traffic, the bell clanging again.

His aunt had lied!

They spent over an hour at the police station giving statements. By the time they had finished Frank had pulled himself together. 'We ought to get over to that hospital and find out how the little lass is doing,' he said.

They had to wait for twenty minutes for Frank's van to be released and then they drove to the hospital, parked, and went in by the nearest door and made their way to the wards.

'How's the Warrener girl?' Frank asked a nurse. 'Is she all right?'

'Are you the father?'

'I'm her brother,' said Jon before Frank could answer.

Jon returned her stare evenly and waited. It seemed an age before she made up her mind. 'Wait here,' she said. 'I'll find out.'

They sat on a bench.

'That was a good 'un, wish I could have thought it up as fast – she was about to send us packin'.'

'She is,' said Jon.

Frank glanced at him, 'Geroff with you!'

Jon didn't answer.

Frank stared at the far wall for a moment or two, 'The one that was adopted?'

Jon didn't trust himself to speak.

'Bloody Hell! And I've gone and nearly killed her.'

There was nothing to say. They sat and waited for the nurse to return. Jon chewed his thumb. He'd travelled halfway around the world to find his sister and then he was in the van that ran her down. It didn't make sense, none of it, Kathy, his aunt, the accident, it seemed that fate was stacked against him. Nothing ever came easy; life was one setback after another. It wouldn't have happened if he'd stayed in Australia. Kathy would still be safe, not lying in a hospital bed, her life in the balance.

'Mr Warrener?' the nurse touched him on the shoulder. 'Mr Warrener.' She smiled. 'Your sister's making steady progress, she's very badly bruised, she has a couple of cracked ribs and concussion. We'll be keeping her in for a few days and—'

'But she'll be all right?' interrupted Frank.

The nurse nodded. 'In time. She's a very lucky girl.'

'Where is she?' asked Jon. 'Can I see her?'

'She's on Ward 6. Visiting times are between half past six and half past seven in the evening, and half past two and half past three in the afternoon.'

'Can't I see her now?'

'I'm afraid not, Mr Warrener. You'll have to wait until half past six.'

'But she's going to be all right?' said Frank.

'Yes, there's no reason why she can't make a full recovery. Now will you excuse me, I've patients to look after.' Her shoes squeaked on the tiled floor as she turned away from them, her stiff white apron rustled as she brushed against the chair and the sound reminded Jon of mulga bushes bending in a breeze.

'That's a relief, I can tell you,' said Frank, 'I thought I'd killed her.'

'It wasn't your fault,' said Jon. 'She just stepped off the pavement.'

'I know, but I've got kids of my own. I could see our Mary lying there on the road.' He shuddered. 'What if…'

'She isn't,' said Jon. 'She's going to be all right.'

'Yeah!' Frank picked up his sopping overcoat. 'I suppose there's no point in hangin' round here. Doris will be wonderin' where I've got to. I'll call back tomorra, see how she is then.' He looked at Jon. 'You comin'?'

'No. I'll wait until visiting.'

Frank patted him on the shoulder. 'I'm sorry, Jon.'

It's all right, he wanted to say, but the words stuck in his throat. He didn't believe he was all right. He felt a bit like the Jonah fella in the Bible who got swallowed up in the whale – jinxed! Everyone close to him died: his mam, Freddie, Curly and now Kathy, except she wasn't dead, but you couldn't trust hospitals. He knew all about head injuries, they were the worst, left you impaired in all sorts of ways and even dead.

He made his way along the main corridor to Ward 6. Even from a distance he could make out Marg from her angular form and wavy hair. He guessed the chap sitting next to her was Harry Warrener, the new husband.

She looked up at the sound of his feet, surprise momentarily wiping the worried look off her face.

'What are you doing here?'

'I've come to see Kathy.'

'What? How—'

'I was in the van that knocked her down.'

She leapt to her feet and grabbed his jacket lapels, her face contorted with rage. 'You're not fit to be in charge of a vehicle, you're a maniac, running down innocent children.'

She shook him till his teeth rattled even though he stood several inches taller than she did.

'You should be locked up,' she shouted.

He didn't have the strength to argue, he felt as if all the stuffing had been knocked out of him, as if he'd been flattened by the Karundah quarry stone crusher.

Harry pulled Marg off him and gently eased her back onto a seat. 'Kathleen's going to be all right, Margaret. She's all right, the ward sister said.' He half turned to Jon. 'I think it is better if you go. You're upsetting my wife.'

'We don't know that for sure though, do we?' Marg said, her words muffled by sobs.

'Why didn't you tell me you'd adopted Kathy?'

'Margaret, what's this lad on about?'

'You could have said, but you didn't, you just let me think—'

Harry turned to him, his face a tight mask. 'What are you saying, son?'

Jon stared at Harry open-mouthed, his brain struggling to get the words out. He didn't know, Harry didn't know.

'I'm Kathy's brother.' He looked in Margaret's direction. 'And she's my aunt…my mother's sister.'

'I thought you'd emigrated to Australia?'

Jon ignored him.

'He was always rude, even as a kid,' said Margaret bitterly, forgetting herself. 'He was a snotty-nosed brat with his arse hanging out of his breeches. He'd ignore you then if the fancy took him. Spoilt he was, spoilt rotten, our Sarah thought the sun shone out of his backside.'

'I was sent,' said Jon, 'they shipped out boatloads of us and made us build an orphanage.'

'He told lies too,' said Margaret, her voice shrill. 'I always told our Sarah that she should wash his mouth out with soap when he lied.'

Jon sat on the spare seat. He didn't want to get into an argument.

'You needn't think you're seeing our Kathleen,' Marg said, 'because you're not. She's nothing to do with you now and I don't want her upset.'

'She's my sister, you can't stop me.'

'Oh yes, I can. All ties with her old family stopped when she was adopted, that means you.' Marg snapped the words out in a shower of spit. 'Kathleen's mine now, mine and Harry's and what we say goes until she's twenty-one.'

'But—'

'But nothing.'

'You're still my aunt.'

'That's as may be, but as of now you're not my nephew.' She turned her back. 'Tell him to go, Harry, I can't bear to look at him a moment longer.'

'You can't stop me seeing her.'

'I shall call the police if I catch you hanging round, do you hear me?' she screamed. 'You…you coming here, spoiling everything.'

'Quiet!' bellowed a female voice.

A woman in a navy uniform with a starched white cap perched on her head, walked towards them. 'This is a hospital,' she said, 'I won't have my patients disturbed.' She glared at Margaret. 'I suggest you continue this…this conversation outside.'

'Sorry, Sister,' said Harry, 'my wife's overwrought.'

'I can see.' The sister sniffed and drew herself up straight. 'But that's no excuse. I've already told you, Kathy is recovering well and she'll be as right as ninepence if she gets a good night's rest.' She glared at the three of them, turned on her heels and stalked back to the ward.

Jon glanced at his watch, quarter past six.

'There's no point in waiting, son, they only allow two visitors at a time,' said Harry.

Jon wavered.

'The rule's unbreakable. Sister won't allow it, so you'd be better off going home. Kathleen's going to be fine, you heard what the sister said so there's nothing for you to worry your head about and Margaret's right, we can't have you upsetting Kathleen, not after all she's been through.'

The man was wrong, all wrong. He had a right. His mam had told him to take care of Kathy, not them.

'You understand, don't you?' said Harry. 'You want what's best for your sister, don't you?'

Blackmail, thought Jon; it's nothing short of blackmail. He opened his mouth to protest.

'The shock might set her back, no telling what it might do to her in her present state. The authorities know what they're talking about. And, like Margaret said, Kathleen's old family doesn't count now and it's better for her if it's left that way.' He turned back to Margaret. 'Are you all right, love?'

Jon heard her sniff into her handkerchief – he'd once overheard his mother say Marg was manipulative – and knew he was wasting his time, but he didn't believe Harry. Kathy would be pleased to see him, he knew she would. He was sure she'd missed him as much as he'd missed her, more probably, her being younger and a girl and all, but now wasn't the time or the place to argue, he turned from them. They might think they'd won but they hadn't, he wasn't about to give up, not after travelling halfway around the world.

CHAPTER 21

Elsie looked up as Jon entered the kitchen.

'You're late.'

'I've found Kathy.'

'Why the long face?'

'She's in hospital. She stepped right off the pavement without looking and we hit her.'

'Oh my goodness, is she all right?'

'Badly bruised, broken ribs and she has concussion and shock.'

'Have you spoken to her?'

Jon slumped onto a kitchen chair and told her everything that had happened.

'Who does the woman think she is?' said Elsie finally.

'Kathy's mother,' said Jon, unable to keep the bitterness out of his voice, 'and now she won't let me see her.'

'Can't you sneak in when she's not looking?'

'You haven't seen the ward sister, she's a real dragon. She nearly threw the three of us out for arguing.'

'I bet Marg was mortified. She never was good at taking advice. Here, you'd better have your tea; I've been keeping it warm.' She picked up the oven gloves, lifted the plate out of the oven, removed the covering plate and placed it on the table. 'Careful, it's hot.' She stood back while Jon took a forkful. 'My Ted always said you think better on a full stomach.'

The Spam fritter and mash sat on Jon's stomach. He belched to ease the discomfort and leaned back in his chair.

'It always gave my Ted wind too,' Elsie commented as she poured the tea. She cleared away the empty plate and sat opposite Jon. 'Strange, Marg never mentioned Kathy the other day. I wonder why?'

Jon wondered too. There was so much he didn't understand, although he was beginning to piece things together.

'Harry reckons it'll unsettle her.'

'Can't see how.'
'Neither can I.'
'So, what're you going to do about it?'
Jon looked across at Elsie. She was absentmindedly stirring a hole in the bottom of the mug with a teaspoon.
'Nothing.'
'Didn't take you for a quitter.'
'You sound like Scally.'
'Who's Scally when he's at home?'
'Just a bloke I met in Australia.' Jon pictured Scally's scowling face, recalled his harsh, grating voice, and his dislike of the British. 'He hates Poms, reckons we're the scum of the earth.'
'Does he,' said Elsie. 'With a name like Scally he's probably half Pom himself.'
Perhaps she was right. One of Rachel's grandfathers had been a Pom so he couldn't hate them that much, and then there were his parting words on the quayside. Maybe Scally had changed his mind, and maybe not. Perhaps he was just pleased to see the back of him.
'I think there's more to it than that,' she said, 'you fancy the same girl or something?'
'No.'
'Elsie looked at him sharply. 'No?'
Jon felt himself redden. 'Don't be daft,' he said, 'Scally's old enough to be my dad.'
Elsie grinned. 'What's her name?'
She was like a dog with a bone. 'Rachel.'
'Scally's daughter?' She chuckled when he didn't answer. 'So, what time's visiting?'
'Half past six to half past seven.'
'You should get there at quarter to seven when there're plenty of people about so you don't attract attention to yourself, then, when it's lights out and everything quietens down you should be able to sneak in and have a word with her.'
Jon was doubtful; the ward sister didn't miss much.
'You'll have to find somewhere to hide yourself for a couple of hours or so, a broom cupboard or something,' said Elsie.
'And just how am I going to do that without getting caught?'
'It shouldn't be too difficult. All the wards are built to the same plan,' said Elsie, 'a short corridor with a broom cupboard, the sluice, and a linen cupboard on the left and the toilets and bathroom on the right. Then you've got the main ward with the parti-

tioned off sister's office with a window so the nurses can see all the beds down each side of the ward.'

Jon considered Elsie's suggestion, it was risky but he had to chance it, he couldn't turn back now.

The next night Jon got to the ward at twenty to seven and joined the small group waiting in the corridor. People were coming and going all the time as they swapped visitors, only two to a bed he heard a nurse say more than once.

He identified the linen store by the label over the door and through the next doorway he could see sinks, taps and shelving stacked with stainless-steel bedpans and other hospital equipment – the sluice. When no one was looking he opened the door adjacent to the sluice – the broom cupboard. Swiftly he sidled into the cramped space and pulled the door closed. In the dim light he took stock of his surroundings. An electric floor-polisher handle dug him in the back as he turned round. Stacked in the corner were brooms, fluff catchers, dustpans and brushes. On the shelving were containers full of liquid polish and disinfectants and, pegged to a row of hooks, six pink rubber gloves hung down like amputated hands.

The smell of polish and disinfectant burnt the back of his throat and tickled his nose. He held his breath and concentrated on not sneezing. He shuffled round on the spot until he faced the door again and resigned himself to a long wait in the cramped, hot, airless cupboard.

First step completed he planned his next move. He'd considered stealing a green coat from a linen store and dressing himself up as a porter, but decided against it. Then there was Hawkeye in the sister's office with her desk pushed up against the observation window and her full view of the ward, not to mention the other nurse on duty that Elsie had warned him about.

After nine o'clock the toilet over the corridor flushed less often and he listened for the sound of rubberised soles on the polished floor. He checked his watch, ten o'clock; the nurses were on the prowl again, he could hear them in the sluice. 'Coffee', he heard a woman say. 'One sugar,' said the other. The kettle hummed as the water came to the boil, then came the clink of a spoon against glass and then pot, the burbling water gushing from the spout, murmured conversation, more clinking, then two pairs of shoes squeaking back to the sister's office and the door clicking to.

It was now or never, quarter past ten, all was quiet, sister and the other nurse were having a coffee break. He eased open the door and slid through the narrow gap like a shadow. On shoeless feet he moved swiftly to the ward entrance then dropped down to the floor, crawled along under the viewing window and shuffled across to the first bed. His plan was to crawl under the beds checking each patient as he went, but he hadn't allowed for drainage tubes and urine bags dangling down from the occupants, or the metal frames and wheels that made moving beds easier for the nurses. It was harder than he thought; the space between bed and floor was less generous than he'd expected.

He found her three-quarters of the way down the ward; she was deeply asleep, he could hear the quiet *huff* and *shluff* and then the silence between each intake of breath. He crawled under her bed and surfaced on the other side. He sat on the floor with his back against her locker concealed from sister's office by Kathy's pillows and prayed that everyone else was asleep too. He reached over and gently stroked her arm, he didn't want to startle her, she might call out.

'Kathy,' he whispered, 'Kathy, it's me, Jon, your brother.'

She seemed to stir and flapped her arm as if shaking off a fly. He persisted.

'Kathy, it's Jon, your brother. Remember?' He stoked her arm more firmly, recalling the time he'd last seen her when she was a five-year-old child with tears streaming down her face.

'Kathy, can you hear me?'

She stirred and turned towards him and her eyes widened, her pupils suddenly huge with fear.

'I'm Jon, your brother,' he whispered urgently, terrified that at any minute she'd start screaming.

'Jon?' she said in a panicky voice.

'Hush, they'll hear you. You've got to whisper.'

'Jon?' she whispered.

She scanned his face looking for clues and he saw her anxiety, he wasn't the kid she remembered.

'I promised I'd come home, Kathy. I said I wouldn't forget you.'

She eased herself onto her side, her teeth gritted, her face grey with pain.

'You okay, Kathy? Shall I get a nurse?'

She shook her head and gingerly settled back against the pillows. 'You went to Australia.'

She wasn't as he remembered, her red hair had darkened to auburn and her face had matured, it was longer, heart-shaped, but the questioning look was the same and the dimple that matched his own. Livid bruising covered most of the left side of her face and she had nasty grazes on her cheek and chin. 'Are you all right?'

She nodded solemnly, watching him, still uncertain. 'Sore, it hurts to move.'

'But you're all right?'

'Why didn't you come back? You promised you'd come back…I waited.'

Her words reminded him of their last morning together when she was crying, her podgy fingers stuffed in her mouth.

'I couldn't, they sent me to Australia, I thought we were both going,' he said miserably. 'They said there was no room left in the children's home for us older kids, and that we could come back if we didn't like it.'

'But you didn't.'

'They lied,' whispered Jon.

'They made me eat my porridge every day even when it made me sick.'

This wasn't what he'd expected; he thought she'd be pleased to see him, not resentful. Couldn't she see what an effort he'd made for her? 'I was an eight-year-old kid,' he said, 'only eight, Kathy. What could I do?'

'You promised.'

'I know and now I'm back, like I promised.' He tried to smile. 'I came back as soon as I could.'

'Did you come on an aeroplane?'

'No, on a boat.'

'When did you get back?'

'Two months ago.'

'So why didn't you come and see me then?'

'Because I didn't know where you were.'

The sister's office door opened, he heard the mutter of conversation and ducked down. 'Pretend to be asleep, Kathy.'

She grinned at him. 'Oh, righty.'

'They won't let me see you,' he whispered.

'Who?'

'Marg and Harry.'

Her eyes widened. 'Why?'

'Look, I've got to go, but I'll come and see you when you're out of hospital, all right?'

He slipped under the bed and held his breath.

The sister stopped at Kathy's bedside, picked up the chart and studied it in the dimmed light. 'You still awake?'

He listened to the brief conversation, his heart pounding. As soon as she moved off he slid under the next bed and the next and then waited. When Hawkeye re-entered her office he made his escape and headed for casualty, the lights, and the people, where there was less chance of being stopped and questioned.

He called at 34 Kilbride Avenue the Saturday after Kathy arrived home from hospital and rang the bell. He stood outside her house and straightened his tie, and glanced at his reflection in the bay window. Inside he could hear raised voices and Kathy crying. When Marg opened the door he knew the worst before she spoke, it was written all over her face.

'I thought I made it plain at the hospital,' she said. He noticed the tension in her jaw, the pale complexion and the way she gripped onto the door post barring the way to him. 'Kathleen doesn't want to see you.'

'She does.'

Marg ignored him. 'It was quite wrong of you to steal into her ward and wake her up. You took advantage.' Her voice was sharp. 'And I've made a complaint to the hospital authorities, now, please leave, or I shall call the police.' She slammed the door in his face.

He stood for a moment, shocked by her reaction, staring at the wood-panelled door. She always made him feel like a piece of dirt stuck to her shoe. He hammered on the door. When no one answered he walked down the path backwards, scanning the windows, and caught sight of Kathy's white face at the smaller upstairs window, distress carved into her features, her hand pressed against the windowpane.

He gave a small wave and received a half wave back. She did want to see him; he knew she did despite what Marg said. He'd just have to bide his time. Marg couldn't hold out on him forever.

Not far from Kilbride Avenue he called in at a newsagent's and bought a daily paper, while he was there he asked about the local schools. It didn't take long to find out which one Kathy went to and where it was.

He made his way to the bus stop. She'd be back at school before too long; he'd wait for her at the school gates.

CHAPTER 22

Elsie was out. He let himself in, made a cup of tea and took it upstairs to the spare room. He needed time to think. He lay on the bed staring at the dirty light bulb and its garish red shade. At night it tinted the room pink. It casts a rosy glow on life Elsie had said when she'd first shown him the room.

There was nothing rosy about his life in Liverpool except Merle; he had a boring job, an aunt who wanted nothing to do with him and a sister he'd been banned from seeing, on top of it all he was permanently hungry and cold. Compared to Jarrahlong it was pretty grim. He wished he'd had the sense to appreciate what he'd got when he had it.

He sat up, drank his tea and then pulled out his old haversack from the wardrobe. He held the stiff fabric to his nose and fancied he could smell the heat and dust of the outback, but he knew he was fooling himself as he wiped off the mould that had grown on the fabric.

He took out the tin he'd found in the wrecked plane and flipped the lid. The bean-sized crescent of raw gold he'd panned for glinted in the grey light, and the remaining black-opal nugget flashed red, purple and green. He rolled it over, absorbed by the glowing facets changing colour like the feathers on parakeets, blue wrens and red-tailed black cockatoos, birds as brilliantly coloured as black opals, sparks of brilliance against the intense blue sky, red earth and grey-green gums. Sparrows and blackbirds didn't compare, only the robin struggled to brighten up the back streets of Liverpool. He snapped the tin shut and then remembered his mam's favourite saying: The grass is always greener…

Carefully, he lifted out Curly's tjuringa and unwrapped it. The dirty cloth smelt musky, like peppery eucalyptus. Tears pricked his eyes, he blinked them back and ran his fingers over the incised patterns that Curly had memorized as a kid.

Stan had frightened him when he'd asked his advice. He'd refused to even look at it; he'd said white men had been killed for less. And when he suggested taking it back to Curly's family Stan had told him not to be an idiot, that they might think he'd killed Curly to get his hands on it.

Now, from half a world away, he knew Stan was wrong. Jimmi would have told him who the tjuringa should go to; instead, too much had happened too quickly, he'd been in too much of a rush to leave Australia and get back to civilisation, to Liverpool, to escape everything that had happened out in the bush.

A wry smile creased his cheeks as he thought of Marg's pristine home and compared it to Curly's mob living in humpies close to the land with only the possessions they could carry on their backs.

His fingers drifted over the wood, it felt warm to the touch, like a living thing. He half expected it to throb and pulse with the monotonous beat he'd heard Curly and the others chanting round the campfire and it occurred to him that it was the tjuringa triggering his bad dreams, that Curly's ancestor, Perentie Man, was refusing to let him go because of it. That would explain why he couldn't sleep some nights, why he was still having occasional flashbacks of Curly's death. Perhaps Stan was right, perhaps he needed to let go of the guilt he still felt about Curly's death, but would taking the tjuringa back help him to come to terms with everything that had happened in the outback? He wished he knew the answer.

Jumbled thoughts tumbled around his brain, plans to return the tjuringa to Curly's folk, half-baked schemes to get rich quick, and plans for himself and Kathy.

The tjuringa drew his eyes. It was only a lump of wood and yet it was Curly's most prized possession, his key to the land. In Liverpool tjuringas were valueless, only money counted...money meant power and people respected wealth. He could see why Pete wasn't interested in going to university, and if he'd been rich Marg wouldn't have dismissed him, she'd have respected him, wouldn't she? She valued wealth more than most he reckoned what with her new Formica kitchen units, polished parquet flooring and fancy cake forks. But how to get it? He'd been out of the country too long. He didn't know his way around like Pete did and, besides, his skills weren't exactly useful in the middle of a city.

'Jon! You awake?'

Elsie's yell startled him; he hadn't heard her come home.

'Val for you.'

Val? What was she doing here? And then he remembered, he'd promised to go with her to Bob Robertson's birthday party the night they'd gone to the cinema, the day he'd killed the damn cat.

'Jon, are you coming down?'

He could tell by Elsie's tone she didn't approve. He glanced at his watch – half past six, he must have dropped off. He rubbed sleep out of his eyes and licked his lips, his mouth felt as dry as a billabong in a drought. He rolled off the bed, splashed cold water into the china bowl, washed his face and pulled on a clean shirt. That was one thing about Val, she was persistent, it didn't matter how often he turned down her invitations she was always back with another. He'd told her he was seeing Merle and she'd laughed. You and me, we're just mates, she'd said and you're not engaged so what's the harm. You should be playin' the field, like me. Merle won't mind, she'd added.

Jon wasn't sure about that because ten days back, when Merle had mentioned Bob's birthday party and he'd told her he'd have to go with Val because he'd promised her, she'd been cool about it. I'll see you there, she'd said, and the next time he'd invited her out she'd turned him down flat. Damn Val!

He wrapped the tjuringa carefully in its cloth, buried it in the bottom of his haversack and banished the sudden, unbidden image of the green pool that Curly had taken him to in his first month at Jarrahlong. Life had been simpler then!

'Jon?' called Elsie. 'Where have you got to?'

'It's Bob Robertson's birthday party, remember?' said Val as soon as she saw him.

He'd not seen Bob since he'd got back but he remembered him well enough. Bob had carroty-coloured hair and buck teeth and had been in the same form at school. They'd never been mates and Bob had only invited him because of Baz, so he'd been inclined to give it a miss until Val mentioned that Pete and Merle were going.

'Got your key?' called Elsie.

Jon patted his pocket, 'Yeah, ta. I won't be late.'

Once in the street Val threaded her arm through his and scurried along beside him in her sister's fancy crocodile-skin courts.

'How's Kathleen?' asked Val.

'She's fine, thanks.'

'Elsie says she's back home and recovering, sez she's a lucky girl.'

'That's right, she is.'

'Elsie doesn't like me, does she?'

'She's all right,' said Jon.

'Not with me, she's not.'

They walked in silence for a while with only their footsteps echoing down the street. 'I suppose she's told you about me mam and me sister?'

Jon felt colour start to rise up his cheeks and was glad the street lights made their skin look pale.

'I'm not like them,' she said. 'I'm goin' to make somethin' of me life. I might even get on a boat and go to Australia.'

He stopped and faced her, 'I've told you already, I'm not going back, not now I've found Kathy, and Australia's not all it's cracked up to be.'

'All right! Keep your hair on, but I'm decided. I'm savin' up. I'm going to start me own business.'

'Doing what?'

'I don't know yet. I'll think of somethin', a dress shop or a hat shop maybe.'

'That'll go down well,' said Jon sarcastically.

'What do you mean? Aren't there any women in the outback?'

'Not many.'

'Don't they wear dresses and hats?'

He shut up. He didn't like the edge in her voice.

'Well, in that case I'll open one in a town.'

'Yeah!'

'Or a city,' said Val, refusing to let the subject drop, 'you just see if I don't. I always get what I want when I put me mind to it.'

Jon scowled.

'What's eatin' you tonight?' asked Val. 'You're like a—'

'Nothing.'

'You still keen on Merle, is that why you won't go to the flicks with me?'

'What if it is?'

'She's no good for you.'

'And what's that supposed to mean?'

'There's only one person Merle cares about, and that's Merle,' said Val.

'Don't talk rubbish.'

'I've known her a damn sight longer than you, hon.'

'You're just jealous.'

'Maybe,' admitted Val. 'But at least with me what you see is what you get.'

She pulled open the Social Club door and the noise hit him like a wave, grandparents, parents and teenagers sat at tables around the edge of the room, chatting; little kids were making nuisances of themselves running across the dance floor with drinks of squash and packets of crisps. The quartet: two saxophones, a double bass, and a piano, was playing Glenn Miller tunes; it was the sort of entertainment he'd imagined going to when he was stuck in the bush and now he'd got it he didn't want it. Val led the way across the dance floor to an empty table and he noticed her normally open, pretty face had a closed look about it. They sat down facing the band, the silence heavy between them.

'Do you want a drink?'

'Coca Cola,' she said without looking at him.

When he got back she'd moved. She waved at him from the corner of the room where she was sitting with Barry, Pete, Bill, Dorothy and Merle.

'How did you get that?' asked Pete, nodding in the direction of the pint.

'Asked for it,' said Jon, conscious of Merle's presence. She was wearing green, a sort of soft moss that accentuated the colour of her eyes and the coppery lights in her hair.

'Jammy bugger,' said Barry.

'I bet they think he's ex-service,' said Dot.

'Val say's you've found your sister, that your auntie adopted her,' said Barry.

'And he never knew,' said Val. 'What do you think of that?'

'*He* doesn't think anything,' snapped Jon. 'Why should he?' He took a quick sip of beer then swivelled in his seat and concentrated on the dancing – silly bitch!

'I was only sayin'—'

'Well, don't. Kathy's adopted and that's the end of it.' He ignored the confusion in Val's eyes and glanced at his watch – eight o'clock – ten o'clock he'd leave, she could make her own way home if she wanted to stay longer.

Val tentatively touched his arm. 'Dance?'

He shook his head.

'Please yourself then,' she said and dragged Barry to his feet. Dot and Bill soon followed which left him with Pete and Merle.

'Take it you're not the dancing type,' said Pete dryly.

'I didn't get much chance in the outback.'

'You know what they say: what you don't have you don't miss.'

'What's that supposed to mean?' snapped Jon still irritated with Val.

'Calm down,' said Pete, 'just making conversation.'

'Sorry,' muttered Jon.

'So, what are you going to do about Kathy?' asked Pete in a more serious voice.

'Pete, me old pal!' A chap of about forty hunkered down and draped his arm over Pete's shoulder. 'I've got family up next weekend, any chance of some rabbits or a brace of pheasants?'

Pete glanced about, then stood up and the pair of them moved across to the far end of the bar.

'Val's really annoyed you, hasn't she?' said Merle. 'What's she been saying?'

'Oh, nothing much, you know Val. So, have you forgiven me?'

'For what?'

'For bringing Val.'

Merle smiled at him from beneath lowered lashes. 'I could be persuaded.' She sipped her lemonade while watching him over the rim of the glass. 'What are you going to do about Kathy?'

'Wait for her after school.'

'Is that wise?'

He glanced at her, a hard look on his face. 'Maybe not.'

She covered his hand with hers and squeezed it and he suddenly felt better.

'Why won't your auntie let you see her?' she asked.

'I dunno. She thinks I'm a bad influence, I suppose. She never really liked me even when I was a kid. She always said Mam favoured me, but she didn't, Mam loved us both.'

'I think you should write your aunt a letter and tell her how much you've missed Kathy, and ask her permission to see her.'

'Why should I? She's my sister.' He took another pull of beer and licked the froth off his lip. 'In any case, what good will it do?'

'It'll show her that you've changed.'

'You don't know Marg, and it doesn't alter the fact that she knew I was being sent to Australia and she didn't do anything to stop it. She could have taken us both in.'

Merle frowned. 'Perhaps she was still grieving.'

'Grieving?'

'Think about it. According to my mother your Uncle Fred's merchant ship was torpedoed not that long after your mother died.'

Jon cast his mind back, trying to recall the details, but so much had happened then, Gran on oxygen, Mam in hospital and then her dying, he couldn't even remember when he'd first heard about Fred's ship going down with all hands. As far as he could recall, they'd never had that much to do with Marg and Fred at the best of times, and in any case it was Mam he'd been concerned about and what was going to happen to him and Kathy.

The band switched tunes to *In the Mood.* He smiled wryly. A blast of wintery air hit him as the door on the far side of the room swung open. Merle looked up and waved at her parents as they slipped off their overcoats.

'Won't be a minute,' she murmured so quietly he barely heard her words. She stood and rested her hand briefly on his shoulder as she stepped behind him. A frisson rippled through him. He held the feeling as she crossed the dance floor, dodging couples, her green dress accentuating her feminine shape as she sidestepped Val and Barry.

Was Merle right? Was his aunt too absorbed in her own troubles and grief to be worried about them? Maybe his going to Australia sorted a problem for her. Either way, it hadn't taken Marg that long to find another fella, he thought bitterly.

He drained the last of his beer and watched Merle talking to her parents, conscious of the anger draining from him. How many others would have tried to make him see his aunt in a kinder light? Val had got it all wrong, Merle was a fine and kind person, and she had feelings for him, he knew she did, otherwise she wouldn't have given him the chrysanthemums, or told him of her hopes and dreams of becoming a doctor, and she certainly wouldn't have kissed him like she had if she didn't care. He put down his glass, crossed the dance floor, and touched her elbow.

'Would you like to dance?'

She turned from her parents and smiled. 'I thought you said you didn't know how.'

'I didn't say that. I said I didn't have much opportunity.'

'Aren't you going to ask Val? You came with her.'

'She's with Baz,' he said, taking her hand.

Merle's body was soft and supple in his arms as they waltzed around the floor, he could smell her perfume and a surge of emotion flooded through him. Did she feel the same? When the music stopped he stayed on the dance floor, his arm around her, ignoring the hurt on Val's face as she and Barry made their way back to their table.

'I'm not very good at the foxtrot,' said Merle when the music started.

'Neither am I,' said Jon, 'but we'll manage.'

'What about Val?'

'What about her?'

'She looks upset.'

'I keep telling you, Val and me, we're just mates. In any case, she told me to play the field, and you're the only field for me,' he said, feeling bold.

She looked up at him and blushed and his heart seemed to skip a beat.

CHAPTER 23

On Monday Jon told Frank he was handing in his notice.
'Why?' asked Frank.
'Because I can't be in two places at once.'
'Is this about your sister?'
'What do you think?'
Frank ignored him and watched the windscreen wipers struggling with the snow. 'If this gets any worse we'll be forced off the road,' he muttered as he manoeuvred the van around an abandoned car. 'Worst winter in living memory, blizzards, ice storms, floodin' and, on top of all that, unemployment at an all-time high and you want to hand in your notice!' He nursed the van along icy tracks in the snow. 'Damn stupid thing to do if you ask me. You don't know how lucky you are to have a job.'
Jon kept his arms folded and stared straight ahead.
Frank sighed. 'Go on then, tell me what you're up for doing.' He listened while Jon outlined his plan. 'Right!' said Frank. 'First, there's no need to hand in your notice. Second, you'll be wastin' your time for the most part. That aunt of yours won't let Kath out of her sight. Pound to a penny she won't, so I'll tell you what, I'll cover for you between three and four one day a week until you sort things out. Will that do you?'
'Yes,' said Jon, 'and thanks, Frank.'
'Don't mention it; it'll cost you a packet of fags though.'
The following Wednesday Frank waited a discreet distance from the school gates and Jon saw he wasn't the only one waiting for Kathy. Marg was there in her tweed coat, fur hat, thick scarf and gloves, hovering at the school gates, stamping her feet to keep warm. When Kathy joined her he could tell his sister wasn't pleased by the distance between them and the way she pulled away every time Marg tried to link arms.
They watched the pair of them for a moment or two. 'She'll be

like a cat on tin tacks for a week or two, terrified Kathy'll step under another van, or run off with that no good brother of hers,' said Frank. He grinned. 'I'd give it another week then try again, give those jittery nerves of hers time to settle.'

A fortnight later Frank pulled up within sight of the school gates. Jon glanced at his watch, nearly half past three.

'Looks like your auntie's had enough of the bad weather, you're going to get a chance to put over your point of view after all.'

Jon stripped off his overalls and put on his jacket. 'Thanks, mate.'

'Don't be late, I've a couple of drops left to do so I'll pick you up here in thirty minutes, all right?'

'You going to introduce us?' asked the girl at Kathy's side. She hitched her satchel higher on her shoulder and flashed him a dazzling smile.

'He's my brother,' said Kathy.

The girl's eyes widened, but she recovered fast. 'I'm Jill, Kath's best friend. She's told me all about you. You're the one that's been living in Australia, aren't you?' She fluttered her eyelashes at him and looked at him coyly. 'I thought she was romancing.'

'Can we talk, Kathy?'

'Can't, Mam's expecting me.'

'She's not your mam.'

'You seen any kangaroos and platypuses?' asked Jill.

'Kangaroos, not platypuses,' said Jon, wishing she'd shut up.

The three of them continued walking for a few minutes.

'If I'm late she'll come looking,' said Kathy.

'But we've got to talk. I *am* your brother.'

'I know.'

'What about koala bears?' asked Jill.

'Well, when?' he asked, ignoring Jill's question. 'I haven't seen you to talk to properly since you were five, for God's sake.'

Jill stopped and grabbed Kathy's arm. 'How about next week, choir prac. Tell your mam you'll be home late.'

'She'll—'

'I'll tell Miss Wynford that you're not feeling well and that you've had to go home early.'

'Where?' asked Jon before Kathy could change her mind.

'The park,' said Jill, pointing over his shoulder. 'Cor, isn't this exciting, I wish I had a long-lost brother.' She flashed him another smile. 'Right, that's fixed, quarter to four near the bandstand.' She nudged Kathy. 'Gorrit?'

Jon arrived early and leaned against the frosted bandstand railings. He watched Kathy as she walked towards him, her satchel slung over her shoulder, her hat perched on her head, a thick scarf around her neck against the cold. She was tall and slim, like Merle, and almost grown up, old enough to know her own mind. He suddenly felt shy.

'Hello,' she said and leaned against the railings next to him. 'Have you been here long?'

'No, just arrived.' Why had he lied? It was a daft thing to do, she was his sister; he didn't need to lie to her. 'I brought you some chocolates.' He pulled out a small paper bag containing a few unappetitizing chocolates that Pete had got for him from a mate he knew who dealt in black-market goods.

Kathy's face lit up. 'Ooh, goody.' She took one, bit into it and wrinkled up her nose. 'It tastes funny.' She held out the half-eaten chocolate for him to try.

He bit into the dark confection; it didn't taste anything like the chocolate he remembered. 'You don't have to eat them if you don't want to,' he said, regretting the time and the money he'd spent on getting them.

They sat together on a nearby bench not speaking for a moment.

'Tell me about Australia,' she said. 'Mam says it's a nice place, lots of sun and nice beaches.'

He didn't want to talk about Australia; it was the last place he wanted to think about. He wanted to move on and get a new life that included her. 'It's hot and big, and where I was living they raise sheep on stations.'

'Stations? Do you mean railway stations?'

'No, you dummy, farms. They call them stations in Australia.'

'You mean like ranches in America.'

'Yeah, farms, ranches, stations, they're all the same thing.'

'Oh.' She twiddled with the tassels on her scarf.

What was he doing, their first proper conversation and he'd called her a dummy? He racked his brain trying to think of something interesting to say. 'What are you going—'

'I cried after you left,' she interrupted, 'I told them I wanted to go to Australia too and they shouted at me, told me that if I cried they wouldn't be able to find anyone to adopt me.'

He stared miserably into the distance. There wasn't anything to say to that. Things were getting worse. He wished he hadn't come.

'They said I'd be better off with a new home and a new family, and then Mam…Auntie Marg and Uncle Harry turned up, and they said I could live with them. So it all worked out all right, I suppose.'

'How long have you been with them?'

Kathy's brow furrowed and then she counted off the years on her fingers. 'Nearly seven years.'

Jon did a rapid calculation. Marg must have adopted Kathy a year after he was sent to Australia. Why had she waited so long? Why hadn't she turned up earlier, before they sent him away? Was Merle right? Had she been grieving for Uncle Fred? Had he been unfair? Truth was, he didn't like Marg and the feeling was mutual, but they could have been a family. He'd have been good, grateful.

'She ever mention me?'

'Yes. She told me you'd gone to a better life and that you wanted to go, that it was an adventure, and she said a boy of eight couldn't look after a five-year-old child properly.'

She was right on that point, Jon conceded, but he really wished she'd been quicker off the mark and had thought about them sooner. He could have done without his adventures as Kathy put it.

'Well, I can look after you now.' He glanced across at her when she didn't answer. 'Don't you want us to be together?'

'Yes, course I do, but Mam…Auntie Marg won't have you in the house.'

'She never did like me much.' He grinned. 'What's she been saying?'

'Oh, just stuff. You know?'

'What stuff.'

'That going to Australia didn't do you any good. That you're rough and uncouth.' She giggled.

'What's that supposed to mean?'

'Rude.'

'I'm not rude. She's the one who's rude.' Kathy played with the tassels on the end of her scarf, plaiting and unplaiting them. 'Anyway,' said Jon, 'we don't have to live with her. I've got a job, I can support us.'

'Auntie Marg's my mam now.'

'Yeah, but Marg's not your *proper* mam, is she? And I'm your brother and Mam told me to look after you, remember? And I promised I would.'

'Well you didn't, did you? You left me and went off to live in Australia.'
'I know, but I'm here now.'
Kathy squirmed and Jon sensed her unease. 'You fancy a walk or something?'
She looked at her watch. 'No. I don't want to be late. I'm supposed to be home for half past four on Wednesdays. Besides, it's too cold.'
'Can I see you next week?'
She hesitated.
'Go on, Kathy. I haven't seen you, hardly at all. We've got a lot to talk about and sort out.'
'But—'
'Come on, Kathy, next Wednesday, same time, same place.'
'I can't miss choir again. Miss Wynford will write to Mam.'
'Auntie,' said Jon.
'Auntie, then,' said Kathy. 'Look, I've got to go. Thanks for the chocolates.'
'What about Saturday? Can't I see you Saturday?'
'I go to ballet Saturday mornings with Jill.'
'After ballet then. Tell Marg you're going to Jill's place then you can meet me here.'

Saturday morning Kathy was already waiting for him, her hat and coat white with the falling snow.
'Sorry I'm late,' he said, seeing the scowl on her face. 'I didn't think you'd come with the weather and all.'
'I hate her,' she screamed at him.
'Who?'
'Mam.'
Jon opened his mouth to correct her and then closed it.
'Do you know what she's done now? She's keeping me in…for the whole weekend. Can you believe it?'
Jon laughed. 'So what are you doing here?'
'I'm at ballet.'
'Why is she keeping you in?'
'Just because I said I wanted you to come to tea.'
'Is that all you said?' He watched the way she scuffed the toe of her shoe in the gravel, disturbing the pristine snow, avoiding eye contact. 'Kathy? Come on, Kathy, what else did you say?'
'Only what you and Jill said…that she isn't my real Mam, just

my auntie and that you're my brother and she can't stop us seeing each other...and she said she could...that she's my legal mother and what she says goes...and she said I'm a silly, selfish brat who could do with a smack, and she sent me to my room, and I hate her.' She paused for breath. 'Do you hear me? I hate her.'

Jon saw the rage on her face and struggled to keep the grin off his own. He hadn't had to do a thing; Marg had done it for him. Good old Marg.

'And she won't let me meet my friends after school. She says I've got too much to do with my ballet and homework...that there'll be plenty of time for gallivanting when I'm older...and she doesn't like Jill...she says she's common.'

Jon brushed snow off the nearest bench and sat on it. Kathy flopped down next to him.

'I've been thinking,' she said. 'We could run away. We could find somewhere to stay, a flat, like you said. I could change schools, and you could get another job. I'll be old enough to leave school soon and then I can get a job too. What do you think?'

Jon didn't know what to think, it was all going too fast. He hadn't considered running away. He'd done enough running away already – enough to last a lifetime, and aside from anything else he liked working with Frank even though the job was boring.

'I suppose you could come and live with me at Elsie's for a while.'

'They'd fetch me back.'

'I don't—'

'It'd be exciting, an adventure. You like adventures. Mam said. What do you say?'

'I—'

'You know all about running away – you ran away from that orphanage, you said.' She waited with an accusing look in her eyes. 'We can go to Blackpool, Blackpool's big, plenty of places to stay in the winter. No one will look for us in Blackpool.' She grabbed his shoulders and shook him. 'What do you think? Say something. You said you wanted to look after me.'

'Yes, well...'

'Yes, well, now you can. We'll go Tuesday.'

Tuesday! He'd arranged to go to the cinema with Merle on Wednesday night.

'Why Tuesday?'

'Mam's going out for the day, with a friend.'

Jon stared at her, she had it all planned!

'I'll forge a note. Jill'll hand it in and we can catch a bus. We can be in Blackpool by one o'clock; that'll give us plenty of time to find somewhere to stay and then we can find me a school after a couple of weeks when everyone's forgotten about us and you can get yourself a job. Yes?' She jumped up. 'That's arranged then, but we mustn't tell anyone.' She brushed the snow off herself. 'See you Tuesday.'

He watched her heading towards the gates. What was he doing listening to her? He was the eldest. He was the one who should be organising things. He couldn't think straight. 'What about Jill?' he shouted after her.

'She won't say anything. She thinks Mam's a stuck-up cow,' she shouted back.

CHAPTER 24

Jon sat next to Kathy on the bus worrying the skin at the side of his thumb with his index finger; at least she'd had the sense to change out of her school uniform. He turned to listen to her excited chatter, conscious of her duffle bag on the floor jammed between them taking up more space than they could comfortably afford, his own, a haversack, had fitted into the luggage rack overhead.

Running away this time felt different; this time he couldn't rid himself of the unease; would his luck hold out or had he used it all up in Australia? This time there were two of them to look out for and he doubted whether there'd be a Mrs Macarthur in Blackpool.

The one advantage in England was the sheer number of people – it was easy to get lost in the crowd, but in Australia it was the space; a man could get away with murder and never be caught, but if folk did see a stranger they remembered. He forced himself to think positively and to plan.

They'd find somewhere to stay, an out-of-the-way place, maybe a bed and breakfast, and they'd need a story, he couldn't say they were on holiday, not in the middle of winter. Perhaps they'd be better off with rooms – more anonymous. He'd keep to the truth as far as possible, it was easier. They were orphans, his dad was killed in the war, his mam dead from cancer and he'd come to Blackpool to find work and a place to live. Once they were settled, Kathy… No! Kathy was no good, they'd need different names.

Merle! Had she received his note telling her he couldn't see her Wednesday night? He wished he could have seen her on Sunday, talked things through with her, but the McGhees had been away visiting family, and then he'd decided it was probably wiser to tell no one. But what would Merle say when she knew what he'd done? He suddenly thought of Alice sitting in her rocking chair on the verandah, at Jarrahlong, smoking a cheroot. She would call him an idiot with fewer brain cells than a gnat. She'd tell him it was about time he grew up. But Elsie wouldn't, Elsie would have understood had he told her. She wouldn't think he was an idiot. Well, he didn't care what anyone thought. He was only putting right a wrong. Sometimes it was right to go with gut feelings.

'You've gone red,' said Kathy. 'Do you feel sick? I always get sick in cars, but not on buses.'

'No, I'm just a bit hot, that's all.'

She gave him a funny look. 'It's flippin' freezing!'

Blackpool looked grim in the grey winter light.

Jon shouldered his bag. 'Remember what we agreed.'

Kathy looked about her, 'Where are we going to stay?'

'I don't know yet.'

'That looks nice.'

Jon followed the line of her finger. She'd picked out the best-looking hotel within sight of the bus station. 'We'd be better off with rooms,' he said, leading them away from the town centre.

'My feet are hurting,' said Kathy after an hour. 'What's wrong with these?' She stood in front of a row of small boarding houses.

'Too dear.'

She flopped down onto a low wall. 'I'm not going any further, and I'm starving.'

'Wait here,' said Jon. He'd have to start asking otherwise they'd never find anywhere to stay. He stepped into a grocer's shop and returned five minutes later with a couple of apples. 'Here!' He chose the reddest apple and handed it to her. 'That'll keep you going until teatime. We need Carson Street.'

It was gone seven before they were fitted up. It cost more than Jon had expected and it wasn't anything special, just two tiny rooms with a shared toilet and bathroom on the landing below, and he'd had to pay up front, a month in advance, but the landlord hadn't asked questions. For once he was glad that he looked older than his years.

The smaller room had a double bed, a set of drawers and a wardrobe, the other had a table, two chairs and a sofa. On a shelf in the curtained off alcove were two plates, two cups and saucers, cutlery, a couple of enamel dishes and three chipped enamel pans, and, below the shelf, a stoneware sink with hot and cold running water, and next to that an electric hot plate that had seen better days.

The flooring was worn linoleum covered with a couple of grubby scatter rugs and at the windows were flowered curtains that barely met in the middle. In the corner of the room was an electric, coin-operated meter and above it a single wall-mounted bar heater.

'Where are you going to sleep?' asked Kathy, flopping down onto the bed. 'I don't like this, there aren't any sheets and blankets, and it's freezing in here.'

'We'll get some tomorrow.'

'And I'm hungry.'

'For pity's sake, give me a chance, Kath.'

She rummaged in her bag, pulled out a small brown ration book and dropped it on the bed.

'Whose is that?'

'Mine.'

He glanced at the front cover and saw her name. Why hadn't he thought about ration books? He hadn't even remembered to collect his own from Elsie. Just who was looking after who he wondered as he scanned through the information page? He dropped the booklet back on the bed. He wasn't even sure they'd be able to use it. The local butcher and grocer might not accept the coupons seeing as they weren't registered with them, and then they'd have to buy everything on the black market or eat out in cafés. It was all a right mess! He shivered, lowered his haversack to the floor and went to find the lavatory.

Down a flight of stairs, on the landing, was a door marked WC in white paint which opened into a bathroom. A large enamel bath on claw feet stood against the far wall, next to it was a sink and a next to that a lavatory with a thunder box high up on the wall. A long chain dangled down with a white porcelain pull at the end of it. He used the lavatory and pulled the chain. The cistern hissed and rattled like a train and refilled with such force that water gushed over the edge and doused him. He shook off the water. What the hell was he doing here? Kidnapping was a serious offence, even in Australia. He retched, but the empty, sick feeling stayed.

In the tiny flat Kathy sat huddled on the sofa, shivering. Jon rummaged in his pocket and found some coins to feed the meter. He pulled the cord attached to the wall heater and watched as the single element glowed red. Kathy dragged the kitchen chair over and sat underneath it, holding her hands out for warmth.

'It'll soon warm up. You get the plates ready and I'll go and see if I can find us some fish and chips.'

'It smells funny.'

'Damp,' said Jon, 'it'll soon go.'

'I don't like it here.'

'It'll be all right as soon as we're settled. Look, I won't be long. Do you like mushy peas?'

Jon woke early – it was a habit instilled by the Catholic Brothers designed to utilise the cooler part of the day, especially for those working in the quarry. He left Kathy sleeping and went out to find something for breakfast.

'What are we doing today?' asked Kathy as she finished her porridge.

'I've got to find a job, my savings won't last forever.' While Kathy was sleeping he'd reviewed his financial situation. After paying the rent he had enough for two weeks maximum, if they were careful.

'What about me?'

'You'll have to stay here.'

'Why?'

'Because Marg will have reported you missing. Knowing her she'll have said you've been kidnapped or something.'

Kathy giggled.

'It's not funny, Kath. We must be careful. If we get caught I'll be in a lot of trouble, and I mean a lot.'

'What? Do you mean jail?'

Borstal, he thought. That's where I'll end up.

'What am I going to do while you're out?'

'I don't know.'

She sipped the remains of last night's left over orange squash and wrinkled her nose. 'I didn't bring a book or anything.'

'I'll go and get you a comic.'

'Two.'

'Two what?'

'Comics, and some apples, I like red ones.'

'All right, two comics and red apples.'

Kathy brightened. 'I want a *Girls' Crystal* and a *School Friend* please.'

After three days Jon got a job with Eddie Cooper, fish wholesaler. He had to be at Eddie's shop for three-fifteen in the morning to get to Fleetwood in plenty of time for the fish auction. There was a half an hour wait while Eddie did the bidding and then he loaded up the truck while Eddie had breakfast. The cold, backbreaking work numbed his fingers and his brain.

When he got used to the routine the early start suited him. They were back in Blackpool for six and after a couple of hours filleting fish, sorting out the orders and the delivery rounds to fish and chip shops, small hotels and local businesses, he was free to go. Most days they were finished by lunchtime, which left the afternoon for Kathy.

Eddie always paid up front and didn't ask questions. The arrangement meant he had spending money, but Jon knew they couldn't play the arcades forever. Kathy needed to be in school, she'd already missed a week, but he was wary, Blackpool wasn't that far from Liverpool.

Kathy's restlessness irritated him and going out every afternoon bored him, there were only so many cinemas and arcades a fella could take. Their claustrophobic life depressed him; he was back living on his nerves, waiting for people to challenge them. He was tired of explaining why Kathy wasn't in school, he was sick of avoiding the police, of giving people in authority wide berth, of keeping away from places where they might attract attention. It was like Charlestown all over again when every person he met was a threat, where anyone and everyone could turn him in, report him to the police or hand him back to the Catholic Brothers.

He dumped his coat on the back of the bentwood chair and poured himself a glass of water.

Kathy came through from the bedroom. 'What are we doing today, Jon?'

'For God's sake, Kathy, I've only just got in.'

'I can tell. You stink.'

'I always stink after being with the fish.'

'We could go to the promenade and see what's happening.'

'I'm tired, Kathy.'

She glared at him, arms akimbo, tapping her foot. 'I'm tired too. I'm tired of living in this dump; it's boring, sitting here all morning while you're out enjoying yourself.'

'Enjoying myself! You mean busting my guts to try and earn enough to—'

'I never asked you to.'

'It was your idea,' shouted Jon. 'You were the one who wanted to come to this stupid place.'

'You said you'd look after me.'

'I am.'

'No you're not, you just go to work every day. There's nothing to do here. I've no one to talk to, there's no ballet, no music lessons, no nothing.'

'No Auntie Marg,' sneered Jon. 'Go on, say it, say you prefer Marg.'

Kathy's lip trembled, fat tears rolled down her pale cheeks. 'I didn't say that.'

Jon didn't want to hear. He pulled himself to his feet. 'Look, Kathy, I'm sorry. I didn't mean it.'

'You did,' she sobbed, turning her back on him. 'You don't care about me.'

He wiped the exasperated look off his face. 'Look, I'll go and wash and then we'll go to the promenade, all right?'

'All righty,' she sniffled and, seconds later, turned towards him again, a smile on her face.

Jon glanced away. He couldn't look at her, afraid she'd read the shock in his expression, his realisation that she was a selfish, manipulative, spoilt brat who was nothing like the little sister he remembered.

Jon lay on the sofa, the blanket that barely kept him warm at night tucked under his chin. His feet felt like frozen cod and he couldn't sleep, two o'clock his watch read, he had to be up in an hour.

A draft from the ill-fitting window frame ballooned the flimsy curtain and the street light wove purple patterns on the wall, blotches, nothing like the purple roses of the print. He shivered. He hated purple, purple dredged up memories, Perentie Man's purple tongue flicking as he ran beside him, just out of sight, his heavy presence looming over him like a malignant shadow.

He rolled on his side, curled up like a baby and closed his eyes but the purple shadows still flickered behind his lids and he could hear the rhythmic beat of Curly's chanting, Curly calling to him from beyond the grave…

…Curly turns towards him and his black face splits into a wide grin. They are standing on a grassy knoll just beyond the last of the docks looking at the choppy, murky waters of the Mersey, the tide pushing the water inland. The sooty smell of the sleeping city prickles his nose, the clouds part and moonlight sparkles on the water.

'What you doing here, mate?' Curly asks.

He smells the lanolin from Alice's sheep on Curly's britches, smells his familiar musky odour, feels the warmth of him. 'It's my home.'

'Nah.'

'It is. Liverpool's a bonzer city.'

'Nah.' Curly hunkers down and pulls out a sod of earth. 'Y'smelt it?' He holds the tuft aloft, sniffs it and hands it over. 'Have y' really smelt it?'

He takes the clay sod from Curly and sniffs the sour scent of damp and decay. 'It's just soil,' he says.

'Death,' says Curly, 'it smells of death.'

'The outback's death,' he says. 'Remember all those sheep?' He looks across at Curly. 'Remember dying?'

'You haven't seen it after the rain,' says Curly, 'when it sprouts flowers, masses of them, as far as the eye can see, when the wattle's yellow. It's beaut. Nah, Jon, here's death.'

They squat together watching the rippling water, conscious of the cool breeze lifting their hair. A screech owl calls from the thicket away to their left and soon after its ghostly shape skims the rough ground in its hunt for mice.

'You got my tjuringa safe, Jon?'

He leans into the bottom of Elsie's spare wardrobe and takes out his haversack. He unbuckles the strap and pulls out his old jackaroo britches and the check shirt that he bought in Simpson's store. Finally, in the very depths, his fingers brush the rough, grimy fabric that wraps the plank of wood he is searching for. He tries to lift it but the plank is as heavy as lead. Sweat prickles his brow as he struggles to free the tjuringa from his bag. The wood throbs in his fingers, the rhythmic beat of an Aboriginal chant thumps in his head. When he looks up the enormous shadow of Perentie Man looms over him, his purple-pink tongue flicking his face. He drops the tjuringa, his heart pounding, and flails his arms warding off the shadow, screaming at it to let him go…

'...Jon?'

He opened his eyes and saw Kathy standing over him shaking him awake.

'Wake up, Jon.'

He sat up. 'What's the matter?'

'You were shouting and hitting. You frightened me,' she said, standing well back from the sofa now that he was awake, an eiderdown wrapped around her.

He looked at his watch – half past two! He must have slept. He rubbed his arms, shrugged away the stiffness from his back and shoulders and the fingers of fear that still tickled his spine. He shivered. 'Go back to bed, Kathy. I've got to get ready for work soon.'

'Are you all right?'

'Yes, it was just a bad dream.'

Jon climbed the stairs, exhausted after the sleepless night and the tiring shift gutting fish, and pushed open the door.

'Sorry I'm late, Kathy, I've got us some ham,' but his words were swallowed up in the empty space, and her bedroom door was closed. Was she ill? 'Kathy, are you in there?' He knocked then opened the door and saw the bed, a tussle of blankets and discarded clothes. She was in the bathroom.

He took out a brown paper bag from his coat pocket. He'd been lucky to get the sliced ham. A friend of Eddie's had sold him it. A late delivery the chap had said, soon as the word's out there'll be a queue down the street and round the corner, and Jon knew he was right. He'd been home long enough to see the queues outside grocers' shops.

He put the kettle on to boil and sniffed the last of the milk. On the turn, it would probably curdle in the hot tea, but it would be warm and wet even if it tasted a bit peculiar. He cut two rounds of bread and smeared margarine over them. He hadn't had ham in years. Mam was partial to ham with Colman's mustard. He'd tell Kathy, he'd talk to her about Mam, remind her about the old times she was too young to remember. Pity he didn't have any photos. Had Marg got them? He remembered the small, oblong prints with white deckled borders that Mam stuck into the album with black gummed corners. Her favourite had been the one taken on the day trip to North Wales. Mam and Kath and him standing in front of the lighthouse in the dunes at Talacre while Dad snapped them with his box camera. The kettle whistled and he made the tea. Where the heck was she?

He dropped down the flight of stairs and hammered on the bathroom door. 'Kathy, are you in there?' Ear pressed to the door, he strained to listen. 'Kath?' A sick feeling gripped him as he turned the handle. 'Kath?'

Empty! Where the hell had she gone? He rushed back to their rooms and yanked open the wardrobe door – her coat was missing and her shoes. She couldn't have gone far, he reasoned, she hadn't bothered to lock the door. He grabbed his coat and raced down-stairs. She knew not to go out, he'd drummed it in every day. He'd warned her that the police would be on the lookout, maybe even have a photo of her. He scanned the street. Where would she go, the beach, the arcades, the promenade? She could be anywhere, knowing Kath.

The front was busy for a Wednesday afternoon. He started at the South Pier and did a recce of the fairground, asking blokes doing maintenance if they'd seen a red-headed girl hanging round the place. Arcades're your best bet, one had said, it's too cold to be hanging round in this weather.

On the main drag he dodged the trams and crossed over to the business side of the street, his belly churning as he worked his way through every likely draw; by the time he'd reached the North End his breath was coming in short painful stabs and his ears ached from the cold. Had she gone into a café or to the cinema? Thing was she could be anywhere. It was like searching for gold in a pan full of sludge and just as tiring. He'd kill her when he caught up with her, the selfish brat!

He crossed the road again and leaned against the railings along the seafront, his frustration a choking lump in his chest. She wouldn't be daft enough to go off with a stranger, would she? Or had she caught a bus and gone home to Marg?

Along the beach a way stood a solitary figure looking out to sea. Kathy? No, she was too big for Kathy and she had a dog. He watched her throw a ball and the dog chase after it. Closer to him an elderly couple, well wrapped up against the chill wind, strolled on the firmer sand and, way over, near the water's edge, two kids where skipping stones across the water. He turned away. Did he go home and wait or go to the police? He whipped round again. There was something familiar about the taller of the two figures. He watched intently at the way the figure threw the stone and heard a sharp shout of triumph carried on the wind. Kathy! It was Kathy, he was sure.

He leapt down onto the sand and hared across to the two of them, air whistling in his lungs and burning his throat with each dragging breath. 'Kathy,' he yelled, the call whipped away even as he spoke.

She saw him then, smiled and waved with both hands. He stood before her, bent over, catching his breath, unable to speak.

'This is Alan,' she said, 'from over there.' She pointed to the South Pier and the funfair beyond. 'He's with a travelling circus.'

'What the bloody hell do you think you are doing?' he ranted, flailing his arms about in sheer frustration at the gormless look on her face.

'I'm not doing anything wrong.'

'Haven't you listened to a word I've said?' he raged, ignoring the lad next to her. 'Do you want to go back home or something?'

She stood before him, arms akimbo. 'Yes,' she yelled back. 'I'm sick of being here and it's boring being on my own all day.'

'You're not on your own all day, I'm back by twelve.'

'Not today,' she shouted.

'One day, Kath, just one day.'

'It's boring,' she screamed at him. 'Boring!'

'I don't care; you've got to do as you're told.'

'Why?' She stamped her foot.

'Because I say.'

'Because I say,' she mimicked. 'You're not my dad. I don't have to listen to you.'

'Yes, you do,' he raged. 'Mam said, she said I was to take care of you.'

'Well you didn't, did you? You cleared off to Australia. You didn't look after me then, did you? You left me in that children's home, didn't you?'

Alan dug his hands deeper into his pockets. 'Is he your brother or something?'

'He says he is,' snapped Kathy.

Jon took a step back, wounded by her words, shocked by her defiance. 'I've had enough of this.' He grabbed her by the arm, dragging her after him.

'Let go,' she yelled, lashing out with her foot. 'You're horrible and I hate you.'

He dodged another well-aimed kick, turned to shout at her and ran straight into Alan's fist. Splinters of light burst in his brain; he staggered and fell face down on the beach. He lay prone, his world spinning, the individual grains of sand shifting in a kaleidoscope of muted shades. After a while, when the nausea passed, he raised his wobbly head and saw them sprinting across the foreshore, fast as they could run, to the far pier.

In the bathroom he checked for damage in the mirror and felt the bruising near his temple. The blow had poleaxed him – it was lucky it hadn't finish him off. He splashed cold water over his face and rinsed off the dirty sand.

In their rooms he flopped down on the hard chair next to lunch, his eyes drawn to the ham sandwiches now dried and curled on the plates, and the cold tea topped with a scummy film. Tears pricked his eyes. Where had he gone wrong?

She didn't come home until gone ten o'clock. He heard her opening the door quietly so as not to wake him.

'Are you all right?' he asked.

She nodded. 'Are you?'

He rolled off the couch and sat on the edge, his blanket wrapped around him for warmth, not knowing what to say.

'I'm sorry,' she mumbled. 'I didn't mean all those things I said.'

'I'm sorry too.' Least said, soonest mended, Mam always said. He looked up at Kathy, weary to the very core. 'Have you had any tea?'

'No.'

'There's a ham sandwich over there, it's a bit dry but it'll fill a hole.' He heard her cross to the table and sit down. 'We'll go home in the morning, Kath.'

'I don't want to go home. I want to stay here with you.' She started to cry, tears rolled down her cheeks and dripped off her chin.

He patted the couch and she came and sat next to him, her body racked with sobs as he held her close to him.

'I'll...I'll stay...stay in now...I promise...Jon.'

He felt in his pocket and pulled out a handkerchief. She blew her nose.

'Eat your sandwiches before they go off.'

She managed a watery smile. 'Is that a joke?'

'Sort of.'

A wet blanket of depression leached his energy. He didn't speak as Eddie drove to Fleetwood, dawn still hours away. The steady drone of the engine lulled him into reverie and gave him the opportunity to reflect on his stupidity. Eddie wasn't a talker. Frank would have asked what was wrong before they were halfway to the fish market, but not Eddie, Eddie was too wrapped up in doing his sums to notice. Jon worried the skin at the side of his thumb and tried to think himself into a more positive frame of mind.

Back at the Blackpool premises Jon gutted the fish, his mind at Jarrahlong, wondering how Alice was coping, wondering whether she'd sold up or decided to stick it out. He didn't rate her as a quitter. Alice would die at Jarrahlong. She'd have herself interred with Jack next to the great jarrah trees by the creek. Too late he'd realised he should have stayed in Australia; he should have listened to Alice, and to Stan.

That morning they finished at eleven. Eddie had a box booked at Haydock and wanted to be away early. He'd studied form for a week and believed he was set fair for a big win on the horses.

'Mind if I drop you off here?' said Eddie as he pulled out of the traffic and parked next to a greengrocer's shop. 'You can catch a bus outside the bank; it's not too far out of your way.' He felt in his pocket and pulled out a wad of notes and peeled off a fiver. 'I'm feeling generous,' Eddie said as he rammed the gearstick into first. 'It's a one-off mind, so don't go getting ideas that I'm a soft touch.' He waited while Jon got out, glanced into his rear-view mirror and joined the traffic again.

Jon shoved the money into his pocket. He should have been feeling pleased, elated by the unexpected bonus, instead the depression remained. He looked about him, got his bearings and headed for the town centre. Eddie had dropped him off in the older part of town where big, red-brick buildings dominated the street. People hurried past him, heads down, bundled up in their drab greys and blacks, muffled against the bitter spring wind. He stuffed his hands deeper into his pockets and didn't see the woman who stepped across the pavement in front of him until he almost knocked her over. He grabbed her sleeve and managed to stop her falling.

'Look where you're going,' she snapped. Her eyes narrowed as she glared at him. She shook his hand free of her sleeve and retied her headscarf. Two other women clattered down some steps after her. 'You all right, Rita?' he heard one of them ask.

Jon glanced to his right and read the gilded words on the board behind a set of iron railings, *Church of Mary, the Mother of Christ*. His feet carried him up the steps to the large mahogany door. He hadn't been inside a church since Karundah; there, they'd had to attend mass regularly in the makeshift chapel.

Half of him knew it was pointless to enter; there was nothing for him in church, no solace, only painful memories. But it hadn't always been that way.

Inside the building the smell of candle wax and incense transported him back. He was with his mother lighting the votive candles for Granddad, he could hear the mumbled words of blessing, the rustle as people knelt to pray or cross themselves and the click as people fingered rosary beads.

The church was gloomy; someone had switched off the lights in the main body of the building. Jon stepped into the aisle and looked towards the altar that was still illuminated by flickering candles, the golden cross glinting in the light; the gold jewel-bright against the dark wall. Before the altar rail a priest knelt briefly in prayer, then he disappeared off to the left, into the vestry, Jon supposed, to divest himself of his stole and alb.

Jon slid into a pew and crossed himself. He bowed his head but no words came and a massive lump seemed to fill his chest, he could feel it rising up his throat threatening to choke him. He stared at the cross; it doubled and then tripled and seemed to grow large even as he stared. He'd made a mistake, what he wanted he couldn't find in church, he made to leave just as he felt a hand rest gently on his shoulder.

'Everything all right?' asked a middle-aged voice.

Jon nodded, the lump still sticking in his throat, the scent of incense and candle wax on the priest's clothing prickling his nose.

'I'm Father Matthews. Do you mind if I join you?'

Jon slid further along the pew to make room for the priest.

'I always think the altar looks beautiful from the back of the church when it's the only part lit. It seems to draw me into it.' The priest sat, his hands clasped loosely in his lap.

Jon cursed himself. He was an idiot. He should have avoided the place, now he was trapped. He couldn't answer the priest and he couldn't slide out of the pew and leave, that wasn't how his mam had brought him up. He felt sick.

'Do you want to talk?'

Jon shook his head.

'Are you Catholic?'

Jon nodded, a *so-what* look plastered on his face.

The priest continued to sit, his whole manner calm and relaxed.

There wasn't going to be a harangue. Jon's nausea subsided and the muscles in his neck eased, the triple cross gradually settled back into one. 'I think I've done something wrong,' he said finally.

'Do you want to tell me about it?' asked Father Matthews.

Jon thought for a moment, he wasn't sure. Did talking help or would it make it worse? Confession hadn't made any difference in his life as far as he could tell, and that was a form of talking about it.

'Did you mean to do it, or was it an accident?'

'I meant to do it, and it's not wrong, not really…at least I don't think it's wrong, but I think I might be in trouble.' Jon thought for a while. 'Will you have to report me to the police?'

'Not if it's a confession.'

'I don't want to go in there,' he said, looking directly at the confessional.

'We can do it here,' said the priest. He leaned forward and pulled a stole out of his pocket and placed it round his neck.

The priest reminded him of Father William; he had the same unhurried air about him. He waited while Jon gathered his thoughts and then listened while he explained about the children's home, about his promise to his mother, about his aunt and Kathy's adoption and running away.

'I know it's hard,' the priest said at last, 'but legally Kathy is your aunt's responsibility now, not yours. I think deep down you know that.'

The cross shimmered as Jon kept his eyes fixed on it.

'She'll be very worried, your aunt. I think you should let her know that you are both safe.' Father Matthews let the words sink in for a moment. 'Can you persuade Kathy to return home?'

'It's not how she thought it was going to be,' said Jon. 'She's only a kid, she thinks life is all about fun.'

'That's how it should be for a child.'

'It doesn't seem to be much fun from where I'm standing, either,' said Jon.

'I can see why you think your aunt has treated you badly, you feel hurt and rejected, but she and her new husband have done their best for Kathy and it's clear they love her. That must take a great weight off your shoulders. Perhaps you should see it as a blessing, and think about what you want for yourself.'

'What I want is my sister, for us to live together like we used to,' said Jon.

'Sometimes we can't go back, only forward. Perhaps you need to lower your expectations for a while. When Kathy's twenty-one she'll be able to do what she wants to do.'

'But that's years away.'

'Would you like me to speak to your aunt for you?'

'No.'

'You will contact her and sort this out?'

Jon focussed on the priest's black serge cassock, the threadbare cloth darned with thin wool where he knelt to pray. Weariness addled his brain. He needed rest, he needed to sleep, he'd lost everything and now he'd lost Kathy's respect. Had he a choice? 'Yes.'

The priest murmured the words of absolution and removed his

stole. 'Have you a rosary?'

Jon shook his head.

Father Matthews pulled one from his pocket and gave it to him. Jon felt the priest's hand resting lightly on his shoulder.

'Will you be all right?'

'Yes,' said Jon. 'Thank you.'

It was snowing when he stepped out of the church, huge big flakes that drifted down and settled on his coat. Jon turned his face to the spring sky and felt the softness on his skin, the cold, warm melt. His fingers brushed against the rosary beads in his pocket, he twisted the string around his fingers, comforted by the memory from his childhood when he'd played with his mother's beads. Today would be his last day with Kathy. They'd go back to Liverpool in the morning.

CHAPTER 25

It was eight o'clock by the time he left the Police Station. The interrogation had lasted hours and he'd been on his own most of the time until Harry arrived and spoke on his behalf. When Marg turned up, spitting fire, Harry had made her listen to reason and he'd talked a lot of sense to both of them. He told Marg she'd drive a wedge between herself and Kathy if she didn't ease up a bit, and Harry told him that Marg was a good mother who loved Kathy, that she didn't deserve all the worry and anguish he'd put her through. Apologising had been the hardest. The words seemed to stick in his throat, but he'd done it, he'd done it for Kathy.

He pulled his coat tighter about him, concentrated on putting one foot in front of the other, fighting off the overwhelming exhaustion. He'd been a fool, too obsessed with his own wants and idea of justice to see the bigger picture. While for Kath it had all been one big adventure that turned sour in the end. But at least some good had come out of it all; Marg had grudgingly agreed he could visit now and again, and Kathy would be happier too, happier with all the things he couldn't provide.

Half an hour later he stood at the top of Bridge Street and his spirits lifted. He didn't deserve Elsie in his life. Alice had been good to him too and yet they were as different as sliced white and damper; Alice, big boned and heavy, with a tongue that could lash at thirty paces, and bird-like Elsie, busying about, taking in washing, doing a bit of cleaning here and there to make ends meet, and whose kind words were balm to a troubled mind.

'Thought you weren't coming back,' she said. 'I was beginning to think they'd locked you up and thrown away the key. Everything go all right?'

'A caution, and borstal if I put another foot wrong, the Sergeant said, but Marg didn't have me guts for garters if that's what you're on about.'

'You look a bit washed out. Had any tea?'

Tea? He tried to remember when he'd last eaten, breakfast probably. 'Harry spoke for me, he knew the sergeant – they're in the same lodge. What does that mean?'

'I don't really know, some sort of men's club, I think.' She passed him a mug of Ovaltine and a slice of bread and dripping. 'Here, have some bread and scrape, it'll make you grow a bit.'

He forced a smile. 'Six foot one'll do me; I don't want to grow any more.' He bit into the bread dripping with hot pork fat – scrape? 'Where are you from, Elsie? You're not from Liverpool, are you?'

Elsie laughed. 'No, lad, I suppose you could say I'm a bit of a mongrel.'

'What's that supposed to mean?'

'Well, I've been about a bit. I was born in Yorkshire, then Da got a job in a Lancashire cotton mill when I was about seven, so we lived there until I met and married my Ted. I met him on a day trip to Southport and we were married within the year and that's when I moved to Liverpool. I've been here ever since. Why do you ask?'

'It's your accent.'

'What's wrong with me accent?'

'Nothing, it's just that it's...it's...'

'Mongrel.'

Jon laughed. 'Yeah, mongrel.'

Elsie licked the frothy milk off her top lip. 'Aye up, I nearly forgot.' She eased herself out of her chair and crossed over to the mantelshelf above the old range. She took down an envelope from behind a brass candlestick and passed it to him. 'This came last week. Looks to me like it's from Alice.'

Jon turned it over and saw an Australian stamp on the right-hand corner. 'No, it's from Stan Colley.' Airmail! It must have cost him a bit. He slit it open and took out the single sheet of paper. Twenty pounds in English five-pound notes dropped onto the table.

Elsie whistled. 'Is Stan that prospector you were telling me about? He must have made a killing, sending that sort of money.'

The top left-hand corner had a pale stain and the paper smelt of rum. He imagined Stan sitting at his deal table swigging the stuff and penning the letter, dogs curled at his feet, the stove burning sweet-scented mulga logs, with a billycan bubbling on the heat.

Dear Jon,

I'm glad to hear that you arrived safe. Sorry things haven't worked out over that sister of yours but no doubt something will turn up. It usually does when you're least expecting it.

You're probably worrying about Alice. Well, there's no need, the rebuilding is going on a treat. She's had a bigger place built this time. The kitchen's looking good but Belle still does most of the cooking outside. Alice shouts but it doesn't make a ha'pennyworth of difference. Old Alan Bynon from Merredin finished rebuilding the barn last week and he's starting on the store sheds next.

The drought broke just after you left, we had plenty of rain, the heaviest for over twenty years. It made a fine crop of grazing for Alice's sheep. She still hasn't got a manager. Adie does his best but he isn't a manager, and you know Alice, stubborn as an old camel and more difficult to manage than a cut snake. She throws me own sentiments back at me, says something'll turn up.

You're probably wondering about the money, thinking I've found the reef. Well, no such luck. Alice said I was to sell the nugget you left. Took it into Perth, I did, and bumped into a chap who deals in opals. He rated it a fine specimen, wanted to know where it came from and all. Anyway, he paid top whack. I reckon it'll be enough for you to hire someone to track down your sister. Look well if she got sent out too and she's up at the girls' orphanage at Geraldton. That'd be a right bugger.

Stan.

p.s. O'Leary, turned up just after you left. He said he wanted to shake the hand of the bloke who saved his life! I said I'd pass it on.

Jon handed the letter across to Elsie. Odd, Stan hadn't mentioned Rachel, Scally and the others. It would have been nice to have had news of them. And there was no suggestion he should go back. He swallowed his disappointment.

'He doesn't know you've found Kathy?'

'No.'

'What are you going to do?'

'I don't know.'

'Strikes me you'd be a fool to let the opportunity go by.'

'What opportunity?'

'There's none so dim as them as will not see,' she said tartly. 'What have you got holding you back here? Only Kathleen, and she's happy where she is, but you're not, it seems to me that without you realising it you've carved out a niche for yourself in Charlestown.'

'You don't know what you're talking about,' said Jon.

'Don't I? How often do you think about the place? Bet you ten bob it's oftener than you care to admit. I know what I'd do if I were a youngster your age, foot-loose and fancy-free – you wouldn't see me for dust. And, come to think of it, I was wrong about Val, she's got her head screwed on. She isn't like her mother, or her sister. She wants more and I wouldn't be a bit surprised if she doesn't up sticks and emigrate as soon as she's twenty-one.' She chuckled to herself. 'Knowing her she'll probably lie about her age and go before then.'

'I thought you didn't like her.'

'I didn't, but I've got to know her a bit better.'

Jon looked at her sceptically.

'She called round most days wanting news of you. It seems she was worried you'd get yourself thrown into jail. She told me you're a nice fella, that you didn't deserve prison.'

'She did!'

'Aye, and she reckoned she'd have done the same had she been in your boots.'

'Did Merle call round?'

'Merle? No, haven't seen a lass called Merle. Is she the one you've been courting?' She saw the look on his face. 'Maybe she hasn't heard about your escapade.'

Perhaps Elsie was right, he hoped so.

A week later Jon stepped off the bus and walked towards the cemetery, a bunch of spring flowers in his hand. Nothing had turned out as he'd expected. What was Frank's favourite saying? – Nothing stays the same. It was the sort of thing Stan would say. As usual Frank spoke a lot of sense, and it was true, Liverpool and England weren't the same, they had changed. The city depressed him, even the streets that were still standing were different, more closed in, meaner than he remembered, it didn't feel like home anymore, he didn't even have a home, he was rootless just like the refugees he'd read about in the papers. At least Kathy was settled even if he wasn't. He could live with the fact that there was no home for him with Marg and Harry; it wasn't what he wanted anyway, even though they were all the family he had.

No, he knew now what he was going to do, he'd finally decided. He'd thought about it more and more over the days since he'd got back from Blackpool, since Elsie's terse words and the Saturday he'd met with Merle and told her everything that had happened between him and Kathy.

It hadn't been an easy decision. At first he'd kept pushing the idea out of his mind, but it kept on returning and he knew he had to go back, if only to return Curly's tjuringa, he'd have no peace until then. But it was more than that, Australia was a young country but its Aboriginal roots were ancient, Curly had shown him that, and he knew now that it was the outback that had made him what he was, if he belonged anywhere it was there.

He pictured Jarrahlong as it had once been, before the fire, Alice sitting on the verandah with her sulphur-crested cockatoo and Adie and the other blackfellas working the sheep. He saw the great jarrah trees alongside the creek, the vast expanses of bush and the wildlife – it was the closest he'd got to a home. But if Alice didn't want him he'd get a job as a jackaroo somewhere else, he could go to the Northern Territory or Queensland to one of the big stations, two million acres and more. He breathed in deeply and fancied he could smell the heat of the place. He could make money in Australia, enough to set himself up, enough to support a wife and a family one day.

He walked taller, straighter, his step lighter, satisfied with his plan. He'd apply for assisted passage and if they didn't give him one he'd get a job on a banana boat to start with and then work the rest of the way around the world on tramp ships. He could be back in six months, perhaps less, and even if it took a year, so what, he'd get there in the end. Queer how life turns out, he thought as he turned into the cemetery.

He cleared away the rotted remains of the chrysanthemums that Merle had arranged weeks ago and tidied up the graves. He sat back on his heels and thought of their trip to New Brighton, the evenings he'd spent with her at the cinema, the strolls in the parks and the long walks home from town, and the kisses, and pulled himself back to the present. He was going to make something of himself, for Merle, so that one day, after she'd qualified as a doctor, they could be together.

He arranged the daffodils he had brought with him. Would Mam understand? Did she know that Kathy was settled and happy? He hoped so. And he wasn't abandoning Kathy, he'd write regularly and, when he'd got some money behind him, he'd come back for visits to see her and Merle. He wasn't leaving England forever.

He stood looking at the gravestones, trying to recall the old feelings, his mother hugging him, his sense of loss when she died, but there was nothing. He felt drained of emotion, weary, and relieved that he was free of the burden of responsibility for his sister and free of England. He was ready to go back, but first he needed to see Merle and tell her of his decision.

It was mid-afternoon by the time he got to the McGhee house and the sun was out. Merle answered the door.

'Will you come with me to the park?' he asked.

She hesitated.

'Please, Merle, there're things I need to tell you, to talk to you about?'

For a brief moment he thought she was going to refuse, but then she smiled.

'Let me tell my mother,' she said, leaving him standing on the step. She was back in no time, her gabardine belted and a scarf wrapped around her against the chilly wind. 'Is something wrong?' she asked as they set off for the park.

He took her arm and felt the warmth of her through the fabric. How did he tell her he was leaving? Would she think he didn't care? The other day she'd accused him of not trusting her because he hadn't told her he was going to Blackpool with Kathy. He didn't want to upset her again; he wanted her to understand his reasons, to see the sense of it and not think badly of him for leaving. He took a deep breath. 'I'm going to go back to Australia, Merle.'

She didn't look at him or comment and they walked the rest of the way in silence. He guessed she was angry, or hurt, and he knew he shouldn't have dropped the bombshell like that, he should have thought it through, told her more gently.

When they reached the park they crossed over to the lake and began walking along its edge.

'I like spring,' she said finally, her hands thrust deep in her pockets. 'The daffodils really cheer the place up, crocuses are my favourite though, I like the yellow ones the best, but the birds always eat them. I wonder why that is? Perhaps it's the colour.'

Why was she talking about flowers and birds? Hadn't she heard what he'd said? He tried again. 'There's nothing for me in England apart from you; Kathy's happy and I can always come back for visits and—'

'Your horizons have changed. Liverpool's too small after the wide open spaces. Is that it?'

'That's about it, but it's more than that. You'll be at medical school soon, so I'm going back to make something of my life. I can earn more there, enough to get a place of my own.'

She bent down, picked up a stone and skipped it across the water. 'Where will you go?'

'Back to Jarrahlong, and if Alice doesn't want me I'll go north and get a job on one of the big stations there, after I've taken Curly's tjuringa back to his family and seen that Alice is all right.'

'Tjuringa?'

'Yes, it's a map, sort of, like a kind of title deed to the land. Jimmi, Curly's uncle, will know who it should go to. Curly gave it to me just before he died.'

'Who was Curly?'

'An Aboriginal mate.'

'Maybe he wanted you to have it. Maybe he was giving his title to the land to you.'

'No, Curly wouldn't do that. This is Aboriginal stuff.'

'Can't you just post it?'

'No, it's sort of sacred.'

'What, like a Bishop's ring or something?'

'Yeah, and I promised.'

'Do you always keep your promises?'

'If I can.'

'Even if you have to travel halfway around the world to keep them?' She dipped the toe of her shoe in the water and made the surface ripple. The two of them watched how the tiny action rolled out across the lake disturbing the water, bouncing leaves and bits of stick as it passed under them.

'Life's like that,' she said as they watched the ripple. 'The things we do affect the lives of other people. If you hadn't met Curly you wouldn't be going back to Australia.'

'Perhaps, but if I hadn't met Curly he wouldn't be dead,' he said.

'And if you hadn't met him you might have been, and you wouldn't have met me, so we can't go round thinking like that, all these *what ifs*.'

He kicked a pebble into the water. 'You know what I think, Merle McGhee?'

'What?'

'We'll be married one day,' he said lightly, catching hold of her hand, 'when you're a qualified doctor and when I've made some money.'

She laughed. 'That'll be the day!'

He stopped walking and turned to her an idea forming even as he spoke. 'You could come with me.'

‘What do you mean?’

‘To Australia, we could get married and go together,’ he said, adjusting his plans even as he spoke.

‘Hey! Hey! Slow down. We’re too young. We hardly know each other, and my parents wouldn’t give permission and—’

‘You want to go to university first and become a doctor,’ he said, concealing his disappointment.

‘Yes, and that’ll take years, and in any case,’ she said, ‘you might change your mind and meet someone else.’

‘No, I won’t.’

‘You might,’ she insisted. ‘You never know.’

He let go of her hand and turned away, getting married now was a mad idea, but he knew he’d never change his mind. ‘Will you write to me?’

‘Can you write?’ she joked, lightening the mood.

‘A bit.’

‘When are you going?’

‘Soon, as soon as I can organise a ticket.’

‘What does Val say?’

‘What’s it got to do with her?’

‘She’ll be upset; you know she’s sweet on you.’

‘She’ll get over it, and no, she doesn’t know. No one knows except you. I haven’t even told Elsie yet.’

‘Kathy?’

He shook his head. ‘She’ll be all right. I reckon she’s seen enough of me to last a lifetime and she’s happy enough with Marg and Harry.’

‘We’ll have more time together before you leave, won’t we?’ she said.

‘Of course, you can’t get rid of me that easily, and I still have to buy a ticket.’

It was dusk by they time they got back to Merle’s house.

‘It was nice walking in the park,’ she said, leaning forward to kiss him, ‘and I’ll see you tomorrow,’ she added, a smile creasing her cheeks.

He sailed out of Southampton on the tide bound for Fremantle eight years after he’d last left England with the other orphans. He leaned against the railings and fixed his eyes on the horizon as England thinned to nothing and the sea melded with the sky. The old life faded; the new life drew him on.

Six more years and he'd be rising twenty-three. He had six years to make something of himself at Jarrahlong, if Alice would have him, and then he'd be back for Merle. By then she'd be a qualified doctor and he'd be rich and in between there'd be letters, lots of letters.

Giant turbines thrummed beneath him, driving the ship south through pewter-grey water, putting sea miles between him and the land of his birth. Above, seabirds mewed, their calls mingling with the tumbling water in the ship's wake. Ahead lay Australia and a new beginning. He picked up his haversack and slung it over his shoulder, conscious of Curly's precious tjuringa pressing against his back. He tilted his head and listened, convinced he could hear Aboriginal chanting, and smiled.

PART III

CHAPTER 26

Jon hitched a lift on a truck bound for Kalgoorlie six weeks after leaving England and at Southern Cross he picked up another truck heading north. Now, as they neared Charlestown, his eyes swept the horizon looking for familiar landmarks – the emergency airstrip beacon, the water towers and the wind pumps and, higher than the rest, The Grand, the only two-storey building in town, an ornate Victorian hotel built in the late 1890s in the middle of the gold rush. When he finally caught a glimpse of its corrugated-iron roof shimmering in the heat his spirits lifted, he was home.

'The hotel do ya?' yelled Sam Tennant above the engine noise.

'Yeah,' Jon yelled back, 'it'll do fine.'

Sam pulled up next to its fancy cast-iron verandah, the engine idling while he waited for Jon to collect his gear.

'Bit different to Liverpool,' Sam commented. He lit a cigarette. 'Reckon you'd do better in Kalgoorlie, most folk can't take the life in these dead-end towns.' He slipped the truck into gear as Jon patted his haversack, feeling for Curly's tjuringa.

Jon grinned. 'Better not let the locals hear you say that.'

'Defensive are they? They reckon it's a bonza place to outsiders and crook to each other, eh?'

'Something like that. Thanks for the lift.' Jon got out of the cab and slammed the door shut. He thumped another *thank you* on the metal and stood back as Sam pulled away. The truck was soon swallowed up in a ragged cloud of red dust and Charlestown was quiet again, dozing in the midday heat the same as the first time he'd seen it.

Nothing had changed while he'd been away. Wes Chapman's petrol pumps still stood like red and white sentinels on the fore-court with the garage doors wide open, catching what little breeze there was. Closer to him the sign over the bank creaked softly as it swung gently on rusting hinges, while over the road Charlestown Agricultural Supplies and General Store's double doors gaped wide as ever. Inside, Les Harper would be making up orders, writing out invoices, waiting for Ed Scally or Gerry Worrall to arrive back for the next delivery run.

Jon's attention drifted to Simpson's Clothing Store. Rachel would be surprised to see him although he suspected Scally wouldn't be too happy about it, he'd never liked the idea of his daughter growing up.

Behind him a couple of trucks were parked next to the old hitching rail in front of The Grand. Lunchtime! There'd be folk in there taking a break, waiting for the cooler part of the day.

It was good to be back. He hitched his haversack onto his shoulder, everything he owned was packed inside: twenty-five Australian pound notes, Curly's tjuringa, two pairs of trousers, three shirts, a spare pair of boots, a couple of changes of underwear and the false documents Alice had given him. Did he call himself Jon Cadwallader or Jon Macarthur now? He didn't know. He'd have to play it by ear and see how things panned out.

He stepped into the gloomy hotel lobby, took off his hat and pushed his way through the half doors into the saloon. Two blokes he didn't recognise were perched on stools, their elbows resting on the bar; both glanced in his direction, no acknowledgement in their eyes. Connie's back was to him, her arms up to her elbows in sudsy water, washing beer glasses.

'Be with you in a tick,' she said without looking up.

Jon eased himself onto a bar stool down along from the other two and breathed in the familiar smells of scrubbed wood, polish, and malty beer. On the walls were the same old faded prints and behind the bar, beneath the huge fly-blown mirror, a glass shelf crowded with lumps of dusty minerals donated by prospectors over the years.

Connie grabbed a towel. 'What can I get for you?' The smile faded.

'Beer, please, Connie.'

'It's Mrs Andersen to you.' She picked up a glass and a bottle and flicked off the cap in one smooth movement. She concentrated on pouring, a frown creasing her brow. 'I thought you'd gone back to England?'

'I did,' said Jon.

She thumped the glass down and the near-empty bottle next to it. He paid for the beer.

'Reckon you've got a nerve showing your face here again,' she muttered, slapping down his change on the counter.

The terse words and cool reception wasn't what he'd expected. The last time he'd stood in the bar she wouldn't let him pay, said he deserved a drink on the house after what he'd done for Alice when the bush fire was raging through the outback like a train.

'Is something wrong?'

'You seen Ed yet?'

Ed Scally? What was she talking about? 'No, I've just arrived. I hitched a lift on a truck heading north out of Southern Cross.'

'Are you planning on staying this time?'

Jon frowned, puzzled by the hostility in her tone. Ed Scally never had had a good word to say about him, better if he changed the subject.

'How's Stan, Stan Colley?'

'Okay when I last saw him.'

He frowned, talking to Connie was hard going. 'Is there any chance of a meal?'

'I suppose. Steak and eggs do you?'

'Yeah, nicely thanks.'

She didn't stop to chat but took her time wiping down the bar on her way out to the kitchen. He heard her yell the order at the cook.

Jon nodded at the bloke nearest to him, slid off the stool and crossed to a table by the window. He sipped his beer, confused by Connie's reaction and the chilly atmosphere. He didn't understand Aussies. Fifteen months ago, after the fire, everyone accepted him. When he was leaving most of the locals turned up in the bar, there'd been plenty of drinking and backslapping, offers of jobs if he fancied staying – and now the cold shoulder. He guessed the problem was his nationality; Poms weren't exactly popular in Australia. Well, he'd just have to work his way back in.

Ten minutes later Connie dumped a plate of steak and eggs in front of him along with a knife and fork. She didn't reply to his thanks and went back to the bar.

The steak was huge; it filled the plate and was topped with two fried eggs sunny side up. His stomach rumbled in anticipation. One plus about Australia was the food; there was no shortage of mutton and beef, or eggs.

He savoured the smell and cut himself a generous mouthful, the golden yolk running off the meat as he carried it to his mouth. While he ate he decided against asking Connie for a room, instead he'd go over to Wes Chapman's garage and hire a utility truck for a few days; he'd visit Alice and see whether she'd got fixed up with a manager. At least he knew where he stood with Wes. Wes would treat him right and so would Alice. No doubt she hadn't changed much; she'd drive a hard bargain and would only take him on if it suited her. Hard, but fair, that was Alice.

The saloon doors swung open and banged against the walls. Scally, his face an ugly shade of red, strode over to the bar.

'Where's the bastard, then?'

Connie glanced in Jon's direction and continued drying glasses.

Jon swallowed the piece of beef he was chewing, readying himself to greet Scally, but he was too slow. Scally crossed the room, his face contorted with rage, his arm outstretched. He grabbed Jon's collar and dragged him off his chair, kneed him in the face and dropped him on the floor.

'Reckon y'can make a fool of me, do yer?' Scally snarled and kicked him in the ribs. 'Get up, y'scum.'

Jon staggered to his feet, his eyes blinded by the stinging pain and Scally hit him again, this time on the jaw with a sharp left hook, snapping his head back, sending him sprawling over the table. The table hung for a long moment on the edge and then toppled, decanting the half-eaten steak and eggs onto his chest.

He lay on the floor, dazed, looking up into Scally's face, at the fury making the older man's features pinched and tight. The two at the bar watched with mild interest. Connie continued polishing glasses.

'Get up, y'bastard,' growled Scally, his voice low and menacing.

Jon rolled onto his side and leaned on one elbow, coughing, unable to making sense of what was happening. Fear knotted his stomach. He was three inches taller than Scally and a good stone heavier, but winded he was no match for the man who loomed over him with murder in his eyes. What was wrong with him?

Scally kicked him again. 'Get up, y'hear me?'

Jon gasped. 'Have you gone stark staring mad?' he yelled as pain shot along his spine. 'What the hell's wrong?'

'Y're coming with me.'

'Why? What have I done, for God's sake?'

'Belt up,' snapped Scally. He picked up Jon's haversack and flung it at him, then waited while Jon gathered himself, his hands fists and the veins along his arms like cords.

What the hell had upset Scally? Jon tried to think, his addled brain struggling to recall a slight, something he'd said or done that had festered in the older man's mind. Was Scally planning to kill him? He discounted the thought – too many witnesses – so whatever had angered the bastard the sooner it was sorted out the better.

Scally's truck stood idling at the bottom of the hotel steps, the passenger door open. 'Get in,' said Scally. 'You think y're a man, eh? Well, y'can bloody well start acting like one.'

'Where're we going?' mumbled Jon through a thick lip.

'Alice's place.'

Scally definitely wasn't planning to murder him then. The pain in his back eased, but his nose and jaw throbbed and he could taste salt blood on his tongue where his teeth had ground into the flesh. He glanced across at Scally's stony face. Was it Alice? Was Scally worried that he'd come back to take over Jarrahlong? Did Scally have plans to manage the station himself? Was that what it was all about? He thought about the passport in his haversack – Jon Macarthur's. But Scally had been party to the deception. Was that why Scally was afraid, afraid he'd claim Jarrahlong when Alice died?

'Is Alice all right?'

'What's it to you?'

'Just wondering.'

'Planning on tecking over the place, are ya, lad?' asked Scally with a sneer.

'He was right! That was the problem! Scally was afraid he'd lose out when Alice died.

'Alice is as fit as a flea on a mad dog; she'll outlive the lot of us. I wouldn't go banking on anything if I was you. Now shut y'mouth before I shove me fist down y'gullet.'

He'd never liked Scally, even in the early days when Scally did the monthly deliveries of dry goods and cooking fat to the orphanage at Karundah. He recalled how Scally ignored him and Freddie Fitzpatrick as they'd unloaded the provisions, how he'd wander over to the canteen to have a natter with Brother Francis, a roll-up cigarette between his fingers. He'd been a shit even then.

He had to admit that Scally's attitude wasn't unique, he wasn't the only one to refer to them as Pommie bastards, there'd been others, some among the Catholic Brothers who'd been hostile. But it was Scally's behaviour that puzzled him the most, something had made Scally hate the British, prejudiced him against lads like him, lads who'd had been dumped in Australia by the British Government.

Thinking made his head ache. He gave up the effort and concentrated on the landscape, watching out for familiar landmarks, the edge of the escarpment and the big old salmon gum at the turn off for Jarrahlong.

The truck bounced along as the corrugated graded road gave way to even rougher track. Scally followed the marker posts that indicated the route. The track was as wide and potholed as ever while the bush either side had regenerated – only blackened scorch marks on the trunks of the bigger trees gave an indication of the inferno that had destroyed huge tracts of land fifteen months earlier.

Jon felt his lip and winced then, conscious of Scally staring grimly ahead concentrating on the road, he turned his attention back to the open window.

A haze hung over the bush – the silvery-grey vegetation cooking gently in the heat had released its oil, thickening the air and tinted it blue. He squinted at the passing scene, red earth and blue sky, colours so vibrant they were painful to the eye after the drabness of Liverpool. He closed his eyes and breathed in the scent of the place, the oily, peppery stink of eucalyptus and turpentine bushes, the smell of the earth, unlike any other smell he'd ever known and overlaying it all the odour of hot engine oil and petrol.

During the seven years he'd lived in the orphanage he'd barely paid any attention to the outback. It had taken Curly to challenge his feelings about the land and the people. Until then he'd made assumptions – he'd been as guilty as Scally in that regard. He thought he knew about the place, but now he knew he didn't. He was an outsider. Maybe that was how it would stay. Perhaps he would have to move on and make a new start further north, or head for the Northern Territory, or Queensland, to one of the bigger cattle stations Alice had once mentioned, with their two thousand square miles of bush.

Jarrahlong came into view. Jon took in the homestead, rebuilt on the old foundations, bigger that the last one but of a similar design with a short flight of steps up to a wide verandah, twelve feet deep. The iron roof was painted white this time. The huge silver gum, that had miraculously survived the fire, drooped in the heat, the silvery-grey leaves casting a dappled shade on the dusty earth.

Stan Colley had told him Jarrahlong had been rebuilt. It looked a lot different to the last time he'd seen it when only the stone supports and the chimney were still standing and everything else was blackened and charred, so where had Alice found the money? Rebuilding didn't come cheap even if you used wood and corrugated iron. A half smile twisted his battered face. He'd always thought she was better off than she claimed to be. She must have saved a packet during the war years when wool prices had been at a premium, that and a Scrooge mentality; he'd only ever known her to buy a bottle of bourbon whiskey now and again and a box of cheroots at Christmas, not exactly enough to break the bank.

Scally parked next to a brand new utility truck in front of the old barn and jumped down from the cab.

'Alice!' he called. 'Y've got a visitor.'

Jon heard the familiar tap-tapping of Alice's stick on wooden boards before he saw her appear on the verandah steps. She hadn't changed either, the same weather-beaten, lined face like a dried out conker, the same thick, white hair. Faded blue eyes as sharp as butchers' knives and as cold as the steel they were made from peered at him, her lips a thin, tight line.

'Thought you'd come back, did you?' she said finally.

'I wanted to see that you were all right,' said Jon.

'And what about Rachel?'

He didn't know what to say. Alice had always had a thing about Rachel, was always trying to pair the two of them off. But Rachel wasn't Merle.

He pictured Merle as he'd last seen her standing on the steps of her family's terraced house. Merle McGhee with her long, dark hair, her green eyes like emeralds – the girl he'd left behind in Liverpool, the girl he was going to marry as soon as she'd qualified as a doctor and he'd made enough in Australia to set himself up with a sheep or a cattle station of his own.

Scally crossed to the truck and leaned on the horn. A few minutes later Rachel appeared from round the corner of the big barn clutching an untidy bundle in her arms. She was plumper than he remembered. She had her hair tied back from her face and wore a floral shirt-waister dress with padded shoulders similar in style to the wool dress Merle wore when they'd last walked in Sefton Park together.

Washing, thought Jon. She must have been doing the laundry out by the water tower.

When she saw him her face blanched under her tan. Even from ten yards away he could see the apprehension in her eyes.

'Look who's back,' said Scally in a voice heavy with sarcasm. 'The libertine returns.'

Rachel stopped, her face stricken with misery.

All eyes focussed on the bundle as a small fist fought its way out of the blanket and waved in the afternoon sun.

Scally glanced across at Jon, anger darkening his features. 'Aye, lad! He's six months old now and I'm buggered if I'm going to have a bastard for a grandson, so the sooner you and Rachel get yerselves sorted out the sooner he'll be legitimate.'

Tears streamed down Rachel's cheeks.

The baby wailed.

Jon did a quick calculation. He'd been on a tramp ship for over eight months after leaving Fremantle, so the kid must have been born soon after he arrived in England. No wonder Scally thought he was the father, the dates fitted.

'I'll leave him here then, Alice,' said Scally, nodding in Jon's direction.

The three of them watched Scally leave, the truck churning up a low plume of dust as he drove back to Charlestown. And all Jon could think about was Merle.

CHAPTER 27

Jon stood in Alice's front parlour, glaring at her lined face as she squinted against the thin ribbon of smoke rising from the stub of a cheroot. Her pet cockatoo, perched on a new stand, fixed a knowing eye on him.

'You do the right thing by Rachel and you can be my manager,' she snapped, her pale eyes never leaving his face.

'It's not mine,' he shouted.

'What do you mean?'

'The baby, it's not mine. Why won't you damn well believe me?'

Her eyes narrowed into slits and her mouth tightened. 'Are you saying Rachel's had a fling with some passing ringer?'

He felt himself redden under her penetrating gaze, frustration and anger twisting his guts. Alice knew he didn't mean that, but Rachel had been with someone else because he hadn't.

'According to Ed you caught her attention the first time she clapped eyes on you. She didn't talk about anyone else. I can't think why,' she muttered, 'you're no great catch. I reckon she'd have been better off falling for Jake Forest's lad over at Cavanagh's Creek or one of the Samuels' boys, but you're the one she wants, there's no accounting for taste, is there! Anyway, she says he's yours and that's good enough for me.'

'I've told you, it's not mine,' he yelled, exasperation making his voice crack. 'Just ask her, can't you?'

Alice ignored him. 'You can stay with Rachel seeing as how you're to be married. Accommodation's free, so's your grub, same as before, and I'll pay you the going rate plus any bonus due you if wool prices do well. I can't say fairer than that. It's a damn sight more than you deserve.' She regarded him for several moments. 'Of course you could always clear off up north, leave your mess behind you, or you can face up to your responsibilities. So, what's it to be?'

Her cold eyes watched him, like a cat with a mouse. He had no answers. She was as bad as Scally; she'd already made up her mind. Now he was cornered, as trapped as he had been at Karundah. He wished to God he'd never stowed away on Scally's truck in the first place. He should have waited for the quarterly Merredin delivery and headed out Perth way, and then he wouldn't have ended up in Charlestown, wouldn't have met Alice, or Rachel. What the hell would Merle think when she heard about the mess he'd got himself into?

His head ached from thinking, his brain chasing solutions to an insoluble problem, a way out of the mire. He needed time. Stan Colley always said, given time, things have a habit of working out. Perhaps Rachel would tell Scally and Alice the truth once he'd had a word with her. He'd make her, damn it!

'Well! What is it to be? You want the job or not?'

'Thanks,' he muttered.

'Is that a yes?' snapped Alice.

'Yes, I suppose so,' he said grudgingly. 'But just one thing.'

'And what's that, Jon Just?' She cackled at the old joke, his habit of using *just* too often.

'I've got to find Curly's family.'

'What for?'

'I need to return Curly's property.'

'And how are you planning on finding them?'

'I thought I'd drive over towards Mullin Soak. Curly said that's where his folk spend a lot of time.'

'No certainty they'll be there. You know blacks.' She took another long drag on the foul-smelling cheroot, contemplating him. 'You can wait until after the shearing, things are quieter then, but you make sure you clear it with your wife.'

Wife! The word shocked him.

'Rachel,' she said, 'she'll be your wife by then if Ed has his way.'

Over my dead body, he thought. He didn't want to marry Rachel; he didn't want to marry anyone except Merle. He tried to think where the nearest church was, Karundah probably, or Pilkington. Well, he didn't care what Scally said or did, nothing would induce him within twenty miles of the place, so Scally could forget it. He breathed easier.

Alice smiled a grim, knowing smile that brought him up short.

'The bush brother'll be around come summer. Reckon that gives you a few months or so to get used to the idea.'

He frowned. What was she talking about?

'The priest, he marries folk, baptises babies, even does a funeral if someone's had the presence to die at the right time.' She chuckled mirthlessly. 'Reckon, come December, a visit to Charlestown will be worth his while, a wedding and a baptism...or a funeral,' she added after a long pause. 'Do you still play chess?'

'No.'

'Well, you do now. Friday, six sharp, same as before. You'd better sort things out with Rachel and get to know that son of yours. And go easy on her. She's had a hard time and the birth was none too easy either, I thought we'd lost the both of them at one point.'

Behind the barn, in the shade of the eucalyptus trees, were the newly built stockmen's quarters for the single men and, along from them, a simple two-roomed shack Alice had had built for Adie to replace the one that had burnt down in the bush fire. Belle sat on the verandah, her huge buttocks folded over the edge of the wooden stool like a cushion, peeling spuds into a galvanised bucket. She dipped her head briefly when Jon raised a hand in greeting and returned to her chore. She'd aged in the time he'd been away, her hair was now as grizzled as Adie's had been when he'd last seen him.

Further along, closer to the creek and set aside from the other buildings, was a larger dwelling. Four rooms, Jon guessed from the look of it, and where Rachel was living if the row of nappies hanging limply from a washing line was anything to go by.

Both dwellings, the smaller and the larger, were raised off the ground on stone piles with short flights of steps leading up to their verandahs. Alice had clearly given Rachel and the baby a place to stay, but why wasn't she in Charlestown, living with her father? He couldn't imagine Scally being happy at the thought of Rachel living at Jarrahlong with only Alice and Aborigines for company.

Rachel was waiting for him, pacing the verandah, rocking her fretful baby in her arms. When she saw him she stopped and waited, anxiety still written on her face.

'I didn't think you'd ever be coming back,' she whispered, fresh tears rolling down her cheeks. 'You said you were going to make a home for you and your sister.'

Jon looked at her appalled. 'I was, but when I got back she was living with an aunt.'

'But I didn't know that.'

'Why the hell didn't you tell them the truth?'

'Dad. He was furious, he assumed it was yours. It was easier to let him think that.'

'Why don't you marry the father?'

She chewed her lip.

'Who is he?'

'You don't know him.' Her words were spoken so low he had to strain to catch them.

'Does he know?' he snapped.

'No.'

'Why don't you tell him?'

'Because I don't want to,' she spat back.

'But—'

'I was upset after you left. Lonely…I was lonely out here with no one my age to talk to, and he seemed nice at first.'

'I bet he did,' said Jon savagely. 'If he's that nice why don't you marry him?'

She didn't answer.

'And now I'm expected to marry you. Is that it?'

'No,' she whispered. 'I don't want to marry anyone.'

'Try telling that to your dad. Knowing him he'll have us both at the end of Alice's twelve-bore shotgun. One of the shearers was it?'

She coloured up as scarlet as the tail flashes on a black cockatoo.

'So, how are you going to make it right, Rachel? As far as I can see there's only one way out of this. You have to tell your dad and Alice the truth. You should have done it first off,' he said bitterly.

'I need time.'

'How much?' he raged, furious with her for lying. 'You've already had over a year, for God's sake!'

'I don't know…until Dad accepts the baby.'

'What do you mean?'

'He won't speak to me. He thinks I've let him down, made him a laughing stock, and he's got this thing about bastards.'

'So I've noticed,' said Jon sarcastically.

'It's because he's one.'

'You're too right there,' said Jon with feeling.

'No,' she said. 'He *is* a bastard. His parents never married and Granddad, Mum's dad, gave him a hard time. He never accepted Dad into the family and then when Mum died he refused to have anything to do with us.'

'History repeating itself, eh! So, my life gets ruined just so your dad can feel better, is that it?' he yelled. 'Well, if you can't tell your dad, you could at least tell Alice.'

'I thought you liked me?'

'I do, but I don't love you, and I don't care what anyone says, I'm not marrying you.'

He watched her face crumple and regretted the way he'd said it, regretted shouting at her. But she needed to know. She had to realise that marriage to him was never going to happen.

The baby started to cry.

'He needs feeding,' she said and disappeared indoors.

Jon sat on the verandah waiting for her to return, listening to the wind pump clanking quietly behind the stockmen's quarters, and caught the smell of smoke drifting on the breeze. He'd noticed one of the humpies had been repaired and extended, seen kids running about scrounging vegetables off Belle earlier in the day while she was working in the garden with another Aboriginal woman he hadn't seen before. That was one thing about Alice; she didn't mind blacks squatting on the edge of the homestead. They come and go, she'd said once, the men do a bit of work and sometimes the women, they don't cost much and it keeps everyone happy.

Old Yella, Alice's dingo-cross bitch, sniffed her way across the yard and flopped down at his feet. He reached over and scratched her ear, remembering when she'd been heavily in pup and pathetically grateful for the titbits he'd saved for her. At least the old dog had been pleased to see him. Why couldn't human relationships be as uncomplicated?

He leaned back against the top step, watching dead leaves eddying in the light breeze, letting the balmy evening calm the turmoil he'd been in since arriving back in Charlestown. He'd forgotten how quiet the bush was after his time in Liverpool where the city never seemed to sleep. Indoors he could hear Rachel singing softly to the baby; she wouldn't be back out that night.

He remained where he was for a while watching the sun sink behind the great jarrah trees that gave the place its name, then he called to Old Yella and together they made their way across to the stockmen's quarters.

At five sharp came the clanging of Alice's brass bell followed by Belle's heavy tread alongside the bunkhouse. Jon listened to the *sluff sluff* of her slippered feet as she shuffled across to Alice's bungalow. He washed and dressed and followed her across the yard.

The kitchen was much bigger than the last one and everything in it was brand new: tables, chairs, sink, cooker, refrigerator, shelving, cupboards, meat safe and the inevitable spiral of golden flypaper, as littered with dead and dying bluebottles as the last had been.

'I bought a new generator,' said Alice when she saw him looking at the equipment. 'It's push button, not like the old one that you had to hand crank half a dozen times, and I've got an inside bathroom with a proper septic tank. I decided I was getting a bit too old to be going down the yard in the pitch-dark.'

Belle thumped down a plate of steak and eggs in front of Alice and gave him the same. She stood a huge brown teapot on the iron trivet alongside three mugs and a tin of condensed milk.

'Thanks, Belle,' said Alice as the old Aborigine waddled out of the kitchen.

'You've still got Adie then.'

'Yes, but Jimmi and Sammo left soon after you did. A couple of weeks after the shearing they upped sticks and went. I've seen neither hide nor hair of Sammo, but Jimmi came back after six months or so and he's been here ever since. We had to take on a couple of new stockmen, Big'un and Mick – it's Mick's family living in the humpy out the back. Adie'll introduce you soon enough.'

Jon poured out two mugs of tea.

'By the way, while you were in England I increased the number of cattle and bought in some Herefords.'

'For your own use?'

'Yes, and for fattening. I've always liked Herefords – pretty faces. I'm thinking of buying a pedigree bull from my sister-in-law to maintain the quality.'

She'd never mentioned a sister-in-law before.

'Beryl Morton. She runs Thornwood Farm in Lincolnshire.'

'England?'

'Yes, in South Sutton.'

The name and place were familiar and then he remembered the letter she'd asked him to pick up for posting once, Thornwood Farm had been the address on the envelope. At the time he'd wondered who Mrs B. M. Morton was. 'That'll cost a packet.'

'No point in running pedigree cows with scrub bulls is there?'

'Do you know much about cattle, Alice?'

She laughed. 'A bit more than you could put on a postage stamp. Why do you ask?'

'Just wondered.'

She watched him over the rim of her mug for a few moments. 'How're Rachel and Joe this morning?'

So that's what Rachel had called the baby! Jon chewed on his steak. Alice wasn't going to let the subject drop and he was damned if he'd let her railroad him into anything. 'How are the sheep?'

Alice gave him an arch look. 'All right.'

Neither spoke as they finished breakfast. When Belle came in to clear away the plates Alice broke the silence, 'Rainfall is a bit down this year but nothing like as bad as the drought, it's nothing we can't handle. When you ride up to the east quarter follow the creek bed, I'm thinking we might dam it in a couple of places, try and extend the grazing up there, maybe even sink a bore.'

'Expensive.'

'I know, but I don't want to go through another drought like the last one. Do you?'

Jon recalled the crows pecking at the eyes of dying sheep, the bloated carcasses, the maggots, and above all the sweet, sickly stench of death heavy in the air as he killed the doomed sheep. He shook his head.

'I think I can run to it, so long as you're not looking for top-rate pay.'

He could feel her eyes on him, waiting. He wasn't even sure he wanted to stay at Jarrahlong now.

'You could always have a word with Jeb Samuels for me. His boys sank a new bore about four years back. Why don't you drive over to Jindalee and ask him how deep we have to go.' She pushed a set of keys across the table. 'Take the utility, but be careful with it, I don't want you holing the sump.'

'Today? You want me to go over there today?'

'Why not? You haven't anything else planned, have you?'

'No.' If he did decide to stay then the sooner everyone knew the better and a trip to Jindalee would suit him just fine, it would give Rachel a chance to tell Alice the truth and him the opportunity to call on Stan on the way back. 'How are things over there?'

'Not good, I gather. It wasn't only the buildings for them, it was all their sheep. And, according to Jeb, losing all the irreplaceable stuff, photographs, heirlooms and the like was too much for Mary.'

'It was the same for you.'

'No,' said Alice, 'I put all my keepsakes in a box in the chimney stack. The fire didn't touch them, poor Mary lost everything.'

Jon cast his mind back to the day of the bushfire when he'd seen

Alice and Belle messing about in front of the hearth. 'So that's what you and Belle were doing.'

Alice smiled. 'Jack built in an asbestos-lined cavity behind the big oblong stone. It's where I keep family photographs, certificates and my bits of jewellery and such, so don't go blabbing about it.'

'Mrs Samuels didn't think to save her stuff?'

'No, she and Jeb were on their way back from Merredin. They'd been visiting family and the boys didn't think, too busy trying to save the stock and battling the fire to worry about knick-knacks.'

Alice's comment to watch out for the sump hadn't been lost on Jon. She knew he'd take a detour and visit Stan on the way back from Jindalee.

He spun the steering wheel. He'd forgotten how much time and patience it took to inch along the winding valley, to negotiate a way around the boulders and avoid the deepest ruts. The mallee was worse than he remembered – the shrubby eucalyptus was thicker and more impenetrable, it lashed the windscreen and sides of the vehicle, rattling along like rain on the metal roof. It wasn't like Stan to let it get so overgrown, no doubt he was too busy prospecting for gold to attend to housekeeping duties.

Once through the thickety scrub the disused adits came into view. The horizontal shafts leading into the mines that littered the valley still punctuated the edge of the cliff, their piles of yellow scree tumbling down as far as the valley floor looking like jaundiced tongues amongst the brush. Over the years the scree and rubble had become overgrown with weedy bushes and rank grasses which added to the air of decay – nature already reclaiming the land, the scars buried under new-growth bush. Closer to Stan's shack was an old mine with a vertical shaft – the rusting derrick and rotten pulleys a tangle of wires, frayed ropes and rotten beams that still clanked and creaked in the breeze.

The place always reminded him of scenes from old western films he'd seen as a kid in Liverpool with Billy Wainwright – ghost towns in California from the gold rush days. He leaned out of the window, glad of the draught, still hot but not like the first time when he'd been intent on dumping Father O'Leary's unconscious body down a disused shaft; then the temperature had been close to a hundred and twenty degrees and fear had made him sweat even more in the heat. Hard to think that the old fella who'd held a gun to his head on that occasion was now his best friend.

The wooden shack with its stone chimney stack and corrugated-iron roof didn't look any different, nothing had changed then – Stan hadn't found El Dorado. The old Bedford parked next to it listed drunkenly, a broken spring by the look of things, so how was the old fella doing for tucker if he couldn't get into Charlestown for supplies?

Bess and Bonny met him, circling around like a pair of porpoises, sleeker than when he'd last see them. He rubbed their ears, unease growing by the minute.

'Where's Stan?' he said to the dogs.

Bonny tilted her head and half wagged her tail.

'Where's Stan?' he repeated.

The dog made for the verandah, scattering the chooks scratching in the dust. She nosed the door open and disappeared inside. Jon followed.

At first he thought the room was empty but gradually his eyes became accustomed to the gloom. 'Stan?' He spoke tentatively, not sure of what he was seeing as the bundle on the bed in the alcove stirred.

'Stan, are you all right, mate?'

The old man sat up, his white hair spiky damp from sleep. 'Who's there?' he challenged, his voice sharp.

'It's me, Jon.'

'Jon? Jon who?'

'Cadwallader, the Pommy bastard, remember?'

'What're you doing back here?'

'I couldn't keep away from the place, Stan, and I also need to find Curly's family and give back the tjuringa.'

'You've not still got that, have you? I thought I told you to get rid of it.' He swung his skinny legs over the side of the bed and hauled himself to his feet.

'Are you all right, Stan?'

'Me? Yeah. Just taking five minutes, I must have dropped off.'

Shocked, Jon stared at Stan's lean frame. The old man had always been as thin as a lath but now his clothes hung off him, his skin had a pallor about it, a greyness that didn't look good. 'Have you been overdoing it, looking for that gold reef, Stan?'

'What do you expect at my age? I'm no spring chicken.' He shuffled across to the blackened stove and shoved in a couple of logs. 'Fill the billy, son, and I'll make us a brew.'

While they waited for the water to boil Stan splashed an inch of rum into two tumblers, handed one to Jon and tossed his own back.

The fiery liquid made him cough, harsh racking coughs that were painful to listen to.

'It's the dust,' said Stan when he could speak. 'It gets into my lungs, makes breathing hard.'

Jon sipped his rum. 'When did you break the spring on the Bedford?'

'A month back.'

'What are you doing for supplies?'

Stan grinned. 'They're getting a bit low, son. I'm down to me last tin of bully beef. I've been meaning to get more in, but—'

'Do you want me to tow the truck into town for you, get Wes to fix it?'

'No, I've a shed full of spares out the back, that's why I didn't trade the old gal in years ago.' Another spasm of coughing racked his frame. Rum splashed on the deal table as he refilled his glass. After a while he breathed more easily. 'When did you get back?'

'A few days ago.'

'Good to see Scally hasn't strung you up.'

'It's not from want of wishing to,' said Jon.

'Aye, there's been some pretty harsh things said, that's for sure. Have you sorted things out with Rachel?'

'Not yet.'

'I wondered whether you'd come back. I reckoned you would, the place has got into your blood. It does that to some, grabs them by the balls and never lets them go.'

'I wouldn't say that, Stan.' Truth to tell he was beginning to regret it, what with Scally breathing down his neck and Connie and Alice giving him a hard time. Then there was Rachel and all her lies, and the baby – not that it was Joe's fault.

'What did Alice say?'

'You know Alice.'

'Aye,' said Stan, 'I know Alice right enough.'

'He's not my son, Stan.'

'If you say so, but the problem is everyone thinks he is.'

Jon tossed back the last of his rum. 'I better go and get those supplies for you, Stan, and while I'm in town I'll ask Connie to radio Alice on the evening schedule and tell her I'll be staying over till I've got that back spring fixed on the Bedford.'

'I'm not an invalid.'

'I never said you were.'

'While you're at it, bring me another bottle of rum...better make it two.'

* * *

The sun had gone down by the time Jon drew up at the shack. He'd bought in enough for a month: dried and tinned food, liquor and kerosene, and he'd also arranged a regular delivery until Stan was back on his feet.

'Alice'll be needing you,' worried Stan.

'No she won't. She knew I'd be gone a couple of days. I stayed over at Jindalee last night. By the time we'd been out to look at the bore it was late. Besides, she knew I'd stop by for a natter.'

'How are they over there?'

'The Samuels? Surviving; they've been busy rebuilding, same as Alice.'

'I heard they'd sold off part of their lease.'

'Why?'

'To cover the cost of replacing stock and rebuilding, I suppose.'

'I don't know, Stan, they didn't say.'

'Well, that's what I heard – sold the lease on thirty thousand acres to Alex Bartokas over on Wanndarah Station.'

With supper heating on the stove Jon set to by the light of a hurricane lantern and washed up the dirty dishes in the sink. He scoured out pans with steel wool and then swept out the accumulated dust until they were both coughing their lungs up.

'Cack-handed way of going about things, isn't it? Couldn't the sweeping wait till morning?' grumbled Stan.

'Not if you want your van fixed,' said Jon. 'Here, have a slug of this, it'll put hairs on your chest.' He gave Stan an inch of rum to steady the coughing and then dished up the stew he'd bought off Connie.

Later, after they'd eaten, Stan dropped his irons back onto the enamel plate. 'You're not a bad cook.'

'No need for the sarcasm. You know full well where it came from. Han Sing, Connie's new Chinese cook made it, and I have to take the skillet back.' They were both sitting on hard kitchen chairs, feet propped up on the logs either side the stove, mugs of tea resting on their bellies.

'How is Connie?'

'Icy…she only let me borrow the skillet because it was for you.'

Stan chuckled. 'She'll come round. Now, tell me about that sister of yours and what happened in England.'

'Not a lot. Kathy was adopted by Aunt Marg and her new husband a year after the superintendent at the children's home sent me to Australia. Bottom line, she's happy enough with them.'

'And what about you?'

'Oh, I'm all right with it now, although it took a bit of getting used to at the time.'

'I'll bet,' commented Stan.

'I found out that Gran died a few years back, so I stayed with a friend of hers, Elsie. And while I was there I got a job – delivery boy.'

'Delivery boy!'

Stan was right to be scathing. He'd hated it, humping goods out of the van and into houses, at the beck and call of everyone, no responsibility, no freedom and boring as hell – the same thing day after day – it was enough to drive a sane man mad; the only good thing about the job had been working with Frank.

'Did you catch up with your mates?'

'Some of them.'

'How did that go?'

How had it gone? The old camaraderie had been there and it was good seeing them again, but somehow he no longer fitted in. He'd moved on and they hadn't, apart from Pete, the spiv. He smiled as he thought of Pete's plans for a grand house like the one out at Speke, and there was Merle who wanted to be a doctor. They were the only ones who talked of the future with real enthusiasm. He frowned…apart from Val with her silly plans for a dress shop, or was it a hat shop, he couldn't remember.

'That's the trouble when you experience things others haven't, it changes you in ways they can't understand,' said Stan. 'It was like that after the trenches in France. I reckon what you've been through has marked you and it'll be the same for those lads returning from the war.'

They both stared into space for a while, sipping rum, letting the big meal they'd eaten settle.

Perhaps Stan was right and he'd been unfair on the others. They'd lived through the bombing of Liverpool, knew of people who'd been killed. Billy Wainwright's gran had died as the result of a direct hit on their home. Vince Tully's father had been killed in Germany and Dorothy Kershaw's dad had been posted missing, was still missing. Had he been too wrapped up in his own business to notice?

'What about you, Stan, have you found gold? Is that why you've been working yourself into the grave?'

'Still waiting to jump my claim, are you?'

'No, I've told you before, I wouldn't do that.'

Stan fixed his pale blue eyes on him for a long moment. Jon returned his gaze, waiting for the opportunity to suggest he see a doctor in Merredin or Kalgoorlie.

'Might have,' said Stan cagily.

Jon grinned. 'And you might not, so there's nothing stopping you taking a break, getting a once over on that chest of yours.'

'If you think I'm going to let a bloody quack anywhere near me then you're more stupid than you look,' said Stan. 'There's nothing wrong with me that time won't sort.'

Jon stayed a couple of days fixing the back spring on the Bedford van and cutting a pile of logs to keep Stan going. They didn't move far from the shack but Jon did manage to get Stan out of his bed and onto the swing seat he'd rigged up for him on the verandah.

'It's about time you got yourself a radio transceiver, Stan.'

'What do I need one of them things for?'

'In case you get sick and need a doctor.'

'I get sick and I get better, or I don't, and that's the end of it. You think I'm made of money?'

'Well, it certainly isn't stashed under your bed.'

'And what have you been doing looking under my bed?'

'Sweeping up the muck and dust,' said Jon. 'Anyway, Stan, I'm off now, but I'll be back next week sometime to see how you're doing.'

'Ask Alice if she's any more books for me,' said Stan. 'I've read the last lot.'

CHAPTER 28

A month later Jon drove a utility truck, belching blue smoke, onto Wes's garage forecourt. He stepped out of the cab and patted the bonnet of the old Ford he'd bought off Les Harper for next to nothing because it needed work on the engine.

'A head gasket's no problem,' said Wes as they moved into the gloomy workshop.

Jon blinked, allowing his eyes to adjust after the brilliant sun. 'The clutch is dodgy too, seems to be sticking a bit. Can you fix it?'

'Nothing so sure, just so long as I can get the parts.'

'How long?'

'A week, ten days, it depends. You need me to run you back?'

'No thanks, Wes. Rachel followed me into town in Alice's ute; I reckon she'll be having a natter with Connie by now.'

'You've time for a cuppa then?'

Jon smiled; Les Harper reckoned Wes drank two dozen in a day. He watched as the huge bear of a man filled the aluminium kettle and stood it on the burner to heat. Wes had always been light on his feet despite his size, and quiet, there was nothing brash about him.

'It's a bit of a bugger about those blacks,' Wes said, wiping his hands clean on a dirty rag and finishing them off on his overalls while he waited for the kettle to boil.

'What's that?'

'Haven't you heard? A couple of them bought it on the way to Southern Cross, out Cavanagh's Creek way. There's talk of murder but I think it's more likely to have been an accident. Anyway, whoever did it didn't stop.'

'Slow down, Wes. Who are you on about?'

'Buni, one of Jeb Samuels' stockmen. Him and his lad, Wally.'

Jon frowned. One of Alice's stockmen had family, cousins or

other, working out at Jeb's place. Were they related? And Jimmi had taken off without so much as a word – walkabout, he had assumed. You never knew when an Aborigine would up swag and disappear for a week, or even a couple of months. He hadn't given it much thought at the time.

'Seems they were out on the graded road, walking down it, crossing it...we'll never know. They were hit by a wagon. Pretty big un, I'd say...made hell of a mess of Buni. The wheels went right over his head, bust it like a melon, it did, blood and brains all over the road. But it seems the kid wasn't killed outright, he'd crawled off into the bush – they found him twenty yards away, dead, of course. Poor little bugger, he was only a kid, ten, maybe eleven.'

'What do the police say?'

'Nickson went out there and had a good look around; he's been to all the garages asking us to look out for damaged wings and bumpers, but I doubt they'll catch who did it. Another week and it'll be forgotten; you know what people are like when it comes to blacks.'

Jon did know. There were too many people who saw Aborigines as vermin. Quite a few would view the tragedy as a blessing. 'You've no idea who did it then?'

'No,' said Wes. 'Scal and Gerry drive the route regular, they say they saw nothing. Constable Nickson says it probably happened at night – black skin don't shine out like white. The driver would have been on them before he knew it and probably panicked, he might not have known he'd hit them, or he might have thought it was a kangaroo.'

'Can't see it myself, Wes. Not unless the bloke fell asleep at the wheel.'

'Neither can I, but anything else don't bear thinking about.'

Jon left Wes to it and wandered down the street, passing Simpson's Store and Charlestown Agricultural Supplies and General Store. Scally's truck was parked outside so he crossed over the road and walked along the raised pathway under the verandah. He didn't feel up to another run in with Scally, not with Rachel and Joe in town. It could turn ugly.

When Jon entered the hotel Connie glanced at him and then looked pointedly at Joe asleep in his carrycot next to Rachel.

'He's a bonny son,' she said, 'and Rachel's doing a fine job of raising him.'

Jon didn't comment but he noticed a faint flush creeping up Rachel's neck.

‘How’s Alice?’ asked Connie when the silenced stretched.

‘Planning on sinking a new bore up on the east side of the property,’ said Jon.

It was all she’d talked about for weeks now. He’d been writing off for quotes from firms with drilling rigs. Jeb’s son, Tom, had drilled further north at the bottom edge of the same incline and found water at a hundred feet. If they did the same they could create a new permanent water supply and keep sheep up in the east quarter for longer, into the months when water was at a premium. At the south end they’d already started damming the creek, holding the water back for longer, extending the supply into the dry months when it was needed the most. Alice eventually wanted to increase the flock to seven thousand head and planned on having enough water and grazing to see them through, no matter what the conditions. I’ve had enough of sheep dying to last me a lifetime, and there’s nothing worse than seeing your life’s work food for crows and dingoes, she’d said on more than one occasion.

‘She’s had a new lease of life since the fire,’ said Connie. ‘I think it’s having something to do, something to think about for a change. And having the three of you out there makes a difference too. It’s all too easy to get set in your ways when you’ve got a few years under your belt.’

Connie stood up and handed the carrycot to Jon. ‘Now don’t you go waking him, he’s all in.’

‘Did Wes tell you about those blacks?’ asked Rachel as they drove home to Jarrahlong. ‘Connie says whoever did it will keep quiet, no one’s going to own up to a hit and run. Wonder what those Abos were doing there anyway. They were probably up to no good.’

‘What’s that suppose to mean?’ asked Jon sharply.

Rachel regarded him. ‘They’ve no respect for anyone’s property. They walk where they will, take what they want.’

‘Who told you that?’

‘Dad.’

‘Well, your dad doesn’t always know what he’s talking about.’

‘And I suppose you do!’

‘There’s nothing wrong with Aborigines. They’re no different from you and me. Some’re good and some’re bad, same as us.’

‘And what about the sheep they kill for tucker?’

‘What about them?’ said Jon. ‘What about all their land that the whites have taken?'

'Now who's talking rubbish? The land's leased legally from the Crown. You can't just step onto land and take it.'

'Can't you?' snapped Jon.

Her face barely contained her frustration. 'I don't understand you. Why are you so defensive about blacks? What are they to you?'

He didn't answer. How did he explain to her how things had changed out there in the outback when he'd gone walkabout with Curly nearly two years ago? Seeing Curly's family, living with them, seeing the mine at Murrin Murrin where the Dreaming had been destroyed, where Curly's people couldn't sing the land anymore…and seeing Curly die.

'Well?' she said.

'Forget it, you wouldn't understand.'

'There's no need to snap my head off,' she said.

'I'm not.'

'I know what your problem is, you're still angry, aren't you? Well, I've already told you, I'll tell everyone about Joe.'

'When?'

'Soon. When the time's right.'

Jon didn't answer; instead, he concentrated on the track, on avoiding the deepest ruts. He hadn't even been thinking about Joe.

The next day Jon rode out with Adie and the boys to the top end to muster the sheep and lambs and drive them south into the holding paddock. They set off at first light with their swags and the gear for a protracted stay lashed to the saddles of the pack horses.

The plain stretched out ahead of them, the spring flowers so numerous it was difficult to make out the red earth that produced them after the rain.

The day was cooler – the blue sky patterned with white cloud created moving jigsaws of light and shade over the landscape. A perfect day! He leaned back in the saddle and closed his eyes, feeling the sun on his face, soaking in the warmth of the place. A bloke could breathe here, under the big skies.

He liked being with the men, liked their silent companionship as they rode out over Jarrahlong Station. They didn't ask questions or probe like the whites did. He kicked his horse in the flanks and moved closer to Adie. 'We'll camp near the well up the top end and start mustering tomorrow. When the mob's big enough we'll drive them down to the holding paddock and then quarter the next section. All right?'

Adie's lined face creased even more when he grinned. 'Reckon we'll have good bush tucker tonight.'

'Roo tail,' smiled Jon.

'Nah, goanna,' said Adie, 'if we can catch a big bugger.'

They arrived at the well mid-morning and brewed up a billy of tea to have with Belle's doorstop sandwiches of leathery fried meat that made the jaws ache.

While the others slept off their meal in the shade of the old eucalyptus tree, Jon set off on foot for the green pool.

It was two years since he'd last been there with Curly and he wanted to capture the moment again, to see the cool water hidden in the gorge, to swim, and to remember the first time the country had got under his skin.

Jon pushed his way through the mallee scrub, following the line of the rock that marked the edge of the outcrop. There were no people or sheep, only the wildlife and a few feral goats that melted away at his approach.

The climb was not as tiring as the last time. He was bigger, fitter and he knew the way. After an hour he stood at the top of the steep incline and looked down at the pool, the water green and inviting.

This time he walked down the track quietly as Curly had taught him to do, watching out for birds and creatures, noticing what was about him; the galahs and corellas resting in the midday heat like pink, grey and white blossoms in the bigger trees; the small flocks of finches flitting from bush to bush following his route; and lizards, whose names he didn't know, basking on warm rock, scuttling for shelter when they felt the first vibrations. The gorge was as breathtaking as ever, a jewel glittering in the still, shimmering air.

The spicy aroma of eucalyptus oil evaporating in the heat tickled his nose and made him want to sneeze. He held it back and stepped onto the flat rock jutting out over the pool and stripped off. Curly had stood in the same place once, stark naked, poised to dive. He took his time, remembering Curly's grace, curled his toes over the lip and leaned forward, his knees bent, his arms stretched above his head and pushed off. The wind whistled past his ears and then came the cold, cold water sliding over his body as he dived down deep beneath the surface.

He curled around in the water and pushed up, surfaced and smiled, a near-perfect dive – as good as Curly's had been. Teeth chattering against the chill, he swam fast to warm up, circling the pool twice until the icy water turned to warm velvet against his skin. Then he rolled onto his back and floated, feeling the weightlessness, the lap of water in his ears, looking at the rock formation around him, the jagged edge of the cliff top, the bright splashes of green as a flock of twenty-eight parrots flew overhead, bright as English kingfishers as they darted from tree to tree.

It was a beautiful place, to his mind more beautiful even than Paradise Canyon, and as secluded as the other place, but smaller, more intimate, a place he could call his own, as Curly had done before him.

A movement away to the right and on the edge of his sight line caught his eye – a rock wallaby! Hands feathering, enjoying the moment, the weightlessness, the cool warmth of the water, he watched intently, curious, hoping for a glimpse of the smaller kangaroo-like marsupials that favoured this type of terrain. But the shape was wrong and so was the colour.

Alert now, he peered at the figure and blinked. About three-quarters of the way up the rock face, forty feet above him, sitting on a rocky ledge was an Aborigine!

Gooseflesh stood out on his arms — Curly?

You stupid fool! Course it wasn't Curly, what had made him think that? The person was too small. Whoever it was sat in shadow, watching him. Conscious of his nakedness he twisted in the water and drifted closer to the edge, his eyes fixed on the figure, feeling less exposed once he was partially concealed by the eucalyptus fronds overhanging the pool.

She moved then, a young Aboriginal girl, her skin lighter than Curly's, her nose straighter, her unsmiling lips fuller than his had been. She hesitated, scanning the rocky shelf, looking for a safe route. The limp, faded fabric of her dress clung to her body as she turned away from him and her chin-length hair, reddish-brown and wavy, gleamed, the curls golden in the sunlight. She looked back over her shoulder briefly, her brow furrowed against the sun. She was pretty, prettier than any other Aborigine he'd met, and then she was gone, scrambling up the track towards the summit.

Jon swam to the pool edge and hauled himself out of the water; he dragged on trousers and ran along the track after her. She wasn't one of the station kids; she looked six years older than Mick's eldest girl. So, who was she? And were there others? He gasped for breath as he climbed after her, stubbing his bare toes and cutting his feet on sharp quartz, and cursing for forgetting his boots.

He reached the spot where he'd seen her disappear, but she was no longer in sight. Below him the vast plateau stretching as far as the horizon and the rocks to his right and left were empty. She'd vanished, secreted herself away in a crevice somewhere to wait him out. He could keep a watch until nightfall and never catch a glimpse of her.

He turned his back on the plateau and retraced his steps. How long had she been watching him? He blushed. She was thirteen or fourteen, he guessed, and attractive for an Aborigine. Not that he'd met that many, only Curly's sisters who were older, and they weren't good looking, not to his eye. Mick's kids were pretty, but they were kids.

He dressed quickly, his mind full of plans for the next day, thoughts of the Aboriginal girl forgotten as he made his way back to the camp. Tomorrow, at first light, they'd begin mustering the sheep and lambs, a task that involved days of searching the vast tracts of bush for them and driving the first of the mobs back to the holding paddock. A week, maybe longer, before they'd rounded them up, then there would be days of eating the dust and flies kicked up by the flock as they worked with the sheep. He shuddered at the thought of insects settling on his eyes, nostrils and mouth, sucking the moisture from him, driving him crazy as they corralled the lambs ready for docking, castrating and notching – a tiring job but nothing like lugging heavy ewes, wethers and rams about come shearing time.

CHAPTER 29

Two weeks later Rachel drove Jon into Charlestown to pick up his utility truck from Wes's garage. Joe slept soundly on Jon's lap undisturbed by the rattle and roll of the vehicle as Rachel negotiated the deeper ruts.

'Connie's asked me to stay,' said Rachel.

Jon didn't answer. Things weren't easy between them. They saw each other at meal times and he'd fixed a couple of things for her, a curtain rail and a sticking door, but apart from that he'd kept away, annoyed by her continued delay in telling everyone the truth, angry that people still believed he was Joe's father.

'Have you seen your dad recently?'

'No.'

He knew why she was staying in Charlestown; she was hoping Scally would come round and accept his grandson. The bastard was one pig-stubborn bloke. Jon couldn't understand how a fella could turn his back on his own flesh and blood. He felt the colour rise in his cheeks. He was a good one to think that way after what he'd done to Kathleen, leaving her behind in the Liverpool children's home when he'd been seduced by Gibson's glib and glowing descriptions of Australia and the opportunities to be had there. Except it had all been a lie, and he'd been a kid of eight who didn't know any better and couldn't be expected to shoulder the responsibilities his mother's death had placed on him. But, at least he'd tried to do the right thing when he was old enough. He'd gone home to England and seen that she was all right. No, he wouldn't have done what Scally had done, not to a baby.

Rachel glanced at him. 'Why do you ask?'

He pulled back to the present. 'No reason.'

The silence that followed weighed heavy between them. Gone was the relaxed, carefree relationship they'd briefly enjoyed; now everything was tainted by her lies. He was relieved when they reached Wes's garage.

Joe woke as Jon got out of the utility and the baby's blue eyes focussed on him, the look direct and intense, and then he smiled. Shocked by the penetrating gaze, the wide, baby smile, Jon beamed back as he made the carrycot secure on the vacated passenger seat and placed Joe in it.

'See you in a few days then,' said Jon and closed the passenger door.

Rachel didn't bother to answer; she gave him a curt nod and was away without a backward glance. He watched her drive down the main street and pull up outside The Grand.

'She's a fine lass,' said Wes. 'You're a lucky bloke. Not enough good-looking girls about here and you've got yourself the best.'

Jon spun round but the mechanic was already walking towards the garage.

'Pity you don't appreciate it,' Wes added over his shoulder.

Wes didn't miss much and Jon sensed he didn't approve of his behaviour. 'Have you ever married, Wes?'

'No, I never met the right woman, not one who would contemplate living out here.'

'You could have had a garage in Perth.'

'Could have, but, for me, this is the place. I like the space. Reckon life's a trade off. Sometimes you can't have everything. You ready for a brew?' Wes poured a mug of dark brown tea, added a generous dollop of condensed milk and stirred until the tea took on a khaki shade. 'How're the blacks out at your place?'

'All right. Why?'

'Jeb Samuels says his black stockmen are restless. That business the other week, over Buni and his lad, has unsettled them. Nickson still doesn't know who's responsible.'

Jon considered the Jarrahlong mob. Adie and Belle hadn't changed but the others were more taciturn and uncommunicative than usual. After work they'd taken to sitting together in the shade of the bunkhouse verandah, and on a couple of occasions he'd had the feeling they'd been discussing something serious. When he'd joined them for smoko conversation had dried up. He hadn't been welcome, and Jimmi wasn't back either. Was there a connection?

After the tea he paid Wes and rolled his utility off the ramp. He pulled a shopping list out of his back pocket and drove over to the Agricultural Supplies. He needed more sheep dip, tar for dabbing on cuts at shearing time, and mineral licks, amongst other things.

Jon parked next to Gerry's truck, and swore; Gerry was the last person he wanted to see. He couldn't stand the bloke; he was a nasty piece of work, a drunk who used his fists and his foul mouth too freely, and Gerry had a long memory – he'd never forgotten the fight they'd had a couple of years back.

'Look who's dragged up,' sneered Gerry, 'Mrs Macarthur's Pommy bastard.'

Jon ignored the jibe. Gerry wasn't exactly bright, he'd soon run out of snide comments so long as he didn't let him needle him into giving a smart answer. 'What sheep dip have you got, Les?'

'Gamalene or Cooper's? Don't reckon there's that much to choose between either of them,' said Les.

'Cooper's will do, and I need tar.'

Les disappeared into the dark recesses of the store and returned some moments later with a couple of two-gallon tins. 'One or two?'

'I'm not sure, Les.'

'Two,' said Les. 'It'll keep if you don't use it all.'

'Have you done a delivery for Stan this month, Les?'

'Aye, last week. Gerry took it.'

'Quite a place he's got there,' said Gerry.

'What do you mean?' asked Jon.

'Never realised there were so many old mines for him to go at. The old fella must be worth a packet. Met fellas like him before, stingy as hell and up to their ears in gold. If you ask me, he'll have it hidden away in that shack of his.'

'It's none of our business either way, so long as he pays his bills on time,' said Les. 'Are you going out that way any time soon, Jon?'

'Why?'

'Stan ordered a box of cartridges for his shotgun – an old sixteen bore. I don't carry sixteens only twelves. The order arrived last Monday, is there any chance of you dropping them off?'

'Yeah, no sweat, put them with Alice's stuff and I'll see he gets them.'

'And you tell him to be more careful where he goes pointing that bloody gun,' said Gerry.

'Now what are you on about?' asked Les.

'Threatened to blow my head off if I set foot on his land, he did, silly old sod.'

Jon smiled. The first time he'd came across Stan he was slithering down a mound of spoil, the shotgun trained on him. 'What were you doing?'

Gerry scowled. 'How's that little lad of yours? Keeping you awake at night, is he?'

Jon ignored him. 'Mineral licks, Les. How many does Alice usually order?'

Les scratched his head. 'Blessed if I know. I'll have to look in the invoices but I should think you'll need a couple of dozen or more for Alice's mob.'

'What about Rachel?' leered Gerry. He made an obscene gesture. 'She keeping your bed warm enough for you?'

'I'd watch what you say,' said Les. 'Scally walks in here and hears you talking about his lass like that and your life won't be worth living.'

'I ain't afraid of Scally, this young pup, neither. Still wet behind the ears, he is.'

Jon clenched his fists, the bloke deserved a thrashing.

'Has the constable caught up with you yet?' asked Les.

Gerry bristled. 'What're you getting at?'

'That wing and bumper you've had straightened. I hope you've got a good alibi.'

'I told you, it was a bloody kangaroo.' He glared at Jon. 'And what're you looking at?'

'Nothing,' said Jon, but he'd caught the fleeting, shifty look on Gerry's face, had seen him avert his eyes when Les questioned him. The man was hiding something – had it been a kangaroo or the Aborigines that had been run down the other week? He moved closer to the double doors for a better look at Gerry's truck.

It was identical to Scally's with its flatbed trailer and wooden sides that let down for easier loading and unloading. The nearside wing had been clumsily hammered out and repainted and he could see a kink in the hefty metal bumper where someone had pulled it straight. It looked like an amateur had been at it.

'Nickson's fine about it,' said Gerry. 'I told him what had happened and where he could find the carcass.' He hitched up his pants and leaned on a barrel of sheep dip, watching Les make up the order for Jindalee Station. 'And I told him we were well shut of them. Too many blackfellas about anyway – the buggers breed like rabbits.'

'One was only a kid,' said Les.

'I reckon it was one of them pit props lorries, them boys drive all hours, foot down all the way. Don't stop for nothing, they don't. It's easy done in the dark, that's how I hit the bloody kangaroo,' said Gerry, 'bounced onto the road right in front of me, it did. I didn't stand a chance.'

'Still not right, leaving the kid to die like that. Whoever it was should have stopped and checked.'

'You're welcome to your own opinion, Les. I didn't take you for an Abo-lover.'

'I'm not,' said Les. 'They don't do themselves any favours, but dead's dead when all's said and done, and that youngster was only a kid. And if you want my advice, Gerry, you'd be better off keeping your opinions to yourself until this mess is sorted. It doesn't do to go bad-mouthing blackfellas when the constable's doing his investigations.'

'Old Nickson's all right. He's no Abo-lover either; he told me himself it was most likely an accident.'

Les shrugged. 'There's a delivery due Jindalee,' he indicated the goods stacked by the double doors. 'Old man Samuels wants it today and I said I'd do my best.' He glanced at his watch. 'If you get a rift on you'll manage to get there before dark.'

'Can't it wait until the next mail run?'

'No, it can't. Not this time. It's a spare part for an artesian bore and he needs it now, not in a fortnight.'

Gerry spat out a gob of tobacco juice.

'And watch for roos,' Les muttered. He folded the sheaf of invoices in his hand, glanced at Alice's shopping list and turned to Jon. 'Are you taking this with you, or do you want it delivered tomorrow?'

'Now, Les, if it's no problem,' said Jon.

'No sweat,' said Les. 'I'll just give Gerry a hand with the loading.'

CHAPTER 30

Early on the following Sunday morning Jon pulled up and parked next to Stan's van. The old fella was sitting on a kitchen chair outside the door shaded by the overhang of the narrow verandah. Bonny and Bess stirred themselves and wandered over to him.

'Fine day for a visit,' said Stan.

Jon glanced at the sky – deep blue with billowy, white clouds scudding across it and a breeze keeping the edge off the heat. 'How are you, Stan?'

'Not too bad as far as things go.' The effort triggered a coughing fit. Eventually Stan hawked up a gob of bubbly phlegm and spat it in the dust.

'I see you're coughing better,' commented Jon.

'There's nowt wrong with me, so you needn't go on about me seeing a quack.'

'Would I do that, Stan?'

'Yes, you would, if I gave you half a chance. Blokes like me who end up in hospital never come out.'

Was Stan right? His mother had gone into hospital saying she'd be out in quick sticks and she was dead within three weeks. Elsie had told him she'd been ill for months, but at eight years old he hadn't noticed, all he knew was that his mam was dead and that she'd died in the hospital where she was supposed to get better.

'How's Alice?' asked Stan.

'Same as always.' Jon handed over a couple of books. 'She recommends *Gold Fever*, says it's set in the Californian goldfields at the turn of the century.'

'She still belongs to that book club?'

'Yes, one arrives every month like clockwork, and Les got you your cartridges.'

'I could have done with them a fortnight ago. I can't stand that Gerry. He really sticks in my craw.'

Jon grinned. 'He is a bit of a bastard.'

'Caught him poking around, seeing what he could find.'

'He says you're sleeping on a mountain of gold, Stan. He says he's met your type before – a stingy old git.'

'He used those words?'

'More or less.'

'He comes sniffing round here again and I'll blast him to smithereens.'

'Do you want me to have a quiet word with Les and get him to send Scally instead?'

'Yeah. At least you know where you are with Scally.'

'Yeah,' said Jon, the word heavy with meaning.

Stan regarded him for a long moment. 'You two never have got on, have you?'

'He can't stand Pommy bastards, especially lads like me – scum, he calls us, the dregs England wanted rid of.'

'Bit of an understatement, isn't it?' commented Stan. 'Last time I was in town your name was lower than a snake's belly.'

'Still is. Wes's all right, and Les, but Connie won't speak to me unless she has to and Scally says if I don't make an honest women of Rachel, then, before I know it, my bleached bones'll be markers in the outback dust.'

'What about Alice?'

'She's laid it on the line, no marriage, no job, take it or leave it.'

'I didn't know you and Rachel were such good friends.'

'We're not.'

Stan raised a bushy eyebrow. 'You don't beget kids at a distance, son, leastways, not when I was a lad you didn't.'

'I've already told you, Stan, Joe isn't mine. Don't you believe me?'

'I don't know what to think,' said Stan.

Jon worried the skin at the side of his thumb nail. What more was there to say, even Stan believed Joe was his son. Until Rachel admitted the truth it was his word against hers, and it was clear who everyone believed. He tried to ignore his disappointment. He'd expected more of Stan, and Alice. He thought they, at least, would have given him the benefit of the doubt and listened to his side of the story.

'So, who is the father?' asked Stan after a long moment.

'I don't know. Rachel won't say.'

'She's admitted the baby isn't yours?'

'Yes, but only to me.'

'So, what's the problem?'
'Her dad.'
'I think it's about time we had a drink, don't you, son?'
Jon fetched them both a couple of inches of rum and the spare kitchen chair for himself. He sat down next to Stan with his feet propped on an old kerosene drum, the tumbler of rum resting on his belly, watching the changing pattern of light as intermittent cloud obscured the sun.
'Scally's not a bad man,' said Stan, 'and I meant what I said earlier, you know where you are with him, he tells you straight.'
'He already has.'
'And you can't blame him for wanting to protect Rachel.'
'But he won't have anything to do with her…or Joe.'
'Give him time.'
'But he's had time, plenty of it.'
'Put yourself in his boots. How would you feel if she was your daughter and the bloke left her in the lurch?' asked Stan.
'But I didn't.'
'I know, but that's what he thinks, that you got what you wanted and then cleared off home to England, leaving your mess behind for him to sort out.'
'But why did he think it was me? I'm not the only young bloke around here. There's Will and Tom Samuels for a start.'
'You reckon one of them's the father?'
Jon shook his head. 'Don't reckon so, but there're other blokes passing through, ringers, shearers, maybe she had a fling with one of them.'
'Maybe,' said Stan, 'but the trouble is, if she's not saying you're damned. Everyone in the town knows she was soft on you and she never looked at Will, or Tom, as far as I know.'
Jon tried to think about what it would have been like back home. He didn't know of any girl that got into trouble except for the O'Gready's daughter. She'd been sixteen or thereabouts when she was sent on holiday to stay with an aunt in Norfolk. Rumour was she was having a baby and then she came home without one. She never went out much after that, except with her parents. And no one ever saw her smile after that either. At least Scally hadn't sent Rachel to live on the other side of the country.
Stan sipped his rum. 'She's a pretty lass.'
'What's that got to do with it?'
'You could do a damn sight worse. There aren't a lot of women to choose from around here and if she already fancies you…well!'

'Well?'

'You can take it from me; it's a hard and lonely life out here in the bush. Few women settle for long. Say what you like, it's still frontier country and at least with Rachel you know she's used to the life, she'd settle and be happy.'

'Alice came out here with Jack.'

'Aye, she did, but Alice wasn't some simpering slip of a lass, she was a strong woman with a mind of her own and she was used to a hard life. She'd worked on her father's farm before she came out to Australia, they hand-milked sixty cows morning and evening. And then there was the harvesting, bagging up the wheat and barley, carting bales and stacking them, and in winter there were the turnips, spuds and sugar beet to lift. Ever done any harvesting?' asked Stan.

Jon shook his head.

'Hard work, I'm telling you. How many lasses do you know who would be up to that? Farming never was an easy option, even at the best of times.'

Jon thought of Merle, tall and willowy, fastidious about her appearance, and elegant. Stan was right, it was a hard life out in the bush, and Merle wasn't the type. A niggling doubt that had dogged his thoughts ever since he'd left England wormed deeper into his brain. Was he expecting too much? But he wasn't the sort to ask Merle to get her hands dirty, except for tending a vegetable patch perhaps. And before too long there'd be children. Children made a family and he wanted a family about him. And if Merle wanted a career, so what? He could look for a position some place else, closer to a hospital or a clinic, but that was in the future. It'd be years before Merle qualified, plenty of time for him to make his fortune and get a nice place for them to live in. He frowned. He'd written to her when he was on the boat but, so far, there'd been no reply. Had his letter gone adrift? Did she think he'd forgotten about her already, that he didn't care?

'You like her, don't you?'

'Who?'

'Rachel.'

'She's all right.'

Stan raised an eyebrow.

'She has some funny ideas.'

'Like what?'

He couldn't tell Stan about their argument over Aborigines. 'Bottom line, Stan, I'm too young to get myself tied down – in five or six years perhaps and as I've already told you, Joe isn't mine.'

'There's nothing more to say then, is there,' said Stan, 'except you'd better hope that Rachel tells the truth sooner rather than later, otherwise you might find yourself married younger than you'd like to be if Scally has his way. And there's another thing, she'll find it harder to tell the truth the longer she leaves it.'

Jon spent the rest of the morning sawing up logs, sweeping out, washing up and doing the bulk of Stan's laundry in the old tin bath with a wooden dolly similar to the one his gran used to use.

Later, they sat down together with plates full of Stan's bully beef and potato stew washed down with strong tea.

'Have you ever regretted coming out to Australia, Stan?'

'No, can't say I have.'

'How old were you?'

'Thirty-two. I made my way out to Kalgoorlie then hitched a lift on a bullock wagon to Gwalia not long before they built the railway. I pegged a claim along with dozens of other prospectors aiming to get rich quick. Folk were throwing up shacks as fast as they could from bush timber, corrugated iron and hessian. I'm telling you the place looked like a vast shanty town full of people from all over the globe, especially Italians and Jugoslavs. It was a real melting pot of a place. A thousand of us living in Gwalia and a similar number in Leonora, all of us digging away, and hoping to find a mother lode.'

Stan poured himself a measure of rum and swallowed it.

'That's where you met Alice, isn't it?'

'Aye, through Jack. He was manager of a cattle station out beyond Gwalia. Making a packet, he was, selling beef. Gwalia and Leonora were expanding fast; the prospectors and their families needed feeding. Anyway, after they built the State Hotel in Gwalia he took to drinking there once a week and that's where I met him.'

'And what about Alice?'

'I only met her once or twice when Jack brought her and David into town for supplies.'

'So how did you end up here?'

'I came back after the war. I knew Jack had taken a pastoral lease at Jarrahlong so I moved into the Pilkington area and then when I heard about Hardman's lapsed lease I took it on, and I've been here ever since.'

'What? Since after the war?'

'Yeah, the First World War, 1919.'

'Twenty-nine years.'

'It's a long time when you say it like that.'

'Too right it is, Stan. And you're still looking for that reef.'

'It's out there somewhere.'

'You can feel it in your bones, can you?'

'I hope you'll remember me and this conversation when I'm dead and buried and I'm proved right.'

Jon grinned and slapped Stan on the back. 'Stan, I'll never forget you. You're me best mate, gold or no gold.'

'It's about time you cleared off, isn't it, before Alice starts breathing down my neck?'

'Why don't you come back with me and stay at Jarrahlong until you're better?'

'What, and risk some smart bugger jumping my claim?'

'Like you did with Hardman? Did he ever come back?'

'No,' said Stan, 'he never did. He died a broken man without a penny to his name, or so I heard. Talking of dying, I want planting next to the creek on that flat bit below No Hope mine.'

'The one you took me down?'

'Aye, that's the one. Anyway, under my bed there's a trunk.'

'Where you keep your mountain of gold?'

'Aye. There are a couple of nuggets in it that'll pay for a headstone and maybe a bit left over for a drink.'

'Don't talk daft, Stan. You've got years yet.'

'Maybe, maybe not, but if you're around I'd appreciate it if you'd see it done.'

The old fella was serious; there wasn't a hint of a smile on his face, just an intense look in his faded eyes. 'All right, Stan, I'll see to it for you even if I have to sail halfway around the world to do it. What year were you born?'

'1871.'

Jon did a quick calculation. 'You don't look your age.'

'I bloody feel it right at this minute,' said Stan. 'Now bugger off, you smooth-talking Pommy bastard, and leave me in peace.'

On the drive back to Jarrahlong Jon went over his conversation with Stan and his funeral plans. There were worse places to be buried and the spot Stan had chosen was nice enough, and it was within sight of his No-Hoper. Twenty-nine years Stan had wasted on that mine. He couldn't think of anything more unpleasant than being cooped up for hours, deep underground, with a mountain of rock above his head, digging out a seam and praying for the golden moment that would make him richer than Croesus, with a life long enough to enjoy it.

His headlights lit up the old salmon gum as he turned off onto the track to Jarrahlong and soon after the beam caught a figure in the distance – an Aborigine. The man's gait was familiar. Jon smiled. Jimmi! Where had the fella been over the last few weeks?

He pulled up. 'Lift?'

Jimmi hesitated, one hand on the utility roof the other holding on to his traditional weapons, the ornately carved spear and woomera that he always carried with him whenever they were out in the bush.

'Kill any kangaroos?'

Jimmi shook his head, dropped his weapons in the back and got into the passenger seat.

'I'm glad you're back,' said Jon, 'we've got a big job on. Alice wants a new well sinking over at Cranston Gap. She was thinking of drilling but it's too expensive. And Adie's been complaining that he's getting too old for digging.' He glanced at Jimmi. 'Have you been visiting family?'

'Nah, blackfella business.' Jimmi looked straight ahead.

Puzzled, Jon concentrated on driving. Jimmi had changed. Gone was the camaraderie, his sense of humour and the big grin that showed his missing front tooth. Perhaps he was lonely with Curly dead and Sammo gone. Behind the impassive face Jon sensed frustration and resentment, or was he reading too much into what Curly said when they'd stood at the edge of the old mine at Murrin Murrin, looking at the desecrated land – that once the land is gone you've destroyed the dreaming. He wondered what it was like for Aborigines living with white people who had taken their land.

CHAPTER 31

Jon led the way on his horse. Adie and Jimmi rode behind, while Big'un and Mick, the two new Aboriginal stockmen Alice had hired while he was in England, led the packhorses laden with equipment and food for a lengthy stay. They were making for the north-east section of the station, over by Cranston Gap, to dig a new well after Alice decided drilling was too expensive.

Red, Jon's big chestnut gelding, picked his way carefully between the boulders, keeping to the smoother ground. Jon let him have his head; he knew the horse would find the safest route better than he could. Red was bigger than Daisy, much younger, and more of a handful to control. Jon liked his liveliness, the way he twitched his ears when he spoke to him. He still enjoyed riding Daisy but Red was a challenge, and although he was a big, rangy-looking horse he was a smooth ride, as smooth as Daisy, but more importantly, Red was his. Alice had given him the horse. Regard him as an early bonus, she'd said. If you're working for me full time you'll need your own horse and your own dog. Then she'd given him Smoky, Old Yella's dog pup, two years old now and as rangy looking as Red. He swung round in his saddle and checked that the dog was following with the others. Satisfied that he was in the middle of the pack, close by the horses' heels, he settled back to enjoying the scenery.

Adie caught Jon's glance and thumbed in the direction of the dog. 'He's a nice looking animal.'

'Thanks.'

'He'll work till he drops so you'll need to pace 'im while he's still a youngster.'

'Yeah, he's still a bit brash.'

'Give 'im time, he'll quieten.'

Over the months he'd come to respect the old Aborigine. Alice had once told him there was nothing Adie didn't know about stock and she'd been right. Adie could look at an animal and tell you what was wrong with it. He'd come to realise that Adie noticed things others missed. He listened to the way an animal breathed, watched the way it moved, looked at the state of its coat, its eyes – it was second nature to him. If he could be half as good a stockman as Adie one day, he'd be satisfied.

Once they were clear of the home paddock Jimmi rode ahead.

'Is anything bothering him, Adie?' asked Jon.

'Nah, he's right.'

Jon frowned as Jimmi picked a route over the rough terrain. For the last fortnight Jimmi had kept himself to himself, he hadn't joined in any of the usual banter, preferring his own company. Jon mulled it over. Maybe Jimmi had family worries, but whatever was bothering him he hoped it would sort itself out soon so that they could get back to the easy friendship they'd had before Curly died. 'I don't think so, Adie. Can you have a word? See if there's anything we can do.'

'Won't do much good. If blackfellas don't want to talk they don't talk.'

Behind them Big'un and Mick were yattering away to each other in their own language, their voices barely audible above the sound of the horses' feet on the hard ground.

'Not like them blackfellas then!'

Adie grinned. 'Talk the back leg off a dingo, them two.'

'What's your name, Adie, your Aboriginal name?'

'Adijiri.'

'How come everyone calls you Adie?'

Adie shrugged his shoulders. 'Mister Macarthur called me it, he say Adijiri too much of a mouthful.'

'You want me to call you Adijiri?'

'Nah, I've been Adie too long now.'

'You related to them two?' Jon indicated over his shoulder.

'Nah, them belong over Leinster way.'

Big'un and Mick were family. Jon hadn't worked out their exact relationship, same as he had never really worked out the family bond between Curly, Sammo and Jimmi, but he thought of them as cousins. Mick was the elder by about ten years, Jon guessed. Big'un, a half-caste, was the one with the most to say, the one with the quirky sense of humour. Both men took off from time to time to spend a few days on family business whereas Jon had never known Adie go walkabout. Adie never had time off; he worked seven days a week for months on end and seemed content living at

Jarrahlong with Belle.

'Your mob from round here, Adie?'

'More or less,' said Adie, refusing to be drawn.

They set up camp at midday, collected a stockpile of slow-burning mulga wood and got the billy going for a brew. While Big'un and Mick saw to the domestic arrangements, Jon, Adie and Jimmi rode alongside the dried-up creek, inspecting the lie of the land and looking for a billabong.

'This'll do fine,' said Adie finally. 'Reckon the water's not too deep.'

They returned to camp and supper, damper and cold, roast mutton and billy tea. Tomorrow the boys would catch bush tucker, goanna, or bungarra as they were called locally, maybe even a kangaroo if Jimmi was accurate with his spear, just so long as they didn't bring back a feral cat – he'd never acquired a taste for cat.

Later, Jon leaned back against his swag listening to the murmur of Aboriginal voices, the movement of the hobbled horses, and the station dogs cadging titbits, their eyes bright in the firelight. He liked camping out under the vast night sky, particularly on cloudless evenings. The open view of the Milky Way above him more than compensated for the colder, clear nights when the temperature could drop below freezing.

After he'd finished eating he refilled his enamel mug and made his way towards the limestone ridge overlooking the creek bed. Smoky followed at his heels, nuzzling his hand as he trotting along at his side. Alice didn't like Smoky's name. What do you want to call the dog that for? Should have called him Blue, she'd said once in a querulous moment. He didn't agree, too many grey-blue dogs were called Blue and he wanted something distinctive, different, and the dog did look like a streak of smoke if you caught a glimpse of him haring over the ground as fast as a greyhound after a rabbit. Smoky was intelligent for a dog. He picked up things quickly and was already fully trained.

Jon hunkered down and sipped his tea, the dog squatting at his side. They were able to see along the whole of the valley from their vantage point. Behind them the red sky bathed the land in an eerie light while before them, to the east, the sky was already darkening from azure to slate; soon the light would go and darkness last until the moon rose casting silver over the land.

Smoky stiffened, his nose twitched, his hackles rose and a low growl rumbled in his throat. Jon squinted trying to make sense of the shapes in the dwindling light. The dog continued to rumble quietly as two figures approached.

They were dressed native style, loin cloths slung low on the hips, woven headbands tied at the forehead. The older man carried a staff made of dark wood. He reminded Jon of an image he'd once seen in an illustrated children's bible they'd used in school – Moses about to strike the rock in the Sinai Desert to bring forth water.

The older man had a peculiar gait, he strode along delicately as if each pace was measured and deliberately placed, and even from a distance there was something about him that created an air of authority that he wore like a mantle. Was it his bearing or the way he carried his head? Or perhaps it was because the younger Aborigine carried both swags and walked a couple of paces behind.

Jon guessed they'd seen him long before the dog had spotted them. Closer to he noted the older man's grizzled hair and spare body, the musculature honed by a lifetime of living off the land. And then there were his legs – thin, with terrible scars in the muscles. What on earth had happened to him that he should be so mutilated? Jon looked into his face and saw quiet watchfulness in his eyes, a look that made him hesitate, and inspired respect and a degree of caution.

Jon nodded his greeting.

The younger Aborigine spoke first. 'You want stockmen?'

'Could do,' said Jon. 'Are you looking for work?'

'Y'right.'

'What can you do?'

'Anything y'want.'

'What about digging?' Jon looked at the older fella, but his face was impassive.

'We can dig. You makin' a well?' asked the younger man.

'That's about it. Have you eaten?'

'Not since mornin'.'

'What're your names?'

'I'm Dave, he's Yildilla.'

'And where are you from?'

Dave swung round and nodded in the direction they'd come, from across the desert. When he turned back he was grinning. 'Any more where that come from?' he said, gesturing towards the enamel mug.

'Mick will make a fresh brew.' Jon threw the bitter dregs over the rock. Yildilla's silence was unnerving. 'I'll come with you, time to turn in anyway.'

He followed the pair back to camp and found the others sitting around the fire, nattering. Mick rose to his feet when he saw the newcomers and handed over a couple of mugs of tea and hunks of damper and cold mutton.

Jon smiled to himself, how had Mick known to bake extra? Had the three of them communicated telepathically? He recalled how Jimmi had found him, two years back, in the desert, suffering from dehydration and heat exhaustion after Curly died from snakebite. He reckoned that had involved telepathy. When he'd asked Jimmi how he'd known where to find him he'd said he'd just known, but telepathy or no Jimmi's action had saved his life that day.

The newcomers sat by the fire, eating and talking. He couldn't make out their murmured conversation or the hand movements, nods and looks that made up their language.

Jon unrolled his swag and settled down for the night. He looked at the sky again, at the sprinkling of stars, listening to the low-pitched murmur of blackfellas' voices and the dogs whimpering in their sleep. What would Merle make of all this? Could a city girl settle in this part of Australia? Would she grow to love it as he had done? Alice had, but there and again, according to Stan, Alice hadn't been a city girl.

Doubt niggled away. Merle still hadn't answered the letter he'd posted in Colombo on the way out to Australia, and he remembered what Wes Chapman and Stan Colley had said, that the outback was a crook place for a woman. But it didn't have to be, not if he provided a decent home with nice furniture, curtains, pictures and books – something like Alice's new place, with an inside lavatory, and fans to cool the air, and a refrigerator. He was still planning for the future when sleep overtook him.

Adie set to with a pickaxe and a spade and marked out a rectangle two yards long by two and a half yards. He dug until the sweat beaded his brow and took a breather while Mick and Jimmi took their turns.

Big'un went off into the bush with Dave and Yildilla to cut some mulga wood props, the scrubby, iron-hard acacia that created an almost impenetrable thicket. The wood took some hewing but once it was in place it would last a lifetime and longer.

Digging wasn't easy and constructing the lining of the well was a slow process. Each piece of wood was chosen for dimension and straightness and cut to length and the ends prepared to lock at right angles. Once Mick was satisfied that the wood was fitted and couldn't move, he dug out the next layer of earth and rock and constructed another frame of wood underneath the last. The deeper Mick and Jimmi dug, the harder the going was, rubble and earth had to be lifted out of the ground in buckets and dumped, the wood cladding had to be carried from further and further afield and by the end of the week they were still only twenty feet deep.

Jon stood at the top looking down into the hole at Mick hacking away at the compacted earth. The only thing holding back the sides was the ladder-like timber held in place and braced against each other. If it collapsed now Mick would never get out alive and they'd still got another ten feet or so to go.

The sky was darkening to the east and over to the west the sun was a huge orb in the sky glowing like a Chinese paper lantern. He calculated they'd got a few more days of digging and then they'd have to construct the wind pump over the well.

'Time to call it a day,' said Jon into the hole.

Mick signalled that he was ready and three of them hauled him up with his safety rope.

Jon grinned at the sight of Mick's face. It was as red as the wattle on a turkey cock. 'Hot down there, isn't it?'

'You bet ya,' grinned Mick, 'and him gettin' hotter by the day. Reckon we'll reach water tomorrow. I can smell it.'

At the camp Dave was roasting a kangaroo that Jimmi and Big'un had killed earlier. Jon breathed in the aroma of the sizzling meat, the billycan tea simmering, and the damper baking in the cast-iron ovens. He was ravenous and so were the others.

While he ate he watched the stockmen, particularly Yildilla. He noticed that Dave had given Yildilla the choicest piece of meat, he certainly needed it; the old fella was lean, not an ounce of fat on him.

Later, his belly full, Jon dozed, conscious of the stockmen talking amongst themselves, their faces glistening in the light from the campfire, sharing stories of hunting exploits. One by one they got to their feet and described through words and mime some great feat of tracking, of killing for the pot. Now and again they intoned a refrain, accompanying the beat of the clap-sticks Dave had pulled out of his swag.

It was still early, the moon had barely cleared the horizon; it was going to be a clear night and a cold one. Jon pulled a blanket round his shoulders and was thinking about bedding down when he heard the old fella chanting in a low and monotonous voice, the indistinct words repetitive and haunting. Then, Yildilla rose to his feet in a smooth, sinuous movement and began stamping his feet to some inner rhythm, circling on the spot, his body crouched low. The others joined in, chanting to the hypnotic beat.

Yildilla began to mime a journey, an ancestor journey. The old man's arms and legs took on the angle and pose of a lizard. His fingers became claws, the limbs were lifted, one after the other, in short staccato movements, each time halting momentarily as if waiting for something. He tilted his head, listening, and scented the air with a flicking tongue. Perentie Man! Yildilla was a giant monitor lizard! Jon's blood seemed to chill in his veins. He felt the shivers start as, mesmerized, he watched the old fella continue his journey around the camp.

The Aborigine turned back towards the fire, panting, gasping in his final death throes, his limbs flung back exposing his belly, his head twisted as he writhed, his movements growing weaker and weaker as the life ebbed from him. Finally, his tongue lolled out of his mouth and his eyes rolled in his head, and he breathed his last.

After a few moments dead the old fella got to his feet and resumed his place among the others.

No one spoke. Mick tossed more acacia twigs onto the fire and the flames flickered brightly throwing long shadows – purple shadows – into the bush.

Perentie! The old man had resurrected Perentie Man! Now the totem animal's spirit seemed to be around them, crouching in the shadows, his breath fanned by the night breeze.

Jon turned his back on the others, and on the fire. He drew his blanket closer to him. Yildilla knew. Had he come to avenge Perentie?

That night he couldn't sleep for thinking about the dying moments of the infant monitor lizard, and the horror on Curly's face when he held up the carcass for him to admire, when it cast long purple shadows on the red earth. He'd killed Curly's totem and it had cost Curly his life. Curly's ancestor had come for him on the journey home to Jarrahlong, demanding atonement as dawn slid over the landscape, but still the debt was not fully paid. Perentie Man now haunted him. He had followed him to Liverpool and turned up in dreams and nightmares, and appeared in shadows when he'd least expected it. Perentie wanted retribution, or was it Curly's tjuringa that he wanted, the title deed to the land, the ancestor footprint?

The night brought no rest. Jon rose before dawn, cold and stiff, and revived the fire. He filled the billycans and waited for the others to wake, and still the purple shadows haunted him, and he knew Yildilla's eyes were following him from under his half-closed lids.

They found water the next afternoon. Mick called up from the well bottom, thirty feet down, to say that he'd hit the water table. Mick dug deeper, two feet deeper, and Jon hauled out the sludge and rock that he had hewed even as water collected in the bottom. The last of the mulga-wood frames was hurriedly lowered down the well and by evening all was finished.

Yildilla and Dave had left them earlier that day and Jon wasn't sorry to see them go, particularly the old fella with his reptilian stare and skin as dry as a lizard.

Over the next two days they fitted the galvanised pipe work they had brought with them, and then they put together a simple wind pump with its own windmill and weathervane over the well head.

Later that day they listened to the tick and clank as the wind pump lifted the water out of the well and they clapped each other on the back as water pooled at their feet and trickled down to the billabong a few yards away. By the time they had packed and loaded the axes, spades, shovels and buckets the billabong was a large wet patch and water was starting to collect in the depression – all they needed to do now was build the holding tanks and water troughs, but that would come later, after the shearing.

Adie tilted back his battered bush hat and scratched his furrowed brow. 'Good week's work, it'll keep the mob in water for a while.'

Jon agreed. No more starving, dehydrated sheep – not this year, he thought. He saddled Red and whistled Smoky then he, Adie, Jimmi, Big'un and Mick travelled back to Jarrahlong across the sandstone escarpment carpeted with pink and white everlasting flowers, yellow billy buttons and green mulla mulla. On the long ride home, under the blazing midday sun that cast no shadows, Jon buried his unease. The old fella and Dave had gone, as they'd come, like wraiths, and he was glad of it.

From a distance the homestead iron roof gleamed and the sun glinted on the new glass. The gum tree towering over the homestead shimmered in the breeze. He imagined Alice sitting in its shade, watching the dust kicked up by their approach, telling Belle to put the kettle on, and perhaps…perhaps there'd be a letter from Merle. The thought cheered him and he geed on his horse, his eyes fixed on the homestead, and then he caught sight of a stranger waiting for them in the yard.

Jon stood up in his stirrups, conscious of the hairs prickling on the back of his neck. He shaded his eyes and swore under his breath. There, leaning against the post and rail fencing over by the new barn, was Yildilla.

CHAPTER 32

Dave and Yildilla had repaired one of the humpies from pieces of spare wood, canvas and discarded corrugated iron, next to the one Mick had commandeered for his family. Jon mentioned it to Alice over breakfast one morning, but she didn't seem concerned.

'Blackfellas have camped on that part of the homestead for as long as I've lived here,' she said. 'They turn up from time to time looking for work, like Mick and his family. They're not hurting anyone, are they?'

'No, it's just—'

'Just what, Jon Just? As I see it they either work or they don't. I don't mind them helping themselves to water, but they only get tucker if they earn it. Belle knows the score. Mind you, I'm not saying she doesn't do free handouts with the left-over grub, but better that than it be wasted.'

He didn't comment on the amount Belle cooked – always enough for everyone – in any case, there wasn't a problem with Mick and his woman, Doris. Doris helped Belle in the cookhouse preparing and serving tucker at meal times and she did her fair share of the men's washing. And Mick was a grafter, when he wasn't out on walkabout. He was better at selecting a young bull for slaughter than Adie and good at butchering them. Then there were Mick's kids, nice kids, all four of them, the baby, the two lasses and the little lad, aged ten now and already helping out with the sheep.

Jon frowned as he finished breakfast. They'd been busy since Yildilla and Dave arrived, mustering the sheep and treating them for parasites. Of the two Dave had done the bulk of the work, but Yildilla had been out hunting and brought back a half-grown euro, one of the wallaroos common in the area. The meat had made a welcome change from mutton and beef.

'Isn't it about time you called on Stan again?' asked Alice, interrupting his reflections.

He'd been thinking that too; it was over a month since he'd last visited. Scally reckoned Stan was doing all right, getting over his chest infection and thinking about doing a bit of prospecting again, but hearing about him wasn't the same as seeing the old fella for himself.

'Why don't you take a ride over this afternoon,' Alice said. 'There's not much going on here. I reckon we can spare you for a couple of days.' She handed him a parcel of books tied up with string. 'I've had Belle roast a leg of mutton, and she's baked some damper. That should keep him going for a while, save him having to cook.'

'Why don't you come with me?'

'Why would I want to go visiting?'

'You and Stan have been friends for years.'

'I've things to do.'

'Like what?'

'Mind your own business.'

Jon shut up, momentarily surprised by the warning tone in her voice. 'But you play chess together, don't you?'

'Not recently,' snapped Alice. 'He's a bad loser.' She hauled herself to her feet and crossed towards the parlour door. 'Tucker's over there.' She waved her walking stick in the direction of the laden wicker basket and disappeared into the parlour.

Jon heard her talking to the cockatoo, the words indistinct, the tone peevish. He didn't understand the woman – a leg of mutton, the damper and books but she refused to visit. Maybe Stan would explain why.

Jon chose the direct route and only twice did he have to get out the sand mats – his own fault for taking the short cut across the low sandhills rather than the longer route on the main tracks.

Rachel had once told him about the trips she'd occasionally made with her dad on the mail runs, delivering post and essentials to homesteads in the area, to Jarrahlong, Stan's place, the Samuels at Jindalee, the Bartokas family on Wanndarah Station, the Kentons on Harrison Station, Kit Kennilworth and his family at Reef Hill and Jake Forest and his family at Cavanagh's Creek Station – seven homesteads spread out over an area bigger than Lancashire and Yorkshire combined. She'd said her dad refused to take her along after heavy rain or when there was a drought. Too risky, he'd say, break down in the outback and there was no certainty they'd make it home alive even if folk were keeping a watch out for their arrival and relaying information over the radio transmitter.

Like them or not, Scally and Gerry did good work delivering supplies and mail to the outlying homesteads. It was Scally who had delivered Merle's first long-awaited letter; he could have kissed him when he handed it over. There was no doubt about it, Gerry and Scally were lifelines for a lot of people, breaking the loneliness of those living on isolated stations like Jarrahlong. It was a pity they were such bastards when it came to him.

He batted at the flies crawling over his face and over the inside of the windscreen. He glanced at the cloth wrapping the leg of mutton and hoped it didn't come adrift otherwise the meat would be fly-blown before he got there.

A euro bounded across his path, he swerved, and then swore – any closer and he'd have been taking it home for supper.

Yildilla had killed one a few days back. He shivered as he remembered the old Aborigine returning with it, the carcass dangling down his back, his sinewy fingers gripping the thick tail. But it was Yildilla's piercing, deep-set eyes that gave him the willies. Ever since the Perentie Man mime he'd known that the old fella was at Jarrahlong for a reason other than work, but his discreet enquires had got him nowhere. Adie hadn't known anything while Jimmi had been tight-lipped on the subject and Alice said he was reading too much into normal Aboriginal behaviour. Perhaps he was, perhaps it was the guilt he still carried over Curly's death; he spat out a fly and concentrated on the track ahead.

Stan wasn't in his shack and neither were the dogs. Jon followed the well-worn trail along the valley, the sun high overhead beating down into the airless gorge. When he reached No Hope Mine he crossed over to the shady side and sat on the flat rock Stan favoured and waited with the dogs, their presence a sure sign that Stan was deep underground.

He didn't like mines. He hated the narrow passageways, the thought of tons of rock and earth above him held up by flimsy wooden props, and the prospect of getting lost in the labyrinthine tunnels scared him. Even thinking about it brought back the feelings of panic and claustrophobia he'd felt the time Stan had taken him into old No Hope when he'd been considering becoming a prospector. He switched his attention to the dogs and minutes later felt a tremor underfoot.

Dust gushed out of the mine.

A collapse!

Stan was in there!

He reached the entrance, his heart pounding, feeling sick with fear as Stan emerged from the adit covered in muck and coughing up his lungs.

'You bloody, stupid idiot,' yelled Jon. 'Haven't you any sense?'

Stan slapped the worst of the muck off his clothes, cleared his throat and spat a gob of dust-laden mucus onto the rock beside him.

'What happened?'

'The blasted roof caved in.'

'What were you doing?'

'Nothing much. I was chipping away at a likely spot and must have leaned too hard on a rotten prop.'

Jon stared at him, open-mouthed.

'It's all right. I reckon it's a worked-out seam anyway. Don't know why I was wasting my time on it.' Stan whistled to his dogs and set off back along the valley leaving Jon behind him.

Alice was right the old fella was a lunatic; his obsession would be the death of him. 'Is gold more valuable than your life?' yelled Jon, his voice strident.

Stan turned on his heels and walked back to where Jon was standing. 'That's the first collapse I've had in ten years and more. I'm careful. Of course I value my life.'

'Alice says you don't.'

'Well, if that's what you think, then you're a fool, son. It isn't just the gold that's keeping me here.' Stan set off walking again. 'Why did you come back?' he shouted over his shoulder. 'Why didn't you stay in Liverpool?'

Jon opened his mouth to answer and then closed it.

Stan stopped and turned back again. 'Because this place gets under your skin…like the people,' he yelled.

Back at the homestead Stan filled an old tin bath from the standpipe, built a fire outdoors and propped the bath over it, supported on a pair of makeshift cast-iron trivets. Then he sat on a kitchen chair, sipping his rum, watching the water heating.

'I don't like to bathe in cold water these days; it doesn't do my arthritis any good.' He tested the water. 'That'll do. Grab that end and lift it over there.' He indicated in the direction of an empty patch of ground by the sawing horse. 'There's a bar of soap in the sink…mind getting it? And there's a towel on the hook over by the stove.'

By the time Jon had found everything the old fella had stripped down to his long johns and was in the tub, knees up against his chest, splashing water over himself. 'Soap me back will you? I can't reach so well these days.'

Within minutes the water was grey and scummy from soap and grime but Stan continued to soak in the soup, washing his long johns even as he was wearing them. 'Easier this way,' he commented as he stood up to rinse off the soap.

'Why don't you play chess with Alice anymore?' asked Jon.

'Because she cheats.'

Jon laughed. 'That's what Alice said you do.'

'I don't cheat!' said Stan in an affronted tone. 'Pass me that towel.' He dried himself and his long johns as best he could, emptied the bath for the chooks to paddle in the water and sat on a kitchen chair to dry off in the last of the sun.

'So why won't Alice visit you?'

'I've told you.'

'No you haven't.'

'It's a long story and one that's better forgotten. Now what did you say you'd got in that basket?'

'What am I going to do about Curly's tjuringa, Stan?'

They were sitting on Stan's tiny verandah, Bonny and Bess at their feet as they supped rum out of enamel mugs and watched the antics of the kookaburra family in a ragged eucalyptus tree. The sun was low in the sky and the last fingers of light played on the rock face creating deep purple shadows that reminded Jon of the giant monitor lizard that haunted his dreams and demanded the return of Curly's tjuringa.

'I'd forget about it if I were you, or I'd burn it.'

'I can't do that, I promised Curly.'

'There you go then.'

A kookaburra bashed a small snake senseless on the branch it was sitting on and then started to swallow it, head first.

'Trouble is, Stan, I can't shrug off the feeling that I'm being watched.'

'Who by?'

'Yildilla. There's something about him.'

'Like what?'

'The way he is, the way the others are with him.'

Stan looked up, his eyes alert, questioning.

'It's like he's the boss.'

'Maybe he is, maybe he's a lawman.'

'What do you mean, Stan?'

'Blackfellas have laws, same as us, and they have elders who mete out punishment when the law's broken, like our judges. Have you ever seen him naked?'

'You mean the scars on his legs?'

'Yup, he's a lawman right enough, he's an important fella in Aboriginal society. You won't find any blackfellas going against what he says. You know how he got them scars?'

'In an accident?'

Stan chuckled. 'Rite of passage. He stood still while tribal elders threw spears at him, part of his initiation into office. It's symbolic; it shows he's a man worthy of respect and strong enough for the job.'

Jon shuddered.

'Aye, you're right to be uneasy,' said Stan. 'You ever heard of bone pointing?'

'Yes, you mentioned it once before.'

'Yeah, well, it don't hurt to hear it twice, them fellas can sing a man to his death. They don't look as if they can, do they? They sit doing nothing much, but they've got power over minds. Anyone who's had the bone pointed at them is doomed, black or white.'

'It's not the Middle Ages, Stan.'

Stan didn't reply and Jon thought that was the end of the conversation. He finished his rum and balanced the enamel mug on the upturned bucket that Stan used as a table.

'Not that long ago there was a blackfella taken sick on a station north of here. The manager brought in the flying doctor. The doctor gave him medicine, said he'd be right as ninepence in no time, but the bastard didn't believe in Western medicine, he reckoned he was a goner. He lay down on his bed and died. Gave up on life, he did, because someone put the influence on him to punish him for some blackfella crime.'

Jon considered Stan's words. Did people still believe in all that stuff?

'You don't believe me, do you?' said Stan.

'It seems a bit weird in this day and age.'

'Well, that's not all of it. There are some who say they have power over white men's minds too, especially people daft enough to get themselves tangled up with blackfella business. I've heard tell of a white fella from Perth who took a piece of Ayers Rock home as a souvenir. He had it on his mantelpiece. After, nothing went right for him, his wife got sick, he lost his job, he got sick, his dog died, so he posted the rock back, sent it airmail and, sure enough, things improved. Blackfella's magic, that's what he believed. He shouldn't have stolen a piece of sacred rock.'

Jon blanched; he felt light-headed. Tjuringas were sort of sacred, weren't they?

'And there's something else,' said Stan. 'Think long and hard before you take up blackfella friendship. They're not like us; they have a different outlook on life. What's theirs is yours and what's yours is theirs. No exceptions. They'll expect you to share all your worldly goods and as you're likely to own more than them you're the one who'll lose out. Aborigines are great ones for not owning stuff. They're the least materialistic people I know.'

'What about Jimmi?'

'What about him? Has he got scars on his legs?'

'Don't think so, but he's related to Curly.'

'Then I'd ask his advice about that tjuringa thing of yours, but take care how you ask and make sure you are on your own at the time. You don't want other blackfellas to overhear. As I've told you before, white fellas have been killed for walking off with sacred objects.'

'I can't do that, Stan. Jimmi's changed. He doesn't speak much, he seems preoccupied.'

'Then I don't know what to suggest. I'd wait and see. Things usually have a way of working out.'

'You've said that before as well, Stan.'

'Have I? I must be getting forgetful in my old age.'

CHAPTER 33

Jon left Stan at midday. It was chess night – it didn't do to be late on Fridays. He picked his way along the valley, avoiding scrub and rock, thinking of Merle and the letter he'd received earlier in the week.

He eased the utility onto the graded road leading to Charlestown and the old salmon gum that marked the turn-off for Jarrahlong.

The graded road between Charlestown and Pilkington wasn't too rutted, it didn't carry much traffic and was a legacy of the old days when Charlestown and Pilkington were gold rush towns and trade was brisk. In the old days water and consumables had to be brought in by bullock and cart, or camels, and merchants made fast money travelling between Southern Cross and the two centres supplying the basics to the miners. But all that had changed. Now, apart from the mail run and locals like him, the road was quiet.

He was mentally replying to Merle's letter, trying to get the wording right about Rachel and Joe, when a young kangaroo bounded out of the bush in front of him. He swerved and braked, stalling the engine. As he restarted the vehicle he noticed a truck parked in the middle of the spinifex plain. Scally's wagon! He let the engine idle, scanning the open country. What was Scally doing so far off the road? He leaned on his horn. Nothing moved. Was Scally in trouble? He shoved the utility into low gear, pulled off the road and followed the tyre tracks, avoiding the rougher patches as Scally had done and parked next to the other vehicle.

Gerry's truck, not Scally's! What the hell was the bloke up to? Gerry didn't seem the type to go hunting. Jon switched off the engine, stepped out of the cab and warily crossed over to the other truck. Gerry was nothing short of unpredictable at the best of times and Gerry with a gun was a lethal combination. There was no kangaroo carcass in the back. Jon scoured the ground looking for clues and noticed the scuff marks and footprints leading away – Gerry's and another set that looked quite different.

A hundred yards further on he found Gerry lying spreadeagled on his back, a spear buried deep in his chest. A cloud of flies flew up as he knelt by the body. He felt for the pulse.

Nothing! Gerry felt cold to the touch – he'd been dead for a while. Jon rolled him on his side. The spear must have gone straight through his heart, there was no blood to speak of, death must have been instantaneous.

Jon sat back on his heels looking at the surprised expression on Gerry's face. Revenge! Whoever had killed Gerry had demanded blood for blood. He'd suspected all along that Gerry was responsible for killing Buni and Wally and he wasn't the only one to think that by the look of things. Gerry loathed Aborigines. He'd beaten up Curly a couple of years back for no good reason. And there had been others.

Jon stared at the spear. The pattern on the shaft was familiar. The hair on the back of his neck prickled. It was Jimmi's, the same one he'd thrown into the back of the utility the day he'd picked him up on the way home from Stan's place.

He looked about him, scanning the horizon. Where was Jimmi now? Hidden among the scrub, watching? Or had he gone back to Jarrahlong? He looked at the spear again. He didn't suppose anyone else would recognise it, apart from Adie and the other stockmen, but if someone did then Jimmi would be arrested, charged with murder and locked up, or even hanged, and what good would that do? It would only stir up resentment among the Aborigines. There'd been no justice for Buni and Wally. He didn't see why it should be any different for Gerry.

He swallowed the sick feeling rising in his gullet. He needed help.

Jon and Stan stood looking down at the body, the spear sticking out of Gerry's chest like a tent pole.

'You want to do what?' said Stan, disbelief making his voice crack.

'Hide the body,' said Jon.

'Why, for God's sake?'

'I know who did it. He's a good bloke and Gerry deserved it.'

Stan gave a long, low whistle. 'Criminal offence to conceal a crime,' he muttered.

'I know, but what happens if we don't.'

Stan took off his battered bush hat and scratched his scalp, his thin hair spiked by the action. 'I don't know, son. It's a hell of a thing to do.'

Jon didn't comment. Stan needed time to think a bit, to get used to the idea.

The spinifex plain seemed quieter to Jon as he waited, only the muted rustling of needle-sharp scrub stirred by the breeze and the high-pitched drone of the blood-crazed flies, disturbed the peace. What he'd proposed was illegal, but then Gerry's killing of the Aborigines was too. That had been murder, he was sure of it, and no one seemed to care – a few questions here, a few written details filed there and the constable was away again, off to investigate cattle rustling from the Kennilworths at Reef Hill Station. Sometimes rough justice was the only way, also he owed Jimmi. Jimmi might have been a miserable so-and-so recently, but he had once saved his life. He remembered the smell of him, the sensation of his head lolling against Jimmi's chest as Jimmi carried him to his horse and held him in his arms on the long ride back to Jarrahlong after Curly died. Alice told him that if it hadn't been for Jimmi he'd have been a goner, his bones picked clean by crows and dingoes and left to litter the outback. No, as far as he could see there was only one option. He scuffed his feet in the dust, poking at a lump of rock with his toe, waiting for Stan's response.

'Who did it?' asked Stan.

'Better if you don't know, Stan, because I'm not a hundred per cent sure.' And he wasn't lying. He didn't know for definite who'd done it. He hadn't seen the killing, he hadn't heard anything recently, but he was absolutely positive about the ownership of the spear. The binding was distinctive. The Aborigines would know who it belonged to.

'What're you planning on doing with Gerry's truck?'

He hadn't thought that far ahead. 'I don't know.'

'You can't leave it here,' said Stan. 'Once it's spotted there'll be a hue and cry. Men will be out looking for him.' He glanced at the ground and scratched his brow. 'You've trampled the place about a bit. Even a good tracker'd be hard pressed to make sense of this lot.'

'There are only the two sets of prints,' said Jon, 'Gerry's and ones that look like someone was wearing slippers.'

'What the heck are you on about?'

'I'll show you, if I can find one.' Jon hunted about for a footprint that he hadn't trampled on. 'There, that's what I mean. Peculiar, isn't it.'

Stan stared down at the mark in the dust. 'Bloody Hell, son!'

Jon winced at the shock in Stan's tone. 'Now what?'

'Exactly,' muttered Stan. 'Now what?' He hunkered down next to the print and examined it for a long moment. 'That,' he said, pointing at the print, 'is a kaditja shoe. They're made of eagle feathers and grass and they're oval in shape so anyone who sees them can't tell which way the kaditja man is travelling. A glimpse of that footprint is enough to make a blackfella's blood run cold.'

'I don't understand what you are getting at.'

'A kaditja man is a tribal executioner,' said Stan, pushing himself to his feet. 'It's his job to act on the instructions of the tribal elders. When a blackfella does something wrong according to Aboriginal law the kaditja man is sent out to exact punishment.'

'But Gerry's not an Aborigine.'

'No,' said Stan, 'that's the odd thing about it. And the other thing is that most kaditja killings are hard to prove anyway. They're skilled at making an execution look like an accidental death. Over Cavanagh's Creek way, five years ago now, a black stockman was found dead in a burnt-out utility truck. It'd crashed into a tree and in the cab were the charred remains of the poor sod and a couple of empty bottles of grog. The official line was that he'd crashed while under the influence and the vehicle had burst into flames on impact. But the police were pretty certain it was a contract killing. Word was he'd messed with another man's wife, violated a sacred tribal law. Anyway, he paid for it with his life.'

'So why did he leave the spear?'

'God only knows – a warning maybe, and if that's the case whoever did it will have long gone. He'll be back on his own tribal lands.' Stan scrubbed at his stubbly chin with gnarled fingers. 'You still want to protect this blackfella?'

Jon nodded.

'I suppose you could drive the truck overland to Galston Gorge on the east side of Jindalee, run it over the edge and hope no one finds it for a time. Old Samuels doesn't keep any sheep or cattle up that end, it's too dry. You'll have to scrub out your tracks and pray to that God of yours that no one spots you.' Stan looked him in the eye. 'It'll be found sooner or later though.'

'Can I get away with it?'

'I reckon so; Gerry won't be the last one to go missing in mysterious circumstances. It's still a lawless place, the outback. They say there's more murder out here than there was in America during prohibition.' Stan leaned on the trailer side. 'Well, son, you've two choices as I see it, dump the bastard down a shaft and conceal the truck or take him into town.'

Jon hesitated briefly. 'Which shaft, Stan?'

'Old Faithful. The structure's rotten to the core; the weight'll collapse the lot in on top of him – that happens and he'll never be found.'

Jon got into the driving seat and, following Stan's directions, drove his utility truck along the track to Old Faithful.

'Why Old Faithful?' asked Jon as he picked a route between the boulders.

'Because it could be relied on to produce nothing no matter how hard the men grafted – that's Aussie humour for you,' said Stan dryly.

Jon backed the utility as close to the mine as he could get without nudging the fragile structure above it.

The kookaburra family cackled softly in the heat and to Jon's ear their muted calls sounded like a rebuke. He shivered and eyed the housing over the shaft, uneasy at its rickety state – a gust of wind and the lot could go. As if to confirm his fears the whole structure creaked ominously, threatening to topple down even as they looked at it.

'Better get on with it,' said Stan.

Neither spoke as they carried Gerry's body to the shaft edge and laid it carefully in the dust. Jon looked down into the mine and smelt the tainted, sour odour of decaying wood and damp rock.

'We get one chance,' said Stan, the sweat slick on his sallow skin. 'Back swing and let go on the forward swing, right? Then scarper because the whole shebang will go.' He glanced up at the rotting timber ravaged by white ants.

Jon followed Stan's glance. 'Ready then?' He bent down and lifted the body under the arms.

Gerry had been a big fella and his body was a dead weight; Jon could feel moisture prickling his forehead as he took the strain. 'Can you manage, Stan? He's heavy.'

Stan coughed up phlegm and spat it out. He grasped Gerry's heels. 'Right, back swing…' he grunted with the effort, '…forward swing…' his breath hissed through clenched teeth, '…go!'

Gerry's body described a ragged arc. It seemed to hang for a moment before it dropped, hitting the props holding the shaft sides as it went.

They both turned and ran for it, listening as the body fell, the dull thud, thud…thud, thud as it bounced off the rotten timber. Then, after an age, came a low creaking sound followed by a sharp crack and a long, slow rumble that built to a crescendo. The rotten structure above the mine shivered like a dying tree felled by an axe. The deep rumble underground belched a sour stench. Dust billowed. Muck spewed out of the hole. Then, the decaying timber sighed and collapsed, wood and metal splintering and grinding as it fell in on itself, burying the shaft head in a jagged mound of lumber and twisted metal.

They stood silently, watching the dust subside, listening to the dying moans as rock and wood settled in an uneasy peace a hundred feet beneath them.

Jon wiped his brow on his sleeve, conscious that he had the shakes. He clenched his fists. The man was already dead. Did it matter where they buried him?

Stan turned away and walked across to some scrubby bushes. He snapped off half a dozen branches and threw them into the back of the utility truck.

Late afternoon they were back at Gerry's truck.

'Better get a move on,' said Stan. He placed an old twelve-bore shotgun in the passenger footwell of Gerry's truck and threw an empty rum bottle onto the seat.

'What you doing?'

'Gerry was out hunting, wasn't he?'

'Was he?' said Jon.

Stan slammed the passenger door shut and walked across to Jon's ute. 'Here.' He handed over half the scrubby branches. 'You know where you're heading?'

'Galston Gorge,' said Jon.

'The south end, it's narrower there, dog-rough terrain and lots of thick scrub. No one's likely to go sniffing around and it should buy us time if nothing else. Park Gerry's truck on the lip, get out, then shove her into gear, let the handbrake off and jump clear. If anyone finds it they'll think he was hunting and accidentally drove over the edge. Can you do that?'

'Yeah.'

'Then make your way back here. Scrub out your footprints, the tyre tracks, everything, and let's hope time does the rest. I'll take the ute to the road and wait for you. All right, son?'

'What happens when they don't find a body?'

'It won't be the first time. They'll think he tried to walk out and died in the bush or else they'll think dingoes ate him. Either way we'll be in the clear.'

The gorge was half a mile away. Jon gentled the truck across the plain, avoiding the bigger rocks and the worst of the spinifex. He concentrated on driving, keeping an eye on the sun sinking in the west, conscious of the size of it, bigger as it reached the horizon, a huge vermilion ball, fire-red in a turquoise sky. Once the damn thing set he wouldn't be able to see the bloody tyre tracks, never mind scrub them out.

At the gorge edge he halted the vehicle and got out, leaving the engine idling. Then, standing on the running board, he reached in with his left foot and pressed down on the clutch, slipped the truck into gear and jumped clear. The truck lurched forward, hung for a long moment on the lip then toppled, engine growling as the whole lot nose-dived the short distance to the gorge floor.

It landed with a deafening crash. Finches and budgerigars, settling for the night, exploded out of bushes, shrieking their alarm calls. Below him the vehicle shuddered, held its position for a few seconds and toppled sideways, its free wheels spinning, the engine dead as the vehicle was swallowed up in a sea of mulga, leaving only the nervous magpies and butcher-birds disturbing the quiet.

He set off back to the road, scrubbing out his footprints and the tyre tracks, threading his way between low-growing saltbush, spinifex, cassia, and small bushes with needle-sharp thorns that shredded skin faster than a cut-throat razor in the hand of an amateur. It wouldn't do to leave bloody marks on a job like this!

At the murder site he rubbed out all the footprints he could see taking extra care over the place where Gerry's body had lain. Then, when he reached the road, he flopped onto the passenger seat, sweating and exhausted. 'It's no good, Stan, you can tell.'

'Maybe, maybe not. It depends on whether it rains and on how long it is before anyone drives out this way looking for him. Seems to me you did a good enough job this end.'

'What if someone else saw Gerry's truck?'

'You'd better pray to that God of yours that they haven't.'

Stan drove them back to the turn-off for his place and did a three-point turn. 'I'll make me own way back; I need to clear my head.' He stepped out of the utility. 'I wouldn't want you to be late for Alice's chess.'

'Already am, Stan.'

'Then you'd better tell her I delayed you.' Stan gave him a half salute as Jon slid into the driving seat. 'Be seeing you, son.'

At Jarrahlong Jon went straight to the stockmen's quarters. Big'un, Mick and Dave were sitting on the bunkhouse steps, smoking, their conversation muted.

'Jimmi inside?'

'Nah,' said Mick.

'Is he in the barn then?'

'Nah, ain't seen him for a couple of days.'

Jon opened the door and scanned the room – empty. 'Where's Yildilla?'

Dave pointed to the paddock.

Yildilla was over by the great jarrah trees. From a distance it was difficult to make out detail in the moonlight. 'What's he doing?'

'Sitting,' said Dave.

Jon hesitated, sensing their unease, their reluctance to be drawn. He crossed to the corral fence and leaned on it, watching the old Aborigine sitting with his back to the homestead, looking out towards the bush. Who was he waiting for? Was he mixed up in Gerry's killing?

Was Stan right? Was Yildilla an executioner? Had he been Jimmi's accomplice in Gerry's death or was there another reason for his presence? It was clear to everyone that Yildilla wasn't used to working with stock, and he wasn't comfortable on a horse, but he was good at tracking. He'd heard Adie tell Alice that the old fella could track a bilby in a sandstorm, and the others respected him. There were things about the bloke that didn't add up.

Jon glanced up at the moon. Alice would be waiting.

'What kept you?' she asked when he sat down.

'Stan,' said Jon, opening the bottle of cold beer she had put ready for him.

'Don't know why that silly old bugger doesn't give up and move into town,' said Alice.

'Perhaps because he's as stubborn as you are,' said Jon too tired and distracted to be polite.

Alice looked askance but said nothing and made the first move.

Jon found it hard to concentrate. He kept hearing the mineshaft collapsing in on itself and imagining Gerry's body mangled and crushed beneath tons of rubble, but worst was the spear sticking out of Gerry's chest, and the sucking noise and soft hiss of escaping air when Stan removed it.

Jimmi's spear! He'd thrown it into the back of the utility. He should get rid of it, snap off the shaft, burn the wood and bury the head. He wished he'd thought to drop it down the mine along with Gerry's body.

Alice conceded the game.

'Why?' he asked.

'Because you're not concentrating.' She leaned back in her seat. 'Has he had you down that mine of his?'

'No.'

'Well, you look like you've had a hard day.'

'It's the beer, Alice. It's gone to my head.'

'Haven't you eaten?'

'No.'

She peered at him over her glasses. 'Anything you want to tell me?'

'No.'

'Then get yourself something to eat and go to bed. You look done in.'

In the kitchen he cut himself a few slices of cold roast beef and a couple of rounds of bread. He slapped the whole together into a sandwich, carried it across to the utility and laid it on the bonnet while he went to get the spear, but the weapon had gone.

He spun round and peered into the moonlight. Was someone watching from the shadows? But the night was quiet, only the ticking of the windmill turning gently and the trickle of water overflowing from the holding tank disturbed the peace.

Silently he pushed open the bunkhouse door. Jimmi's bed was empty. The others were sleeping. He closed the door convinced that Yildilla was awake and watchful. Had Jimmi come back after all, or had Yildilla taken the spear and hidden it?

He found Old Yella sitting by the front wheel, the sandwich long gone.

'You thief,' he muttered and pulled at the dog's ears. She licked his hand and followed him over to his lean-to. Before he got into bed he checked that Curly's tjuringa was still where he had hidden it. He rewrapped the carved mulga-wood board and put it back into its hiding place. Was that why Yildilla had turned up, to retrieve the tjuringa? Would he be the next one to die, a spear through his chest? He shivered. There was so much he didn't know about Aboriginal law.

That night he couldn't sleep and by morning he knew he couldn't put it off for much longer, the sooner he was rid of Curly's tjuringa the better. It had to be returned, and soon, otherwise he'd never have peace of mind.

CHAPTER 34

Jon scrutinized the horizon looking for signs of sheep, a frown creasing his brow. They found a small mob mid-morning over by Corkwood Bore with only a handful of lambs, well down on the numbers they'd docked and castrated earlier in the year.

They spent the rest of the day looking for other mobs which had followed their noses away from the main flock, seeking fresh grazing. Now, late in the day, Jon realised they had a problem, and they hadn't even reached the main flock. Two smaller mobs had yielded the same results, ewes without lambs, dozens of them.

'At this rate it'll take ten years to restock,' said Jon. 'Alice won't be pleased. What do you think has happened to them?'

'Dingoes,' said Adie.

'How can you tell? We haven't found any carcasses.'

'One of the stockmen at Jindalee said they'd moved south. It's the drought,' said Adie. 'Dingoes do well then, plenty of meat. It don't take long for the numbers to rise. Need to get the dogger over quick.'

'Dogger? What the hell's a dogger?'

'Bloke who goes after dingoes,' said Adie.

Jon was busy replacing damaged paddock fencing with Adie in readiness for the shearing when Constable Nickson arrived.

'What's he after?' muttered Adie.

Jon dropped his hammer into the bucket of nails; he'd wondered how long it would be before the police turned up. 'I'll be back in a minute or two, Adie.'

Nickson was talking to Alice. He looked up as Jon approached. 'Just the fella I came to see!'

Belle appeared on the verandah carrying a pot of tea, mugs and sugar.

'Black and sweet, that's how I like it,' commented Nickson.

Jon poured and handed round the mugs of tea.

'So, what can we do for you?' asked Alice.

'It's about Gerry Worrall. He's been missing for ten days now and his mate, Josef Kowalski, from over Pilkington way, says he wouldn't take off without telling anyone. He thinks something's happened, and that's what other people are saying too. Les for one. He reckons it's not like Gerry to leave his wages behind and I'm inclined to agree with him.'

'So, what's this got to do with us?' asked Alice.

'Well, it seems Gerry had a run in with one or two people, young Jon here, for one.'

'That's right,' said Alice. 'Gerry beat Jon up when he was drunk, a couple of years back.'

'What was it over?'

'He was shoving Curly around,' said Jon.

'Curly?'

'One of my black stockmen,' said Alice. 'He's dead now.'

Nickson inclined his head. 'I'd heard about that. Not long before the big bush fire, wasn't it? You were lucky to get out of that alive, I hear – that right?'

'Yes,' said Jon, 'but I never had anything to do with Gerry.'

'I'm not saying you did. All I'm doing is seeing people who might have had a grudge.'

'I didn't like the bloke, anyone will tell you that. But I wouldn't kill him if that's what you're getting at.'

'Now, why would I be thinking he's dead?' asked Nickson.

'Stands to reason,' said Alice, 'if he's been missing for ten days.'

Jon bit his lip and wished he'd kept his mouth shut.

'Well, it's a possibility, I can't deny that, but I'm hoping he's gone on a bender and forgotten to come back,' said Nickson.

'Can't see that,' said Alice, 'not Gerry, he likes his home comforts too much.'

'When did you last see him?'

'Me?' asked Jon.

'Yeah.'

'When I was last in Charlestown picking up supplies for Alice, about a month ago. He was in the Agricultural Supplies loading up his wagon for a trip out to Jeb Samuels' place. Les was there. He'll tell you.'

'You didn't meet up with him at Stan's place later?'

'No. Why?'

'Some say Gerry was interested in the gold that Stan keeps about the place.'

'Whatever Gerry was, he wasn't a thief,' said Alice. 'I can't see him stealing from Stan.'

'No, perhaps not,' said Nickson. He finished off his tea, picked up his hat and stood up. 'I'll be getting along. There are a few more people I want to see.'

He took his time sauntering down the steps. At the bottom he hitched up his trousers and lit a cigarette before getting into his vehicle.

'Do you know anything about Gerry's disappearance?' asked Alice as they watched the dust from Nickson's ute settle.

'No.'

'What about Stan?'

'How should I know?'

He didn't like the way she watched him as he went back to his fencing. That was the trouble with Alice; he didn't know what she was thinking half the time.

The dogger rode into the homestead yard on a rangy, dun-coloured horse with a wall eye, leading a nondescript-looking pack horse, a week after Alice sent out word on the bush telegraph.

The dogger dismounted in the yard, tethered his horses to the post and rail fencing, flapped his battered bushman's hat against his thigh and walked across to the bungalow looking like a bloke who had spent all his life in the saddle.

'Hello there, Mrs Macarthur, me dad sends his regards.' He turned to Jon and appraised him openly. 'Whatcha mate,' he said. He wiped his hand down his chaps and extended it to Jon. The handshake went on forever. 'Nice to meetcha,' he added. 'Nice to meetcha.'

'Take a seat,' said Alice. 'How's your father?'

'Can't complain,' said the dogger, 'stiffens up ever since he fell off his horse and did his hip in. He hasn't been what you'd call right since, but he'll live.'

'This is Jon,' said Alice, 'Jon, this is Ty.'

'Ty?' said Jon, the beginnings of a quip on his tongue.

'Yeah, me mam liked the films, named me after a bloke called Tyrone Power…senior,' he added belligerently, staring Jon in the eye, daring him to smile.

Jon kept his face straight. He'd never met a Tyrone before.

Tyrone Henderson looked all of twenty-two and like most of the fellas in the area he was a big bloke, six foot something and broad with it. He'd have been pretty if he hadn't had a long scar crossing his cheek diagonally from his left eyebrow down towards the corner of his mouth, as it was the scar gave a sardonic cast to his features. The disfigurement, together with tawny eyes and the thatch of sandy hair, was unsettling. There was something of the wolf about him.

'Gather you've got a problem, Mrs Macarthur,' said Tyrone.

'Lost over a third of the lambs,' said Alice.

Tyrone nodded. 'They've the same problem over at Wanndarah and Jindalee as well as at Cavanagh's Creek Station. You're right to get a grip on things before it gets out of hand and they start killing off your breeding stock. Okay if I sleep in the bunkhouse overnight and get me stuff sorted out for an early start?'

'What exactly are you planning to do?' asked Jon.

'Kill the bastards. Shoot, trap, poison, any ways I can.'

'Traps legal?' asked Jon.

'Too right they are. Government wants rid of vermin and they don't mind how you do it. You want to take a ride? See how it's done?'

'That's not a bad idea,' said Alice. 'You can teach Jon and then I won't have to pay your extortionate rates.'

Tyrone chuckled deep in his throat. 'Takes more than a bit of poisoned bait to catch dingoes. I reckon me job's safe for a few more years, don't you, Mrs Macarthur?'

'So,' said Alice, her eyes watchful, 'how would you like a couple of weeks off, Jon?'

He remembered the last trip, when she'd sent him on walkabout with Curly. He hesitated too long. She took it as a yes.

'You could do with a break. Give you time to think things through,' she said pointedly.

She was alluding to Rachel, waiting for them to name the day. Well, she could wait, but a couple of weeks hunting dingoes would get him out of the way for a while, until the Gerry business blew over. Two more weeks and Gerry would be old news, especially when they didn't find a body. 'Suits me,' he said.

Ty led the way on his horse, leading the pack animal. Jon followed on Red. They crossed the creek at Sandy Spit and headed deeper into the bush.

'We'll be away for a month, maybe more,' called Ty over his

shoulder. 'You okay with that?'

'Yes.' A month was even better, and anyway he could hardly turn back to Jarrahlong now, word would soon get out on the bush telegraph that he didn't pass muster as a dogger's assistant.

They reached the mob late in the afternoon and set up camp not far from a billabong.

'You want to see what dingoes do to sheep then folla me,' said Ty. He set off on foot, skirting the mob, his eyes inspecting the undergrowth. 'See here?' He pointed to broken vegetation and a few tufts of wool caught on broken branches. 'And this.' He hunkered down and cleared away debris, revealing deep prints in the earth, the toes splayed where there had been a struggle.

'Not much blood,' said Jon.

'Doesn't mean anything,' said Ty.

They moved on to open ground and watched the sheep grazing. At the back of the flock a ewe hobbled behind the rest of the mob.

'You reckon she's injured?'

'Maybe,' said Jon, 'it's hard to tell. She could be lame.'

'I reckon she's got a bad injury. You can see dried blood on her. The buggers go for the rear end. A bite near the bum soon gets infected and the animal dies a slow death. He raised his rifle, took aim and felled the animal where she stood, as if poleaxed. The rest of the mob scattered.

Ty took a knife from his belt and cut her throat. Blood arced into the dust. He skinned the animal. Deep bite marks punctured the flesh on the flanks. 'I'm surprised it didn't die from shock,' he said as he butchered the meat.

'Why do they go for the rump?' asked Jon, avoiding the sheep's dead eyes. Already the bright blood had darkened, attracting flies crazed by the sweet, metallic smell. Jon shuddered, remembering what Merle had once said, that killing was always killing at the end of the day. Would he ever get used to it?

'They don't usually, except for rams who'll turn and face them and fight. They normally go for the throat and the windpipe where all the vital blood vessels are, but if the sheep are running away from them then they bite at the back legs, that's when you see the sort of damage on the ewe.'

Back at camp they unpacked a skillet and Ty opened a tin of steak, added water, tossed in a pinch or two of salt and a cube of dried meat extract. 'Makes for better gravy,' he said. 'Flour's in the saddlebag and the camp oven is over there.' He pointed to a wooden box that he'd unloaded earlier in the day.

'What's wrong with that?' asked Jon, indicating the slab of meat Ty had carried back from the carcass.

'Nah, mate, it's for bait, can't eat that, it'll be tainted from the dog bite.'

While the stew simmered Ty opened up another, smaller box made of galvanised steel and lifted out a tightly wrapped package.

'You be careful with this little wrapper, Jon. Leave you with your lips drawn back from your teeth like a long-dead corpse.' On a piece of flat rock he chopped up the mutton and laced it with poison. 'Strychnine,' he added. 'It gives the buggers belly ache.'

Over the next ten days they set traps and laid baited meat. They shot a couple of dingoes that got within Ty's gunsight, and tracked the pack deep into the outback, travelling on from Alice's land over Jindalee and Wanndarah and on to the Harrison Station.

Ty only spoke when spoken to and Jon wondered why he'd agreed to let him tag along if he didn't want the company, until he realised the dogger had got out of the habit. Adie too was the silent type, not big on conversation, not like Curly who could have talked a camel into submission.

He tried to imagine the life Ty led, month after month, year after year, a solitary bushman hunting dingo and feral dogs, travelling the vast outback tracts with only his horses for company. Was it any life for a young fella? Perhaps he should try harder, find out more about Ty and what made him tick, how he coped with the loneliness.

'That it?' asked Jon as Ty finished baiting the last trap of the day.

'Nah, mate, tomorra we head back the way we come and check the traps.'

'For dingoes?'

'Yep, and for kangaroos, crows and bungarras. Bet you a bob that some other vermin's got himself caught. Need to shift them pretty quick, every time we catch a wrong un it's one less dingo scalp.'

Scalping – he'd nearly thrown up the first time he saw Adie scalp a dingo. He hadn't been expecting it and watching him take off the ears along with the scalp between them as well as a strip along the backbone including the tail had reminded him of a western film he'd seen at the Majestic with Billy Wainwright, when an American Indian had scalped a white settler. He hadn't seen the deed done, just the Indian grasping the settler's hair, and the knife, and then the scalp held aloft in a bloodstained hand. He'd had nightmares for a week after. Too vivid an imagination he'd heard Gran say to his mam one night when he couldn't sleep for fear of getting slaughtered in his own bed.

'Why do you scalp them? To keep a tally?'

'No, the Government pays a bounty. Dingo predation's a real problem, and not only in Western Australia but all over the country. They built the dog-proof fence back in the 1880s because of it.'

'In Western Australia?'

'Nah, from Dalby in Queensland to the Eyre Peninsula in South Australia. It didn't work. Still plenty of dingoes. They tried the same thing over here with the rabbit fence. That doesn't work either.'

'How much does the Government pay?'

'A pound a scalp.'

So that was why Adie had done it, no doubt he sold the scalps on to doggers like Ty.

'My dad made a fair living trappin' dingos,' volunteered Ty. 'He started out in the Northern Territory and then moved on into Western Australia. He'd trade with the Aborigines: sugar, flour, tobacco and tools for scalps. On one trip he traded several hundred scalps. That was a lot of money in those days.'

'When was that?'

'Pretty late on. He'd been a stockman out Oodnadatta way in South Australia, travelling from station to station, mustering, crutching, shearing, digging wells, that sort of thing. Then came the depression in the twenties and thirties. Lots of blokes abandoned their stations in the Great Depression. Dad found himself out of work so he bought himself a camel and went off for months at a time, travelling through South Australia and then in the Northern Territory, trapping and trading. Then one day he decided to move further west, he settled near Coolgardie first and then moved north to Wiluna. Western Australia paid a bigger bounty, a pound over against seven shillin' and sixpence.'

'He still a dogger?'

'Nah, got sick of it in the end. He sniffed out a good spot south-east of Pilkington. Reckoned water wasn't too deep and dug a well. Government granted him a hundred square miles leased for next to nothing and gave him a two hundred pound cash reward. He used the money to buy stock. Been there ever since.'

'On his own?'

Ty shook his head. 'He's livin' with Gracie, an Aborigine woman. They got a bunch of half-castes between them.'

'What about your mam?'

'She died having me.'

Jon drank his tea, looking into the embers of the fire, thinking about having half-castes for family. Ty didn't seem that bothered. He thought of Liverpool and attitudes back home, when he was a kid. Albert White, his best friend, was Jamaican. And he knew several half-caste kids from his primary school days, but neither the blacks nor the whites really approved of mixed marriages. He seemed to recall lots of tutting going on when Annie Chambers went out with Albert's elder brother and in the end they split up – family pressure from both sides.

He tried to imagine what it would be like married to an Aborigine and couldn't. The only Aboriginal women he knew were Belle, old and ugly, and Mick's wife, Doris, younger and, he supposed, better looking, and Curly aside, none of his family had been what he'd call pretty.

His thoughts drifted to the time he'd been at the green pool, where he'd seen the Aboriginal girl. She'd been a looker. She hadn't been what you'd call dark-skinned, and her hair was light, a copper-blonde. He'd wondered then which mob she belonged to because he hadn't seen any Aboriginals living in the area or crossing Alice's land at the time.

'You got a problem, mate?'

'No,' said Jon, a shade too quickly.

They sat in silence for a while, Jon not knowing how to break the tension.

'It's a harsh place, the bush,' said Ty eventually; he swept his mug of tea in an arc taking in the whole of the country before him, 'not enough women to go round.'

'That's what Wes says, he reckons it's a crook place for a woman.'

'He's not wrong there,' agreed Ty.

'You married?'

'Nah. Not met the right Abo yet,' said Ty sarcastically. He threw the dregs into the sand, rolled onto his feet and disappeared into the bush.

Jon heard Ty relieving himself. What was wrong with the bloke? Why was he so touchy?

* * *

A week later Ty led them into a broad valley. It reminded Jon of Stan's place with its abandoned mine workings.

'What's it called?'

'Gilbert's Find,' said Ty.

'Made a bloody mess of it, didn't he?' commented Jon.

Ty turned towards him, his look long and penetrating, his brow creased in a frown. 'What d'you mean?'

Jon couldn't understand Ty's prickliness especially when it came to anything about the land or family. Thin-skinned, that's what he was. Graham Eastham, one of his old mates from Liverpool was the same, took everything the wrong way, saw slights where none had been intended. Well, pussy-footing around wasn't his style. 'Gilbert a relative of yours or something?'

'What if he is?' snapped Ty.

'Still doesn't make it right, digging up a place and leaving it like a bloody wilderness.'

'It is a bloody wilderness, mate – far as you can see – the whole bloody Never Never's a wilderness.'

'You don't know what you're talking about,' said Jon.

The scar on Ty's face puckered when he pulled his lips back and spoke through gritted teeth. 'You're a bloody newcomer, mate, don't you go tellin' me I don't know what I'm talkin' about.'

Jon pulled up his horse. That was it! He'd had enough! Just because he was a Pom didn't mean he didn't have a right to a point of view. 'For God's sake look at the place…that Gilbert fella has chewed the guts out of it…rusting metal, mangled machinery, spoil all over the place it looks like a…a…' He flung his hands up in frustration at the closed look on Ty's face, and his inability to explain how he felt about the devastated valley. 'Sod you, Ty!' He spun his horse round and followed the trail back the way they had come. What would Curly have said? He remembered the old mine at Murrin Murrin. It was well named. In the book of Exodus God sent murrain on the land, killing the Egyptian cattle and Murrin Murrin had been destroyed too. Whoever had named the place had probably been thinking of the Bible passage, but there and again Murrin Murrin was more likely to be an old Aboriginal name and had nothing to do with God's plagues. He crossed himself as he left the valley behind him.

After a time Ty overtook him and resumed the lead, checking the traps as they went, emptying them of dead animals, and killing those that were still alive, scalping the dingoes and re-baiting the traps. When they reached the border between Jarrahlong Station and Jindalee they set up camp.

'Follow me,' said Ty after Jon had put the damper in the camp oven to cook. Jon dusted off his hands on his trousers and followed.

Ty led the way along the line of the limestone ridge that overlooked the plain they had recently crossed. Underneath an overhang Jon noticed the faded marks of Aboriginal paintings, but Ty didn't comment and if he saw them he gave no indication.

They climbed higher, gradually ascending the outcrop. Below the summit of the ridge Ty stopped and patted the rock face. There, clearly visible, was a wall of Aboriginal art. Elongated human figures hunting with spears, animals in x-ray detail depicted in red ochre. It was like Paradise Canyon all over again, except these figures were faded; no one had visited to retouch the images and leave new hand prints behind.

'Who did these?'

'No one knows, maybe an Aboriginal tribe that's died out, no one's been here in a long while, but I reckon it was once an important place sometime in the past. There are drawings everywhere on this stretch of rock, but these are the best.'

'Why're you showing me these?'

'Reckoned you'd appreciate them.'

'What makes you think that?'

'Gilbert's Find.'

Jon glanced at Ty, surprised by his reply.

'He wasn't no relative, just a bloody vandal, like you said,' said Ty. He held out a hand. 'Mates?'

Jon shook it. 'Mates,' he said.

Jon stayed with Ty over the next three days and on the last night over a meal of spit-roasted bungarra and damper Jon asked him about his Aboriginal family.

'Learnt everything I know about dingoes from Gracie's family and about the land. Dad's the same. He reckons you can't beat an Aboriginal tracker.'

'How come your dad ended up with an Aborigine?'

'Not enough white women to go round,' said Ty, 'not in the bush…lots of blokes finished up with black women and had kids and then abandoned them when they found themselves white wives. Dad's not like that though, he reckons married is married whether it's blessed by the priest or not. Mind you, Gracie's good-looking, taller than most and with light skin, and me half-brothers and half-sister are all better looking than me. And then there's the law. It's caused right upset in our house. Dad's got away with it so far, but no telling how long that'll last.'

'What do you mean?'

'Constable Barnes, Dad and him go way back. Dad pays him a backhander not to mention his domestic arrangements.'

'Why?'

'So they don't take Bindi away.'

'Who's Bindi?'

'My half-sister. Gracie's youngest.'

It was getting complicated. Curly had mentioned something about his aunts being taken away to Settlement School because they were half-castes. He changed the subject. 'How did you cut your face?'

Ty ran his fingers down the scar. 'Happened out Oodnadatta way, when I was a kid. Dad had had a skinful in the bar and got into a brawl. The other bloke pulled a knife on him and I stepped between them. The bloke sliced my face open. Dad took the knife off him and stuck him in the guts with it, then he scooped me up in his arms and did a runner, heading north-west to Alice Springs, and then later we left the Northern Territory and travelled south-west to Coolgardie. Stitched me up himself, he did. Got me drunk on grog, washed out the wound with it and took a needle and thread from his housewife for the sewing. He reckoned I was as good as new within a week.'

Ty flung the tea dregs into the ashes. 'You think you'll make a dogger?'

Jon grinned. 'Nah, I reckon your job's safe for the time being.'

'That's all right then, I wouldn't like competition.'

'Does the job ever take you out Mullin Soak way?'

'No. Why?'

'I've got to go out there sometime soon and find an Aboriginal family and return something.'

Ty glanced up sharply. 'What sort of something?'

'A tjuringa. A mate of mine was dying and he gave it to me to look after, but I think it should go back to his family. You know about tjuringas?'

'Not much.'

'Stan says I've to watch my back. He reckons Aborigines can be funny about white folk having their stuff.'

'Don't know about that, but according to Dad you have to be

pretty careful about having anything to do with a Kulpidji.'

'What's a Kulpidji?'

'It's the most sacred object of the Western Desert tribes.'

'Is it like a tjuringa?'

'Nah. Tjuringas are small. Kulpidji is a piece of carved board, twelve foot or so long and about eight-to-ten inches wide and an inch deep and it's carved with lots of symbols. It's a sort of recorded history of the tribe that contains all the knowledge of the ancestors and the rights to their lands that other tribes respect and honour.'

'What? Like a kind of tribal title deed?'

'Suppose so. And the women aren't allowed to see it. It'd kill them if they did, they'd sort of wither and die. And if one tribe steals another's kulpidji they destroy the tribe's right to life.'

'What about tjuringas?'

'I don't know much about them.'

Ty's information put a different slant on things, maybe taking the tjuringa to Curly's family was the last thing he should do.

Ty unrolled his swag and was soon asleep.

Jon leaned back against a rock and finished his tea, thinking about Curly's tjuringa. Should he do as Stan said and burn it, or was there a better option? Bury it in Curly's grave perhaps, or return it to the place Curly got it from. He was still trying to make up his mind when he fell asleep.

CHAPTER 35

A month or so later, after his trip with Ty, Jon was sitting on the verandah with Alice watching the sun sink behind the great jarrah trees.

'Hear that?' said Alice.

'What?'

'Circadas. It's a pretty sound.'

He sat, sipping a cold beer, listening to the chirruping out in the bush. 'There's nothing like it in England, except grasshoppers.' Not that he could recall ever seeing or hearing a grasshopper.

Alice chortled. 'Nothing like.'

'Why did you come out to Australia, Alice?'

She lit up a cheroot. 'It's a long story.'

Stan had told him a bit, but that didn't explain why she'd left home so young, she hadn't been that much older than him, and then there was the farm back in England where her family lived. He smiled as he recalled Stan's words.

'What're you grinning at?' asked Alice.

'Something Stan said.'

'And what was that?'

'He said you were as pretty as paint...that you had a slick, silver tongue and liked a bit of banter.'

'Did he now.'

The muted light from the kerosene lamp in the parlour cast a soft glow on Alice's face, illuminating a gentle smile.

'I was only a girl in those days, and with a baby, but it was Jack who was the sticking point, my father didn't approve of him. He was dead set on me marrying Thomas Challinor's son.' She took a sip of whiskey. 'He owned the farm down the road. The fact that he was twenty years older and a confirmed bachelor didn't come into it. Anyway, I fell for Jack.'

'Was Jack a farmer?'

‘No, according to my father he wasn’t much better than a gypsy.’

‘So how did you meet him?’

‘He turned up for the harvest. In those days you hired a man with specialist equipment for however long it took, and when Harry Johnson retired, Jack took over his business. I remember the day he arrived in our yard driving a great steam traction engine and pulling a threshing machine and an elevator behind him.’ She smiled at the memory. ‘It was a stinking hot day in late August. Father had been panicking because the barometer was dropping. Anyway, Father took against Jack from the first, called him a cocky so-and-so, and perhaps he was, but Jack was a grafter, there was no doubt about that, he could do the work of two men and not break out in a sweat.’

‘I don’t know anything about harvesting,’ said Jon.

‘Threshing is backbreaking, dusty work. By the end of the day everyone looks like a black, and by the end of the week you’re glad to see the back of it, and then the party begins, too much ginger beer for your health, never mind your senses. Anyway…’

He waited. Why had she stopped telling the tale? ‘Did you do something daft?’

‘You could say that. I got myself in the family way.’

‘What did you do?’

‘Ran away with Jack. Dad threatened to run him through with a pitchfork. He said I was to give Jack up, that they’d raise the baby. When I refused he told me to leave. So I left. After a few months on the road Jack sold the steam engine and all the threshing equipment and we emigrated. Been here ever since.’

‘What made you decide to come here?’

‘Jack had a distant relative in Western Australia and he also knew a bloke in Perth doing road building. The plan was for him to get a job driving a steamroller, but it didn’t work out. We ended up on a station over near Gwalia working for a meat company. Jack was manager, talked himself into the job, he did, and we made a packet, then, later, in 1908, we took a lease on this place. We decided we’d learn about sheep as we went along. We thought it would be easy.’ She laughed. ‘Trouble is the outback isn’t for the faint-hearted.’

‘When you took out the lease, Alice, who did you take it over from?’

‘What do you mean?’

‘Who owned Jarrahlong before you?’

‘No one. It was virgin territory, bush as far as you could see.’

'So, what did you do?'

She drew on the cheroot, held it for a moment and then exhaled slowly. 'Well, Jack turned to me and said: What d'ya reckon, gal? And I said, if it's all right by you then it's all right by me, so Jack went along to the Land Registry and took out a pastoral lease, then, when he got back, we built a shack right here where we are now. It was pretty basic, dirt floors at first, tin walls and roof; we were baking during the day and freezing at night. We had water from the creek and a shovel for a dunny, then, after we'd got a roof over our heads, Jack went and bought breeding ewes and some rams and a few cattle for our own use and we turned 'em loose and prayed.'

'What about the Aborigines?'

'What about them?'

Jon hesitated, put off by the sudden aggression in her voice and the hostility in her eyes.

'Well, lad, what you getting at?'

He was treading on shaky ground, he hadn't expected her reaction.

'Well?'

He breathed deep and then said what was on his mind. 'Didn't you and Jack think it might belong to someone?'

'Like who?'

'The Aborigines.'

'Don't talk daft, blackfellas don't own land, they only move across it hunting kangaroo, and my sheep when the mood takes them, and picking berries and wild yams.'

'But they were here first.'

'Government wouldn't have leased it to us if it wasn't Crown land to lease,' she snapped. 'And I've a piece of paper to say I'm the lessee and that's the end of the matter.' Alice dragged ferociously on her cheroot, the tip glowing crimson against the brown stub until she'd smoked it down to her fingertips. 'Time I turned in, and you've got an early start. Shut the door after you.'

Jon put his empty beer bottle on the table. 'See you in the morning, Alice.'

She didn't answer.

Jon strolled across to the home paddock fence and stood watching Daisy and Red and the other horses dozing over near the barn. He'd upset Alice and really rattled her asking about the land and the Aborigines.

Her reaction surprised him. All the stockmen at Jarrahlong were Aborigines until he turned up and he knew she wouldn't have gone looking for a white manager despite what she'd once said. She paid them well too, more than the going rate and she didn't mind Aboriginal families squatting in the humpies down by the creek. Was it guilty conscience? Was that what had made her voice sharp? Deep down did she know that the land wasn't the Government's to lease to anyone?

He looked up at the Southern Cross. There were matters he didn't fully understand, prejudices that he hadn't considered. Alice and Jack probably hadn't given the Aborigines a thought, probably hadn't even seen any when they signed the lease. It might have been years before she realised Aborigines lived on the land she called hers.

It wasn't an easy situation, Aborigines on the one side, Pastoralists on the other; people like Jack and Alice who'd sunk their own money and their whole lives into creating a viable station, in good faith, to raise sheep on marginal land far out in the bush. Jon's head throbbed thinking about it, but one thing was certain, there was no way of resolving the dilemma. Someone would always lose out. He turned away from the paddock. Across the way the light was on in Rachel's bedroom. Rachel wasn't keen on Aborigines, neither was her father. Had he been unfair to Alice?

At dawn they rode out to muster the sheep for shearing. It was always a big job bringing them back to the homestead and the paddock adjacent to the shearing shed. Mostly, when there was work to do with the flock they created temporary yards and didn't always bring them back to the home paddock.

As usual the sheep were spread over a large area. They had separated out into smaller mobs and had wandered off into the bush but he knew where the sheep preferred to graze and so did the station dogs.

He quite liked rounding up the sheep. Riding had become second nature to him over the months and he couldn't imagine the days when he hadn't been comfortable on a horse. There wasn't much more a bloke needed than a horse, a good dog and a job that occupied his mind and his time. Adie was the same, happiest when out in the bush working with the sheep.

Adie had told him all about the shearing, how the men were booked year on year, arriving like clockwork, a blast of fresh air, bringing their rough humour and news from other stations – a highlight in the year, according to Alice. And after the shearing was the party. Alice wouldn't be drawn on the party. You'll find out soon enough was all she'd say.

Jon inspected the sheep. Merinos – good lambing sheep with a heavy clip. He thought the fleeces looked all right, but he couldn't tell whether it was a good year for wool or not as some of the sheep had lighter more open coats and others close ones. A couple of old wethers looked as though they'd missed the last shearing, overlooked on the muster, no doubt.

Once in the home paddock it would be easy enough to bring the animals down to the holding pens and the shearing yards in batches.

Alice was leaning against the fence with Rachel and Joe when they got back, keen to see the first of the flock. The men, tired, but cheerful, raised their hats as they rode their horses towards the unsaddling corral. Jon reined in next to Alice.

'You got them all?'

'No telling, Alice. We must have missed a few.'

He dismounted and saw Rachel's troubled face. The next few days should be interesting, he thought, perhaps by the end of the shearing he'd know who had fathered Joe.

CHAPTER 36

Early next morning Jon leaned on the yard fence next to Alice looking across the home paddock at the Merinos they'd brought in from the bush. A flock of crested pigeons, top-knots, Alice called them, their metallic-purple wing flashes glinting, muttered over their heads and landed in a wet patch near to a water trough. He liked this time of the day when it was still cool. He glanced briefly at the lone currawong greeting the day from the top of the old gum tree and turned back to the sheep.

'Nice mob,' he said, 'it should be a good clip.'

'It needs to be to pay off my debts,' said Alice, 'rebuilding doesn't come cheap.'

'At least you didn't have to rebuild the shearing shed.'

'No, thank goodness, we'd have been back to shearing in the open air otherwise.'

The shearing team arrived soon after on the back of a wagon. The day promised hot for autumn and there was no breeze. The men jumped down and greeted Alice. She introduced him to Cadge Coles, the boss, while the rest of the men lugged their kit across to the shearers' quarters, a bunkhouse as basic as the stockmen's over by the barn.

The huge shearing shed and the shearers' quarters, together with a self-contained kitchen, were situated away from the main block of buildings. For a few days Belle, Doris and Rachel had been hard at work preparing the sleeping quarters, the kitchen, and the lean-to furnished with trestle tables and benches. They scrubbed out the bunkhouse, aired the mattresses, bleached the trestle tables and benches, rubbed down the old cooking range with steel wool, and restocked the woodpile for cooking and hot water. Wes Chapman had driven over from Charlestown to overhaul the generator and inside the shearing shed the pens had been repaired, the powered sharpening disk covered with new emery paper and all the cogs, gears and shearing equipment checked.

Jon walked over to the shearing shed, the biggest building on the homestead, and flung open the huge double doors to create a through draught. A strong whiff of tar-based creosote used to kill off mites and lice prickled his nose. The smell wouldn't last, not once there were sheep in the building.

He'd missed the previous two shearings. For the last one he'd been in Liverpool thinking about returning to Jarrahlong, but the year before that, not long after the big bush fire that had done so much damage, he'd been on a tramp ship working his passage to England and that was about the time Rachel got pregnant.

He'd noticed that as shearing time approached she'd become quieter, more withdrawn. She smiled less, did her tasks and disappeared back to her bungalow at the first opportunity. She hadn't been around when the men arrived either. It all stacked up, one of the shearers was Joe's father, but which one?

A series of short whistles distracted him, and then came the familiar sound of animals' feet on baked earth as the sheep jostled together. He joined Adie and the others and drove the first of the sheep into the inside pens, eight in all, each pair adjacent to a shearing station. As the front pens emptied the animals behind were moved forward and the back row of empty pens filled providing a constant flow of sheep for the shearers.

Once the sheep were ready and all the hand pieces sharpened the graft began. Berry, Sid, Rosie and Ray, in the four-stand team, leapt forward. They each dragged an animal out onto the board, upturned it and held it firmly between their legs, a quick yank on the cords and the shearing began – belly first, then the chest, neck, head, sides, flanks and back.

'Bloody hell,' cursed Rosie within the first couple of minutes. 'First bloody animal and I've gone and cut it. Tarboy, where are ya?'

Willie carried over a pot of tar and painted the viscous mix onto the cut while Rosie held the struggling animal.

'You want to slow down a bit,' commented Cadge. 'More haste, less speed.'

Rosie let the ewe go and, like the others, it escaped through the hatch door behind the shearer into the safety of the counting-out pen.

Jon wrinkled up his nose at the stink of the tar, a harsh treatment but better than the animal suffering blowfly strike later.

While the shearers were getting the next animals into position, Dusty, one of the rouseabouts, picked up the discarded fleeces, flung them onto a table and swept the board. Wheat was busy skirting the fleeces of daggy, sweaty bits, while Willie classed others and Dusty bundled them up and threw them into the appropriate bays depending on the quality.

All the men knew their place in the team and worked well together, but there was no doubt that shearing the animals was backbreaking work, and he was getting in the way. Jon left them to it and headed outside, into the yards, to help with sorting the sheep into ewes, weaners, wethers and rams ready for the shearing lines. And then there were the sheep out in the home paddock that needed bringing down to the yards ready for the next day's shearing.

When Jon wasn't out in the yards sorting the sheep into pens, he was in the shearing shed watching, learning the routine and the unfamiliar words, and helping out where he could while eyeing up the men, trying to decide who Joe's father was.

'Pass a pannikin of water, will yer, mate,' yelled a chap called Berry, nodding in Jon's direction. He stretched his back between sheep, sweat pouring off him while he waited for the water.

'On the table, over there, Jon,' said Cadge Coles, indicating the water bucket.

Jon guessed Cadge was sixty if he was a day and he was called Cadge because he was forever cadging cigarettes. Cadge had been in the game all his adult life. He'd been a top gun in his youth shearing two hundred sheep day after day in the season. According to the boys he'd got enough in the bank to retire, but he liked the life and set himself up with a lorry and a shearing team. Now, he oversaw the job and kept the tally book that recorded the number of sheep each shearer shore during each two-hour stint.

Jon found the pannikin, filled it and passed it over.

Berry downed the water, wiped his mouth on the back of his hand and grinned. 'This how you do it in England?'

'Don't know,' said Jon, 'never worked with sheep till I came here.'

'You want a go?'

'No, reckon I'll leave it to the experts.'

Berry shrugged, a self-satisfied smile on his face. 'Nice to be appreciated,' he added in a droll voice, handing back the pannikin.

Jon didn't take to Berry. There was something about the bloke's manner that got under his skin. The fella was too full of himself. He was the best shearer in the team and he knew it and he was forever tossing throw-away comments in Ray's direction. Ray, a new member of the team, was learning on the job. Berry referred to him as a dragger, the slowest shearer in the shed, but despite his frequent joshing Ray kept right on shearing and refused to rise to the bait.

'How you doing, Ray?' asked Berry between sheep.

'Don't you worry,' Ray said, 'I can only get better and those at the top of the tree have only one way to go.'

'You reckon, do you?' said Berry as he took a long blow from tail to head along the back of the sheep he was shearing. 'Reckon you're no better than a bloody Pom.'

Jon ignored the humour, not quite sure whether Berry's comment was barbed or harmless.

'How long to smoko?' yelled Sid as he upturned another ewe. 'My back's killing me already.'

'Half an hour,' shouted Cadge. 'Stop yapping and get on with the job.'

Jon moved to the end of the shed where Slim was pressing wool. Slim was a couple of fleeces short of a bale but he took the jesting he got from the others in his stride. He couldn't imagine Rachel with Slim, even though he was a nice enough bloke.

'How's it going?' asked Jon as he watched Slim take a huge tent-peg of a needle, stitch up the canvas sacking with string, stamp the bale with the Jarrahlong mark and roll the bale of wool over to the rest awaiting shipment to the coast.

'Not so bad,' he said in his slow, quiet voice. Slim was about twenty-five and six foot two or three with a barrel chest and arms like tree trunks. He was good at pressing wool and not much good at anything else except bale rolling, according to Berry.

After two hours' graft Cadge carried in a large bucket of tea that Doris had prepared. Each man ladled himself a mugful and moved outside to the shady side of the building, glad to get out of the heat and the smell of the shearing shed.

'Any news on that Gerry fella who went missing a bit back?' asked Cadge after he'd completed the tally.

'No,' lied Jon, 'but the constable's been around asking questions.'

'Bit of a bummer, him disappearing like that,' commented Rosie, one of the older shearers. 'He always seemed a nice enough fella. He liked his game of two-up.'

'And his grog,' said Berry. 'He's probably got himself a woman somewhere.'

'Nah,' said Cadge, 'Gerry ain't interested in women, he's a confirmed bachelor, always has been.'

'He'll turn up when it suits him, his sort always fall on their feet,' said Berry.

Jon avoided Berry's eye. It was a long drop down Old Faithful – cats were supposed to fall on their feet, was that true of bodies? He dismissed the thought. It didn't do to dwell on the past, he shouldn't think about Gerry and the mine, he'd end up having nightmares about it. 'What's this bale rolling Berry mentioned earlier?' he asked.

'Everyone wants Slim on their team for the bale rolling,' said Sid. 'Don't know any other station daft enough to come up with the idea.'

'They're a bit heavy to shove around, aren't they?'

'You're not wrong there, mate, but there's a twenty pound bonus for the two blokes that can roll a bale fastest round yon far tree and back again.' Cadge pointed to the gum standing on its own halfway to the creek. 'It was Jack's idea. He wanted something to cheer Alice up and came up with the bale rolling. You should have seen Alice laugh the first time we did it. The winners that day were as ruddy as the flashes on a red-tailed black cockatoo by the time they'd got back to the start line – ever since it's become an institution, the end of shearing entertainment. You going to have a go?'

'Maybe,' said Jon as he followed Cadge into the shearing shed and another two-hour stint.

At the end of each day, after a wash and change, the shearers sat down for the evening meal with Alice presiding at the head of the table. Every evening she'd been there, sitting like Jon imagined Queen Mary sitting, her white hair brushed and pinned up. Regal, that's what she looked like when she made the effort. Jon recalled Stan's words about how Alice looked when she was young, how she scrubbed up well, and how all the young bloods in the district had an eye for her. The fact was Alice liked male company, she enjoyed the jokes, the men's ribald sense of humour, her cold blue eyes sparkled, the brain behind them sharp as ever. Alice was sixty if she was a day but Jon reckoned that in her head she was young.

Was that how it was when you got old, he wondered? Did you still feel the same as you felt at eighteen?

Belle placed huge platters laden with roast beef and boiled vegetables on the table. Bottles of cold beer were handed round and soon the only sound was that of men eating their way through a mound of food that would have fed a battalion. No sooner had they finished the meat course than Belle cleared away and placed a steaming pudding on the table – Rachel's. Jon could tell by the texture and the smell. She was a better cook than Belle, had a lighter touch. He wondered where she was, whether she'd put in an appearance and thought it unlikely. He studied each of the men again.

The team was the same as last year apart from Ray who was new. Cadge, Rosie, Sid and Willie were all too old, Slim was too slow, that left Wheat, Dusty and Berry. But who would Rachel have gone for? Which of them was her type? Truth was he didn't have a clue.

According to Cadge the shearers were based around Charlestown every autumn. Alice's mob was the first to be sheared, and then they moved on to Wanndarah, Jindalee and Cavanagh's Creek Stations. Weekends they'd descend on Charlestown, spending their money on beer and playing two-up in Les's lean-to. There would have been the opportunity.

The men leaned back in their seats, stretching their bellies, belching away the excess wind from eating too fast.

Alice handed round the box of small black cheroots she ordered every Christmas. Jon passed the box on and a little while later watched while Ray turned green under his tan.

'Don't they suit you, lad?' said Berry, a smug smile on his face. 'You'd better get used to it, smoking and beer and a game of two-up is all you'll get in Charlestown. No lasses to speak of, only the one and you're not her type.'

Jon caught the movement when Alice cocked her head to listen.

Wheat grinned and nudged Jon in the ribs. 'There's no one like Berry for getting inside a girl's knickers, is there, Berry?'

'At least I don't go poking gins like some I know.'

'There's a lady present,' said Cadge. 'There'll be less of that, lads, if you don't mind.'

Jon took a swig of beer, so Berry was Joe's father! No wonder Rachel was keeping out of the way. He didn't blame her, she'd probably realised what a puffed-up shallow bloke Berry was. No wonder she didn't want to marry him. He'd met men like him before, blokes with the gift of the gab when it came to girls, the soft voice with a silky edge to it. Berry was a good-looking fella, no doubt about that, but he was the sort who didn't rate women. With Alice he turned on the charm, but with the men he was different, with the blokes he was who he really was.

'It's our last day, you lads ready for the bale rolling?' said Cadge, stubbing out the remains of his cheroot. 'Slim's with me, you lot can sort yourselves out.'

'Howsaboutit, Dusty,' called Berry, 'you and me a team?'

'Too right,' said Dusty. 'We'll give old Cadge a run for his money, even with Slim.' He turned to his boss. 'You're long past it, old man,' he said.

'Who you calling past it?' growled Cadge. 'There's life in the old dog yet. Come on, Slim, pick out five bales and make sure Berry's is the heaviest.'

'I'm standing down on this one,' said Willie. 'I've eaten too much. But Sid and Rosie, they'll give it a go, won't you lads?'

'You can count me out,' said Wheat. 'I've got a bone in my arm.'

'It don't stop you quaffing beer though, does it?' said Cadge dryly. He turned to Jon. 'Looks like you've no choice; we need you to make up a team with Ray.'

'Hold fire a minute,' said Alice. 'Belle,' she yelled.

Belle stuck her head round the canteen door.

'Belle, fetch Rachel, tell her she's to come across for the entertainment.'

Belle shuffled off.

Jon hung back while the others limbered up and retied his boot laces curious to see whether Rachel would cry off. But she didn't. She joined them, flushed with embarrassment, or from the heat of the kitchen, he couldn't tell which, and Joe wasn't with her.

'Hello, Rachel,' said Cadge, 'I didn't know you were living out here now?'

'It's only temporary,' said Alice. 'She's been giving me a hand since the fire.'

'Aye,' said Cadge, 'and it's a bit of company for you, Alice.'

Ray coloured up crimson when he was introduced, while Rosie, Sid and Willie shook her hand in turn. Dusty tipped his cap and continued helping Slim with the bales, Wheat called his greeting and got on with finishing his beer, only Berry held her hand a shade too long, his grin wider than necessary. Rachel's reaction too confirmed his suspicions, she wouldn't look Berry in the eye and her flushed face reddened further.

Cadge carried Alice's chair across to the starting line and then offered his arm and escorted her to her seat. Belle, Adie and the rest of the black stockmen and Mick's kids sat on the fence behind Alice, waiting for the fun to start, the station dogs milling at their feet.

'Toss the bloody coin, Cadge, and make sure it's an honest one,' called Berry.

'Want to check it?' asked Cadge, spinning the coin.

'Trust you, mate,' said Berry. 'Heads!'

'Tails it is.' Cadge tossed the coin again and again until the second, third and fourth positions were decided.

'Lucky bugger,' muttered Berry. 'Reckon you fixed it.'

Cadge and Slim had the inside, pole position, Berry and Dusty and Rosie and Sid the middle slots, and Jon and Ray the outside position.

'On your marks…Go!' called Alice before Jon had time to spit on his hands and lean into the bale.

Rolling the bale was like pushing a granite boulder up a hill. Before they were halfway to the gum tree sweat was dripping off all of them. All Jon could hear was men grunting and cursing and a low-pitched rumbling in his ears as his heart tried to keep pace with his efforts. Cadge and Slim were in the lead, with Berry and Dusty, and Rosie and Sid, neck and neck. Despite Ray's efforts they were last, struggling hard to set up a rhythm and keep the bale rolling straight. By the time they reached the tree Berry and Dusty had taken second place and were on the return straight. But neither his bale nor Berry's were following a true line. They hit, corner to corner, winding all four of them.

Berry recovered first.

'You Pommy bastard, get out of my way.' He shoved Jon aside and shouldered the bales free.

'Foul!' yelled Ray. 'Keep your hands on your own bale.'

The incident disrupted what little rhythm he and Ray had established and starting the bale rolling again hurt, veins stood out on their arms as they shoved together, their chests burning from the effort as they rounded the tree.

Ahead, Berry and Dusty were gaining on Cadge and Slim, taking the inner, shorter line, bent on winning.

Jon realised that he and Ray didn't stand a chance of being placed. Suddenly it became important to close the gap, to make a respectable fourth.

'One…two…three…roll,' he grunted, 'one…two…three…roll.'

He kept up the rhythm, forcing Ray to up his pace, turning the bale marginally faster than the other three teams.

As they all neared the finishing line Wheat and Willie were bashing their bush hats against their thighs, yelling for their favourite, not wanting to lose money on a bet. The row of Aborigines sitting on the fence watched the proceedings with mild interest, apart from Mick's kids who were clapping with excitement. While Alice, as far as Jon could tell, was still sitting on her chair puffing on a cheroot, watching their antics with more than a little interest.

Sweat poured off his face in rivulets, stung his eyes and dripped off his chin, Ray's face, equally slick and red, showed the strain and the effort, but close the gap they did. They were still last, but it was a respectable fourth considering their start position.

Ray flopped onto the dust, legs and arms spreadeagled, drawing in great gulps of air. 'I want a rerun, we was impeded,' he gasped between each intake of breath.

'You can forget that idea, Ray. I'm not up to the job twice and I don't reckon Jon is either,' said Cadge, panting. After a few moments he slapped Jon on the back. 'Not bad for a Pom, not bad at all.'

Berry grinned, 'Told you we'd got the beating of you, Cadge. You're past it, old fella, reckon you should retire.'

'Next year you'll need to be watching out for Jon and Ray,' said Alice. 'They were nipping at your heels today, once they'd got the hang of it.'

'Not likely,' said Berry, looking at Rachel as he spoke, 'it needs a real man to roll a bale.'

Rachel turned crimson and looked away.

Alice drew on her cheroot, savoured the smoke and exhaled slowly, her cold, blue eyes fixed on Berry's flushed face. 'They haven't finished growing yet; they're still laying down muscle. I'm telling you, they'll out-roll you next year. I'll put money on it.'

Berry scowled. He saw the look on Alice's face, shrugged and smiled, the flicker of dislike masked as soon is it appeared.

Alice considered Berry for a few moments, an inscrutable look on her face, then she turned to Cadge. 'Not bad for an old 'un.'

'Thanks.' Cadge flopped against his bale still trying to catch his breath. 'Isn't it about time you stopped this tradition?'

'What, and miss out on the highlight of the year,' said Alice, her tone tinged with sarcasm. 'Not on your— '

'That's okay, Alice, I get your drift.'

Jon stripped off his shirt and mopped up the sweat on his face and body conscious of Berry striding round the place like the cock of the walk, joshing Alice and his mates. He'd been too harsh on Rachel. He looked for her, wanting to offer a friendly word, but she'd gone. It was then he noticed Alice watching him, a contemplative look on her face.

CHAPTER 37

When Jon got back from a trip to Charlestown Ty's horse was in the yard next to the post and rail fencing. He parked up and unloaded the rolls of barbed wire, staples, stretching ratchet and other equipment that he'd bought to repair and extend the fencing in the top paddock for Alice's Herefords.

He washed up, put on a fresh shirt and strolled over to Alice's place with the invoices. Belle was in the kitchen.

'Missus is out the back catchin' the late sun,' she said without bothering to look up.

'Thanks, Belle,' said Jon.

'Suppose you want a mug of tea.'

'Wouldn't say no.'

Belle picked up the billy stewing on the stove and poured him a mugful of dark brown liquid and handed it across. When she slammed the billy down tea splashed onto the hot plate, beads splattered and rolled spitting to the edge.

Jon took a sip. 'This'll put hairs on me chest, Belle.'

'You complainin'?'

'No, just commenting.'

Belle gave him a dour look and turned back to Alice's washing.

Jon stepped back out onto the verandah and walked round to the west elevation. Alice was sitting in her usual chair while Ty lolled back on the swing seat he usually favoured.

'Take a seat,' said Alice, indicating the bench seat over by the wall. 'Ty here's got a problem. Or rather his family has a problem.'

Jon greeted Ty, sat down and took another sip of the scalding hot brew, filtering the tea through his teeth as he drank. He spat out a couple of leaves.

'We've been discussing the best way to deal with it,' said Alice. 'Maybe you can help.'

It was clear from the look on their faces that whatever it was they'd been talking about it was serious.

'What's the problem, Alice?'

'It's Ty's half-sister, Bindi.'

'What about her?'

'Constable Barnes, on behalf of Jepthson, the so-called Protector of the Aborigines, picked up Bindi a couple of weeks ago and shipped her off to the Native Settlement north of Perth.'

'I thought you said your dad had a deal with Constable Barnes?' said Jon.

'He did,' said Ty, 'but then Dad fell out with Barnes playing two-up. Dad called him a worthless, good-for-nothing, cheating, Catholic bastard and that was that. As soon as Mrs Kenton from over on the Harrison Station wrote a letter to Barnes complaining that Bindi was running wild, accusing her of setting a bad example to her girls, teaching them Abo ways, it was all the excuse Barnes needed. He set the wheels in motion and got his revenge.'

'How old is she?'

'Fourteen.'

'They'll not keep her long. She'll be out before you know it.'

'Isn't that simple,' said Alice. 'They send them to other states as maids, separate them from their families. She won't be allowed home. She'll have to work for a white family.'

'Gracie's beside herself,' said Ty. 'Bindi's all she's got now – all her boys are working as stockmen in the Northern Territory.'

Jon sat drinking his tea. What did the two of them expect him to do about it? It was none of his business. 'Where is this place?'

'To the north-east of Perth. It's a fair old way,' said Alice.

Why was she telling him all this? Was she expecting him to volunteer to go and fetch Ty's half-sister home or something? It was madness. What could he do anyway? He wasn't about to go kidnapping a half-caste even if Alice said it would be all right. He'd had enough of kidnapping in England when he and Kathy had run away to Blackpool, and where had that got him? Very nearly in Borstal, and now that he was older it'd be jail.

Alice cogitated, gazing out over the scrubland at the blood-red sun sinking heavily towards the horizon before shifting her focus to the willy-wagtail catching flies in the patch she called her garden.

'Waldron Griffiths lives over Wanneroo way,' she said.

'Who's Waldron Griffiths?' asked Jon.

'He's a distant relative of Jack's, but he's also a retired Government Officer. Pretty high up he was – a representative of Western

Australia in Canberra.'

Jon frowned, dredging his memory for an earlier conversation. Alice had mentioned a relative in Perth once before. Was he the same fella?

'I think he can help us.' She sat for a while watching the wagtail eat more flies. 'That's what we'll do,' she said at last. 'I'll write to Waldron and ask him to go with you to the Settlement. They won't ignore my letter if Waldron is there with you.'

'Will it make any difference?' asked Ty.

'It will if I say that Bindi's my maid and that Constable Barnes had no right to take her while she was visiting her family. I'll tell them I'm taking a personal interest in educating her. That should do it. Anyway, the more I think about it the more I realise I could do with a maid in my old age; I need someone to dress my hair in the morning and iron my linen.'

Jon looked at her askance.

Alice looked straight back at him and winked. 'Aye, lad, I like my drawers pressed.' She laughed at him and Jon felt his skin turn scarlet. She turned to Ty. 'The point is we've more stockmen here than we've had in a good few years so Belle and Doris could do with some help in the cookhouse and with the vegetable plot. Rachel can't do as much these days; she has her hands full with young Joe. How do you think your sister will feel about working at Jarrahlong?'

'Seems to me it'd suit everyone and Jarrahlong isn't that far from our place,' said Ty. 'Bindi could save up her days off and visit for a spell, provided she can have the loan of one of your horses.' He laughed. 'But knowing Bindi she'd walk it. Knows the area like the back of her hand, she does. Dad says she's a wild thing, more Aboriginal than her mother, or her granddad come to that.'

'Didn't realise Gracie was from round here,' said Alice.

'She isn't. She's from a mob over in South Australia. Dad met her when he was on his travels as a dogger, before he worked in the Territory.'

'You staying over, Ty? Or do you need to talk to your father?'

'I'll stay the night if you don't mind, Mrs Macarthur, then I'll head off home and put it to Dad, see what he says. He's bound to be all right about it – it was his idea to come over to see you in the first place, fact is, he can't stand Gracie's keening. She's sitting on the step, rocking and cutting her arms with sharp stones, and Dad says there'll be no peace until Bindi's back safe and sound.'

Jon left them nattering. He didn't want to go off to the Settlement with Ty but he'd been in the same hole once and if someone had stepped in to help him and Kathy when their mam died then maybe he wouldn't have ended up living at Karundah with the good Catholic Brothers.

He felt anger surge at the memory as he made his way over to the lean-to. That was the trouble with governments and institutions; the people running them always believed they knew best, that splitting up families and riding roughshod over people's feelings was the only way.

He recalled the orphanage at Karundah, an austere place like the children's home in Liverpool. Did the people looking after them ever think about what the children needed? He supposed some of them had been decent enough, like Father William, but then there were the others, the ones who'd left little boys terrified and unable to sleep for what the night would bring. Was that what these Settlements were like? He guessed they probably were and, knowing that, did he have a choice?

CHAPTER 38

The following week Alice handed Jon a letter addressed to the Superintendent at the Native Settlement. 'Give this to Waldron. He'll know best how to handle the situation. Have you got everything you need – water, fuel, sand mats, spare tyres?'

Jon nodded. 'Checked everything last night.'

'Know the route?' She handed over an old school atlas by way of a map. 'Take the road south from Charlestown to Southern Cross. Once you meet the Perth-Kalgoorlie highway head west to Perth then take the coast road north towards Wanneroo. Ask for directions to Waldron's place there. I wrote to him, he'll be expecting you. Have you a change of decent clothes?'

Jon grinned. 'My strides do, and my checked shirt?'

'Indeed they won't,' snapped Alice.

He caught her eye and she laughed.

'It's a serious business,' she said. 'You of all people should know that.'

'I know.' He recalled his interview with Superintendent Jones at the Liverpool children's home when Jones told him Kathy had been adopted. Then there had been no way around it, the law was the law – intractable, maybe they'd be up against the same rigid attitudes. He glanced at Ty's grim face and hoped not. Splitting families up wasn't the answer to problems, all it caused was resentment and heartache. He imagined Gracie sitting on her verandah crying and cutting herself to take the pain away. What was it Stan said? – Life can be a bitch. Well, Stan wasn't far wrong there.

At Wanneroo a local directed them to Waldron Griffiths's place north-west of the town. When they arrived Waldron and his wife were taking afternoon tea on the terrace, looking out over the Indian Ocean, watching the sun glinting on the water and listening to the waves lapping on the beach.

They both stood ram-rod straight to greet them and directed them to sit and take tea in fine bone-china teacups reminiscent of the type Marg used back in Liverpool, but there the similarity ended. Mary was a warmer personality. She chattered away, discussing their journey, the weather, and Alice until evening when the main meal was served informally by a half-caste maid.

'This is Ginny,' said Mary. 'She came to us from the Settlement a couple of years ago, didn't you Ginny?'

Ginny wasn't expected to answer and she didn't.

'Her family live east of Carnarvon, near the Ethel River.'

Ginny placed plates of roast chicken before them and disappeared into the kitchen.

'So what part of England are you from?' asked Mary.

'Liverpool.'

'Did you come out to Australia with your family recently?'

Jon glanced at Ty and hesitated. Did he tell the truth or lie? The truth – Ty had been pretty honest with him. 'I was sent out to Karundah when I was eight.'

Ty looked up from eating, a query creasing his brow.

'Ah, yes,' said Waldron, 'I visited there once to see what Father O'Leary had achieved. Marvellous, giving all those orphans a fresh start. Marvellous!'

Jon stopped eating. 'I wasn't an orphan.'

'Pardon?'

Already the anger was tightening his chest. 'And kids died building that orphanage, did he tell you that?' His voice was barely under control. 'And things happened to them.'

'What sort of things?' asked Mary.

Jon blushed, how could he tell Mary what some of the good Catholic Brothers did to little boys late at night.

'Oh, you know how these stories spread, Mary,' said Waldron equably.

'But it's…' Jon caught Ty's piercing look, the almost imperceptible shake of the head – a warning, and he was pulled back to the present, their reason for being there. He steadied himself, lowered his voice. 'Alice says you are a relative.'

'Yes,' said Waldron, 'distantly so. When Alice and Jack first arrived in Australia I was able to help them secure their first position and then later the pastoral lease. How is Alice?'

'She's well. There was a bad bush fire a couple of years back, most of the homestead burnt down, but she's had it rebuilt and decided to increase the cattle – add some Herefords.'

Waldron laughed. 'So she finally did it. Jack always promised her a herd of Herefords. He said she'd never be happy until she had a few white faces in the paddock to remind her of England.'

'It was one of the things she missed the most; the family back home kept Herefords as well as a dairy herd,' added Mary. 'Waldron and I couldn't have done what they did. We like our home comforts too much, don't we, Wal?'

'Oh, I don't know.'

'You don't even like it when you get mud on your shoes, so heaven knows how you'd be—'

'Knee deep in sheep,' finished Ty for her.

Mary laughed. 'And the rest of it. Let's take our coffee on the terrace. We usually do. We like to look at the moonlight over the ocean, particularly on nights like this.'

Ty and Jon followed them out of the dining room with its heavy mahogany furniture and dark oil paintings to the cooler terrace and the rattan furniture. They sat overlooking the sea, the air heavy with the scent of blossom and the sound of fruit bats in the palm trees.

'Best time of the day,' said Waldron.

They drank their coffee and enjoyed the balmy evening until bedtime.

'We'll be off straight after breakfast. We should be back here by tea tomorrow, with a fair wind,' said Waldron. 'It's not that far.'

That night Jon couldn't sleep. Mary and Waldron were a nice enough couple but it was hard keeping his mouth shut, especially when Waldron was going on about Karundah. Why was it people never looked below the surface? Never asked what Government actions meant to people like him and Bindi, people on the receiving end? Fortunately, they weren't all like Waldron Griffiths; there were plenty like Alice and Stan, people who, even if they didn't exactly question the Government, didn't always feel comfortable with what was happening, otherwise Alice wouldn't have stuck her neck out over Bindi. But that was Alice all over, a one off, someone who didn't give a damn what anyone else thought.

The Settlement, situated on a sandy plain overlooking a creek, was a collection of squalid, dilapidated, wood and iron buildings: dormitories, a communal canteen, classrooms, and a building Jon took to be a church hall – the newest building as far as he could tell.

Overlooking the compound was the superintendent's house, a big place double the size of Waldron's home. Waldron parked a short distance away under a stand of pine trees that dominated the skyline.

'You'd better stay in the car, Ty,' said Waldron. 'Caldecott might take exception to Alice's request if he thinks Bindi's going back to her family.'

'But she's not.'

'I know, but we don't want to complicate the situation, do we?'

Jon followed Waldron across the hard-packed driveway to Caldecott's place. The *scuff scuff* of their feet on gravel matched the thump, thump of his heart in his rib cage. He was back in Liverpool, in the children's home, preparing to meet Superintendent Jones again, and he hated the feeling. The only plus this time was that Waldron led the way and Waldron didn't seem to be a man you messed with.

They sat in the parlour taking tea while Charles Caldecott read and re-read Alice's letter.

'And who's Mrs Macarthur again?' he asked, looking directly at Waldron from under black, bushy eyebrows.

'She's a relative's wife. They came out to Australia at the turn of the century and eventually took a pastoral lease on land north of Southern Cross.'

Caldecott frowned.

'She's a good woman,' said Waldron, his tone reassuring. 'She's in her sixties now and still running the station with the help of Jon here. You'll see from the letter that she employed young Bindi as a maid a couple of months ago and she's taken responsibility for educating her herself, teaching her reading and writing and domestic skills, you know the sort of thing. Anyway, she had allowed the girl home for a couple of days and that was when Constable Barnes picked her up. Of course Mrs Kenton wasn't to know that Bindi had been taken on by Mrs Macarthur, had she known that then I'm sure she wouldn't have contacted Constable Barnes.'

'Quite,' said Caldecott.

'So, are we able to return her to Mrs Macarthur?' asked Waldron.

Caldecott hesitated. 'I suppose it can be arranged.'

'Excellent!' boomed Waldron.

'I shall require a few more details about Mrs Macarthur and your signature on the release forms. I will clear it myself with the relevant Authorities, should the need arise.'

'Nice to know the wheels run smoothly here, as well-oiled as always. You remember our Ginny?'

A bemused look flickered across Caldecott's face.

'The girl from up near Carnarvon, over by the Ethel River.'

'Oh yes, I remember.'

He doesn't, thought Jon. He can no sooner put a face to the name than Alice can rope a poddy.

'She's a fine girl, you should be proud of what you do here, saving youngsters from a life of ignorance,' said Waldron. 'Ginny settled in well, she's as happy as a chook in dirt and she's a real help to my wife, Mary.'

'Good,' said Caldecott, 'now, if you'll step this way we'll go and find Bindi.'

Caldecott led the way to where groups of youngsters were playing in the dusty yard. All around them boys and girls, aged from five to fifteen, stood about the place. Jon looked for the feelings he'd experienced, despair, hopelessness, stubborn resistance and rage, but their faces were expressionless. He unclenched his fists and controlled his anger. There were so many of them and the conditions they were living in looked far worse than those at Karundah. He followed behind Caldecott and Waldron, his unease growing at the familiar and yet unfamiliar surroundings.

Caldecott beckoned to one of the women supervising a group of the younger children in the shade of some eucalyptus trees.

'Mrs Todd, I'd like to introduce you to Waldron Griffiths, perhaps you recall he and his good wife have Jenny—'

'Ginny.'

'Ginny, in their care. And this is Jon.'

She extended a hand to Waldron and then to Jon.

'It seems there was some mistake with regards one of our newest girls, Bindi. She was already working for Mrs Macarthur on Jarrahlong Station.'

'Indeed,' said Mrs Todd. She scanned their faces with unsmiling eyes.

She doesn't believe a word of it, thought Jon, any minute now she'll call our bluff and then what do we do?

'Perhaps you would be good enough to find Bindi for us and get her to pack her things. She'll be leaving with Mr Griffiths.'

Mrs Todd inclined her head towards them and crossed over to one of the large iron and wood buildings to the right of the compound – dormitories, Jon guessed. The place was run down and depressing, not at all like Karundah with its brand new pristine buildings that he and the other boys had helped to build.

They didn't have long to wait. Mrs Todd returned with Bindi trailing along behind her, carrying a simple canvas bag. A small crowd had gathered around asking what was happening. Bindi shook her head, bewilderment creasing her brow.

'Well, Bindi, it seems Mrs Macarthur can't do without you. You've made a big impression,' said Caldecott. He turned to Waldron. 'We'll keep an eye on things, of course. Constable Barnes will call on our behalf from time to time to check that everything is running smoothly, that Bindi is behaving herself and that her education is coming along. Mrs Macarthur understands, I presume.'

'Indeed she does,' beamed Waldron, glancing at his watch.

'Quite,' said Caldecott. 'You have a long journey ahead of you. Now, Bindi, you behave yourself and you are to do as Mr Griffiths says. He'll soon have you back with Mrs Macarthur.'

For a long, horrible moment Jon thought Bindi was going to say she'd never heard of Mrs Macarthur, but she didn't. He watched her out of the corner of his eye – downcast, copper curls falling forward obscuring her face, scuffing her bare feet in the dust, her hands clasped behind her back clutching the bag.

He'd seen her before. He racked his brains trying to think where it could have been. Was it Charlestown? It was the most obvious. He'd never been to Ty's place so it hadn't been on her own patch. So where?

Caldecott patted her on the head. 'You are to go with Mr Griffiths and Jon.'

She looked at him then and he saw a flicker of recognition in her eyes that vanished as soon as he saw it.

'Thank Mr Caldecott for having you,' said Waldron.

She muttered a barely audible 'thank you' and then the three of them walked with Caldecott towards the car. At the gate Waldron and Caldecott shook hands.

'Thank you, Superintendent. It's been a pleasure seeing you again and do pass on my regards to your wife.'

Jon took Bindi's arm and led her over to the car. It wouldn't do if she decided to make a dash for it or gave the game away when she saw Ty. 'Don't say a word, you understand? Sit on the seat and look straight ahead – got it?'

She didn't answer but her eyes widened in shock when he opened the car door. Without a word she sat beside her half-brother, perching on the back seat and looking straight ahead as instructed. Jon shut the door after her and got into the front passenger seat as Waldron started the car.

Jon breathed an audible sigh of relief as they pulled onto the road. 'For one moment there I thought Caldecott was going to change his mind.'

'Caldecott's a decent bloke,' said Waldron as the car gathered speed.

Ty gave his half-sister a playful punch on the arm. 'Nice to see you, Bindi. Did you think we'd abandoned you?'

Tears rolled down her cheeks and dripped on to the thin dress she was wearing as they headed back to Waldron's place.

'Hey,' said Ty, putting an arm round her shaking shoulders. 'What's Jon and Mr Griffiths going to think seeing you bawling like a nipper?'

Bindi barely spoke a word on the journey back to Jarrahlong. She listened tight-lipped while Ty explained the arrangement he'd made for her.

She gulped back her tears. 'Who's Mrs Macarthur?'

'The lady who owns Jarrahlong Station south of our place. She's nice, you'll like her.'

Depends on your point of view, thought Jon. He recalled his first week at Jarrahlong painting the corrugated-iron roofs while he was still recovering from his saddle sores. There weren't many harder taskmasters than Alice if she didn't take to you. And then he remembered where he'd seen Bindi – at the green pool. She'd seen him swimming without a stitch on. She'd stood on the ledge looking down on him. He felt a hot flush creeping up his neck. That was where he had seen her!

'And it looks like you're going to have to brush up on your reading and writing,' Ty said. 'No more sloping off into the bush for days on end. Right?'

She swallowed hard.

'You'll be fine with Mrs Macarthur.' Ty's voice was over enthusiastic. 'Jon likes it there, don't you, Jon?'

'Yes,' said Jon.

She turned a stony face to the window and refused to speak.

'So, how come you're working at Mrs Macarthur's place?' Ty asked, after a lengthy silence.

'I ran away from the orphanage at Karundah and ended up at Jarrahlong. Alice guessed straight off, but she was short of stockmen and once she decided I was a worker she offered me a job.'

'Don't they have orphanages in England?'

'Yeah, but the Government decided to send some of us to Australia...to help populate the Empire,' he added wryly.

'I thought you told Waldron you weren't an orphan.'

'I'm not. I've got a dad somewhere. The bastard ran off with a woman from the next street and when Mam was taken sick she put me and my sister in the children's home, temporarily, while she was in hospital having an operation.'

'Yeah!'

'Yeah. We weren't the only kids waiting for their mams and dads to get back on their feet.'

'Didn't you have any other relatives?'

'Gran, but she was ill with emphysema so when Mam died Kathy and I stayed in the children's home.'

As he drove he remembered the ciné-film they'd been shown of kids living on a farm school in Australia, smiling, laughing and healthy looking, and the superintendent asking who wanted to go there to help build the Empire. There'd been plenty of sun, he thought bitterly, but that was about it, the food wasn't anything to shout about and there wasn't much laughter, and they'd had to build their own bloody orphanage.

'So how long were you at Karundah?'

'Seven years.'

Ty gave a long, low whistle. 'Why didn't you leave at fourteen?'

'They wouldn't let us. They needed big, strapping lads for the quarrying, carting the rock and the building and then Freddie Fitzpatrick got killed,' he added quietly.

'And you left.'

Jon nodded. 'I thought I'd better get home to England, to my sister, while I still could.'

'Why didn't you stay there?'

'Kathy had been adopted, she was happy, and Liverpool...Liverpool—'

'You missed the heat, the dust and the flies.'

Jon grinned. 'You could say that.'

The miles slipped by, the country changed from green and lush to outback arid. As the bush became sparser so Jon felt the tension slip away. He was familiar with this kind of landscape. He preferred the big open spaces. His heart raced when he saw the great salmon gum at the turn-off for Jarrahlong. Almost home!

They pulled into the yard late in the afternoon, dusty and tired after the two day journey. Alice was sitting on the verandah awaiting their arrival.

Ty introduced Bindi.

'Do you want to work for me, Bindi?' asked Alice, leaning back in her chair.

Ty nudged his sister.

The stony face remained; Bindi stared at the ground refusing to look at anyone.

'She's a fast learner, Mrs Macarthur. She's not—'

'Aye, I know, it takes a bit of getting used to. Well, I suggest you take her home for a night or two. Let her mother see that she's all right, then bring her back in a couple of days when she's used to the idea. Take the utility, we won't need it and I can always use Jon's if necessary.'

'I thought you might have let them stay for a bite to eat,' said Jon after they'd left, 'we've all had a long drive.'

'Another two or three hours won't hurt them, and you'll have enough to think about without worrying about Ty and his half-sister. You've got a visitor. You didn't tell me you'd invited your...'

Jon could see her searching for the right word, an unusual enough experience for him to be surprised.

'...friend,' she finished.

'I don't know what you're talking about, Alice. I haven't invited anyone over.'

She jangled the brass bell hanging from the beam above her. 'You'd better take a seat then, you'll be needing it.'

Jon sat. What had upset Alice? In recent weeks she'd mellowed towards him, especially after the shearing. Whose arrival had annoyed her so much? Was it Stan? He didn't think so. Alice liked Stan despite her acerbic remarks about his No Hope mine. Father O'Leary? Had the priest finally tracked him down? Well, what if he had, O'Leary couldn't take him back to the orphanage now. He glanced at Alice's grim face, her eyes fixed on the yard next to the stockmen's quarters, waiting.

Rachel appeared carrying Joe and with her was a young woman. She was taller than Rachel and blonde, and she was wearing a floral dress with white high-heeled shoes that were badly stained with red earth. He blinked his eyes. Val? Surely not!

They'd almost reached the verandah steps before Val spotted him sitting in the shade. 'Hi ya, hon,' she called in a cheery voice. 'Surprise!'

Jon sprang to his feet. It *was* her! 'What are you doing here?'

'Aye,' said Alice, 'I'd like to know the answer to that too.'

'I told you I was goin' to emigrate, get one of those ten-pound-Pom tickets.'

'But how?'

'Well, it wasn't easy, hon,' she laughed. 'Aren't you pleased to see me? Elsie sends her best. She said she'd like to see your face when you clapped eyes on me.'

'I bet she did,' muttered Alice. 'Who's Elsie?'

'The woman I stayed with in Liverpool. I told you...remember?' said Jon.

Val smiled broadly. 'I caught a boat out of Southampton bound for Fremantle and two weeks out I dropped dead lucky, one of the kitchen staff got took sick so I offered to help out.'

'Doing what?' asked Alice.

'Workin' in the galley,' said Val, 'I'm not a bad cook when I turn me hand to it...and I got paid.'

She glanced at Jon and then at Alice. 'When I got to Fremantle I hitched a lift with one of the drivers goin' to Kalgoorlie. He did a detour and he dropped me off in Charlestown.'

'Nice of him,' muttered Alice.

'That's what I thought. Anyway, I got to Charlestown and stayed at the hotel for a couple of days...Connie's nice.'

'Bet she knows your life story by now,' said Alice dryly.

'Then I managed to get another job.'

'In Charlestown?' said Jon not able to keep the shock out of his voice, even Rachel's eyes widened.

'Yes, I'm workin' for Mr Simpson, as of next week. He's a sweetie, isn't he?'

All three of them stared at her as she tried to dust off her shoes, but her sweating hands made the stain worse. She mouthed a swear word, abandoned the effort and beamed at everyone. 'Gets every-where, don't it?'

Jon pictured Simpson wearing his trademark suit and patent leather shoes. They didn't come any more dapper than Simpson even allowing for his scrawny neck, rotten teeth and stinking breath. 'Simpson?'

'Yes, Mr Simpson. He said the ladies prefer to do business with a woman and he thinks I'm the right person for the job.'

'The only person,' snapped Alice.

'I told him I couldn't start until next week though. I wanted to see you first. See where you live an' all, and meet Alice.'
'Mrs Macarthur to you,' said Alice.
'Aren't you pleased to see me, hon?'
'I suppose,' said Jon, still in shock. He never thought she'd do it, thought it was all talk.
'Tea's ready,' said Rachel, catching sight of Belle carrying food across the yard from the cookhouse. She handed Joe across to Jon and helped Alice out of her chair.
No one spoke while Belle served up the usual roast mutton and boiled carrots and potatoes. Overhead, the fan Alice had imported from Perth churned the humid air making Jon feel hotter than he had when he'd stepped out of the utility half an hour earlier.
'Mam won't believe me when I tell her about the food,' said Val.
'What's wrong with the food?' snapped Alice.
'Nothin', Mrs Macarthur. Back home everythin's still rationed, even bread. You don't see joints like this, at least, not where I come from.'
Belle cut the meat into slices and flopped a thick slab of mutton onto each plate and slapped a pile of potatoes and carrots on the top. Once she'd served up the food she shuffled out of the kitchen and back to the shack she shared with Adie.
'How long are you staying?' asked Jon.
'Is Sunday all right? Mr Simpson said he'd pick me up Sunday afternoon.'
'You what?' said Rachel. 'Simpson's driving out here to pick you up?'
Val nodded, her mouth full of mutton.
'Where're you planning on living?' asked Alice. 'The Grand?'
Val swallowed and wiped her chin with the back of her hand. 'No, Mr Simpson's offered me his room over the shop.'
Jon stopped eating.
'The storeroom!' said Rachel.
'Yes, the front one overlookin' the street. He said he'll gerrit fixed up right smart for me.'
'Did he now,' said Alice.
'He said he'd take the rent out of me wages.'
'Wonders'll never cease,' muttered Alice.
Val turned to Rachel. 'You used to work for Mr Simpson, didn't you? What's he like?'
'He's all right,' said Rachel, warily.
'Smarmy,' said Jon, 'with a healthy respect for Rachel's father.

That answer your question?'

'And his wife cleared off with a fencing contractor in 1932,' added Alice.

'Well, he seems a nice enough fella to me,' said Val. 'He likes a bit of banter. There an' again, don't most men?'

'Know about men, do you?' asked Alice.

'You learn,' Val said, an odd expression on her face.

'Well, I'm glad you've come,' said Rachel. 'It'll be nice having someone my own age to talk to. What are the fashions back in England?'

'Fitted waists and full skirts, everyone's sick of utility wear. The trouble is you still need coupons for a lorra the stuff.'

Alice harrumphed, picked up her stick and walked towards the parlour, her head held erect, her spine stiff and unyielding.

The three of them listened in silence as the door clicked to behind her.

'She doesn't like me, does she?' said Val.

'Don't take any notice,' said Rachel. 'It's her way, she'll come round.'

'How is everyone back home?' asked Jon meaning Merle. 'And how did you manage to emigrate on your own, at your age?'

'Lied through me teeth, didn't I. Got a passport in our Evelyn's name and then I forged Father Gregory's signature on the back of the photograph. Easy! Besides, all me friends say I look older than eighteen.'

'And they let you do it? Your mam and Evelyn?'

'Don't be daft, course not. I told them everythin' in a letter I posted before I jumped on a train to Southampton. They won't care; they're too busy with their own lives to bother about me.'

'You realise you could go to jail?'

She giggled. 'For what? Coming to Australia?'

'No, the passport, you dummy.'

'You goin' to report me or somethin'?' She grinned at him. 'You can close your mouth, hon. It's not that much different to what you did. Just because I'm a girl doesn't mean I don't have dreams.'

He wished she's stop calling him honey, it really got on his nerves. He glanced at her. At least she'd stopped smoking. 'I didn't say that.'

'No, but that's what you thought, isn't it?'

'I wish I had your courage,' said Rachel. She mopped up spilt rusks from Joe's bib.

'It's not courage,' snapped Jon, 'she hasn't got a brain, that's her problem.'

'Rubbish,' said Val. 'It's my pioneerin' spirit. It's what made Britain great, Elsie said.'

'Elsie wouldn't say that,' he said, knowing full well it was exactly the sort of thing Elsie would say. He recalled her comments about Val not long before he returned to Australia, that knowing Val she'd up sticks and emigrate under age or no. Blast Elsie!

'She did,' said Val. 'She told me to go for it, said if she were my age she'd be off like a shot; Liverpool wouldn't see her for dust. Those were her exact words.' She held her foot out and turned her ankle to display the stained suede shoe. 'These cost me a whole week's wages and look at 'em.' She giggled. 'Elsie's red dust. Only thing is I didn't come prepared for this place, any chance of me borrowin' a pair of your britches and a shirt?'

'They wouldn't fit,' said Jon, dropping his plate in the sink for Belle to see to.

The next morning, early, Val was waiting for him wearing his khaki strides and a check shirt.

'Gorr 'em off the line in the wash house and Rachel lent me the boots. I want you to teach me how to ride.'

'I'm busy.'

'No you're not, not that busy.' She followed him across to breakfast. Belle plonked down plates full of steak and eggs and Jon watched amazed as Val quickly demolished the whole plateful and downed a mugful of strong tea. 'Thanks, Belle.'

'You're welcome,' said Belle, a beam plastered on her broad face. 'Nice to be appreciated,' she commented, looking pointedly at Jon.

'Alice says I can learn to ride on Daisy, that you'll teach me.'

'Did she,' muttered Jon. 'Since when?'

'Since before you were out of bed,' said Alice from behind him. 'I like a lass who knows her own mind so you teach her right.'

'Thanks Alice,' beamed Val. 'And after I'll come over and cut your hair and give you a manicure.'

Jon's mouth dropped and he closed it quickly when he caught a bemused look on Belle's face. She probably doesn't know what a manicure is, he thought. And what was Alice up to wanting a manicure at her age? Alice caught his eye and he reddened. He scraped back his chair, stepped out of the room and clattered down the verandah steps. Val followed a couple of paces behind. From the kitchen he heard Belle mumble something and Alice laughing.

'What do you want to learn to ride for anyway?' he snapped. 'You're not stopping.'

'You can't live out here and not ride,' she said.

'Rachel doesn't.'

'Well, she's gorra bairn to look after. Have you asked her if she can ride?'

'No.'

'Well, there you go then. Bet she can.'

He'd never had occasion to ask and Val was right, ever since his return to Jarrahlong Rachel had been busy caring for Joe. It didn't leave much time for riding.

He entered the barn and crossed to the wall where the spare hats were and took one off the peg. 'Here, you'll need one of these.'

Val held it at arm's length, inspecting the dark, greasy stain all around the hatband then leaned forward and sniffed it. 'Do I have to?'

'No, not if you don't mind getting sunstroke.'

Jon picked up Daisy's saddle and took it out to the home paddock, whistled, and waited for Daisy to trot over. He saddled her up and went back for Red's saddle.

'Right,' he said, 'grab the bridle and the pommel and I'll give you a leg up.'

Val stood with her back to him, holding on to Daisy's mane and the pommel, waiting for him to help her into the saddle.

'This is all right,' she said, wriggling her bottom into a more comfortable position. She leaned down to peck him on the cheek.

He stepped back, avoiding the kiss. You won't think that after a morning's riding, he thought, a tight smile plastered on his face.

'Where do me feet go?'

'In the stirrups.' He put her left foot into position and wondered when she'd given up smoking. The last time he'd seen her she'd smelt like an ashtray.

Val hung on to the bridle for grim life and leaned back in the saddle as Daisy took a step forward.

'Sit upright,' said Jon, 'and keep your hands low, near the pommel. She'll not bolt. Give her her head and she'll follow my horse.'

'Where we goin'?'

'We're going to check one of the bores, make sure the sheep have water and that they're all right for grazing.'

Jon led them towards the creek, past the jarrahs and into the acacia scrub bordering the creek bed.

'This is easy,' said Val, making exaggerated movements, matching the horse's gait. 'You can't fall off, can you?'

'Not if you don't go and do anything daft,' said Jon, smiling to himself. He'd show her. She wouldn't want to go riding again in a hurry, not after a morning in the saddle. A couple of hours should do it, three and the cramp would set in and the muscles in her legs seize up. He whistled to himself, feeling quite cheerful.

'How're Pete and the gang?' he asked casually after half an hour's riding.

'They've all gorr'emselves jobs now, 'cept for Pete. He's gone into the supply and demand business.'

'You mean he's still a spiv?'

'Yes.'

'And what about...' He hesitated not wanting to ask outright about Merle.

'Merle? She's got a place at university. Pete says all she does is study.'

He already knew that. Merle had told him all about it in her latest letter. He frowned. She'd also asked about the nearest cinema and gone on about the heat in Australia and about the flies, wanting to know whether it was true. He batted away the insects buzzing around the brim of his hat. The flies weren't that bad and after a while you got so you could ignore them most of the time.

They reached the bore mid-morning and prepared to set off back to the station once Jon had checked the water supply and that the sheep were all right, that there had been no dingo predation.

'White, aren't they,' Val said while waiting for a leg up.

'What do you expect? They've not long been shorn.'

'Oh! Right!' She gentled herself into the saddle, biting on her lip as she did so.

'You okay?'

'Yes. Is that it? Is that all you're goin' to do?'

'Yeah, for today.' He glanced at her, satisfied to see the pinched look on her face and the way she was trying to hold her bottom off the saddle, taking the weight on her arms. 'You sure you're all right back there?'

'I'm fine.'

Jon grinned at the lie and the strangled answer. He recognised the sound of words spoken through clenched teeth.

When they got back to the station Jon slid off Red, unsaddled him, rubbed him down, watered and fed him while Val watched from Daisy's back.

'You going to get down?' he asked.

'Can't. I don't know how.'

He helped her off the horse and watched as she staggered stiff-legged across to the post and rail fence. He'd done exactly the same after his first ride on Daisy, except then it had been a longer trip, six hours instead of four. 'You all right? You look a bit pale.'

'I'm okay,' she said, her teeth gritted into a smile.

'You go and wash up, I'll see to Daisy.' He watched her totter round the side of the stockmen's quarters towards Rachel's place. That'll teach her, he thought. She won't want to do that again in a hurry.

Rachel accosted him before he'd finished with Daisy. 'You're a right bastard, Jon.'

'Now what?'

'You know what... Val.'

'What about her?'

'Did you have to take her so far on her first ride?'

'Oh, that!'

'Yes, *Oh that*! The poor girl can hardly walk. What got into you?'

'Nothing.' He couldn't bring himself to look at her.

'Nothing! Some friend you are.'

Jon hid his exasperation. He couldn't begin to explain his anger with Val, that he resented her presence. It was Merle he should have been teaching to ride. 'She'll get over it,' he snapped, irked by the furious look on Rachel's face. He picked up Daisy's saddle and, cursing under his breath, left Rachel standing in the yard, fuming.

CHAPTER 39

When Jon arrived back tired after the week-long trip up to the top end of the station he wasn't surprised to see Ty's horse hitched to the post and rail fence and Will Samuels' utilility truck parked next to it.

Val was sitting on a small upturned barrel, bouncing Joe on her lap. Next to her, on the verandah steps, was Rachel talking to Will, and Alice was laughing at something Ty had said. It was quite a gathering. The sight annoyed him. A bloody tea party! All they needed was a plate of cucumber sandwiches!

He took off his bush hat, wiped his brow, flapped the hat against his thigh, flopped it back on his head and dismounted. Red stood still as he removed the bridle, unbuckled the girth and carried the tack into the barn. He picked up the curry-comb and brush, returned to Red and rubbed the horse down vigorously. As he worked he could hear conversation and more laughter drifting across the yard. Irritation niggled like an itch, didn't folk round here have anything better to do?

Out back, next to the wash block, he stood under the galvanised shower, letting the cold water cascade over his head and body, washing off the dust and grime, easing the tension in his neck. He couldn't be bothered to light the donkey, the boiler made from an old oil drum that they used to heat the water for washing.

Jon shivered as he soaped himself and rinsed off the lather. The place had changed beyond recognition and it wasn't simply the new buildings Alice had had built. There were the new breeding ewes, and the Hereford bull she was importing to run with the cows she'd bought while he was in England. There were more black stockmen too, and Alan Bynon from Merredin had been back to build the purpose-built butchering room and a new cookhouse. Now, instead of seven of them the number of people living on the station had doubled, plus the occasional Aboriginal family that turned up from time to time and stayed briefly in one of the humpies beyond Rachel's place.

Jon sawed the rough towel over his back. Hardest to take were Val's visits every weekend, and those of Tyrone and Will – Ty supposedly to see his half-sister, Bindi. He scowled. It was nice for Alice to have the extra company, but did she need so much?

Smoky yapped, pulling him out of his thoughts. The dog lay a few feet away in the shade, watching him, his tail half wagging in the dust. He forced the scowl off his face and grinned at the dog. Jealousy – that was his problem! He couldn't blame Ty and Will for visiting. Rachel and Val were young and attractive and it wasn't their fault that Merle was nine thousand miles away in Liverpool training to be a doctor. He roughly dried his hair. But which bloke was interested in Val and which in Rachel? Or were they both after Val? He'd ask Alice, she'd know.

Jon pulled on clean strides and a shirt and looked in the mirror. He needed a haircut. Val was handy with scissors, she could do it. He dragged a comb through his hair. He couldn't believe how fast she'd settled in Charlestown and how quickly she'd got everyone wrapped around her little finger. Wes Chapman, for one, offering the use of his second-best utility and teaching her how to drive, and Simpson letting her finish early on a Saturday so she could visit Alice. And Alice was as bad as the rest of them, sitting on the verandah, foot tapping, watching out for the plume of dust that signalled Val's arrival.

Ever since Val turned up Sundays had taken on a very different pattern. Girly time – that's how he thought of it, the three of them, Alice, Rachel and Val, friendly as a mob of kookaburras, laughing their way through the day. Alice and Rachel looking through fashion magazines, while Val trimmed, washed and styled first Alice's hair and then Rachel's. And the three of them painting their nails pink! What the hell did girls want pink nails for, especially out in the bush?

'Would you like a glass of lemonade?' asked Val as he approached the group.

'Thanks.' Jon clapped Ty on the back. 'Caught many dingoes recently?'

'Got another dozen scalps last week, reckon I'm about on top of them here and over at Cavanagh's Creek.'

'Yeah,' said Will. 'Jindalee's pretty free of them too.'

Val stepped lightly along the verandah in pretty shoes, carrying a large jug and seven glasses on a tray. 'Lift that table over here, if you don't mind, Bindi,' she said. 'It's a nice name for a station, Will, what does the word mean?'

'Jindalee? Haven't a clue. It's probably an Aboriginal word.'

'Have you lived there long?'

Will smiled. 'All my life. It used to belong to a bloke called Jackson, but he never lived there; he always had a manager looking after the place. When he died the family sold off their holdings, that's when Dad and Mum bought the lease.'

Val poured, and Bindi handed out the drinks.

Will sipped the lemonade. 'This is really nice, Val. Did you make it?'

'Yes, Mam's secret recipe.'

'I didn't know your mother was domesticated,' sneered Jon.

'Oh, you know Mam,' said Val lightly, 'she always did know how to make a man happy.'

Alice caught his eye and raised a questioning eyebrow. He took a long draught, savouring the taste. He hadn't told Alice about Val's mother and sister. He wondered what she'd say when she learnt they were on the game.

'Guess what we've decided to do next Sunday,' said Val.

'I've no idea.' He wasn't into guessing games.

'We're havin' a picnic.'

'Don't be daft,' he said.

Rachel looked at him sharply. 'What's wrong with a picnic?'

'Yes,' said Alice, 'what's wrong with a picnic?'

'Where are you planning on having it?'

'Alice says there's an ideal spot along Jarrah Creek,' said Val.

'You mean Sandy Spit?'

'That's the spot,' said Alice. 'The creek's deep there, it's a good place for swimming and there's a flat rock overlooking it. It's ideal for a picnic, nice and shady. Jack and I often used to go there.'

'Alice ain't wrong,' said Ty. 'It's a beaut spot, right enough.'

'Well, I think it's a good idea,' said Will. 'Ty and me are up for it, aren't we, mate?'

'I suppose you're planning on riding out there, Alice,' said Jon, ignoring Will's endorsement.

'No need to be sarcastic, young man. You're going to drive me there in the utility. It's passable if you pick your way.'

'It'll have to be your utility, Alice, mine needs a new sump. Wes says he can't get it fixed before next week at the earliest.'

'See what happens when you drive an old banger,' said Val.

'We can go in my ute, if you like,' offered Will.

'It's got nothing to do with its age,' snapped Jon. He glared at Val. 'I clouted a rock crossing the creek. Anyway, I think it's a cockeyed idea, especially in this heat.'

'Thank you, Will,' said Alice. 'I'll take you up on that offer.' She turned to Jon, her look withering. 'What's got into you these days?'

'Nothing.'

'You're as bad-tempered as a cut snake.'

Jon bit back a sharp retort and felt his colour rising. He deserved Alice's comment. He'd been very quick on temper for a while now. Too much work and not enough sleep had taken its toll. It was Curly's tjuringa weighing him down, leaving him washed out even before the day started, and since Val arrived he'd missed Merle more than ever. She kept turning up in his troubled dreams, like Curly, Perentie and the tjuringa did, no wonder he was tetchy all the time.

Val chuckled. 'Is *cut snake* a local expression or an Aliceism?'

'Local,' said Rachel, 'and Alice is right...anyway, you don't have to do anything, Jon. Alice is providing the food and Val and I are preparing it, and all you lot have to do is lug it out to Sandy Spit for us.'

He forced a smile. 'I take it we are all going?'

'Yes, all of us,' said Val, a sunny smile lighting up her face. 'It'll be fun.'

Friday night Jon sat opposite Alice, concentrating on the next move. If he wasn't careful he'd lose his bishop.

'While you're here I want to talk about the Hereford bull I've bought. Eric's sending Greg with it.'

'Who's Greg?' asked Jon.

'Greg is my great-nephew, Eric's younger son – Beryl's grandson. Anyway, Eric thinks Greg should see a bit more of the world. And Beryl, remember, my sister-in-law?'

'Yeah.'

'Well, she thinks Jarrahlong'll do him good. I've said I'll be pleased to have him to stay. He's twenty-three now. Not much older than you. He should be company for you.'

'Right,' said Jon, wondering where it was all leading. 'You mean your sister-in-law is hoping Greg'll fit in here and run the place for you one day?'

'Inherit it after I'm dead? I suppose she does. It's a reasonable assumption. They are my only living relatives. Francis, the elder one, won't be interested; Eric says he has grand plans for expanding the farm, but Greg's rootless, needs to be channelled. Reading between the lines things were difficult between Greg and his ma. He wanted to fly spitfires in the war, but she wouldn't have it.'

Jon moved his knight and Alice took his bishop with her rook. He should have seen it coming, would have, had he been concentrating.

'Take it you're not keen on the idea of another Pom on the place?'

'It's none of my business, Alice.'

She poured herself an inch of whiskey. 'Tell me about Val.'

'Nothing to tell,' said Jon.

'You don't like her, do you?'

'She's all right.'

'What about her sister and mother?'

'You know the type, working women,' he said tactfully.

'Like me?'

'No…not—'

Alice chuckled.

'Now what?' he challenged. 'What's so funny?'

She relit the stub of her cheroot. 'I know all about Valerie's mother and sister. She told me. So on Sunday you're to behave yourself.'

'What's that suppose to mean?'

'I see your temper hasn't improved! And you know damn well what it means. You be nice to her. She's as sunny as the day is long and all you do is pick fault.'

'I thought—'

'You thought what? That I didn't like her? Well, I wasn't over keen at first, until I got her measure, but since she arrived the place has come alive. We get visitors again.'

'Ty and Will?'

'Yes, and she's good company, for Rachel and me. It's like the old days when Jack and I were—'

'You've got Bindi. I thought you said Bindi was going to be your companion?'

'There's none so dense as those who don't use their brains, is there?' said Alice. 'Checkmate!'

Jon finished his beer. No wonder he'd lost. He couldn't concentrate with Alice going on about Val. How did she do it? First Elsie, now Alice! What did they see in her?

He put his empty beer bottle in the kitchen. So, he was to behave himself at the picnic and then, to add insult to injury, there'd soon be another one! The blessed Greg! So much for his plans to manage Jarrahlong! Along comes Beryl's blue-eyed grandson and his plans are scuppered. He scowled as he made his way over towards his lean-to in the moonlight.

When he rounded the store sheds he caught a glimpse of Bindi over by the vegetable patch with Yildilla. What were they doing out so late?

He pulled back into the shade of the buildings and strained to pick up their conversation, but he couldn't make anything of it – an Aboriginal dialect probably.

He frowned. It wasn't the first time he'd seen the two of them together. Only last week he'd seen them sitting with Mick and his family around the glowing embers of a campfire, engaged in earnest conversation until they'd both looked up and their tawny eyes had locked on him. Neither had smiled at his approach, their faces remained flat, without a hint of expression to soften the intensity of their gaze. The scene had disturbed him. He'd thought about it on several occasions since and still couldn't work out why he was so unsettled.

The water sparkled in the morning sun. Jon lifted Alice's wicker chair from out of the back of the utility and carried it over to a patch of deep shade. Val threw a couple of ex-army blankets on the ground next to Alice for Rachel, Joe and the others and busied herself carrying baskets of picnic food and drink over to the flat rock Alice had mentioned.

Sandy Spit lay in the middle of a short, wide gorge south-west of the homestead and, according to Alice, it was a favourite place for picnics and swimming in her younger days. The water, warmed by the sun, was still cold but not the bone-numbing cold of some pools he had swum in. Either side of the creek were spits of sandy grit, beaches for Joe to play on. The site was perfect for a picnic.

Val, Will, Rachel and Joe were soon swimming and paddling.

'It's freezin',' said Val. She stood waist deep in the water, shivering.

'Swim,' ordered Will who had already done several lengths, 'you'll soon warm up.'

Rachel stood in the shady shallows with Joe.

'Why don't you three join us?' said Val.

'Too cold,' said Ty, leaning back against a rock, his legs stretched out before him.

Jon squatted next to him, sitting as he'd seen the Aboriginal stockmen do, on one heel with the other leg extended for better balance, watching the others enjoying themselves. He looked around for Bindi and saw her further along the gorge.

The girl puzzled him, when he was out with the sheep he'd catch sight of her deep in the outback, running across the red earth like a flickering flame. When she wasn't working for Alice she covered miles. Twice he'd seen her at the green pool, a full day's ride from the homestead, and there had been other occasions when he was sure she'd been watching him. He'd get a prickling sensation when the short hairs on the back of his neck stood erect.

'Where's Bindi going?'

Ty looked over his shoulder and caught a glimpse of her disappearing over a rockfall further along the gorge, carrying a dilly bag slung over her shoulder like a satchel. 'Looking for leaves and stuff – roots and berries.'

'What for?'

'Aboriginal medicine, dyes and the like.'

'Why?'

'I dunno. Bindi's always been different, asking Gracie about her family, pestering the old man about his Aboriginal knowledge.'

'Your Dad?'

'No, Gracie's dad – Yildilla.'

'Yildilla's her grandfather!'

'Yes, I thought you knew.'

Jon leaned back against the rock. That explained a lot, but did Alice know that Bindi and Yildilla were related? He didn't think so, she'd have said something to him. And it didn't explain what Yildilla was doing at Jarrahlong; the old fella wasn't to know that Bindi would end up working for Alice.

'He has the same effect on me,' said Ty.

'What?'

'Knocks me speechless. Yildilla's not an easy fella to get to know, or like, not that we see much of him, he doesn't approve of Gracie living with Dad. According to Gracie, one of her relatives had to take tribal punishment for what she did when she ran away with Dad, and even now when Yildilla's hanging around the place it puts the wind up her. She's jittery for days after he's gone. But Bindi, she took to Yildilla from the first, screamed her head off whenever he left. Don't know why but the old man took to her too, he's taught her things he never taught Gracie even though Bindi's a half-caste. Dad goes on about her being more aboriginal than a full-blood.'

Jon pondered the information not sure whether it eased his mind or added to his anxiety.

'How's our Bindi doing with the reading, writing and arithmetic, Alice?'

Alice tilted back her hat. 'I can't keep up with her. She's a damn sight better than David was at her age. She's almost worked her way through all my books, so I'll be needing the rest of those encyclopaedias, Jon.'

'What are you doing with encyclopaedias?' asked Ty.

'Using them to prop up my bed! What do you think I'm doing with them?'

'He's getting himself an education,' said Alice. 'Pity there aren't a few more like him.'

'Are you two goin' to sit there all day?' called Val.

Ty got to his feet. 'I'll have Joe while you take a dip, Rachel.'

Jon stripped down to shorts and joined Val and Will, the chill taking his breath away when Val splashed him with the icy water, but even the shock of the water didn't fully take his mind off Bindi.

Val, Will and Jon lay in the shade, drying off, full of the picnic lunch that Val and Rachel had prepared, while Alice dozed in her chair, and Rachel, Ty and Joe made mud pies at the water's edge.

'What are those birds in the trees over there?' asked Val, propping herself up on her elbow.

'Where?' asked Will.

'There.' She pointed to a stand of black-trunked gidgee.

'Twenty-eight parrots,' he said.

'That's a funny name for a parrot.'

'It's because their call sounds like twenty-eight.'

The birds flew over them, green flashes against the blue sky.

'Pretty, aren't they?' she said, shading her eyes against the glare. She flopped back and rested the back of her head on her hands. 'If they could see me now.'

Will rolled onto his side and looked at her. 'Who?'

'Mam and our Evelyn, they'd be green. It might even be snowin' in England.'

'I've never seen snow,' said Will.

'Chilly stuff,' said Alice. 'But it's not the worst of it. It was the winter east wind that I couldn't abide – it chills you to the very marrow.'

'Smog,' said Val. 'Can't stand smog, it stinks, you can taste it and feel it burnin' the back of your throat, and it's so thick you can't see your hand in front of your face. Talking of Liverpool, have you heard from your sister recently?'

'Not for a couple of months,' said Jon. 'She's not one for letter writing.'

'Have you told her about this place?'

'No, but I will.'

'She'd be made up with this. When she finishes school you want to get her to come out for a visit, she'd love it.'

Jon didn't think so, all Kathy talked about in her letters was ballet, or the new tutu Marg had bought for her, and what was on at the cinema. She'd never commented on any of the things he had written about, the birds and the animals, his work with the sheep, or the people at Jarrahlong.

'At the rate we are going,' said Alice, 'we'll have to think about renaming Charlestown "New Liverpool".'

'Well, if it brings in more women, then I'm all for it,' said Will. 'The place needs more women, it civilises the men, that's what Dad says.'

Val giggled. 'You need civilisin', do you?'

'Now, now,' said Alice, 'we'll have less smutty talk, if you don't mind.' She looked up at the sky. 'I think we should be making a move. By the time we've got this lot packed away it'll be getting on.'

Val rolled onto her stomach and propped herself up on her elbows. 'This has been the best day, Alice. We should do it again.'

'David always enjoyed a picnic,' said Alice. 'Jack taught him to swim in this pool.'

'Who's David?'

'Alice's son,' said Jon. 'He was killed in the Gallipoli Campaign in the First World War.'

'Oh, Alice, I am sorry,' said Val.

'No need to be,' said Alice, 'it was a long time ago.'

'Do you have any other children?'

'No, there was only David.'

Jon packed away the blankets and baskets aware, for the first time, of how lonely Alice must have been living alone at Jarrahlong. Trust Val to come up with an outing that would lift her spirits, he would never have thought of it.

'Is Bindi back?' asked Ty.

Everyone scanned the gorge for a glimpse of her.

'No worries,' he said. 'I'll wait for her.'

Ty loaded up Alice's chair and helped her into the passenger seat, and by the time they were ready to leave Bindi was back with a full dilly bag.

'What have you got in there?' asked Val.

'Leaves and things,' said Bindi.

And the rest, thought Jon. Had Yildilla sent her to get poison berries and roots? Was that the plan?

CHAPTER 40

Wes and Jon sat drinking tea on an old baulk of timber that Wes used as a chock.

'You're not looking too good these days,' said Wes, 'too drawn in the face, anything wrong?'

'No.'

'This business with Scally not getting to you?'

Jon smiled. 'No, I'm just a bit tired, Wes.'

'Too many picnics, is that it?' said Wes.

'Who told you?'

'Will Samuels, he said it was Alice's idea.'

'Is that what he said? It's more likely to have been Val putting her up to it.'

'Oh, I don't know. Alice has had a few rare ideas of her own over the years.' Wes sipped his tea staring fixedly into the dust. 'You know, I'll never understand Alice if I live to be a hundred.'

Jon grinned. 'You're not the only one…so, what's she gone and done now?'

'No, it's not that…it's…well, how old would you say she is?'

'Sixties.'

'Exactly! You'd have thought she'd have cut her losses after the bush fire and got herself a nice little place in town. She deserves to take it easy at her age, but, hell no, she has to go and invest her savings rebuilding the place and buying in new stock. And then what happens, Rachel moves out there and you come back from England and that friend of yours, Valerie, turns up, likes the place and gets herself a job and suddenly Charlestown's on the up.'

'That's a bit of an exaggeration, Wes.'

'I don't think so. Two blokes were round here last week looking for work. I'm telling you the town would be a sight different if we had a few more good-looking women about the place. It'd put Charlestown on the map. You any more lasses up your sleeve that you haven't mentioned yet?'

Jon laughed. 'There's Merle, she's studying to be a doctor in Liverpool, but I'm hoping she'll come out to Australia once she's qualified, and my sister, but she's still a kid.'

'We could do with a doctor; they're pretty few and far between. Imagine, three young women all with babies.'

'Hold on, Wes, Merle hasn't said yes yet, and Val's not stopping, she'll soon get sick of the place and then it'll just be Rachel again.'

'That's what you think, is it?'

'Yes. It was you who said the outback is a crook place for a woman.'

'Yeah,' said Wes, 'but that's only because there aren't enough of them. We need women. They're a civilising influence.'

'That's what Will said.'

'It's true, and it's up to us to make the place appealing.'

Jon grinned. 'And how are you going to do that, Wes?'

'I'll have a word with Connie, see if she knows where the old ciné-projector is. I think we should dust it off and show a film. That'll bring them in, and it'll make a change. Yes, that's what I'll do. I'll get Connie to order a film for us.'

'And where are you going to show it?'

'In the town hall; it's about time we used it again, and it has blackout curtains. Cato said we'd need them if the Japs took to bombing the place. He got the wind up when they bombed Darwin in February 1942.' Wes chuckled. 'He thought it'd be Charlestown next.'

Jon stood up and rinsed his mug in the sink. 'Thanks for getting the sump fixed, Wes. I don't like being without wheels.'

'Talking of the Japs have you heard the latest about Gerry?'

'No. What about him? And what's he got to do with the Japanese?'

'Hates them more than blacks.'

'Is there anyone he does like?'

'Not many, anyway rumour has it that Stan knows something. A mate of Gerry's is agitating, claims the last anyone saw of Gerry he was doing a delivery out Pilkington way, over beyond Stan's place. People speculate, you know how it is, and apparently Gerry had been shouting his mouth off about Stan being worth a packet, a stash of gold hidden somewhere in that shack of his.'

The hair on Jon's neck prickled. Who'd been talking? Les? No...he couldn't see it...Les wasn't the type to stir, and Gerry had got about a bit; there was no telling who he'd been gossiping to or who'd been listening in. 'People are clutching at straws, Wes. Can you imagine Stan doing Gerry in?'

'Stan was a fiery so-and-so in his day. He was always one to stand up for a fight. I've seen him square up to a fella twice his size so I wouldn't underestimate him if I were you.' Wes hauled himself to his feet and dusted off his pants.

'They've got it all wrong, Wes.'

'Maybe, but Constable Nickson called on Stan last week, he had a look round the place, checked out all those decrepit sheds of his.'

'And he didn't find anything, did he? I told you, Wes, Stan wouldn't do a thing like that.'

'No, I don't suppose he would, but if he had, the old fella's canny enough to get rid of the evidence. Nah, I reckon Gerry went shooting roo, had an accident, set off walking and collapsed in the bush somewhere.'

'Maybe they'll never find him.'

'Perhaps. Nickson had Aboriginal trackers out for days after Gerry first disappeared and that's three months gone, but they were working blind. No one knew for sure where Gerry had gone missing. Trouble is it's a long time for a body to be out there. I should imagine the dingoes will have done a fair job by now. Odd though, they haven't found his truck.'

Jon chewed his lip. It wasn't a closed case after all. 'No doubt he'll turn up sometime, Wes.'

'Aye, reckon you're right,' he tossed Jon the ute keys. 'Now you take care, don't go holing that sump again anytime soon.'

Jon set off for Jarrahlong worrying about Stan and how he'd hold up under questioning if Nickson decided there was something to investigate.

He thought back to the day he'd found Gerry's body with Jimmi's spear sticking out of his chest like a tent pole. He could still hear the sound of Gerry's body tumbling down the mineshaft, the rotten timbers collapsing and the rumble deep underground before everything settled into silence. They'd never find the body so there was nothing to implicate them if they kept their mouths shut, and Jimmi could be anywhere by now – South Australia, the Northern Territory, although that didn't mean he'd be safe from arrest if Stan talked.

He stifled a yawn, Stan wouldn't talk and there was nothing to link Jimmi with Gerry's disappearance. He couldn't see anyone in Charlestown making a connection between Buni's and Wally's deaths, Gerry's disappearance, and tribal justice.

Jon shook his head to clear it and took long blinks, glad that he was on the Jarrahlong track and not on the graded road otherwise he'd have turned the ute over in one of the run-offs. The need for rest overwhelmed him. He pulled up and killed the engine, leaned back in his seat and closed his eyes – a ten minute nap should be enough – but sleep eluded him. Yildilla's face appeared in the blue lights behind his eyelids – an aged face, as old as Methuselah's.

He stared at it, mesmerised by the pulsating image that faded and brightened even as he looked. He shivered violently and opened his eyes, wide awake now and all hope of rest gone.

Yildilla was a lawman. Stan said. Since the day they'd met, the Aborigine's watchful, tawny eyes had given him the jitters. He'd see them in his mind's eye even when Yildilla wasn't there. Was that what Stan meant when he talked about bone pointing? Was that why he couldn't sleep at night for headaches and disturbing dreams?

Nausea rose up his gullet. He stepped out of the vehicle and vomited into the dust. He didn't believe in bone pointing. It was his imagination running away with him, nothing more.

'You should have more sense you Pommy bastard!' he said to himself, the sound of his voice blotted out the unwelcome thoughts. 'Just think things through, what does Yildilla want?' he muttered.

He sat on the running board and chewed his thumb nail. It couldn't be revenge for killing Perentie; he'd have been punished by now, so it must be the tjuringa Yildilla was after. Was that why he had stayed on at Jarrahlong? Was the Aborigine waiting for an opportunity to claim it back?

What if I give it back to him? he wondered.

But he already knew the answer – it was too risky, and in any case, he didn't know enough about Aboriginal law. If Yildilla believed he'd violated a sacred object he'd have to punish him.

There was only one solution – return the tjuringa to Paradise Canyon, put it back where Curly had got it from and then he'd be able to start over with a clear conscience knowing he'd done the right thing. Yildilla would probably leave him alone then, and he'd be able to sleep at night.

He felt better having arrived at a decision and, with Nickson breathing down his neck, now was as good a time as any to make the journey.

CHAPTER 41

Jon stood in the shadow of the old gimlet tree at Denman Creek listening to the muffled hoof beats as Adie rode back to Jarrahlong with Red on a lead rein; where he was going a horse would be a liability.

Damp shirt clung to his skin; he shrugged, letting air circulate and squinted at the overcast sky, looking for a break in the cloud. The atmosphere had been muggy for days and with the oppressive heat the nightmares had returned – Perentie's hot breath fanning his face, the smell of him – or was it Curly's in his dying hours when the stench of gangrene gagged him? – And mixed up with the images of Curly and Perentie had been Gerry's dead body bloated and rotting at the bottom of Old Faithful mineshaft, and Jimmi and Yildilla implacably determined to uphold tribal justice.

He hawked up phlegm and spat it into the dust, his thoughts turning to the long walk ahead. Would he remember the route? For weeks now he'd dredged his memory of the journey he and Curly had made to the place he thought of as Paradise Canyon. He'd sketched a map of the markers he remembered, the king brown rock, the salt pans, the sandhills and the approximate distances they'd travelled in days. It wasn't perfect by any means, but it would have to do, and this time there was no drought. This time it would be easier to find water, wouldn't it?

Fourteen days it would take. Seven days there and seven days back. He was better prepared now. He knew the land, had a healthy respect for it and with all his outback experience it shouldn't be a problem.

He lifted the haversack onto his back. It was well stocked with Belle's dried meat and hard-tack biscuits – two weeks' worth at least, as long as he was careful; then there was the flour for damper, and salt, a hunting knife, and snares, and Curly's tjuringa wrapped in its scrap of dirty cloth just as it had been when Curly handed it into his safekeeping.

Night travelling was best, cooler, but the overcast sky had put paid to that – with two hours of daylight remaining he struck east at a brisk pace, following the watercourse before crossing the ridge and the scrubby land beyond that gave way to the vast spinifex plain where Jimmi had found him dehydrated and delirious.

He shivered as he recalled the last time, crossing the plain in the blazing summer heat, searching for the babies, the smooth rounded rocks that looked like babies' bottoms. There had been the terror of knowing that time was fast running out and the horror of the delirium, when the intense colours – red, blue and orange – seared his retinas, and the dry heat sucked the moisture out of his lungs making each breath agony, when he believed he was dying and when he wanted an end to it all.

This time he'd skirt the plain – legs shredded with the razor-sharp grasses and prickly scrub, and trousers reduced to bloody rags flapping round his ankles a quarter of the way into the journey, wouldn't do. If he'd calculated right the babies would be smooth mounds on the horizon.

Curly's grave first – he needed to go back and pay his respects; it was Curly's due. Perhaps it was a stupid idea, but that was the way he saw it, and that's what he'd decided in the small hours when he couldn't sleep and Perentie was breathing in his ear.

If only he could turn the clock back. If only he'd stayed in the camp at Mullin Soak with the others and hadn't seen the infant monitor lizard, a perentie, dozing on the rock. But he had, and the chance to show Curly he could provide an evening meal had been too good an opportunity to miss. He'd killed the lizard, he'd slaughtered Curly's sacred totem animal, his Dreamtime ancestor, and Curly had died, punished for the violation done in his name, for his benefit. All Jon's arguments, his reasoning, counted for nothing – Curly hadn't listened. Curly believed that he was the one ultimately responsible for Perentie's death, and he believed in his dying moments that Perentie's revenge came in the snakebite that ended his life.

So much had happened on that journey and somehow he had to make things right. But what if he couldn't? He blotted out the worrying thought and concentrated on the route ahead.

While Jon walked he tried to emulate Curly's chanting, but without the Aboriginal words it was difficult. He made up his own song describing the land, chanting the same refrain over and over in a monotonous sing-song intonation reminiscent of Curly's two and a half years earlier.

That night the cloud cover cleared and he saw the stars again, a net of diamond points in a midnight-blue sky. He built a fire, threw on extra wood, hung a billy on to boil, then rubbed his arms against the chill – he still found it hard to believe how cold it could get in the desert once the sun had gone down. That was the trouble with Australia: the extremes. His foggy breath clouded the air. The temperature was already dropping after the muggy days and balmy nights under the thick cloud cover.

After supper he took out the tjuringa, Curly's title deed to the land, and examined it by the firelight. The wood felt heavy, the grain fine and smooth to the touch except where the carvings cut deep into the wood. Jon ran his hand over the surface and felt its patina. With his index finger he traced the footprint – the ancient tribal route through the outback – the spiral at one end leading on to a necklace of circles joined by rows of parallel lines, the string of salt pans Curly had talked about. A groove crossed the line at right angles and then came a squiggle – king brown rock; and after that another circle, the vast claypan; then there were the wavy marks of the sandhills and, finally, an oval with zigzags incised within it, Paradise Canyon, his destination.

The remaining marks meant nothing to him. Had Curly carried on to Murrin Murrin using someone else's tribal route? Curly had said something about sharing. What was it he'd said when they stood looking at the huge scar in the landscape at Murrin Murrin? We've all got our own route that we have to memorize and share with others…I know my brother's bit and he knows mine, and we share them with cousins and uncles and people from other tribes. Is that what he'd said? He wished he'd taken more notice.

He caressed the wood that lay in his lap as delicately as he would a baby's cheek. Was he doing the right thing? He wished now that he'd talked to Jimmi. Jimmi would have advised him, but he'd left it too late, Adie said he'd gone back to his own people over Emu Field way.

Jon held the wood against his chest. Waiting wasn't an option any more; the nightmares were more frequent now, more intense and the responsibility laid on him by Curly in his dying moments weighed too heavy – the sooner the tjuringa was returned, the better. Carefully, he rewrapped the title deed and stowed it in the haversack, rolled out his swag and settled in for an early night – two more days travelling to that God-forsaken gorge in the back of beyond where Curly's grave lay – he'd still a long way to go.

At dawn tendrils of pale-grey light brightened the sky to the east. Jon rolled out of his swag and stretched his aching bones, conscious of the deep unease that had been dogging him for days, the feeling that he was being followed. He glanced about him and saw nothing out of the ordinary. Perhaps it was the remnant of a nightmare, but he didn't think so. Worry about the trip? That neither. He had enough food. Curly had shown him how to find water and the drought had broken months ago. He was fit and healthy. The trip was manageable – barring accidents.

He revived the fire and put the billy on to boil while thinking of Smoky. The half-breed cattle dog would have sniffed out a stranger straight away, and the animal would have given him something else to worry about, would have helped stop Perentie breathing down his neck.

He tried to ignore his unease and wished he hadn't listened to Adie. Adie had advised him against taking the dog, said the arid land wasn't good for domestic animals. But, either way, it was too late for regrets, and in any case, he was on a pilgrimage of sorts; he wasn't on a jaunt. He was here to atone, to put things right as far as it was possible. And even if he couldn't do that then he'd be honouring Curly's life, the Aboriginal's love of the land, and the knowledge Curly had imparted to him in the few short months they'd been friends. All he had to do was remember everything Curly had said and live as he'd been taught on their journey to Paradise Canyon, and if he could find some way of showing his respect to Curly's ancestor, his totem, then all to the good. But how the hell did he go about showing a monitor lizard respect?

The hurried breakfast of dried meat and hard tack sat heavy in his stomach as he doused the campfire and shrugged the bulky haversack onto his back. Ahead, the land looked as if it was carpeted in dirty snow, the eerie morning light bleaching colour from the faded pink and white everlasting flowers that grew profusely on the escarpment – only the vibrant billy buttons, splashes of yellow, punctuated the landscape with their vibrant hue. He stood for a moment taking in the scene and then set off east, anxious to cover as much ground as possible before dark.

The spinifex thinned and the ground became increasingly stony and uneven. Overhead an eagle soared on an early thermal, searching for sluggish reptiles, easy prey until the sun warmed their blood. On the horizon was a thin blue line, the edge of the escarpment – a day's walk away. It would take another day to cross it to the gorge and the dried-up river bed where Curly's bones lay.

Two days later he built a campfire close to Curly's grave not far from the rotten eucalypt where he'd seen a python taking the air. The valley was quiet in the late afternoon, just warbling magpies and the occasional raucous calls of crows and bush parrots. He went about his task, gathering wood for the night, checking every piece before picking it up. Pythons were all right, but Curly had been killed by a death adder, or maybe it was a king brown – the mulga snake.

That evening, by the light from the fire, he cleared away the leaves and twigs that had collected on the grave while thinking of Curly lying beneath the rocks and red earth, wrapped in his grey blanket, facing the morning sun.

Jon tried to pray and couldn't, Catholic words didn't seem right for an Aborigine, but they were all he had. He whispered the familiar Hail Mary, and crossed himself. Did it matter which words were used, Catholic or Aboriginal? He supposed not. They all worshipped the same God to his way of thinking despite what Father O'Leary said, but the Catholic words brought him no comfort and he wondered what Curly's ancestor spirit had made of them.

That night he kept a vigil, remembering the times they had spent together hunting goanna, the bungarra as he'd learnt to call them, watching western greys, euros and big reds grazing on the edge of the scrubby brush, following animal tracks, camping in the bush, and swimming at the green pool.

The night noises distracted him making it harder to focus on his thoughts. He fished in his pocket for the rosary he still carried from habit and found among the beads the rough marble-shaped tobacco ball Ty had given him. Ty had made it from dried and powered pituri leaves mixed with acacia wood ash and he'd used threads of the native flax plant to make the concoction stick together.

Jon looked at the grey ball covered in fluff in the palm of his hand. Ty had expected him to chew it there and then, but he hadn't fancied it, he'd said he'd keep it for later and had forgotten about it.

Curly also chewed the stuff, had even offered him some once and had laughed when he'd shaken his head. You don't know what you're missin', mate, he'd said, and afterwards he'd stuck the masticated lump behind his ear for later.

Jon wiped off the bits of lint and sniffed it. The smell was distinctive but not like anything else he'd come across before, it wasn't anything like chewing tobacco or his mother's favourite cigarettes. He leaned back against the nearest boulder, put it in his mouth and held it there for a while conscious of its smooth grittiness. The ball softened. He chewed it tentatively.

Saliva flooded his mouth and he swallowed. The Elders had given it to Curly before his initiation ceremony. What was it Curly said? – Couldn't cope with that stuff, mate, not without pituri. Curly grinned when he'd asked him about the rite of passage. Private stuff, he'd said, it's more than me life's worth to tell you. But Stan had already told him about Aboriginal circumcision, and the rest of it. He shuddered.

The boulder cradled him softly, like a pillow. Strange thoughts peppered his brain, colour was brighter – eye squintingly bright – and his mind was out there somewhere, floating, watching his body relaxing against the rock, feeling the pituri juice trickle down his throat, smelling the acrid odour of it, absorbed by the weirdness of being in two places at once. Was it the pituri, or his imagination?

He drifted into a waking sleep, his memories of his time with Curly clear and unclouded and he heard Curly's voice murmuring in his ear telling him about pituri…

'...It makes you feel good, mate. It staves off the hunger pangs and keeps you going long time. Good for catching emus, parrots and kangaroos at waterholes. The smell attracts them and dopes them, makes 'em easier to catch.'

And then they're travelling along a dried-up watercourse, heading into the bush, hunting for kangaroo, leaving the other stockmen looking after the sheep at Corkwood Bore. Curly strides ahead carrying his boomerang, his spear and a throwing stick, his woomera, with him and, after a time, they turn west towards the grassy plain on the edge of densely-wooded land bounding Jarrahlong Station, following the eucalyptus line, keeping in the shade, eyes scanning the glades and open patches for kangaroos.

Curly drops down to his haunches and signals him to do the same. They squat in the long grass watching a mob of big reds grazing, lazing and squabbling on the far side of a clearing.

A female kangaroo lopes towards them, one rolling hop at a time, a joey hanging out of her pouch. Behind her a couple of half-grown males are sparring with each other, vying for position whilst keeping a weather eye out for the big adult males. Other roos lie in dust baths grooming themselves, nibbling the under-fur on their bellies and rubbing their ears with their paws.

'Which one're we going for?' he asks.

Curly indicates in the direction of the half-grown males.

They skirt the mob, keeping down wind. Silently, Curly raises his throwing stick and slowly and deliberately takes aim, his left hand pointing towards the kangaroo and his right drawn back until his hand is level with his shoulder. Then comes the thrust. The spear sparkles through the air, the sun glinting on the metal tip. The kangaroos scatter, but too late. The spear reaches its mark and sinks deep into the animal's haunch – the shaft describing an undulating line with every bound.

Curly is after it, following where the injured kangaroo leads. He follows too, ploughing through the undergrowth, half his thoughts on venomous snakes that might be lurking underfoot.

They run through dappled shade, the mulga and mallee snatching at their clothes and whipping their faces, dead twigs and sharp grasses scratching their legs. He can feel his chest tightening, the effort to drag air into his burning lungs harder with every step, his legs heavier, the air rasping in his throat. Through blurred vision he catches glimpses of Curly's lithe, athletic body increasing the distance between them, of Curly pacing himself like a long-distance runner as he follows the track of the maimed creature.

How much longer? Will the animal escape only to die in the bush? His rubber legs give way and he hits the ground hard. Red mist clouds his vision as he struggles to draw oxygen into his burning lungs and starving brain. He flops onto his back, gulping warm air, waiting for the sparkling pinpricks of light behind his eyelids to settle.

After a while the dizziness subsides and he rolls onto his belly and crawls to his knees. He listens, but the bush has returned to normal, he hears only the sounds of insects and birds scuttling, chirruping and scratching about in the scrub, there are no pounding feet, no crashing noises in the undergrowth. On his feet again he follows the trail, slowly, so as to miss nothing, and finds Curly butchering the kangaroo...

...The remembered smell of the fresh meat, and the sound of the blade as it sliced through the muscle and sinew, cut through the drug-induced memory and pulled him out of his reverie. For a moment he didn't know where he was and then it came to him – the pituri. He smiled. He'd forgotten about the kangaroo hunt, of seeing the excitement in Curly's eyes, the satisfaction as he'd handed over the meat to Jimmi for the evening meal and his pride as they'd eaten the food he'd provided, but it had been Curly's ability to run long distances without flagging that had impressed him the most. Was pituri the secret of Curly's stamina, his endurance? He took the masticated ball out of his mouth and stuck it behind his ear like Curly had done. Better not waste it, he might need it later.

Over the next few days he followed the route to Paradise Canyon, crossing the string of salt pans with their shimmering mirages and then, later, the vast claypan, and after that the sandhills, a red sea of sand dunes too high to look over. He chewed on the pituri ball when the going was hard and came to believe it gave him extra strength, the ability to sustain a steady pace even when the muscles in his legs were screaming for rest. A day behind schedule he reached the huge ironstone escarpment and labyrinthine gorges carved deep in the mass of rock that led into Paradise Canyon – the green oasis with its abundance of wildlife, an Eden in the middle of the desert.

From a distance no one would have suspected the gem hidden within, from a distance the ironstone looked like any other range, but Curly had taught him otherwise. Curly's Eden was Aboriginal insurance against the hard times, a place where water could always be found, where there was game to be had, and bush food: yams, seeds, and berries. Curly had taught him to respect it, to take only the absolute minimum from the land, to leave the plants, animals and birds to reproduce for future use.

The canyon was sacred to several Aboriginal mobs, not just Curly's. It didn't lie within one tribe's domain but lay on the old routes of many. As Curly had once said, it was a crossroads in the desert complete with its Aboriginal equivalent of an Aussie roadhouse.

Jon followed the same gorge into the valley, the sheer sides casting deep shadow, the route as rough and littered with boulders and stones as before. He picked his way carefully, mindful of the need to avoid a twisted ankle, anticipating the view from the plateau. As the gorge narrowed so began the climb up the old foot trail until he was back in sunlight.

He crossed the tableland and stood where he'd stood two and a half years earlier with Curly looking down into the great gash in the ironstone that curved around out of sight. From above its shape was like a giant question mark, the sheer sides punctuated with fissures – the narrow gorges that petered out into the vast escarpment or provided other routes out of the valley. Compared to the barren rock upon which he was standing and the vast rolling sea of sandhills that stretched as far as the eye could see, the gorge below was a jewel reminding him of a sliver of fire opal. The flashes of scarlet, purple, indigo and viridian – the bright plumage of birds – contrasted dramatically with the grey-green foliage of acacia and eucalyptus and the thread of glittering blue water far below.

Jon gazed down on the Perentie footprint, the clear, small pools now linked in a long sparkling zigzag of water that ran the length of the gorge. He looked for the sandy spits of land that punctuated its meandering route in among the mallee and mulga that grew in profusion along both sides of the water. He recognised the smaller trees: gidgee, kurrajong, currant and sweet quandong and the huge ghost gums and other eucalypts that soared above the scrub bush, and smelt the wattle-scented air that wafted up on the gentle breeze.

Away to the right, at the base of the sheer rock face, he searched for the ruined remains of the plane he'd found last time and thought he saw a flash of sunlight bouncing off glass, but he couldn't be sure, perhaps it was his imagination.

He followed the winding path downwards and set up camp. There he lit a fire, put the billy on to boil and went fishing for yabbies, the crayfish Curly had taught him to find. Afterwards he searched for yams, looking for the thin tendrils of growth that twisted up through the open bush. He followed the stems back to the ground and started digging – two good sized yams washed and cooked in the burning embers would be delicious.

Later, replete, elbows resting on raised knees, sucking the meat out of the last yabbie claw, the late afternoon sun warming his skin, Jon considered his position. This was the life, like being a boy scout only better. Above him parakeets and twenty-eight parrots settled for the night, squabbling and fighting for prime perches. In the undergrowth cicadas rattled and chattered. He was glad to be back. Curly would have approved, he was sure.

He threw more wood on the fire, refilled the billy and hung it from a stick to heat overnight. Tucked into his swag, keeping close to the rock for warmth, he sat awhile looking at the starlit canopy above. It would have been nice to have shared the moment with Merle, to have had her sitting next to him, eating the best of the bush tucker and warm damper, drinking strong billy tea. Their life together would be good. He fished in his pocket and took out her most recent letter, dog-eared and battered from re-reading and read it again, remembering their time together in Liverpool and imagining the future they would have once she was qualified. There was talk of a new hospital wing being built at Merredin and that wasn't so very far from Charlestown, a few hours or so, not too far to drive over and see her at weekends. Then, after they were married and the babies came she'd be busy; they'd both be busy building a new life for themselves. He remembered the smell of her, the soap she used, the softness of her hair against his cheek. 'Night, Merle,' he murmured, pocketing her letter and then he settled down for the night, waiting for sleep to overtake him.

Jon woke early, before the dawn chorus, sure that he was being watched again, that someone else was out there. Gooseflesh stood out on his arms and he couldn't shake off the uneasy feeling. He lay for a while surveying the gorge through half-closed eyes, hoping to catch a glimpse of the watcher but saw nothing except the native birds, preening and stretching, fluffing their feathers as they warmed up in the chill morning air.

He tried to convince himself it was an animal, but his anxiety grew as he breakfasted on stale damper and dried meat. Perhaps he was mistaken, not an animal but Aborigines who had arrived overnight.

After eating he picked up his haversack and took a walk down the length of the gorge, looking for fresh signs of human activity, but found nothing – only the remains of several old campsites, ashes, grinding stones and broken cutting tools; and small piles of broken pits from the quandong fruit; and gashes in the trunks of the biggest trees where Aborigines had removed large slabs of bark to make coolimans for carrying food and water.

There was no sign of recent occupation. Except for him the canyon was empty, an over-active imagination then, that was his problem. The sooner he returned Curly's tjuringa to the sacred cavern the better, he'd have done the right thing and the guilt triggering his unease would go.

On the way to the cavern he stopped to look at the plane wreckage. It didn't look any different; the same bush still scrubbed the windscreen clean, the old webbing from the seat belt still dangled down inside the cabin. It wouldn't have been comfortable hanging upside down in the seat still strapped in from when the plane flopped over on its back, belly-up. Had the pilot been conscious, afraid the whole lot would catch fire? Or had he been mercifully oblivious to it all, knocked out by the impact? Jon looked up and saw the scarred rock where the plane had nosedived from eighty feet above him. Unconscious! The pilot had probably been out of it for hours – weird though, the way the windscreen had survived intact when the rest of the plane was matchwood.

He inspected the remains, looking for clues he'd missed before and found nothing new, only the partial number of the plane in black paint. Satisfied there was nothing more to discover he jumped down, collected the haversack and made for the hidden gully, following the route Curly had shown him.

The shaded passageway was as cold as ever, the sheer rock oppressive. Above, a ribbon of cobalt sky narrowed to nothing as the sides closed in and became a cave.

Jon stopped for a moment, taking in the smell and the sounds of the place, the damp, dank, metallic tang of rock that never sees the sun, the drip, drip of condensation and the muted bubbling of running water deep underground that had sounded like a purring cat the first time he heard it. Now he thought of it as the heartbeat of a sleeping reptile even though it existed only in his imagination.

This time he knew the way and was not afraid. He edged forward, willing his eyes to adjust, watching for the grey pearl of light at the end of the tunnel, feeling his way with his feet, listening to the rock sighing, its measured breath tickling his face, knowing where the draught of cool air came from, from high on the plateau, sucked in through the collapsed cavern roof.

Soon the darkness lightened and the grey pearl grew larger until he stood at the edge of the cavern looking up into the shaft of sunlight streaming down from the gaping, ragged hole some seventy feet above. This time Curly was not standing in the sunlight to welcome him, this time he was alone with sleeping Perentie and the cloud of midges dancing maniacally in the sunbeam.

He stepped further into the cavern, his eyes drawn to the reef of pure gold running diagonally across the cavern wall – a bolt of golden lightning frozen in time. He remembered the momentary elation when he thought he'd found Lasseter's famous reef, and the awful realisation that the pilot had got there first, had despoiled the pristine seam, had violated a holy place.

At the edge of the sunbeam the spoil glinted. Even from a distance he could see the gold nuggets he'd handed back under

Curly's watchful gaze. He could still remember the feel of the gold, the hardness of the nuggets pressing against his thigh, their rough edges under his fingertips as he took them out of this pocket, and Curly's words – not from here, Jon – when he handed back the two opal nuggets that Stan later said had come from the mines at Coober Pedy.

He stepped forward, bent down and picked up a piece of the discarded gold and weighed it in his hand as he had Stan's gold nugget. A dozen nuggets, and the rest, enough wealth for a lease on a sheep station like Alice's and money left over to build a home with pretty curtains and rugs, enough comfort for an English girl a long way from home. He reached over the spoil and caressed the reef, running his fingers up the jagged streak until it was out of his reach.

Thou shalt not covet – Father William's words came back to him, the priest's teaching from the Old Testament, the tenth commandment. Truth was he *did* covet. He wanted the gold. The Aborigines didn't, that was obvious, had they done so it would have been long gone. Jon thought of the gold cross and the gold candlesticks on the altar in the Catholic Church in Liverpool that he used to go to with his mother when he was a kid, and the silver-gilt paten and chalice used by the priest in Holy Communion. That was holy gold, so what was different about this?

Nothing!

He replaced the nugget and turned away, troubled by his desire and his need, troubled by his sense of regret at having to leave a dream behind him.

The golden rubble rattled under his feet as he turned his back on fabulous wealth and crossed to the other side of the cavern with its painted wall, its huge monitor lizard, Perentie Man, Curly's clan ancestor, chasing the tail of the golden reef. The ancient paintings danced before his eyes, the salt pan circles, the king brown rock squiggle in red ochre, the x-ray images of the wild life, the bandicoot, wallaby, kangaroo, lizards, birds and fish; the handprints, hundreds of them in red and yellow ochre – some ancient and others brand new, the paint barely dry. This was where Curly's tjuringa should lie? This was where it had been two and a half years earlier when Curly retrieved it from its hiding place.

He searched the rock face for the place where Curly had stored the mulga-wood panel. Gradually, his eyes acclimatized to the gloom and he picked out irregularities in the rock. High up, not far from Perentie's head, was the spot, a natural fissure, the niche where he would place the tjuringa safe from harm but within reach should Curly's people wish to reclaim it. But there was nothing to stand on, nothing that he could use as a ladder, and he wasn't as nimble as Curly had been. He would have to go back to the gorge and find something.

The sun's heat warmed his skin and he shivered after the chilly cavern. A crow watched him from a rotting eucalypt and the old sensation, that he was being stalked, returned. He shivered again. He was getting paranoid, too much time spent on his own with not enough to occupy his mind – that was the problem. 'Shoo,' he shouted, waving his arms.

The bird lifted, beating the air with outstretched wings like a black demon in the Book of Hours in the orphanage library. He dragged his eyes away from it and found a piece of mulga that would do as a ladder, strong enough to take his weight.

Back in the cavern with the wood jammed against the rock face and secure he shinned up it and placed Curly's tjuringa in the fissure, resting it on its long edge, like a book on a shelf, and ran his fingers over it one last time. Perhaps he'd been wrong to take it to England, but he had kept his promise to Curly, he had looked after it and now he'd returned it to the only place he knew. He'd done his best, he could do no more.

Jon dropped to the ground and looked up at Perentie's image for a long moment, and then he solemnly asked forgiveness and promised to guard Perentie from harm as Curly had done. But did an English lad's promise mean anything to an Aboriginal Perentie? He doubted it, so he added a Hail Mary for good measure.

CHAPTER 42

The light was fading fast by the time he left the gully. Parakeets and finches squawked and chattered as he pushed through the brushwood. Underfoot, small reptiles and insects, their tiny feet and claws scratching the sandy rock, scuttled for safety – from him or the watcher?

Jon crossed himself, listening for unfamiliar sounds and sniffed the air for woodsmoke and cooking. Then he laughed out loud, Val would have given him what for, she'd have chewed off his ear and told him a good lass was worth two blokes any day of the week. Val wouldn't get rattled. He recalled how she reacted when he'd put the dying cat out of its misery on the waste ground in Liverpool. Of all his friends she was the only one with the courage to question his actions, the only one who gave him the opportunity to explain himself.

His stomach rumbled, breakfast was hours ago. He collected an armful of tinder-dry acacia wood and lit a fire. Soon, the scent of baked damper and the sound of boiling water filled the air, and only then did he notice the marks on the sandy spit in full view of the camp – footprints, two of them, side by side as if someone had stood there watching, but in what direction? He stared mesmerized by the oval shapes as a shudder rippled down his spine.

He sat with a big rock firm against his back, waiting, watching for the executioner to appear, dread chilling him to the marrow.

The kaditja man was after him, but why? Was it for killing Perentie or for taking the tjuringa? He still wasn't sure. Was he being punished for what he'd done or for something Curly had done? Had taking responsibility for the tjuringa meant that he had other responsibilities – ones Curly hadn't been able to tell him about before he died?

He drank his tea and ate the damper and some of the dried meat, chewing over the unfairness of it all. It wasn't right. Aborigines had no jurisdiction over whites; an Aboriginal lawman couldn't punish him for something he had no understanding of or knowledge about.

Jon drew his blanket closer to him and waited.

The night hours dragged. Periodically he flung more wood onto the fire, he watched the sparks flare, heard the wood crackle, smelt the acacia scent as the timber burnt, while above him the stars moved across the night sky. By three o'clock his eyelids were heavy, staying awake increasingly hard, was the executioner waiting for him to sleep so he didn't have to look him in the eyes when he killed him? He wondered what Gerry had done when faced with death. Had he pleaded with Jimmi for his life, or had he toughed it out, threatening to shoot the Aborigine, leaving his carcass for the dingoes as he'd done with Buni and Wally? But he wasn't Gerry. Gerry had deserved to die. Gerry had killed Aborigines, he hadn't. Perentie didn't count, did he? All he'd killed was a monitor lizard…perhaps if he pleaded his case…pleaded ignorance…

Dawn – a magpie warbled its beautiful melodic song, nothing like the harsh rattle of Liverpool magpies…one for sorrow, two for joy Mam always said…he searched the bush for its mate. And where was the kaditja man? Was he playing a waiting game…wearing him down…instilling fear in him, was that it?

'I know you're out there,' Jon shouted, the words echoing down the gorge, disturbing the galahs and budgerigars that exploded into the air like confetti at a wedding. 'What do you want?' *Want…want…want* bounced back, echoing his alarm. He tried to ignore the fear twisting his guts, the sweat on his brow, the clamminess prickling his skin in the early-morning chill, and then a pebble clattered and rattled above and behind him. He twisted his head to look up at the rock he was leaning against – nothing – only an animal or a bird, not the executioner.

He turned back and the kaditja man stood before him, his face painted white, dressed native style, a spear clasped in his hand, its shadow a diagonal slash across his naked chest.

Jon gasped, the sharp intake of breath punctuating the silence. Yildilla!

Jon stared at the Aboriginal in horror. From the first Yildilla had seemed different, remote, aloof, a man apart and the other Aborigines feared him, treated him with deference. Did they know? And what about Bindi, did she know her grandfather was a kaditja man?

'What do you want?' asked Jon, rising slowly to his feet. 'Why are you here?'

The Aboriginal didn't answer. He stood there in his feather and grass slippers and began a muttering that Jon could barely hear.

Then Yildilla crouched, his arms and legs taking on the characteristics of Perentie Man, his feet stamping the red earth.

So that was what it was all about – his killing of the totem! Except Perentie wasn't his totem, he was Curly's.

'Perentie's not my totem,' he yelled. 'You hear me?'

Yildilla continued the mumbling chant.

Did Yildilla believe Curly had made him a clan member when he showed him the sacred cavern and handed the tjuringa into his safe keeping? Had he signed his own death warrant by returning to the sacred place?

The skin tightened on his scalp. He licked his lips. He was going to die, just as surely as Gerry had, run through with an Aboriginal spear.

Yildilla's eyes never left his face. The chanting and the stamping to the mesmerizing rhythm continued. There was nowhere to run. He knew that. The old man was fast and he had stamina, like Curly. Jon closed his mind to the Aboriginal and blocked his stare. He thought of his sister, of Merle, the people he loved and who loved him. They would never know what had happened. By the time Alice realised he wasn't returning to Jarrahlong, and Stan had persuaded her to send out a search party, his body would be long gone, his bones scattered in the dust.

The chanting stopped. The Aboriginal stood as still as the rocks behind him, his spear raised to shoulder height and drawn back, a feather on his headband fluttering in the breeze. The tension increased in Yildilla's arm muscles, his body twisted, the spear pointing at Jon's chest.

This was the moment! Jon wanted to close his eyes and couldn't.

Yildilla dipped the point – the moment too fast to register – and the weapon hissed like a snake, the mean head cut the air and pierced his thigh. Jon gasped. His lips drew back as the iron sliced through skin, nerve and muscle and lacerated the bone. Fire leapt the length of his body spreading like a dark stain, and wet warmth seeped through his britches as he lost control.

Like a man in a dream he sank to one knee, the injured leg stretched out, one hand splayed in the dust supporting his body, the other clutching the spear and leg. Blood bloomed like a rose under his fingers and mingled with the urine.

He could hear moaning.

When he looked up Yildilla filled his world, looming over him, his face an impassive mask, oblivious to his agony.

He heard a rushing in his ears and his sight blurred. Blackness crept in around the edges of this vision.

Was this death?

When Jon regained consciousness the sun was high overhead, the heat burning his face, the ground digging into his back. For a moment he didn't know where he was.

He moved; pain exploded through his body, every nerve screamed in agony, turning his stomach. He vomited half-digested meat and damper and brushed sand over the mess, waiting for the pain to ease. Getting comfortable was impossible. Every movement jarred the spear, compounding the agony. Tears pricked his eyes as he sort to ease the pain, to drag himself into a more comfortable position.

What was he doing in this God-forsaken place? He was a city boy. He shouldn't be in the outback dying because of some stupid Aboriginal law that meant nothing to him. He thought of Pete in his smart suit doing black-market deals, raking in the cash, and wished he'd never left Liverpool.

He swore and flopped back onto the sand and stared blindly into the distance cursing Yildilla, Aborigines, Australia and the magpie sitting on a dead stump watching him, its head cocked to one side, waiting for dinner.

Somehow he had to remove the spear, but how? His pocket knife wasn't sharp enough to cut through the spear shaft; it was barely sharp enough to cut through his trousers.

Underneath the cotton the flesh was blackened and puffy and already he'd suffered fly strike. The blowfly eggs, yellowish rice-like seeds, were ugly and it chilled his blood just to look at them. He gritted his teeth and scraped off what he could – there'd be more where the spear had exited. How long before they hatched – five days? He'd seen what maggots did to sheep and shuddered.

He batted at the cloud of flies circling overhead like carrion crows, waiting for him to give up the fight, and then he lay back carefully, avoiding any movement that would jar his leg. What did he do now?

There was no chance of walking out, and Yildilla wasn't coming back, not unless he planned to finish him off after he'd suffered sufficiently to appease Perentie. But even as the thought formed he knew that wasn't likely to happen. Dying would be a slow, protracted process from dehydration, starvation, infection or animal predation – from dingoes.

Well, he wasn't about to give Yildilla the satisfaction. Somehow he'd survive, but first he'd have to remove the spear and give the wound time to heal. He stared at the weapon and then looked down beyond it to his foot and tried to wriggle his toes to assess the nerve damage, and couldn't.

He licked his lips. Of course he'd be able to walk, no point in considering the alternative. He eyed the spear shaft, three feet long one side and at least six inches protruding out of the back of his thigh at the other. He had no choice. He had to cut through the shaft as close to the leg as possible and pull the remainder through from the back.

He started sawing before he could change his mind, panted to disperse the bright spangles of light flickering behind his eyes, concentrated on his breathing, forcing back the black edges crowding his vision.

Sweat made the knife slip in his hand, tears trickled down his cheeks.

He couldn't do it!

He stared at his hand, at the knife, watching the shake he couldn't control, waiting for the next wave of nausea and blackness to descend.

Hours later, or perhaps it was days, he thought he could hear voices, see people out of the corner of his eye. Keeping his thoughts ordered grew harder; he was losing the thread, and his skin had taken on a grey tinge – it felt cool and moist, and cramp added to his misery.

He reached over for his water bottle and shook it – empty – the distance to the water inches and yet miles away. He licked dry lips and tried to swallow, but couldn't, his tongue thick in his mouth. Water, without it he'd die. He buried the thought and dragged himself across the sandy patch, gritting his teeth against the pain, his right hand gripping the spear, minimizing movement.

At the water's edge he sucked in the smell, buried his head in its cool sweetness and drank deeply. Did water always taste this good? He rested, drank some more, filled the water bottle and dragged himself back to the dead campfire.

Exhausted, he lay as close to the big rock as he could for warmth, wrapped in a blanket, and ate the hard tack and dried meat, and drank more water.

Rest – tomorrow was another day. Tomorrow the spear would have to be removed, somehow.

That night his dreams were kaleidoscopes of people he knew: his mother, Jimmi, Father O'Leary, Alice, Stan and Rachel, all clamouring to give their advice, berating him for his stupidity. He searched in his dream for Merle and got angry when Val interrupted, her shoulder-length hair bouncing as she laughed at him, mocking his helplessness. He thought he could smell Perentie from time to time, the stench of carrion on his foul breath. And there were sounds – Aboriginal chanting, the rhythmic clap-sticks, the rattle of an old utility truck bouncing over rough ground, and sheep bleating in the distance.

In the early hours he woke, his leg throbbing, the flesh puffy, red and angry. Already the shaking chill that came with fever had a hold. He'd been a fool to wait so long. The spear shaft had to be pushed through his leg. It was his only chance.

He rolled onto his side, grabbed the shaft with both hands and pushed. A loud gasp scattered the sleeping birds. He panted to clear his head, clamped his teeth together and pushed again and again. Fresh blood trickled down his leg from the wound and down his chin from his bitten lip. Tears of pain and frustration rolled down his cheeks. He couldn't do it! He couldn't block the pain.

Pituri! He stuffed the ball in his mouth and bit into the bitter half-chewed baccy, grinding it like chewing gum, swallowing the saliva until he felt the drug kick in. When his head stopped spinning and the blackness receded he dragged himself to his knees, the muscle deep in his thigh tugging against the shaft sending jagged pain through his body.

He swore and chewed on the pituri like fury, then, kneeling upright, with both hands gripping the spear shaft and teeth clenched against the pain, he took several deep breaths, letting the drug and the hyperventilation bring on the light-headedness he needed, and pushed.

Three times he repeated the process, blacking out between each effort, and every time the shaft moved a few more inches.

Finally, with breath hissing through his teeth, he knelt upright again, this time grasping the spear from behind. He chewed the pituri and breathed in deeply, filling his brain and lungs with drug and oxygen. 'This time,' he muttered, 'this time…this time!'

He curled his fingers tighter round the shaft and yanked.

Breath exploded from his mouth. Bright lights seared the backs of his eyes. Black spots danced before him and gasping, ragged breath roared in his ears.

He flung the shaft away, heard it clatter on the rocks and flopped forward, taking the weight on braced arms, his elbows locked until the faintness passed. Then he crawled to the creek and sat in the deepest part letting the flowing water wash away the blood, sweat and grit, and clean the fly-blown flesh.

CHAPTER 43

The next days passed in a shivering daze, his body burning up, craving cool water one minute and a warm blanket the next. Overhead the sun travelled across the sky three times, or was it four?

Eventually Perentie Man visited less often, the nightmares dwindled, colours separated out again, lucid moments during the long days and nights lengthened, he recognised the birdsong, his surroundings, the sound of cicadas at dusk, and he knew he'd make it. The infection that had racked his body for days was receding; the puss seeping from the awful wound less profuse. A week after the injury he made himself a crude crutch, built a fire and made his first brew of tea for eight days. He needed to eat, needed to get his strength back. His clothes hung off him, he'd lost weight and his face felt gaunt under the thick stubble. He scratched his itchy skin, easier than shaving and less effort.

A week passed, and then another. The wound healed leaving deep craters where the spear had gone through his leg. Walking was painful and he limped. His situation too had deteriorated, he was out of hard tack and dried meat and there wasn't a deal of flour left, soon he would be reliant solely on what the valley could provide, and by his calculation it would be another week at least before anyone at Jarrahlong would really begin to worry.

Five weeks after he'd left Adie at Denman Creek he dug down into the rock-hard earth after a goanna he'd been trailing. He needed meat. He was sick of yabbies, and in any case, he'd eaten most of them.

Behind him a flock of twenty-eight parrots chattered in the top of an old eucalyptus tree. He ignored the commotion and kept digging. Sweat poured off his brow and dripped onto his shirt already stiff with dried perspiration. When he'd dug as far as he could he got down on his good knee, his damaged leg extended, and started digging again, using his hands to clear a wider entrance, then he leaned over and pushed the whole of his arm down the hole, reaching for the lizard.

He knew it was down there. He'd seen it scuttle down the burrow. He felt for it again, shoving his shoulder deeper, the earth rough against his cheek, sandy soil running down his neck, wishing the bloody parrots would shut up; their chattering was getting on his nerves spoiling his concentration.

Finally, his fingers felt smooth, dry skin – the goanna. He felt its hissed warning when he clamped his hand around the thick tail and back leg and gave a tug. But the lizard wasn't going anywhere, it braced itself against the tunnel walls, its feet digging in, resisting him. He pulled again, harder this time and felt the animal shift. 'Got you,' he muttered, pulling the animal out of its burrow tail first.

Jon rested for a moment, getting his strength back, and pulled the creature clear of the hole. He thwacked it hard on the head with his digging stick and watched with satisfaction as its legs and tail twitched and then curled involuntarily – a goanna, not a monitor lizard, there'd be no nasty repercussions, no retribution this time.

Jon pictured it roasting in the ashes, succulent hot flesh, juices dripping off his chin, his first real meal in weeks.

He left the animal on the ground and stood up, his head spinning from the effort. He thought he saw Bindi – a mirage? He closed his eyes and shook his head to clear the fuzziness and when he opened them she was chasing after the goanna as it tried to escape. She grabbed it by a back leg and swung it hard against a rock. This time the animal flopped limply against her bare leg as she walked towards him.

He grinned. 'Am I pleased to see you!'

She acknowledged his words with a slight tilt of the head and strode off towards the camp. By the time he caught up with her she'd buried the animal deep in the hot ashes.

Jon poured her a mugful of stewed tea and watched her drink the bitter liquid, wondering what she was doing in the canyon and how she'd known where to find him.

'Yildilla sent me,' she said.

She'd read his thoughts!

'I got tucker in me bag.' She studied the cobalt sky dotted with small billowy clouds and smiled. 'Good travelling tonight.'

Bindi finished the tea and handed back the mug. He refilled it and sat back against a big rock, nursing the mug and watching her as she busied herself making damper. He hadn't realised how fearful he had been of making the journey home on his own. It was something he'd shoved to the back of his mind, but with Bindi he'd be all right. Ty reckoned no one knew the outback like she did, that Yildilla had taught her all the bushcraft he knew.

Bindi was different. His gran would have described her as fey. She had an otherworldliness about her as if she lived in another space half the time. Alice called her a dreamer, but he didn't agree – she just marched to a different drum. That's what his gran used to say about mad Gladys Watts who kept cats and lived on Prince Street. Well, that summed up Bindi exactly, not that Bindi was mad, she just had other priorities and worked to Aboriginal time.

He must have dozed because when he woke the meal was ready. Later, after they'd eaten roasted goanna and hot damper, Bindi divided the left-over food between their bags and refilled the water bottles, and together they set off for Jarrahlong. By the time the sun had gone down they were clear of the gorge. His leg ached from the effort and his head throbbed, but he wasn't going to admit to Bindi that he couldn't do it.

Jon chewed on the pituri ball aware that its potency had dwindled that the sensation of being one step from reality had gone. Only the bitter grittiness remained. He laughed at his stupidity when he thought of what he had done. Perhaps if he'd burnt Curly's tjuringa as Stan suggested then none of it, the long journey, the punishment, would have happened, and he would not have been in the sacred canyon miles from anywhere at the mercy of Yildilla and Aboriginal justice.

They rested a while in the thin ribbon of mallee scrub between the ocean of sandhills and the sandstone ranges. Bindi built a fire and filled the billycan with enough water for a brew from the hole she had dug in the earth, just as Curly had done a lifetime ago.

Jon leaned back against his haversack, closed his eyes and focussed on the long trek ahead, refusing to think about the walk out of the gorge and the pain in his thigh. Keeping up with Bindi had been tougher than he'd expected, nothing like his movements in the canyon when he could take his time and rest.

He heard her throw more sticks onto the fire, heard the crackle, smelt the familiar scent of burning eucalyptus, felt the heat of it on his face. He kept his eyes closed, afraid to open them in case she read the doubt there, and straightened his leg, feeling for the damaged muscle to pull. When he flexed his toes sweat prickled his forehead. The sandhills lay ahead – a three-day walk, five in his condition – a sea of gritty ridges rising up like swell on the ocean.

He tried not to think about the sheer effort it would take to haul himself up ridge after monotonous ridge, and the sense of despair he'd feel while standing on the top of one looking out across the land, seeing nothing else for as far as the eye could see.

Jon concentrated on the warmth from the fire, listening to Bindi moving around the camp.

When she woke him the moon was already up and the stars were bright. He rubbed away the sleep chill from his arms and legs and accepted a mug of gritty tea. After the fire was doused they set off, heading south-west, using the stars as a guide.

Mind over matter, he kept telling himself as he toiled up one sand ridge and flapped down the other side. Walking down was bad but it didn't raise the sweat or the heart rate like toiling up them when the strain on his damaged muscle was at its greatest. He muttered half-remembered passages from the Bible that he'd learnt in school, and playground rhymes, and thought about his friends back at home in Liverpool and, when all else failed, he thought of Merle, but even thoughts of Merle didn't block the aching, stabbing agony in his leg.

Later still he kept his eyes fixed on Bindi's track, following her footprints, quelling the panic when he lost sight of her familiar figure, afraid that she'd abandon him. But time and again he'd find her waiting for him, sitting on the top of one of the ridges. He wondered what she did as she waited. Was she resting, watching the stars, or listening to the night noises? Probably all three knowing Bindi!

Jon wished he could rest and contemplate the stars; instead, he had to be content listening to the air whistling through his gritted teeth, and to the *sluff, sluff* of his measured tramp up and down the interminable hills.

He became increasingly troubled as the night progressed. They were following a different route to the one he'd used, but he wasn't completely sure because he hadn't taken that much notice at first. He'd been too busy putting one foot in front of the other, concentrating on his breathing, on keeping the agony at bay, and on willing the night to end. The only time his attention deviated was to scan the horizon for a glimpse of Bindi whenever he reached a ridge top.

Then, she was nowhere to be seen, not on his ridge top or the next. Anxiety balled in his stomach like the time he thought he'd lost his mother in Lewis's the Christmas he was six and Kathy was a babe in arms. He breathed in slow and deep, controlling the fear.

Had Bindi tired of his slow pace and abandoned him to certain death? Had that been part of the plan all along?

Across to the east the sky was brightening. It would soon be dawn. He sniffed the air and thought he could smell woodsmoke, but the moment was fleeting. He trudged up another sandhill, and another, and another. He'd been walking all night and he needed rest. It was all right for Bindi. She rested every time she waited for him. A stub of resentment flared and died. She'd come for him hadn't she? It wasn't her fault he was struggling; it was that grandfather of hers – Yildilla – the bastard!

A bout of hysterical laughter convulsed him. He wished he'd never ventured into the outback, had never met its people. Then there would have been none of it. No Curly. No tjuringa. No Yildilla. No retribution.

Jon smelt the smoke before he saw the fire. Bindi had lit it on the edge of a scrubby clump of trees in the hollow between two large sand ridges. The smoke had rippled along the depression before curling over one of the ridges, drawn along on the early morning breeze.

After a breakfast of cold goanna meat, hot damper and billy tea they slept under the stunted trees shaded from the fierce, midday sun. As the shadows grew shorter the fever returned; he pulled his blanket closer to him, shivering uncontrollably, and later came the sweating as the heat went out of the sun. Fearfully, he felt the wet patch on his trouser leg where the wound had seeped and was too afraid to investigate further. There was no point. There was no spare water for washing away pus.

They left the sandhills as the stars came up and as moonlight flooded the first of the claypans. They were south of the course he had taken. This time they were skirting the great claypan, not crossing it as he had. Travelling was easier although his limp was more pronounced and the pain was too great to put much weight on his damaged leg.

They journeyed during the cooler parts of the day and during the night, making the most of the full moon and the clear skies, and they stopped at water holes to refill their bottles whenever they could. Soon, he lost track of time. He ate and drank when they rested, slept when he could and refused to look at the darkening stain on his trouser leg.

The light-headed feeling returned and with it came an English voice gabbling away and an Aboriginal voice responding. When he realised it was his own voice and Bindi's he tried to make sense of the words.

'We're going the wrong way,' he heard himself say. 'You're trying to kill me, aren't you?'

Bindi didn't answer; she walked on ahead, her back ramrod straight. He knew then he was done for. He'd got her measure. She was leading him out of the canyon on a trek she knew he'd never survive. She'd see that he didn't.

She turned towards him. He could see her mouth working; he heard her voice but couldn't decipher the words. Then, as he watched her lips, she took on the look of perentie's mate, a female perentie, mother of the perentie he'd killed and he was afraid. He blinked and saw Bindi. This time her mouth was closed and she was waiting for him.

He turned to run but the ground seemed to grip his feet and his leg gave way. He hit the claypan hard, winded, he gasped for air, tears of fear and frustration rolling down his cheeks.

The perentie mother's hot breath fanned his cheek as she leaned over him and lifted him by the arm. Then they were moving forward, slowly, like some ungainly creature. She'd tucked her shoulder under his armpit and her arm supported his back. She was smaller than he'd realised. He tried to take the weight off her and couldn't. He staggered on conscious of her warm body pressed against his, her smell, the softness of her hair against his cheek and he thought of Merle and the letter in his pocket – the last letter he'd received from her, the one he'd read over and over until the folded edges were frayed and thin.

Hours later, or so it seemed, Bindi, or was it the perentie mother, lowered him to the ground, wrapped a blanket about him and built a campfire. He could smell the strong billy tea long before the water boiled but by then his exhausted body craved sleep more. He clutched Merle's letter to his chest for comfort, closed his heavy eyelids and felt himself drifting...drifting...

...The creek is dry except for the wet patch over by the red gums – the billabong – the reason he'd built the homestead on the high ground overlooking the old soak.

He leans back in his chair, feeling the verandah boards give a little as he sips his tea. Seven years it has taken and he's done well for himself – his own pastoral lease and three thousand sheep out there breeding and growing wool. If everything goes well they'll see a profit within a couple of years.

Behind him, in the kitchen, Merle wails. 'Jon, the pilot light's gone out again.'

He puts his cup down and goes into the kitchen, his dog at his heels.

'How many times do I have to tell you to keep that mangy animal out of the kitchen,' she yells. She flops down on a kitchen chair, strands of dark hair sticking to her forehead. She bats her hand at the flies circling overhead. 'This heat,' she says, 'how do you stand it?'

He crosses to the stove and relights the pilot. 'Why don't you go outside and sit on the verandah and I'll finish the tea,' he says, the spiral of flypaper littered with the bodies of dead and dying insects catching his eye. He tries to recall where he's seen it before and its significance. Mesmerized, he watches it twisting lazily in the sultry air then hang for a moment and untwist the other way.

Is this what life is all about? Is everyone trapped by their needs? It doesn't make sense, desires and needs spinning in space, three spins one way and three back.

He shuts his mind to his worries and finishes off the meal Merle started, clears away the dirty pots and pans and serves up tea – roast mutton, potatoes and tinned carrots. And that is another worry – the vegetable plot. Merle hates gardening even though he's had Bindi show her how to look after the patch.

'Remember fish and chips?' she says at the end of the meal. 'From the fish and chip shop in New Brighton – one the German's didn't bomb.' And he did. He remembers the smell of fat chips cooked in lard and soft white fish coated in golden, mouth-watering batter with lashings of salt and vinegar and eaten with fingers out of old newspaper – one of the pleasures that wasn't rationed even during the war.

'After the muster I'll take you to Perth,' he says. 'We can get fish and chips there.'

They sit together on the verandah looking across to the red gums and beyond them to the fence that he has half built.

'It's the best time of the day, this and early morning, before the sun gets too hot. Tomorrow we can ride over to Sandy Spit for a swim. It's nice there, plenty of shade. We can pack up a picnic.'

'No,' says Merle.

'You'll be safe on Daisy.'

'No.'

He looks at her, shocked by the hard tone in her voice. 'But I fetched Daisy from Jarrahlong especially, and the old saddle. She's a hundred per cent reliable.'

'You said that about the other horse.'

He doesn't answer. He'll give her a minute or two and let her get used to the idea.

'What if I'd broken my neck?'

'But you didn't.'

'A quadriplegic, that's what I'd be by now, stuck out here in the back of beyond in the heat with all these flies.'

'But you didn't.'

'But I might have. We'll go in the utility.'

'We can't go in the ute,' he says. 'It's rough country, better if we go on horses.'

The light fades, darkness descends and he continues sitting, listening to Merle sobbing in the bedroom.

'This place is all wrong for some people,' says Alice.

He glances at the chair Merle has vacated and sees Alice's profile, sees the end of the cheroot glowing redly when she draws on the pungent tobacco, and he smells the sweet, bitter smell of the smoke she exhales.

'She'll get to love it. It's early days,' he says.

'No she won't,' says Alice.

'I did.'

'You're different.'

'No, I'm not. No one hated the outback more than me, the dust, the heat, the flies. Like Merle says, you can't escape.'

'You're wrong, Jon, you only thought you hated the place,' says Stan who's appeared from nowhere, like Alice has done. He is sitting on the top step of the verandah, a tumbler of neat rum in his hand. 'Your mind was in a rage over your mate dying under God's altar stone at Karundah. You were in shock. It would have turned anyone's mind.'

He glares at Stan. 'And what about the drought and the death, sheep belly deep in putrefying mud, their eyes pecked out?'

'And what about it, son? It's not the land's fault. Drought has been part of the cycle of things since time began. It's what makes the outback the Outback. There're the good times and the bad and if folk choose to try and tame the frontier then you take it on its own terms: good and bad.'

'You'll have to let her go,' says bird-like Elsie, her arm resting on the back of Alice's chair. 'Merle's not made for this place.'

'You're wrong, Elsie, she'll settle, I know she will.'

'And what about the cat?'

'What cat?' asks Stan.

'What cat?' asks Alice.

'The cat on the waste ground,' says Elsie.

'I wish I'd never told you,' he says.

'The poor thing was injured – dying from gangrene. Know about gangrene, do you?' asks Elsie.

'Tell me about it,' says Stan. 'Men dying of gas gangrene in the trenches, the stench, their agony.'

'Jon here put it out of its misery and his friends didn't understand. Merle didn't understand, she couldn't see it was a kindness,' says Elsie.

'Yes, she did,' he says, 'later, she did.'

'And what about when its tens of sheep and cattle that need putting out of their misery? My Jack couldn't cope with it, in the end,' says Alice.

'He took a gun and shot himself,' says Stan. 'Poor bugger. It turned his mind.'

'I didn't know that,' says Elsie. 'Does Merle?'

'But you love the place,' he says. 'You and Jack built a life for yourselves. You didn't leave when Jack died, did you?'

'No,' says Alice. 'By then the place was in my blood like it is with you, but it comes at a high price.' She breathes in the warm night air. 'Smell the mulga after the rain,' she says. Smell the heat of the place. See the wide, open spaces, the land further than the eye can see with its red-ochre earth, cobalt-blue skies and grey-green eucalypts. See the saltbush and spinifex, the skinks, thorny devils, kangaroos and emus. I'm telling you, once you've lived in a place like this nothing else will satisfy your soul.'

'You're wrong, Alice,' he says. 'Merle and me, we could go back to England, make a go of it there.'

'In Liverpool?' asks Elsie. 'What about the last time?' She looks at him, her deep-set eyes piercing, penetrating, digging into his memory, making him recall the stench of the city – the petrol fumes, the smog that caught in his throat and blocked out the sun and the stars, and the muddy, turgid waters of the Mersey. 'You hated it.'

'There's the countryside. I could get a job on a farm.'

'One, two hundred acres, maybe four hundred if you're lucky, and working for someone else,' says Alice, 'after this?' The lighted tip of her cigar zigzags brightly as she indicates the land before them. 'Listen,' she says.

Out in the bush cicadas rattle, nocturnal animals skitter and scuttle through the dry grasses. Frogmouths call to each other – the soft oom-oom-oom repeated a dozen times even as they listen.

'The city is for Merle,' says Stan, 'but it's not for you. You have dreams, plans for the future, for a life in the outback, here, beyond the Black Stump. But that's not what Merle wants. She has dreams too, but not of here. She's unhappy, Jon.'

'You have to let her go,' says Alice.

They all sit on the verandah listening to Merle sobbing.

He closes his eyes, he stops up his ears, feels the warmth of Merle's letter in his pocket. 'You're wrong,' he says finally, opening his eyes.

Perentie Man sits in Alice's chair, his yellow and brown skin like beaded cloth in the half-light. The ancient reptilian eyes turn towards him. He sits there like Alice had done, his front feet resting on the chair arms, one back leg crossed over the other like a crazy cartoon from a Punch magazine.

Perentie opens his mouth to speak and the stench of death wafts on the air. 'She's right, mate,' he says in Curly's voice. 'You should listen to Alice...'

...Sweat poured off him. Someone – was it Alice, Stan or Elsie? – stripped off his clothes, rubbed his skin with oil then wrapped him in a coarse blanket. You're all wrong, he thought he said. What's gone before doesn't count. Merle and me, we're together, that's all that matters.

No one answered; instead, someone lifted him and tilted his head over a steaming pot. He held his breath for as long as he could and then took in great gulping lungfuls of the aromatic steam. Soon he felt sick and dizzy. Was he in the canyon with the spear through his leg? Was he dying all over again? It felt different from the last time. Then he'd been afraid, now, the peculiar sensation gave way to forgetfulness, his brain became sluggish, sleepy, his thoughts slowed, were less important. He wanted to sleep, to rest, to forget his worries. Then he seemed to be floating, and the throbbing in his leg slowly eased and gradually faded into nothingness.

Jon woke long before dawn unsure of his surroundings. The embers had turned to white ash but he could still feel the heat of them through the blanket.

He wriggled his arms free and unwrapped himself, then he rolled on to his side and propped himself up on his elbow. On the other side of the campfire Bindi lay as still as a log and as silent as death. Fear rippled down his skin and made the short hairs prickle. And then he saw the soft rise and fall with her next breath. Relief coursed through him. He wasn't alone.

Across on the eastern horizon pale peach bands of light leached upwards, staining the night sky, bringing the day. He looked around him. He didn't recognise the place. Behind him was a low range and ahead a vast plain with a huge claypan – all that was left of a lake that once dominated the land. At his feet were bones, feathers, charred sticks and old ashes. They'd been camped awhile – a week at least, maybe longer by the look of things. Above him was a stunted tree, long dead, its branches skeletons decorated with green and yellow bunting – budgerigars, dozens of them, still dozing as night became day.

Where the hell had Bindi brought him to? Had she led him round in a circle back to the canyon? He tried to sit up but the effort was too much. He looked down at his arms, his stick-thin body, the skin greyish in the morning light. He felt his face – a beard – two weeks then, at least.

Jon staggered to his feet and bent to rub the stiffness from his muscles and saw he was stark naked. He grabbed the blanket at his feet and wrapped himself while keeping an eye on the sleeping Bindi. Where had she put his clothes?

He checked his leg. The wound had stopped festering; the hole had healed over again. How long would that have taken? When he straightened up Bindi was watching him.

'Where're my clothes?'

She indicated the mulga bushes behind her.

He hobbled over to them and, using the blanket as a screen, pulled on his jocks, khaki pants and then his shirt. They hadn't been washed only aired and the fabric felt thick and sticky as the cloth warmed against his skin.

'No spare water,' said Bindi.

'It's all right,' said Jon. 'Where are we?'

'Kitigirri,' she said.

'And where's that?'

She shrugged.

'Where are you taking me?'

'Jarrahlong,' she said, surprise widening her eyes. 'You hungry?'

Jon nodded not completely sure that she was telling the truth. The muscles in his belly tensed and he could hear his stomach gurgle and squish at the thought of food.

She rolled up her swag, then picked up her digging stick and proceeded to rake out the fire. Soon she'd removed a thin layer of earth and Jon could see a bird buried under the hot ashes.

'Emu. Caught him yesterday.'

She tore away the feather and skin and revealed the cooked flesh beneath; the aroma drifted on the air and Jon's mouth flooded with saliva.

The bird lay on a flat stone and the pair of them ate the hot flesh with their fingers, the juices dripping off their chins, grease running down their arms to their elbows.

'Slowly,' she said when Jon wolfed down a piece of breast. 'Eat slow or you'll get bellyache.'

He kept on eating.

'You've hardly eaten for a week.' She put a restraining hand on his arm. 'Have more later.'

He wiped his chin with his forearm, nausea rising in his throat. He belched, his belly uncomfortably full even though he'd hardly eaten anything. Exhausted, he lay back on his blanket and slept.

Over the next week Bindi made him eat and sleep. She brewed a concoction to reduce the fever from leaves from the turpentine bush which she carried in her dilly bag. When she caught a goanna she cut away the fat and crushed strong smelling leaves into it, and then she smeared the mess onto his leg and massaged the weakened muscles. Before she went hunting and gathering she gave him a ball of the tar-like substance Ty had once given him, processed pituri leaves, to chew. Helps pass the time, she'd said.

One evening he'd watched her as she made the balls from acacia ash, pituri leaves and flax tassels.

'Your brother gave me some of that once.'

A smile split her face and Jon noticed her teeth, white as milk and perfect like Curly's had been. 'I taught him to make it.'

'And who taught you?'

'Yildilla.'

He'd already guessed the answer but he'd wanted to see her reaction. 'You know he did this?' He tapped his thigh.

She nodded as she kneaded the mixture on a flat stone.

'Is he coming back?'

She shook her head this time, concentrating on rolling out the paste into small balls.

'Why did he do it?'
'You broke a tribal law.'
'Which one?' He watched as she lined up the balls in neat rows and put them to dry by the fire.
'I dunno, but he won't come back. The punishment is over.'
She might think that, but he didn't. He couldn't see his leg ever being right again. He noted the guarded look. She wasn't anything like Kathy. 'I've a sister your age.'
She looked at him, her eyes wide. 'She live in Perth?'
'No, in Liverpool, with my aunt.'
'That's all right then, my aunties sometimes looked after me when I was little. What's she like, your sister?'
'She's about your height with auburn hair, darker than yours, and freckles across the top of her nose, and she likes ballet.' He waited for the question about ballet.
'Does she dance like Anna Pavlova?'
'Who's Anna Pavlova?'
He thought he saw a smug look flit across her face. 'She was a famous ballet dancer. I read about her in a book Alice gave me to read.'
Jon grinned. 'You're not just a pretty face then?'
She smiled back. 'They look silly, don't they, in those little frocks and funny shoes.'
He considered her with fresh eyes. Alice said she was sharp, that she was better at reading and arithmetic than David had been at her age. 'What do you want to be when you grow up?'
Bindi picked up a couple of pieces of wood, put them on the fire and sat down next to him, watching the flames lick around the branches and ripple along their dry edges. 'I dunno. I've been thinking about it.' She sat watching the flames again. 'I don't think it's right the way people like me get taken into the Settlement. It was horrible, we weren't treated right. Alice says I should become a lawyer.'
'Does she!'
'She says I'm bright enough, but I've got to take exams.' She swept her hand before her, indicating the landscape, taking in the whole of the plain before them. 'This sort of education doesn't count.'
'What?'
'Blackfella knowledge. How we live out here like Yildilla does, in the old way.'
The flames were brighter now, the heat from them burning his

face. They'd been travelling across the outback for three weeks, or thereabouts – he'd lost track of time – living in the old way, relying on the land. 'I wouldn't have made it home without you, Bindi.'

'I know,' she said. 'That's why Yildilla sent me.'

Early mornings, after Bindi left to look for food, he'd make his way up the cliff side to the tableland where he'd sit in the shade of an overhang decorated with Aboriginal stick figures and fish. It looked out over the vast plain laid out before him like a jigsaw puzzle. Away to the north on the edge of the great claypan he could make out splashes of verdant green – clumps of desert kurrajongs sustained by the water deep below the clay surface, and next to them groves of beefwood, corkwood and mulga. And, along from those, huge swathes of wanderrie grass growing in the dips and hollows where Bindi was hunting for animals attracted by the promise of water. Then the other patches he couldn't recognise, ochre and grey, pink and orange, plants at various stages of growth or maybe it was the bare earth – it was difficult to tell at a distance.

Jon chewed on the pituri, tempted to spit out the bitter juice except its essence had already slipped down his throat and the warm sensation was beginning to flood his brain.

His mind floated, enjoying the vibrant colours, the smell of the place, the gentle breeze on his face and the soft whistle of the wind sighing through the rocky places.

He remembered an earlier conversation with Curly – or had it been in a dream? He searched his memory, knowing it was flawed, that the memory *had* been a dream because Curly was dead, had been dead months but, nevertheless, he recalled them sitting together on the bank of the silty Mersey river, smelling its stench and the sour earth, and Curly's words: "This place death, Jon."

'Too right,' whispers Curly in his ear.

Was Curly right? Would returning to Liverpool to be with Merle be the death of him, the death of his soul?

He chewed the bitter concoction some more and swallowed the potent saliva, looking out across the landscsape.

'See it in the spring after the rain,' murmurs Curly.

He'd always thought that the landscape was at its most beautiful in the spring when everywhere was a Persian carpet of colour, the yellow billy buttons, the white and pink everlastings, the pink and blue fairy orchids, the wattle, the bottlebrush and banksia and the green mulla mulla. It was then that the sandflies danced in the steamy heat and he'd see skinks, lizards and snakes hiding in the grasses, and kangaroos, dingoes, brumbies and feral camels crossing the vast plain. And then there were the dragonflies and butterflies, hundreds of them.

'And Perentie Man,' murmurs Curly. 'Don't forget the Perentie.'

Jon smiled as he remembered the monitor lizard almost as big as a man when fully grown. He flexed his leg and felt the pull of his scar. No, he'd never forget Perentie Man.

'You belong here, Jon,' the voice says loud in his ear. 'You part of the land, it part of you. Your blood spilt in its dust. You bury your dead here.'

Shocked, Jon turned to speak, but there was no one – just him and the landscape and the mewing call of a wedge-tailed eagle overhead, circling on a thermal high above the claypan.

'Me, Jon, you buried me, and soon you'll bury Stan, and, in years to come, you'll bury Alice.'

Jon held his head in his hands, remembering the grave he'd dug for Curly, more real to him than Mam's or Gran's graves. And what of Stan? Stan was sick; he hadn't considered the old fella dying. Could he bear it without Stan? His hand dropped to his pocket and he felt for Merle's dog-eared letter that he'd read and re-read, and he took comfort from it.

He knew Curly was right, that death stalked Stan – death was in his eyes, in the colour of his skin, and on his breath.

And Alice! Well, Alice was Alice. She'd last years. Too afraid of dying to let go on this world Elsie would have said. And there was nothing wrong with that. Mind over matter, that's what kept people going when the odds were stacked against them.

Jon gazed at the decorated rock face, at the fish and the figures, faint outlines thousands of years old and imagined Curly's people sitting, as he was doing, looking down on the claypan full of water, a huge, blue lake teeming with fish, painting the bounty on the ancient sandstone. Had the artists been whiling away the hours painting what they saw before them, or was there a greater significance to their art – charms to ensure future supply, thank yous to the ancestors perhaps, and did it matter which?

He supposed not, but he wasn't an Aborigine. He didn't see the land the way Curly had, he didn't understand the Aboriginal mindset, but the place was in his heart, he'd missed the cruel beauty of the outback, and its people, when he was in England. In Liverpool he'd been half alive, living a grey life, in a bomb-wrecked city, where the people were dressed in drab clothes and were worn down by war and rationing. Was that the life he wanted?

Over the next week when Bindi went hunting he went walking, building up his strength and his stamina. He explored the huge plain, crossing and re-crossing the claypan, digging out frogs as Curly had shown him. He thought about his life so far and his friends in England and Australia. He thought about the good things and the bad, and tried to see himself ten, twenty, thirty years in the future. And each night he sat in front of the campfire and ate Aboriginal food under an immense Aboriginal sky, conscious of the vast land that had been inhabited by Curly's and Bindi's ancestors for millennia, aware that he was part of it now, and that, like them, his destiny lay in the land laid out before him like a patchwork, that the outback had, in some strange way, brought meaning and purpose to his life.

CHAPTER 44

They reached Denman Creek late in the afternoon under an overcast sky and travelled west along the watercourse. Another day and they'd be home.

Jon saw the campsite from a distance, the horses hobbled under the trees and a figure sitting, leaning back against the fluted copper-coloured trunk of the old gimlet, a bush hat tilted forward, dozing in the afternoon heat. Adie! What was he doing out here? Jon looked for sheep, for signs of station work, but nothing caught his eye. He squinted against the light. It wasn't Adie, just some fella on walkabout. He quelled the unreasonable feeling of disappointment. Why should anyone come all the way out to Denman Creek to meet him, he'd been gone weeks, they'd probably given up on him long ago.

As they neared the camp a second figure stepped out from the shade. Jim Sandy, a young stockman they'd taken on six months earlier when they'd been extending the fencing around the top paddock for Alice's Herefords.

The figure by the tree looked up as they approached and a slim hand tilted back the hat. Val!

She got to her feet and stepped forward to meet them, a smile lighting up her face.

'What are you doing here?' His words sounded like an accusation.

She raised an eyebrow. 'What? No *it's-nice-to-see-you, Val*?'

He didn't answer; he couldn't get the words out.

'Rescuin' you,' she said, the smile now gone from her face. 'Hiya, Bindi. You okay?'

Bindi grinned. 'I'm good.'

'Where's Adie?' asked Jon.

'Jarrahlong, Belle's lookin' after him.'

'Why? What's wrong?'

'Concussion. He took a nasty fall. Seems the horse shied – they say it saw a snake. Anyway he came a cropper and Alice said he wasn't fit to go on a mercy mission so I said I'd ride out to meet you. You might not realise it but you've had Alice worried. She's had a man camped out here for weeks waitin' for you and Bindi to get back. Then when you didn't show she kept snapping everyone's heads off.'

So, Alice had missed him. He had wondered. 'Where are the rest of the men?'

'Roundin' up the sheep Alice is sellin'.' Val turned her back on him and busied herself making tea. Later she dished up pannikins of stew and slabs of damper.

'Nice,' said Jon when he'd finished the meal. 'Thanks.'

'It's only stew,' said Val, 'and damper.'

'And thanks for the horses,' he added.

'My pleasure,' she said dryly. 'Alice told us to follow the creek to the old gimlet tree and Adie told us what to pack.'

'Alice didn't try and stop you?'

'Why should she? I'm not a complete dimbo you know, I've gorra brain.' She turned her back on him and unrolled her swag.

'Sorry,' he said.

'Don't mention it.' Her tone was clipped. 'I'd have done the same for anyone.'

Jon shut up. Why was he such a bastard when it came to Val? But he already knew the answer – she wasn't Merle.

It was barely fifteen months since he'd last seen Merle. She'd hinted in her letter that they were too young to be tied down, that five years was a long time and feelings could change, that he shouldn't make long-term plans.

He knew they were young, but he knew his own mind. He knew she was the girl for him; it was just difficult, not being able to see each other. On the journey to Paradise Canyon he'd mentally drafted dozens of replies to her most recent letter, describing the people, the land and the opportunities. He'd thought of telling her more about Charlestown and how much Val liked the place and dismissed the idea – Merle wasn't keen on Val, she was the last person he should mention, but he'd decided to write more about Alice and his life at Jarrahlong.

He frowned. He hoped Merle would keep an open mind, maybe even change it once she knew of the plans for a new hospital wing at Merredin and the need for doctors in the outback.

'Anyone told you, you look like death,' said Val. 'And you could do with a shave.'

He scratched his chin through his beard. 'You'd look like death if you'd been through what I've been through,' he said.

'Hasn't improved your temper, has it?' she said lightly as she pulled a blanket over her ears and settled down for the night.

Two hours into the ride home Jon brought his horse alongside Val's. 'Were you there when Yildilla got back to Jarrahlong?'

'Didn't see him.'

'So what happened? Did Bindi go to Alice?'

Val grinned. 'Did she heck! Alice spotted her crossin' the paddock…said she was lookin' purposeful, so she called her back and interrogated her.'

'Interrogated her?'

'Yeah, kept askin' her questions, pickin' her up on things.'

'What do you mean?'

'How should I know, she was talkin' Aboriginal half the time.'

'Aboriginal?'

'Do you always repeat everythin'?' asked Val.

'I didn't know Alice knew Aboriginal.'

'Well, she does. Bindi said that Yildilla had told her to go to a gorge called Kitigirri – I think that's the name she used, said you'd be needin' some help, that you'd hurt your leg.'

Hurt his leg! That was an understatement if ever there was one – the bastard had left him there to die, nothing less, but then Yildilla must have changed his mind, had decided he didn't want a white man's death on his conscience.

'So what did you do to your leg?'

Her question jolted him. 'What?'

'I said, what did you do to your leg?'

'I didn't do anything.'

Val looked at him and waited.

'It'll take too long to tell.' He wished she'd shut up. It was hard blocking the pain; the scar tissue, stretched by his unaccustomed position in the saddle, was making him sweat. He swallowed the nausea rising up like bile, and resisted the weariness numbing his brain by focussing on the route ahead.

'Please yourself,' she said and gave her horse a swift kick in the flanks.

Jon pulled his horse back and let her ride ahead. How much did he need to tell Alice? The truth or could he leave some of it out?

Then there was Alice's ability to speak an Aboriginal language, Bindi's language, which meant Yildilla's. He smiled grimly. It didn't do to underestimate Alice, the truth then and to hell with it.

They were in Alice's parlour drinking whiskey after the evening meal. Jon yawned.

Alice's hooded eyes glittered as she watched him over the rim of her glass. 'Well, lad, what was it all about?'

'You tell me, because I'm damned if I know.'

She didn't probe; she sat very still, listening to his account of events out at Paradise Canyon. When he'd finished he looked down into his glass, swirled the last of the whiskey and drank it down in one swallow. 'I should have left the tjuringa wrapped up in its filthy piece of cloth instead of trying to do the right thing.'

'Wouldn't have saved you, kaditja would have got you in the end. Anyway, honour is served, those who need to know, know and that'll be the end of it.'

'So what did I do wrong?'

'Broke some clan law by the sound of things, a taboo, your guess is as good as mine.'

'Yildilla still about?'

'Doubt it. His job's done. He'll have gone back to his own patch, wherever that is. What did he do to you?'

'Threw a spear at me.'

'Your leg.'

Jon nodded. 'It hurt like hell, but getting it out was the worst.'

'If you want my advice you should put it behind you and let it be a lesson. Don't get involved in Aboriginal affairs in the future. Be friendly, but keep your distance, and whatever you do don't go trampling into their business, or over their sacred sites.'

'What sites.'

'Any of them. You ask Adie. He'll tell you where the local ones are and what their Dreaming is. Now, get yourself off to bed, you look done in, and tomorrow I'll get Rachel to drive you over to Pilkington.'

'What for?'

'To get that injured leg checked out at the clinic.'

'What good will that do? It's healed now.'

'What about the limp?'

'No guarantees they'd be able to fix it. It looks to me like I've got to live with it.'

'It's your leg,' said Alice.

'Any news of your Hereford bull?' asked Jon. 'I thought it was due any day.'

'Came in five weeks ago. He's a fine looking animal. Greg hired a cattle transporter and a driver in Fremantle.'

'Where is Greg?'

'Up the top end. With Adie crook and you on walkabout he's had plenty to do.'

He could feel Alice's eyes watching for a reaction. He kept his face neutral.

'He's keen to learn more about raising sheep.'

I bet he is, thought Jon.

'I should imagine you'll get on fine,' commented Alice, 'and it'll be good for you to have another Pom about the place.'

It was another three days before he met Greg. He turned up one afternoon with Jim Sandy, ahead of the rest of the stockmen, covered in sweat and dust. Jon watched with interest as he dismounted and yelled at Jim to see to his horse. Greg gave it a hefty slap on the rump and crossed the yard, had a brief conversation with Alice, then disappeared into the building to return minutes later with a change of clothes and a towel – the bloke hadn't even noticed him.

Jon strolled over to Jim Sandy.

'You all right doing this?'

'Yes,' said Jim.

The horse, lathered in sweat and wild-eyed, pulled away as Jim Sandy unhitched the girth and lifted off the saddle. Across the horse's flanks were large welts. Jon frowned. The horse had been ridden hard and with a heavy hand. What the hell had been going on out there?

Half an hour later the rest of the stockmen arrived united in their tiredness, the sheep mustered and collected into the home paddock ready for transportation to the stockyards near Perth.

Jon strolled over to Alice. 'Chatty, isn't he?'

'You know what the muster's like, dirty, tiring, it takes some getting used to,' said Alice.

Cooking smells of beef and root vegetables wafted over the yard from the kitchen block and Jon's stomach rumbled.

'They're back then,' said Rachel, watching as the other stockmen unsaddled in the yard. She picked up Joe and balanced him on her hip. 'Have you met Greg?'

'Not yet.'

The four of them went into the kitchen and Jon noticed the high chair.

'Nice, isn't it?' said Rachel. 'Val ordered it for me, from Perth.'

Greg arrived as Belle put the food on the table, a scowl still plastered on his face.

'You're going to have to get rid of those blacks, Alice. They're no damned good.'

Greg was slimmer than most blokes Jon knew and his shock of carroty-red hair was nearly as bright as his skin where he'd caught the sun. His peeling nose was sharp and the lips thin, but it was his eyes that were arresting, grey, flecked with green.

'You met Jon yet?' asked Alice. 'Jon, this is my nephew's youngest, Greg.'

Jon nodded a greeting and Greg looked him up and down. 'We could have done with you this last fortnight, can't run a place this size short-handed.' He flopped down on the chair next to Rachel, leaned across the table and helped himself to a slab of beef and a generous helping of vegetables.

'Never had any trouble with the men in the past,' said Alice.

'They won't do as they're told,' said Greg.

Rachel passed the plate of meat to Jon.

'Are you talking about Dave, Big'un and Mick?' Jon asked as he took a slice of beef.

'If you want me to manage the place for you, Alice, then you're going to have to give me a free hand,' said Greg, ignoring the question.

Jon looked at Greg shovelling food into his mouth, his eyes fixed on his plate. It wasn't often he took against someone, but Greg was one of them. 'There's nothing wrong with the stockmen.'

'And who are you?'

'If you'd listen for a minute, you'd know,' snapped Alice. 'Jon here has been managing the place for me.'

Jon stopped eating. Was that how she saw it? She'd always resisted the idea of a manager before.

'And if he says the men are all right, then they are. He's worked with them a damn sight longer than you have.'

Greg looked up from his plate and appraised Jon through narrowed eyes.

'Alice says you're from Liverpool, that right?'

'That's right.'

'Didn't know they had farms in the city.'

'They don't,' said Jon. 'I've learned on the job, just like you're doing.'

The atmosphere was tense, even Joe started grizzling.

Greg shrugged. 'Is it all right to use the utility, Alice?'

'Where are you going?'

'Charlestown.'

The kitchen was quiet after he'd left. Rachel settled Joe. Alice finished eating and retired to her parlour.

'Nice fella,' said Jon.

'He's not usually like that,' said Rachel. 'He's always seemed nice enough and he gets on well with Alice. Maybe something's upset him.'

'Well, now he's upset Alice,' said Jon.

At breakfast Greg was eating when Jon arrived and Alice was smiling at something he'd said.

Greg felt in his pocket and flapped a coin onto the table. 'Cato reckoned it was his last brass farthing.'

'Cato,' laughed Alice, 'everyone says he's more tight-fisted than a monkey with a nut in its paw.'

Greg grinned broadly. 'He lost his shirt last night.' He glanced up as Jon pulled out a chair. 'I owe you an apology.' He stood up, leaned across the table and offered his hand. 'Nice to meet you, Jon.'

They shook hands.

'Alice says you've had a rough time over the last few weeks. Are you all right for a bit of light work after breakfast? We need to sort out those sheep going to the stockyards and those we are keeping.'

Later, Jon joined them in the paddock, but sorting the sheep took it out of him and in the end he had to leave Greg to oversee the loading while he returned to the barn.

William Samuels drew into the yard as he was repairing Red's tack. Will waved a greeting to Alice and hunkered down next to him.

'Good mob there,' he commented, looking across to the men loading the sheep. 'They should do well in the sales.'

'That's what Alice is hoping,' said Jon. 'She has to pay for all these new buildings somehow and she says she wants to buy in more breeding stock.'

'Me old man's forever going on about costs, a bad bush fire takes a lot of getting over.'

'Take a seat,' said Jon.

Will picked up an old bucket, upturned it and sat down, watching as Jon punched a neat row of fine holes to take the stitching.

'How are you? Word is you've had a bit of a do.'

'That's right, but I'll mend.'

'I'd give up going walkabout if I were you,' said Will. 'It isn't good for your health.'

'Too right it isn't.' Jon looked up from his stitching and grinned. 'Your visit business or pleasure?'

'We were wondering if we could borrow your bloodless castrators – one of our stockmen drove a wagon over ours and bent them.'

'How did he manage that?'

'God knows.'

'They're on the bench.' Jon glanced over to the end of the barn. 'And while you're there bring me the tin of saddle soap and a rag, if you don't mind.'

'Thanks, mate,' said Will. He sauntered over to the bench and returned with the equipment he needed and dropped the soap and rag at Jon's feet. 'I suppose you'll be going to the races next month. It's the Cathay Cup.'

'Alice mentioned it,' said Jon. 'She says everyone for miles around descends on Charlestown, says all the rooms are booked up from one year to the next.'

'Aye,' said Will, 'she's not wrong there. Race Day makes a change for the ladies. Rachel mentioned Race Day?'

'No.'

'You ask her about the Cathay Cup. She picked the winner last year, a real outsider.' He chuckled. 'She won't want to miss the spectacle for anything. You tell her from me I'll bet her a bob she can't pick this year's winner.'

'Yeah, I'll tell her.'

'Tom and me'll be there, and my mother and the old man. We've already invited Val to join us.'

'You've invited Val?'

'Yeah, we must look after the ladies. While I think on, how's that little lad of yours doing?' asked Will.

'He's not mine,' snapped Jon, the words were out before he'd even thought about them.

'Sorry, mate, only I thought…'

'No worries, you're not the only one; everyone else hereabouts reckons he's mine,' said Jon, aware of Will's embarrassment.

'Whose son is he?'

'No idea,' he lied.

Will flapped his hat in the direction of the tack Jon was working on. 'Pretty neat stitching for a Pom.'

Jon laughed. 'Thanks, I always did like needlework. You time for a cuppa?'

'No, I won't, if you don't mind. Dad's waiting on me. You know what he's like when he's ear-marked a job to be done.' He picked up the castrators and bashed his bush hat against his thigh, knocking off the dust that had collected on the brim. 'Be seeing ya, mate.'

Jon watched him leave, finished his stitching and then saddle-soaped it to soften the leather. He ran the bridle through his fingers, feeling for irregularities, and then hung it on the peg next to the other tack, satisfied with a job well done. By the time he'd cleared everything away Alice was sitting in her favourite spot on the verandah feeding nuts to her cockatoo.

'What did the Samuels' lad want?'

'Bloodless castrators.'

'Haven't they got any of their own?'

'Will says a stockman drove over them and bent theirs.'

'Careless of him. Any news?'

'No. Will mentioned the race meeting. He wanted to know if I was planning on going.' The parrot picked up a foot and scratched its ear, its head tilted to one side, its yellow crest erect like a row of curls. Jon indicated the bird. 'Where did he come from, Alice?'

'Jack won him in a game of poker, years ago; he thought a talking parrot would be company.'

'I didn't know Charlie could talk.'

'He can't. Want a cup of tea?'

'I'll get it.'

The kitchen was empty. Jon poured himself a mug of tea and added a dash of condensed milk and joined Alice on the verandah.

'Where's Bindi, Alice?'

'Working the vegetable plot, at least that's what I told her to do.'

Jon sipped the tea heavy with tannin and a tad tepid. Still, it was warm, wet and welcome. He sat in the spare rocking chair enjoying the quiet moment. He liked these sorts of days, just a slight breeze, enough to dry the sweat without making the hair stand on end.

'So, what else did Will have to say?'

‘Not a lot, he asked how I was.’ He batted at a mob of flies that had landed on his shirt. ‘And, as I said, he mentioned Cup Day at the races.’ Over in the paddock he could hear the whistles and shouts as the last of the sheep were herded into the cattle wagon.

A smirk split Alice’s face. She pressed her toe against the floor-boards and set the chair rocking. ‘Good place to meet the ladies,’ she said. ‘Everyone from miles around will be there, eyeing each other and the horses. There’s more than one marriage has its origins at Race Day, there’ll be plenty of drinking and romancing going off on that Saturday, that’s for sure.’

‘Will said something similar,’ said Jon. ‘The Samuels have invited Val to join them.’

‘I’m not surprised.’

‘What’s that supposed to mean?’

‘You haven’t got a clue, have you? Every red-blooded male in the district has an eye for her.’

Jon considered Alice’s comment. Val was pretty enough, he supposed, but nothing to shout home about.

‘Anyway, what’s so special about this Cathy Cup?’

‘Didn’t Will tell you?’

‘No, he didn’t.’

‘You’re in for a treat then. Best race in the State,’ said Alice.

CHAPTER 45

A couple of weeks after his return from Paradise Canyon Jon left the stockmen finishing the main meal of the day and limped over to the post and rail fence beyond the barn. He leaned on the topmost rail looking out over the new paddock.

In the far distance he could make out one or two white faces – Alice's Herefords. He hadn't realised how much the animals had meant to her until he'd found her sitting in the utility truck watching them resting near the bend in Jarrah Creek. It had been a balmy evening with frogs croaking in the shallows, and the warbling, melodic calls of native birds contrasting with the rattle of cicadas. He'd ridden out on Red, looking for her, following the tyre tracks, wondering if she had gone to the place where Jack was buried. Instead, she'd driven into the bush to the far end of the home paddock half a mile from the homestead. He'd found her sitting in the cab, the driver's door wide open, a silver flask of the bourbon whiskey she preferred in her hand, listening to the bush calls and watching the cattle, their tails switching away the flies as they chewed the cud or nuzzled each other in friendship. He had tied Red to the tailgate and sat in the cab with her sharing the amber liquid when she offered the flask.

Reminds me of home, she'd said.

He hadn't agreed – the tatty ribbon-bark eucalypts with their copper-coloured bark and silvery-green leaves were nothing like any English tree that he knew of except perhaps willows. They'd sat together looking out over the land, its colours muted into rich cobalt blues, oxide reds and grey, as the light faded. And then there'd been the smell of the place, a hint of eucalyptus, acacia blossom and the warm smell of the cattle, nothing like England, and yet he had known what she meant. Make a nice scene for an oil painting, he'd said after a while.

She'd looked at him then. Didn't know you liked art, she'd said.

He'd felt himself colour up and was glad that the light was beginning to go. Gran used to go to the Walker Art Gallery in Liverpool, he'd said, feeling the need to explain. She liked to look at the paintings and the sculptures.

And what was your favourite?

George Stubbs, he'd said, except he painted horses standing under trees, not Herefords.

You never cease to amaze me, Jon Just, she'd said presently. Then she'd leaned forward and turned the engine over. When we get back there's something I want to show you.

He'd remounted Red and walked the horse the half mile to the station, thinking about the changes he'd seen in Alice. Ever since he'd arrived back from England she'd been more active, doing things, going places, dressing better and he couldn't decide whether it was the shock of nearly losing Jarrahlong in the bush fire or whether having Rachel and Val around the place was what had made the difference. Perhaps it was a combination, you could never tell with a woman like Alice.

She'd waited for him on the verandah while he'd unsaddled his horse, and when she ushered him into her bedroom he'd felt his face turn scarlet – until he saw the paintings. There were two of them, large oils with carved, gilded frames like the paintings in the Walker Art Gallery in Liverpool.

You like them? she'd asked.

And he did.

The one above the bed head showed an Australian scene, a billabong surrounded by four majestic eucalypts. On the other side of the track was a simple two-roomed shack with a verandah on the front elevation. The dirt road running between the shack and the billabong disappeared into the distant mulga and on it was a dray pulled by a team of eight oxen. The other was an English scene, after Stubbs, with long-horn cattle standing under English oaks and in the distance a rolling scene of English countryside.

That was Jack's wedding present to me, she'd said, pointing to the English scene, and that one he bought in Perth after David was born.

They're nice, he'd said, conscious that the words were inadequate the minute he'd said them.

She'd agreed. Which do you like the best?

The billabong, he'd said without hesitation.

She'd looked at the painting, lost in the detail of it. Mine too and it was always Jack's favourite.

Afterwards they'd sat out on the verandah drinking whiskey,

enjoying the warm evening, alone for once as Greg had taken a few days off, something he had taken to doing with increasing frequency.

Thoughts of Greg dragged him back to the present. Greg had been at Jarrahlong for three months and didn't look like leaving. He'd been right about Greg from the first – a shirker, too ready with excuses when there was work to be done with the mob. He'd taken to finding vague reasons for trips into Charlestown or Pilkington where he'd spend his time drinking and gambling, playing two-up with his new mates, Cato, of all people, and blokes from off the stations.

Then there was Greg's attitude towards Alice – always solicitous but with an edge there that he couldn't put his finger on. Greg still hadn't realised that Alice and Jack had put in equal hours building Jarrahlong from nothing. Neither had he until Stan told him, but he'd never taken Alice for a fool even at the very first meeting after he'd run away from the orphanage at Karundah, and he couldn't help feeling that Greg didn't appreciate the steely side of her nature. Alice too was wearing blinkers; she didn't hear the insincerity behind the flattery? Why didn't women see through good-looking blokes like Greg and Berry? At least Scally, much as he disliked the fella, treated Alice with respect.

He sensed Adie's presence before he heard him. 'Mrs Macarthur wants a word,' said Adie as he leaned on the fence next to him. 'Fat aren't they?'

They looked across to the Herefords, their ghostly faces and white chests all that could be seen of them in the dying light.

'Yes, but will they survive a drought?'

'Even scrub cattle die in a drought,' said Adie.

'Yeah, I suppose you're right,' said Jon. 'I better go and see what Alice wants?'

Alice was sitting in her easy chair, reading in a pool of light cast by an old kerosene lamp that she used when the generator was switched off. The light cast an eerie yellow glow on everything and softened Alice's features.

'Take a seat,' she said. 'Beer?' She leaned forward and picked up a bottle off the occasional table next to her.

'Thanks,' said Jon as he took the proffered bottle.

'Are you feeling up to a trip?'

'What sort of trip?'

‘To Leonora. Stan asked for you while you were away.’
‘Leonora?’
‘I said you would, but that was before. Do you think you are up to it?’
‘I should be all right.’
‘What about that leg?’
‘I won’t have to do much walking, will I? When does he want to go?’
‘He asked for you about a month back so sooner rather than later I should think.’
‘How long for?’
Alice drew on her cheroot. ‘A few days should do it.’
‘What about the—’
‘The sheep? Greg can oversee things here. It’s about time he had more responsibility and he’ll have Adie with him. Ed says that Stan’s crook.’ Alice studied the glowing end of the cigar for a moment. ‘How crook?’
‘Pretty bad, I’d say,’ said Jon. ‘He won’t go to hospital. He says he’s having no quack doctor prodding and poking him about and taking blood off him. He reckons there’s nothing wrong that time won’t sort.’
‘Did he? So he’s pretty sick then?’
‘Yes, and stubborn with it.’
Alice laughed. ‘That’s Stan for you.’ She crossed to her bureau, took out a package and gave it to him. ‘That’s to cover your costs, and I want change back.’
Jon opened the package…pound notes.
‘Make sure Stan gets a few square meals in his belly, and keep him off the grog, it isn’t doing him any good.’

A few days later Jon and Stan, with Stan’s dogs in the back of the ute, bounced along the graded road corrugated by traffic, heading towards Leonora. ‘How much did you get for that die-shaped nugget you once showed to me, Stan?’ asked Jon.
Stan rummaged in his pocket and pulled out a paisley handkerchief. He flipped the cloth and tossed the nugget in the air. ‘This one?’
Jon caught a glint of gold.
‘Had it for years,’ said Stan. ‘It brings me luck. Gold attracts gold. You carry that piece you found?’
Jon shook his head.

Stan glanced at the nugget and rewrapped it in his handkerchief. 'You should. Keep it somewhere safe and forget about it. It doesn't do to be too obsessive when it comes to gold.'

'According to Alice you're pretty obsessive about your prospecting,' said Jon.

'Maybe she's right.' Stan slipped the nugget back into his pocket. 'But if you want something too badly you'll never get it – the need jinxes it.'

'That's superstition, Stan.' He didn't see how wanting something badly could make a difference. 'What would you do if you found a Lasseter's Reef?'

'I'd hop along to the Department of Minerals as fast as a big boomer outrunning a bush fire and lay me claim real quick.'

'And what if it was in the middle of an Aboriginal sacred site?'

Stan looked at him and blew a long, low whistle. 'If you've got any sense you'd forget you ever saw it.'

'Yeah, that's what I thought.'

'You remember the run-in Hardman had with the Aboriginals I told you about?'

'When?'

'Just before I took you down old No Hope?'

'You mean when I was still a kid and keen on getting rich quick from prospecting?'

'Wasn't that long ago.'

'Getting on for three years now, Stan.'

'Is it that long?'

'Yes,' said Jon.

'Well, that was over a sacred site – remember those paintings high up on the rock face?'

'Yes, but you never did show them to me.'

'That's because they're pretty inaccessible, you need to be a bit more agile than me to get to the ledge.'

'What about them?'

'Well, it seems Hardman once started to mine that side of the valley in the early days. Pretty soon blackfellas appeared, dressed up to the nines in paint and feathers, waving spears around and threatening anyone who approached that bit of rock. Anyway, it seems Hardman eventually decided it wasn't worth risking a spear in the back. Apparently there was more than one set-to between the Aborigines and Hardman's men until they came to an understanding.'

'Is that why you've never bothered to mine the rock on that side of the valley?'

'You could say that.'

'Do you think there's gold there?'

'It's possible, and there and again it could be another No-Hoper, I never reckoned it was worth the risk to find out.'

Stan lapsed into silence and they drove for the next hour through miles of thick acacia and eucalyptus forest under a grey, oppressive sky. Once through the forested area the bush became sparser and, after a time, Jon pulled off the road and followed a track for a short distance and stopped next to an old mineshaft with a collapsed and higgledy-piggledy wooden structure over it similar to the ones out at Stan's place.

'Home from home,' said Jon, killing the engine.

While he set up camp Stan dozed, propped against the sloping edge of an abandoned trench – the remains of someone's search for alluvial gold.

Jon looked about him, assessing the place. Whoever had tried their luck had long abandoned the project. It was impossible to gauge the depth of the shaft, and the precarious state of the wooden shuttering made it far too dangerous to investigate.

'Pound to a penny the fella found a lump of alluvial gold lying on the surface and staked everything on it,' commented Stan.

'He could have struck it rich,' said Jon.

'Could have, there were a lot who did. At the turn of the century Coolgardie was a boom town with a population of four thousand and more.'

'Did you do any prospecting there, Stan?'

'No, I was there a couple of weeks or so, but it was too crowded for me. When they built the railway line it brought in prospectors by the coach load, there were twenty-six pubs in its heyday, not to mention all the spin-off businesses associated with the gold rush: hoteliers, proprietors of gambling dens, teamsters, blacksmiths, quacks and whores all wanting to make it rich on the back of the gold.'

'And what about those who didn't?'

'Aye, tell me about it,' said Stan, 'there're plenty of them in the Coolgardie cemetery.'

After their meal they sat waiting for the night to close in, gazing unto the embers, sipping Stan's favourite tipple, the dogs at their feet.

'You ever regretted spending your life chasing a dream, Stan?'
'No.'
'What about a wife and a family?'
'Lots of blokes out here do without,' commented Stan. 'It's still frontier country, even now...anyway, there was only ever one woman for me and she was married to someone else.'
'Alice?'
'Aye, Alice.'
'Didn't you get lonely?'
'Had me dogs.'
Jon sipped the spirit, letting the brown liquid slip down his throat and warm his stomach. There were plenty of fellas like Stan in the outback, old fellas who lived alone, eking out a living prospecting or making a better living on the stations. Some were confirmed bachelors; a few lived with Aboriginal women like Ty's father. The number of half-castes working on the stations was testimony to the liaisons that had occurred over the years. No wonder Val's arrival at Jarrahlong had caused a stir, both she and Rachel could have their pick of eligible blokes. Then there was Stan's earlier comment about not getting too obsessed with gold. Did jinxes apply to other aspects of life? Did he want Merle too badly, like Stan had wanted Alice? Stan was a one-woman man and he was the same. He knew Merle was the one for him but it was clear from Merle's letters that her feelings didn't run as deep. He tried to imagine himself old and couldn't. If Merle refused to marry him would he end up alone, like Stan, and if he did would he regret it?
Stan's coughing interrupted his thoughts. He thumped him on the back, helping to clear the phlegm in his chest. The old man's skin had turned a sludge colour and sweat pricked his brow. Stan was crook, no wonder he wanted to travel into town and sort out his affairs, it wouldn't do for him to die leaving his business in a muddle. 'You ready to turn in, Stan?'
Stan nodded and wiped his brow and chin on his sleeve. 'I meant to tell you. Old Nickson was over last week sniffing round again. You know they found Gerry's truck over at Galston Gorge.'
Jon coughed on the rum he'd been sipping. 'When?'
'No need to panic, son, but putting my old twelve-bore in Gerry's truck wasn't such a bright idea after all,' said Stan, a wry smile on his face. 'Seems a mate of Gerry's reckons he had a thing about shotguns ever since a barrel blew out and nearly took off his hand. According to Nickson that incident scared the hell out of him and now some folks are saying it wasn't misadventure but murder –

that someone killed him and then tried to make it look like an accident.'

'Does Nickson think you did it?'

'Seems like it, and I'm not surprised, not after he searched all my sheds for Gerry's truck two or three months back.'

Jon pictured Old Faithful, the head frame collapsing, the rumble of props and stone, the stench of foetid air and dust as Gerry's body tumbled to its grave.

'Any chance he can link the gun to you, Stan?'

'It's possible. I had a repair done on it once, years ago, over in Pilkington. If he thinks to check with the gunsmith he'll be back.'

'How did they find the truck?'

'One of the Samuels' stockmen was doing a sweep of Galston Gorge looking for sheep. He found a couple of them holed up in the same patch of thicket.'

Jon swore under his breath. He hadn't expected anyone to find the truck. He remembered the satisfaction he'd felt as it tipped over the edge, bounced off an outcrop and disappeared into the dense bush at the bottom of the gorge, the most inaccessible part, all rocky outcrops and thick brush, totally unsuitable for stock – the bloody sheep!

'And there's another thing, Nickson called round while you were away asking after you, it seems someone told him that Gerry had been needling you over Rachel and the kid.'

Who'd blabbed? It wouldn't have been Les; it was more likely to have been Gerry shooting his mouth off on the mail run. No telling who he'd talked to, and once it was decided Gerry's death wasn't an accident people talked and speculated.

'Don't you go worrying about it,' said Stan. 'It'll all blow over, you just see if it don't and without a body what can they prove?'

Jon wasn't convinced it would blow over, not if Gerry's mate was out to stir trouble. He glanced across at Stan and saw him sagging, done in by the effort of conversation. He rolled out the old man's swag and built up the fire with keepers for the night and soon Stan's rattling snore competed with other night noises, but it seemed a long time before his own eyes closed in sleep.

While Stan was with the solicitor Jon took the dogs and walked down the town's broad street that looked like something out of an American western, with a road wide enough to turn a bullock cart. On the corner of Rajah Street and Gwalia Street was the police station. The name 'Gwalia' caught his eye, it was a name he was familiar with, a Welsh name, he racked his brain trying to remember where he'd seen it; perhaps it was a village name he'd seen when they'd gone on day trips into Wales when he was a kid. Further along, on the corner of Gwalia and Trump streets, was the court-house – an imposing building, and over the road from that the Masonic Lodge – they'd had those in Liverpool too, and fire stations, and Catholic churches. He stopped in front of the fire station and looked across to the church. The door was open and he was tempted to enter. He recalled the old, stone church in Blackpool, the last time he'd been inside God's house. The pull was strong. Gran had been a good Catholic and Mam had gone as often as she could, but what good did religion do anybody?

He turned his back on the church and followed the road towards Tank Hill and there he flopped down on the ground and watched the comings and goings in the town. He thought of Stan's hunched frame and hesitant gait. What was he doing? Writing his last will and testament?

The old fella's condition had deteriorated since he'd last seen him not that long before his trip to Paradise Canyon. He'd tried to keep the shocked look off his face but he could see in Stan's eyes that the old man had missed nothing. He glanced at his watch. Time he made a move; the old fella would be through at the solicitor's by now.

Stan was waiting for him in the bar when he got back to the hotel. 'Here, son, get that down you and then I'll shout you a plate of steak and eggs.'

'You celebrating?'

'Could say that.'

'Cheers, Stan.' Jon took a long pull on his beer.

'What do you think of the place then?'

'It's big, bigger than Charlestown.'

'You should've seen the place in 1911. There were over a thousand souls living here then and a similar number in Gwalia. The whole area was like a gypsy camp – prospectors' and miners' huts made of bush timber, corrugated iron and hessian were scattered all over. And the place was full of families, kids and chooks scratching in the dust and the women busy washing, cooking and tending veggie plots. Opening the railway line at the turn of the century was what did it. It brought in migrant workers by the dozen, especially Italians and Jugoslavs. Mind you, it's still a busy place, but not like it was in its heyday.'

'Is this where you worked, Stan?'

'Too right. It's where gold got in me blood. I was here right up to when I went to Europe to fight in the bloody war.'

Stan leaned across the counter and spoke to the woman behind the bar. 'We'll have your special – your best steak and eggs for two and a refill.' He slid across the empty glasses.

Stan leaned back in his seat and belched. 'I take it you took your punishment like a man? That Yildilla fella was it?'

'Yeah.'

'Well, if I were you I'd put it behind me and write it off as experience.'

'I haven't much choice, have I?'

'Not a deal.' Stan slid his glass across the table. 'Your shout.'

'Beer's better for me guts,' Stan said after quaffing half of the fresh glass. 'So tell me about this great-nephew of Alice's. What do you make of him?'

'Brags a bit.'

'Aye.'

'He doesn't like Aborigines.'

'Nothing unusual in that,' said Stan.

'Alice likes him.'

'And what about you?'

'I'm not over keen. He's not right for Jarrahlong. He spends too much time playing two-up, and drinking.'

'That's what I heard.'

'Scally?'

'No, Scally likes the bloke. Les mentioned something the other day.' Stan leaned back in his seat, lost in thought for a moment or two. 'What will you do if Alice decides to let him manage the place for her?'

'Find a job in the Northern Territory.'

'You wouldn't go back to England?'

'I might have to eventually if Merle doesn't like Australia.'

'Who's Merle?'

'The girl I'm going to marry. She's studying to be a doctor in Liverpool.'

'So Rachel's definitely not the one?'

'She's nice enough.'

'But she doesn't set your loins on fire.'

'I suppose you could say that.'

Stan sipped his beer savouring the last of the pale liquid. 'This Merle, is she worth giving up everything for?'

'Was Alice?'

'Touché.'

Jon grinned. 'That a word you learnt in France?'

Stan thumped his empty glass down onto the table. 'Finish your beer. I'm about ready for me beauty sleep.'

At Stan's place Bess and Bonny milled about, scampering around in circles like pups, glad to be home, while Jon lit the stove, set the billy on to boil and sorted out the makings for a meal: boiled potatoes, bully beef and beans, all thrown into the pot together. While it was cooking he saw to the chooks, chopped some wood, swept out the shack and poured Stan a couple of fingers of rum. As he handed over the drink he noticed Stan's pallor and his slumped shoulders – the old fella was done in; the journey had drained the strength out of him.

'I could stay a bit longer, Stan.'

'I'll be all right in a day or so. I'll take it easy, rest up a bit, be back on my feet in no time.'

They ate their meal and afterwards Jon cleared away and made up Stan's bed.

'I can stay the night if you like, Stan.'

'No need.'

Jon gave him a searching look.

'And you can take that wifey look off your face. I'm as fit as a flea on a mad dog.'

When Jon heard the belligerence in Stan's voice he knew he was wasting his time arguing. 'Anything else you need? I can drop it by later in the week.'

'I'm a bit low on rum, a bottle or two wouldn't go amiss and some more books, if Alice can spare them – helps pass the time.'

'I'll bring them over tomorrow.'

'There you go again doing your wifey thing. Next week'll do fine. I've still got a full bottle stashed away so there's no hurry.'

Jon arrived at Jarrahlong in the late afternoon. The homestead was quiet in the waning heat. Chooks fluffed in the dust under the old gum tree, while the horses stood idly by in the shade and Alice dozed in her chair on the verandah.

He stepped out of the cab and heard voices in the barn. He glanced at his watch, too late for smoko. He listened and recognised Rachel's voice, the words indistinct, and Greg answering.

He grinned. He didn't want to disturb them although, for the life of him, he couldn't see what Rachel saw in Greg, but there and again he wasn't a lass and he supposed Greg was a good-looking bloke.

He turned to leave and heard Greg's voice. 'I thought you liked me?'

'I do,' said Rachel.

'So why won't you?'

Rachel's answer was muffled. Jon stepped closer to the doorway.

'Playing hard to get?'

'No.'

'I've met your sort before, and it's not as if you haven't been around.'

Jon heard the slap as he crossed the threshold and saw Rachel, her cheeks flaming, and Greg standing a couple of feet away, a sheepish look on his face.

Rachel recovered first. 'Have you seen Bindi, Jon?'

'No,' he said. 'Is she busy down the vegetable patch? Anything wrong?'

'No, nothing at all,' snapped Rachel. She stalked past him without a backward glance.

'Fiery, isn't she?' grinned Greg, rubbing his cheek.

'If I were you,' said Jon, his tone chilly, 'I'd be very careful what you say to Rachel. Alice is very fond of her, and so am I.'

Understanding dawned on Greg's face. 'Joe's your kid then?'

'No, he's not and that's got nothing to do with it.'

'It was only a bit of fun.'

'Oh, yeah?'

'Don't get yourself steamed up.'

Jon clenched his fists.

Greg took a step backwards. 'I didn't know she was spoken for?'

Jon let it drop. If Greg thought he fancied Rachel perhaps he'd leave her alone.

'Never was interested in used goods anyway,' said Greg when he reached the doorway.

'Pommy bastard,' muttered Jon under his breath.

CHAPTER 46

Charlestown was packed to overflowing with race-goers and Jon was lucky to find a place to park close to The Grand. He recognised Ty's horse with its distinctive colouring hitched to the railing, and Will Samuels' utility parked alongside others belonging to folk from stations as far away as Southern Cross.

According to Alice, Race Day in Charlestown had been abandoned in 1947 following the bushfire – not that he'd been around at the time, he was already on a tramp ship working his passage back to England, and he'd missed the 1948 meeting too.

Val called and waved to them as he helped Alice out of the passenger seat. Jon looked up and saw her leaning out of the small window built into the gable end of Simpson's store. He pitied Rachel and Joe staying in the hot, airless room, but he knew Rachel wouldn't reconsider asking her father if she could move in with him, not while he was still bitter about Joe, so she didn't have much choice, every available bed in the hotel had been booked months ago.

'Come on over,' Val called down. 'I'll put on a brew.'

Rachel swung Joe onto her hip, picked up her canvas carryall and walked towards Simpson's. Jon gave Alice his arm and guided her towards The Grand and the room that she had booked for the duration of the race meeting.

The bar in The Grand was three deep and he had difficulty getting Alice through the throng and up to her room. He left her there to unpack and change and arranged to meet her in the saloon later.

Jon wandered out to the makeshift racecourse. The organisers had cleared away new growth from around the circuit, replaced the marker posts that had been eaten by white ants, and constructed a grandstand from forty-four-gallon drums and planking lashed together with rope in the only shady patch on the course, not far from The Grand. Faded bunting decorated the lower branches of the shade trees, and trestle tables had been set up ready for the sale of food and beer. Despite everyone's best efforts it was as far removed from Aintree and a society event as he was from Merle.

Back at the hotel he met Alice and escorted her to a table beyond the worst of the crush in the saloon.

Scally joined them. 'Your usual poison, Alice?'

'Thanks, Ed.'

Jon watched Scally fight his way to the bar. 'He doesn't mellow with age, does he?'

'Well, you know the solution,' said Alice.

'Is that what you think I should do, marry Rachel?'

'No. Two wrongs never did make a right, but I'm not the problem, am I? You've got to sort things out with Scally if things are to improve around here and it looks like it's up to you to make the first move.'

Scally returned with a double whiskey for Alice and a beer for himself. He sat down opposite Alice and passed her a race card. 'I thought you might like to study form, Alice. Looks like the first race tomorrow should be a good un. Kit Kennilworth reckons his gelding's got the lot beat in the first race.'

Jon left the pair of them to it and crossed over to the bar and ordered a beer from Al.

'Bad limp you've got there. You fell off your horse?' asked Al.

'Something like that.'

'No chance of you having a go in the rodeo then? You don't fancy your chances poddy roping?'

'Nah,' said Jon, 'never was no good with poddys.'

'Or Scally,' commented Al, glancing over towards Alice's table. He placed a beer on the counter and Jon paid.

Nothing like being alone in a crowd to make you feel welcome, thought Jon. He sipped his beer while watching Scally and Alice over the rim of his glass. Alice was right, if the situation wasn't sorted soon it never would be. Rachel was unhappy, and Joe was already rising two. He put his glass on the bar, left the hotel and walked rapidly in the direction of Simpson's store.

The stairway up to Val's room was stifling and climbing the steep stairs pulled on his leg. He could hear Val's voice and Joe laughing. He tapped on the door and opened it when Val called and saw her sitting on a threadbare rug playing with Joe, the two of them building a tower of bricks.

'Where's Rachel?' he asked.

'She's over at her Dad's place pickin' up a few of her things while Scally's at The Grand.'

'So she's not planning to patch things up with her Dad?'

'No, I don't think so,' said Val.

Jon swore under his breath. Rachel was never going to tell her dad the truth.

'Are you going to help us with these bricks?'

'No, it's Joe I want. Is it all right if I take him out for a few minutes?'

'It's his bedtime.'

'I won't be long; I want to show him the town.'

Val gave him a quizzical look, and he could feel the heat rising up his neck. 'I'm not his dad if that's what you're thinking,' he snapped.

'Never crossed my mind, hon.'

Liar, he thought, angry at the terse exchange.

'I'll come with you.'

'No.' He spoke too quickly and saw the enthusiasm fade from her face. 'No, just Joe and me…maybe next time.'

'Ten minutes then.' She slipped a cardigan on the little boy and handed him over. 'And you look after him or you'll have me as well as Rachel to answer to.'

'Ten minutes,' repeated Jon, bending down to pick up Joe.

The toddler was heavier than he'd remembered. He supposed children were like lambs and calves, fast growing. Joe's hair and cheek brushed against his nose, he still had a baby smell. Joe chuckled with pleasure and Jon smiled.

'Guess where we're going,' he murmured in the child's ear.

He pressed his way through the overspill crowd in the foyer, through the double doors into the saloon and across to where Alice and Scally were sitting. Alice saw them first and Jon noted the look of surprise on her face and the quick glance in Scally's direction.

He sensed Connie's eyes boring into his back and wondered how long he'd got before they were both thrown out.

'Scally!' said Jon, his tone firm, decisive.

Scally put his glass down and didn't bother to look up. 'Now what, you Pommy bastard?'

Jon lowered Joe onto Scally's lap.

Scally's shocked reaction gave Jon his opening. 'He's not my son, Scally, and Rachel and I are not getting married, not now, not ever, and it's about time you got to know your grandson.'

'No kids in the bar,' said Connie.

'Sort it out with Scally,' said Jon. 'It's none of my business.' He turned on his heels, but not before he saw the wry amusement in Alice's eyes and the shock on Scally's face.

Once out of The Grand he crossed to the shaded side of the street and sat down on the walkway steps and waited. Would Scally relent, or would it be Connie he'd see carrying Joe? He tried to imagine the consternation in the bar, Joe's bottom lip trembling when he sensed the unaccustomed lap and hostile atmosphere, Alice putting in her pennyworth, and Connie demanding Joe's removal from the saloon. Instead he saw Rachel hurrying towards The Grand, a worried look on her face.

'Rachel!'

She stopped. 'Jon?'

He beckoned to her.

'Where's Joe? What have you done with him?'

'He's all right. He's with his granddad.'

'Dad?'

'Yeah.' Jon grinned. 'I dumped Joe in his lap and told him to get to know his grandson.'

'You should have kept your nose out of my business.'

'It's mine too! How do you think I feel knowing everyone thinks I'm a scoundrel, and worse, a bludger, living on Alice's charity because of you and Joe?'

'Alice doesn't think that.'

'I know, but everyone else does.'

She flushed and turned away.

'Rachel! Wait! Nothing's going to happen to Joe. Alice is there and so is Connie. Let's wait and see, all right?' He grabbed her arm and felt the tension drain out of her. He sat down again and patted the step next to him. 'Sit here, next to me and watch.'

Ten minutes passed, and another ten, Rachel getting jumpier by the moment.

'It's past his bedtime,' she said, and then they heard the hotel double doors swing open.

Scally appeared carrying Joe. He stood for a moment on the hotel steps and then he stepped onto the verandahed walkway and adjusted Joe's position against his shoulder. 'Let's go and find that mother of yours,' they heard him say.

Jon put a restraining hand on Rachel's arm. 'Let's see what your dad does.'

They could hear Scally talking to Joe all the way down the street. Jon and Rachel followed at a distance, keeping in the deeper shade. When Scally reached Simpson's Jon nudged Rachel. 'Go and ask your dad if you can stay with him tonight. Make some excuse if you have to.'

'Like what?'

'I don't know; say it's too crowded at Val's, too stuffy for Joe…anything. I'll square things with Val.'

Rachel looked doubtful.

'It'll be all right, you'll see. Go on.' He gave her a gentle shove and stepped into deeper shadow. He was the last person Scally would want to see.

He heard Rachel call and saw Scally turn towards her, Joe still in his arms.

'What do you think you're doing letting that Pommy good-for-nothing look after Joe?' he demanded.

Jon grinned.

'Sorry, Dad. Jon said he wanted to take Joe out for a few minutes.'

'Well, it's not good enough, Rachel. What does he know about raising kids, the little fella needs regular hours.'

'I know.'

'Here,' Scally handed Joe back.

Go on; ask if you can stay the night, willed Jon from the shadows, ask him, for God's sake.

'Dad, is it all right if Joe and I sleep in my old room tonight, only there's not a lot of space at Val's…and…and…'

Jon strained to catch Rachel's words, conscious of Scally's rigid posture.

'I suppose so…so long as the pair of ya don't keep me awake,' said Scally grudgingly.

'Thanks Dad. He'll be no trouble, I promise.'

The two of them stood facing each other, the strain between them palpable.

'I've missed you, Dad.'

Jon heard the catch in Rachel's voice and knew she was crying. Scally stepped forward and put his arms around her and Joe. After several moments he gave her his handkerchief. She wiped her eyes and blew her nose. 'I'll go and get our things,' she said at last. 'You go to your granddad, Joe.'

Scally took the toddler and held him at arm's length. 'You'd better hurry up, he needs his nappy changing.'

Rachel looked back to the shadows, the beginnings of a tremulous smile on her face.

'Hope you don't mind, Val, only I had to do something.'

'Too right you did, so no worries,' said Val in a broad Aussie accent. She switched back to her normal Liverpool dialect. 'You did the right thing, hon, but will Scally take them back?'

'I think so. It looks like it.'

'So who is Joe's dad?'

'Your guess is as good as mine.' He wasn't about to tell Val he suspected Berry, he had no proof. 'Has Rachel said anything to you about it?'

Val shook her head. 'No. Closed-mouthed, she is. If you ask me she really regrets havin' anythin' to do with the bloke. He probably took advantage. Rachel's not exactly worldly-wise.'

'No,' said Jon.

'And what's that tone of voice supposed to mean?'

Jon grinned. 'Not like us Liverpudlians.'

'You fancy a cuppa?'

'Wouldn't say no, it's been a busy couple of hours.' He sat back in a battered easy chair, watching her make the tea on a portable stove. 'When are you thinking of going home?'

'I'm not, I like it here.'

Her answer took him aback.

'Why are you lookin' at me like that? Are you plannin' on goin' home, or somethin'?' asked Val.

'No, my home's here.'

'So, what makes you think it'd be any different for me?'

'What about your mam and your sister?'

She carried the tea tray over to the tin box that she used as a table and balanced it carefully. 'And what about your family?' She poured the tea. 'Sugar?'

'No thanks, gave it up for Lent.'

'Since when?'

'Since ten or so years back, when I first came out on the boat with all the other kids.' He grinned broadly. 'Truce?'

'Truce,' she said.

'So, what are your plans? This place is a bit limited for the likes of you.'

'I'll ignore that comment, Jon Cadwallader.'

'Well, it isn't exactly a cosmopolitan city like Liverpool, is it?'

'Maybe limited is a state of mind.'

'Getting philosophical all of a sudden.'

'No, but in case you haven't realised it, there is scope for improvement.'

'Like what?'

'This place for a start. I've persuaded Larry to stock nicer, more fashionable clothes, swanky stuff, for the women. He's says I can go with him to Perth next time and help with the buyin'.'

'He'll be asking you to marry him next.'

'He already has,' she said dryly.

Jon choked down the mouthful of tea he was about to swallow. 'And are you going to?'

'What do you think?'

'He must be worth a bit.'

'What's that gorra do with it?'

'Depends what you want.'

'What I want is to fall head-over-heels in love with a fella who feels the same way about me,' she said lightly.

'And what about getting rich? I thought you said you wanted to be wealthy?'

'Well, that'd be nice, but I'd sooner be with someone I fancy.'

He watched Val sipping tea, her face in shadow, and found it difficult to read her expression.

'What about Merle?' she asked.

'What about her?'

'You think she'll like it out here?'

'Why wouldn't she? You do.' He was suddenly conscious of Merle's recent letter in his pocket.

'I'm not Merle.'

'Has she said something to you?' he asked after a long moment, wondering if Val had heard about Paul Vincent, a physicist at the same university who had taken Merle to a concert in the Philharmonic Hall.

Val laughed. 'Merle doesn't write to me, hon. She never did have time for the likes of me and Dot, and she was always one to keep her own counsel.'

He hadn't considered tact to be one of Val's strengths, but her assessment was pretty accurate, especially Merle's views about Dorothy. Neither he nor Merle had liked Val's best friend, they'd found her shallow, a bit of a good-time girl.

He looked down at the empty mug and frowned. Merle hadn't wasted any time making new friends at university. He wondered what the Vincent bloke was like.

'Do you reckon there's more than one person you could make a go of it with?' asked Val.

'You having second thoughts about Larry Simpson?'

'No.'

'So what do you mean?'

'Well, suppose Merle doesn't want to live in Australia.'

'What sort of a question is that?'

'Well, what would you do? Stay here and marry someone else, or go home to England to be with Merle?'

'I suppose I'd go back.'

Val finished her tea.

'Anyway, what's it to you?' asked Jon.

'Nothin', just makin' polite conversation.' She stood up and held out her hand for his mug. 'Have you finished your drink?'

'Yes,' said Jon. 'I suppose I'd better be getting back, me being here won't do your reputation much good if you're planning on hooking yourself a rich pastoralist at the races.'

'No,' said Val quietly, 'I don't suppose it would.'

Out in the street he looked up at Val's attic room. The light was already off. It wasn't like Val to be so quiet, so reflective. He ran through his conversation with her. Maybe she wasn't feeling too good. Maybe the place was wearing her down after all.

The first race ran at midday and by then the whole town was at the track plus every station owner and stockman for two hundred miles. They'd travelled in by truck and horse, some with their wives and families, to drink the bar dry, to make a killing on the tote, to play two-up in the evenings, to swap news and gossip, and eye up the single women.

Alice was comfortably installed in a wicker armchair in a patch of deep shade down by the finishing post. Rachel, Joe and Val sat on a picnic rug next to her while a group of younger stockmen were standing drinking, betting on the first race and keeping an eye on the two prettiest women present.

A hand clapped him on the back – Will Samuels, and behind him was Greg.

'What ya doing, mate?' Will raised his hat in Alice's direction. 'G'day Alice. You placed a bet yet?'

'I'm still studying form, Will. Have you any tips?'

'You know Alice,' said Greg. 'She likes the gee-gees.'

'Don't we all?' said Will.

'We've got sure bets,' said Val. 'I've half a crown each-way on Blackbird and Rachel has the same on Outback Lass.'

'Lost it already,' said Will. 'You should have put it on Cracker, reckon he's set fair to win this race. What about you, Jon?'

'I'm with Alice, I'm still studying form.' He watched the horses collecting near the start line for the first race. The animals, all working horses off local stations, were beginning to lather up. The riders, wearing bright racing silks over singlets and strides, were keeping the animals calm, waiting for the order to move forward.

'Cracker looks all right, but if I were you I'd put ten bob on Ken Hammond's horse,' said Tom Samuels as he joined them.

'Which one's that?' asked Jon.

'The little chestnut.'

Jon studied the horse. It wasn't much to look at, leggier than some with a finer head than most of the stock horses he'd seen. Her rump was covered in mud from where she'd been rolling.

'You reckon?' said Jon.

'Only fit for the knacker's yard, if you ask me,' said Greg.

'Aye, she might look it, but Ken says she has what it takes, stamina and a turn of speed in the final furlong, and if it loses I'll shout you all a beer, can't say fairer than that,' said Tom.

'What's its name?'

'Rough Diamond.'

Jon crossed to the tote and put ten bob on the horse to win.

'Sensible,' commented a bloke called Dave Janek who was running the tote. 'You don't want to blow all your money on one scraggy nag, do ya?' He smiled away the barbed comment.

Jon's horse came in second having been impeded by the winner, Blackbird, a big, black gelding that failed to keep to a straight line. Out of the corner of his eye he'd seen Val standing next to Will, jumping up and down, shouting for the horse as it came into the home straight.

Val smiled broadly. 'Which did you back, Tom?'

'Rough Diamond, lost fifty bob, and Jon lost ten.'

'You should have asked an expert,' said Val. 'Mam taught me. She always was lucky on the horses; she used to take me and me sister to Aintree on race days when we were kids.'

'Aintree?' said Will.

'Where they run the Grand National,' she said. 'Not that I've been to any races recently, the war put paid to that. There were Yanks campin' on the turf till forty-six.'

'You can't beat a flat race,' said Greg, 'less of a lottery than over the sticks.'

'But nowhere near as excitin',' said Val.

'The Melbourne Cup, that's the big flat race here,' said Will. 'Everyone has a few bob on that one.'

'Anyone made a killing then?' said a voice from behind them.

They all turned and saw Berry standing with a thumb tucked into his trouser belt, the other hand holding a bottle of beer; behind him stood Dusty, Wheat and Ray talking to Wes Chapman.

'Where's Cadge?' asked Will.

'Propping up the bar,' said Berry. He held out a hand to Greg. 'Take it you're a relative of Alice's.'

'Yeah, that's right.'

'If we ain't careful we'll be knee-deep in Alice's relatives.' His eyes fixed on Jon for a moment. 'Are you going to introduce me to your lady friend?' he said, looking pointedly at Val.

'Yes,' said Val, 'aren't you goin' to introduce us, Jon?'

'This is Valerie Rayner, from England,' interrupted Will before Jon could answer, and then he indicated Berry, 'Berry Greenall.'

'Which station do you work on?' asked Val, watching Berry openly, a half smile on her face.

'We're shearers, we work on all the stations hereabouts, and you work for old man Simpson, that right?' said Berry. 'Are you planning on staying?'

'As long as I'm welcome,' said Val.

'You're welcome, right enough. Every bloke in the area'll be beating a path to your door.'

'Not so far, they haven't.' She ignored the wounded look on Will's face. Alice harrumphed and Val turned to her and smiled broadly. 'Now then, Alice, don't you go spoilin' me chances with this nice young man.'

Ray joined them, grinning from ear to ear. 'I heard that – nice young man, eh! Berry's a dissolute, womanising, no-hoper. You're better off with me, I'm a gentleman,' he said. 'What you doing tonight?'

'What you offerin'?' quipped Val.

'How about the picture show? You up for it?'

'You bet,' said Val, 'Rachel and me, we like the pictures.'

'We'll all go,' said Berry. 'What about you, Alice?' He caught sight of Joe. 'I heard you'd had a son, Rachel. What have you called him?'

'Joe,' said Rachel.

Berry looked at the toddler chewing on a piece of crust. Jon noticed Berry's taut jawline, heard the clipped edge in his voice and saw that he wasn't the only one watching and listening. While Val chatted to Ray, Alice was keeping an eye on Rachel and Berry. Berry's unasked question hung in the air.

'He's a fine looking kid,' said Berry at last.

'Thank you,' said Rachel, scarlet stained her cheeks. She didn't look up as she busied herself straightening the rug where Joe sat.

Berry leaned over and patted the little lad on the head. 'He looks just like you, Rachel,' then he turned back to Val and the others. 'You want a shandy, Val? My shout.' He brushed past Jon on the way to the temporary bar. 'It's about time you made an honest woman of her,' he murmured.

'What did you say?' said Jon, catching sight of Rachel's white face.

'Nothing,' said Berry.

'Exactly,' snarled Jon, 'it's none of anyone's business, except Rachel's, got it?'

Berry grinned. 'If you say so, mate. I'm only saying what everyone else is thinking.'

'It'd be better if ya kept y'views to yourself, Berry,' said Scally coldly.

Jon swung round. He hadn't heard Scally's approach.

Berry shrugged. 'If you like, Scal.'

'I do like.' Scally stood his ground glaring at Berry, hostility ironed on his face.

Val had heard every word and Jon caught the speculative look in her eyes. If she said anything to him he was ready for her. He waited for the comment, a sharp reply hanging on his lips.

Val turned away, fanning herself with a race card. 'Have you picked a horse for the next race yet, Alice? I'm goin' for Silver Cloud, Wes reckons he's a dead cert.'

'Can I shout you a beer, Scal?' offered Berry.

'Maybe later, mate.'

'Suit yourself.' Berry sauntered over to Ray and the others at the bar.

The exchange momentarily put a damper on things until Joe dropped his half-chewed crust and wailed loud enough to distract everyone. Val knelt down and retrieved it, dusted it off and handed it back to him.

'Thank's Val,' said Rachel, the colour fading from her cheeks.

'Have you got your mount sorted for the Cathay Cup, Will?' asked Alice when the awkward moment passed.

'You bet, and so has Tom. We've been in training this last month.'

'I didn't know you were that interested in racing,' said Jon. 'What's the name of your horse? I might put a couple of bob on it.'

Will grinned. 'Brown Jack.'

'What's that about Brown Jack?' asked Jeb Samuels.

They all turned. Jeb Samuels and his wife, Mary, stood behind them, dressed in their best.

'Who's putting money on it?' asked Mary.

'Hello Mary,' said Alice. 'Jon's thinking about it. Come and sit by me. We haven't had a good old natter for months. Jon, go and find another chair for Mary.'

Jon found one and placed it next to Alice.

'What's Tom riding?' asked Alice.

'Big Boy.'

Alice smiled. 'Is it any better than Pot Luck?'

Mary laughed. 'You'll have to ask him.'

'How's the rebuilding coming on at Jindalee?'

'Slowly, you know how it is,' said Mary.

'Changing the subject, I've heard that Stan's not too good,' said Jeb.

'That's right,' said Alice. 'Jon keeps an eye on him. He called at Stan's place yesterday to see if he wanted a lift into town, but he wasn't up to it. The trip to Leonora the other week took it out of him.'

'All this business about Gerry's disappearance can't help either,' commented Jeb.

'As if Stan could have done it,' said Mary. 'I don't believe that for a moment.'

'No,' said Alice, 'but when all's said and done, there's something strange about Gerry's disappearance.'

Jon didn't want to hear any more. 'I'm going over to the bar, Alice. Can I get you a drink? Mrs Samuels? Mr Samuels?'

'No, thank you,' said Alice.

'Not for us,' said Jeb. 'Not long finished one.'

When Jon saw the crush around the bar he changed his mind and wandered over towards the rodeo yard where people were gathering for the poddy roping and joined Val and Berry at the rails.

'You not having a go?' asked Berry, his arm draped around Val's shoulder.

'Never roped a poddy in my life,' said Jon.

'What's a poddy?' asked Val.

'A calf that hasn't been branded,' said Berry.

She looked across to the charcoal brazier. 'You mean that's what they're goin' to do, catch a calf and brand it?'

'That's right.'

They all watched the first of the calves lassoed, brought to the ground, a back and a front leg roped, and branded.

'Smell that,' said Berry, taking in a deep breath, 'singed hair and flesh.' And it was all over, the animal released and back with its mother in less than two shakes.

Val gave a long, low whistle. 'They don't do that in Liverpool.' And the crowd around them laughed.

The last race of the day was the Cathay Cup.

'About time, I hope it's worth waiting for after all I've heard about it,' said Jon as they all made their way over toward the rails.

'Oh, it is,' said Rachel. She caught Val's eye and laughed.

'You mean you haven't heard about Charlestown's famous race?' said Berry.

'I've heard about nothing else, so who's Cathy?' asked Jon.

'Cathay,' said Rachel. 'Not Cathy.'

'Funny name for a race?'

'It's named after Connie. Cathay was her maiden name,' said Alice.

'Didn't know she was married.'

'She isn't any more. Vince drank himself to death years ago. Anyway, when she came up with the idea for the race it was decided to name it after her.'

'What are you putting your money on, Alice?' asked Berry.

'Pot Luck,' she said, and everyone laughed.

Jon frowned. What was going on?

'And mine's Brown Jack,' said Val. 'Berry's is Sir Loin, and Rachel's is last year's winner, Old Soap.'

'All jockeys for the Cathay Cup make your way to the starting post,' announced Wes Chapman over the loudspeaker.

A great cheer erupted from the crowd.

Jon looked about him, everyone was moving forward to the rails, laughing and waving their hats at the jockeys as they strode down the track to the starting line.

'What's happening?' asked Jon.

'Beats me,' said Greg, 'some sort of Aussie tradition by the look of things.'

The cheering got louder. Rachel leaned over the fence, shouting encouragement. Jon pushed his way to the front to see what she was looking at. There, at the start line, were the jockeys, each mounted on a bullock, hanging on to home-made bridles, whips at the ready.

'And they're off,' yelled Wes.

The stampede gathered momentum as the jockeys flapped their bush hats and whips against the animals' rumps. It was nothing like anything he'd ever seen before, no rules, no line on the race-course, just a free-for-all, every man and animal for themselves, and all of the jockeys out to win. The sound of six bullocks, weighing half a ton each, pounding down the track was drowned out by the cheering and shouting. The jockeys, oblivious of the crowd, focused on the winning post, determination in the set of their jaws as they urged the animals onward.

Dust consumed the crowd as the animals thundered past only feet from where they were standing.

'Who's winnin'?' shouted Val. 'Brown Jack?'

'No,' yelled Berry, 'Will can't get him to run in a straight line, look.'

They all looked.

Brown Jack wasn't going anywhere. He was locked into a tight circle with Will flapping his hat against the animal's side, his face red from the effort and from swearing.

'What about Old Soap?'

'Can't see him,' yelled Berry, 'I can't see a bloody thing for dust.'

'And the winner, by a short head...is...Old Soap,' announced Wes over the loud speaker.

A huge cheer went up.

Rachel hugged Alice. 'I did it! I told you it'd win, I told you,' she shouted to all and sundry.

'And what about Big Boy?' asked Alice. 'Was he placed?'

'No,' said Berry, 'he came in second to last. I'd tell Tom to send him to the knacker's yard; he's not even fit for stew.'

'I'd have thought you'd have been in among that lot,' said Alice. 'It's not like you to miss an opportunity.'

'No, not me, Alice. I've got more sense.'

'What, value your dignity too much, do you?' said Val.

'No. Imagine what riding one of those does to a fella's tackle,' said Berry.

Rachel blushed.

Val laughed and caught hold of Berry's arm. 'We better be off otherwise we'll not get a seat for the picture show. Are you coming, Alice?' she called over her shoulder.

'No thanks, Val. I think I've had enough excitement for one day.' Alice picked up her hat and accepted Jon's offered arm. 'The Grand, if you'd be so good, and I'll shout you a cup of tea.'

'Don't mind if I do, Alice.'

'What about the others?' asked Alice.

'They've all gone with Val and Berry, except for Rachel.'

They stopped and waited for Rachel to catch up.

'Tea?' said Alice, 'or are you going to the picture show?'

'Tea would be fine, Alice. I'll go and find Dad and Joe.'

After the dust settled the five of them made their way to The Grand and Alice ordered tea for four and a bottle of milk for Joe.

'I don't know where Greg's got to,' said Alice as she poured the tea.

'Last time I saw him he was at the racecourse,' said Jon.

'He's over at Les's place playing two-up,' said Scally. 'If I was you, Alice, I'd have a word in his ear. It's all too easy to lose y'shirt in the ring and some blokes never learn when enough is enough.'

'Better two-up than drinking,' said Alice. 'Greg needs a break from sheep now and then.'

'Y'too soft on him, Alice.'

'No, I'm not,' she snapped.

'All I'm saying is that gambling don't suit some,' said Scally.

'I heard you the first time,' said Alice in a clipped tone.

Jon kept out of the argument, but, for once, he agreed with Scally. Alice was too soft. He finished his tea aware of Scally's frustration. Did Scally know something about Greg's gambling that Alice didn't? 'I'll take a wander over, Alice. See how he's doing.'

'Thanks, Jon. I wouldn't like him to make a fool of himself.'

Some chance, thought Jon, Greg was the type to come up smelling of roses no matter what.

Cato was the spinner. He stood inside the ring holding the kip.

Jon barely heard Les's greeting for the raucous crowd betting furiously before the ringie placed the coins on the kip for the next toss. The room quietened as he passed the kip to Cato.

'Are you ready?' called the ringie. 'Come in spinner.'

Jon had seen two-up played often enough but had never been interested in the game – it was too easy to lose money by risking everything on the toss of two coins. He knew it was stupid to get involved, but the atmosphere in the lean-to was charged; he'd been drawn in against his better judgment, and he was now in the thick of it, betting with the best of them. He watched Cato's coins spinning in the air and catching the light as they tumbled.

'Tails.'

A groan went up from the crowd. He'd lost his bet too. The amount wasn't large but it was big enough to bring him up sharp.

A mug's game his gran would have said. A bet to win on the National and the same for the Derby, the Oaks and the St Leger and that was it. Anything else and you're paying the tote, she'd say.

Cato stepped out of the ring and handed the kip to the next bloke, a middle-aged stockman Jon didn't recognise.

'Are you ready? Come in spinner.' And they were off again, coins spinning time and time again, the wagers higher with every pair of heads thrown.

Greg was yelling encouragement and laying bets, sweat glistening on his brow as he threw ten-bob notes into the money tray between each toss of the coins.

Les's face was a picture of concentration. He was a two-up champion from way back and now he organised the games in the lean-to shed with its purpose-built two-up pit.

The stockman was on a roll; he headed the coins three times and collected his winnings from Wes, and then he handed the kip on to Greg. 'I'm off for a beer. Leave you lot to lose your money,' he said.

'Let's see how the Pommy bastard does it,' yelled someone from the back of the shed.

Jon tried to leave, but he was hemmed in by the crowd pushing forward to see the Pommy spin.

'Ten feet high and no less,' said the ringie, 'otherwise it's a bum toss.'

Greg's first toss was good – heads. So were the next two.

'You can make your own bet now,' said the ringie.

'Double up then,' said Greg, gripping the kip so tightly his knuckles showed white under the skin.

'And another three,' yelled the ringie after Greg tossed three sets of heads.

'Beginner's luck,' yelled someone. 'Bet ya can't do that again.'

Greg grinned. 'You watch me, you Aussie bastard.'

On the next toss the coins feathered.

'Foul toss,' called the ringie, catching the coins.

Betting was fierce. The tray was full of coin and notes. The ringie replaced the coins in the kip and handed it back to Greg.

'Come in spinner.'

Up went the coins. Everyone was silent as the coins spun, all betting suspended on the outcome of the toss.

Greg had doubled and doubled again. He had to throw heads or lose the lot. Down they came, a head and a tail. Les paid out on those who'd bet on tails and Greg passed on the kip, his demeanour less cocky, the excitement gone from his eyes.

Jon saw Greg talking to Les, and saw Les briefly glance in his direction. By the time he'd pushed his way out of the crush Greg was at his shoulder.

'I'm a bit short on cash,' he said, 'any chance I could borrow a few pounds? I'll pay you back.'

Jon took out his wallet. 'How much?'

'Forty'll do,' said Greg, his colour higher than usual.

Forty! Jon took out his wallet shocked at the amount. 'I've only got twenty, but you're welcome.'

'Ta, I owe you,' Greg said, taking the notes.

Jon stepped out into the street. Forty quid! Didn't Greg have any sense? He stuffed his hands into his pockets, the loan had cleaned him out, he couldn't go back to The Grand without a pound or two in his wallet. He glanced at his watch, half past seven. Damn Greg and his gambling! And he'd missed the picture show.

He stood for a moment listening to the laughter coming from the direction of the town hall and the cheering from the two-up ring, and thought of Stan, sick and alone. He needed to check-up on him, see that he was all right, and there was nothing for him in town, it was still fairly early, he could be at Yaringa by nine.

CHAPTER 47

As soon as Jon saw the light on in Stan's shack he knew something was amiss. The old fella always went to bed early, and he was a stickler for making sure the kerosene lamp was doused. Don't want to be burned alive, he'd once said – not a pretty way to go to me Maker.

When Jon entered the shack he could smell the burning kerosene and overlaying it an odour he couldn't define but knew as illness; he'd smelt it before when his mother was sick, in the days before she'd gone into hospital.

Stan was on his bed, fully clothed, with Bess at his feet and Bonny lying on the floor only inches from his shoulder. Stan's breathing was laboured and his skin felt hot to the touch. Jon pulled Bess off the bed, then he wrung out a cloth in cold water and laid it across Stan's brow. The old man opened his eyes.

'How are you doing, Stan? Can I get you anything?'

The eyes, bright with fever, looked at him without recognition. 'Rum,' he said.

Jon poured him a tot, lifted him up and supported him while he swallowed it down. Stan's coughing was painful to listen to, his whole body racked by the effort to clear his lungs. When the moment passed Jon laid him back on his pillow and wiped the sweat off his brow.

All night he kept a vigil, wringing out cold compresses when Stan's temperature raged, and wrapping him in blankets when the shivers set in. He made Stan drink tea, or water laced with rum when the old man refused anything else.

During the long hours till dawn Jon thought of Curly's dying moments and prayed that Stan would pull through. Stan didn't deserve to die yet, not until he'd found his gold, and that aside, he'd miss Stan's dry sense of humour, his wisdom, having someone to turn to for advice. He listened to Stan's rattling breath. Pity there wasn't a doctor in town. Perhaps that's what he should write to Merle about, convince her of the challenge, of the opportunity to set up a clinic to care for the stockmen and their families, and old prospectors like Stan.

Illness and accidents were what everyone feared, and the flying doctor service at Kalgoorlie was still their best hope of quick treatment, despite the distance. But there were still limits – a plane needed a landing strip, and the nearest was Charlestown, a two-hour drive from a station like Jarrahlong, longer when the creeks were up. On remote stations, when the creeks were swollen and the roads impassable, then the sick and injured either recovered or died, there was no middle ground if the plane couldn't land in the bush. Maybe if Merle knew how much people like her were needed in the outback she'd want to give it a go.

He made himself a brew, fretting on the matter. It would be a while before Merle qualified and, as she'd written in one of her earlier letters, a lot can happen in a few years.

At dawn he stretched his stiff muscles walking with Bess and Bonny along the valley in the direction of Stan's No Hope mine. Everywhere and everything looked greyish in the early morning light, even the brightly coloured birds stirring in the bushes and trees bordering the creek bed. He enjoyed the invigorating morning chill, glad to be out of the shack and the stink of illness. As soon as the sun was up he'd check on Stan again, make him comfortable and set off back to Charlestown to pick up medicine and arrange for someone to take Alice back to Jarrahlong, a four hour round trip, plenty of time before the night drew in.

It was quiet in The Grand, only one or two in the bar.

'Where's Connie, Al?'

'She's out in the back with Han Sing organising things.' He jerked his thumb in the direction of the side door.

Connie was in the kitchen sitting at the big deal table, writing. She looked up when the door opened.

'And what can I do for you?' she asked, her voice chilly.

Jon took a deep breath. 'Can I buy one of your boiling chooks and some vegetables, Mrs Andersen?'

Connie stared at him, a bemused look on her face, and Han Sing looked up from preparing vegetables.

'And have you a couple of old sheets you aren't using at present?'

Connie recovered first.

'Is this some sort of—'

'It's Stan. He's really sick.'

'How sick?'

'Fever, chills. He's got a bad pain in his chest. It hurts him to breathe and he's coughing up a lot of rubbish.'

'Sounds like pneumonia,' she said. 'Any blood in it?'

'In what?'

'The stuff he's coughing up?'

'No.'

That's good then. Han Sing will sort out what you need in the food line and I'll get some old sheets. What about blankets?'

'I'd be grateful, only Stan's stink a bit.'

'I bet they do. How long has he been like it?'

'Well, he wasn't up to a day at the races, but I thought he was on the mend, then when I called by last night he was burning up.'

'Have you ever looked after someone with pneumonia?'

Jon shook his head.

'Bathe him with tepid water when the fever's bad and keep him warm when he gets the shivers. Put a pan on to boil and keep the air steamy, it'll help him to breathe. Wring out a towel in as hot water as you can bear and put it on his chest to loosen it and get plenty of fluids down him, water, tea and no alcohol. Are you planning on staying with him?'

'Yes, he's a mate.'

'What about Alice?'

'Once I've got the stuff for Stan I'll arrange for someone to drive Alice home.'

'Alice isn't here; she's over at Val's. You go and see her and Han Sing and I will get what you need.'

'Thank you, Mrs Andersen.'

'Connie,' she said. 'Call me Connie.'

'Don't you bother about me,' said Alice. 'I'll stay at The Grand for another couple of days.'

'I can drive you back to Jarrahlong,' said Val. 'Larry won't mind, in any case, after the weekend, business will be slow, everyone bought what they needed while they were in town for the races.'

'Thanks, I'll take you up on that,' said Alice. She turned back to Jon, 'And you get back to Stan's place, he'll need looking after by the sound of it, but he's a tough old fella; he'll pull through with a bit of nursing.'

'Will you be all right, Alice?'

'I'm not in my grave yet! And I've got Val here, and Greg can manage the place while you're at Stan's. Do you know how to look after him?'

'Yeah, Connie told me.'

'Connie, eh!'

Jon grinned. 'Yeah!'

At The Grand a box of clean sheets and blankets stood ready, and next to it another of vegetables and a cast iron cooking pot with a lid.

'Han Sing has prepared a chook and vegetables, all you need to do is add water and simmer it until it's cooked and the meat falls off the bones. Got it?'

'Thanks, Connie. Can I pay you later, only—'

She waved his words away. 'Stan's been a good customer over the years; it's the least I can do. Have you got soap?'

'I think so.'

'Han Sing,' called Connie. 'Get a bar of soap and a couple of towels.' She turned back to Jon. 'I'll send someone over tomorrow to see how he is and whether you need the doctor.'

'You know Stan and doctors.'

'I do, but that doesn't mean we can't call one if he needs one.' She placed the soap and towels on top of the blankets. 'Give him our regards. Tell him I'm keeping a cold beer on the bar and if he gets any worse, or you are worried, get back here and we'll radio the doctor and get him into hospital.' She gave him a small bottle of tablets.

'What are these?'

'Aspirin, it'll help reduce the fever and provide pain relief.'

At Stan's place Jon added water to the cooking pot and put it on to simmer. Outside he built a small fire and set a tin bath full of water over it balanced on makeshift trivets. While Stan slept Jon rummaged through his belongings and found a worn but clean pair of long johns and a singlet. By the time Stan roused the bath water was hot enough. Jon carried it inside, adjusted the temperature, tore up an old towel he'd found and persuaded Stan to sit on the edge of the bed.

'What for?' grumbled Stan.

'So I can give you a wash. You'll feel better.'
'I'm all right,' said Stan, making to lie down again.
Jon stopped him. 'You stink worse than a nest of ferrets. Hold your arms up.'
Stan did as he was told and Jon gently removed his shirt and singlet, then he soaped the flannel and washed the old man's body, noticing the sunken chest and the effort it cost him to breathe. Was it pneumonia, or was it something else? 'How long have you been like this, Stan?'
'Three or four days.'
'Why didn't you tell me before that you were feeling crook? I'd have stayed.'
'It was the Cathay Cup.'
'There was always next year.'
'Did you back the winner?'
'Did I heck,' said Jon. 'Here, slip this over your head,' he held out the singlet, 'and then stand up.'
Stan stood and Jon helped him out of his trousers.
'I've never had a bloke wash me tackle before.'
'And you're not now. Here, wash yourself, you old goat.' Jon handed him a soaped flannel and then, after he rinsed it for him, he handed it back.
Jon finished washing Stan's legs and feet and then helped him into his long johns and supported him over to the kitchen chair.
The bedding was damp with sweat. Jon held his breath against the rank odour as he threw the bedding out onto the verandah and remade the bed.
'These aren't mine,' said Stan as Jon helped him back into bed.
'Connie's,' said Jon. 'They're on loan so no smoking.'
'I don't smoke,' muttered Stan, 'only ever chew the stuff.' He coughed and hawked up phlegm into a stone jar at the side of the bed.
'Feel better?'
'Not much.'
Jon saw the strain on Stan's face, washing him had taken the sap out of him. 'Here, take this.'
'What is it?'
'Tea and aspirin.'
'Can't I have rum?'
'No, maybe later, this is better for you.'
'Who sez?'
'Connie.'

He watched Stan drink the brew down and wished he knew what Bindi had used when he'd had a fever. It wasn't pituri – she'd said so, although it had the hot peppery taste of pituri. She called the herb she'd given him wild tobacco and after he'd taken the stuff he'd been out of it for a time, oblivious to the fever raging in his body. If Stan didn't improve he'd have to drive over to Jarrahlong and bring Bindi back with her dilly bag of Aboriginal medicine, the wild tobacco, the turpentine leaves and the other stuff she used. He didn't want to upset Stan by calling in a doctor if native medicine would do the trick.

Later, when the soup was ready, Jon eased Stan into a sitting position and fed him chicken broth. Stan slept then, his breathing as laboured as the night before, the sweating and the shivering unabated. All night long Jon made hot compresses for Stan's chest, cold compresses for his fevered brow and kept the atmosphere as humid as a Chinese laundry.

Someone was shaking his shoulder pulling him up from the depths. He tried to shrug off the hand, unsure of where he was. 'Stan?'

'No, it's Val,' said a calm voice.

When he opened his eyes he saw her silhouetted against the open doorway, her blonde hair, back lit by sunlight, looked like a halo. He blinked and licked his paper-dry lips.

'What time is it?'

'Ten o'clock.'

He'd slept for four hours! He staggered to his feet – 'Stan?'

'He's all right, his breathin' seems okay.'

Jon looked down at Stan. His colour was still bad, but the rattling, rasping sound in his chest had eased.

'What are you doing here?'

'Rachel was goin' to come but Joe's got the sniffles so I offered. Connie had Han Sing prepare some beef stew. Have you eaten?'

'Not since last night.'

She ladled out a couple of bowls full and cut two thick slices off a loaf she'd brought with her. 'Here, eat this. It won't do Stan any good if you get sick too.'

Jon ate, too exhausted to argue.

'What you plannin' on doin' with the beddin' on the verandah?'

'Wash it.'

'In what?'

'The tin bath.'

'If you show me where things are I'll do it while you get some sleep – on that bed in the corner this time, not propped up at the kitchen table.'

When he woke she'd gone. On the line were the sheets and the blanket, she'd also washed up the dishes and a note said she'd fed Stan more of the chicken broth. He thought he could still smell the scent of her on the air, but knew he was imagining it. He ladled out another plateful of beef stew, ate it and then poured himself a stiff measure of Stan's rum.

'She's a fine lass, that Merle,' said Stan, hours later.

'It wasn't Merle,' said Jon, rousing himself from a doze. He checked his watch – two in the morning. 'It was Val. Merle's in Liverpool training to be a doctor.'

'The English girl living in Charlestown?' asked Stan.

'Yeah.'

'Les mentioned her...she has capable hands,' Stan said as Jon helped him to sit up. The effort triggered a bout of coughing and soon Stan was spitting out great gouts of yellowish-green phlegm. When the spasm passed he leaned back against the pillows, his body bathed in sweat. 'Pour me a drink, son – a real drink.'

Jon handed him a measure.

'That's better,' Stan muttered after he'd swallowed it down in one gulp. 'She's a good-looking woman,' he said after a moment or two.

'Who?'

'Val.'

'I suppose she is,' said Jon. Truth was he'd never taken that much notice of her and apart from her blonde hair and blue eyes, he couldn't easily have described what she looked like.

'Is she from Liverpool too?'

'Yes.'

'So, what's she doing out here, in the back of beyond?'

'She's got this mad idea about opening a shop selling dresses and hats and stuff.'

'In Charlestown?'

'Yeah, but I don't reckon it's a goer, there're not enough women around to buy them.'

Stan held his glass for a refill and Jon measured out another two fingers of rum.

'Alice likes dresses and hats,' he said. 'Blue is her colour, it matches those eyes of hers.' He coughed as he drank, choking on the fiery liquid.

'That's what Val said. She brought Alice a couple of dresses to try on, and a fancy hat. Seems she browbeat old Simpson into getting more stock in, and told him his dress sense was appalling.'

'What has Simpson got to do with it?'

'She works for him. She says he's already asked her to marry him.'

Stan wiped his mouth with the back of his hand. 'Larry's no fool, and he's a good judge of character.'

'That's not what Alice says. She said his wife ran off with a fencing contractor.'

'That's right, but a bloke's allowed one mistake.'

Stan dozed off again, Jon took his empty glass and tucked the blanket around his frail body.

CHAPTER 48

The new day dawned bright, the sky clear after a spell of overcast, humid days.

Stan woke early, hauled himself into a sitting position and wobbled to his feet.

'Steady,' said Jon as he helped him to the table.

Stan ate the bowl of stew Jon placed before him then leaned back in his seat and belched. 'I need some fresh air; this place stinks like a brothel.'

Jon smiled.

'Ever smelt a brothel?' Stan asked.

'Yeah, once.'

'And where was that?'

'In Jakarta, the crew on the tramp ship I was on got me drunk. They said I needed educating.'

'All sweat and perfume,' commented Stan.

'Can't smell a deal of perfume in here.'

'No, maybe you're right on that count,' agreed Stan as he made to stand up.

'Where are you going?' asked Jon.

'I told you, I need some fresh air.'

'I don't think you're up to it yet, Stan.'

Stan struggled to his feet and leaned against the table. 'I need to go and have a look at my mine.'

Was the old fella mad? Jon ignored the stubborn determination in the set of Stan's jaw. 'It's too far, Stan, maybe tomorrow when you're a bit better.'

'You missed your vocation, nurse,' said Stan. 'Pass me my cardigan.'

Jon hesitated and then reached for the garment. 'You're a stubborn old fool – you know that, don't you?'

Stan managed a weak smile. 'It takes one to know one.'

They followed the path alongside the creek, Stan leaning heavily on Jon's arm as he shuffled along the uneven surface, each small step an effort.

Jon read the track ahead looking for resting places, large rocks close enough to the path for Stan to sit on. By the time they reached the first Stan's face was grey and he was bathed in sweat. Jon handed him a handkerchief. 'Shall I fetch the trolley, Stan?'

'Stop fussing,' rasped Stan. 'I'll be right as rain in a minute or two.'

Jon hunkered down, listening to Stan's laboured breathing. He might make the mine but then there was the getting back to consider. Could Stan cope with the heat in his condition?

'Are we ready,' said Stan, holding out a hand to Jon.

'Ready,' said Jon. 'How about a piggy-back ride?' but Stan's look was answer enough. Jon extended his arm for the old man to lean on and helped him cross the bridge over the creek to the shady side of the valley.

It took another half an hour to cover the short distance to No Hope Mine and by the time they reached the flat apron of scrubby grass in front of it Stan was wheezing like a clapped-out engine. They sat together on a flat rock, not speaking, while Jon waited for him to recover.

'I see I've had visitors,' said Stan at last.

'What do you mean?'

Stan pointed across the grassy area to the opposite side of the valley, to the odd shaped rock with the curious overhang. 'See?'

'What am I looking for?'

'Fresh paint.'

It was over three years since Stan had first mentioned the drawings and the trouble Geoff Hardman had encountered with the Aborigines.

'They've been back touching up the drawings. Once a year they come with their yellow and red ochre to freshen up the pictures and add a few hand prints. I reckon there must be some powerful dreaming linked to that rock.'

'You never asked them?'

'Never see them to ask. Only once, but they melted away like shadows in the night. I don't touch their rock and they leave me be. I reckon there's room for both of us in the valley, so long as there's respect.' A fresh spasm of coughing racked his body. He pulled a small silver hip flask from his back pocket and sipped the rum, letting the liquor trickle down his throat; then he offered it to Jon.

'Not for me, thanks.'
'Don't blame you, but it's good for clearing the throat when it's clogged with dust down in the mine. Have you remembered what I told you?'
'About what?'
'My grave.'
'You're not going to die, leastways not yet, and this time next week you'll be out prospecting again.' He glanced at Stan and saw the waiting look. 'I haven't forgotten, Stan. Over there do you?' He pointed to the flattest piece of land that provided a good view of the head of the valley and of the entrance to the mine on one side and the Aboriginal site on the other.
'That'll do nicely, son.'
'And you want a headstone.'
'Yeah, that's right. I've left a sealed envelope with Cato in the bank. It's got your name on the front. There's enough cash in there to see it done right.'
'What words do you want on the stone?'
'Anything you think fitting will do.'
By the time they'd got back to the shack it was late afternoon and Stan was in a bad way. His face was grey and coughing brought up great gobs of phlegm streaked with blood. His breathing was even more laboured and with every breath he held his chest against the pain.
Jon gave Stan aspirin and helped him into bed; he made a cold compress for the old man's head and a hot one for his chest. Jon frowned, worried by the deterioration in Stan's condition, and prepared to leave for Charlestown.
'No doctor,' said Stan when he could speak. He dragged himself into a semi-seated position, his eyes fierce. 'I want no bloody quack, and no hospital – understand?'
'But—'
'No buts. I mean it, no doctor, and no hospital.' Stan flopped back on the bed, exhausted by his efforts. 'Now pull that trunk out from under my bed.'
The trunk made of ironbark and cross-banded in metal squealed as Jon dragged it out from under the old bedstead.
'In the bottom there's a blue leather box.' Stan lay back, his eyes closed, dragging air into his lungs, his face contorted in pain despite the aspirin.
'This where you keep your gold?' asked Jon, doing his best to sound cheerful.

A faint smile creased the old man's cheeks until another spasm of coughing turned it into a rictus grimace.

The trunk smelt musty and contained old documents, a copy of the title deed to the mineral lease, letters dating back to the First World War and after – some in a writing he thought he recognised. There were silk embroidered postcards from France similar to the ones his granddad had sent Gran before he went missing in action, and photographs, and diaries – dozens of them, all kept in a neat copperplate hand – but no gold. Then in a corner he found what Stan wanted, a small box covered in blue leather.

Jon wiped off the mouldy bloom with his sleeve and held it up for Stan to see. 'This what you wanted?'

'Aye, that's the one. I want you to have it.'

Inside the box was a three-stone ring.

'Diamonds,' said Stan as Jon looked at them. 'The best that money could buy – all three carats of them.'

'I can't take this,' said Jon.

'Why not?' The old fella's feverish eyes flashed.

'Because—'

'Because nothing. Give it to…to…your girl.'

'Merle?'

'The pretty blonde one.'

'Merle's not blonde, she has auburn hair and…' But Stan had dozed off before he'd finished the sentence.

The ring was worth a fortune from what Stan said, more than he could afford to pay for one, but who had Stan bought it for, and why was it still in the trunk?

He put the ring on the table, pushed the trunk back under the bed and sat back on his heels. Bonny crept up beside him and licked his hand. The dogs needed feeding. He saw to their needs and then to his own, made himself a mug of tea and settled in front of the stove, listening to Stan's rattling breath.

Hours later, while he was placing a cool cloth on Stan's brow, the old fella opened his eyes – the pupils were dilated with fever and his hands were dry and hot to the touch.

'Alice,' said Stan. 'The ring was for Alice.'

Shocked, Jon sat back on his haunches.

'Two years after Jack killed himself,' said Stan.

When they were old, Alice in her fifties and Stan in his sixties! Jon didn't know what to say. He couldn't imagine anyone that age being in love, wanting to marry and…and…

'Shut your mouth, son. Love's got no claim on youth.'

‘She said no?’ said Jon stupidly.

‘You don’t choose who you love,’ whispered Stan, ‘and guilt is a terrible thing.’

What was Stan talking about? It didn’t make sense.

‘Tell Alice I shouldn’t have taken no for an answer,’ muttered Stan.

‘All right, if that’s what you want,’ said Jon.

‘I do want,’ said Stan, his eyes suddenly fierce. ‘And don’t you forget.’ The effort drained him and his eyelids drooped, his body burning up with fever.

Jon sat at the side of the bed changing the cold compresses and cooling Stan’s body with tepid water. He wished Val was with him.

Capable hands Stan had said she had. Capable they were, but it was the company he needed, someone to sit with him during the long hours ahead – someone who knew when to be silent – someone to be there for him.

Stan was dying. He knew it and Stan knew it, but the knowledge didn’t make it any easier. Stan had once talked to him about dying when he spoke of the war in France, of the horrors he’d seen in the trenches and in no man’s land when they’d gone over the top. He’d spoken of the kindnesses to the mortally wounded when the dying was beyond bearing. It had been like that for Curly at the end – tears pricked his eyes – except he hadn’t had the courage to provide the ultimate kindness for Curly. But during those final hours of agony he’d discovered one truth: there were worse things than death. He brushed away the tears, glad that it would be easier for Stan.

He wiped Stan’s brow, his sunken eyes, pinched nose and mouth. It was hard to imagine Stan in his prime, when he’d been young with his life before him.

The old man’s hand grasped his own. ‘It’s been a good life.’

The whispered words jolted him, and a frisson rippled down his spine – had Stan read his mind?

‘I shouldn’t have taken no for an answer,’ muttered Stan. The lucid moment passed and he drifted again, the rasping breath more rhythmic as his exhausted body slipped into twilight sleep.

Alice! Stan was still thinking of Alice!

He tried to picture them as they had been when they were young with their futures ahead of them, living in the back of beyond as Stan called it. There’d been old photographs in the trunk, sepia ones from the turn of the century. He’d recognised Alice holding a baby in one of the photographs, and in another Stan with a bloke, Jack Macarthur probably, standing in front of the new hotel in Gwalia, the one that Stan said cost seven thousand pounds to build. He tried to imagine the contrast of living in a place like Gwalia with hundreds of other people packed together, all searching for the elusive gold reef, and then this place with its loneliness and isolation – at least for Alice and Jack there'd been others living on their homestead even if they were Aborigines. It wasn't surprising that Stan had taken to talking to his dogs.

They know what you are thinking half the time, Stan had once said – couldn't live out here on my own without dogs, they're life savers.

But it was Stan who had been his life saver. When Stan had caught him with O'Leary, Stan hadn't known he'd changed his mind about killing the priest that he was already on his way back to Charlestown with the injured man even though he hadn't quite worked out how he was going to manage the situation. But Stan had never held that against him. The old fella had taken him in, as Alice had done, and offered him friendship, had become like the grandfather he'd never had. Alice had done the same and then there'd been Elsie in Liverpool, all of them looking out for him in their separate ways.

Nine o'clock and the sun was streaming in through the shack's open door, a diffused light filtered through the dirty windows. He felt bone weary, his head ached, but he couldn't sleep. Stan was fading fast. He'd given up the fight for life. It was in his eyes.

Jon looked at the sunbeam through unfocussed eyes and saw dust motes, like ash, swirling and turning in the light – ashes to ashes, dust to dust, were the words used over coffins. He'd heard them often enough at Karundah as they'd buried Jeremy Hodges and Father William and Freddie Fitzpatrick. And that's what he believed, dust to dust, that and nothing more.

He hadn't always thought that way, but Curly's death and, more recently, when he was laid up in Paradise Canyon with the fever burning in him, things had become glass clear. Dust: that was his destiny, as it was Stan's, you only lived on through your children and in the minds of people who knew and loved you.

Jon smiled wryly; there was barely a day when he didn't think of Gerry lying not two hundred yards away at the bottom of Old Faithful. He turned towards the bed and looked down at Stan's shrunken body – had Gerry's burial place haunted him? Somehow he didn't think so. Stan had taken a colder slant on Gerry's death, had shared his sentiments that the bloke was dead, that it didn't matter where he was buried.

He wiped Stan's face again and moistened his lips. Stan would live on in his memory long after he'd forgotten about Gerry. It was Stan's kindness, his generosity, his dry sense of humour and his love of the land that he'd adopted as his own that he would always remember.

A vehicle grinding along the valley disturbed his thoughts, then a door slammed and he heard light footsteps, footsteps he'd recognise anywhere, coming closer – Val.

She crossed the threshold.

'How is he, Jon?'

'Failing,' he murmured. 'He won't see a doctor.'

She put a cast-iron pot on the stove. 'From Connie – do you want some now?'

'No.'

'What about Stan?' She crossed over to the bed and sat where he'd been sitting all night. Jon stood next to her looking down at the old man's frail body. Stan's breathing was less ragged. Was he going to surprise them both, get better, laugh at them for their morbid belief that he was drawing his last? Even as he looked at Stan's tired face he opened his eyes. This time they were lucid, no longer clouded with pain.

'What time is it?'

They had to strain to catch his words.

'About ten o'clock in the mornin', Stan,' said Val.

'Where are me dogs?'

'Down here at the side of the bed,' she said.

Jon bent down, picked up Bonny and placed her on the bed next to Stan. The dog crouched down close to the old man, licked his hand and then pressed her nose against his chest. Val moved to let him pick up Bess and he put her on the other side of the bed.

'Nice old girls,' muttered Stan as he stroked their noses. 'You'll take care of them, won't you, Jon?'

'Of course I will, Stan.'

'You won't take them out and shoot them?'

'No,' said Jon. 'I'd never do that.'

The old man drifted then, his eyes closed, his hands resting on his dogs.

'Thank you, Merle,' said Stan, his breathing easier.

'I'm Val,' she said gently, resting her hand on the top of his.

He opened his eyes and gave her a long, penetrating look. 'Yes, I know who you are. You're Jon's Merle.' He closed his eyes again.

'It's the fever,' she murmured.

'He's not going to make it, is he?' said Jon, tears pricking his eyes.

She shook her head.

They listened to the soft *luft luft* of Stan's breathing. The wooden shack, expanding in the early summer heat, seemed to breathe with them, listening as they listened to the old man's soft wheezing, to his rippling, tired breath.

Let it be a gentle death, Jon prayed, thinking of Curly's tortured end.

The minutes stretched to an hour and more and Stan's panting was easier, softer and shallower, the spaces between each intake longer.

Later, Val leaned across and felt for Stan's pulse. She looked at Jon, saw the question in his eyes, and nodded her head briefly.

They carried kitchen chairs out into the sunlight, and mugs of tea. Bess and Bonny followed and flopped down at their feet.

'Are you all right, hon?' asked Val after a while.

'Yes.'

'I liked Stan,' she said, 'not that I knew him like you did.'

'See that kookaburra?' said Jon, pointing across to an old gum tree, straggly and tattered amongst the mulga.

'You mean the bird?'

'Father William told me that they don't belong in Western Australia. They're from the east, New South Wales, Victoria, that side of the country. Someone brought them over in the eighteen-nineties.'

'Who's Father William?'

'Was…he was a priest at the orphanage. He hung himself.'

'Are you sure you're all right?' asked Val after a long silence.

'Of course I am,' said Jon, looking at the old bird watching them. 'One of them stole Stan's sandwich once. He said the bird eyed it up from its branch, closed its wings in tight to its body, flattened its feathers, launched itself like a dart and took the sandwich clean out of his hand. Imagine that! And now a few of them are settled this far in land, as if they've always lived here.'

'They're a bit like you then, aren't they?'

'What do you mean?'

'Well, you're an import too, just like them.'

Jon frowned. 'And they've a peculiar call, they sort of laugh like a donkey.'

'Do they!'

'Yeah, Stan calls…called them laughing jackasses.'

They drank their tea sitting in the heat of the day, letting the chill of the long night seep from their bones, watched over by the alien bird.

Val glanced at Jon then looked up again at the kookaburra, at its cream body, the speckled-brown back and blue flashes on the wings, at its large beak, and the head cocked to one side as it kept an eye out for the main chance. 'Do you want a tot of rum or something? It might do you good.'

'No, thanks,' said Jon. 'I'm fine.'

They sat, not speaking, watching the fleeting patterns on the valley floor cast by wispy clouds intermittently blocking the sun.

'What do we do now?' asked Val.

'Bury him.'

'Can we do that?'

'Of course!'

'I didn't mean that, I meant where?'

'Here,' said Jon. 'He's chosen the place.'

'Don't we have to tell the authorities?'

'The constable, I suppose.'

The kookaburra preened itself and was joined by a mate trailing a snake.

'They eat snakes then?'

'Yes,' said Jon, a crack in his voice. 'I'll…I'll go and dig the grave.' He looked up at the sky. Cerulean, his gran would have called it. She knew lots of fancy words for colours. Vermilion was her favourite. She liked to wrap the word round her tongue. 'Ver..mil..ion, ce..ru..le..an' he said aloud, copying his gran. He hadn't thought about Gran and her love of colours for years, not until Alice showed him her oil paintings.

'You what?' said Val.

'Nothing,' said Jon. 'It's something Gran used to say.'

'What's vermilion anyway, some sort of bird?'

'A colour…' said Jon, '…red.'

'Is cerulean red too?'

'No, it's blue.'

'Outback colours,' she said.

Jon looked at her, and then looked away, perplexed. 'You drive back to Charlestown and let the constable know, and I'll make a coffin and dig the grave.'

He glanced up at the sun, feeling the bite on his skin. By mid-afternoon the heat would be stifling in the valley. 'I'll need to bury him tomorrow at the latest,' he said.

After Val left, Jon made a coffin from the wood he found in one of Stan's sheds. It wasn't much of a coffin by anyone's standards, just a rectangular box, but it was the best he could do. Then he returned to the shack and Stan's body.

Gran had spoken about laying out bodies – she'd done it often enough. While water heated on the stove he gathered together soap, a flannel, and a towel. He talked to Stan as he washed him while Bonny and Bess lay at his feet watching, and then he dressed Stan in clean clothes and laid his body back on the bed.

All night he kept vigil, sipping the last of Stan's rum and talking to him about life in Liverpool, about Merle and his plans for the future, about the outback and Alice, and the others he'd met. Some of the time he sat stroking Bess's and Bonny's ears; at others he recalled the things that Stan had told him over the months they'd known each other. When he stopped thinking he dozed until dawn and then breakfasted on cold stew, wrapped up the last of the bread, and stood at the side of Stan's bed looking down at his body for a moment or two, at Stan's face, placid in death, at the bushy eyebrows and wispy hair.

'I need to dig you a grave, Stan, before the sun hits its peak, be seeing you, mate.' Then he set off for No Hope Mine with a pick and a shovel and the dogs trailing behind him.

Digging a grave for Stan was harder than sinking a well. Four foot down he reached solid rock. 'Some place for an burial,' he muttered as he hacked at the rock, but even as he worked and swore at Stan's decision he knew that of all the places in the valley that Stan could have chosen, this was the prettiest – at the head of the valley – the worst of the ugly mining activity obscured by a dog leg in the rock strata.

At five foot deep he stopped for a breather and ate the last of the bread, and then he took a long draught of water, wiped his mouth with the back of his hand and screwed the top back on the bottle. He glanced up at Stan's mine. The entrance, part way up the valley side, had a sloping apron of spoil. From below it looked like a yellow mouth waiting to swallow up the next prospector looking for gold, just as it had Stan.

He smiled at Stan's sense of humour, at his choice of plot. How many years had Stan grafted in old No Hope searching for the seam that would make him rich? And how many hours in the rest of the valley, systematically working through each old mine working in turn, hoping to find what others had missed? He couldn't imagine anything worse, the dust and the claustrophobia, the knowledge that the tons of earth and rock above were liable to collapse.

It had been bad enough the first time Stan had taken him into No Hope. He recalled his fear, the terror of the close, confined space, his relief at being back in the open air again. But Stan had spent thirty years down the mines. Was it a kind of madness? He decided it was and he knew that mining wasn't for him. He wanted his life above ground in the heat and flies. He'd sooner swallow insects and breathe in dust kicked up by sheep than that kicked up by a pickaxe deep underground.

He resumed digging. Stan had been one of a dying breed, the lone prospector hoping to make it big, hoping to find the mother of all lodes, but times had moved on. Big business had taken over gold mining, companies with vast resources at their disposal. Now they carved huge swathes out of the earth – chewing the guts out of the land was how Curly put it. He tried to imagine Stan's valley as a vast hole in the ground, unrecognisable after the mechanical diggers and machines had had a go: no more distinguishing marks, no No Hope, or Old Faithful where Gerry was buried. No wheel houses, nothing to show for the work of decades by men who refused to believe there was no gold.

Thinking grew harder as the hole grew deeper and the sun hotter. Soon all that kept him going was single-minded, dogged determination to see things through, to ensure that Stan was buried where he wanted to be, in a place that meant something to him.

At mid-afternoon, as Jon was lifting Stan's coffin onto a trolley, a utility truck drew up and Wes Chapmen stepped out followed by Val and Connie.

'They wanted to come,' said Val.

'Where are you going to bury him?' asked Connie.

'Down by his favourite mine.'

'Old No Hope?' said Connie.

Wes laughed. 'Trust Stan! He always did have a rare sense of humour.'

The burial party made their way along the valley, following the path beside the creek that Stan had worn over the years, Jon pulling the trolley, the other three steadying the coffin, and Bess and Bonny following behind. At the graveside Wes helped place Stan's coffin into the ground and then the four of them, and the dogs, stood around the grave looking down at the crude box.

'What are the words?' asked Wes.

'Damned if I know,' said Connie. 'This is where we could do with a priest.'

'Was Stan religious?' asked Val.

'No. He'll be turning in his grave at the very mention of a priest,' said Connie. 'He always said religion was wasted on the likes of him, that if there was an afterlife it'd come as a pleasant surprise.'

'Do you want me to say a few words?' asked Wes.

'If you wouldn't mind,' said Connie.

The three of them listened as Wes spoke about Stan's cavalier attitude to truck maintenance, and his ability to drink rum in quantities that would have killed a lesser mortal. He spoke of Stan's dry sense of humour, his generosity and his love of prospecting, of the outback, and of his dogs. When he had finished there was nothing else to say.

'Ashes to ashes,' murmured Jon as he dropped a handful of earth onto the coffin.

'And dust to dust,' added Connie.

Around them the bush was quiet, the native birds silent in the late afternoon heat. The other side of the grave from Jon, where Val stood, the sun was sinking in the sky, a red orb, vermilion, he realised, in a cerulean sky, outback colours Val had called them. It was a fitting display for a man who regarded the outback as his home.

Val and Connie stepped back while Jon and Wes filled in the grave and set up a cairn of stones, a temporary marker until Stan's headstone could be carved. Then together and alone they made their way back along the valley.

Later, after the others had left, Jon called Bess and Bonny to him and they walked back to the grave. He felt the need to be there alone, with only the dogs for company, to say a private goodbye to Stan. He sat on a flat rock overlooking the site, soaking in the feel of the place, the evening noises, birds settling for the night, and scuttling reptiles already hidden from view. What would happen to the valley now? Would another prospector move in or would the bush encroach still further, the rotting, collapsing winding gear and engine housing returning to the dust, the earth reclaiming its own?

At his feet Bess stirred, she sniffed the air looking in the direction of the rock face over to his right. For a split second Jon thought he saw movement and then decided he'd imagined it, that the white marks he could see in the gathering dusk were not eyes but spots of white paint reflecting the last of the light. The dog settled. Jon relaxed. So what if he was being watched – the Aboriginal guardians would be watching over Stan's grave too, just as they must have watched over Stan's comings and goings for three decades. He stood up and saluted the invisible watchers, called the dogs to his side and followed the track back along the valley, on the old trail, as Stan had done for the last thirty years of his life.

The next day Jon spent his time tidying up, burning soiled blankets and linen and building a carrying crate for Stan's chooks. When he'd finished he collected up Alice's books and carried Stan's trunk across to his utility. As far as he could see the trunk contained the only things he needed to keep safe until he knew who Stan's letters and diaries should go to. Stan would want him to do that. And then there was the ring – his to keep Stan had said. He tried to imagine Merle's surprise and delight at such an expensive engagement ring, but the image wouldn't come, the fleeting picture he formed in his mind faded even as he thought of her. He wondered why it was so difficult to hold a mental image of her when they were apart and wished he'd got a photograph. He whistled Stan's dogs and lifted them into the utility truck, and then took one last look around Stan's shack and closed the door.

'So Stan's dead,' said Alice in a quiet voice, her face expressionless as she took in the news.

Jon sensed the sadness in her words.

'Did he say anything else?'

'He said to tell you that he shouldn't have taken no for an answer.'

She sat on her chair, smoking, looking out into the bush for a long time. Jon sat next to her, waiting for her to come to terms with his news.

'Anything else?' she asked presently.

'He said that you don't choose who you love.' She wanted to ask more, he could tell by the way she sat with her hands clasped tightly together, rolling one thumb around the other, a sure sign she was thinking. Finally, Alice unclasped her hands and the tension drained from her and he was glad he hadn't told her the rest. He didn't know the whole truth of her relationship with Stan, but he knew enough to know that his knowing would cause her real distress. Sometimes it was wiser to say nothing. She was an old woman and, like Stan, she deserved consideration.

'If I were you I'd get some sleep. You look done in.'

'Thanks, I will,' he said, aware that neither of them could face a game of chess that night. He finished his drink, called to Stan's dogs and made his way across to his own small place by the bunkhouse.

'What are those dogs doing in here,' snapped Greg, poking Bonny with his foot. Jon looked up at the sharpness in his tone.

'They're Stan's dogs,' said Alice, 'and I don't mind them under the breakfast table.'

'Stan, the old bloke who died?'

'Yes,' said Jon, catching the irritated look on Alice's face. Was Alice beginning to see through Greg? He hoped so; she didn't need his type in her life even if he was her own flesh and blood. He'd met blokes like Greg before – his dad for one. He'd seen the way his mam had hidden the housekeeping money so he couldn't hand it over to the bookie's runner down the pub. Money runs through his hands like water he'd heard her say to Gran on one occasion. He hadn't understood what she meant at the time, but he did now. His dad had always been a drinker and a gambler, a self-centred loser, a bloke who always wanted more. Maybe he should have pitied Rose Butler instead of hating her when his dad ran off with her leaving them fatherless just when Mam needed him most. He smiled grimly. Alice would be lucky if Greg cleared off and went home to England.

'We're moving the sheep up to the top end today,' said Greg.

'Sorry,' said Jon, 'I have to go to Charlestown and sort out Stan's affairs.'

'Can't it wait?'

'I suppose it—'

'But it won't,' snapped Alice.

Greg shrugged.

'He wants a headstone, Alice,' said Jon, 'any idea where I can get one made?'

'In Pilkington. Mike Tunstall, he's your man. If you ask in the Commercial Hotel they'll direct you to his place. What does he want on the headstone – did he say?'

Greg finished his breakfast and scraped back his chair. 'I'll be seeing you, Alice.' He picked up his hat. 'Some of us have work to do,' he said pointedly.

'Don't let the fly door slam.' Alice cocked her head, listening, and smiled when the door snicked to. 'He's learning,' she said. 'Now, what are you going to have inscribed on the stone?'

'I don't know. I was going to put his name and dates – "Stanley Gerald William Colley 1871 to 1949", but I want something more. What do you think?'

'How about "who never found El Dorado"?'

He was surprised by the bitterness in her voice. 'You know what, Alice. I've been thinking these last few days and I'm not so sure about that. Maybe he did, after a fashion.'

'You mean he found a reef?'

'No, but he did find a sort of gold, didn't he?'

'What do you mean?'

'Well, it strikes me that Stan liked living where he did. He panned and mined enough to get by, and he had his dogs and his rum; it seems to me he was pretty contented at the end.'

'He wasn't like that when he was younger; he was always chasing the dream.'

'We have to have dreams, Alice, especially when we are young. You and Jack had a dream and you built this place on the back of it. You achieved yours, didn't you? I think life would be pretty bleak without them – just so long as you don't let them become an obsession,' he added, remembering Stan's words on the way to Leonora.

'What makes you so philosophical all of a sudden?'

Jon grinned at the surprise on her face. 'Life – isn't that the stock answer?' He leaned back in his seat waiting for a tart reply but Alice was silent for once. 'Out there, in the outback, when I had Yildilla's spear through my leg, I wished I'd stayed in Liverpool, and then later, on the journey back, I got to thinking and I realised it was about time I appreciated what I had got, that I shouldn't let setbacks kill my dream. I thought about my mates in England and what they'd been through in the Blitz and what they had to look forward to, and then I thought about all those with no prospects, lads not much older than me who were killed in the war, and I knew for sure that my life is here. Australia is where I belong. Have you ever been to Liverpool, Alice?'

'No.'

'Well, it's a great city, a rich city, or it was, now a lot has happened to it with the bombing and everything...but what I really learnt, out there in Paradise Canyon and on the journey back with Bindi, was that I've changed. Before, I'd always thought of myself as a city lad. But I'm not, am I?'

'No.' she said. 'And you're not a lad anymore. You've left those days behind you in that canyon of yours.'

'It's not my canyon, Alice, and if anyone has a claim on it then it's not white folk.'

'You sound like Stan,' said Alice, 'that's the sort of thing he'd have said. But maybe you are right. Maybe you should put that on the stone.'

'What?'

'That he loved the place.'

'Yes, that's what I was trying to say earlier. Stan made the most of what he did have, and he didn't let the hankering after a dream poison his soul because the living he was doing was enough.'

'But he never gave up the dream, did he?' said Alice.

'No.'

'And what's your dream?'

Jon grinned. 'A place like this, Alice. One day I'll have my own station: a place like Jarrahlong.'

'Are you prepared for the work, and the heartbreak?'

'Yeah, I reckon I've seen the worst of it.'

Alice pushed her breakfast plate away and sat back in her chair. 'Perhaps you're right. Any more tea in the pot?'

Jon refilled her cup and his own and they sat in companionable silence, each lost in their own thoughts, finishing their tea.

'About this gravestone...who's going to pay for it?' asked Alice.

'Stan,' he said, 'he's left an envelope with Cato and enough cash to cover the cost and a bit spare to buy a round of drinks for everyone.'

'And what about his belongings?'

'There isn't much. Did Stan have any family?'

'He does have distant relatives back in England, but no brothers or sisters, I do know that.'

'Well, there are his war medals and a few letters and diaries.'

'Letters?'

'Yes and a few photographs. Do you want to have a look through them?'

'No, burn the lot, best thing to do with stuff like that,' said Alice. 'It's not going to be of interest to anyone else.'

'Is there anything you want me to get while I'm in town?'

'I can't think of anything...but while you are there you might as well call in at Simpson's and pick up the pair of shoes I've ordered. Val knows which they are.'

Cato greeted him with a polite nod and ushered him over to the desk in the corner. 'Take a seat. I take it you're here about Mr Stanley Colley's business, Mr Macarthur.'

'Jon, call me Jon,' he said, still uneasy about using Alice's surname. Cato was the only person who insisted on calling him Macarthur, and one of these days Greg or Val would overhear him and then there'd be ructions right enough and he'd have to explain to everyone why he'd assumed a name and why Alice let him use it. He should talk to Alice and sort it out.

Cato disappeared into the back room and returned with a metal box. He blew a thin layer of dust off the top then opened it with a key he'd selected from a bunch he carried on a long chain.

'Mr Colley said it was to be opened in your presence,' he commented. He lifted out three envelopes. 'There is one addressed to you, one to me and...' Cato frowned and placed the third envelope on the desk, '...and one for posting.'

Jon opened his and took out a wad of fivers and a letter. 'For the headstone,' he explained. 'Stan asked me to get one made for him.'

'Mr Tunstall, over in Pilkington, is a mason.'

'Yes, Alice mentioned him.' Jon opened the accompanying letter.

Dear Jon,

Enclosed is the money you will need for my headstone. Choose something that will last a long time and tell the mason to cut the letters deep. Buy a round of drinks for everyone and any money left over is yours to do with as you please.

Thank you for looking after my dogs. Bess is old, going on eleven but Bonny has a few good years left in her.

Please yourself what you do with the contents of the trunk. I'd like you to take a moment to look through everything before you throw it on the fire. Alice might like the photographs of her and David when he was a baby, and the ones of Jack. She'll tell you which they are if you're not sure.

I've no family to speak of – only distant relatives who probably don't even know I exist, so whatever is left is yours. Not much, I know, a few bits of chipped china, a couple of utility lamps, a stick or two of furniture and a valley full of worked-out mines.

It has been nice knowing you, son. And for what it's worth you are the type of Pommy bastard this place needs.

Your friend,

Stan.

Jon finished reading the letter and sat quietly while Cato finished reading his.

'This is Mr Colley's last will and testament, Mr Macarthur—'

'Jon,' said Jon.

'Jon,' repeated Cato, 'and, according to this, you are his sole beneficiary.'

'What does that mean?' asked Jon suspiciously.

'It means he has left everything to you, including the mineral lease at Yaringa Creek.' Cato opened out a map. 'That is this area marked in red,' he said helpfully.

'You mean the whole valley?'

'Looks like it.'

'What the hell am I going to do with a valley full of worked out, useless mines?'

'You could sell the lease.'

'I suppose the lease will lapse anyway if I don't work it.'

'Well, there is that,' agreed Cato. 'Anyway, according to this you've inherited all Mr Colley's worldly possessions and he's made provision for the transfer of the mineral lease to you. I've received instructions and payment from him to deal with the legal side for you.'

'Is that it?'

'Yes, for now. I may need to see you again for a signature after all the legal ends have been tied up. Now, would you like to open an account of your own?' He indicated the money on the table between them.

'No thanks, not at the moment. Most of this will go on a headstone and a round of drinks in The Grand.'

'Of course,' Cato stood and extended a hand, 'always nice to do business with you…Jon.'

'You look like you've lost half a crown and found sixpence,' said Connie as he sat at the bar with Les, sipping beer.

'Stan's left me his mines.'

Connie laughed. 'What, Old Faithful and that No-Hoper of his?'

'And the rest of them.'

'Are you going to chase after the gold too?' she asked.

'No, I've got more sense.'

'Well, Stan made a living from it. He wasn't rolling in gold but he had enough for his needs,' she said.

'According to some he had a pile of it stashed away. Gerry always said he was worth a bob or two,' said Les.

'Take it from me,' said Jon, 'there's no gold stashed anywhere...only a trunk full of old photographs, letters and personal papers, nothing worth anything to anyone.'

'Who's looking after his dogs?' asked Connie.

'Me, along with his chooks and his lease,' said Jon. Connie opened another bottle of beer each and passed them across. 'I suppose we should welcome you to our town, seeing as how you are a lease holder and we're stuck with you.'

Jon grinned. 'Nice to know I'm welcome.'

'As welcome as if you'd never come at all,' said Les.

'Thanks both.' He tilted his bottle towards Connie and then to Les and took a swig of the cool, amber liquid.

Jon drove back to Jarrahlong, spoke to Alice and told her of his plans to stay at Stan's place for a while until he had decided what to do about the lease. He collected his belongings, Stan's dogs and the trunk, loaded up the chooks in the carrying crate again, and set off back to Yaringa Creek.

The dogs were pleased to be home, they milled about his feet as he unloaded the provisions he'd bought in town: cooking oil, flour, tinned food, kerosene, and all the other things he'd need until he'd decided what to do with his inheritance.

Over the next couple of days he swept the shack, and sorted out Stan's belongings, keeping the useful stuff and throwing out the rest. Then he looked through the rest of the ramshackle sheds along from the shack. The closest was the woodshed, and then the hen house where Stan's chooks were kept. He refilled their water bucket, fed them some grain and collected the eggs. After the hen house was the shed with all the spare parts for the Bedford van as well as spares for the various winding frames. In the last were mining tools, spades, pickaxes, pit props and pans for washing gold. Behind the sheds was Stan's abandoned vegetable patch, a spade rusting in the earth where he'd left it a decade ago, at its base a pile of hen droppings, testimony to its most recent use. He smiled, he hadn't taken Stan for a gardener, and by the look of it he was right.

That night, after a meal of bully beef, damper and tea, he dragged out the ironbark trunk from under the bed. No time like the present for going through the boring stuff.

He placed what he found in piles on the kitchen table, letters in one, assorted bills and invoices on another, photographs on another and the diaries laid out in year order. In the bottom he found a new envelope with his name on the front – so that was why Stan wanted him to sort through the trunk!

Dear Jon,

I've one last favour to ask. I want you to chisel S. Colley 1871-1949 in old No Hope, under the lightning-strike mark. I know it sounds daft but I want my name in that mine for posterity. The bloody place used up thirty years of my life and I'm damned if I'm leaving without recording the fact. I always meant to do it myself but never got around to it. You'll find the tools in the shed.

Cheers, Stan.

Jon shuddered. It was a long way down the mine to the lightning-strike mark. He still vividly remembered the time Stan took him down there, the time he realised he didn't have it in him to be a prospector, the time Stan told him the mine had tantalised men for nigh on fifty years with just enough gold to keep them interested, but not enough to justify the time and effort needed to extract it.

He remembered the oppressiveness, the weight of the rock pressing down even though the roof of the gallery was a clear inch above his head, and the claustrophobia. He shuddered violently. Stan's request could wait, it was a lot to ask and he wasn't even sure that he could do it.

Constable Nickson, Les and a bloke Jon didn't recognise turned up at Stan's place a week later. Jon had heard the truck churning along the valley, picking a way around the rocks and the scrub, before he caught a glimpse of Constable Nickson's snub-nosed vehicle. He stepped out onto the verandah and waited for them.

'G'day,' said Nickson. He extended a hand, smooth for a bloke. 'This is Josef Kowalski from out Pilkington way; he was a mate of Gerry's.'

'Was?'

'That's right; it seems your friend, Stan Colley, shot him.'

A cold hand seemed to brush Jon's spine. Somehow he stopped

the shiver, the giveaway, even so the chill rippled down his arms and back and he felt the hairs start on his scalp and then lie down flat again. The airless valley suddenly seemed icy despite the mid-day heat.

'Stan wouldn't do a thing like that,' said Jon.

'That's what I said,' commented Les. 'You'd better show him the letter, Constable.'

Letter? What was Stan playing at? Had he decided to tell the truth when he knew he was dying? Had conscience got the better of him? But why hadn't Stan warned him?

Jon crushed the instinct to flee. Running away from his part in concealing Gerry's murder wasn't the answer, not any more. If his involvement in things meant jail, then so be it. He wished now he'd kept Stan out of it, but he hadn't realised just how sick Stan was at the time.

Nickson unbuttoned his top pocket, pulled out an envelope and handed it to him.

Jon looked at the familiar handwriting conscious of Nickson's impassive face with not even a flicker of emotion, just a steady eye watching his every move, his every expression. He felt sweat prickle in his armpits.

'It's Stan's handwriting,' Jon said as he unfolded the single page.

Constable Nickson,

By the time you get this I will be dead and buried, but there is something you need to know. I shot Gerry Worrall and dropped his body down Old Faithful mineshaft.

I caught Gerry snooping around my place looking for gold. I warned him off, but be came back one night, drunk and ugly. There was no reasoning with the man. It was him or me. So I shot him.

After I got rid of his body I threw the shotgun in Gerry's truck and then drove it over the edge at the top end of Galson Gorge to make it look like a hunting accident.

Stanley Gerald William Colley.

Jon replaced the letter in the envelope and handed it back to Nickson, his mind spinning.

'Do you know anything about this?' asked Kowalski, aggressively.

'Don't reckon he does,' commented Les, 'not by the look on his face.'

'Well?' asked Nickson.

'No,' said Jon.

'Stan didn't say anything to you, not even after my last visit?'

'He did say you'd been over asking after Gerry, that you'd taken a look around the place. And I told him you'd spoken to me about the fight Gerry and I had three years back, but that was all.'

'It's a bad business,' said Les. 'I know Gerry could be unpredictable when he'd had a skin full, but I still don't believe he'd have touched an old fella like Stan.'

'Where is this mine?' asked Nickson.

Jon led the way up the valley until they stood in front of the remains of the wheel housing collapsed in a tangle of wood and iron.

'Don't suppose there is much hope of getting him out of there,' said Les.

Nickson scratched his head. 'Is there any other way into the mine?'

'I dunno, if there is Stan didn't say,' said Jon.

'You'd only be risking other lives,' said Les. He picked up a large stone and hefted it into the shaft to smash through the tangled wood and metal. The four of them stood listening to its slow descent, the splintering, grinding sounds as it fell through the debris in the shaft, followed by a deep rumble and then, moments later, came a plume of muck and dust rising like smoke. Nickson batted it away with his hat.

'Is there any chance Stan was lying?' asked Kowalski.

'Why would Stan lie about a thing like that?' said Les.

'To protect someone.'

'Like who?'

'I don't know.'

They all stood in silence, looking at the mess before them, listening to the final settlings deep underground.

'What about a marker?' said Kowalski.

'A marker?' queried Les.

'Yes, to say that Gerry is buried here. A man should have a marker.'

Nickson turned to Jon.

'If Mr Kowalski wants to put up a marker for Gerry then I don't mind,' said Jon.

'Don't know how you'll do it,' commented Les. 'You won't catch me tidying up the top of that shaft. What are you going to do, cap it and put a grave stone on top, or what?'

'Yes,' said Kowalski.

'Well,' said Les. 'I still owe Gerry a week's wage. I suppose that can go towards it.'

'Thank you. I'll get Mike Tunstall to carve one for him.'

'Yeah,' said Les drily, 'while he's making Stan's.'

'You old bugger,' muttered Jon. He was sitting on the rock overlooking Stan's grave. He smiled. Stan had laid Gerry's ghost to rest, there'd be no more talk once word got out.

But what did he do about Stan's legacy? He looked along the valley to the bend in the creek. Stan always said this was the pretty bit and he was right. Apart from the spoil spilling down from No Hope entrance the place was unmarked, whereas further along was a decaying industrial landscape – a depressing mess where no thought had been given to planning or order. It was a hotchpotch of aborted diggings, heaps of yellow spoil, old shafts and wheel housings – the rusting, rotting remains of gold-fever days.

His thoughts shifted to Jarrahlong. Had there been no Greg on the scene the answer would have been easy. He wouldn't be sitting pondering his future, but now things were different. Greg was here to stay. Greg had seen the rebuilding Alice had done after the bush fire, he had ridden over the land, seen the opportunities and weighed up the income from the four thousand sheep that Alice currently had, and he would have assessed the money that had been made in the war years when wool was selling at a premium.

Unlike Greg, it had taken him a long time to realise Alice was comfortably off, that the run-down station was more valuable than he'd thought, whereas Greg with his farming background and his knowledge of wool prices had soon appreciated that keeping Alice sweet would pay dividends long term.

Greg was no fool – at Jarrahlong he wasn't in his brother's shadow and he was free of his mother's suffocating influence and, more importantly, it was clear he expected to inherit one day. But for him the situation was more complicated. He still needed to keep his options open. There'd been no pressure from Alice for a decision, although Greg had made his feelings clear. Greg didn't like him about the place and he resented his friendship with Alice, the Friday night chess, and the easy banter. Then there was Alice's offer, outstation – that had been the word she'd used. There's nothing stopping you prospecting and working for me, she'd said. Stan's place is close enough to Corkwood Bore and the sheep graze mainly over on that side of the station, you can save yourself hours of riding. Build yourself a paddock for a couple of horses and work out from there. Ride out every other day or so and check the bores and wells in the north-west quarter, otherwise you'll only be needed for the big jobs, shearing, and the like, that way the mineral lease won't lapse and you'll have a wage to live on until you decide what you want to do. Her only stipulation had been the weekly game of chess on a Friday night.

Think about it, she'd said, things are quiet here at the moment; I'm in no hurry for an answer.

What about Greg? he'd asked.

You leave Greg to me, she'd said, besides he still has a lot to learn about running a sheep station, and about the outback.

He'd looked at the place with fresh eyes when he'd got back to the valley. Stan's shack wasn't anything to shout about, only a single room, but it was dry and it was a roof over his head. It was also bigger than the lean-to he'd been living in, and if he cleared away some of the old sheds there'd be space for a small corral. Alice's offer wasn't such a bad one after all!

CHAPTER 49

Two months after Stan's death Jon was sitting in Alice's parlour sipping a nightcap after the Friday night chess game.

'How are you liking living on your own?' she asked.

'Lonely, but I've got Smoky and Stan's dogs and the horses to look after.'

'Done any prospecting?'

'A bit of panning.'

'Find any gold?'

Jon grinned. 'No.'

'I'm not surprised. I kept telling Stan he was wasting his time, but you can't talk to some folk.' She finished her whiskey and stubbed out the remains of the cheroot. 'Are you planning on staying there, or would you rather move back here?'

He looked up from his glass and saw Alice was serious.

'You know you can move back, don't you?'

'What about Greg?'

'What about him? As I said the other day, he's a lot to learn. He's not ready to take over as manager yet.'

Jon knew better than to argue, but Alice wasn't getting any younger and although she hadn't said so in as many words he'd gathered she'd been thinking about retirement. He caught her watching him. 'Wouldn't you like to take it a bit easier, Alice?'

'One day, when the time is right, but Greg's not ready for the responsibility, and he'll need more time before he understands the vagaries of the climate and the hard reality of running a station on marginal land. You don't see animals dying of drought in England,' she said, 'drowning in floods maybe, but not the slow starvation that we see here from time to time.'

'Where is he tonight?'

'Charlestown. He took off this afternoon; he said he was meeting Cato and the others for a game of two-up.' She put her tumbler back on the table. 'Give me a hand up will you, Jon?'

Her use of his name both pleased and surprised him.

'What's the film tomorrow?' she asked.

'I don't know.'

'You know, that girl never ceases to amaze me,' she said as Jon helped her to her feet.

Jon didn't need to ask who she was referring to, and he was inclined to agree. Wes, Connie and Val had got together following the Cathay Cup weekend and revived the monthly film show in the town hall. Mary Samuels had been asked to repair the blackout curtains and Wes overhauled the projector and fixed the curtain poles. Val had persuaded Scally to sell tickets on the mail run and she'd organised refreshments in the intervals, whilst Connie ordered in the films.

'You know what Val did last month? – Drove over to Pilkington and put up posters advertising this month's film. Connie says they may need to have two showings if the numbers get any bigger,' rattled on Alice.

Jon smiled. It was good to see Alice looking so well and enthusiastic about a trip into Charlestown to see a film. She was better dressed too since Val had ordered some new dresses for her and cut and permed her hair in the latest style.

'You still think she'll go back to England?' Alice cast a sidelong glance in his direction.

'Give it a few more months. She'll tire of the place. Val's the sort who likes the bright lights, dancing and parties. One film show a month isn't exactly the high life, is it?'

'It is for round here,' said Alice drily. 'Did you go to the last showing?'

'You know I didn't,' said Jon.

'Well, I think you're wrong about Val. Did she ever tell you that she rode out to Denman Creek and camped there every Saturday night for three weeks?'

Jon glanced at Alice to see if she was joking, but she wasn't, she was looking directly at him, a serene smile on her face. 'What did she do that for?'

'You tell me, I'd already got a stockman in the area keeping an eye out for you, but she insisted, said it was in case you and Bindi were in trouble and needed help getting home.'

'We didn't need help.'

'That's what I told her, but she wouldn't listen.'

He'd forgotten about his surprise at seeing Val and Jim Sandy waiting for them at Denman Creek. At the time he hadn't given it a thought, his only feeling had been irritation, and with hindsight he'd been less than grateful. No wonder she'd been so short with him.

'The fact remains that Val has fitted in like a native,' said Alice. 'She's settled into the life here, and she's thriving on it and I'll bet you five pounds she stays.'

He pictured Val at the Cathay Cup meeting, laughing and joking with Berry. He recalled the way Larry Simpson doted on her, and how easily she got on with everyone in Charlestown, particularly Wes and Connie, and the way she'd driven over to Stan's place when he was dying, and then there was the unobtrusive support she had offered after Stan's death.

'Well?'

'I'm not a betting man,' he said.

Charlestown was busy. Utility trucks were parked all along the length of the street and in The Grand the bar was crowded. Jon and Alice went over to the town hall where Val and Rachel were putting out chairs and Wes was setting up the projector.

'Nice to see you, Alice,' called Val. 'I've got a job for you.' She handed over a sheet of paper. 'This is the membership, they've all paid up front and everyone else pays on the door. You know most of them, don't you?'

Alice looked at the list. 'Most of them.'

'And here's the price list – children and adults.'

'What about retired folk like me?' asked Alice.

'We have to cover our costs.' Val grinned. 'And you're not retired yet, and if you're that hard up, Alice, I'll shout your ticket.'

Alice laughed. 'What about the float?'

'Connie has that organised. Jon, run over to The Grand and collect it, and ask Berry to hurry up with the water heater. It should be on by now.' Val disappeared into the back room to help with the refreshments.

Berry! Since when had she taken up with him? He wouldn't have thought he was her type. He caught Alice looking at him.

'Val's a good-looking girl. She can have her pick.'

Alice's comment rankled. Did that mean Berry was going to be a fixture in the town from now on? He pushed open the double doors into The Grand, still irritated by the thought.

'She's roped you in too,' said Connie when he asked about the float and about Berry. 'He's in the kitchen with Han Sing making cakes.'

'What?'

'Only joking, Han Sing's a dab hand at making Victoria sponges; he won't let anyone else have a look in.'

When he got back to the hall most of the seats were taken and there was a queue forming outside the door.

'Second showing at five o'clock,' announced Wes as Jon slid onto a back bench. The place was packed, men mainly from stations up to two hundred miles away, and people he didn't recognise, probably from Pilkington if the film had been advertised there, as Alice had said. A sprinkling of women dressed in their best brightened up the place like flowers in a desert.

Jon looked for Greg but couldn't see his distinctive red hair – playing two-up, no doubt. He'd seen men making their way over to Les's lean-to. He caught a glimpse of Will sitting with Mary and Jeb, a set look on his face. So that was how the land lay! Will had had his eye on Val, and Berry had beaten him to it! A pity! Will was a much nicer bloke than Berry, but some women were too blinkered to see what was in front of their noses.

'Shove along, mate,' whispered Ty in his ear.

Jon inched along the bench seat.

'Alice said I could squeeze in next to you, otherwise I'll have to wait till five.'

'How come you get priority treatment?'

Ty caught Rachel's eye, smiled and waved. 'Because I'm helping to clear away later.'

After the film Jon made his way over to The Grand, spoke to one or two of the stockmen from Jindalee and had a drink with Wheat who had driven over with Berry from Pilkington for the film. At six he'd had enough and decided to go home. The second showing had put a damper on things. Alice, Val, Rachel, Ty and Berry were all involved in setting it up and by the time it was over there wouldn't be that much of the evening left. He checked that Alice was booked into The Grand, told Connie he'd pick her up on Sunday afternoon, and got into his utility.

He liked driving at night. The landscape always seemed friendlier and more intimate in the headlights and so long as he could avoid kangaroos he had time to think.

Greg hadn't turned up for the film, too busy playing two-up. Les had let something slip about Greg's bottomless pocket; Jon hoped it was his own money he was losing and not Alice's.

Lonely as it was, living alone had its advantages; it kept him out of Greg's way and gave him breathing space to think about the future. Then there was his promise to Stan. He still had to erect the headstone and iron railings he'd ordered for the grave. A few more days and his promise would be honoured, and then what? Did he stay and work for Alice part-time and do a bit of panning for gold now that the creek was flowing again, or move on to a station up north like the Samuels' lads were thinking of doing and take on a manager's job? He'd got enough experience under his belt, more than some, and although Alice wasn't keen on the idea she'd agreed to write letters of introduction and a reference if he needed them. He didn't know what to do and decided to follow Stan's advice and wait and see how things panned out.

A week after the film show Scally arrived at Stan's place and had started to unload the headstone and railings before Jon had returned from checking Alice's sheep.

'What do y'want me to do with them?' Scally asked when Jon arrived.

'They need taking down to Stan's grave, just give me a minute to see to the horse and I'll be with you.'

Scally waited while Jon unsaddled and released the horse into the corral, then together they loaded the heavy stone onto a trolley and leaned the cast-iron railings against the shack wall.

'You'll want some help with this, won't ya?'

'If you wouldn't mind,' said Jon.

Scally grasped the trolley handle and together they dragged and pushed the cart along the track, Jon steadying the load so that it didn't come adrift.

'Trust Stan to want to be buried here instead of Charlestown cemetery like everyone else,' commented Scally.

'Oh, I don't know,' said Jon, thinking of Curly's lonely grave, and the wooden marker for someone called D. W. Berridge dated 1824 over on Jindalee Station, and Jack Macarthur buried under the great trees at Jarrahlong, 'there are worse places to be buried.'

'Aye, I suppose,' conceded Scally, 'but you'd have thought he'd have seen enough of that bloody mine.'

Together they lifted the headstone off the trolley and propped it up against the rock Jon usually sat on.

Scally stood back, read the wording carved deep into the granite, and scratched his head.

Stanley Gerald William Colley
who found gold.
1871-1949

'What's that supposed to mean?' he asked. 'Did he find a bloody reef after all?'

'No, but Alice and I agreed he'd sort of found his El Dorado here.'

Scally grinned. 'Yeah, I suppose y're right…Stan'd like that, it'd appeal to his sense of humour.'

'That's what Alice said.'

They dragged the trolley back to the shack.

'Look, mate, I've got the time, why don't I help y'with the rest of it?'

Jon hesitated. He'd sensed a change in Scally in recent weeks; it would be churlish to reject his offer. And the company would make a change, he hadn't realised how lonely he'd been feeling until Scally turned up. 'Thanks, I'll get the tools.'

Scally reloaded the trolley with the railings and the carved base stones, pre-drilled for the railings, while Jon collected together pickaxes and spades, and then they made their way up the valley again followed by Bonny and Bess and Jon's dingo-cross cattle dog, Smoky.

Fitting the railing plinths and headstone was straightforward, each piece of stone keyed into the next and formed a rigid rectangle, while the railings slotted into the pre-drilled holes and were held in position temporarily with wire.

Scally stood up and dusted off his knees. 'You'll never get a high enough temperature to melt lead with an ordinary fire, you'll need a brazier. There's bound to be a crucible kicking about the place. Do y'want me to help y'with it?'

'I don't know anything about working with lead.'

'Me neither. It'll be the blind leading the blind.'

In one of Stan's sheds they found what they needed, a portable brazier, bellows, crucible, double-handled pouring tongs and a sack of charcoal. Down by the graveside they built a fire in the brazier and when the charcoal was white hot they took the ingots of lead that Mike Tunstall had supplied, dropped them into the crucible and used the bellows to achieve the temperature needed.

Pouring the lead was delicate work and it overflowed and ran down the sides of the stone, but they got better at it, and faster. Sweat dripped off them in the sweltering summer heat as they concentrated on the task.

'If y're up there watching us, Stan, then I hope y'appreciate this,' grunted Scally as they poured lead into the last hole.

When they'd finished they stood together looking down at Stan's grave. 'What a rigmarole that was,' commented Scally, stretching his aching back. 'When y'bury me y'needn't bother with any fancy railings, got it?'

'Got it,' said Jon as they made their way home to the shack.

The sun was already setting by the time they put everything away. Scally climbed onto his truck to lash down the load and secure everything.

Jon looked up at him. 'It's a long haul to the Harrison place, why don't you stay the night and have an early start?' He waited as Scally tied off another rope. Was this what it was like living alone, hungry for company? Stan had never said, had never tried to hang on to him when he'd visited. He turned away embarrassed by his offer.

'Is y'cooking any better than Belle's?'

'Bully beef and beans.'

'Y'can't go far wrong with that, it'll do me fine. Here, there's a letter for ya, from England.' Scally tossed it down and secured the mailbag again.

Jon looked at the envelope – from Merle. He put it in his pocket for later.

The meal finished Jon handed Scally a mug of tea. 'Sorry there's nothing stronger.'

'Y're not like that Greg then, he likes his grog a bit too much if y'ask me, and his two-up.'

'I thought you said he was all right for a Pom?'

Scally drew deep on his cigarette and the end glowed in the darkened room.

Jon regretted the remark the minute he'd made it. Would Scally retaliate with a scathing comment about all Poms being scum as he had in the past?

'Rachel doesn't like him either.'

'Why, what has she said?'

'It's not what she's said: it's what she hasn't said.' Scally stared into the distance, absent-mindedly stroking Bonny's ears. 'She likes you though.'

'Look, Scal, I'm not—'

'Going to marry her. I know. She told me y're not Joe's father even though she won't say who the mongrel is.'
Jon said nothing; it was up to Rachel to tell him.
Scally stubbed out the cigarette. 'But the fact is, she likes ya, and y'd have been all right as a son-in-law.' Scally's words were spoken so quietly that Jon had to strain to catch them. It was probably as close to an apology as he was going to get.
'Nice of you to say it, Scal.'
'Y'know Ty calls in to see her when he can, and Joe's really taken to him.'
'Ty's a good bloke,' said Jon.
'And while we're on the subject y'should have a word with Val and warn her off Berry. He's a nice enough fella as far as blokes go, but he isn't husband material.'
'Val wouldn't listen to me, Scal. She's a mind of her own.'
'That's what Rachel said, but there'll be tears if she thinks she can tame that one. Wheat reckons Berry's got women spread across the State. Nah, that one's not the settling kind. He's a man's man, sees women as useful for cooking, cleaning, raising kids and a roll in the hay. I wouldn't like to see her hurt.'
Scally hadn't put two and two together after all. He still didn't suspect Berry was Joe's father, but why was Scally so bothered about Val? Jon shifted in his seat, unsure of what to say.
'Val being in Charlestown has made a difference to Rachel,' said Scally.
So that was it!
'Company, y'know. Connie's a good woman but she's not Rachel's age. Y'have to think about these things living out here. I wouldn't like to see Val leave now, it would cause too much upset, and not just from Rachel's point of view, Alice would miss her too.'
'It won't matter, will it, if Rachel's got Ty?'
'Y've got a lot to learn, haven't ya?'
There was no edge to Scally's statement so Jon accepted it at face value and wondered what the bloke was getting at.
'It was the one thing Elizabeth found hardest to do without,' said Scally.
'Elizabeth?'
'Aye, Rachel's mother – she missed the company of other women her own age.'
Elizabeth! So that's what his wife was called. Jon remembered seeing the beautiful face smiling out of the cheap wooden frame on

Scally's kitchen dresser on his first trip into Charlestown for Alice, and Rachel telling him about her mother's tragic death from tuberculosis.

'She was a fine woman and a good mother.'

The matter-of-fact statement couldn't conceal the loneliness behind Scally's words, or the bleak look in his eyes. In that moment Jon saw him as a bereft husband bringing up a four-year-old child on his own with all the hopes and fears that entailed. Had Rachel appreciated that? Had she understood Scally's feelings of failure when she'd fallen pregnant with Joe?

Scally roused himself. 'I'd better get some sleep. As y'said, it's a long drive to the Harrison place. Am I over there?' He gestured towards the truckle bed in the corner.

'Yeah, and you'll probably find Bess curled up at your feet in the morning.'

Jon lay on the top of his bed listening to Scally's snores, thinking about what had been said, about Scally's offer to help with Stan's grave, and their evening together, a couple of mismatched blokes in a shack not much bigger than a garden shed in the middle of the outback. He wondered what Merle would make of it. Her letter! He'd forgotten it was in his pocket.

He rolled off the bed and found a candle stub and lit it, shielding the light from Scally and sat at the kitchen table.

He imagined he could smell Merle's perfume as he opened the envelope and took out the single sheet – blue it would be in daylight, the edges deckled, the handwriting in black ink like spider's marks across the page. He pulled the candle closer.

Dear Jon... He tried to picture Merle writing the words, her auburn hair swinging across her cheeks as she tilted her head towards the desk, a pen in her hand, but the image wouldn't come. He read the letter, chatty, informative about life in Liverpool, the rebuilding of the city, her friends at medical school. He wondered if she was thinking about Paul Vincent as she wrote and quenched the jealous twinge. He read and re-read the letter looking for words of love and affection, but there were none apart from the conventional *Dear Jon* and *Love, Merle.*

He folded the letter, put it back in the envelope and thought about an earlier letter he'd written to her describing his ordeal at Paradise Canyon, about returning the tjuringa, Yildilla's punishment, the long journey back home across the outback, his delirium, and of being cared for by Bindi, and Merle's short, matter-of-fact reply, telling him what he already knew about scar tissue and nerve damage. Her short letter didn't compare with his, pages long, and she hadn't even mention Pete and the others back home in Liverpool, or whether she'd heard how Elsie was doing. Then there was his most recent letter telling her about the Cathay Cup race meeting, and Stan's illness, and the crying need for medics out in the bush. He looked down at Merle's reply, all had gone unacknowledged. He swallowed his disappointment and pocketed the letter. She was busy. It was hard studying to be a doctor, long hours, lots of stuff to learn when she wasn't attending lectures. It wouldn't leave much time for letter writing.

He returned to bed and lay there, his mind in turmoil, knowing that Merle wasn't really interested in his life in Australia, that the world he'd tried to describe in his letters was of no consequence to her. It was understandable, he supposed. How could Merle begin to appreciate the beauty of the outback, its vibrant colours, the scents and smells, and the sheer vastness of a place she'd never visited? He recalled the birthday party he'd been to at the social club back in Liverpool, the time he'd realised just how much he loved her, when he'd held her close on the dance floor and felt the heat of her pressed against him. She loved him too, he knew she did, she wouldn't have melded herself to him if she hadn't, and yet he could feel her slipping away from him and, short of going back to England, he couldn't see how to stop it, or how to arouse her interest in the land he loved.

Bonny crawled up beside him and laid her head on his arm, her mournful eyes watching his face. He stroked her; the soft rhythmic movement felt soothing and restful as sleep overtook him…

'...Nice grave,' says Stan.

The two of them are standing in the morning sunlight looking down on the pristine stone, the words beautifully chiselled into the granite. Stan leans over the rails and takes a closer look.

'Tunstall's done a good job. Who chose the words?'

'A joint effort – Alice and me.'

Stan chuckles. 'That's Alice for you, all right. Did she come to the funeral?'

'No, just me, Wes, Val and Connie, but Scally helped me put the headstone up and the railings.'

'What exactly does the epitaph mean?'

'Do you need me to tell you, Stan? Can't you work it out for

yourself?'

Stan stares at the words. 'So, this place is my El Dorado, eh!' He turns round and takes in the valley, the rock strata and the shale spilling down from the entrance to No Hope Mine, the red earth leeching into the small patch of grass where his grave is, the creek, the birds chattering in the bushes, the irritating, ever-present flies clinging to their shirts, crawling up their noses, taking moisture from their eyes and mouths. 'You reckon, do you?' His eyes light up with silent laughter. 'Are you planning on staying and working my mines?'

'No chance, Stan.' He bats away the worst of the insects. 'You won't catch me down there in the dark and the muck. No imagination, that's what you need to go down a mine.'

'Or more than the average,' comments Stan.

'But I am planning on staying for a while. I can use this place as an outstation and keep an eye on Alice's sheep, and I might do a bit of panning, search for some of that elusive alluvial gold of yours.'

'And keep out of Greg's way at the same time?'

'Something like that.'

'So, what's wrong, son?'

'I dunno, Stan. I'm restlessness I suppose. I'm not sure where I'm going anymore, not now Greg is looking to take over managing Jarrahlong. Things aren't turning out as I'd imagined, and it's hard watching him take over responsibility, giving out orders, and making decisions with Alice. I thought I might move on to the Northern Territory, or Queensland.'

'What about Alice?'

'She'll be fine, Stan. She's got Greg, and Scally will keep an eye out for her.'

'Well, before you go north don't forget to carve my name and those dates I gave you in old No Hope,' says Stan.

'Look, Stan. I don't think I...' He hesitates – listening. Somewhere in the distance he can hear clanking, a starting handle turning, and an engine catch, a cab door slam and gears engage...

...Scally! Scally was leaving! Jon tumbled out of bed and opened the door. It was still dark outside. He watched the truck reversing and heard Scally ram the gearstick into first. When the vehicle swung round the headlights caught him full in the face blinding him momentarily. He blinked sense into his eyes and saw Scally leaning out of the cab window.

Scally shouted above the noise of the engine. 'Y'was sleeping like a baby. Didn't want to wake ya. See ya, mate.' He raised his hand, a salute, engaged the gear again and drove off, the headlights a wavering beam threading along the valley track, the engine rumbling and fading even as the tail lights disappeared from view.

CHAPTER 50

Jon stood at the entrance to No Hope, a chisel and a hammer in his hand, building up courage to face what lay ahead. For months he'd been putting off the task and now Stan was turning up in his dreams again, like Perentie had done, nagging him about the memorial.

'Some mate, Stan, expecting me to do this for you!' muttered Jon. 'You know I hate the bloody mine.' He weighed the tools in his hand, dithering, wanting to turn his back on the task ahead.

How long would it take to chisel Stan's name and dates into solid rock good enough for a future prospector to read? He took a silver hip-flask out of his pocket, the one Stan had always carried with him, and took a long pull of the fiery liquid hoping it would stiffen his resolve. Maybe he should have fetched Tunstall over from Pilkington and paid him to do it. He dropped his tools back into the bucket at his feet wishing he'd thought of it sooner.

Jon turned away from the mine entrance and saw one of Stan's kookaburras sitting on the gravestone, watching him – the old granddaddy of the mob. It tilted its head and fixed a beady eye on him. Jon hesitated, embarrassed by his cowardice.

'All right! I'm going,' he yelled at it and grabbed the tools again, lit the miner's lamp and plunged into the entrance before he could change his mind.

The clammy chill made him shiver. His stomach churned as he inspected the roof and tested one of the pit props, feeling for movement, listening for cracking and creaking, trying to keep a lid on his overactive imagination.

'Pull yourself together, Cadwallader!' He drew back his lips, gritted his teeth and whistled through them to keep his spirits up, but the deeper he went into the adit the eerier the place seemed. He stopped and listened again, sure that he could hear the rock above settling, and realised it was his own panicked breathing that he could hear. He rested for a moment and took several long, slow breaths forcing the fear to a manageable level. Stan had worked the mine for decades – it couldn't be that dangerous.

The lamp lit up fresh timber reinforcements – that's what he liked to see, and the amount suggested the old fella had been busy. He ignored the side galleries, concentrating on the main one leading him deeper into the rock. Gradually, the tunnel narrowed until he could feel the sides brushing his shoulders and he had to stoop lower to clear the roof. Twenty more yards or so and it would open out again. He held on to the memory, trying hard to think of other things as he inched his way along the narrowing space, thinking of blue sky and red earth, ignoring the tightness in his chest, the sweat trickling down his sides. 'Blue sky, red earth, cerulean, vermilion,' he muttered over and over through gritted teeth, using his gran's favourite colours as a talisman against disaster, fighting off the terror that threatened to engulf him.

The dank smell of stale air was rank in his nostrils. Not much further, he thought. Then, at the point when he felt he couldn't go on, the shadows lengthened and he was in the lightning-strike chamber, six feet by six feet, with space to breathe again.

The quartz glistened in the lamp light and the ironstone from which the chamber was hewn gleamed brownish-red. He squatted on his haunches and studied the rough walls, calculating the best place to put Stan's memorial. He looked at the lightning-strike mark, the quartz zigzagging through the ironstone, and identified a likely spot underneath it, flatter than the rest and perfect for the task ahead.

The chisel rang like a bell when he hit it with the hammer and for one long moment he wondered whether the whole roof would collapse on him. He waited until the ringing in his ears stopped and wished he'd thought of ear plugs.

S. COLLEY

Jon shuffled back to look at his handiwork pleased with the uniformity. Stan had it all planned out – easy letters to chisel. Now the dates—

1871 – 194

The second thwack with the hammer on the last 9 drove the chisel deep into the rock. Horrified, he stared at the chisel head. Did it mean he'd have to start on the date all over again? He tried to waggle the chisel free and couldn't. He struck it up and down and side to side with the hammer making the hole bigger, and then the worst happened, the flattish piece of rock that he'd been working on fell to the floor and shattered – hours of work gone in a second!

Jon sat back on his heels not even thinking of further rockfall so angry was he. 'That's it, Stan. To hell with your mark. I've done my best,' he muttered. He grabbed the miner's lamp and made to get up.

Something bright caught his eye in the rock face. He held the lamp higher and squinted at the newly exposed seam.

Gold!

Carefully he pecked at the edge of the fresh rock with his chisel and more stone fell away. He picked up a piece and looked at it closely, at the thin sheet of ironstone with a mortar layer attached. Stan had cemented it to the wall!

'You old bastard!' muttered Jon.

It took half an hour to clean off the rest of Stan's handiwork and there, gleaming like burnished metal in the dimly flickering light, was a gold reef, a horizontal seam about three inches wide. Not as big or as dramatic as the one in the cavern in Paradise Canyon, but sizeable nevertheless.

Jon was certain that it was gold and not iron pyrites. Stan knew what he was about, he wouldn't have spent time and effort when he was dying to disguise the reef as he had, or fit new pit props to secure the entrance and make it safe, had the seam been worthless.

He leaned forward and caressed the golden rock, ran his fingertips over its irregular surface, and shivered.

A pocketful of gold nuggets gleamed in the moonlight – wealth beyond his dreams and a fortune for the taking back down in No Hope Mine. He sat on his favourite stone overlooking Stan's grave and took a swig of rum. He felt the liquid burn its way down his gullet and its spreading warmth in his empty stomach. The irony of it! Thirty years of toil! He picked up a piece of the gold and weighed it in his hand. Had Stan experienced the warm flush of exhilaration, or cold disappointment – sadness at what might have been?

What had gone through Stan's mind when he discovered the reef? Jon couldn't begin to imagine. It was clear he'd said nothing to anyone, too afraid that his claim would be jumped. Stan had talked of that happening to others often enough. Then there was the rest of it, Stan's decision to leave the mineral lease to him, but why hadn't Stan told him? Did Stan want to find out whether he was up to the job, knowing as he did of his fear of confined spaces? Was that why Stan had hidden the reef and left the letter for him to find, sure that if he carried out the last request he would discover the gold?

Jon took a second, longer draught of rum, savouring the taste this time, enjoying the light-headed sensation of alcohol and good fortune.

He breathed in the chill night air and looked up at the clear sky, at the Southern Cross high above him, and felt his euphoria drain away as he considered the future. Gold brought its own problems, not least the mining of it. Could he face working alone, deep underground until the reef was worked out or did he sell the mineral lease to the valley and hope that one of the big gold mining companies would pay top money for the rights?

If he did that there'd be a gold rush. Charlestown would be a boom town again as it had been at the turn of the century. There was real wealth to be made on the back of gold. All the vacant plots would be built on. The Grand would be busy again, more hotels would be built, Val could have her dress shop, but at what price? The valley would be ruined, there would be the muck and the dust, and the noise. It would become a vast hole in the ground like the old mine workings at Murrin Murrin, the Aboriginal Dreaming destroyed and Stan's grave violated. Stan would have to be reburied in Charlestown cemetery.

There was too much to consider to make a decision lightly. He leaned back against the rock, overwhelmed by the moment.

The valley, bathed in silvery light, drew his eyes and the long shadows cast by the railings around the grave stretched almost to the mine entrance – Stan would have liked that.

Jon looked back at the gold. What would Stan advise? Then he realised he already knew the answer – as Stan always said, things have a way of working out. He smiled, there was no hurry. He'd bide his time like Stan had done and continue to work for Alice at Jarrahlong so no one would guess, and, on his days off, he'd conquer his fear, go back down No Hope and mine the seam himself – the incentive was big enough. He could travel to Kalgoorlie or Leonora and sell the gold anonymously, bank the money and play a waiting game. Something would turn up. He was still young. He had the time.

He picked up the nuggets, crossed over to the grave and looked down at the epitaph carved deep into the granite headstone.

'To El Dorado, Stan,' he said as he slipped the gold into his pockets, and then he turned and walked back along the path in the moonlight.

* * *

Acknowledgements

I should like to thank my family and friends for their support and encouragement during the writing of this novel, and my thanks also to those who helped with the preparation of the manuscript for publication.

I am also indebted to Kathy Boladeras and her husband, Malcolm, for their generous hospitality in allowing my daughter and me to stay with them on their cattle station in Western Australia during a cattle muster – the experience was both enlightening and exhilarating and was, without doubt, invaluable in the writing of this novel.

A Place Like Jarrahlong [The sequel to *The Kookaburra Bird*] will be published in 2012.

A Place Like Jarrahlong

S. E. Jenkins

Jon Cadwallader has inherited a rich gold mine but wants to preserve the land and the Dreaming from a gold rush. Chips Carpenter's quest for a lost gold reef threatens Jon's plan and jeopardizes a hidden canyon sacred to the Aborigines forcing him to make a return journey to a place that holds terrible memories for him. Jon's life is further complicated by his friendship with Val, a fellow Pom, and Greg, Alice Macarthur's resentful great-nephew.

A spell in the goldfields provides the cover Jon needs for his new wealth and his future finally looks assured. But, soon afterwards, news from home turns his world upside down and the fallout from a political decision made by the British and Australian Governments affects him, and others, setting in motion a chain of events that ultimately requires him to re-evaluate his feelings towards those closest to him.

* * *

Lightning Source UK Ltd.
Milton Keynes UK
UKOW04f1915190915

258863UK00004B/1/P